Carole –
Thank you for con
to Tell". You'll lo

MW00957849

A
PRECIOUS
STONE

LESLIE M. ARNO

[signature: Leslie M Arno]

ⓒiUniverse®

A PRECIOUS STONE

iUniverse books may be ordered through booksellers or by contacting:

iUniverse
1663 Liberty Drive
Bloomington, IN 47403
www.iuniverse.com
1-800-Authors (1-800-288-4677)

ISBN: 978-1-4917-5647-8 (sc)
ISBN: 978-1-4917-5648-5 (e)

Library of Congress Control Number: 2015900285

Printed in the United States of America.

iUniverse rev. date: 1/27/2015

A
PRECIOUS
STONE

*In memory of Uncle Al,
who always gave me a high~four,
and words of encouragement.*

*The thing to do in life is sail.
Sometimes you sail against the wind,
and sometimes you sail with it,
but you must sail,
not drift nor lie at anchor.*

~ Anonymous

CONTENTS

PART THREE
SOUTH DAKOTA

PART FOUR
THE RANCH

PART FIVE
UGANDA AND WYOMING

PART SIX
HOME

PREFACE

I wrote this book with the idea in mind that no matter who you are, where you come from, or what obstacles you've faced, you will always have battles, but it's not the battle itself that destroys us, it's how we handle them that determines whether we win or lose.

Often, we live our lives thinking, "if only this were different," or, "if only that one thing wouldn't have happened, then everything would be perfect." So we spend our lives thinking about that one thing (or many things) that already happened that we can't change, and we lose sight of what's ahead of us.

Like most everyone else, I've had some hard won battles in my life. Some of them were harder, but most of them were easier than my characters face. What makes my main characters battles get easier is when she starts looking at things differently, and handling pain and unexpected life events with a different outlook. It not only changes her life going forward, it changes how she sees the past.

ACKNOWLEDGEMENTS

A special thank you to my husband and my children for putting up with me when I sat around typing instead of playing, cleaning house, or cooking. I appreciate your support, and I hope you didn't mind eating pizza a little more than usual during especially engrossing parts of my book when I just couldn't put it down.

Thank you to my mom, and my daughter Tori, who read my book as I wrote it, and made me think that maybe it was good enough to publish.

To my entire book club, Sheila, many thanks!

Thank you to my brother Sam, the cowboy poet, for contributing some of his awesome poetry to my book. I've rarely been more excited about anything in my life. Including your creative work in my book means the world to me, and if nothing else comes of it, that one thing will have made all the hours I have into it, all worthwhile.

Thank you to all of my friends and family out there who have encouraged me, made me feel like I was good enough and smart enough to write a book, or do anything else I set my mind to. There have been many of you that I have been blessed to know throughout my life. Many thanks to you. You know who you are!

PART ONE

AN ALASKAN ADVENTURE

CHAPTER 1

FROM THE BASQUE COUNTRY

It had been half her life since Jewel sat still and calm, peacefully lounging in the contentment she'd found in this unlikely sanctuary. She carefully soaked up every moment as she kicked back with a beer, and dared to let her memories run wild, unafraid of them for the first time in a long while.

After the tragic, but anticipated death of her grandfather a few months after her eighteenth birthday, she'd run as fast as she could away from all she knew. She escaped into another world, throwing herself into another life, and forcing herself to be reborn into something more certain. *He was entirely too good to die,* she'd thought, and yet she knew he had been sick. He had been hanging on just long enough to deliver her safely to the front door that would open to the rest of her life.

How incredibly like him to wait until it was a safe time for me, being of legal age, but not too close to my birthday to bring sadness to me when I celebrate it. She shook her head and smiled when she thought of him. He'd always thought of her first, making sure the pain life handed her would be eased as much as possible. He always seemed to find a way to soften the hardness of life before he exposed her to its sharp, jagged edges.

After the unexpected death of her parents when she was eleven, and the subsequent death of her grandmother shortly after that, Jewel had been raised by her grandfather on her family's sheep ranch at the base of the Big Horn Mountains in Johnson County, Wyoming. Domingo Etchemendy had done his best to raise the delicate looking young girl, but despite her fine features, she had most definitely become a tomboy, and she embraced the lifestyle of a young Basque rancher; trailing sheep, hunting, camping, and ranching, always eager to do whatever work was necessary to help her grandfather, and keep their ranch viable.

She had grown up to have the classic look of a Basque, with her black hair and her olive skin, but she inherited the fine French features from her mom, along with her deep blue eyes that sparkled with flecks of violet. She'd grown into a stunning girl, tall and thin, but had somehow managed to grow-up without ever realizing it, always more consumed with the grief following her parent's death than by anything else. She usually threw her hair up in a ponytail or in a braid, and never seemed to notice if she walked around with smudges of dirt on her clothes or face, which by contrast, always seemed to make her attractiveness that more apparent.

She ordered another beer and continued to relax at the table she was sitting at, thinking of her family history, and all they had endured that led her to that one place in life where she sat contently. It was a long history that she knew well, since her grandfather had told it many times before his death.

Her family's ranch had been handed down from generation to generation since her great grandfather, Ismael Etchemendy, arrived in Wyoming from the Basque Country sometime in 1905, during the so-called *Age of the Great Overseas Migrations*, when so many fled Europe in search of opportunity that was available in America.

The Basques were said to be the oldest people of Europe, but they fled the Basque Country, a small area that spans the border of France and Spain between the Pyrenees Mountains and the Bay of Biscay. They ran toward climatically similar land in America that was ideal for their nomadic sheepherding culture, allowing them the opportunity to flourish. The Basque Country itself wasn't a country at all, but rather, a culture of people politically divided between France and Spain, and coming to America meant they would be able to own and work their own land, though it wasn't going to be easy.

Somehow, the Etchemendy family had managed to hang on to their land throughout nearly a hundred years of turmoil. It always amazed Jewel when she thought about it, and that day was no exception. She continued to sip her beer, sitting back contemplating all the obstacles that her family had managed to endure since arriving in America..

The first big threat actually happened before the Basques ever came to America, but it cleared the way for those that would later arrive in that part of the country. The Johnson County War in 1892 pitted settling ranchers against large cattle companies that wanted to keep everything free-range. The mayhem climaxed at the T.A. Ranch that neighbors the land that would later become the Etchemendy Ranch, with only a few miles separating them. The large cattle companies hired several hundred gunmen to kill and intimidate the settlers, making their way from Idaho into Wyoming, and they left a path of destruction in their wake.

The settlers in Wyoming were ready for the hired gunmen, having organized a posse numbering about sixty to protect their settlements, and the gunmen were met with force when they reached the T.A. Ranch. The posse surrounded the gunmen, locking them up in a barn, and things escalated to the point that the U.S. Cavalry were called in to stop the posse from burning the barn to the ground with all the gunmen inside. Tensions ran high for several years after the standoff, but things eventually settled down, so the ranchers in Wyoming no longer had to fear losing their land and their livestock to the hired gunmen, or the large cattle companies.

The Great Depression in the 1930's was the next big threat to the Etchemendy Ranch, during which time a large portion was sold off to keep the family afloat and salvage what they could, leaving a remaining 30,000 acres from their original 60,000 acres. It was near catastrophe for the Etchemendy family, but they welcomed their neighbors, and created a community of fellow Basques that helped them work the ranch, and it kept them all alive. The Etchemendy's provided jobs they couldn't afford to provide, and in return, the people in the community gave back to them by hunting and harvesting hay and grains, and that kept people and livestock fed.

The recession of the 1980's was the closest the Etchemendy family had come to losing their ranch altogether. There were rich trophy hunters, wealthy CEO's, and Hollywood movie stars standing at the ready, snatching up these generations old ranches, as one-by-one, families fell victim to the financial downturn of the economy. Interest was so high that buying equipment and paying mortgages was bankrupting Wyoming ranchers at a steady pace, many of them losing their ranches to the banks, or selling them off piece-by-piece to keep from losing everything all at once.

In the 1980's, her mom and dad's best friends lost their ranch, and in all honesty, had that family not been there to help the Etchemendy's keep their property, they would have likely suffered the same fate. The Landas family and the Etchemendy family had a partnership that ran as deep as the ocean they had crossed together so many years ago, escaping the hardship from the homeland. Since the death of her parents, and with the help of her grandfather until his death, the Landas Family had been managing the Etchemendy Ranch. They had invested what they could to keep it alive, and provide them all with enough income to survive, receiving a portion of the land as compensation.

Troy Landas was just a few months older than Jewel was. She frowned and fidgeted in her seat when she thought of him, taking several large gulps of her beer as she did, instinctively trying to drown them out. The thought of him always caused the pain and guilt she carried with her, creep up into her face, flush it red, and disrupt any contentment she was scarcely able to find.

Troy and Jewel had been raised together, and had been completely inseparable since before they could walk. She often recalled her mom telling the story of them lying together in Jewel's crib with both arms wrapped tightly around each other. They were both the only children in their families, and Jewel had always thought of Troy as a brother, but everyone thought they would grow up one day and get married. They hunted together, trailed sheep together, went to prom together, and spent every spare moment they had with each other. It wasn't until Troy asked her to marry him, scaring her to death, that she fled frantically without looking back, to a place that offered her something that would both deflate her soul, and then make it *feel* again, a state it hadn't been in since before the death of her parents.

She shifted her mind away from Troy, desperately searching for another memory, which always made her think of the path that led her to become a nurse.

For as long as she could remember she had felt an intense pull to heal and help people, and put the pieces of other broken souls back together, even if she hadn't been able to mend her own. Throughout high school, Jewel was always an exceptional student, flying through her classes with such ease that her grandfather never questioned her when she started taking nursing classes at the community college in her last two years of high school. With all the college credits she already had, and her exceptional academic achievement, it had been easy for her to gain acceptance into the nursing program at the University of Wyoming. It was at college where she found her calling, and she joined the Army Reserve Officers Training Program, and finished her nursing degree. She wanted to lend comfort to the men and women in the armed forces that gave the most of themselves, and she remembered her grandfather talking about how important nurses were in lending comfort to the rattled minds of soldiers, when he recalled his own time in the military serving in the Korean War.

College had been a nice escape from everything she had been running from. Her grandfather had always done his best, and she'd adored him, but he was gone, and it was time for her to be out from under the cloud of sadness that followed her around on the ranch. She threw herself into college, finishing the remainder of her nursing degree, and the required internships, in just two years. She excelled in the basic military training that came with the officer's training program, and it launched her toward her future.

At first, Troy was confused and saddened by her leaving, but he knew her well enough to know that getting away from the ghosts that surrounded her in her family home, and on the land, was exactly what she'd needed. Nobody knew Jewel the way Troy did, and he'd been certain she'd be back one day. He had always been fiercely protective of her, always there to comfort her, and make her laugh and enjoy life again since the death of her parents.

She took another large swallow as thoughts of Troy crept back in, as they always did, and she sighed heavily. Her mind wandered forward as she shifted in her seat, as if that would be enough to jolt the memory of him loose, which it would momentarily. Her mind wandered back to college and the path it led her down, forcing the memory of Troy from her once again.

She remembered it was shortly after she graduated from the University of Wyoming, the Army shipped her off to Iraq, just as she hoped they would. She had never imagined what awaited her in the U.S. Military's Medical Center in Balad, north of Baghdad where she had been sent, but she never questioned why she was there. She knew that somewhere in God's infinite wisdom, He knew she would need to feel the pain that someone else carried before she could release her own, and not just the pain from losing her grandfather, but all of it. There was a deep vein of agony she carried within her when she dared to remember the smell of her mother's perfume, the calloused yet gentle hands of her father, or her grandma's warm smile, and it needed to finally heal. She needed to find a place in the world where she could finally *feel* again, and be the person she was meant to be, and she found that in the Army among the suffering that pulled her out of her own tortured mind.

The day she arrived in Iraq had marked nine years since the death of her parents, but the first soldier that came in under her care confirmed to her that the path she had taken was the right one. She had a natural ability to bring comfort to people. She knew that from a very young age when her mom's cousin Mary came to visit them one summer. Her mom was from Denver, and her family hadn't been happy with her when she left her culturally progressive lifestyle to step back in time a hundred years to go live on a Wyoming sheep ranch, and be *just a mom and wife*, instead of the career woman they wanted her to be. Eleanor Martin, or *Ellie*, as her dad called her, didn't mean to fall in love with the charming man from Wyoming, but when she did, there was no turning back, and her family didn't come to visit very often.

The arrival of her mom's cousin had been a bit of a surprise, and in all the excitement and nervousness of her arrival, her mom jumped up and down excitedly, catching the pot handle with her arm, and had accidentally launched a pan of boiling water across the room, hitting Mary square in the chest. It was mass chaos, sending dogs and cats running, her mom standing there screaming and crying, and poor cousin Mary yelling every obscenity imaginable, not knowing or understanding exactly what had happened, or why.

Jewel smiled thinking of it as she sat there, remembering the moment she first thought of becoming a nurse. She signaled to the bartender for another beer, and then got up from her table, making her way into the bathroom, which was just barely large enough for a toilet and a sink. It looked like it had been there for a hundred years or more, though it was immaculately clean and well preserved. She used the restroom and washed her hands, catching a glimpse of herself in the mirror as she tucked some loose strands of hair behind her ears, straightening out the Wyoming Cowboy's tank top she wore, always feeling like it was a losing battle to look presentable.

She walked back to her table in the bar where she had been sitting, and looked around at its quaintness as she sipped her beer. She sat back down, continued with her memory of cousin Mary's unexpected visit, and her time in Iraq.

She remembered standing there briefly after her mom launched the pan of water across the room. She then stepped into action and calmed the situation. She walked straight over to her mom, and told her to go to the sink and draw water until it was freezing cold, giving her mom the direction she needed to help remedy the pain she just caused. She then reached Mary, leading her into the back bedroom to get her undressed to care for her burns as best as a ten year old girl could. When her dad came in later, Mary was quietly lying on the bed, having been given some pain reliever and cold compresses to ease the burns on her chest and legs. Her mom was sitting there holding her cousin's hand, and stroking the poor woman's hair to keep her from running scared from the ranch, never turning back.

Jewel had taken such good care of Mary that she ended up not having burns that were too severe, and they had been able to heal without scarring. Mary was the first person who told her she should consider becoming a nurse one day.

She didn't know how she knew to treat a burn with cool water at such a young age. Perhaps she had read it somewhere, or maybe it was just a natural gift she had to heal and comfort that led her to know that a hot burn would be soothed with something cool. It was more than that though. She had a gift to ease the mind and calm the nerves with just a few words and a caring look. Her eyes told a story long before words could ever form on her mouth, and the story they told comforted people, and made them relax in her hands. As soon as someone was in Jewel's care, they knew they didn't have much to worry about.

Although she grew up hunting, fishing, and raising sheep, she had a gentle and patient hand, which proved to be the best medicine when working with the rattled minds of those who came in from the frontlines of war. After she had gently cleaned, wrapped and comforted them as much as she could, she would simply listen to those who needed to tell their story and confess aloud, probably less to her, and more to the world in general. It was as if they had to confess the ugliness of it all before the memory of it suffocated them to death, seeping into the depths of their minds to haunt them later. The telling of it allowed them to take the next steps toward another day, and with each story, she could feel the hard steel within her own soul soften just a little. Easing their pain healed a part of her she forgot she had.

She sat there contently in all her memories good and bad, still contemplating the last few years that had brought her to Alaska, thankful for the ability she had to help people. She sat with peace and calm in a place she had never imagined herself before. She was far away from her Wyoming ranch, and even further away from the war in Iraq. It was a little bar of sorts; a quiet little place where people gathered to have a beer and eat simple fare, letting life envelope them in the moment. It was in the center of town in a tiny little community just a couple hours away from Homer, Alaska. On that particular afternoon, there were just a few souls in there watching nothing of particular interest on the small television that hung over the bar, each of them quietly sipping their drink of choice, and maybe contemplating their own lives, just as she had been.

It had been unseasonably warm outside, and Jewel had kicked back in her tank top and khaki pants, comfortably slipping off her flip-flops, resting her feet up on the extra chair at her table, occupied by her memories. She took another sip of her beer and thought about the spring in Alaska that had breathed life back into her, and that made her smile again, feeling a peace she hadn't felt in a while.

She felt ready for anything life had to offer, or so she thought.

CHAPTER 2

ANYTHING TO KEEP FROM GOING HOME

The man who had bowled Jewel over earlier that morning, running into her like a freight train, and then grabbing her up as if she were nothing more than a small child, walked in the door of the bar where she was sitting, turning heads from every direction. The man filled up the doorway, entering with a presence that seemed to light up the entire room. The ice blue eyes that nearly drowned her earlier, as her feet fought to find the sidewalk solid beneath her once again, were scanning the room before landing with a smile on her own blue eyes, stealing away the easy breath she had only just recently acquired.

I suppose you could call it love at first sight, except for the fact that it was so cliché and ridiculous that it almost made her laugh out loud, even as she failed to find the strength to look away from him. She found herself sitting up more alertly, and fidgeting nervously, as the blue-eyed man and his friend walked over to a table near her own, sitting down with a nod of hello, and a hint of a smile in her direction, ordering a couple of beers. Jewel, who was normally very sturdy and laid back, was suddenly as rattled and unnerved as she had ever been. Through all her fidgeting and nervousness, she managed to knock over her beer, sending the cool liquid flying in one direction, and her glass flying in the other.

"Oh my gosh! Look what I've done!" She jumped up without thinking before the beer could spill down on her legs as Grady reached over, and just as he had so easily done before, he grabbed her up before she could tumble backwards into their table. That was not exactly the introduction she was hoping for, but it came nonetheless.

"Are ya okay ta stand, or should I plan on carryin' ya around ta keep ya from fallin' anymore taday?" he asked mockingly, but the joke of it got lost as they once again locked eyes with each other.

"I'm so sorry," she stuttered. "I think I'm okay to stand on my own now," she said shyly, with more confidence than she felt, even as her wobbly knees threatened to betray her.

"Here," he said, pulling out a chair for her at his table, "sit here while I get ya another drink and have this mopped up. I wouldn't want ya ta stumble on yer way ta talk ta the bartender, as I might not be able ta catch ya from that distance," he said smiling, guiding her into the chair at his table, over exaggerating the act of getting her safely on the chair, as if all their lives depended on it.

"I'm Jewel," she said with a smile a little broader than she wanted, introducing herself to Grady's friend as Grady went over and talked to the bartender.

"I'm Rudy, and it looks like you've already met Grady. Is there something that I missed? There seems to be more to this story," Rudy said, completely dazzled by the woman in front of him. He was shaking his head, impressed at how smoothly Grady had managed to get a beautiful woman relocated from her own table to theirs, in one swift move.

Jewel could see that Rudy was much older than Grady, who was likely several years older than her own twenty-two years. He was quite tall, though slightly shorter than Grady, with dark hair and dark brown eyes, and he had a friendly smile that complimented the good feeling she had been enjoying moments before. She smiled back at him, and just as she was getting ready to explain what happened earlier that day, Grady cut in, "This woman tried ta tackle me earlier, assaultin' me in broad daylight, probably attemptin' some type of unwanted sexual advancement. Ya know how aggressive women are these days," he said smiling, giving her a wink that melted her from the inside out, making her less steady in her chair.

"I did not!" she laughed. "He came around the corner so fast and furious I saw my life flash before me when he plowed me over like a little bug on the sidewalk."

"Now that seems more probable," Rudy said, giving Grady a knowing look.

"Well I was pretty furious, I'll admit," Grady said with more seriousness. He'd furiously left the hospital where his friend Jared was being treated, knowing that everything he had carefully planned over the last several months was now in jeopardy.

He didn't say anymore, and Jewel could sense that it wasn't a good idea to ask about the cause of his angst. Hoping to bring a lighter tone back to the table, she reached out her hand to Grady. "I'm Jewel Etchemendy. Thank you for at least catching me after launching me off the sidewalk this morning," she said smiling wryly, meeting his eyes once again.

Grady paused for a second nearly forgetting his own name as he took her hand, introducing himself, but never once taking his eyes from hers. "I'm Grady McDonald, and I'm pleased ta meet ya, and even more pleased ta have caught ya." He realized how corny this sounded the moment he said it, and blushed a little as he looked away, trying to recover and figure out why he was so flustered.

This never happened to Grady. He was not shy when it came to women. They flocked to him, and he basked in their attention. At six foot, four inches tall, he was naturally a presence when he entered a room; add to that his ice blue eyes, thick muscular frame, and careless blond locks, and you had a man that attracted more than his fair share of female attention. It was him that caused women to blush, not women who made him blush. Yet, even in his most animated dreams, he could not have imagined a more stunning woman. It wasn't just her looks though; he saw something within her the moment their eyes first met on the sidewalk. As he held l.er, a little longer than was absolutely necessary, trying to keep them both from tumbling into the middle of the street, he felt something he hadn't felt before. He wasn't entirely sure he liked it, and yet, he was certain he wanted more of it.

Rudy leaned back and shook his head. He couldn't believe what he saw happening before his eyes. He had known Grady since he was in grade school. Even then, he had girls following him around like lovesick puppies, and Grady barely seemed to notice. Grady always knew the girls liked him, but he didn't seem to know why, and he often seemed annoyed by all the attention. He never saw himself as especially handsome or attractive, because he simply never thought of it. He lived his life and thanked God for the foolishness of the women who always sought him out. Something different was happening though, and he watched with amusement as his friend stumbled all over himself for the woman at their table.

Rudy started wondering why she was there. A small hunting town in Alaska was not a place you would expect to find someone who looked like Jewel. He wondered if she was there for the competition, and as soon as the thought occurred to him, he asked, "Are you here for the competition Jewel?"

"What competition? What do you mean?" she asked, leaning on the table again after the bartender delivered their beers.

"Oh, I thought that maybe you were here for the competition that everyone's in town for. That's why Grady and I are here, but I'm not sure if we'll be able to do it now that Jared's sick," Rudy said, meeting Grady's now angry eyes. It started to become clear to Jewel why he had been so furious earlier.

"We may have to drop out of the competition entirely if they won't let us continue with a two man team," Rudy explained.

"We have been plannin' this for six months," Grady said, "and just yesterday our friend Jared came down with the flu, and it doesn't look good. We thought we could nurse him ta health ourselves, but we got worried for him last night and took him ta the hospital when his temperature spiked really high. They said there was no way they would clear him in time ta start, and the rules clearly state that each team must start with three men."

"Well, it doesn't exactly say *men*," Rudy said with a wink in her direction. "I believe it says three *person* team. So, what are you doing for the next six weeks Jewel?" Rudy joked, but still, with a little more hope than he realized.

"Geez man! Ya can hardly expect a woman we met not five minutes ago ta go traipsin' through the Alaskan wilderness with two strange men! Give it a break man! It's over unless we can convince them ta let us start with the two of us," Grady said annoyed, and a little embarrassed that Rudy would suggest such a thing.

"So what are you doing here Jewel?" Rudy asked, glancing sideways at Grady with a stern look. "I'm just making conversation now."

"That's a very good question," she said, not sure how much she should tell them without sending them running and screaming from the building. After considering for a second, she finally answered, "After sweating day and night in the ungodly heat of the Iraqi desert, I could think of nothing more refreshing than heading to the cool crisp air of Alaska," and that was exactly the truth, albeit lacking in much detail.

"What in the world were ya doin' in the Iraqi desert?" Grady asked with more interest, soaking every square inch of her up as he looked at her with astonishment.

"I was a nurse in the Army, and I served in Iraq for nearly two years before I came here. I got out on a family hardship, and I'm going home pretty soon, but I could hardly say no when some people I worked with invited me along on this trip."

Grady couldn't have been more surprised, and Jewel knew that he would be. She didn't exactly look like a soldier. Her height of five foot eight inches was the only thing about her that might be perceived as *almost* menacing, but the rest of her was pure delicacy. She had soft fine features, with tiny little fine-boned hands. She looked like she could have been made of fine porcelain, complete with a natural hint of red hue on her lips. She had a thin frame, but it was deceiving, as she was incredibly strong, having wrestled down many a sheep, and baled enough hay to build muscles for the strength of a hundred men.

"We are both ex-military, and Jared is also ex-military. We thought a team made up of men with the discipline that you learn in the military would be unbeatable, and we thought we'd have a pretty good chance of winning," Rudy finally said, coming to Grady's rescue as he sat speechless, mesmerized by her. "We were to be *The Military Team* in this competition I was telling you about. My invitation to have you join us doesn't seem like such a far-fetched idea now that we know you're also ex-military, now does it?" Rudy said coyly, eyeing Grady sideways.

"Well, how long do ya plan on bein' in Alaska then? Where's the group ya came with?" Grady asked, leaning back in his chair while throwing up his hands in surrender, surprising himself, and nearly making Rudy choke on his beer.

"The group I came with is long gone, but I wanted to stay behind for a little while longer. I haven't given it much thought on how much longer I'll stay," she lied, not wanting to reveal that she had been nearly in a panic, wondering how she could manage to delay her return home once again. "I came here with a group of people to go on a two-week camping trip, and when it was over, I found that I wasn't ready to leave. So, I stayed here by myself, and teamed up with another group to go on a mountain climb for a few days, and then a guided hunting trip the last two weeks. Then, I found I still wasn't ready to leave, and so here I sit. I'm not really sure what I'm doing," she said, feeling as if she'd said too much as she rambled on nervously.

"So tell me more about this competition," she said, fumbling to make conversation and divert the attention away from what she just said, "and is that an Irish accent I hear?" she tilted her head at Grady questioning.

"It is. Ya have a good ear, but I'm tryin' ta lose it, though I think the effort makes me sound like a back woodsmen," he said smiling at her before leaning forward and continuing. "They drop ya in the middle of Alaska somewhere, and ya have a pre-determined amount of time ta find a location they've marked on a map for ya. Whoever gets ta the finish line first wins the race, but ya don't just do it once, ya do it six times over six weeks. It's really just more of an adventure than anything else," he explained.

Grady and Rudy both talked about the exciting and adventurous things they would be doing over six weeks of the competition, as they all drank one beer after another. They talked about mountain climbing, and repelling off cliffs. They told stories of snowshoeing, or climbing up and down off large glaciers that most people will only be able to see in photographs. Grady told her about a previous competition he read about where they had to raft down a cold Alaskan river, camping along the way, and surviving off the land as they tried to get to the finish line before the other teams.

The two men questioned her about her outdoor experience, and she offered up information, all three of them starting to think that maybe they had each found a solution to their problems. Grady and Rudy, of course, were hoping to find a way to stay in the competition. Jewel, on the other hand, was looking for another way to stall her inevitable journey home.

She couldn't help but feel the excitement of possibly going on an adventure for six weeks through the Alaskan wilderness. The possibility of being able to delay going home for another six weeks made her want to immediately sign-up without asking another question. *Still...,* she thought to herself, *I don't know these men, and Grandpa would not approve of that, but then... Grandpa's not here, and these men seem safe enough. Surely, they would have had to go through some sort of screening to participate in a competition. Surely, Troy could manage without me for another six weeks.*

"It does sound like fun," she said with excitement showing in her eyes, the thought of facing Troy prompting her to want to stay in Alaska a while longer. They all sat in silence for a few minutes, and they each took a few long draws off their beers, ordering another round.

"Well it's completely absurd!" Grady finally said, breaking the silence. "How would ya feel about campin' out every night in the freezin' cold, hikin' through dangerous bear-infested tundra, and possibly puttin' yer life in danger, while ruggedly livin' with two strange men for the next month and a half Jewel?" he said sarcastically, leaning back in his chair in exasperation, but with a glimmer of hope in his eyes he couldn't seem to hide.

"Look," she said more determined, and perhaps a little drunk, leaning forward with a look of seriousness on her face, "I know how it is. Men form this brotherhood when they become a team. I've seen it over and over. I've seen the men come in from the battlefield, an unspoken pact that says they have each other's back no matter what! It's not the same with women, because men always feel they are the protectors, and they alone carry the burden of survival, but let me tell you something about that... I've had many people's backs. I've had the backs of men whose name I only know because I read it on their dog tags as they were carried unconsciously into the operating room. I've stayed up day and night, and then day and night again, watching over these strangers that are hanging on for dear life, nurturing their very souls back to life again. Everyone serves a role. Maybe equality has less to do about roles, and more to do about valuing each role equally. Do not underestimate the value of sisterhood," she finished, leaning back and eyeing the men intently, daring them to deny the truth of it as she took another long drink of her beer.

"Well, the Adventure Team has a woman," Rudy finally said convinced, looking Grady squarely in the eye, daring him to challenge Jewel's promise of sisterhood.

Grady couldn't challenge it though. He knew exactly what she was talking about, remembering the nurse that brought him back to life a year earlier. After taking shrapnel in a particularly bad gunfight in Afghanistan that nearly cost him his life, he could remember very clearly the gentle hands that cared for him when he was in the hospital. It was as if God Himself had hand selected an angel from heaven to be there to ease his pain, and make him more comfortable. She seemed to know, even before he did, that he would need to change positions or take a sip of water, a task he wasn't able to manage on his own. He knew the sisterhood Jewel was speaking of moments before.

He remembered seeing his nurses face for the first time, after having had his head and his eyes bandaged for several days, or maybe weeks, he couldn't remember. She was nothing like he had imagined. Perhaps the gentle touch of a woman after so long without had stirred his active imagination, for he had imagined a glorious woman of twenty-something, etched from the molds of the most perfect supermodel that had ever graced the cover of Sports Illustrated Swimsuit Edition. Instead, she was a middle-aged woman with thick glasses and a crew cut, and she had the warmest smile he could have ever imagined.

The warm look she had in her eyes as she unwrapped his head, told him everything he needed to know about her. She did have his back, and she was so in tune to his aches and pains, he felt like she had reached in and taken control of his mind. As the weeks passed, he grew to care for her more than he thought possible. It wasn't a romantic love, but it was an unbreakable bond, and it was as strong as any he had formed on the battlefield, with only the two of them ever knowing the depths of his suffering, her as much as him. Jaime, he recalled, remembering the sisterhood she offered, and the brotherhood he gave in return.

"Well, it's not a terrible thought," Grady finally said with a shrug, looking at Jewel with a questioning look in his eyes.

"Ugh... well... I would need to know a little more about it, but it's not out of the question," she said hesitantly, wondering what she was getting herself into. "I don't have anywhere else to go just yet. I'm certainly not ready to go home. I've fallen in love with Alaska, and I need to see more of it. Would they even accept me so late in the game?" she asked with more nervousness, remembering with a twinge of pain that Troy didn't wait for her any longer, and had married her childhood nemesis, Jolene Franklin.

Jolene the name itself sent a shudder down her spine just thinking of it. Jolene hated her, and Jewel was never sure why. She seemed like a nice enough person to everyone else, but when it came to Jewel, there had always been hatred there that she never understood. They were in the same grade, had played volleyball together, had run track together, and had been paired together as lab partners once, but Jolene had always been cold to her. Not outwardly mean or hateful, just cold and distant, but Jewel never cared that much at the time. She had bigger things to worry about than Jolene, but she never understood it, and whenever the thought of Jolene entered her mind, she couldn't help but wonder what all the hate was about.

"Let's find out!" Rudy said excitedly, interrupting her memory, standing up abruptly, and nearly causing another flood of beer on the barroom floor. "There's only one way we'll know for sure! We can go down to the office and see what Jewel would need to do to join the competition. You know this is our only shot Grady. You know they're never going to agree to let us start with the two of us, or you wouldn't be stalling so much. You'd be down there right now getting it all finalized!"

"Well, it's up ta the lady here. I'm game if she is," he said smiling at her invitingly, though feeling a little surprised by Rudy's brazenness to get the woman they just met signed up on their team. They had a lot riding on this though, and neither one of them were ready to just throw in the towel and head home. They would have likely recruited a bum on the street if they needed to, and had even considered that possibility on their way to the bar. Had there been any sitting on a street corner they had passed, they would have probably tried to make a deal, though they were both glad they hadn't, as Jewel seemed like a good fit.

"Alright, I'm up for it. We can at least find out if it's even a possibility," she said shrugging a little reluctantly. Part of her was excited, but another part of her was completely terrified, and she suddenly felt like her life was out of control again.

CHAPTER 3

THE PHYSICAL

The three of them, all nervous for their own reasons, but feeling invincible, as people often feel after several beers, left the little bar together, staggering toward the information office at the recreation center that had been set up for the contestants in the competition. Clearly, Grady and Rudy's situation with losing a team member was well known, and the other teams looked at them sympathetically when they walked through the door, and with a little relief, probably feeling thankful that they wouldn't have to compete with highly skilled men with their military training.

"We'd like to register a new team member!" Rudy said, slamming his hand down on the counter in front of him with a smug look on his face. He looked around at the other competitors, relishing the surprised looks on their faces.

"Well, I mean, what would I need to do if I were to join the competition? What would it entail, and would I need to pass a physical or something?" Jewel started nervously, suddenly feeling sober, and feeling the situation had left her control, giving Grady and Rudy a nervous look.

A surge of excitement and fear coursed through her body. She was having an internal argument with herself that was causing her to change her mind every other second. *What the hell am I doing?* she had asked herself all the way over there. She knew she would do just about anything to keep from going home, despite having gone out of her way to get an early discharge from the military, expressly for the purpose of going home. Yet, she put one foot in front of the other as they walked over there, scolding herself for agreeing to such an absurd notion of joining up with two strange men for a crazy competition in Alaska.

"The first thing you need to do is fill out this application, and if by some miracle you happen to pass the physical," the man behind the desk said doubtfully, "then you're in." He was leaning toward her with a condescending smirk on his face, clearly underestimating the slight, delicate little figure that stood before him. She knew the type well. He was an insecure man with a small body, bulking up his physique as much as possible to make himself feel more powerful, belittling the few people who were smaller than him, which of course were mostly women. This gave her the distraction she needed to put her fears aside, and forget about the uncertainty that was consuming her moments before.

"Let's get started then," she said determinedly, staring the man in the face, not being one to back down from a challenge, like the one written all over the condescending man's face.

Grady gave her a nod and smiled after her as she bravely left the two of them standing there, waving farewell when they called her back for her physical. He watched her long black ponytail sway back and forth as she walked in the back fearlessly, flashing one last smile at him as she turned, making his knees buckle. With that, the two men found a place outside to wait and make plans. It was a beautiful sunny day, and they sat down to lounge in the warmth of the sun.

"Are you going to be able to handle yourself man?" Rudy finally asked after they settled down in a grassy area outside the office, eyeing Grady intently as a father would eye a boy coming to take his daughter out on her first date.

"What are ya talkin' about?" Grady tried to sound nonchalant, but even as he did, it was obvious Rudy could see right through him when he saw the smirk on his face. "Yer the one who started this! We wouldn't be sittin' here waitin' for this mystery woman if ya hadn't opened yer big trap!" he added, trying to muster contempt of the situation that he didn't feel, and trying desperately to hide the smile that refused to leave his mouth. He was thrilled that the woman he had bumped into on the sidewalk earlier was inside; hopefully passing a test that would allow him to spend the next six weeks with her. He hadn't been able to get her out of his mind since their chance encounter on the sidewalk.

"Don't even try it man. I saw the way you two looked at each other, and I don't blame you one bit. In fact, I swear to you man, if you don't go after this woman, I will leave my wife here and now, abandoning children and all the rest to take your place!" he said with a smile, both of them knowing the ever-faithful Rudy would never leave his wife, and would likely end his own life before abandoning his children.

"All I'm asking is that you keep your head through the competition, and maybe wait until afterwards to make your move," Rudy said with more seriousness. "We've got a lot riding on this, and I could really use the money from the winnings." He looked up at Grady from the sprawled out position he found himself in on the grass, enjoying the rare warmth of the Alaskan sun.

Grady and Rudy had both been in the military, and simply being a civilian had proven to be the greatest challenge of their lives. Grady was a former U.S. Army Sniper, having been honorably discharged after recovering from battle wounds that nearly took his life. At the young age of twenty-eight, Grady's military career had ended long before he expected it to, and without a family to tie him down, he had no idea what he wanted to do with the rest of his life. He had earned a bachelor's degree in mechanical engineering as part of the Army R.O.T.C. program through the South Dakota School of Mines, and always had a field to fall back on, but he was still mourning the long military career that he hoped for when he started. He was also systematically avoiding making a long-term commitment to work for his dad in his construction business back home.

Rudy on the other hand, had spent over twenty years in the military. He was a U.S. Navy Seal, and had spent his life serving his country. He was trying to find a way to give his family a more settled life. The winnings from the competition would go a long ways toward starting a business, and buying them a nice little home in the countryside where his wife longed to live.

"I'll keep my head. Ya don't have ta worry brother. I know how important this is ta ya, and I'll not let ya down," Grady said with all seriousness, all the while trying to suppress the memory of those little red lips that had taken up residence in his mind.

Grady did know how important it was for Rudy, as the man was married to Grady's sister. He was a late baby, but even with thirteen years between him and his older sister, they were especially close, and he loved her with a ferociousness that was hard to match. He remembered the smell of her when she would rock him gently after he skinned a knee, or when he broke his arm jumping out of a tree. He remembered the way she would read a book to him, with such excitement and animation that he could practically feel himself being magically transported onto the pages, like an active character in the story.

He remembered when Rudy came along. Grady was about seven, and all of the sudden, a stranger was occupying that special space in time that his sister had reserved only for him. He hated him immediately, but that hatred didn't last very long. Rudy won him over quickly, and Grady worshipped the ground he walked on, modeling every aspect of his life after the man. Rudy was a rare gem, and certainly one of the most-honorable men he had ever known, second only to his own father.

His sister was lucky to have him, and he knew damn well he was lucky to have her. She was chased by every man within a five-hundred-mile radius of their home in South Dakota. Diana was her name, and she was often compared to the late Princess Diana, and not only because they shared the same name. Diana was strikingly beautiful. She was tall, blond, and blue-eyed, and had that constant look of innocence that Lady Di always seemed to have.

Diana never wanted to leave home, but she couldn't resist the dark haired Rudy, dripping with so much charm, she found herself on a plane bound for one post after another, following him wherever the Navy sent him, and giving birth to six children along the way. They met at a military ball, and it was love at first sight, but Rudy had promised to take her home one day and settle down, and it was time to make good on that promise. He was determined to give her the home she wanted, and Grady was there to help him do it.

Grady didn't even care about the money, he was just after the adrenaline rush that he constantly chased, but Rudy, being the man that he was, had insisted they all split the money equally if they should win. That's why Grady loved the man. He always did the right thing no matter what it cost him. Right was right, and wrong was wrong. There wasn't a lot of grey area where Rudy was concerned. He wasn't going to take something that wasn't his fair share.

It was Grady that had stumbled across the Alaskan Wilderness Competition while casually searching the internet one night, looking for something dangerous and hair-raising to do. He'd gone back home to help run his father's construction company, but it was seriously lacking in the exhilaration that Grady had come to expect from his career in the military, and the thought of doing something like that was exciting. When he brought it up to Rudy, he jumped on it immediately, knowing he would need to make some money to keep his promise to his wife.

As the team leader, Grady was no dummy, and he knew he would need to defer to Rudy at times, and take advantage of his vast survival experience. Grady himself was no slouch when it came to survival, having spent two years in Afghanistan and another two years in Iraq, and a total of ten years in the military, but the expertise of a twenty-year veteran was something he knew would be an invaluable asset.

Jared was also ex-military, and the vast experience he acquired in his twelve years in the Marines would have made their team unbeatable. *How would Jewel fit into the picture?* Grady had wondered. She had spent just two years in Iraq, in the relative peace of an Army hospital, not that it didn't come with its own challenges. She hadn't been on the frontlines of war, but certainly, she had fought for the lives of so many others, just as they all did, and that said a lot about her.

Jewel was all they had, and she would have to do. They were quite possibly back in the competition, and he smiled with hope for the first time since seeing Jared's 104-degree temperature on the thermometer at the hospital. Of course, she hadn't passed the physical yet, and he didn't want to get his hopes up.

CHAPTER 4

A TEAM IS BORN

The application had been easy enough, and the physical was laughable at best. *The competition could learn a thing or two from the U.S. Army when it comes to putting someone through a test of physical endurance,* Jewel thought when she redressed herself after showering. Next to boot camp, the endurance test had been easy, lifting small objects, and carrying and pushing them around. Jewel passed the physical with ease, swimming, running, dodging, and enduring a torture chamber of extreme cold that had been nothing compared to the ice-cold winds of the high plains of Wyoming. The climbing had been the only thing that really challenged her, but that's only because she had never been rock climbing or repelling before, and she was still feeling the effects of drinking too much beer. She caught on quickly though, and the instructor was impressed when she told him she'd never done if before, and he passed her without hesitation.

Jewel was used to the look of surprise people got when they realized she wasn't as fragile as she looked, and she smiled to herself when she signed her name as the third member of The Military Team for the competition.

"I'm in!" she ran out excitedly, giving Grady and Rudy both high fives, and hugging them both without a second thought, the camaraderie and friendship already taking shape, with one hug lingering a bit longer than the other. She was surprisingly comfortable around the two men she'd just met. Maybe it was because of their shared military experience. Jewel couldn't quite put her finger on it, but she trusted her instinct. She had a keen sense of reading people, knowing who to trust, and not trust, was something built in her that had never steered her wrong. She felt safe with them, and the three of them quickly fell into an easy friendship.

"Now what?" she asked, looking up at Grady and Rudy with her hands on her hips, not really sure exactly what she had gotten herself into, but excited nonetheless.

The excitement that was coming from Grady and Rudy was more certain, having gone from not being in the competition to having a solid team again, and... it was a solid team, Grady had thought to himself. He could clearly see that the ease at which she passed the physical said something about her strength. His own physical had taken a bit longer than hers had, as the running took its toll on the part of his back that had taken the brunt force of the shrapnel he caught in Afghanistan.

"Well, first things first," Grady said, "let's go get a bite ta eat, and have a team meetin'." He took the lead, and tried hard to resist the urge to put his hand on the small of her back to guide her toward the restaurant across the street, the way he would if he were on a date.

"A quiet table for three please," he said as the waitress grabbed a few menus, and led them to a circular booth toward the back of the restaurant.

"Can I just say one thing right off the bat, and then I'll shut up, and let you lead the meeting Grady. I just want to be clear about this. Jared getting sick and Jewel coming on doesn't change how I feel. We split the money equally if we win," Rudy said absolutely. Jewel could see he was a very passionate man with clear objectives. He saw excitement in everything, but he would only participate in something if it lived up to his moral code.

"Money?" Jewel said, smiling at Rudy's excitement. "I didn't know there was a prize. I guess I assumed it was just bragging rights we were after, being ex-military as we all are. It's not like we did that because we wanted to get rich, right?"

"True enough," Grady joined in, "but Rudy here has gone and produced more than his fair share of off-spring, and has a beautiful wife at home ta keep fed, which is no small feat, let me tell ya. I've seen the girl eat enough ta shame a grown man."

"You two must be good friends then?" she asked settling in, giving Grady a warm look, eager to listen to him speak.

"He's my brother-in-law," Grady said, looking at Rudy, "and the best man I know, second only ta my own father, and that's only because the man gave me life. You'll know him ta be fair and honest, and he'll not take yer share of the earnins' no matter what ya have ta say, so you'll just have ta accept it and move on." He leaned back in the booth, spreading his arms out, resting them on top, and easily taking up the full length.

Jewel watched him, and she could barely speak the words caught up in the back of her head. "Uh, what is the prize then?" she stuttered, shifting her eyes away from him, trying to hide a blush that was threatening to reveal her thoughts.

"It's exactly zero if the two of you don't get ahold of yourself," Rudy chided. "Christ it's like I'm sitting here with my sixteen-year-old daughter and her boyfriend, knowing the second I turn my back, the hormone induced beasts are going to devour each other," he said laughing, but also quite serious. "The two of you need to make a decision. The last thing we need to deal with is romantic complications. I swear to you. I've seen it happen. I'm all for women serving in all aspects of everything, but if people don't keep the romance separate, it causes problems."

And with that, Jewel lost control of the blush that finally consumed her, and Grady was losing his own battle.

"Look," Grady said after contemplating what Rudy said for several moments, leaning forward on the table as if to confide his deepest secrets to the two of them, "clearly the woman is mad for me. I've known it since she first accosted me on the street," he said with an upturned smirk, "but we are a team, and we'll not put the team in jeopardy. Do ya think ya can keep yer hands ta yerself woman?" he joked, looking at her with a half-smile, trying to resist the urge to grab her and kiss her even as he swore to keep his distance.

"I think I'll manage," she laughed, all the while trying not to look into Grady's eyes. *What color of blue is that exactly?*

An awkward silence descended upon the three of them, as Rudy eyed them suspiciously, and Grady and Jewel fidgeted in their seats like two chastened children, trying to avoid eye contact.

"All right then," Rudy said, giving them both a suspicious look and a crooked smile. "Neither of you have ever given me a reason not to trust you," he said looking at Grady, "so, I'll take your word for it."

"The prize is twenty-five thousand dollars each," Rudy finally said, apparently satisfied with their response, leaning over to give Jewel a friendly hug, not at all convinced that they'll be able to maintain their distance from each other. He knew Grady was very logical, and he was honest to a fault. He knew he wouldn't do anything to jeopardize their chances.

"Wow!" Jewel said excitedly, "maybe it's time you guys explained the details of this competition. I had no idea," she suddenly started feeling a little scared, worried that she may be in over her head with such a large amount of money on the line.

"It's goin' ta be challengin'," Grady said with a stone cold look of seriousness, "yer goin' ta be cold and tired probably every day. You'll go hungry some days, and you'll want ta quit a few times before it's over. You'll be climbin' some of the toughest peaks in Alaska, sleepin' with one eye open, lest a bear decide ta invade our camp. You'll be wet, dirty, covered in mud, and layin' in clothes that haven't been washed in weeks. Yer hair will be dirty, you'll be squattin' in the backwoods ta do yer business, and you'll not have an ounce of humility left when yer finally rid of the two of us, and that's sugar coatin' it!" he said dramatically, trying to get a sense of her by watching her reaction.

She never flinched though. Everything he'd said she took in casually, as if it were nothing too unusual. What he described was just another day on the ranch she'd grown up on, and she didn't really see it as anything too out of the ordinary. If he had told her he was going to drop her off in New York City to make her way to a place twenty or thirty miles away, she would have been absolutely terrified, but what he described was something she felt comfortable doing.

He watched her carefully as he described vile conditions, and there was no reaction from her whatsoever except when he talked about the cold. She was a little afraid of being cold, and he must have caught that reaction from her, because he made a mental note to make sure to help her prepare for cold conditions.

As she sat there listening to his speech, Jewel could clearly see who the two men were, what they meant to each other, and she knew she didn't want to let them down. She'd climbed mountains, and endured the cold while trailing sheep, and froze her tail off night after night, camped in the Wyoming Rockies. This would be different though. It would be all that and more, and the two men's livelihoods were going to depend on her, a position she'd never been in before.

She knew twenty-five thousand dollars would go a long ways toward paying off the Landas family, to give Troy his freedom from her and her family's ranch. She also knew it was only a matter of time before he demanded his fair share, and she was forced to come up with the money. *I'm sure Jolene would appreciate moving away from me,* she thought, *though Troy will be lost to me forever, but I guess he already is,* she thought with a twinge of sadness, missing the brother she once had.

They ordered their meals, and they each sipped a beer, quietly contemplating the words and the magnitude of everything Grady had just laid out for them. No matter what you've endured in the past, the future was not guaranteed, and they all understood that very well. They could all find their breaking point, and they each prayed it would not find them over the next six weeks.

The competition started in just a few days, and they didn't have long to get all the gear Jewel would need. The thought had crossed Grady's mind to ask Jared if she could use his gear for Jewel, but he didn't feel right asking him, especially after he was already feeling the sting of having to quit the competition. They would have to do their best to gather everything she needed with what they could buy from the locals.

"Let's head back ta the room, take stock of what we have, and make a list of what we'll need. After that, we'll call it a night, and get tagether in the mornin' first thing ta go on a scavenger hunt, and see what we can outfit the lady with," Grady said, clearly having come up with a plan of attack while he ate. "Jared's wife is meetin' us at the hotel later to collect his things, and I'll want ta go see him one last time before we head out."

It was easy to see why Grady was the leader of the team. While Rudy had more experience, and a good fifteen years on Grady, Grady had a natural ability to lead, and he could clearly see the finish line, and all that was required to get there, long before most people could see the starting line. Rudy was more of a doer, Jewel sensed. Once you put him to a task, you didn't have to think twice about it. He would not only complete it, he would do it in a way that put most other men to shame.

With a leader like Grady, a person like Rudy who could do damn near anything, she thought they might actually have a chance of winning, *provided, of course, I don't screw up,* she thought as she tossed and turned later that night before finally drifting off to sleep, long past the hour when she should have.

CHAPTER 5

A SCAVENGER HUNT

Jewel had always been an early riser, but she was still a little surprised to find Grady banging on her door at six in the morning. How many hours of sleep had she gotten? *Four or maybe five hours?* she thought with a haze, still longing for more sleep as she got up to answer the door without even thinking about it, before remembering that she was wearing nothing more than a long t-shirt and underwear.

"Are ya ready ta head out?" Grady asked completely dazzled by her messed up morning hair and her long, bare legs.

"Are you mad?" she asked as more of an accusation than a question, as she rubbed sleep from her eyes and yawned uncontrollably.

"Time's a wastin', and I don't want ya ta get out there and be unprepared. We'll have breakfast and then find what ya need. You'll be needin' a few things ta get ya through it, and you'll have ta pack a few things that will be needed by us all. We had it all planned out for months between Rudy, Jared and myself, and now we have barely a day ta get everything you'll need ta fill the gap. I just hope you'll be able ta carry as much as we need," he said looking at her small frame doubtfully, but with a certain amount of appreciation, albeit not in a way that helped the situation.

"Ok, well, come in then," she said sarcastically, inviting him inside unnecessarily since he had already helped himself. "Have a seat and give me a few minutes to get dressed and brush my teeth… if you think we could spare fifteen minutes," she said taking a jab at his sense of urgency.

"Well, I can't have ya runnin' around half-naked, though it may be an interestin' strategy ta distract the competition if ya thought ya'd be up for it tomorrow as we head out," he said cheerfully, with more happiness than she'd seen from him since they first met.

She closed the door to the bathroom, quickly running her fingers through her long hair, pulling it up in a ponytail. With her teeth brushed, and after having gotten fully dressed, she was ready to go. She walked out of the bathroom, and Grady stood there looking at her completely speechless, wondering how he would survive the pain of not reaching out to kiss her for even five more minutes, let alone six weeks. With her hair pulled back, her eyes shined all the more brighter, and she was dressed casually in jeans and a tank top before pulling on a fleece pullover and lacing up her hiking boots.

"I've got a list," Grady finally stuttered, holding it up like a white flag of surrender. "Rudy will be out gettin' ya a pack, and a few other things he saw when we were hikin' though the outskirts of town the other day. Are there items you'll need or want that aren't on this list?" he asked, trying to stay focused on the task.

Jewel scanned through the list, surprised at the extent of just how thorough it was, complete with sanitary napkins. When she read that, she looked up at Grady, who was peering over her shoulder, and gave him a smile. "You do think of everything don't you," she said impressed, but still a little embarrassed.

"Ya don't have ta be embarrassed. It's part of life. I've known that since I was a small boy when I first commandeered my sister's box of them ta line my football helmet with. Why, all the other boys were so impressed with the softness of them, having endured bumps, and rashes, I had ta go in search of more of them ta line all our helmets with. They were so handy with the sticky side, that ya could get them all in there just right, but ya can only imagine the coaches' surprise when they found all our helmets lined with sanitary napkins," he said laughing, talking as they left the hotel, heading out to grab breakfast before getting Jewel's gear.

"What did he say when he finally saw them?" she asked laughing.

"Well, our coach was actually a woman, and bein' so, I think she did the only thing she could do, which was ta praise us for our ingenuity, explain their real purpose, and promise ta supply more if we were still interested," he said smiling, clearly impressed by his coaches logic. "Of course, we were all too proud ta continue usin' them, despite the fact that they were the softest head pads available. No! Boys bein' the way they are, we all decided ta endure the pain, rather than admit the need of sanitary napkins."

"There are a few things that aren't on your list that I'm going to need," she said quietly, not wanting to interrupt the memory Grady was caught up in, but also not wanting to forget to mention the items she needed.

"Oh? What is it then?" he asked, surprised that he would have forgotten something after having been up half the night making sure everything was accounted for.

"I am a nurse, and there are things I need to make sure I can do my job if something should happen. I'll need some medicines that I already have in my kit, some more sutures, needles, gauze and bandages, and other things along those lines," she said, looking up at him.

"They have medics with the crew Jewel. They'll have everything ya need there, and more," he said carefully. "We'll need ta carry as little as possible, and only take what we have ta."

"I'm not leaving without those things," she said indignantly, putting her hands on her hips as she did.

Clearly, the determined look on her face told him he was in a losing battle, and they would be taking the items she wanted.

"Well, if it's that important ta ya then I'll not argue with ya, but it may mean you'll have a heavier pack than I intended," he said relenting.

"The medics will only be at the start and the finish of each leg if I read the rules correctly. Wouldn't it be an advantage to have someone who could stitch up a wound if needs be?" she asked, knowing that each leg put them out in the wilderness for three to five days each.

"Yer right. Ya've a valuable skill, and we'd be fools not ta be prepared ta take advantage of it," he said. "It's my greatest weakness. I'm always optimistically thinkin' my crew will never be hurt, even though this has proven ta not be the case on many a journey."

"Really? Many journeys? Are you completely accident prone, or should I be expecting you to put me in lots of dangerous situations?" she teased, flirting despite her best efforts not to.

"Well, ya can't help but find danger in the Middle East. We're not exactly popular there with certain groups, but yes, ya can expect a certain amount of danger. I'll keep ya safe though," he said flirting in return, resisting the urge to wrap an arm around her as he smiled down at her.

Jewel couldn't say as she was completely convinced, but the thought of him trying to protect her and keep her safe was an appealing thought, and it reminded her of the dream she'd had in the few hours she'd actually slept the night before. She smiled at the thought as they continued on their way, finding bits and pieces of what they needed in various places.

The town they were in could barely be described as a one-horse town. They searched through a thrift store, a country store that had everything from a radiator hose to gourmet baby food stocked on its shelves, and several old antique stores, which seemed to be the perfect place to find tools needed to survive in an Alaskan wilderness.

She was pleased to find that Grady had included a rifle, and a handgun on her list of things she needed. These were going to be the other items that she was going to vehemently argue for had they not been on the list. She had a rifle that had been given to her by her father when she turned ten, and she wasn't about to go hiking through bear country without it. It had been in storage during her time in Iraq, and on top of that, she had a pistol that she'd bought before her camping expedition a few weeks earlier, and it proved to be a comfort to her as she made her way through the wilderness. Grady had been a bit surprised when she pulled firearms out of their hiding place beside her bed earlier, but she could see he was also relieved to check something off their list so easily. Those might have been the things they would have had to ask Jared if they could borrow, and he hadn't really wanted to.

"Do ya know how ta use that thing?" he had asked with surprise, clearly not expecting her to have a rifle stored beside her bed as she pulled it out to show it to him.

"Of course," she said, "this thing is nearly an extension of my arm I've had it so long and used it so much. My father, my grandfather, and other friends we knew would take me and my friend Troy hunting all the time. We truly lived off our land. Not a conventional way to raise a girl, but not unusual for Wyoming. I'm sure it must be the same in South Dakota. Isn't that where you said you were from?" she had asked gazing up, admiring the man beside her.

"It is. It's just that, well ya look so tiny next ta it, the stock of it bein' slightly bigger around than yer actual arm," he stumbled, smiling despite himself. "I'd think that thing would kick ya ta heaven and back again," he said, not wanting to insult her, and trying to suppress the urge to feel protective of her, just as she said always happens when men and women are teamed up.

"It's the great equalizer. How tough do you have to be to pull a trigger?" she had said, shrugging at him like that should be completely obvious. He couldn't really argue with her on that point. She had a way of making him completely speechless.

They had spent the day together, going from one store to another, stopping only long enough to have a quick sandwich for lunch, laughing, and talking the whole time. There was an obvious spark between the two of them, and flirting with each other would have been impossible to resist, though they did manage to stay focused enough to make sure they got the items they needed.

"Let's drop off all this stuff at the hotel, and then we'll meet up with Rudy for an early dinner," he said after they checked the last item she needed off their list.

It was just before dinner when Grady and Jewel finally met up with Rudy. After they grabbed some dinner, they headed up to Jewel's room to get all her stuff. She had anticipated having one more night to sleep in her warm bed, but the logic of getting her checked out of there, and having all her remaining items safely stored with Grady and Rudy's stuff before they started out, was undeniable.

Jewel noticed right away that Grady was always a few steps ahead when it came to planning things out. It was as if this magical path appeared before him, clearly showing him options and possible outcomes, much like a road map would. It wasn't a road map though, it was just a brief moment of quiet, and what sprung from that moment was a plan much like a mathematical equation with an undeniable conclusion, though often difficult for mere mortals to grasp at that speed. *The logical decision*, Jewel thought, *was to just do as the man said*, though she'd not let him know that she thought so.

Still, she'd be sharing a room with two strange men she'd just met a day ago. *Am I a fool?* she wondered as she packed her belongings up in her duffle bag. *Should I take off running and never look back? How in the world did I get in this situation?* Just as she felt those thoughts might actually consume her and send her into a panic, she caught site of the man. She looked at him with his back turned to her as he looked out the window thoughtfully, arms stretched up high, resting above the windowpane. She could see the defined muscles outlined through his shirt, and had to resist the urge to reach out and touch him.

Somehow, she just knew who he was... a man of honor defending his country, a brother, a brother-in-law, a friend, and a son. *Surely, I'm safe. If I weren't, wouldn't I be in danger at this very moment? If he was going to hurt me, why didn't he do it right now? We are, after all, alone,* and just then, as if reading her mind, "You'll have no need ta worry about Rudy or me. We'll give ya yer privacy, we'll respect yer space, and we'll defend ya ta the dyin' end. Don't ever fear either one of us," and with that, he turned and looked at her with a seriousness she knew was a promise.

She didn't speak. Words wouldn't have been adequate. She simply met his eyes and accepted his promise, never once taking her eyes off his. For the rest of her life she'd never be able to fully explain how much was said in that brief moment of silence, and just as it threatened to become too much for either one of them, Rudy came in bounding with newfound energy and excitement.

"Fifteen hours from now lady and gentleman! In fifteen hours, we'll be setting off on a life changing adventure, surviving off the land, climbing unimaginable peaks, and crossing icy rivers. I've dreamed about Alaska my whole life! Thank you man," Rudy said, turning toward his brother-in-law, grabbing him for a hug.

"Let's just see if ya still want ta thank me in a few weeks brother," he said smiling and returning the hug. You and Jewel will both want ta have me put ta a firin' squad by then, and I'll need ta kindly remind ya of this moment."

The conversation and excitement waned as they each fell into silence, contemplating their own roles over the next six weeks. Gathering up the rest of Jewel's belongings, and lugging them over to where Rudy and Grady were staying, they each silently prayed for the strength it would take to win the competition. Jewel was glad not to have to be going home for at least the next six weeks. She knew she was once again just stalling, but she was glad for it. She was at a complete loss on what she was going to do once she got back home. She was a young woman who was likely going to be one hundred percent responsible for a huge ranch, and she had no idea how she was going to be able to handle everything on her own. She knew the ranch inside and out, and she knew what needed to be done, but the idea of taking the weight of it on was so overwhelming she couldn't face it.

She was terrified that Troy would never forgive her. At least while she was away she could pretend she had a chance of being forgiven, even though she knew in her heart that she didn't deserve it. Once she faced him, everything would be done. If he walked away, it would be forever. She was certain he would want to take Jolene and leave forever, and she didn't know how she would be able to survive that. She also knew it wasn't fair of her to expect Troy and his family to stay there and take care of her responsibilities, but she managed to convince herself that her Godparents, which were Troy's mom and dad, would want to do it out of loyalty to her parents and grandparents. *What else would they do?*

Anna and Diego Landas, Troy's parents, were two of the greatest people she has ever known. They tried to step in as acting parents for her after her own parents died, but they were lost in their own grief, and Jewel pushed them away when they tried to take her parents place. Diego and her dad, Alex, had grown up together and were best friends. Anna had been an exchange student from Rome, Italy in her senior year of high school when she first met Diego, and after going back home and exchanging cards and letters for six months, he convinced her to come back and marry him. Anna had grown up in a big city, and she was relieved when Alex showed up one day with a woman from Denver. Anna and Ellie had a lot in common, and they hit it off immediately. They would reminisce about the things they missed about living in the city, even though they both truly loved living out on the ranch, and took to it quite naturally. When Ellie came along, a bond developed between the four of them, and they did absolutely everything together. It was really hard on Anna and Diego when her parents died, and that was something she could understand.

She missed them, and smiled when she thought of them, catching herself as she did, remembering that she wasn't alone in the room, but she looked up and could see that Grady and Rudy seemed lost in their own thoughts, and the rest of the evening passed with a careful quiet, each one fighting their own battles inside. They packed their gear, took one final hot shower, stowed away the items they were leaving behind, and finally fell asleep, anxiously awaiting the adventure before them.

CHAPTER 6

THE TEAMS

The morning came far too early, but Jewel wasn't surprised to see that Grady was already awake, as she slowly propped herself up on one elbow, not yet ready to leave the warmth and comfort of a bed, the likes of which she wouldn't be enjoying for a month and a half. Rudy was still sleeping soundly in the other bed, and Jewel could still see Grady's outline in the space next to him where he had slept, indicating that he hadn't been up long.

"What time is it?" she asked sleepily from the other bed where she had slept, looking over at him where he sat drinking his coffee, looking out the window.

"It's just now five o'clock. I'm sorry if I woke ya. We don't have ta be down at the docks until eight, though I'd like ta get there a little early."

"You didn't wake me," she whispered, but it was the feeling of someone looking at her that had stirred her awake, and they both knew it.

"Ya looked like an angel lyin' there sleepin'," he whispered, walking over to where she was propped up, gently sitting down beside her. "I was sittin' here wonderin' just what I'm askin' of ya, and wonderin' if it was simply for selfish reasons that I'd gone along with it."

"Don't we all have our own selfish reasons for being here?" she asked as more of a statement than a question, meeting his eyes.

"I just want ya ta know that if ya have any reservations, we'd not blame ya for backin' out. Rudy and I talked last night, and I wanted ta make sure ya know that. This all happened so fast, we were afraid that ya might feel like ya'd been scooped up on a runaway train before ya knew what hit ya, and didn't know how ta get off... well... if ya wanted off, and I just... well... if ya need ta get off, we'd understand. That's all. I just wanted ya ta know that," he said looking at her, searching her face for answers, afraid she might take the out he was giving her.

"Thanks Grady. I appreciate you giving me an out. I do feel like I'm on a runaway train, but it's not an altogether unpleasant experience. The thing is, I have nowhere else to go right now, I mean... I do have somewhere to go... I just don't *want* to go there just yet. This feels right, not that the thought of disappearing in the middle of the night hadn't crossed my mind a time or two," she said looking up at him with a smile.

"I'll go if you'll still have me, and I'll do my part. You don't have to worry about me. I can take care of myself Grady, but I do appreciate the concern. I'm not used to people worrying about me, but... I guess it's kind of nice actually," she trailed off looking out into nowhere, remembering what it felt like to have the love of her family, and Troy, now all gone.

"Of course we'll have ya," he said relieved, giving her a warm look.

He sat on the bed with her a moment longer and wondered how it was possible she could be there alone, without a family worrying about her back home. He hoped to find these things out about her, but for the moment, he was just happy to have her there, shrouded in mystery or not.

He got up and poured an extra cup of coffee before sitting back down beside her on the bed, handing it to her. She sat up in bed, and the two of them talked quietly for a while longer. The attraction between the two was undeniable, and they both knew it. They had a very comfortable and natural rapport, and they enjoyed the early morning companionship, stopping only when Rudy got up, and made his way to the bathroom for a final shower.

Jewel also couldn't help but take one last opportunity in the shower, lingering a little longer than usual, though feeling a little anxious to get started. She could still feel the warmth of it on her skin as the three of them made their way down to the docks where they would board a helicopter to take them to a remote Alaskan wilderness they'd have to fight to survive.

It was a competition between three teams of three people each. There was The Military Team, The Alaska Team, and The Adventure Team. A helicopter would take all nine of them out, drop them off in the same place, and the teams would split up from there. They had three to five days, depending on which of the six legs they were on, up to five o'clock in the evening on the last day, to make their way to a destination shown on the map they were given. Each team would pick their own route, and whoever got to the destination first would win that leg of the competition. There would be six legs, and whoever won the most legs would win the grand prize of twenty-five thousand dollars per team member who finished. In the case of a three-way tie, the team who beat each deadline by the most accumulated time would be the winner. If your team didn't make the deadline, you were immediately disqualified from the whole competition.

In between each leg of the journey, they were given two to four days of downtime at a base camp that had been set up for them where they could regroup, hunt, and maybe even rest a bit before heading out on the next leg. All six weeks would be spent camping out, living on the meager beans and rice rations they were given, and subsisting on what they could hunt or fish. It was a game of survival, where only the fittest and the hardest working would survive the competition.

In all, there were seven men and two women. The Adventure Team consisted of an older world-class traveler/adventurer who had spent a few weeks every year going on a guided adventure, taking a break from the gridlock of the city where he lived. His name was Gary, and he reminded Jewel of the weekend warriors who came to Wyoming, flying in on their private jets for a long weekend, roughing it a bit before heading back to their luxury apartments in the city. Jewel was afraid this was going to be a bit of a challenge for the man, who confidently described himself as having thirty years of experience in the wilderness, despite his apparent lack of physical fitness.

The woman's name was Angela, she was pleasant, and Jewel liked her the moment she first introduced herself. She was relieved to find a warm smile on her face that came with a welcoming hug, and the two of them hit it off right away. She was a beautiful, middle-aged woman of about fifty-five, and she had a lot of experience living a subsistence lifestyle. She had been a professor at Arizona State University, before starting her own survivalist training school near her underground home where she lived in the most remote part of the Sonoran Desert.

The leader of the team was a very gregarious and deliberate man. He was anything but reserved and soft-spoken, and had an air about him that didn't leave any doubt that he was in charge. His name was Joe, and he introduced himself saying, "My name is Joe, but you can just call me Joe," he'd said laughing and endearing himself to everyone. He had spent his life gold mining, diamond mining, and chasing one crazy dream after another without a seconds thought. While this adventure was a chance of a lifetime for most people, to Joe, it would be just another blip on life's radar. He was tall and handsome, and reminded Jewel of John Wayne's character when he played George Washington McClintock, one of her favorite movies of all time.

The Alaska Team consisted of two brothers in their early twenties, and a young man of twenty-one years old named Aaron, who had grown up off the grid in the backwoods of Alaska. Jewel was happy when she found out she wasn't the youngest one out of the nine of them, though she wasn't exactly sure why he felt it was necessary to tell everyone his age when he introduced himself.

The brothers were Todd and Mark, and they had spent most of their young lives on the Bering Sea working as commercial fishermen where they met Aaron. They were there hoping to win the money to save their families fishing boat from a near certain bank seizure, due to an especially difficult fishing season the year before. The mere thought of fishing on the Bering Sea was enough to make Jewel shiver. She couldn't imagine a rougher or more brutal life, and though she thought they may be lacking in survivalist skill, she knew their ability to endure extreme conditions would make them a strong team. They were a quiet, methodical trio, and Jewel liked the brothers immediately, but there was something about Aaron that gave her an uneasy feeling, and she decided right away to keep her distance from him as much as possible.

She could see Grady and Rudy sizing up their competition, as she herself did, and she knew the other teams would be doing the same as they introduced themselves. It was clear that the other teams found the experience of a well-disciplined military team a bit intimidating, all of them eyeing Jewel suspiciously, as her meager frame seemed barely large enough to carry the gear on her back. It was a doubtful look that she had seen all too often, and she accepted it with pleasure. She knew what she was capable of, and she knew they'd be surprised to find out what that was. They had the same look on their faces her drill sergeant had when she showed up in boot camp. She didn't know it at the time, but all the officers had picked her as the most likely to dropout, and she understood why, and relished the look on people's faces when she would surprise them as she usually did.

They did look a bit intimidating Jewel thought, looking the men over and catching a glimpse of herself in the mirror before leaving the room earlier. While not donning the more obvious camouflage that you would expect from the military, they were decked-out in military style survival gear. They were ready with all-weather layering, and water repellent material. They had multi-pocketed pants, and coats full of various survival implements complete with rifles, shotguns and a few handguns strapped to their backs and hips. The gaiters were a necessary touch that added to their menacing appearance, and would certainly come in handy when hiking through heavy brush, icy water, and mud and muck. Jewel completed the look by putting her long hair in a single braid, and wearing a black wool beanie hat she'd bought for each of them at the country store the day before. Decked out in dark greens and blacks, the three of them could clearly see the mental warfare had the intended effect on the other teams when they walked toward them on the docks.

Just as the introductions were finishing up, it was time to board the helicopter that would take them to the start of their first leg. They loaded up all their packs, and the nine of them climbed in for the journey ahead. It was perhaps the most beautiful experience of Jewels life, having taken the window seat where Grady could easily lean in over her to peek out. The view was breathtaking, and they could see the beautiful and rugged terrain below. She couldn't decide what was more exciting, the journey ahead, or the man pressed up beside her.

CHAPTER 7

THE FIRST LEG

The first leg of their journey started near Lookout Mountain where they would methodically make their way through the rugged, snowcapped mountains, to a destination nearly one hundred miles away. Once they reached the spot on the map, they would be picked up, and taken to a base camp for two days before heading out on the next leg. Having already started out relatively late in the morning, each team was eager to get a start to put some miles behind them.

They were given their maps after landing, and it was clear The Military Team had a slight advantage in getting a quick start, with Grady and Rudy being experts when it came to quickly navigating through hostile country. Their military training included some of the most extensive navigation astuteness imaginable, and it wasn't just theory. These two men had been put to the test in the front lines of war, and lived to tell about it. They both had a quick grasp of the map, and could easily see the most direct route, with the least amount of obstacles and risk to the team. Before Jewel had a chance to find true north on her pocket compass, the two of them had devised a plan, and were ready to start heading in that direction.

It wasn't long before Jewel realized that the long strides of the two men were going to be a challenge, but not being one to fall behind, she quickly caught up and found that pace. The two men had already decided she'd fall-in between the two of them in their military-style, single-file hike. *I suppose men just can't help themselves,* she thought, and after looking out at the vast, wild land that was splayed out menacingly before her, she wasn't the least bit disappointed that the two men felt a need to keep her safe. She couldn't imagine being with a pair of men more capable than the two she was with, and she was thankful for their protective instincts.

She smiled at the strange situation where she found herself. Just a few days earlier, she was looking toward her immediate future with trepidation. She had wondered if she should go back and face Troy and Jolene. She wondered how Jolene would treat her, and she wondered if it would be fair to Jolene to insert herself into the lives of two newlyweds, knowing how Troy felt about her. She didn't know what to expect from Troy. He poured his heart out to her, and she turned and ran away. He didn't deserve that, and a flush of red shame crept up in her face when she thought of it once again.

The invitation she got to his wedding had been a surprise, and had gone completely unanswered. She didn't know what to think of it. Part of her had been relieved to know that his life didn't stop the day she left, but another part was sad that it hadn't. They had planned a life together, or rather, their lives had been planned out together by other people. She could remember from a very young age, their moms planning their wedding, and rolling the name Jewel Landas around on their tongues. It wasn't a life she necessarily wanted, but it was still a life, and I guess a part of her mourned that life that would never be. I suppose there was a part of her that felt guilty for not fulfilling her duty to marry the son of the man that saved her family's ranch. Perhaps she was even ashamed that she didn't marry the great-grandson of the man who had stood beside her own great-grandfather, all the way from the Old Country. She often felt she was ending something that was destined to happen… the two families that had lived and died together for generations were now separated because of her.

The only communication Troy and her had since her first few months at college had been the exchange of a few brief emails, before Jewel finally canceled her email account in an attempt to avoid it altogether, and pretend that it didn't affect her. Troy was always prodding her to give him the words that would decide the rest of her life, and Jewel was giving her answer by not responding at all. She had behaved very badly, and she ached when she thought of him, her oldest and closest friend whom she loved dearly. She couldn't remember a day that had gone by in the last four years, since she left the ranch, that she didn't think of something she wanted to share with him. *If only things could have stayed the way they were before he told me he loved me, and wanted to marry me.*

Why am I running? she wondered for the millionth time, finally knowing the answer for the first time since she first asked it, as she looked up to see the man in front of her. It was the not knowing about life, and it was confusion, and ignorance. Nobody had ever been there to tell her she would know the right man when she saw him, or to tell her about love. Everybody always told her that Troy *was* the right man, and I suppose there was a part of her that had accepted that, but there was a part within her telling her something different that she had never been able to decipher.

It wasn't until Grady ran her over in the middle of the street that she found a small portion of what may finally be an answer. It was a racing heart… a brief moment that made her palms sweat, and her pulse race. It was something she had never felt before. She suddenly wanted to be near someone again, rather than secluding herself. Was this what *knowing* meant? Was this that ill-defined logic that has nothing to do with thinking and reason, but of matters of the heart? She wasn't quite certain, but a piece of life's puzzle seemed to have found her, and she wasn't about to let him out of her sight.

There was the doctor in Iraq that had distracted her briefly, and provided her with some answers. He was beautiful with his tall, dark look that reminded her of her own father. He always talked about his wife and kids so fondly that she couldn't help but become completely infatuated with him. He was the consummate father and husband, and she imagined it was her married to him, and it quickly became her favorite fantasy. It was her first real crush. A feeling that had been lost to her through the grief of her teens, and a feeling that seemed to consume her friends as they obsessed over one guy after another, week after week.

One day, the doctor came to her, and the man she had imagined kissing a million times was finally offering himself up to her for the taking. The man that she worshipped because of his love and devotion to his family, was now willing to betray them for her, and it ended her infatuation with him immediately. After fawning over him for months, he was more than a little surprised when she turned him down. Clearly, he was used to getting his way, and he didn't take the rejection kindly. She blamed it on her Catholic upbringing, and he chastised her like a child, and refused to speak to her again.

The infatuation with the doctor only seemed to confuse her more though. She thought maybe she was only good at fantasy, and the moment it became reality, she would always run. Maybe she was destined for a lifetime of being alone, she thought, when she remembered the moment they shoveled dirt onto her parent's coffins. She had been so completely closed off since then, she wasn't even sure she was capable of loving another person. *Would I run the moment Grady showed interest in me?* she wondered. *Hadn't he already shown interest, and hadn't I immediately run toward him without hesitation? Perhaps there's hope for me after all,* she thought smiling to herself as they continued their hike.

After hours of hiking and getting lost in her thoughts, they reached the hilltop they had been climbing. The magnitude of the wilderness that showed itself before her, was caught up in her throat, and she was so taken in by it, she couldn't find words to speak. They were up high and could see snow-capped mountains up top, with green vegetation covering the lower terrain. There was color everywhere as spring flowers bloomed, and small bodies of water glistened when the sunlight hit it, still melting the winter ice and reflecting the blue sky. The magnitude of it was overwhelming.

Apparently, Grady and Rudy felt the same way, as the three of them stood there together in silence for a long time, looking out at the vastness, and the beauty of the landscape. While Jewel wasn't always the most religious person, having struggled with her faith since the death of her parents, the need to cross herself, and say a little prayer in thanks for this mountainous majesty, was more than she could resist.

After several minutes, it was Grady that finally spoke. "We need ta make our way down there near those trees ta set up camp for the night. There may even be some fish in that stream, and we can have ourselves a little protein ta get us started out right on the days ahead of us."

Even though it was still broad daylight out, it was near nine o'clock, and Grady suspected the other teams had long since bedded down for the night.

"It'll be near half an hour before we get there, and another hour before we can find our racks, but the head start is good for the soul, isn't it?" Grady asked, turning to look at Rudy and Jewel with a broad smile. Jewel could clearly see the man was in his element.

"It does feel good to be in the lead," Jewel said feeling happy and content to be right there in that moment, looking over to see the same happiness in Rudy.

They quickly headed out to what would be their camp for the night, and they each went to work. It was as if they had planned it all out, each naturally falling into a vital role, making preparations for them to eat and then bed down for the night in a makeshift shelter.

"I think I can build us a decent shelter using these trees," Jewel said, finding an area she felt would be her greatest way of contributing for the night.

"Great, I'll see if I can catch us a fish if ya could get us a fire started for the night," Grady said nodding toward Rudy, heading off in the direction of the stream.

Rudy had a talent when it came to getting a fire started, even in the worst possible conditions. With just a flint and a knife, he was able to get it started right away, despite the dampness around them, and he came over to lend a hand in getting the shelter put together. There was a pretty good chance of rain, and the shelter was very important for them. It could get pretty cold at night, and freezing to death in Alaska was always a threat.

"How are you feeling Jewel?" Rudy asked. "We kept a pretty hearty pace. I was impressed with how easily you kept up. Grady and I have hiked together a hundred times. Don't be afraid to speak up if we need to slow down a bit. We get in our habit and forget about anyone else. I don't want you burning out," he said sincerely, smiling at her warmly.

"Thanks Rudy. I feel fine though. I've spent much of my life hiking at higher elevations. The pace was fast, but it felt okay. Don't worry about me. I'm not afraid to speak up when I need to," she said returning the smile.

The two of them worked well together, and by the time Grady showed up carrying a couple of fish, the shelter was up, and Rudy and Jewel were sitting by the fire with Jewel laughing hysterically as Rudy told her a story.

"I was just telling Jewel here about the time when you streaked across the field after winning the state championship football game," Rudy said, as Grady walked up and sat beside them with a few dead fish.

"Were ya now?" Grady said laughing, remembering the moment. "One day I'll look back on that and really laugh, but the ass chewin' I got from my dad is still a little too fresh. Maybe another ten years or so," he said flashing them both a smile. "For now I'd like ta get these fish cleaned and ate, so we can catch some sleep and get an early start in the mornin', but... the two of ya did well taday," he said more to Jewel than Rudy. "We've got us a good team, an' I'm glad ta have ya both here."

The three ate, and then bedded down for the night, but it would prove to be a restless night for Jewel. The cold was her greatest weakness, and she looked at the two men enviously as they slept with relative ease. *Why do men always seem to have a built-in heater and women don't? It really isn't fair at all*, she thought as she laid there waiting for the sun to come up and warm her.

The next three days and nights would go much the same way, with the three of them hiking at a steady pace all day, and then bedding down for the night with fresh fish in their bellies. Each night Jewel found it difficult to sleep with the cold, and one morning she decided to get up long before it was time, so she could stoke the fire and warm herself up a little.

"Can ya not sleep Jewel?" Grady asked startling her.

"Sorry, I didn't mean to wake you. I'm just a little cold, and I'm having a hard time sleeping."

"Is that what kept ya from sleepin' the last few nights?"

Jewel, looking surprised, answered sheepishly with the affirmative. "Did I wake you up each night then?" she asked him, looking over her shoulder at him.

"I'm not much of a sleeper Jewel. That's how ya survive in a hostile country with hundreds of armed rebels eager ta kill ya or take ya hostage," he said looking over at her in the firelight. "For a moment I thought I was dreamin', and must have died and gone ta heaven. This bein' the first time I woke up thinkin' I was about ta be attacked and killed, only ta see a beautiful woman stokin' the fire." He laid back with a smile to gaze out at the stars, as if to savor the memory, "don't ever apologize for that."

"Why don't ya come lay between Grady and I?" Rudy said sitting up, looking at Jewel, longing to fall back to sleep and stop the chatter. "You're practically like a sister to me now Jewel. Come sleep between us, and I promise you'll not be molested. We can use our body heat to keep you warm," he said a little exasperated.

"Well, I definitely don't think of ya as a sister," Grady said smiling at her affectionately, "but ya need not worry about me. I'll keep my hands ta myself. Come lay between us and we'll keep ya warm so ya can get some sleep. Yer no good ta us sleep deprived."

"Alright then," she said, remembering the chill of the last two nights, but feeling a little shy to snuggle up to Grady so closely. The smile on the man's face didn't make it any easier, with her trying hard not to smile herself, but she could feel the warmth of the two men within minutes of lying between them, and she was thankful Rudy had suggested it.

She didn't feel at all shy about snuggling up next to Rudy. They had developed a sibling like bond, much like the one she had with Troy when they were younger. They had an easy relationship, and she never doubted that everything that came out of his mouth was the absolute truth, and could be counted on without a second thought. He constantly talked about his wife and kids, and she didn't have any doubt that he was devoted to them.

It was so much warmer to be mashed up between the two of them that Jewel could feel herself falling asleep pretty easily... warm, and content. Of course, sleeping by two large snoring men proved to have its own challenges, but *anything's better than being cold*, she thought as she fell into a deep sleep.

CHAPTER 8

BY THE RIVER

The next day proved to be more of a challenge for the team as they encountered what seemed to be an impassable river. They walked up stream for a long ways before finding a place to cross. Their plan was to cross, knowing they'd get wet, and then make camp on the other side, giving them the opportunity to get dry and warmed up before starting out again the next day. The threat of hypothermia was constant, and they'd have to plan it out carefully. Just a minute in the ice-cold river would be enough to send them into hypothermic shock. They were going to have to be very careful.

They agreed that it would be best to have Rudy go across first as he could get over there, and get a fire going right away, minimizing the time they would each be exposed to the elements without the warmth of a fire. They thought he might be able to shimmy over holding onto a branch that had fallen across the river, and get over there without getting wet at all. He'd take a long rope across with him that would allow him to pull Jewel and Grady over in their pack rafts.

Jewel would go next, attempting to be pulled across the river in the raft, but expecting to be dumped in the cold water as she was given strict instructions to guard Rudy's gear that he was leaving behind. At the very least, she'd be getting wet up to her knees, and she knew it was going to be a challenge for her to withstand the cold temperatures. The greatest risk was the dam of driftwood that was nearby. If the raft were to become caught in it, the swift current would pull it under, passenger and all, before anyone would have a chance to do anything.

Finally, Grady would be pulled over in his raft, and for this, Rudy and Jewel would both need to be on their toes, pulling as hard as they could to keep him from being washed down river, or taken under in the current. Grady was a large man, and it was going to be no small feat to pull him across, fighting the swift current, and the wind that seemed to be picking up.

The plan started out fine, with Rudy pulling himself hand over hand across the branch, nearly making it to the other side before the branch cracked and submersed him head to toe in the cold rushing water. There was a moment of panic as Jewel and Grady sat helplessly on the far bank, watching him struggle against the white water and rushing currents. Rudy was a strong swimmer though, and he managed to get himself to the other side in relative safety, thankful when he saw that the wind wasn't as bad on the other side of the river, as there was a natural shelter among the trees and some large rocks.

Freezing and shivering uncontrollably, Rudy quickly gathered what he needed to get a fire going, and warmed himself just barely long enough before getting ready for Jewel. Rudy had been hit hard in the shoulder, and had a fairly large gash after tumbling into the water with a large branch. Even from across the thirty or forty feet that separated them, Jewel could see the red stain seeping through Rudy's clothing. He stuffed his scarf inside his shirt to stop the blood before positioning himself on the bank to pull Jewel across. Having seen the blow Rudy took, Jewel wasn't feeling too good about putting herself completely in his hands to pull her across, but she also knew he wouldn't put her in any danger if he felt he wouldn't be able to continue.

"Don't worry about Rudy, Jewel. Two hands or one, you'll never find a more determined man. He wouldn't put ya in harm's way. If he thought he couldn't pull ya safely across, he'd signal ta me and we'd change course. You'll be safe," Grady said, reading her worried face before reaching up and touching her gently on the cheek.

"I know," she said unconvincingly. "It'll be okay. I don't see any other options, and I know he wouldn't put me in harm's way," she said with a little more determination, crossing herself nervously.

The pack raft worked well in getting Jewel and Rudy's gear safely across, once she got up the nerve to get in. It was the look of turmoil on Rudy's face that finally made her put her fears aside and climb in, throwing all caution to the wind. It seemed that the moment she got in and launched herself off the bank, the wind picked up harder than it had since they'd started off on day one, but as promised, Rudy pulled her across with just a little water up to her knees. Once she got her raft and gear pulled up near camp, she quickly readied herself to help get Grady across after checking on Rudy to make sure he was up to the task. Time was of the essence, as Rudy was wet and cold, starting to wear down, and she definitely wouldn't be able to pull Grady across by herself.

Jewel could see that the cold and the blow from the tree branch, had sapped Rudy's energy, and she had to dig deep within her to make sure Grady got across, giving it everything she had and then some. Grady and his pack combined weighed over three hundred pounds, but somehow Rudy and Jewel managed to get him across without incident. Rudy could have pulled him across with relative ease had it not been for his wounded shoulder and the severe cold that was fatiguing him.

With all three of them safely across, and nightfall approaching, they got to work, but Grady and Jewel insisted that Rudy climb in his sleeping bag to get warmed up while they finished setting up camp for the night. Jewel gave his shoulder a quick look to make sure it wasn't gushing blood, but decided to let his core temperature heat up before she took a closer look at it.

Grady built the fire up, and threw some flat rocks in there to get them hot. He was worried about Rudy, watching him shivering uncontrollably. He knew that the length of time he had been exposed to the cold was pushing the limits. The man never knew when to quit, and *that* was his greatest weakness. Hypothermia was their biggest threat in this region, and he needed to get Rudy warmed as quickly as possible. He cut back some of the mossy underbrush blanketing the riverbank, filled it full of the hot, flat rocks, and then covered it back up with the moss, creating a warm surface for Rudy to lie on near the fire. Within a few minutes of getting Rudy pulled up on top of the warm surface, he could see that his shivering was starting to subside.

After making sure Rudy was no longer in danger of hypothermia, Jewel and Grady let Rudy rest a while by the fire, and headed out to see what they would be able to catch for dinner. Grady was a master when it came to catching fish, so he headed downstream looking for a fishing hole while Jewel headed up the hill with Rudy's shotgun to see if she could find a squirrel or other small game. With the threat of bear always present, Jewel cautiously made her way further up into the canopy of the trees, checking the pistol she always wore strapped to her side, as more of a way to scare a bear off than for protection.

It wasn't long before she came across the very thing she was hoping to avoid. She had seen the bear scat and paw prints long before she saw the bear itself, so she wasn't surprised when he poked his head out from a distance, and looked at her curiously. *A young male,* she thought. *Not as bad as a momma bear, but more unpredictable,* she knew the best thing for her to do was to start making noise in hopes of scaring him away. *Of course, that does have a tendency to scare away small game,* she thought, and so she decided to back away slowly, hoping the bear would lose interest in her. Apparently, her backing away just made him more curious, and he got up from his bed in the thicket to follow her. It was then that Jewel saw the hare, decided to take a shot at it, and hoped to scare the bear away in the process. She just needed to get a little further down to the side so that she didn't end up scaring the bear off in the direction of camp, or Grady's fishing hole.

She took a few steps down, quietly creeping away from the hare, getting in a better position to scare the bear in a direction away from camp. Finally, she rose up, took aim at the hare, and fired the shot. The bear went running further up and away from the camp just as she hoped, but she could see him slow-up and stop just a little ways up. She pumped the shotgun again and took a shot in the bear's direction, hoping to scare him, and then she quickly loaded it with a couple slugs in case he decided to come back.

"Damn I hate shotguns!" she yelled as loud as she could, rubbing her aching shoulder, and going over to retrieve the hare when the bear ran away.

Having heard the first shot, and then the next one, Grady couldn't help but get worried. She said she was a hunter, but he hadn't known her long enough to trust the situation, and so he decided to make his way in that direction. "I guess she was right," he mumbled to himself, making his way up in the direction where Jewel had gone, "men can't help but feel protective of the women in their lives, and is that such a bad thing? Aren't we just made that way?" he mumbled some more, adequately justifying it to himself enough to keep going.

She was easy enough to track, and he was able to catch up to her quickly as she made her way back toward camp.

"Were you worried about me?" she yelled down to Grady, flashing him with a big smile as she caught sight of him.

"Yer right Jewel," he yelled back to her, throwing his hands up in surrender, "ya've got men pegged. I had ta come check and make sure ya were okay."

"You know Grady, I must confess," she said as she made her way down to where he was standing, "I don't really mind as it turns out. It's nice to know that someone's looking out for me."

"That's good Jewel, because I can't help myself. The mere sight of ya makes me want ta grab ya up with both hands and carry ya around safely."

"You've already done that," she laughed, both of them thinking about the moment they first met.

"Well, it was the least I could do after mowin' ya over."

"I suppose it was," she said gazing up to meet his eyes, instinctively wetting her lips with her tongue.

"Wow Jewel," he said shaking his head, "ya take my breath away. Ya standin' there, shotgun in one hand, dinner in the other, unbathed, uncombed, and lookin' more stunnin' than ever. Do ya torture all men this way, or am I just special?"

"I didn't know I was torturing anybody," she said shyly, "but you are *special* I think," she joked, looking up at him sideways as they made their way back to camp.

They walked downhill a ways, both of them smiling and just happy to be alone with each other for a minute.

"There was a bear up there, just above where I shot this hare; a young male. I fired the second shot to scare him away. I guess the first shot wasn't enough. We'll need to watch out for him tonight I think," she said breaking the silence between them. It wasn't an awkward silence, in fact, it was quite comfortable, and for a second she regretted interrupting the quiet moment they had shared.

"See? I did have reason ta worry. Ya were out in the woods about ta be eaten by a bear."

"And how were you going to save me from a bear armed only with some fishing line and a few dead fish? Were you planning on being bait?"

"Do not underestimate the versatility of fishin' line, and a man defendin' a beautiful woman."

"Do you really think I'm beautiful?" she asked not feeling very attractive with her dirty hair and dirty clothes.

"Christ woman! Ya take my breath away, lyin' next ta ya night after night. Do ya not know the affect ya have on me?"

"I think I understand," she said smiling shyly, "it's not that easy for me either. I mean… on one side there's a man who's become much like a brother to me. On the other side there's a man I don't yet know, but I feel as if I've known him forever, and I just want to reach up and brush the hair from his eyes in a way that would feel familiar, like I'd done it a million times before, except I've never done it before."

"Ya do understand then," he said stopping to face her while reaching up and cupping her face in his hand, "and I'd really like ta kiss ya right now, but I promised Rudy I'd keep my cool until we finish this. Have ya ever thought about it?" he asked barely whispering.

"I have," she whispered back, drawing in a little closer to him, covering his hand with her own as her heart pounded wildly in her chest, "but I don't want to let Rudy down either," she said looking deep within the blue eyes staring down at her.

"One day I'll kiss ya, and everything else can be damned," he said trying to control the pounding in his own chest as he wets his lips in anticipation of the kiss they both knew they'd have to wait for.

She closed her eyes and put her head down, not able to look up at him for one more second without throwing her arms around him and kissing him. She could feel her heart pounding in rhythm to his, and they could both feel the electricity flash between them as they stood just inches away from each other without touching. They stood there breathing each other in as if the attraction between them was something tangible. Neither one of them wanted to move, but they both remembered she was holding a gun in her hand and the mood seemed to shift suddenly as they each thought of it.

"I never really knew what my *type* was before," he said finally, "probably because I've never met anyone like ya before."

They smiled at each other, and slowly they made their way back to camp. Rudy was up and feeling much like his old self again, aside from the pain radiating from his shoulder. Their camp was near the river in a little clearing that had a large cliff protecting them on one side. They had to hike up and around the large rocks of the cliff to make it up to the mountainous area. It was well protected from the wind, and the canopy of trees overhead would provide shelter from light rain.

"Rudy, I'm so glad you're up and about. You look much better. How do you feel?" Jewel asked, shrugging her pack off and gathering her medical kit before going over to check on him.

"Hungry!" he replied, eyeing the hare and the fish they brought with them.

"I'll get something cooked up for us if ya want ta tend ta his shoulder Jewel," Grady said.

"Let me take a look Rudy. Can you get your shirt off so I can look at the wound?"

Rudy pulled his shirt off and Jewel could see that he'd been hit hard, the bruising already apparent. He'd be sore for several days, but it could have been much worse. Nothing was broken, and nothing needed stitched up.

"You probably don't want to hear this, but the extreme cold was probably the best thing you could have done for your shoulder," she said after checking him carefully, satisfied that he was in relatively good shape.

"The thought had crossed my mind, but I wasn't feeling too appreciative of it at the time," Rudy said with the thought of the cold sending a shiver down his spine.

Jewel got to work on his shoulder, getting the wound cleaned up and wrapped it up in clean dressing the way she had with hundreds of wounds before. Rudy's wound was nothing compared to the wounds that had come in to the hospital in Iraq. She was a surgical nurse, and had treated people from the inside out. She could clearly picture the inside of the shoulder as she felt her way around, gently probing the bones and the muscles to make sure there was nothing that needed more immediate medical attention.

"You're going to be pretty sore. Let's give it a day or two to heal, and then we'll start some heat therapy, and massage it to get it loosened up again. Meanwhile, I found some wormwood. It makes a decent tea, and promotes healing. I'll get some cooking and we can enjoy a nice warm cup of tea," she said smiling with a little extra pep in her step that Rudy couldn't help but notice. He saw Jewel and Grady walk out of the woods together, both smiling, and it was obvious that keeping them apart was going to be impossible.

"It does feel a lot better being all cleaned and wrapped up," Rudy said gratefully, pleased to have her there to help, "thanks Jewel. You're a skilled nurse."

"It's was nothing. You don't have to be a nurse to clean a wound, but if it made you feel better, then I'm glad. Here, take this," she said handing him an Aleve, "it will ease the pain and help with the inflammation. Tomorrow we'll want to tie it down to your side. Keeping movement limited will help it heal faster. Do you think you can manage without the use of one arm?"

"I'll manage."

"Look up there," Grady said pointing up the mountain opposite of where Jewel had seen the bear, "looks like we have some company, and one of them might be in some trouble. I'm goin' ta go see if I can help."

Grady reached the three men of the Alaska Team, and could see that one of the boys was hurting. His foot had been bandaged, and he was walking with the help of the brothers, one on each side of him.

"Are ya alright man? Can we help ya?" Grady called out as he approached the three men, grabbing Aaron on one side, relieving one of the brothers who seemed to be struggling the most under the weight of this large man.

"I cut my foot on something the second day out, and it's starting to get infected

I think. It's hurting pretty good, but I'm not ready to throw in the towel just yet. If I quit now my whole team will be out," Aaron said.

"If a team member wants to quit, they have to do it in between each leg or the whole team is out," Mark added.

"Let's see if Jewel can take a look at ya. She was a combat nurse in Iraq. If anybody can help ya and give ya some answers, it'll be her," Grady said proudly.

"Come sit over here by the fire," she said as they approached, making a spot for the boy, eager to take a look at his foot.

"What happened to you?" Jewel asked him, trying to distract him from the pain as she pried his boot and sock off.

"We were sleeping and I heard something in camp, which turned out to be a bear. When I stepped backwards, an old gold pan we found cut me on the side of the foot. I think it's getting infected," he answered, wincing a little as the boot and then the sock came off.

"It's badly infected Aaron, and very dirty. Have you had tightening or spasms in your jaw muscles, stiffness in the neck, or difficulty swallowing?" she asked with her head down trying to avoid making eye contact with him. There was just something about him that she didn't like, but she was a professional, and she could separate the man from the wound.

"No, nothing like that. It didn't seem that bad, so I just put my shoes and socks back on. I never gave it a second thought until it started hurting this morning, and getting worse and worse all day."

"Well, that's a good sign. Tetanus will be your biggest worry. Do you know when your last tetanus shot was?"

"I had to have one a few months ago when I first started fishing. I guess that'd be the last time I had one."

Grady and Rudy made the other two comfortable, offering up fish and a little bit of warm tea that Jewel had brewed up. They noticed they were doing good compared to these three boys, and were feeling confident with their position. They both smiled proudly as Jewel carefully looked at the wound and determined what she could do for him.

"Any sign of the other team?" Rudy asked Todd and Mark.

"They were a ways behind us last we saw them, but we've been pretty slow today. I imagine they caught up a little. They're probably an hour behind us I'd guess," Todd replied.

"How's it lookin' Jewel?" Grady asked, coming over to see if he could help.

"It needs cleaned out. Do you think you can put some water on to boil while I go get my medical supplies?" she asked while heading off toward her gear.

They all came to gather around Jewel and Aaron as she pulled a needle from her kit, every one of them surprised at just how prepared she was. Up until then, none of them had been expecting actual medical treatment.

"I'm going to have to numb your foot, or it'll be too painful for you as I clean your wound and stitch it up. The down side is that it'll be too painful for you to walk on for about twelve to fifteen hours, and you'll get a late start tomorrow. The good news is that you'll recover, and with a little luck, you may still make it to the finish line in time. What will you have me do?" she asked laying out his options for him.

"Well, I suppose you could just as easily take us out of the competition by doing nothing. If you don't mind fixing it up, I'd owe you one," Aaron said smiling at her salaciously.

Grady could see how taken the boy was with Jewel as she washed her hands thoroughly, and laid everything out in preparation. He couldn't help but feel a stab of jealousy, wanting to go over to her and stake his claim. "What kind of animal have I become?" he mumbled to himself, and just as he thought he might lose his mind entirely, she turned and flashed him with a smile that melted his heart, "and the woman saves me just as I think I may go mad," he mumbled again, shaking his head as he wrestled with unfamiliar emotions.

"I would never leave a person to suffer, competition or not," Jewel told Aaron as she prepared the needle and washed the injection site.

"It's going to hurt a little, and I'm sorry for that, but I'll need you to stay still. Don't look at it. Just lean back and try to think of something wonderful, like a favorite song or a favorite memory. There's a song called *My Favorite Memory*. Do you know it?" and without giving him a chance to answer, she started to sing quietly.

> *The first time we met*
> *Is a favorite memory of mine*
> *They say time changes all it pertains to*
> *But your memory is stronger than time*

Everyone was focused, listening to the beautiful sound coming from her as she worked, and nobody, including Aaron, even noticed when she stuck the needle in him to numb his foot, slowly emptying the medicine from the needle.

"There, now that wasn't so bad was it?" she asked as she pulled the needle from him, looking up to see him relaxed. "Let's give that a minute, and then we'll get to work," she said getting up to go fetch the boiling water, giving his foot time to get numb from the shot.

"Ya surprise the hell out of me woman!" Grady said coming up behind her to help her with the boiling water he had obediently started to boil for her. "Ya should be hundreds of miles away singin' ta millions of screamin' fans, not stuck in the backwoods of Alaska singin' ta a bunch of stinky, unwashed men!"

"There's no place I'd rather be Grady than right here, right now," she said looking up at him with a smile, giving him a look that left him speechless.

"Can you feel that?" she asked prodding Aarons wound, quickly giving Grady a backwards glance that gave him butterflies in his stomach.

"Can't feel a thing, well... not in my foot anyway..." Aaron said as he looked at her seductively, sending a chill through her.

With the foot numb, and all of Jewel's items laid out properly, she was set to get started on the cleaning of his wound. She had to carefully pick out some of the larger pieces of material with tweezers, and then use the boiling water, now cooled just enough to finish cleaning without causing damage to the tissue, getting as much bacteria out as possible. After getting the wound cleaned, she was able to stitch it up, and get fresh dressing on it.

Everyone was watching her intently as she focused in, blocking out the rest of the world, all the while singing sweet and low. It was just something that she did. In Iraq, she would have wounded men come ask her later what the song was she had sung while she worked on them, and she would look at them absently, having no memory of ever singing anything. It's how she steadied herself and reached the part of her brain she would otherwise not be able to access. It allowed her to see deep within the wound, beyond what was truly visible, and find the source of the pain, and what the songs did for her was nothing compared to what it did to those she healed. The songs relaxed a worried and rattled mind, putting people at ease while she prodded and pulled, and did what she needed to make them better. They were usually so focused in on the song, that most people were disappointed when she was finished with the medical treatment.

There would be no need to ask about the song she was singing as she finished, because it would be forever etched in the minds of the men who surrounded her.

Up in the mornin', out on a job,
Work like the devil for my pay...

CHAPTER 9

─────────

THE FIRST WIN

"Are ya sure you'll be okay?" Grady asked as they readied themselves the next morning to get started on the last day of this leg, leaving the three boys behind.

"We'll be fine. Thanks for everything. We appreciate your help, and we've got your back when you need it," Todd said as he and Mark shook hands with Grady and Rudy, and gave Jewel a hug goodbye.

"Bye you guys," Jewel said waving to them, "you'll want to have someone look at your foot when you get to the base camp later today. You'll need some antibiotics," she said checking on Aaron one last time before heading out. Even though Aaron made her uneasy, she did her duty as a nurse regardless.

"You owe us a story later," Rudy called out to them with one arm tied safely to his side, "you never did tell us what happened with the bear."

With that, they headed up the hill leaving the Alaska Team at their camp by the river.

"There was something very special about that camp," Rudy finally said, remembering the soft melody of Jewel's voice, looking back down the hill as they started to make their way over and then down the other side of the hill.

"There was definitely somethin' magical about it," Grady said giving Jewel a smile, "now come on. We've got about six or seven hours of steady hikin', I figure. We'll need ta hump it if we want ta beat the other team. I think our chances of winnin' this leg are pretty good, but without knowin' exactly where the other team is, I don't want ta chance it by lettin' up," he said slipping back into his leadership role.

With their heads down, they fell into a steady pace, each taking up their single file position they had established early on. Grady was always up front leading the way, Jewel falling in behind him about fifteen paces, and then Rudy bringing up the rear. It was the perfect formation, and it hadn't been chosen by accident. It was a carefully constructed plan Grady had decided on before they set out their first day. He needed to make sure they would be as efficient as possible, all the while insuring the safety of his team. The landscape was harsh. They'd be facing many dangers, and it was second nature for Grady to make sure the most logical plan was being executed.

They always tried to stay at higher elevations to avoid the bushwhacking through the tundra that skirted the mountain at lower elevations, but sometimes it was unavoidable, and they would have to change positions so they could each take turns in the lead, cutting through the bush, trying their hardest to make an easy path. Just when they thought they'd found an easy path, they'd reach glacial ice and have to change strategies, putting on their cramp-ons, and tying off to each other, lest they fall or step into one of the ice crevasses.

They hiked about an hour down off a glacier before realizing they'd have to repel off the end of it. There was no other way down without backtracking. It was maybe only forty feet, but the idea of repelling off a glacier had Jewel a little spooked. *This was going to be much different than repelling off a fake wall in a gym,* she thought to herself.

Rudy was the most experienced at repelling, and he quickly went to work drilling into the ice with his hand tool so they would have something to tie off to. He had untied his arm some hours earlier, and Jewel didn't harass him about it. It didn't seem to be giving him much pain, and pain was the best indication if something was wrong. The best part about pain was that it couldn't be easily hidden… not without medicinal help. *I'll take a closer look at it later,* she thought to herself.

After about twenty or thirty minutes, Rudy got the line securely tied off in the ice. They tested the strength of it as best as they could before Rudy finally decided it was safe enough. "I'll go first," he said securing his tools and putting his pack on, "if my anchor isn't going to hold, I don't want anyone else getting hurt because of it."

With that, he started down the foot of the glacier, which had a bit of an overhang to it, and Grady and Jewel quickly lost sight of him, both of them holding their breath and watching the ice anchor carefully.

"Are ya alright Rudy?" Grady called out.

"I'm good," he yelled, "I'm just about down."

They were both relieved when they saw him reach the bottom and come out from beyond the overhang where they could see him.

"Yer next Jewel," Grady said giving her a serious look.

"Ok then. I'm ready. Let's do this," she said trying to get herself pumped up, crossing herself as she said a quiet prayer. With her pack on her back, looking anxiously at Grady, she readied herself to start her descent.

"Yer a brave woman Jewel. You'll be just fine. If I thought there was a chance in the world ya might not make it, I'd grab ya right now and kiss ya 'til we both died," he said smiling at her.

"Another time then," she said smiling back at him as she started her descent, giving him one last look before falling out of his sight.

Rudy watched her from below. She was a brave woman, and she repelled her way down as if she'd done it a hundred times. He was relieved to have her safely on the ground, and hadn't realized until just then how much he'd come to care for her. She was a rare woman, and she was perfect for Grady in every way. Rudy knew it without a doubt, and happily wrapped an arm around her as they both watched anxiously for Grady to appear beyond the overhang.

Grady was by far the heaviest of the three, and Rudy was on edge waiting until he was safely on the ground. Grady wasn't just his brother-in-law. Grady was probably the best friend he ever had next to his wife. Having known him since he was a small child, he naturally felt responsible for him, despite the fact that he was a grown man. He knew that Grady was more than capable of taking care of himself, but with the summer sun melting the top of the glacier, he wasn't sure how long they'd have before the rope broke through, tearing it out of the ice anchor he'd drilled.

"I'm comin'," Grady yelled. They could see him finally pop over the overhang and start to make his way down with ease. Just as they thought he was home free, he came to an abrupt stop about ten feet off the ground.

"I'm stuck," Grady said, "the rope must be iced up. I'll probably be able to yank it free once I get on the ground, but I may need to drop from here."

Ten feet doesn't sound like a lot, but when you're looking up at the distance of ten feet between the ground and a man's feet, it seems like a long ways. The bottom was rough and hard and there was going to be a fair amount of risk. Grady tried to free the rope as best he could.

"Yep. I'm goin' ta have ta drop from here," he said resigned.

Jewel and Rudy cleared the area where he'd be dropping, making sure there weren't any rocks or anything in his path. Grady looked down, systematically planning his drop. He shimmied his pack off and let it drop before carefully unhooking his harness while holding onto the rope with his other arm. He finally let go and dropped. He landed hard on both feet and immediately fell to the ground. His back was his weakest point after taking shrapnel deep in the muscle tissue when he was in Afghanistan.

"Oh crap! My back!" Grady yelled, writhing in pain on the ground, "just give me a few minutes," he said rolling flat on his back and stretching out as hard as he could, "I'll be fine just as soon as the spasms stop, and we'll be on our way. See if ya can get that rope free Rudy," he said still giving orders from his wounded, prone position on the ground.

Rudy was already on it though, and after pulling as hard as he could for several minutes, he was finally able to get the rope free. He wrapped it up and secured it to his pack, readying everything for the final push.

"Are you going to make it brother?" Rudy asked, coming over to where Grady was still lying on the ground with Jewel sitting next to him checking him for other wounds.

"I'll do," Grady said, "I was just lyin' here hopin' Jewel would check me over one last time before we got on our way," he snickered, opening one eye and smiling up at the two of them.

"Oh you big faker," she said swatting him playfully, the three of them laughing.

On their way again, they easily made it to the location shown on the map. It was so quiet and calm when they arrived they thought maybe they'd gone to the wrong spot. After a quick look around though, they found their stash of rations that was their prize for being the first team to finish the leg. They'd won the first of the six legs.

"We won!" Jewel said excitedly, giving both Rudy and Grady a big hug, "I'm so relieved! I was so worried I would slow you guys down!"

"Ya did good Jewel, and we're a few hours early," Grady said, putting one arm around Jewel and another around Rudy, "I suppose there's nothin' ta do now but relax and wait."

"And eat!" Rudy said opening the package of bread and jam they won.

The three of them sprawled out on the beach area and waited for the other teams to arrive. The Adventure Team came in next, and Jewel ran over to Angela to help her with her pack and give her a hug, surprising even herself at just how happy she was to see the woman.

"You made it!" Jewel said coming up to Angela excitedly.

"Yes! We made it!" Angela said, matching Jewel's enthusiasm, wrapping an arm around her.

The three of them were looking happy and excited, but clearly worn out, with the world-class traveler with thirty years of experience, heading up the rear by quite a ways.

"You can hardly beat the military!" Joe said congratulating them for their win, "I knew you'd be a force to be reckoned with," he added looking up at Grady appreciatively.

"Help yourself to some bread and jam. There's plenty, just save some for the last three," Rudy said, inviting them to eat what was left while helping them with their packs.

There was only one hour left to go for this leg of the competition, and there was no sign of the three young fishermen. About thirty minutes left, and they could finally see them off on the horizon. Grady and Rudy decided to run out and help them as best they could. They wanted to win, but helping was second nature to the two of them. "Prizes don't mean much if you can't win by doing the right thing," Rudy had said early on. From the beginning, all three of them understood that, and Jewel was proud to be on a team with them.

The three fishermen were moving slowly, with Aaron's foot slowing them down a bit, "It's sure a lot better than it was yesterday... thanks to Jewel," Aaron said, straining to see Jewel as she sat on the beach near the lake.

Grady couldn't put his finger on it, but there was just something about the boy he didn't like. At first, he took it as pure jealousy on his part. He could see the affect Jewel had on men, and he could hardly hold that against him, but the way he was straining to find her on the beach, and saying her name like they were best friends, really irked him. He helped him with his pack reluctantly, eyeing him as they walked back to the pick-up area.

Jewel noticed the angst on Grady's face as they walked toward them, but brushed it off as she went up to Aaron to check on his foot. "How does it feel Aaron?" she asked as he sat down and let her probe around on it to check it for any fresh bleeding, or signs of infection.

"It's fine Jewel. I think you saved my life. Let me know if there's something I can do for you," he said looking around to make sure no one was watching before grabbing her hand, placing it on the hardness that had been growing between his legs.

Jewel startled immediately, meeting his eyes and shivering at what she saw there. It wasn't unusual for men to become infatuated with the person who was nursing them back to health. Hundreds of men had come through the Army Hospital where she had been stationed, and she was not without skill when it came to graciously thwarting their advancements. The head nurse had warned her about getting involved with any of them, and she had taken that warning seriously. They all came in with promises and one-liners, most of them were seriously lacking in originality, like the one she'd just heard. This was beyond that though. There was something evil in his eyes, and it sent a wave of fear through her.

"Thank you. I will," she said hotly, standing up abruptly. "Have the crew's medic take a look at this later," she said moving away from him, going over to sit with Angela.

Grady was fuming at the way Aaron was looking at Jewel, but he couldn't help but smile to himself, as she seemed to brush him off. Of course, he hadn't seen the whole thing, or Aaron might have died on the spot.

"Christ man! You're wired so damn tightly over here, I'm half worried I'm going to have to tackle you and throw you in the lake," Rudy said to Grady. "The two of you are made for each other man. I'm letting you out of your promise to keep it under-wraps for five more weeks. You'll kill someone before that! Just promise me you won't let it get in the way of us winning this competition," Rudy said, looking up at Grady with a serious look, and a hint of a smile.

"Ya've got my word on it man," Grady said, wrapping an arm around his neck and smiling widely, "I couldn't live with myself if I ever let ya down."

"Yeah... well, that man gives me the creeps, and I'd hate for you to have to break his neck so early on in the game," Rudy said as the two of them gave each other a knowing look.

"Well, that I can't promise ya brother," Grady said as they grabbed their packs, heading toward the helicopter that had flown in to take them to the base camp.

Try as he might, Jewel made sure Aaron couldn't sit next to her as they boarded the helicopter. He knew he'd been blown off, but tried to give it one more chance before she skillfully managed to make sure she was sitting right in between Grady and Rudy, and so did they. He sat straight across from her though, and stared at her the entire flight, with a look of anger on his face. Jewel pretended not to notice, and just sat there concentrating on the view outside the window, thankful for the safety of having the two men sitting beside her. An instinctual fear ran through her with Aaron's eyes boring a hole in her head.

Aaron was not one to be put off though. He always saw himself as quite the ladies' man, and one whore was as good as the next as far as he was concerned. All women were whores according to Aaron. Flash them a few smiles, buy them a few drinks, and they'll all spread their legs, with or without a little help on his part. "This bitch is probably just too damn sore at the moment from bending over for these two jerks," he had commented to his teammates before getting on the helicopter. Apparently, Aaron had been imagining the three of them in a nightly orgy, getting more and more angry as he talked about it earlier.

When you grew up as Aaron did, you didn't learn a whole lot about respecting other people. His father was a loner who moved to Alaska after several failed attempts at living in society. About the only thing Aaron's father remembered learning in his North American Anthropology class, in a failed attempt to educate himself, was how the Inuit women were submissive, and they got money from the government every time they had a kid. To his father, it seemed like a lucrative opportunity for a user and a loser like him.

It wasn't long before his father successfully knocked up a young girl down on her luck. "She wasn't bad to look at for an Indian," he had once told her, which was about the nicest thing he'd ever said to her. One child after another, the money rolled in, and he moved them to a remote cabin out in the middle of nowhere. Most times, he'd be gone, out living like a king spending the welfare checks as quickly as they came in. Those were the good days.

Occasionally, he'd show up, sometimes with other women, or other losers he'd occasionally hang out with. He'd beat his mother so severely, and she'd just take it. She would apologize to him when his knuckles would hurt later on. He hated that woman. She was so weak and pathetic according to him, that he was just a young man of about thirteen when he started abusing her too. The only softness he had in his whole heart had been for his little sister, who he protected at all costs to himself. That softness turned to stone the first time he saw his precious little sister out with one of the boys in town. "What a little whore!" he had screamed at her the last time he ever spoke a word to her.

As the helicopter landed, and they were walking toward the camp where the nine of them would be staying, Aaron apparently couldn't control his anger any longer. "So how does this work with the three of you then? You just take turns fucking her, or does one of you hit it from behind while the other gets blown," Aaron yelled mockingly from behind them as the three of them walked together

"Are ya out of yer fuckin' mind man?" Grady yelled, turning around and grabbing Aaron by the front of his coat with lightning speed. "This woman helped ya when ya were in need man. She picked dirt out of yer wound and stitched ya up so ya could finish this leg, and this is how ya repay her?" Grady's face was within inches of his, "she should have left ya ta fester and rot!"

Aaron was ready to fight though, and he swung up hitting Grady in the side of the head, nearly knocking him down. He had been ready to fight since before he could remember. He was always looking to punch, insult, or otherwise hurt someone in any way he could. A large man himself, Aaron wasn't used to finding a worthy opponent. He clearly underestimated Grady though, and never knew what hit him as Grady grabbed him surreptitiously by the throat, and gave him one swift punch to the face.

"Ya dumb bastard!" Grady yelled at him as he dropped him to the ground, having knocked him out cold. "That's a dangerous man right there, the likes of which I cleanly detest!" Grady shouted, backing away from the boy in disgust.

Everyone gathered around them, and the crew, having seen what was taking place, ran over and started checking Aaron for signs of life.

"Hold it right there! We don't want any trouble from you," one of the crewmembers said to Grady as several of them approached him cautiously.

"Are ya mad? Did ya not see what took place here?" Grady said heatedly, spreading his arms out to show them he meant them no harm.

"He didn't do a damn thing!" Todd said coming forward. "Aaron here is a crazy man! We've been traveling with him for five days, so believe me, we know!"

"He's been going on and on about Jewel, talking about getting her alone, and bending her over a rock and such," Mark chimed in. "Sorry Jewel," he added glancing over at her looking embarrassed. "He threatened to kill us if we said a word. Said he'd killed a man before and got away with it. Our plan was to get back here and turn him in. He's fucking crazy!"

"Didn't you come here with him?" Rudy asked accusingly. "Didn't you know what kind of beast you were dealing with?"

"We didn't know him well. We wanted to sign up and he kinda invited himself along. He was the only one who showed any interest, so it sort of made sense," Mark said in their defense.

With everyone coming to Grady's defense, including the crewmembers who heard the exchange, the focus went from Grady to Aaron as they carted him off, and figured out how to deal with the situation.

"Go with your team to the base camp Grady, and we'll come talk to you in a bit," one of the crewmembers finally said. "Please just go. We'll come talk to you shortly."

With that, they all started making their way back to the base camp with The Military Team walking together in solidarity. Jewel was completely stunned by the confrontation that had just taken place, and was feeling startled by Aaron's anger that came out of nowhere.

"I'd have done the same thing brother, if you weren't so damn fast. I was right behind you." Rudy said letting Grady know he had his support.

As they walked to base camp in silence, all three of them knew that Grady was going to be thrown out of the competition for hitting the man. They had been given strict instructions that throwing punches would mean immediate expulsion no matter the cause. The rules were pretty clear on that, and the realization of it was sinking in pretty heavily with all three of them.

"Sorry ya had ta hear that Jewel. The man gave me the creeps from the start, and now I know why. He's filth," Grady said putting a hand on her back, attempting a smile.

"Well, I suppose I should say thank you for coming to my defense, and, well… I'm sorry. This is awful. If they throw you out then I'm going too! I don't want to be part of something that won't even allow you to defend yourself. I mean, the man hit you in the head. What else were you supposed to do?" she said angrily. "I mean, I don't want to let you down either Rudy, but seriously, I just can't bear the thought of continuing this without the three of us together."

"Let's not jump ta conclusions Jewel. When we were waitin' ta board the helicopter, I heard the crew talkin' about our young Aaron. I've a feelin' they were goin' ta boot him for some reason. They were eyein' him cautiously, talkin' about keepin' him contained until we were back at base camp. I don't know, but it seems that if they put a dangerous man out here with us by not doin' their homework properly, then they might show some leniency. If we defended ourselves against the very danger they subjected us to," Grady said, explaining his logic, and bringing a sense of calm to the trio a little more convincingly then he actually felt, "then they won't punish us for it."

"Alright, but I'm with Jewel. If you go, then we all go. Leave no man behind! Or… woman for that matter," Rudy stumbled, smiling over at Jewel, giving Grady a pat on the back to show his support.

CHAPTER 10

BASE CAMP

Base camp provided them with a fairly good-sized tent, a fire pit, a community bathroom, which was just a glorified outhouse, a picnic table, and a makeshift shower area by the bathrooms where a person could take care of some long overdue personal hygiene needs. Each team had their own tent spread-out over a wooded area of about ten acres that sat near a lake, so they had plenty of privacy. The winning team was rewarded by having the largest tent, complete with the luxury of padded cots, and it was located in the center of the entire acreage, and nearest the bathrooms, but not too close.

As the three made it to base camp, and started setting up their gear, they slipped into their roles, each one quietly contemplating the various scenarios that were about to play out. Jewel couldn't imagine being there without Grady. She'd grown to care for him. *I may even love him,* she thought, which startled her a little. *What's going to happen? Will I ever see him again?* She knew that part of the reason she had even agreed to join the competition was because of Grady. The thought of saying goodbye to another person she cared about was just too much to take. That, combined with lack of sleep, hunger, and fatigue, it all became too much.

"Oh, I can't take this!" she finally said, breaking the silence and startling Grady who was standing in the tent, lost in his own thoughts as Rudy wandered around outside.

"Come here Jewel," he said grabbing her and pulling her against his chest, hugging her tightly.

It was then that years of frustration seemed to flood out of her all at once. She hugged him back tightly and cried as hard as she ever had, and Jewel never cried… not since the death of her parents when she cried non-stop for weeks. It was as if she had used up every last tear she had in her, and she never cried again until just then. She never cried for her grandma, and she never cried for her grandfather. She never cried for the men and women who had been wounded or killed in Iraq, and she often wondered if there was something wrong with her. She missed them, and she felt sympathy, and empathy, but she couldn't ever just let herself cry. She had built up a wall that didn't allow her to access that part in her that could feel anything so deeply, but suddenly, it seemed she couldn't do anything but cry, and he held her there for a long while to let her finish, never saying a word.

"I'm so sorry Grady. I don't want you to go, and I'm just upset right now, I don't know what to do. I don't know what's wrong with me," she said apologetically, feeling embarrassed, wiping her eyes and nose with a napkin she had in her pocket.

"What is it that's upsettin' ya the most right now?" he asked, lifting her chin up to face him a little surprised by her reaction.

"I don't know, just everything...the loss of my parents and grandparents, the loss of my best friend, war, crazy mad men, and now, well, maybe losing you and Rudy too. I just can't take anymore," she said, trying to stop the flood of tears that rolled down her cheeks. "I don't know where I'm going or what I'm doing, and everywhere I go, I just know less and less. I'm a complete mess Grady! I've been running and running, but it's finally just all catching up with me, and I feel like I'm going to drown in it all. I don't know what I'm doing... I shouldn't have let myself get close to anyone again."

He stood there quietly holding her for a minute as she pulled herself back together. She had tried to back away, but he just held her there until she was calm.

"Well, ya can't be accused of not havin' a good reason ta cry darlin', but don't cry about losin' Rudy and I. I'm not lettin' ya go without some kind of restrainin' order, and a team of armed bodyguards surroundin' ya," he said lightheartedly, wiping the last tear that had escaped down her face. "Christ, the thought of never seein' ya again nearly turns my heart inside out. Can ya not see how I feel about ya Jewel?" he said more seriously, grabbing her head with both his hands, hoping she'll see everything he has no words to describe.

"How is it even possible that I feel this way about someone I just met? I don't understand," she said looking up at him, having regained control of her emotions again.

"I don't know Jewel. I've been askin' myself the same question, but there are no answers, it just is."

"Kiss me," she said barely whispering.

What else could he do, gazing down on the magnificent creature that was asking him to kiss her? How could he not do exactly as she asked? and so he leaned down and gently pressed his lips against hers, feeling the warmth and wetness, stopping only when the taste of her threatened to consume him.

"Grady," she whispered when he stopped, "nobody's ever kissed me like that before. Where did you learn to do that?" she asked, not really wanting to hear the answer.

"Shhh, just let me kiss ya for a minute longer Jewel. It's all I've wanted ta do since I first caught ya on the sidewalk."

The two stood like that for several more minutes, one warm kiss after another until Rudy finally came in, and to break the ice, he came over to them and put his arms around them. "I didn't know it was group hug time! Why didn't you guys tell me?" he laughed.

The three of them stood there hugging each other for several minutes. An unlikely team forged among them, and they weren't ready to let it go. They were all wrapped up in the emotions of winning the first leg of the journey, and the notion that Grady was likely going to be kicked out of the competition. Rudy had been outside contemplating the idea of finishing the competition without Grady, and he simply couldn't wrap his brain around it. He felt that the three of them needed to take a stand together. If the crewmembers wanted to throw Grady out, they would have to say goodbye to them all.

"If Grady goes, we all go! Agreed?" Rudy said.

"Agreed!" Jewel replied enthusiastically.

"Ok, well if anyone comes in now, they're goin' ta kick us all out for indecency," Grady finally said, breaking free from the group hug.

"Knock knock! Anyone in there?" someone yelled from outside the tent.

"Wow! That could have been embarrassing," Rudy whispered smiling at the two.

The three of them went out of the tent to see who was there, and were not surprised to find a couple of the crewmembers. *Well at least we won't have to go about not knowing,* Jewel thought, part of her glad to see they had come so soon, and another part of her wishing they'd never come.

"We came to apologize to you, and let you know that you're not being kicked out of the competition Grady," one of the crewmembers said, surprising all three of them, "Aarons out. We got a call from the local P.D. out of Homer just a few hours before we were scheduled to come pick you up. We were hoping to get him back here without incident, but that obviously didn't work out. Turns out, Aaron's wanted for raping a young girl, and stabbing her boyfriend. He'd gone out on the crab boats to stay out of sight, but when we ran him through our system for the background checks, there was a hit. We didn't find out about it until today, because they had a little mix up in Homer. We're glad they called us when they did and nobody got hurt. Or... well... hopefully you didn't get hurt too bad Grady," the crewmember said, looking up at him anxiously.

"I'm fine, but when I think of Jewel lookin' after him ta stitch up his foot, and sharin' our campsite with the man, it makes me sick. Let's hope ya've done a better job checkin' out the others," Grady said scolding them, "meanwhile, let it be known here and now that if there's another mad man ya've got us competin' with, I'll not hesitate ta protect my friends here."

"We understand. You're safe. You've got my word on that, and I hope you'll accept my sincere apology on behalf of the entire organization. This is the last thing we wanted to happen, and we wouldn't want you to be out of this competition," another one of the crewmembers added.

"Did he hurt you, or do anything to you Jewel?" another crewmember asked.

"We need to report everything, and fill out all the proper paperwork to make sure this guy never sees the light of day again."

"Um... not exactly," she answered reluctantly, remembering how he had put her hand to his crotch.

"Would you prefer to talk to us in private?" the crewmember asked.

"No. I mean, it was nothing really. After I checked his foot at the beach, he grabbed my hand, and well... he put it to his crotch," she said looking embarrassed, surprising both Grady and Rudy.

"He did what?" Grady asked angrily. "Why didn't ya tell me? I'd have broken the man's neck!"

"Well, that wasn't really the part that scared me. I mean... I saw evil in his eyes. I've never seen a person with no soul before, but I saw it today. It sent chills down my spine, and it makes me want to wretch just thinking of it," she said, remembering the evil look in his eyes.

"We'll need all three of you to make a statement. Please just take this notebook, write down any involvement you've had with him, and we'll be by to pick it up later," the crewmember asked before leaving to go talk with the two brothers.

"Why didn't you tell us about that Jewel?" Rudy asked, coming over to put an arm around her. "We care about you and want you to be safe. Don't you trust us?"

The roller coaster ride of emotions caught up with Jewel again. She went from being completely closed off, to suddenly caring for people again, and it terrified her. It was welcoming and suffocating, and she didn't know if she wanted to cry more or start yelling, but finally gave into anger and frustration all at once, "Of course I trust you! but for one, I never had a chance to tell you! and for two, I can take care of myself! I was in the Army you know, and this isn't exactly the first time I've had someone put the moves on me! and for three, while we're at it," she added heatedly, "I didn't really need to tell you did I? The two of you circled me like two momma bears protecting her cub! and I...," she swallowed hard feeling frustrated, "I'm not used to being taken care of, and I... I... just need a little time to myself." she said, breaking down and crying again, leaving them standing there as she headed off to the bathroom, never once turning to look back.

Damn! These men are killing me! she thought as she reached the bathrooms. She had been guarded for so long, this rush of feelings she was experiencing were overwhelming her. *Get it together Jewel,* she told herself, splashing cool water on her face when she made it to the bathroom. Her first instinct was to run away and never look back. *Everyone I care for dies,* she thought to herself, feeling overwhelmed and slightly dizzy, knowing she couldn't run this time. She wanted to be able to open herself up and feel something again, but it was so hard for her. She had pushed everyone away, and purposefully grown away from people she had known growing up, so that she didn't have to risk any more loss.

The thought of caring for Grady so deeply terrified her, but the idea of not having the opportunity to let love in was suddenly even more terrifying. There was something about these two men that had immediately caused her to open up a little, in a way she hadn't been able to do in years. She knew she couldn't run. They seemed to hold a key that unlocked a part of her she thought had been gone forever. She knew that even if she wanted to, she wouldn't be able to run away from them. Her feet were firmly planted where she stood, and there was a part of her that liked the way it felt, though it scared her to death.

She was completely wiped out after her emotional outbreak. The first night at base camp was turning out to be bittersweet. She showered and shaved her legs, and it was sheer bliss, but the unfamiliar emotions she had been experiencing were wearing her out. She remembered when her dad had tried taking their homestead and salvaging it as best as he could. For weeks, it never looked like he was doing anything, and day after day, she went out there bugging him, asking him one question after another.

"You've got to put the scaffolding up before you'll be able to repair the house Jewel, and it's usually the most tedious part, but it's the most important, because without it, you'll fall flat on your face," he had said.

That's what this is, she thought. She was building the scaffolding around her broken heart. She knew the brokenness inside her could never be repaired without it, and she knew that she couldn't run forever, and for the first time in a long time, she didn't want to, but it took everything she had not to.

She'd stayed away from Grady and Rudy for a while that night, skillfully gathering her bathing items when she knew they were out, and it seemed they had planned it just so, knowing she needed a little time to herself. Angela and her talked for a while as they bathed, and it was a nice break from the flood of emotions that had engulfed her earlier.

"How are you doing pretty lady?" Angela asked greeting her.

"I'm okay. I could have done without the Aaron thing, but I'll be fine."

"I don't think you have much to worry about with those big men looking after you dear," Angela said giving her a wink.

"They're both like a couple of mother hens, but I can't say as I mind," Jewel said with a smile, "though it might take some getting used to. How are you doing then? How's your team?"

"Joe's great! He has me laughing every step of the way. I finally had to tell him that if I use up all my energy laughing, I'm never going to make it to the finish line," Angela said laughing, and Jewel could see that laughing was Angela's natural state, and it would probably take a lot to keep her from it. "To be honest with you dear, I hope to take the man home with me when we're done here!" she added, giving Jewel a coy look and an elbow to the side.

"Oh really? Do tell," Jewel prodded.

"Well who knows, I don't want to get ahead of myself, but having someone who makes you laugh every day is about as good as it gets."

"How's Gary then?" Jewel asked, curious about the weekend warrior.

"He's fine. He tries really hard, but he's woefully in over his head. We'll see how he holds up over the next two weeks. Poor man lost his wife to cancer, and I think this is a little lonely for him, especially with Joe and I hitting it off so well. He's the one who put our team together through an ad. I think he was hoping to build friendships and just get away awhile... maybe to meet a woman... not expecting Joe and I to have hit it off so well. He's enjoying himself though. Joe and I may be just the thing he needs. A daily laugh and the love of friends can go a long ways toward mending the heart," Angela said before making her way out of the bathroom, leaving Jewel to her thoughts.

Well, I guess that pretty much sums it up, Jewel thought to herself, *I guess everyone is fighting their own battles inside, and you just never know when God's going to send you a little Angel-a to make sure you get the message!*

She walked out of the bathroom, and Jewel could see Grady and Rudy sitting out by the fire. She decided it was finally time to make her way back to camp to face them again. When she got there, it was clear that the two were enjoying a bit of forbidden contraband.

"I'm sorry you guys. I don't know what came over me," she said when she walked up where they were sitting around the campfire in front of their tent.

They both just shrugged it off like it was nothing and smiled up at her. "We all need a good cry every now and then," Grady said smiling up at her.

"What is that you have there, and did you bring one for me?" she asked, eyeing the bottles of beer the men were drinking.

"We brought one especially for ya Jewel, and there's more where that came from," Grady answered, making a space for her to sit by the fire with them.

"We thought you needed a little something to take the edge off the day Jewel. We all needed it!" Rudy said, "and a little celebration is in order I do believe," he added, raising his beer to toast them.

"Topa!" Jewel said in celebration, clinking her beer to theirs.

"What's that Jewel?" Grady asked, looking at her curiously.

"It's Basque. My dad's family is Basque. I've heard my grandfather say it a hundred times in celebration when he was feeling especially happy! I've always wondered if I would ever feel happy enough to say it, and what do you know... there it is," she said taking a long draw off her cold beer.

"Alright then, topa!" Grady bellowed.

"Topa!" Rudy chimed in.

"Wow! You guys look quite handsome with your clean-shaven faces. I have to admit though... I kind of liked the beards," she said seeing the men had made good use of the showers earlier. She liked seeing their amazing transformations the week before as their beards grew out and they took on a more rugged appearance. It reminded her of hunting season back home when all the men would grow out their beards to keep their faces warm while they were out in the woods for weeks at a time. She always liked when Troy grew his out, a feat that he was able to do starting at about age fourteen. It grew into a thick, tangled mess, seemingly overnight, and Jewel always liked the way it made him look. First of all, it made him look about ten years older, which was pretty handy when they needed someone to go buy beer, and second of all, it reminded her of her dad, and that always made her smile.

"And you look mighty fine as well, but I did sort of like the, *I just brushed my hair with a tree branch* look ya've been sportin'," Grady said giving her a playful squeeze.

She laughed as they teased her about the tangled mess of hair she had tried to brush out one morning, and the three of them sat back and enjoyed the evening, laughing and talking as friends, taking pleasure in a light moment. They were all finally at ease knowing that Grady wouldn't be kicked out, and Aaron was in custody. The roller coaster of emotions they had all been on had taken its toll on them, but they washed it all away, one beer after another.

And so the scaffolding goes up, Jewel thought to herself, smiling and enjoying the love and friendship she'd found in her teammates.

CHAPTER 11

GOIN' FISHIN'

The next morning came a little too early for The Military Team. They had come up with a brilliant plan to get up at the crack of dawn to do some fishing, wanting to smoke some meat and get a little extra protein stocked up for the next leg of the competition. Of course, ideas bred from the spirits of beer are usually not as brilliant looking under the early morning sunlight. The three of them were moving pretty slowly, with Jewel raiding her medical kit first thing, handing out aspirin to her teammates.

"Topa," Grady said faintly, still lying in his sleeping bag, holding his hand up toasting the air.

"Oh no, don't remind me of that right now," Rudy said, grabbing his head.

"Food! I need food! When will the kitchen staff ever bring us our breakfast in bed? What kind of luxury resort is this anyway?" Jewel asked, turning around in the center of the room, pretending their camp was the lap of luxury, and she a spoiled patron of said resort.

"She's gone mad Rudy," Grady said, getting up to check her for a fever.

"I'm perfectly well. In fact, I've never been better. I just took a lovely swim in the pool off the lanai, and now I'm getting ready to enjoy a long hot bath, followed by a massage," Jewel said with her hands on her hips, giving Grady a serious look.

"She *has* gone mad," Rudy said sitting up to see for himself.

"I haven't gone mad. I'm pretending. It's a little game my grandpa and I used to play when we were getting ready to go do something we didn't feel like doing. We'd pretend that we were on a wonderful vacation in the French Riviera, or getting ready to go on a luxury cruise. He had a way of getting me out the door, and halfway through my chores, all the while feeling like I was getting ready to go to some fabulous place, and be pampered like the rich and famous."

"Well ya'd better find yer pearls then darling," Grady said, dragging out the *ing* with some effort. "I wouldn't want ta have ta escort ya ta the ball lookin' so drab without all yer jewels and riches," Grady said, playing along while he gathered up his gear for the day.

"Let me just get my top hat and cane then, and we'll be off," Rudy added as he finally made it out of his sleeping bag.

The three of them were finally up and ready to go fishing, having put together some smaller daypacks, and eaten the remainder of the jam and bread from their winnings. Grady and Rudy had talked with a few locals when they were at the liquor store the day before, and had a place mapped out where there was supposed to be some good salmon fishing. It was about a two and a half mile hike on an easy trail, but still, habits being the way they are, they naturally fell into their formation, making it to the fishing spot in just half an hour.

"Wow!" Jewel said, coming over the crest, and looking out over the river where they would be fishing all day, "this is beautiful. I want to build a house and live right here, and never leave," she said looking up at Grady who was smiling over at her.

They walked down into a little clearing where there were some large boulders and a grassy area that looked down at the river. Jewel and Grady sat and rested after spreading out a small blanket they brought with them. The clearing was marked by various colors of greens, dotted by rocks and white cresting water that filled the air with a lulling sound as it rushed downstream. Trees canopied much of the area, except for the area where they sat stretched out on their blanket, lying in the sun.

"What are ya runnin' from Jewel? Tell me somethin' about ya?" Grady asked after several minutes as they kicked back for a little while, Rudy having gone off to do some exploring on his own.

"Um… ghosts, I guess… to answer your question," she said looking out to the abyss and shrugging her shoulder a little, "my parents died when I was eleven. One day I was just walking up the drive after the school bus dropped me off. It was about a mile up our driveway. I could see there was a bunch of cars, and so I got really excited and started to run inside. We lived so far out of town that it was a rare treat to have visitors. I ran in, and everyone just stared at me. My grandma was crying, and I knew something was wrong immediately. I'd never seen her cry before. I just started running through the house calling out to mom and dad. My grandpa finally grabbed me up and just hugged me so tight I thought I was going to break. He said, *Jewel, there's been an accident. Mom and Dad were on the highway heading up the mountain and a truck rounded the corner…* but then he trailed off, not knowing how to finish the sentence," she said, pausing for a moment to choke back the emotions that were stuffed down under the surface where they always were, "he didn't need to finish though. I knew what he was trying to say. I could see the pain in his eyes. I didn't want to make him finish his sentence. I just grabbed a hold of him and we stayed like that for a long time. He just held me and let me cry until I couldn't cry anymore, and after a few weeks, I never did cry again… not ever. Well, not until yesterday," she said, meeting his eyes as he sat beside her silently.

"My life changed forever, and just when I thought I couldn't take one more day of hurt, my grandma died just a few months later. She had been sick for a long time, and it wasn't unexpected. She'd given up on life long before I ever knew her, having given birth to two stillborn babies, and after having several miscarriages. It was pretty hard on Grandpa though, but he was a rock for me. Every once in a while, late at night, I'd hear him cry in his bed. I thought about going in to comfort him, but I knew it would hurt him to let me see him cry. So, I'd just sit by his door and pray for God to ease his pain. My dad was his only child, and Grandma was the love of his life. It was really hard on him, but then, just a few months after I turned eighteen, my grandpa died too. I completely shut down after that. I became completely numb, and I just threw myself into studying and being a nurse. The break from feeling anything at all seemed to give me exactly what I needed to help the soldiers that came in the hospital in Balad. They needed to tell me things... horrible things they saw or did, and I could just listen to them without an emotional reaction. I could just listen without judgment being written all over my face, and I think it helped them."

"Yer grandpa raised ya then Jewel?" he finally asked after several quiet moments, trying to imagine everything she had just told him.

"He did. He was the best person I ever knew," she said remembering the man, smiling as she did. "He always put me first even though it must have been really hard for him. He had heart disease, and he was dealing with his own grief, but he always made it a point to put on a happy face for me. He was really funny too. He always had a look on his face like he was getting ready to tell a funny joke, and he usually was. Every time I saw him, I would start to smile."

"Yer damn tough Jewel," Grady finally said after several minutes, meeting her eyes, and reaching down to give her a kiss on the forehead as he wrapped an arm around her. They sat side by side looking out at the water, "I'm sorry about yer parents."

The two sat there in silence for a while, Grady holding her as tight as he dared, feeling like he needed to hold onto her to keep her from slipping back in the past, beyond his reach where she had hidden herself away for so long. He could finally understand why she always seemed to be holding back a little, though he could sense that she didn't really want to be.

"Thanks for tellin' me Jewel," he finally said turning to her, looking deep in her eyes. "Yer grandpa sounds like a good man."

"Thanks for letting me. I never tell people about it usually, but for some reason, it feels good to say it out loud," she said, softly kissing him and cuddling up to him as he pulled her in closer. They sat that way for quite a while, each of them thinking about the things Jewel had just said. For Jewel, it was a confession that eased her burden a little, and she couldn't explain why, but she knew it felt good, and she sat there smiling despite the sadness of the memory. For Grady it was an understanding of how this woman had come to this place all alone, not eager to go home.

"Now that's an interesting way of catching fish," Rudy said as he walked up over the ridge where they were laying, "I assume you're praying for the fish to jump up on the shore and feed us while we nap."

"We were waitin' for yer endless supply of sarcasm, but we knew we wouldn't have ta wait long," Grady said, smiling up at Rudy.

They both just laid there for a minute before they all started moving simultaneously, as if on cue. It wasn't long before they started catching one salmon after another, stopping only when they thought they'd caught as much as they could eat and carry. The two brothers of the Alaska Team had built a makeshift smoker out of sticks and blankets of moss, and they intended on heading back to their own camp to build something similar. They needed to head back, build a smoker, get all the meat cut up in small strips, and let it smoke a good twenty-four hours before packing it up with their gear. The task seemed daunting as they each struggled with the lingering effects from all the beer they drank the night before.

"Well mi' lady, would ya care ta accompany me ta the masquerade this lovely evenin', after which I shall have the servants draw us a warm bath and feed us grapes and champagne," Grady said to Jewel, offering her his arm, and over exaggerating an uppity accent of an English Gentleman.

"Certainly, kind sir," Jewel chimed in, grabbing his arm and heading toward camp, "but perhaps we should help the poor servant boy carry the fish."

"I'm the poor servant boy now? I don't think I want to play this game anymore," Rudy said, picking up the end of the stick that all the fish were on, as Grady took the other end.

"Sorry Rudy, but being obscenely rich and pampered only works if someone is there to do all the work," Jewel said shrugging her shoulders, as if she were only following the natural rules of the game.

"Isn't that the truth?" Rudy said winking at her.

They made their way back to the base camp where they all worked together, as if they'd been doing the same routine for years. Jewel jumped in right away to build a makeshift smoker, while Grady and Rudy cleaned and cut up the fish. Jewel had even managed to find some baling wire that worked as a perfect hangar to string out the salmon for smoking.

Grady was a little skeptical of the smoker, which was just a teepee covered in moss, but it was the tie at the top that had him puzzled. It was what looked to be a bra, "but I give her points for creativity," he mumbled as he considered the image of her walking around without wearing a bra. It did seem to be working well though, and he had been impressed by how hard she worked on it. He had poked his head in there a few times to check on the fire, and was pleasantly surprised by how well it worked.

They finished their chores and were getting ready to lounge around for a while and have some tea. The few weeks that Jewel had spent with the mountain climbing guide had proved to be invaluable on their journey. He taught Jewel about the flora and fauna they encountered, and she was able to keep the team stocked up with a nice supply of tea, as well as a few other treats they could eat along the way. Tonight they'd be eating well, and just when they thought it couldn't get any better, the two brothers showed up carrying fresh venison for them.

"Good evening," Todd said as he and his brother walked up where they were sitting and resting by the fire.

"Mark! Todd! Good to see you," Jewel said, genuinely excited to see the two brothers.

"How are the two of you doing after losing your teammate?" Rudy asked while offering them a place by the fire.

"Better than ever," Mark answered, "that boy has issues. We're glad to be rid of him. He gave us nothing but trouble, and we spent most of our time taking care of the bastard. He'd boss us around like we were his slaves, and scream and yell all the time. It sucked!"

"We're sorry we didn't say anything when we were in camp with you. We didn't know he was that crazy. We thought he was just a talker. You know how some guys are," Todd said, shrugging as he looked for understanding.

"Not ta worry," Grady said, still a little upset they let him get that close to Jewel without a fair warning.

"We met up with a couple local boys this morning and got us a deer. I hope you'll accept this as a peace offering, and well, just a thank you," Todd said, handing Grady a choice cut of venison.

"It wasn't yer fault man, but we'll accept it and offer ya some smoked salmon in return. As soon as it's ready that is," Grady said, eyeing the makeshift smoker dubiously.

"You owe us a story," Jewel said, "what was the story with the bear in camp that somehow caused Aaron to cut his foot?"

"Well, we never actually saw a bear. I think it was just another story. Aaron liked to make himself out to be some kind of hero, like he was always protecting us from some kind of unknown danger all the time, like there was a bear or poisonous plants lurking around every corner. He grew up roughing it pretty bad, and seemed to have a bit of skill, so we'd listen to him. Earlier in the evening he'd been giving Mark here a hard time about his braid, and said he was gonna cut it off one night while he was sleeping. Mark had told the story about being baptized, and how he liked the braid because it reminded him of that day. We're still not exactly sure what happened. We think he was up sneaking around trying to get to Mark's braid, got spooked, and fell down the ridge we'd been sleeping on, and managed to cut his foot on the way down with the knife he was going to use. Of course, Aaron would never admit to that, so he made up some ridiculous bear story, going on about having saved us from being eaten. I'm glad that bastards gone man," Todd said shaking his head.

"I wondered," Jewel said, "I've seen a lot of wounds, and that didn't look like one that had been cut by a dull, rusty object. Whatever cut his foot was extremely sharp."

"Didn't ya know what kind of man he was before ya came?" Grady asked.

"No. We didn't know man. He was quiet and kept to himself for the most part.

Once in a while, he'd get to talking and telling crazy stories, bragging about himself mostly, but it was just talk. You know how it is," Mark said, searching Grady's face for absolution.

"Well yer safe, and we're all better off. We'll move off from it then," Grady said, granting him what he asked for.

Just as they were all making amends, the Adventure Team showed up smiling and laughing, as they always seemed to be doing. Wherever Angela was, there was always a lot of chatter and movement. She had a larger than life personality, and seemed genuinely excited by just about anything she encountered.

"Hey there friends, did we not get the invitation to the party?" Joe asked, greeting everyone warmly. Joe was an older man of about sixty who looked like he had weathered many a storm. He was rugged looking, and had hands that had one callus on top of another. The beard he had grown over the last week made him look like he had just stepped off the movie set of Tombstone, and Jewel could see why Angela found him so attractive. He was a man's man if she had ever seen one, and for an older man, he was very appealing.

"We heard the chatter over here and thought we'd join you if you don't mind," Angela said, taking her place next to Joe again, the two clearly having established an active romance.

"We're glad to have you. Come sit down with us by the fire," Jewel said, moving closer to Grady to make room for their guests.

"And I've got us a little treat while we're at it." Gary reached into his coat and pulled out a bottle of whiskey, "that is, if you all don't mind. I know we're not supposed to but…," Gary said trailing off with a guilty shrug.

Jewel smiled at the man. He was a smallish man who was a little round in the middle, and she thought the trip was starting to look good on him. He seemed to have come out of his shell a little, and got some well-needed sun on his face. He seemed happy, and Jewel felt a little kinship with him after Angela told him about his wife dying of cancer. The grief was definitely something she could sympathize with.

"Ya've answered my prayers man!" Grady said excitedly, "and ya've even got my brand, straight from the belly of the homeland."

"You're an Irish fellow then?" Gary asked, sitting by the fire comfortably as they passed around the whiskey.

"Well… no. I'm as American as apple pie, but my mom and dad came from Ireland, and so I suppose the love of Irish whiskey is just in the blood," he said smiling, taking the bottle that was being offered, and pouring a little into the tea Jewel had brewed up.

"Please, keep it going around. There's enough for everyone, and there's more where that came from, as I've got a crewmember in my pocket with a sympathetic palate," Gary said with a coy look.

"That same crewmember brought us a little something too," Mark said, getting up to go retrieve something he had hidden in the bush before entering the camp, "we remembered how you said you missed your guitar Jewel, and we'd love to hear a song." Mark walked up and handed a guitar to Jewel.

Mark and Todd were both a little shy around Jewel, especially after what happened with Aaron. Looking at them, she wondered if they were from a Norwegian descent. She knew that there were quite a few Norwegian fishermen in Alaska, and they certainly had the look. They were both of medium height with blond hair and greenish-blue eyes. She guessed they were both in their early twenties, and she looked at them in awe every time they talked about fishing on the Bering Sea.

"It's beautiful! Thank you," Jewel said excitedly, taking the guitar.

"Well, you can't keep it. We just borrowed it, but we'd love to hear you sing again," Todd said feeling a little nervous, eyeing Grady for approval.

"I'd love to." Jewel positioned the guitar comfortably on her lap, clearly feeling at home with the instrument.

"Well, this is for you then," she said, looking at Mark and Todd thankfully, "it's my favorite songs to sing, and as soon as you told me about your braid, I thought of it."

They all gathered around and listened as she started playing the guitar, and sat in awe as the sweet sound came out of her mouth.

> *...And it was down with the old man, up with the new*
> *Raised to walk in the way of light and truth*
> *I didn't see no angels, just a few saints on the shore*
> *But I felt like a newborn baby, cradled up in the arms of the Lord*

Jewel sang on, completely oblivious to the group that surrounded her, digging deep within her soul where music lived, and another building block melded to her heart, slowly, and meticulously making her feel whole again, one small piece after another. Music was the gateway to her heart. When she sang, she reached a part of her that didn't exist at any other time. She just sank into another realm, completely freeing herself from anything and everything that scared her or made her want to run away.

She sang on and on half the night, the group joining in for some jovial favorites, all of them passing the bottles of whiskey around, laughing, singing, and dancing the night away. Rudy had cooked up the venison the brothers had brought over, and they shared it with the group. Friendships were formed, and hearts were filling up and running over as they all laughed and enjoyed each other's company.

They told stories, and they each took turns picking songs, every one of them trying to stump Jewel and pick a song she didn't know, but she seemed to know them all. Even when they picked a song she initially thought she didn't know, she would pull it seemingly out of thin air and come up with the words and music, surprising even herself sometimes. She had grown up learning country songs, and rock songs, but she also enjoyed some rap songs, and even a few grunge songs. It wasn't just the music she loved. She liked to dissect the poetry buried within each song, fully understanding the need to express something for which there are never enough adequate words. Music set her free.

CHAPTER 12

FAQAIWI [FUK' A' WE']

"I'm going to have to restock my supply of aspirin if we keep this up," Jewel said, getting up the next morning and handing out aspirin to her teammates again, as she massaged her temples and tried smoothing out her messy hair.

"You and your damn Irish whisky," Rudy said quietly, giving Grady a stern look with the one eye he managed to pry open.

"Ya didn't seem ta mind it so much last night brother," Grady said, getting up and patting Rudy gently on the head.

"Don't remind me. I plan on blaming you until my head stops pounding. It'll make me feel better," Rudy said lying spread out on the floor of the tent.

"I feel surprisingly well," Grady said looking fresh as a daisy as he got up and got himself dressed, "whiskey is like momma's milk ta an Irishman. Providin' all the right stuff ta make a man ready for another day."

"Well, that explains it. Did I mention I'm not Irish?" Rudy said mockingly. "We drank actual milk in my household."

"What is your heritage Rudy?" Jewel asked a little curious since he had the classic look of a Basque, with his dark hair and dark eyes.

"I'm from the Faqaiwi tribe," he said sitting up, giving Jewel a serious look.

"I've never heard of that. Is it Indian? Say it again," she said seriously.

"Fuk-aw-we," he said slowly, "it's Indian, and Scottish, and Norwegian, and probably a few other things. We're so mixed up we just walk around and ask ourselves, who the fuck-are-we?" he shrugged dramatically, busting out laughing at his own joke.

"Oh you!" she laughed, the three of them laughing as they grabbed at their heads to stop the pain, "Well you look like a Basquo with the dark hair and the olive skin. That's why I was asking," she said still chuckling, shaking her head at Rudy.

"We have some of that in our tribe too," he said getting up, kissing her on the top of the head before heading out to the bathrooms.

"God I love that man!" she said as she gathered her stuff up for the day, still laughing and smiling at the joke.

"And this man? How do you feel about him Jewel?" Grady asked, coming over and standing right in front of her, making her look up to see his face, now more serious. His blond hair was messed up and she doubted he had any idea how attractive it made him as he casually ran his hand through it, gazing down at her with a smile.

"I… well… love… I'd have to say," she said timidly, trying to calm the pounding in her heart, not exactly sure what it all meant until that moment when she stood staring up at him.

"I feel it too. I know it's soon, but I can't help it Jewel. It's just how I feel every time I look at you," he whispered, leaning down to kiss her, softly at first, but then more urgently, wanting to take her all in.

She could do nothing but wrap her arms around him, pulling his head down to hers, kissing him deeper, and suddenly wanting something she'd secretly feared she wasn't capable of feeling. She had never felt like that before. She pulled him to her, wanting more, running her hands through his hair as she kissed him harder.

He wrapped his arms around her, finding her soft skin beneath the shirt she'd slept in. Exploring, wanting, and needing until he'd lost himself, stopping only when he heard her cry out as he found the hard nipple beneath her shirt.

"Oh god Grady… stop… we can't. Rudy will be back soon," she said lost in her own desire.

"Shhh. I know Jewel. I just want ta touch ya and hold ya a minute. It's all I can think of since I met ya," he said kissing her neck, exploring the bare breasts beneath her shirt more thoroughly, "So ya did use yer bra ta tie the top of the smoker then?" he said, trying to find the strength to tear himself away.

"You noticed that?" she asked, pushing herself into his touch.

"God but yer beautiful Jewel. I may need ta go jump in the icy river. How will I keep from goin' mad, wantin' ta touch ya every second?" he said not really waiting for an answer before kissing her again, trying to take as much of her in as possible in the few minutes they had alone.

"It's not easy for me either you know," she said between kisses, "but we should stop before Rudy gets back." She stepped back a little and took his hands in her own. They were both breathing hard staring at each other, both of them wanting something they knew they would have to wait for. They had only known each other a little while, but they had already spent more time together than most people who had been dating for several months, and the feelings between them had been getting increasingly more obvious.

"You'll never believe what's going on!" Rudy said bursting into the tent, anxious to tell them what he had heard; breaking the unspoken exchange they were having as they stared at each other, wanting more than they were able to give at that moment.

"What is it?" Grady asked, letting go of one of Jewels hands, trying to pull himself together.

"They're letting one of the locals from town join up with Todd and Mark," Rudy blurted out.

"That's interestin'. I suppose we can't really hold that against them. We picked up our own stray along the way," Grady said putting an arm around Jewel.

"It was their fault for not vetting Aaron better. I suppose it wouldn't be fair if they didn't give them a chance to find a third team member. They'd be at a huge disadvantage," she said, narrowing her eyes at Grady.

"They're going to be tough to beat. This boy knows his business. He was one of the boys we were talking to at the liquor store the other day. Daryl! The smart one with the headband!" Rudy said giving Grady his most serious look.

"That's goin' ta make this more interestin' for sure," Grady said, rubbing his phantom beard that he'd shaved off a couple days earlier.

"See? You miss it too don't you?" she said smiling at Grady, and squeezing Rudy's arm before heading outside. She needed to cool off after kissing Grady. She loved Rudy, but it seemed like every time they had a moment together, he always walked in, and she was feeling a little frustrated. She wanted something from Grady she had been afraid was missing from her physical and emotional bank. She always heard people talking about wanting sex all the time, or not being able to keep their hands off someone, and she never really understood why that was until that moment. She sat down by the fire that was smoldering from the night before, sipping what was left of the coffee, and listening to the two men inside strategically talking about their new competitor.

The boy they were talking about was born and raised in Alaska. He knew everything there was to know about that part of the world, and he was going to be quite an asset to the Alaska Team. He had a lot of knowledge about how to catch small game, and about edible plants. The Military Team went from a near certain win, to having some pretty stiff competition. Clearly, Daryl was going to be hard to beat. They debated the fairness of it, but in the end, they welcomed the challenge, and agreed that Daryl was going to be an interesting person to get to know, though they thought they had better spend a little extra time getting their things in order to make sure they were ready.

They mended things, packed and re-packed their gear, and readied themselves throughout the day, getting to bed early; wanting to make sure they were in top shape before setting out on the next leg of the competition. Besides, after two nights of drinking in excess, they were in need of some rest, and it wasn't long before they all fell asleep thinking about the next leg of the competition ahead.

Of course, Grady was up just before the sun, sitting out by the fire, thinking about the days ahead of them. He was always planning things out, imagining the next leg of the journey, which the only thing they knew about was they were going to be using their pack rafts a lot, and that added an element of danger.

"What are you doing out here all by yourself?" Jewel asked softly, coming up behind him and wrapping her arms around him. He was warm as he always was, even in the coolness of the early Alaskan morning.

"Jewel, what are ya doin' up?" he asked putting his hands over hers and leaning into her. They both were usually up early, but Jewel usually didn't wake up that early.

"I heard you get up. I just wanted to be alone with you for a minute before the day started," she said rubbing his back, finding the scars beneath his t-shirt.

"Ahhh. That feels good Jewel," he groaned as Jewel rubbed the muscles beneath the raised scars on his back. She closed her eyes imagining him hurt, being carried into the hospital unconscious, under the care of a doctor and a team of nurses. She thought of all the men and women she had treated, wondering if they would have had the same connection if she had met him in Iraq. She had always distanced herself from the men who came through there. She cared for every one of them, but she was happy to send them back to their families, most of them in one piece, but some of them not. She silently thanked those who had taken care of him in Afghanistan.

"Shhh. Rudy's going to think we're fooling around out here," she said probing deeper, massaging the hard nodules she found, making Grady moan even louder.

"Oh! Oh Jewel. That's so good!" he said even louder.

"Quit it!" she said swatting him playfully.

"I owe him! He started datin' my sister when I was seven years old. Ya have no idea how much moanin' and groanin' I've heard over the years. One time when I was about ten, the two of them had been stayin' with me while mom and dad were on vacation. I walked in the house and heard my sister makin' these god-awful noises. I thought she was bein' killed. I ran upstairs without a second thought, grabbin' my baseball bat as I went. Well, ya can only imagine the look on their faces as I broke in ready ta hit a homerun," he said smiling in remembrance.

"I love you two together. You're so close. I'm glad to be a part of it," she said, moving around to face him.

"It's like ya've always been a part of it. It's just... well, like ya've just always been here. It's only been just a couple weeks maybe since I've known ya, but I feel like I've known ya for a lifetime," he said sitting down and pulling her onto his lap.

"How do you do that?" she said gazing up into his eyes, "you always seem to take what I'm feeling and put it into words, something I've never been able to do very well."

"For some things there aren't any words," he said kissing her on the forehead lightly, "but I don't think ya give yerself enough credit. The way ya sat there and told me about yer parents... I'll remember every word of it until the day I die Jewel. Not wantin' ta talk about feelins', and not bein' able ta are two different things. I can see how it's hard for ya."

They sat cuddled up with each other, watching the sunrise together as they had gotten in the habit of doing since starting out on the first leg of their journey. They talked quietly, and enjoyed the time they had alone, waiting for Rudy to come out and say something witty, as he usually did.

"I hate to break up the party, again, but there's work to be done," Rudy said coming out of the tent, dragging his sleeping bag behind him.

"I'm going to head over to the bathroom real quick," Jewel said giving Grady a small kiss before getting up from his lap, "I'm taking a quick shower, and shaving my legs one last time before we leave. I'll be quick! I promise!"

"Yes! Get that mop washed, and get those sandpaper legs of yours cleaned up before someone loses an eye!" Rudy said calling after her jokingly, "Christ! We're not beast's woman! We still need a bit of civility for crying out loud!" he yelled louder, making her laugh all the way to the bathroom, and halfway through her shower.

CHAPTER 13

FIRSTS

Leg two began easy enough, with the helicopter dropping them off for a five-day trek. They knew they'd be spending a lot of time on the river after the helicopter dropped them off in the Denali State Park, making their way toward an old plane wreck marked on the map where they would be picked up when they finished.

The three of them started out quickly again, falling into their single file formation, Grady and Rudy having quickly decided on the path they would be taking. Instead of doing a lot of climbing, this time it was going to be a lot of downhill hiking, which came with its own challenges. It also meant they would likely be doing some more repelling. Jewel was getting more comfortable with it, but it wasn't the most appealing thing to her, and she realized that she had a little fear of heights.

She remembered the long treks they made taking their sheep up and down off the mountain when she was a little kid. Hiking through Alaska reminded her of that, mostly because she felt so happy. The days of trailing sheep were some of the happiest times of her childhood, and she relished it. Her dad was always leading the way, getting everyone set up in their positions. Mom would usually go ahead of everyone, along with Mrs. Landas, making sure they would all have something warm to eat at the end of a long day, usually homemade chicken noodle soup, complete with homemade noodles that she could practically taste in her mouth every time she thought of it.

After they died, everything changed. She never thought she'd feel happy again. *It was almost like a family,* she thought, *Grady... where did he come from exactly?* It wasn't something she'd ever expected to happen. She had been starting to think it would never happen to her, and she often wondered if she were even capable of love. *Maybe my heart is just too broken,* she had thought, watching her friends fall in and out of love, over and over again.

In high school, everyone always thought she and Troy were together, and I suppose they were for the most part, even though they weren't romantically together. He kissed her once, she remembered, stiffening just a bit. It was awkward and made her feel weird. Troy looked horrified when he saw the look on her face, and had run off, and he didn't speak to her again for a month. When he finally did, they both just picked up where they left off before the kiss, and they never spoke of it. It was one of the few things they hadn't discussed in detail.

Sometimes she wondered if Troy had told her he loved her and asked her to marry him just out of obligation. That might have been the one thing she was most of afraid of, though she didn't believe it for a minute, but then, what if he had only asked her out of obligation, and she had to find out that there was nobody alive who loved her, and she really was all alone? He worried about her a lot growing up, she knew. He knew how hard it had been for her losing her parents and her grandma, and he went out of his way to make her feel better. She wouldn't put it past him, and I suppose that really was love, if not the romantic kind it was always supposed to be.

"Let's camp here," Grady said interrupting her thoughts.

"We've made good time!" Rudy said, "I haven't seen any sign of the others since we left."

"I used a few muscles I didn't know I had on that hike," Jewel said throwing off her pack and stretching out.

They quickly set up camp, all three of them falling into their usual roles, getting everything set up for a night in the Alaskan wilderness. It was going to be pretty cold that night so they took a little extra care building an adequate shelter. Having the smoked salmon was a nice treat, and they were able to relax for a little a while around the campfire sipping tea, enjoying each other's company as the sun went down.

"That woman reminds me of my first... well, my first... woman I was ever with," Rudy said trying to find the right words as they all settled in by the campfire to relax.

"What woman?" Grady asked having his thoughts interrupted.

"Angela. Just her personality, and the way she's always laughing. She reminds me of the first woman I was ever with," Rudy said leaning back in his hammock smiling.

"Tell us about it then. How old were ya?" Grady said looking over at his brother-in-law and settling in for a story, surprised he had never heard it before.

"Well, I was seventeen and Karen, that was her name, was my neighbor's best friend several years older than me. She'd spent the night there before, and I would always see them over there playing around all the time. She was a very pretty girl. It wasn't like I could ignore her. I'd hear her laughing all the time as they jumped around on the trampoline, or sat out on the deck, and I'd just have to look out and see what was so funny all the time. There never seemed to be any good reason for her to be laughing, and it intrigued me. The window in my bedroom looked right down into my neighbor's yard, and gave me a pretty good view of bikini clad women out by the pool," he said attempting a lecherous look that he wasn't really capable of making.

"One night, I walked over to look out the window, and there she was sitting quietly all by herself, not laughing or anything. She was just sitting still and quiet, all by herself staring out into the pool as if she were a million miles away. It broke my heart just looking at her," he said with the emotion of that memory written on his face.

"I made my way down the stairs into the backyard, and I stood right beside her without her ever moving a muscle. Well, to make a long story short, she was feeling pretty lonely," he said smiling.

"She had just been dumped by her boyfriend, and offered to take me in the pool house after a little while of talking. I was too embarrassed to tell her it was my first time, acting like I'd done it a million times before. She was obviously quite experienced, and I didn't want her to think I was just some seventeen year old green-gilled kid, which of course I was," he finished, trailing off into a part of the memory he wasn't going to share.

"So what happened to her?" Jewel finally asked.

"Well, apparently her and her boyfriend got back together a few days later. She'd wave to me, or blow me kisses once in a while, but other than that, we never spoke again, and I was sort of heartbroken. If I had known we were only going to have that one time together, I would have treasured it more. As it was, I barely remember it. I was so nervous and scared, and just excited to be having sex!" he said making them laugh.

"It all worked out pretty well though since I married the perfect woman," he said leaning back again more content and smiling, thinking about his wife for a long moment before asking, "Now do you want me to tell you about Grady's first? That's a good one," he said looking seriously at Jewel.

"No! You can't tell that story! I'll lose all respect from the woman," Grady said nearly blushing.

"Oh come on. I'm always up for a good story," she said squeezing Grady's hand that she'd been holding.

"Well, truth be told it's a quick story," Grady said eyeing Rudy sternly, and fighting back the red that was creeping into his cheeks.

"I was sixteen," Grady said narrowing his eyes at Rudy. "I was off visitin' my sister and my *former* friend here," he said sitting up, giving Rudy a friendly jab, "we had gone ta his commandin' officer's house for dinner, and he had a very aggressive little daughter about my age. She flirted with me throughout dinner, and it sort of scared me a little ta be honest. She was kind of a big girl. Not overweight or anything, just large… very tall, and… stocky. I didn't start growin' this tall until I was about eighteen, so she was equal ta my size at sixteen," he added getting his defense in place before telling the story. "After dinner she invited me down ta the basement ta play some video games, and before ya knew it, she was all over me."

He was stalling, not wanting to finish the story, shaking his head in disbelief that he was actually telling it as each word came out of his mouth.

"Well, I heard her dad callin' down ta us, and so I was tryin' ta push her away, but this just seemed ta add ta her excitement," he said clearing his throat, trying to delay telling the part of the story he didn't want to tell.

"Well, I could hear him yellin' for us and she was unbuttonin' my pants and climbin' on top of me like a wild animal, and that was it," he said finishing the story abruptly.

"Wait a minute! That's not the whole story!" Rudy said prodding Grady.

"Alright then," Grady said giving Rudy the evil eye, "next thing ya know I'm on the couch, pants pulled down, the little beast on top of me doin' her thing, and me not mindin' so much at that point, when I look up ta see her dad kneeled down, peerin' at us through the basement window." Grady was fully blushing, and avoiding Jewels eyes.

"I jumped up with what little strength I had left, having just… well… anyway," he said giving Jewel a sideways glance. "I jumped up and ran as fast as I could headin' for the stairs, which isn't very fast when ya've got yer pants down around yer ankles. I smashed head first into the first step, trippin' over my pants, and the next thing I remember was seein' the angry eyes of my sister peerin' over me. I'd knocked myself out cold, and was lyin' there at the bottom of the stairs," he said still fidgeting as he told the story.

"Poor Rudy here was upstairs tryin' ta keep her dad from comin' downstairs and shootin' me right on the spot, all the while bein' nearly beat ta death by the girls mom. My sister pulled me up and marched me out of the house so fast I was startin' ta think I'd rather take my chances with the dad," he said with all of them laughing at the scenario that Grady had just laid out for them.

"So what happened with the commanding officer? I mean, how was it for you after that Rudy?" Jewel asked finally catching her breath after laughing so hard.

"Yes… poor Rudy… let's hear about how rough it was for you," Grady said sarcastically.

"When I walked in the next day, he slapped me hard up against the back of the head and told me if I ever breathed a word of it, he'd have me court marshaled. I believed him too!" Rudy said trailing off, leaving everyone to their own thoughts as they all chuckled and pictured the scene.

"Alright, yer turn now!" Grady finally said eyeing Jewel, trying to stop everyone from thinking about the image he'd just painted in their minds.

"Isn't there some unwritten code of sorts that says you're not supposed to ask a woman that? You know, like you never ask a woman her age. You never ask a woman about her first time… that sort of thing," she said in an attempt to avoid the question and change the subject.

"I fully believe in equality Jewel," Grady said smiling at her.

"Me too! I'm all about it," Rudy chimed in.

"It's really too embarrassing. I don't think I can tell you. I mean. It's just too embarrassing," she said shaking her head.

"Spill it!" Rudy said giving her a stern look.

"Well, I mean, I was a pretty grief-stricken girl," she started, looking like a frightened child who was trying to explain why she didn't make it home by curfew. "I always had Troy. He was my best friend since before we could walk, and everyone always thought we were a couple, but we never were, even though we did *almost* everything together," she said nervously.

"When I went to college I was just lost, and I would just stay in my room all the time and study and play my guitar. It seemed like the only way I could get through the day was to throw myself into not thinking about anything but school, and I finished my degree early because of it..."

"Wow! This is a very romantic story," Rudy said sarcastically, "get to the good stuff!"

"Well, the truth is that I've never even been out on a date," she finally said turning bright red, "I mean... I know I'm a complete freak of course, but there you have it."

"What are you saying?" Rudy asked sitting up suddenly, "you've never...?"

"Oh, this is so embarrassing," she said as Grady pulled her back into him, hugging her, and giving her a place to bury her head to save her from her embarrassment.

"Ya don't have ta be embarrassed by that Jewel," Grady said tenderly, giving her a kiss on the top of her head, "yer not a freak. Ya had a pretty rough childhood," he added, providing her with supportive excuses.

"Weren't you in Balad with hundreds of horny men throwing themselves at you all hours of the day? I mean... Jewel, not that I don't believe you, it's just that... well, you're one of the most beautiful women I've ever seen. Had I been single and wounded, and being nursed back to health by someone like you, I would have been begging you day and night for affection," Rudy said in disbelief.

"Well, I spent most of the time I was in Iraq obsessing over a married doctor," she finally admitted. "When he finally showed interest after I'd fawned all over him for nearly a year, I completely lost interest in him. He always talked so fondly of his wife, and I guess that was one of the things I liked most about him. As for the other men that came through there, there was definitely no shortage of opportunities. There was a man about my age from Salt Lake City. He was pretty cute, and I was sort of attracted to him, but not overly. I think I was mostly just ready to get it over with," she said with exasperation as she frantically tried to explain herself.

"We'd kiss and make out a little, until one day I thought... this is it," she said eyeing the two men who were staring at her, "and so I went to find him in his room, but he wasn't there, but on the way back I thought I saw him out near the fence. So, I went out to find him, and when I rounded a jeep that was parked there, I saw him. He had his pants down, and was in the throes of passion with a P.A. that I worked with who was always going with one man after another. I guess he was just getting tired of waiting for me, and he obviously found a more willing partner," she said finishing her explanation, feeling a little awkward.

"The poor dumb bastard!" Grady said after several minutes, "he'd kill himself if he knew how close he'd come," he said shaking his head with a little sympathy for the man.

"No doubt! He'd shoot himself for sure," Rudy said shaking his head sympathetically.

"Alright then, now that you know my deepest secret, I think I'll crawl up in my sleeping bag, pretend I'm normal and I've had lots of sex, and a great first story to tell," she said slipping down into her sleeping bag where she would be comfortably wedged between the two men. Jewel knew that being a twenty-two year old virgin was absolutely ridiculous. She felt like it was a glowing example of just how broken she really was. She walked around for years wondering if there was something seriously wrong with her. It wasn't as if she hadn't had the opportunity, it was that she'd never really had the desire, and she thought there must be something seriously wrong with her. *Am I even capable of love?* she'd often wondered.

She was lost in her thoughts, still feeling embarrassed and broken when she felt Grady snuggle up closer to her, answering her own question once and for all. *I'm definitely capable of love, and most certainly, desire,* she thought as her heart raced thinking of his touch. Without being able to stop herself, she reached up and touched his face gently as he pressed her hand to his lips and kissed it.

"You don't have to be embarrassed Jewel. You're a good person. I shouldn't have pushed you into telling," Rudy said as he got into his sleeping position.

"I'm not upset Rudy. It's kind of embarrassing, but I would be more upset if I had run off and refused to tell you guys. That's usually what I do. I'm *really* good at running away. I'm actually a little bit proud of myself right now to be honest," she said lying on her back, speaking to Rudy in the darkness.

"Ya can say anything ta us Jewel. We're not here ta judge ya," Grady said squeezing her hand, "my own story's a bit more embarrasin' I'd say."

"That's for sure," Rudy replied enthusiastically, laughing at the memory, "You know I love you like you were my own sister Jewel! Anything you have to say, I will gladly listen to without judgment," he added.

"Thanks. You guys are the best," she said trailing off, falling asleep with a big smile on her face.

CHAPTER 14

FIRST DATE

"When this is over Jewel, I hope you'll let me take ya out on yer first date," Grady said as they sipped their tea by the morning fire while Rudy slept.

"I'd love that," she said looking up into his eyes. "What will that be like I wonder?"

"Well, I'll pick ya up in the evenin', and take ya ta some fancy dinner of sorts, and we'll walk in the moonlight, and things like that," he said hopelessly, clearly out of his element with the whole fancy dinner date.

"Hmmm… okay… that sounds… nice," she said trying to sound excited.

"Okay, ya don't sound too interested. Where did I lose ya?" he asked.

"Well, it's just that I can't imagine anything better than just sitting here with you like this every morning," she said spreading her arms out to include the stars that were still visible in the early morning light, and the snowcapped mountains that surrounded them. "Or what about today? I mean… we're getting ready to go rafting down a beautiful river in Alaska. I can't imagine any first date that could be better than that," she added.

"So, this is like our twelfth date then, not includin' the other times we're tagether?" Grady said, thinking about all the time they'd spent together sipping tea or coffee in the early morning as Rudy slept.

"I suppose so. Isn't this better than a fancy dinner, a walk in the moonlight, and *things like that*?" she asked, mocking his failed attempt at describing a romantic date.

"What I'm hearin' is that we've gone out on dozens of dates, and ya've only let me get ta second base once," he said grabbing her playfully, pulling her onto his lap, and kissing her firmly.

"We can have other firsts," she whispered between kisses as she peered into his eyes, "what will that be like then?"

"Yer goin' ta drive me stark ravin' mad woman," he said before kissing her more deeply, "I'll have ta pray ta God beforehand that I don't turn inta some kind of wild beast, but then… I'll have ya 'til ya beg me ta let ya rest," he said kissing her more fiercely.

"Now that sounds more convincing," she said pushing herself closer to him, running her hands up his chest, feeling him beneath the light pullover he wore. "How will we wait five more weeks?" she said reluctantly pulling away from him.

"I don't know. I can barely think about makin' it through the day without havin' ya, but I have ta try, or I'm goin' ta lose my mind. All I know for sure right now is that we should probably get movin'," he finally said giving her one last kiss.

"Same time tomorrow then?" she asked getting up from his lap.

"I'll be lookin' forward ta it," he said reaching up to run his hand up her leg. "Meanwhile, I think I'll pretend that today's our first date, just so I can think about kissin' ya for the first time all over again."

"You think I'm going to kiss you on the first date? What kind of girl do you take me for?" she laughed, smiling over her shoulder at him as she walked off to get her things together.

He was still smiling to himself when Rudy wandered over. He was finally up, and the three of them started to get ready for the day. They got their camp picked up and their packs ready, and they headed out toward the river that would take them most of the way to their destination on the map. It was a warm summer day in Alaska, but the snow-capped mountains above reminded them where the icy water was coming from.

"Let's get the rafts pumped up, and we'll get on the water to put some serious miles behind us," Grady said rubbing his hands together with excitement.

Grady lived off adrenaline, and he was excited to go rafting down the icy cold rapids that were ahead of them. He was even more excited to see how eager Jewel was. The woman was fearless, and was his match in every way. He himself hadn't been on many dates that included fancy dinners, and moonlit walks. That seemed like a standard dating requirement that he couldn't ever get the hang of. The one's he'd been on had felt like torture, and he sat through every one of them constantly looking at his watch, wondering when it would end. He was pleased when she made it clear that she wasn't into that either.

There'd been women in his life here and there, but most of them wanted something from him that he could never understand. They fell for him, because of who he was, but then immediately when things started getting serious, they would want him to be someone else, wanting him to dress up in a suit and tie to take them places he couldn't stand. He tried to go along, but it seemed too laborious, and always left him feeling empty. He never understood exactly why until he met Jewel.

"Let's do this!" Rudy said as the three of them readied themselves to push off.

First Grady, then Jewel, and then Rudy, just as it always was when they started off. It was a beautiful day. The sun was shining, and it was relatively warm for Alaska. They were all ready to get on the water to put some distance behind them, moving them closer to the finish line, and possibly winning that leg of the competition.

"Woohoo!" Grady screamed as they started to make their way down the rushing water. They were in a deep canyon with high rock walls on either side of the river, and there wasn't a cloud in the sky. Every living thing along the riverbank was turning green with flecks of color made by the blooming flowers in various colors, going from reds and yellows, to purples and blues.

Jewel had been on a few white water rafting trips before, but it was always a group trip, and came with an experienced guide. Her grandpa had taken her and Troy to Yellowstone a couple times, driving them to the top, and of course grilling everyone to make sure it was completely safe before sending them on their way. It would take them all day, and it was one of her favorite things she had ever done. She had always wanted to ask Grandpa to take them again, but she knew how hard it was for him, and she knew he would say yes. She didn't want to put him through it.

This trip would be much different. Grady and Rudy had gone over everything with her as they made their way toward the river earlier, talking to her about what dangers to look out for, and how to pick her path. There wasn't a group this time, and there wasn't a guide. It was just her in her little raft, and of course, all her gear that she somehow needed to make sure she didn't lose. Grady and Rudy had both said multiple times not to lose her gear. They knew if any of them lost their gear, they'd be out of the competition. There was no way they could continue without their supplies. If it were true survival they could live without it, but for a competition, it wouldn't be worth the risk.

It was a warm summer day, and she wasn't too worried about getting wet, but she also knew that if she did end up in the water, she wouldn't have long before the cold would threaten her with hypothermia. Nobody could survive in the cold water very long, and she was especially sensitive to it. Being cold was the one thing she always struggled with.

They'd be going about twenty miles, but they would have to stop a few times to make their way through the brush, around a few areas that were just too dangerous, because of white water or waterfalls. It was going to be a long, wet day, and Jewel couldn't have been more excited. It was the illusion of somehow being able to control water, harnessing it to transport her down the river, that excited her the most. It was controlling the uncontrollable, beating it despite the fact that it could never be beaten, only tamed momentarily, until it decided to turn back into the wild untamable force it was always meant to be.

They made their way down quickly in some areas, and more slowly in flatter areas where the water seemed to stand still. Her arms would get tired constantly fighting the rapids, but she loved the challenge of sticking with it until she thought she wouldn't be able to bear it another second. Finally, relief would come by way of a flatter area, giving her just enough time to rest up and prepare for the next few miles of rushing water.

Toward the end of the day, they got to an area that was rougher than they had seen all day. Jewel watched as Grady went through the rapids, trying to memorize the path he had taken. She needed to go before Rudy came up behind her too fast, and she aimed directly for the same path he had taken. She saw Grady waiting at the bottom ready to toss her a line if she was overturned, just as they'd planned out earlier. *Well, it's not going to get any easier,* she thought before heading downstream.

Just as she started down the chute, she caught sight of the Alaska Team out of the corner of her eye, one right after another, all three of them heading down the rapids together. They didn't see her push off just as they descended, and the four of them ended up in a melee of rafts and gear with arms, and legs, and all four of them crashing into the other, just as the white water pushed them under.

Jewel felt herself crash into them, but there was no stopping it. The water was in charge, and she was at its mercy. She didn't know who was bumping into her, but every time she came up for air, something else would crash into her, sending her back under the water. Her only thought in the world was of her gear, of which she never once let go, and it was the only thing that kept leading her upward where she could find air again, protecting her as she bounced off rocks. She held onto it for dear life, thinking it was only a matter of time before she would finally reach an area where she could make her way to the shore, but it never came.

She thought for a second she heard Grady calling for her, but before she could yell back, something else would knock into her, sending her back under the water that was swiftly washing her down the mountain. It was all happening in slow motion, and after what seemed like hours, she started to feel the cold settle in, and she shivered uncontrollably.

Grady was ready at the bottom, wanting to make sure he could throw a lifeline out to her if she went under, but he sat helplessly searching her out, trying to see where to throw the rope. Which one was her? It was hard to distinguish her from the other three through all the rapids. There were rafts, gear, and people everywhere, and he couldn't find her.

"Jewel! Jewel!" he yelled, calling out to her, hoping she would hear him, and by some miracle, glance his way, but he couldn't see her. He threw the rope, and ran out into the water as far as he dared without being pulled under himself. "Jewel!" he yelled again, feeling helpless as people and gear rushed past him forcefully, with Grady only managing to catch one empty raft.

Jewel could feel the pull of the water. It was so strong and so cold, the shock of it paralyzed her. It was a force so strong she felt like she was being buried under a thousand seas. The pressure on her chest crushed her, and she knew she would die if she didn't find air, but all she could do was fight helplessly against a force a million times stronger than she was, and she knew she couldn't make it. She couldn't fight it any longer. The cold overtook her, and she gave into it as it took her deeper into an icy prison.

"Jewel! Jewel! Where is she? Where is she Rudy?" Grady yelled out. The two of them quickly organized, and they started following the river downstream, one on each side looking for any sign of her. They had seen the three boys get to shore, and knew they would take care of each other, so they immediately headed out looking for Jewel.

Grady's heart was thumping out of his chest, calling out to her, the eyes of a sniper on full alert, scouting out every crevice of the earth, looking for the smallest hint of something that was out of the ordinary. The thought of never again holding the soft, fragile little hands of hers between his own, was more than he could bear to think of.

Walking down alongside the river was its own challenge. There wasn't always a shore to walk on, and they would have to hike up a bank, calling out to her, and scanning every inch of ground looking for her. Rudy could see the worry and strain on Grady's face, even from the distance of the river that separated them.

He had never seen Grady like that before, well... not since he'd seen him in action in Afghanistan. The two had ended up there at the same time. Not a huge coincidence given the fact that there were thousands of troops there from all branches of the military, and they were both career soldiers. Grady had been given an assignment that required he drop-off behind enemy lines to recon a particularly bad area they believed to be a safe haven for Al Qaida terrorists. He saw Grady go into a near trance studying the map, and preparing his gear. Grady and his team slipped off, getting in and out of the area with relative ease, and with more intelligence than anyone had hoped for. He knew that once Grady was given a task, he wouldn't let up, and he knew that Grady would never rest until he found her.

Rudy was frantic with worry himself. He had come to care for Jewel. She truly was like a sister to him, and he knew that Grady would be a broken man if something happened to her. He steadied his eye, glassing the landscape every few steps, calling out to her as he went. He was worried. He didn't know how it would be possible for her to survive in the water as long as she had been in there. He remembered the few minutes he had spent in the river during the last leg, and how quickly the cold sapped his strength.

"Where is she God? Bring her back to me," Grady yelled, crossing himself as he continued down the river, determined to find her.

CHAPTER 15

HYPOTHERMIA

Jewel couldn't feel a thing. Her mind seemed to float above her without a body attached to it. *I suppose this is what death feels like,* she thought to herself, but she knew she wasn't dead as soon as the shivering started, and her teeth started chattering uncontrollably. *Surely, you don't shiver in heaven,* she thought as she snuggled into what she thought was Grady. *Why is Grady wearing a tarp? Why am I sleeping when I'm supposed to be in surgery?*

The shivering started shaking her so hard she forced herself to open her eyes to stop the confusion of it all. She opened one eye, and then the other, the light piercing her brain as she let it in, and forced her eyes to open even wider. She looked around through the haze, seeing the riverbank, and then the mountains, trying her hardest to make sense of it all, but she couldn't quite figure it out. She could sort of feel water rushing over what she thought might be her feet, but that didn't really make sense, and she wasn't even sure they were really her feet. *Oh, it must be a picnic. I remember now. We were on a picnic, and I decided to take a nap,* she thought to herself. *That doesn't seem quite right though. When were Grady and I on a picnic?*

She laid there for a long time, her eyes having finally adjusted to the sunlight, but she could see that the sun was starting to go down, and her teeth were chattering so hard she felt like someone was hitting her in the head with a hammer. Something deep in the subconscious of her brain told her she needed to get up to get a fire started. She wasn't sure why it was necessary for her to start a fire, but she knew that she wanted to feel its warmth, and forced herself to sit up. It wasn't until she finally managed to sit up that she realized it wasn't Grady she had been snuggling up to, but her gear that she'd been hanging onto for dear life. She carefully fished in one of her pants pockets with her hands shaking uncontrollably, looking for her flint and knife. She started crawling further up the bank looking for dried wood, and kindling that she could use to start a fire.

After I get this started, I'll just go up to the house to get some blankets, she thought to herself chattering, and using her flint to get a spark going. *That doesn't really make sense either, but I'm not sure why?*

It didn't take long before she was able to get the fire going, but keeping enough fuel in the fire was getting to be a challenge. She could barely feel her legs and her hands, and her feet seemed like dangling bits of excess that just seemed to be getting in her way, hampering her progress as she crawled around looking for more driftwood. *Why didn't someone just turn up the heat?* she thought feeling annoyed, not really sure why nothing seemed to be making any sense.

Once she got the fire going as well as she could, she crawled back over to her pack looking for her sleeping bag. Grady had insisted their sleeping bags be wrapped in plastic bags at all times, and she was feeling very thankful for the man an hour or so later when she started warming up, but at the moment, she was annoyed at how difficult it was to get to something that could help her get warm. After struggling with her bag, with her numbed fingers and chattering teeth, she finally got to her sleeping bag, and crawled back up to the fire dragging it with her as she did.

She woke up sometime later curled up in her sleeping bag feeling confused as to why she was there, and how she had gotten so cold. She forced her eyes open once again, and started all over as she tried to piece things together. Nothing was making sense to her, and she was starting to feel angry and a little scared.

"I'm so hungry!" she said loudly, the noise of her voice sounding out of place in the quiet emptiness where she laid. The sound of it startled her, and she looked around cautiously to see if there was anyone else around who may have been alarmed, but there was no movement other than the water.

She immediately fell back to sleep, but awoke sometime later, the hunger pangs were more persistent, and little pieces of what happened to her were flashing through her mind whether she wanted them to or not. Her stomach growled louder, and she saw her pack still lying down by the river, and was finally feeling good enough to climb out of her sleeping bag to go get it. She stoked the fire, reaching over and pushing more driftwood in the flames before climbing out of her bag. It was only then that she noticed she was naked, which confused her even more, having no memory of how she got that way.

"Well who cares anyway?" she said loudly, daring someone to hear her and come find her, the realization that she was completely alone having set in.

She could feel her feet again, but they ached, and as she walked on them, it felt like shards of glass were sending lightning bolts of pain up her legs, making the walk to her pack an enormous undertaking. She tried lifting the whole pack, and dragging it all back with her, but she was too weak, and gave up immediately when the cold hit her again as she carefully made her way back toward the fire.

Damn that man is so logical, she thought to herself as tiny pieces of the world started to make sense to her again, as she devoured the smoked salmon, and thawed out by the fire. They had divided their rations amongst them equally, and she was eagerly shoving it into her mouth as quickly as she could. She had argued that they should divide things up by category, as it would have made it easier to carry and store, but Grady insisted they each carry a little bit of everything in case they were ever separated. She thought he was being overly cautious, never imagining a circumstance where they wouldn't all be together.

"This isn't war you know?" she had said teasing him when he divided everything up equally, carefully planning out every detail as he always did.

"They thought of everything, and probably saved my life in the process," she said to herself savoring every bite. *They must have skipped that part when I was in basic training*, she thought, feeling cheated. She snuggled back into her sleeping bag, trying to recall exactly what had happened, but it was all too confusing still. She remembered small pieces, but none of the pieces seemed to fit together logically. Whatever it was that had brought her to that river bank, naked in a sleeping bag, was a total mystery to her, and every time she would come up with what seemed like a logical explanation, a dose of actual logic would kick in, leaving her even more confused than she had been before.

She dozed off for a little while more since her stomach was no longer growling. The weakness from the hypothermia sapped her energy. It made it difficult to stay awake very long, but every time she dozed it was restless, and she kept opening her eyes to check on the fire. The fire had become her lifeline. Its warmth was feeding her with energy again, and it was slowly bringing clarity back into her mind. The fire became the only other thing that was living and breathing, and she got as close to it as she dared.

It was starting to get dark, and the reality that she'd be sleeping out in the open by herself at night was setting in. She had slept outside half her life, but this would be the first time she had ever done it alone. She was thankful to have her pistol and rifle, but it would take another trip to her pack, and she wasn't looking forward to getting out of the warmth of her bag again.

She briefly thought about getting dressed to go look for someone, but she knew that was a bad idea. Once when she was little she ran away from home, but as the sun went down she quickly decided that maybe doing the dishes wasn't so bad compared to sleeping alone in an area where she frequently saw predators roaming around. *It wouldn't be smart to go traipsing along the river at night,* she thought as she made her way down to her pack again to retrieve her rifle and her pistol.

Finally settled in, having warmed herself considerably, fed herself, and retrieved her means of protection, she fell asleep almost immediately. This time she sunk into a deep sleep, unable to fight the fatigue any longer. Even the fear of sleeping out by herself wasn't enough to keep her from closing her eyes.

~~~~~~~~

"Jewel! Jewel wake up!" she could hear him and feel him all at once, and she wrapped her arms around him as he lifted her up against him, sleeping bag and all. At first she was confused, not knowing exactly who it was that had lifted her up, but she clung to him instinctively, knowing that whoever it was, they were there to help her.

"How did you know I was here?" she asked, still half-sleeping, but thinking more clearly than she had when she went to sleep, the memory of the rushing water coming to the forefront of her mind as she held onto him.

"God woman ya scared me half ta death," Grady said kissing her face, squeezing her tightly, "do ya know how far down the river ya are? I was startin' ta think I'd missed ya or…," he said trailing off not wanting to finish the sentence.

"Grady," she finally said, suddenly realizing who was holding her. "I barely remember anything. I woke up shivering, and I thought I was snuggling up next to you at a picnic, but as it turned out, I was really just snuggled up to my gear. I held onto it just like you said," she said trying to fight back tears.

"Ya did good Jewel. Ya went about three miles I think. Rudy stayed behind when it started ta get dark, in case I missed ya he'd be able ta see ya in the daylight. He'll catch up with us tomorrow."

"Didn't anyone tell you it's not a good idea to go traipsing around the forest at night Grady?" she said kissing him frantically, not wanting to let go of him.

"I was goin' mad woman. I couldn't bear ta think of ya out here by yerself freezin' an' starvin'. I know how sensitive ya are ta the cold, and I didn't know if ya had yer pack, or had put the flint and knife in your pockets as I'd said. I had ta find ya. There was no way I was stoppin' until I found ya."

"You saved my life. All your careful planning. All the little things you have me do every morning that annoys me, and feels like a waste of time," she said smiling at him, pulling him down to kiss her again.

"Are ya alright then?"

"I'm bruised in places I didn't know existed, and I have a few minor scratches, but nothing serious. Plus, reality is starting to come back to me. I was really confused for a while. I didn't know why I was here. It was strange. I was definitely hypothermic."

"I've never been more scared Jewel. I'm sorry I couldn't catch ya. God when I realized ya'd gone past me, and I couldn't find ya right away, I thought I'd go crazy."

"How could you have possibly caught me Grady? It's not your fault," she said grabbing his face with both her hands.

"I can't help it Jewel. I can't help but feel like I need ta take care of ya ta keep ya safe. I can't change it. It'll always be that way, and if ya don't like it then tell me now."

"It's all I've ever wanted," she confessed, hugging him tightly, the two of them falling into quiet thought for several seconds, glad to be wrapped up in each other's arms.

"Yer startin' ta think the fancy dinner and a walk in the moonlight is not such a bad idea now, aren't ya?" he asked playfully.

"Not a chance."

He squeezed her harder, and held onto her, looking around at their surroundings. "With all yer clothes lyin' out on the rocks over there, what's it yer wearin' under that sleepin' bag darlin'?" he asked feeling excitement run though him that nearly took his breath away as he held her tight.

"Well… I'll leave that to your imagination," she said raising an eyebrow at him seductively, "I must have taken them off before I climbed in my sleeping bag, but I have no memory of it. I was trying to figure out why I was naked when I was eating earlier, and couldn't come up with a logical explanation. I guess I took them off because they were wet," she said pulling him down until their lips met, the sleeping bag falling down to uncover her bare breasts.

Urgently, he laid her back against the hard ground where she had been sleeping, wanting to explore her more thoroughly. He couldn't stop himself from touching her, allowing his hands to roam freely across the parts of her that he had often pictured in his mind. One breast, and then the other, his warm mouth took her in, softly at first, and then with more urgency. Both of them were pulling the other closer, the need of the other growing stronger with each kiss.

He kissed her thoroughly, just as he imagined he would when he was searching for her, remembering every detail of her face, and the blue of her eyes. She could feel that he was aroused, and she raised her hips in anticipation, pulling him down to her as she did.

"Ouch!" she cried out, "there's a rock or something poking me in the back."

"Oh god Jewel," he said coming back to his senses, forcing himself to lift himself off her. "Not like this Jewel. Not here. I won't have ya like this; lyin' out in the dirt with sticks and rocks pokin' ya. Not the first time," he said sitting back, cursing himself for saying the words that were coming out of his mouth, "yer first time should be… special." He was barely glancing at her.

"Oh Grady, I don't want to stop. I was starting to think I was incapable of feeling this way, and now I do and…," she trailed off looking over at him pleadingly.

"Jewel, ya have no idea what this is doin' ta me. Ya lyin' there naked in yer sleepin' bag, pleadin' with me ta do exactly what I've been dreamin' of doin' since first I laid eyes on ya. If ya were just some girl, and not *the* girl, I'd have ya flat on your back with yer legs in the air by now."

"I think that's supposed to be a compliment right?" she asked, "it's kind of hard to tell right now."

"Yeah, it is Jewel. It's the only way I know how ta show ya exactly what ya mean ta me darlin'," he said looking at her more seriously, taking hold of the fragile little hands he'd longed to kiss again.

"You say the sweetest things Grady. Why do you have to be so logical all the time? I swear I don't know what makes me feel more dazed and confused, hypothermia or you."

"Is that supposed ta be a compliment Jewel?" He looked at her with a raised eyebrow.

"Yeah, it is Grady. It means I love you too."

"Sayin' I love ya doesn't seem adequate. It's just not enough of a word. I feel like I might lose my mind. It's crazy Jewel. I can't even begin ta tell ya," he said feeling exasperated and at a loss for words, so he just sat there shaking his head.

"Wow. You really were scared," she said tenderly, reaching up and stroking his face.

"I thought I'd lost ya darlin'. I've never been more scared in my life. It's one thing ta be on yer own fearin' for yer life, and it's another thing ta be helpless, the whole of yer beatin' heart lost ta ya, and ya swear ya might never breath again."

"I'm sorry you were so scared. Thank you for finding me," she said reaching to kiss him more tenderly. "Will you sleep with me by the fire then? I'm so tired."

"I'm goin' ta get a bigger fire started ta make sure ya stay plenty warm, and then I'll come lay with ya," he said getting up to start his task. "Are ya hungry? Do ya need some water, or maybe some hot tea?"

"Oh! Hot tea. I would love hot tea," she said smiling to herself as she snuggled in, enjoying the feeling of having someone take care of her. It wasn't something she was used to, but she also knew that it was something he needed to do. She understood it. She remembered seeing the soldiers that came into the hospital. The helplessness she felt seeing men and women coming in, one after the other, injured, traumatized, and broken. It was something that could only be relieved by bringing as much comfort to them as possible. She would imagine every one of them, and how they must have looked and felt before the war. They were all so proud to serve their country, and it overwhelmed her, filling her with so much emotion, she would need to get up again to carefully check each patient to make sure she had done all she could to make them rest as peacefully as they could, if only for that one night. She knew Grady felt bad about not getting to her faster, and the only way he was going to feel better was to take care of her for a while.

Grady got the fire going sufficiently to last them through the night, and she sat watching it, happily sipping her hot tea as he finally laid down beside her. She snuggled up as close to him as she could when he slipped into his bag, and he pulled her to him as she did. She was lying comfortably between the fire and Grady; feeling blissfully warmed from the inside out, and fell into a deep sleep, the exhaustion of the day finally taking her once and for all.

~~~~~~~~

The early morning light finally woke her up, hours after Grady had already been up as he usually was. She couldn't believe she had slept so long, but she was feeling surprisingly refreshed, albeit a little sore from hitting her arms and legs on a few rocks on her way down the river. She was really lucky, and she crossed herself thinking of the faint dream of her father that arose briefly in her memory. She closed her eyes trying her hardest to remember the dream, but it didn't feel like a dream at all. She could almost feel his presence, and she laid as still as possible, eyes closed, trying to soak it in.

"Should I call room service ta have them fetch ya breakfast in bed?" Grady said seeing her finally stir.

"That would be great actually. I could use a strong cup of coffee while you're at it," she said stretching out, turning toward him where he was standing by the river.

"Unfortunately I don't have either, but I could offer ya some salmon and tea... Rudy has all the coffee."

"What? Why didn't you divide the coffee equally?" she asked teasing him.

"It's not exactly a survival item, though I've been wonderin' the same thing as I sat here watchin' ya sleep."

"Coffee not a survival item? Are you serious? Have you gone completely mad?"

"Maybe a little, but Rudy should be along soon. Ya might want ta get some clothes on darlin'," he said letting his eyes roam over her, clearly imagining her naked body within the sleeping bag.

"Alright then," she said climbing out of her sleeping bag, never once taking her eyes off his. She watched him, as she stood before him completely naked, never moving despite the cool morning air that made her nipples spring forward. She had never stood naked in front of a man before. In fact, she had never stood naked in front of anyone before, not since she was a child, but it didn't scare her or make her feel uncomfortable, it felt perfectly natural, and she was enjoying the tease.

"Wow. I've never seen anyone look so beautiful," he said softly, meeting her eyes, but resisting the urge to move toward her. She had taken her hair out of her braid the night before so that it could dry out, and she stood before him with her long black hair blowing softly in the breeze, part of it covering one breast. He looked at the other breast, round and supple, remembering how it felt in his hand the night before. His eyes made their way down the length of her. She was tall and thin, and he longed to pick her up and wrap her long beautiful legs around him. His heart thumped in his chest as he took every inch of her in, wanting to remember every detail... the soft patch of dark hair between her legs, her full, round breasts, and her skin that looked like silk.

As the two stood there staring at each other, they both suddenly heard voices, and she immediately grabbed her sleeping bag, and headed further into the forest to hide behind some bushes. She poked her head out, and could see that it was Mark, Todd, and Daryl that she heard as they were making their way down the river. *They must have camped out near the area where they all crashed,* she thought. She was hoping they would go on by, but as soon as they saw Grady, they pulled up on the shore. She glanced over toward the rocks near where she and Grady had camped out and saw her clothes lying there, and realized there was nothing she could do to go get them. Grady must have thought the same thing, because he went over to where they were laying, and picked them up smiling coyly at her, waving them in the air.

"Do ya want these?" he mouthed to her, holding them up and pointing to them mockingly.

By this time, she really was cold, but she couldn't help but smile at him as he made his way toward the bushes where she was hiding, holding her clothes in his hands.

"That's what ya get for teasin' me woman!" he said jokingly. "I would have made ya come get them yerself if I wasn't so damn jealous."

"Well thank God for small favors," she said eyeing him playfully while snatching the clothes from him, swatting him away as he reached for one of her breasts, "now get."

She got herself dressed, and then made her way down to where the four of them sat talking, but before she could reach them, they ran up to her and started hugging her, each making their apologies, several times each, before she was able to finally get away to go get her morning rituals taken care of. She brushed her teeth, and braided her hair the way she liked to keep it while she was hiking. She grabbed a few chunks of the smoked salmon, and sat watching as Grady sat with the three boys down by the river. She could tell he was still miffed with them for nearly drowning her. He towered over them, and she could see their reaction to him as they looked up at him, making more apologies.

"Jewel! Is it you?" Rudy said rushing over to grab her up and hug her, swinging her around as he did.

"I'm so glad to see you!" she said hugging him as hard as she could.

"God we were worried about you. Grady was nearly insane. He wasn't going to stop until he found you sweetheart," Rudy said, taking her face in his hands, kissing her on the forehead.

"Did ya get the smoke signal then brother?" Grady said coming up to meet Rudy. They had worked out a smoke signal ahead of time, so Rudy would know whether or not he'd found Jewel, and could quit looking for her to make it more quickly in their direction.

"Yeah, I did. As soon as I saw it, I just put my head down and went as hard as I could. I was so relieved. I was just praying to God she was in one piece. I can't believe how far down the river you went," he replied, feeling happy to have the team together. "What's the Alaska Team doing?" he asked seeing them ready their pack rafts. Clearly, Rudy was still a little upset with them too.

"They're waitin' for us ta get started. They said they didn't want ta win like that knowin' they'd caused all this in the first place. They stopped and apologized nine hundred times, and hugged her, and kissed her, and fawned all over her for so long I thought I was goin' ta hurl," Grady said rolling his eyes. "Christ it was like watchin' a bunch of grovelin' pigs, she had them eating out of her hands so much."

"Stop it. It wasn't like that," she said swatting him, eyeing him narrowly. "They were just being nice. They felt bad for nearly drowning me."

"I seriously thought I was goin' ta throw each one of them in the river if they didn't stop droolin' all over themselves," Grady said putting an arm around her, pulling her in close to him.

"I'm just glad you're safe, and I might hug you a few more times myself," Rudy said happily.

"Are ya ready ta get back in that raft Jewel?" Grady asked, giving her a questioning look.

"Well, thankfully there's not much about the last few miles that I really remember, so I guess we may as well get going," she replied.

"Let's do it!" Rudy said patting both Jewel and Grady on the back.

Jewel hadn't been completely honest when she said there wasn't much she remembered about her trip down the river. She remembered when she quit breathing, and she was ready to hand herself over to the other side until she felt herself floating above the water. It was as if she were just a small child again, being carried up to bed for the night. She could feel the loving hands of her father wrapped tightly around her, placing her down gently, softly kissing her on the cheek before leaving her there. She could still smell him. He always smelled like fire and fresh cut wood, and it was the sweetest smell in the world.

"I want to stay with you Daddy," she had told him.

"You can't Jewel. It's not your time. You'll stay with Grady, and you'll see us again one day, but not now."

"Where's Momma?"

"She's right here with you. She's always with you Jewel. She's always watching over you honey."

"Why did you have to leave me Daddy?"

"We've never left you baby. We've always been right here," he said lifting her hand, laying it over her heart before leaving her to rest.

The memory of it filled her heart so completely she thought she would burst, and she wasn't ready to share it with anybody. She didn't know what it meant. She didn't know if it was real or imagined. She only knew how it made her feel, and that feeling belonged to her forever.

There was no fear inside of her as she got back in her pack raft. She looked around her wondering where they were, wondering if they were watching over her that very moment, blushing a little as she remembered standing there naked in front of Grady, teasing him. She breathed in deep, still remembering the smell of her dad. She closed her eyes for a second, savoring the gift she had been given for a moment longer, before pushing off for the rest of their journey down the river.

CHAPTER 16

GRADY'S CABIN

It was the last day of the second leg, and Grady was fairly certain the Alaska Team was far ahead of them. They had managed to navigate the river the last two days without further incident, and he hadn't seen them since they left them there, but he was sure their new team member knew a better way around the massive falls that had been ahead of them. He shuddered when he thought about what would have happened if Jewel hadn't ended up on the riverbank where she did.

"No wonder they wanted ta let us go first. The bastards didn't want ta see them cut across land to learn their secret," he said to his team members.

"Well, they would have taken it whether I had been dumped in the river or not," Jewel added, coming to their defense a little, knowing Grady had been annoyed with them. "How much further do we have to go do you think?"

"About five miles I'm thinkin'. We'll get there in plenty of time. I wonder where the Adventurers are," he asked more to himself.

"Let's hump it brother. We may still have a chance," Rudy said optimistically.

In their standard formation, the three dug in, sticking to a slightly faster pace than they normally hiked at. They had left the river several hours earlier, and were back to hiking across land. The wind was hitting them right in the face, but they kept their heads down and pushed on. They were in a clearing that offered little protection, and the sudden gusts of cool air would come up, hitting them like a hammer, pushing them backwards as they leaned into the wind. The sun was up, and trying to push through the clouds that hung low in the sky, but it did little to warm them.

Jewel was feeling the effects of her trip down the river, and she was looking forward to a few days at base camp. The breezy conditions were doing little to lift her spirits, combined with hypothermia from the river days before, and everything was sapping her energy. Plus, she was excited to see Angela, and get everyone back together again. They were a fun group of people, and she was excited to see every one of them since Aaron was gone. She assumed he was well on his way back to Homer to face charges, and that gave her comfort as she remembered the way he made her hair stand up on the back of her neck.

"There they are. The rotten scoundrels! They beat us. I wonder when they got here," Grady said shaking his head, but smiling nevertheless, as they finally approached the destination marked on their map.

"Dammit!" Rudy said.

"Hey guys!" Grady yelled as the boys came out to greet them, each of them jockeying to see who would get to help Jewel with her pack.

"Any sign of The Adventure Team?" Jewel asked.

"They're here. They beat us. They got here hours before we did and set up camp. They're over there napping. They hiked all night thinking they were far behind. They thought they had a good eight hours left to go when they accidentally stumbled across the plane wreck," Daryl said.

"Well, sometimes it's better to be lucky than good," Rudy said shrugging.

"What was the prize then?" Grady asked.

"They won't say. They said they were saving it for later until we were all together," Mark said.

They all settled in until the helicopter came to pick them up, and they could head back to base camp. Jewel had never been so excited to be going to a tent in all her life. She couldn't wait to hit the showers, and then tuck herself in for a long nights sleep.

"Are ya alright Jewel? Yer not lookin' so good darlin'," Grady asked, helping her carry her stuff to the tent after they arrived.

"You're such a sweet talker. You really know how to flatter a girl," she said playfully, smiling up at him.

"Ya always look good. Ya know what I mean."

"I'm just a little tired. I want a warm bath and a soft bed, but since I have neither of those things, I'm going to go shower and get in my bag early. No beer drinking for me tonight," she said, readying her things for her shower.

"I'd like ta join ya for that shower, but Angela might not appreciate that, so I'll bid ya goodnight," he said before kissing her thoroughly. "We're goin' ta sneak inta town again and see what we can find."

"See what kind of trouble you can get into, is that it?" she asked a little annoyed, feeling left out.

"What do ya mean? Do ya not trust me?" he asked a little startled, standing back to eye her carefully, a little surprised by her reaction.

"Of course I trust you. I'm tired. I'm grumpy. I'm frustrated. I love being on this adventure with you and Rudy, but at the moment, I just wish I could take you to a quiet place and have you all to myself for a while. That's all," she said shaking her head, not really understanding her own reaction.

"Come on then. Come on a little hike with me. I've got a surprise for ya," he said. "I was savin' it 'til ya were more rested, but now seems like the perfect time."

"A hike? Are you out of your mind? Do you really think more hiking is the cure for being tired, grumpy, and frustrated?"

"Yeah, I do. Trust me on this," he answered, grabbing her shower bag, and throwing it into his daypack. "Come on darlin'. You'll not regret it."

"What about Rudy? I thought you were heading into town?"

"Rudy will be fine. He'll head inta town with or without me."

"You're mad, and I'm equally mad for following you," she said grabbing his hand to follow him.

"Rudy! Good timin' man. We're headin' out ta that place we found the other day," he said, giving Rudy a knowing look, patting him on the back as they walked past him. "Don't wait up for us brother."

"Oh good. I get the whole palace to myself. I'm going to lay around naked, and scratch myself a lot," Rudy joked as they walked toward a trailhead.

"What place did you find? Where are you taking me? What are you up to?" she asked completely intrigued.

"One time when I was a teenager," he said falling into a slow hike, "not long before I'd joined the Army, my dad and I came ta Alaska on a huntin' trip. It was a pretty special time for me. My dad is a hard workin' man, and he rarely takes time ta stop and enjoy life. He knew I was wantin' ta join the Army, and I think it scared him. He suddenly wanted ta make up fer years of lost vacations, or weekends he'd spent workin' rather than playin' with me. My mom and dad moved ta South Dakota shortly after they'd been married... tryin' ta escape all the turmoil in the 1960's that was dividin' Northern Ireland. They were both from a small town just outside of Belfast, and had come from families that spent generations at war, fightin' for their freedom, and fightin' each other. They were from opposite sides of the fence, and the only way they were goin' ta make a life tagether, was ta start over somewhere else. So, they left there ta go and live a peaceful life, and finally stop the madness that plagued their families for centuries, but then here I was, joinin' the most powerful Army in the world," he said trying to convey the exasperation his parents had likely felt.

"Anyway, we spent nearly a month here hikin' all over the place, huntin', and just enyoyin' life, takin' planes, boats, and helicopters. We went everywhere. It's one of my happiest childhood memories. I'd never seen Dad so relaxed, and laughin' so much. One night we'd put up our hammocks and bedded down for the night, only ta wake a few hours later ta blowin' snow and sleet. We were in trouble. It was a late storm we hadn't been expectin', and we were likely ta freeze ta death if we didn't find shelter soon. We packed up as best we could, hopin' ta make our way deeper inta some brush ta find protection from the wind. Just when we thought we wouldn't be able ta take another step, my dad said *Look over there son. It looks like a little cabin or somethin'*. It was a ways off, but when we finally made it ta the cabin, we knew we'd been saved. We were near froze ta death. I swear I'd never been so cold in my life, and my dad was startin' ta mumble, and talk about things that made no sense at all. We'd found salvation."

"Yes. The early stages of hypothermia, I think I understand," she said, remembering the weird thoughts she had after waking up by the cold river.

"So we got inside, started up a little fire in the wood burnin' stove, shared a bottle of Irish whiskey my dad always carried with him, and we talked for hours. We'd never talked like that before. My dad never wanted me ta know about his troubles. He always wanted ta make himself out ta be like some kind of rock, wantin' always ta be strong for us, but that night, he just talked and talked, and I sat and listened ta every word, takin it all in, relishin' every last syllable that came from the man's mouth."

"Well, anyway, when we were tryin' ta find somethin' ta do ta give ya a little space last time we were at base camp, I thought we might be close ta that cabin, so Rudy and I hiked around lookin' for it. I admit, I thought about bringin' ya here the second we found it. It was all I could do ta keep myself from runnin' back and draggin' ya up here like a caveman," he said smiling at her. "I was plannin' on surprisin' ya and bringin' ya here tomorrow night when Rudy was plannin' ta be gone, but I thought maybe ya needed somethin' ta make ya feel better tonight."

"Where's Rudy going? Why was he planning on being gone?" she asked.

"My sister Diana is flyin' in here. The two of them can't keep away from each other very long without goin' mad. Ya'd be surprised if I told ya just how far the woman's gone ta fly in for conjugal visits wherever it is that Rudy happens to be," he said giving her a knowing look.

"How did they arrange that?"

"That was the main reason for sneakin' inta town last time. He wasn't goin' ta stop 'til we found a phone so he could call her. They planned it all out then."

"You're not really supposed to go into town you know. That's against the rules, and it was in big bold letters when I signed the agreement. We could get kicked out."

"I know darlin', but if they really wanted ta enforce that rule, they shouldn't have accepted a former Navy Seal, and an Army Sniper. It's what we do. Do ya know how many times I've slipped in and out of areas I wasn't supposed ta be without ever bein' detected?" he asked rhetorically.

"Oh. I suppose that's a good point," she said, imagining him in all his Army gear dangerously creeping around in enemy territory.

"Here. Yep. Here it is Jewel. Come on," he said excitedly, grabbing her hand and pulling her toward the cabin.

Jewel couldn't see what he was talking about, or what they were running toward, but she ran behind him feeding off his energy. She couldn't see anything, but after running for a few more minutes, Grady pulling her eagerly up a small hill, she could finally see a little cabin hidden in the side of a bank, camouflaged by the thick brush.

"Wow! This is amazing. If you hadn't pointed it out to me, I would have walked right by it."

"Look here Jewel," he said pointing to the sign on the door when they made their way onto the deck.

Rest here and be safe.
Take what you need.
Leave what you can.
<u>*Honor the Gift!*</u>

"That's beautiful. I love that," she said thoughtfully, looking up at Grady.

"Come on. Let's go in. I want ta show ya somethin'," he said opening the latch on the door, leading her inside.

The cabin was small, but not nearly as small as Jewel thought it would be when she saw it from the outside. Inside she could see a wood burning stove, a bed, cabinets stocked with blankets, canned goods, and a fairly large round tub off to the side as they entered.

"What is this?" she asked, going up to look at the large round tub that sort of looked like a stock tank they kept in their pastures to water their horses.

"It's a bathtub. Look!" he said, pulling the top off to set it aside.

"Ya fill this side up with water where ya sit and bathe, and ya make a fire over here, heatin' up the water ta give ya a nice warm bath," he announced proudly.

It was pretty rustic looking, made of aluminum, complete with rust and a few jagged edges she'd have to be careful of while getting in and out. It had garden hoses running in and out of it that she presumed would run to the creek. One side of it looked like a fire pit, but the other side where you bathed was decent, and had some sort of lining in it. Jewel had to admit that the idea of taking a warm bath was very appealing.

"Sit here darlin'. Let me pamper ya a bit," he said, pulling out a dusty chair for her that was sitting in the corner.

It was no time before Grady figured out the hand pump to get water pouring into the tub, and he got a fire started in the other side right away, using some logs that had been stacked outside the door. Jewel sat watching him, thanking God for him in a silent prayer she'd said to herself. She had never been able to imagine her future. She would try over and over, but after the death of her parents, nothing ever made sense. She was too lost. Nothing she ever thought of seemed to fit. She would think about being on the ranch, or on one of the exotic vacations she and her grandpa had pretended they were on, but it never seemed quite right.

She envied all those people who seemed to have it all figured out. They would talk about their future and all their plans excitedly, knowing exactly where it was their life was headed. She always wondered how they could be so certain. Of course, she had known she wanted to be a nurse, but where, and what would the rest of her life look like beyond that? She never had a clue. She once had to write a college paper about what her life would look like in twenty years, and she was so puzzled by it, she finally interviewed a girl on her floor, and wrote her plans down as her own. She wanted to graduate college and marry her boyfriend, move to the coast and have two kids, take wonderful vacations while making her way to a powerful position in a swanky law firm, still madly in love with her husband, and her two perfect children. To Jewel it didn't seem like a great plan, but at least it was a vision. It was a glimpse at the future that Jewel seemed to be completely void of imagining.

Certainly, never in a million years, did she think of being in a dusty old cabin in Alaska, about to take a bath in something that looked like a glorified stockpot she would have used to boil potatoes in. When she looked at it, she could imagine Elmer Fudd cutting potatoes and carrots up, ready to boil Bugs Bunny for dinner. She looked at Grady and watched him, smiling, and working so hard, trying to do something to give her comfort. She couldn't have imagined anything more perfect. She dared to dream about the future.

"Let's give it a bit ta get warm. The water from the creek is still pretty cold, but it's clean. You'll have a nice bath. Come here. Let me show ya somethin'," he said taking her hands, pulling her up from the chair, talking excitedly, eager to share the cabin with her.

He pulled her toward the wall in the back of the cabin to point at a skull hanging on a nail, smiling proudly as he showed it to her.

"What's it from?" she asked, looking at the skull that was unlike anything she had ever seen before.

"It's a polar bears skull. My dad hung it here, wantin' ta show his respect for the place. I was surprised ta see it was still here. We'd been ta a little town when we were in the Aleutian Islands, and a man we met gave it ta my dad. They'd taken us out on a hunt, and we didn't have much luck. For dad and me it was just a bad hunt, but ta these people, it was a matter of life or death. They truly live off the land Jewel. They need the meat, or they don't eat all winter."

"Well, just as we were calling it quits for the day, my dad had gone off ta take care of business," Grady said giving her a knowing look. "All the sudden we hear screamin' an yellin', and all this commotion, and then a single shot. My dad had walked up on a juvenile male moose that charged him, and caught him completely off guard. His rifle had gone flyin' and laid about ten feet from him, but he managed to get the forty-five off his hip and shoot it right in the heart before the five hundred pound beast fell right on top of him, nearly crushin' him ta death," Grady said smiling, enjoying the memory.

"Oh my gosh! Was he all right?" she asked, imagining a man being crushed by a large moose.

Grady shook his head answering that he was, smiling as he did. "We ran toward him when we heard the screamin', and when we got there, all we could see was dad's head and an arm stickin' out. The rest of him was buried under this massive moose. He was lucky, because the beast's legs kept the full weight of him off Dad just enough ta keep him from bein' crushed. It took every last one of us ta move him off my dad," Grady said laughing.

"One of the men we were with was so thankful ta have the meat, he'd given this ta my dad as thanks. My dad didn't want ta take it, because he knew how special it was ta them. It had been hangin' as the centerpiece in their home, but he had ta accept it. It would have been disrespectful if he hadn't, but after we came here, he thought this is where it belonged. The polar bear is very sacred to the Native Alaskans. They believe that the polar bear gives them the ability to navigate, hunt, and provide both physical and spiritual nourishment, and that's exactly what it did for us. It belongs in Alaska, not South Dakota."

"That's an incredible story," she said looking up at him. "Your dad must be a really good man. I think I would like him."

"You will like him, and he'll love you," he said leaning down to kiss her thoroughly, lingering every time their lips parted, not wanting to let her go. "Come on Jewel. Yer bath should be about ready. It heats up faster than ya might think."

He led her back to check on the temperature of the water, dipping his hand in. "Should I just give ya some space then Jewel?" he asked, suddenly feeling a little unsure, not wanting to feel like he was pushing her.

"No. I've had plenty of space. Space is not what I want at all," she said, slowly taking off her boots, and then her pants, never once taking her eyes from his. "I finally know exactly what I want, and besides, we could help each other get washed."

"Are ya sure about this?" he asked, not really waiting for an answer before lifting her shirt over her head, kissing her as he did, his heart pounding wildly.

"I've never been more sure of anything," she whispered in between kisses, her heart pounding in rhythm to his, returning the gesture by helping him lift his shirt off over his head.

They stood there kissing each other heatedly, both of them knowing that the time had finally come where they could be alone, and not worry about interruptions. They didn't have to explore each other hurriedly before their brief moment alone passed by too quickly. They slowed down, wanting to make the time they had together last as long as possible.

"God yer beautiful," he said taking her hand, helping her down in the tub, both of them having stripped down to nothing. "Come let me wash yer hair Jewel."

He helped her pull her long hair out of the braid she always wore, combing it out between his fingers as he did. He had imagined it many times hanging loose, and he savored every moment, running his hands through it. Long and black, a breathtaking contrast to the deep blue eyes that sparkled with violet flecks, taking his breath away every time he looked at her. Her olive skin looked and felt like silk, as he slowly ran his hands along her curves. He had never imagined someone so beautiful, with her dirty face, and her dirty hair going wildly in every direction without a care in the world, but it was more than just her appearance that always startled him. She had something beneath her eyes that pierced his very soul, a look she seemed to have just for him. He saw it as he slowly washed her hair, moving his hands down the rest of her, not wanting to rush a single moment, breathing every ounce of her in.

"Now it's my turn," she said breathlessly, as the anticipation made her heart race. She poured shampoo out in her hands, and started washing his hair slowly, pressing herself against him as she did.

"Yer toyin' with me woman... like a cat plays with a little mouse. Quiet, methodical, and seductive, like a lethal weapon... dangerously enticing. The sky could start fallin', and the only thing I'd be thinkin' about is getting ya inta bed," he said rubbing his hands on her skin as she rinsed his hair, stopping every so often to kiss his lips or his neck.

"Take me to bed then," she whispered, pressing against him harder, kissing him more urgently.

"God give me the strength ta keep from actin' like a wild animal," he barely uttered, more to himself, picking her up, and lifting her out of the tub as she wrapped her legs around him.

"Let me just lay these blankets out," he said setting her down, wrapping a towel around her before quickly making a comfortable bed for them.

Jewel stood back watching him as he shook the blankets out across the bed, taking him all in from head to toe. She could finally see the muscles she'd felt beneath his clothes, the perfect silhouette of his body outlined in the dimly lit cabin. She watched as long as she could before reaching out to touch the shiny scars that were scattered across his broad back, kissing them gently, and running her hands up the length of him.

She felt the strength of him as he turned to grab her, wrapping her in both his arms, laying her down gently on the bed as he climbed on top of her. He kissed her softly, starting with her lips, propping himself up over the top of her, wanting to take her all in, kissing every inch of her as he made his way down the length of her, stopping to kiss each breast, and feel the softness of her stomach.

"Oh my gosh Grady! What are you doing?" she startled as he made his way down further, gasping as his tongue found the place between her legs. She'd heard her friends in college talk about men doing that, but she could never quite imagine why anyone would do it until just then.

"Shhh. Just close yer eyes Jewel," he whispered as she writhed beneath him, tipping her head back in pure ecstasy, her body making movements and feeling things she'd never felt before.

She could feel his need as he worked his way back up, kissing her stomach, her breasts, her neck, and then her lips. It instantly became more urgent. His breaths came faster, matched by her own. She longed to touch every inch of him, running her hands over his chest as he propped himself over the top of her. She arched back instinctively as he took her nipple in his mouth again, feeling a need wash over her that she had never known before.

He took her hand, guiding her to feel between his legs, gasping as she grabbed a hold of him, both of them suddenly bound by the other. He skillfully parted her legs with his own, finding the wet slippery place within her. He gently eased himself in, both of them lost in their own desire. She arched back instinctively, wanting to feel him deep within, a primal, instinctual move that invited him in more urgently.

"Just a little further Jewel," he gasped, trying to keep control of himself. He had never been with a virgin before, but he knew enough to be gentle with her. He wanted to make her first time memorable for the right reasons.

She knew he was trying to make it easier for her, trying to answer his own prayer he'd said to himself as he carried her to the bed, so she grabbed him, pulling him into her until the length of him was deep within her. Another thrust and then another, both of them getting lost in the other, until finally crying out, reaching the ecstasy that had been driving them. A flood of yearning they'd felt since they first met, nearly drowning them only moments before, was finally releasing them.

"Are ya alright Jewel?" he whispered several minutes later, still kissing her, running his hands down the length of her.

"I'm perfect," she said sighing, smiling up at him still lost in her own desire.

"Yes ya are darlin'," he said looking down at the woman still lying beneath him, neither one of them wanting to let go of the other.

"I definitely have the best story of the three," she said, remembering the stories Grady and Rudy had told her about their first times.

"I'm glad ya think so."

"I'm glad you brought me here Grady. I can't think of a more perfect place."

"Ha. Yer somethin' else Jewel," he said moving to lie beside her, gathering her up in his arms as he did. "Most women would not think a dusty old cabin in the woods was a perfect place. They'd want the Ritz Carlton, or some high-end resort with bath salts and room service."

"I'm probably not normal. I remember my friends getting all excited to go shopping for prom dresses, and I'd try to be as excited as they were, but I never was. We would all pile into my friend Jeannie's car, drive two hours to Billings, everyone chatting about the kind of shoes and dresses they wanted, and which accessories to buy. I'd find myself staring out the window wanting to go running out onto the plains, across hills, and rivers, just to see what was out there. Troy knew I didn't like shopping that much. He would tell me beforehand what color of dress to buy. I would just buy one in that color, and be done with it hours before anyone else. It was then that I realized I was probably crazy," she said trying to make a joke of it.

"Yer not crazy Jewel. Yer everything I ever wanted in a woman. A friend that I could hike with, camp and hunt with, and then make love with at the end of the day. Ugh! That sounded terrible!" he said grimacing.

"Well, it didn't sound that bad. I mean, I know what you're trying to say. Troy was my best friend. We spent every day together hunting, trailing sheep, and hiking all over the countryside. Everyone always thought we would get married one day.

They expected it actually. It might have been planned from the very beginning for all I know. All I really know for sure is that I had this wonderful friend, a boy that loved me unconditionally, and I couldn't love him back, well... not in that way anyhow. I just didn't feel that way about him," she said, turning to wrap an arm around him, kissing him softly on the lips.

"So what happened with Troy then... if ya don't mind me askin'?" he asked meeting her eyes.

"Nothing. I need to go back and talk to him. He told me he loved me, and he said he wanted to marry me, but I ran away. I didn't return phone calls, emails, or letters. I owe him an apology. His family runs my family's ranch... well... my ranch, I guess," she said with a heavy sigh, feeling the heavy weight of the burden she had been avoiding. "He married a girl we went to school with... a girl who hates me, but I miss talking to him," she said a little sadly.

"Do ya think ya might take me there someday Jewel? I'd love ta see where ya grew up," he asked, kissing her lightly on the forehead when he saw the sadness.

"I would love to. It's actually the most beautiful place in the world. I don't know why, but for the first time since I left, going back doesn't seem as scary anymore," she said, feeling a piece of the heavy brick wall that guarded her heart, suddenly fall away.

"Are ya ta go back and run yer ranch then, or will him and his family keep runnin' if for ya?"

"I don't really know. I mean, he wouldn't leave without telling me, but I suppose he wants to go live his own life. I haven't been fair. I just left. I mean... I just ran away, and I never thought of the consequences. I had to leave," she said with the weight of it suddenly hitting her.

"Well, ya don't have ta go this second do ya?" he asked, feeling her tense up.

"No, but I suppose I'll be ready when we're done with the competition. What about you Grady? I mean... where are you going after we leave here?" she asked awkwardly, not sure she wanted to hear the answer to her question.

"I don't really know," he said with a heavy sigh, searching the ceiling for answers. "I thought I'd still be in the military, but now... I don't know..."

"We're both a little lost aren't we?" she asked rhetorically.

"Not anymore Jewel," he said turning to her, smiling. "It seems we've found each other. It's the least lost I've felt in a long time, because at least we can maybe be lost together."

She shook her head when she heard him say that, unsure how to respond.

"What is it? Ya don't want ta be lost together?" he asked carefully, his pulse quickening a little, albeit for a different reason than it was a moment before.

"It's not that... I just... well, we've only known each other for a short time, and I've been wondering how I can be so sure of how I feel, and to hear you say all that so certain yourself, I just... I'm scared of it a little maybe."

"It scares me too, but it feels damn good."

"Yes it does… ugh… have you ever felt like this before… I mean, just the way everything happened so fast between us from the very beginning?" she asked timidly.

"No. Never. Nothing even close to this. I would have relentlessly harassed any friend of mine that was fallin' all over himself, and talkin' all lovey-dovey the way I've been. I'm not even sure I believed in this sort of thing before, at least not for me… right up until I bumped inta ya on the sidewalk."

"Really? How come? You said you'd been with women before… what makes me any different?"

He propped himself up to look at her more closely, scrutinizing every inch of her thoroughly, before shaking his head with a hint of an upturned smile, finally answering. "I don't know. You're really pretty ordinary come to think of it, with your shiny black hair and piercing blue eyes, and let's not even talk about that voice of an angel ya have, and the way ya always want ta care for everyone. You're really pretty disgustin' now that I look closer."

She swatted him playfully, even as she pulled him in for a long, lingering kiss as he wrapped his arms around her solidly, pulling her on top of him.

"The fact that ya don't know Jewel, is what makes me love ya darlin'," he finally said, reaching up to brush the hair from her face when she stopped kissing him, "and I don't know what it is that makes ya love me in return, but I thank God fer yer foolishness."

"I do love you Grady. I don't know how, I just know that I do."

CHAPTER 17

DIANA

"Did ya sleep okay Jewel?" Grady asked when she woke up, knowing they hadn't done much sleeping.

"Not exactly. I've never slept naked next to a man before, and especially not one who periodically wakes me up for another round of love-making that I'm completely unable to resist," she said, wrapping a blanket around her naked body, smiling up at him as he handed her a cup of hot coffee.

"Coffee? You are simply the best!" she said, blissfully sipping and smelling the aroma.

"I ordered room service. Do ya like it?"

"Hmmm. It's wonderful. I have to go brush my teeth so I can kiss you. How long have you been up?"

"Maybe half an hour. Ya were sleepin' pretty hard. I'm sorry if I woke ya."

"You are? You didn't seem sorry the first time you woke me, or even the second or third time. I'm not sure I believe you," she mumbled while brushing her teeth, giving him a playful wink.

"Yes, well... I can't keep my hands off ya. If I could have found the strength ta wake ya one last time, I'd have done it. Come here woman," he said pulling her onto his lap as she made her way back to the bed moments later.

"Ouch! Careful. I'm a little... sore I guess."

"Sorry. I'm a little sore too. I can't help myself Jewel," he said kissing her softly. "I'm completely unable to resist you. You're my kryptonite and my strength, all at the same time."

"I'm not complaining. Don't ever be sorry for waking me up in the middle of the night for that," she said leaning back into him contently.

"I'd like ta introduce ya ta my sister," he said casually stroking her hair as she laid up against him. "She'll love ya. Rudy told her on the phone that I'd fallen madly in love, and she can't wait ta meet ya. Said she'd have ta see it with her own two eyes before she'd believe it."

"Really? I would love to meet her," she said sitting up. "When is she coming?"

"Well, that's the bad part. If we're goin' ta make it in time before the two of them run off ta their little love nest, we'll have ta leave here pretty soon."

"I don't want to leave yet, but I would really like to meet your sister. Maybe we could come back here again sometime," she said nuzzling into him again, kissing his neck.

"I'd like that," he replied, kissing her thoroughly before getting up to get ready for the day.

~~~~~~~~

"I'll admit that when you got up last night to wash out our clothes, I thought you were a little crazy, but I'm pretty happy about it at the moment," Jewel said, pulling on the fresh clothes Grady brought in from outside. He had them laid outside on the bushes to dry overnight.

"I said I was goin' ta pamper ya a bit Jewel. Washin' yer clothes out in dirty bath water, and throwin' them up ta dry on the bushes, is just the sort of luxury ya can come ta expect," he said smiling at her.

"Well I require only the best you know."

"Besides, I didn't want us smellin' like beasts the first time ya meet Diana. Not that she'd mind, but I didn't want ya ta feel awkward or anything," he added.

They'd gotten ready, both of them helping to empty the bath tub and get everything cleaned up, wanting to make things cleaner and better off than when they arrived. Jewel felt like she belonged there in some strange way. She felt like there was a part of that place that had lived within her since before she ever knew it existed. She wanted to leave what she could, and honor the place just as the sign said. *I did leave something here*, she thought smiling to herself, feeling breathless just thinking about it, *but that probably wasn't what they were thinking about when they wrote the sign.*

"I brought some MRI's I had in my pack. I wanted ta have somethin' ta leave behind. They aren't the best things in the world, but it sure beats goin' hungry," Grady said as if to read her thoughts, walking around anxiously.

"Are you nervous about me meeting your sister Grady?"

"I guess a little. I've never introduced her ta a girl before. I mean, it's a big deal for me Jewel. My sister is very important to me. I remember ya sittin' across from us in the bar when first we met ya. I knew then I wanted ta introduce ya to her. That's all. I don't really know how ta say it, I just knew," he shrugged, searching for the right words.

"I know what you're trying to say I think. Grandpa would have liked you a lot. I've thought about that a lot since we met. I suppose if he were alive I'd feel the same way."

"Ya don't have any family then Jewel? No cousins or aunts?" he asked cautiously.

"My mom's family, but I don't really know them. They didn't approve of my dad, and I never really knew them very well. They thought I was a hideous little kid after they saw me walking around with a rifle on my back one summer when they came to visit. They didn't approve. They kept talking about how I needed to be sent away and educated, as if I were some ignorant country girl that needed them to enlighten me. When we would go to Denver, they would want to dress me up and have my hair done, and it was actually pretty fun. I think I would have really enjoyed it if they could have done it without acting like they were doing me some huge favor. Plus, I didn't like the way they treated my dad. I like you too much to introduce you to them," she laughed nervously, giving him a half smile. "Trust me… according to them, we're probably beneath them."

"I can't imagine how hard it's been for ya," he said, pulling her in for a hug, holding her close to his chest. "You're the toughest person I've ever met."

"Well no worries," she said bravely. "We should probably go. I don't want to miss meeting your sister."

They left, carefully latching everything tightly behind them, making sure the next guests would find comfort there. Jewel was lost in her thoughts trying to shrug off the loneliness of not having a family. Everywhere she went people talked about moms, and dads, and siblings. Most of her friends back home had an abundance of siblings and cousins. It seemed like everyone was related to someone except her. Whenever someone brought up the subject of family, she felt immediately excluded from the conversation. She loved hearing about everyone's family, but she always dreaded how she would respond when it circled around, and people asked her about her own.

How will Grady's sister react to him falling in love with a homeless girl? Well… not homeless, as I do own a rather large ranch, but certainly orphaned. Ugh! she cringed when she thought of that word. *Orphan.* It was a word of abandonment and sadness. It was a word that summed up to the rest of the world that she was alone, and didn't have people back home who worried about her, or people who invited her home for Thanksgiving, or Christmas. She usually spent holidays dishing out meals to other lost souls, all of them gathering to find comfort in each other.

"Ya don't ever have ta worry about not havin' a family again Jewel," Grady said, interrupting her thoughts as they slipped into a silent hike. "I mean, ya've got Rudy and I, and all that we come with. Will ya let us be yer family darlin'?"

She knew he must have been thinking about her growing up without much family. It was hard for some people to imagine.

"How do you always know what I'm thinking?"

"I was just thinkin' about what ya said. I was thinkin' about my own family. I don't know Jewel, I mean… we haven't known each other that long, but it's just… I can't think of my family or my life anymore without ya in it. I see them, and I see ya right beside me," he said stopping to look her in the eyes.

"Grady," she started, but then stopped, a tear bubbling up, escaping from one eye, slowly making its way down her cheek.

"Shhh. Yer not alone anymore Jewel. Just know that," he said wiping away the tear, before hugging her tightly. "Come on now. I can't wait for ya to meet Diana."

They made their way back to the base camp, both of them lost in their own thoughts. Jewel thought about all that Grady said to her, and she knew it was true they hadn't known each other very long. She never imagined it was possible to fall so in love with someone she hadn't known her whole life, but then there he was offering himself up as family. It terrified her and comforted her all at once. She was still lost in the onslaught of thoughts racing through her mind when Grady started yelling and running.

"Diana! Ya made it!" Grady yelled to her, running up to lift her up in a big bear hug, sweeping her off her feet.

"There he is. It's good ta see ya brother!" Diana said hugging him tightly. "Oh my gosh, is this Jewel?"

"Hi! Yes, I'm Jewel," she said coming up to Diana, getting caught up in all the excitement. Diana and Rudy were both beaming and full of so much energy, she could hardly escape feeling all of it lift her up, and she became part of it.

"Oh come here!" Diana said excitedly, grabbing Jewel and hugging her. "The woman who stole my brother's heart... I never thought I'd see the day, and I can certainly see why. Look at ya! Yer lovely!"

"Wow. Rudy said you looked like Princess Diana, and he wasn't kidding. It's so nice to meet you!" Jewel said, holding her out with both arms to pick out the features that resembled her brother.

"Rudy is nothin' but a charmer. Can ya not love him though?" Diana asked rhetorically, wrapping her arms around him as he came up beside her.

"I do love him. He's like the brother I never had," Jewel said, the phrase suddenly feeling less cliché and more certain, remembering her and Grady's earlier conversation.

"She's a fine wee lassie, as yer daddy would say," Rudy said, putting an arm around Jewel, exaggerating the heavy Irish accent of Diana and Grady's father was something Rudy did well, and they all laughed.

"Come over here. I brought ya all a picnic. I didn't know what ya liked Jewel, but Rudy said ya'd grown up on a sheep ranch, so I brought lamb, and sheep cheese, and some red wine, and a few other things. You'll not go hungry, I promise!" Diana said, grabbing her by the arm, leading her toward their tent.

"You brought lamb? How incredibly thoughtful of you," Jewel said, feeling a little overwhelmed.

"Diana yer a good sister," Grady said, coming up to put an arm around her, kissing her on the top of the head.

"And a fine wife!" Rudy said grabbing her away from Grady and Jewel, "and I'll be stealing her away before too long, so enjoy her company while you can brother."

"I know! Don't remind me. I know what horny little bastards the two of ya are.

I've heard it a time or two," Grady said rolling his eyes, narrowly dodging a blow from Diana.

"Jewel, Rudy said ya were in the Army... a nurse?" Diana asked as they settled around the campfire for an early picnic.

"Yes. I love being a nurse. My grandpa wanted me to be a doctor, but nurses are the ones who take care of people, I mean... beyond the physical wounds. They listen. Doctors never listen," Jewel said shaking her head with a smile, savoring the lamb and wine that Diana brought.

"Oh my! Mom and Dad are goin' ta love ya! I've heard Dad say that exact thing a hundred times. Grady aren't ya glad ya didn't marry Mrs. Pinker?" Diana asked Grady laughing.

"Mrs. Pinker? Do tell. I need to hear this story," Jewel said smiling at Grady.

"Here we go. Let the stories begin!" Grady smiled.

"Mrs. Pinker was his fourth grade teacher. She was a very pretty lady, and he was madly in love with her, swearin' he was goin' ta grow up one day and marry her. He'd go cut her lawn or bring her flowers. It was really pretty sweet," Diana said smiling at her brother. "One day somethin' occurred ta me, and I sat Grady down and I told him that Mrs. Pinker and I were the exact same age. Well, ya'd thought I just stabbed him in the heart. He wrinkled up his nose and got the most horrible look on his face, like bein' my age was the most terrible thing in the world. It nearly broke his heart."

"It was pretty heart breakin' when I realized what an old sot she was!" Grady laughed, going in a defensive pose to dodge another playful blow from Diana. "She was a very pretty lady though. She smelled like sugar cookies all the time, which is a very appealin' smell ta a nine-year-old boy. I'd imagine us goin' ta the park and eatin' sugar cookies all over town, and all the other boys bein' jealous," Grady said laughing. "I suppose I should thank God for unanswered prayers." He flashed a smile at Jewel and squeezed her hand.

"Yeah, I met your Mrs. Pinker a few years ago," Rudy said eyeing Grady sideways," she smelled like rotten milk and applesauce. You dodged a bullet my friend! You don't want to be falsely lured by sugar cookies only to find sour milk!"

"Well, thankfully, Jewel here smells like rotten fish, dirt, and wet grass most the time. There's no false advertisement goin' on here," Grady said, wrapping an arm around Jewel.

"Ahhh. That's so sweet. Can you see why I fell for him?" Jewel asked Diana sarcastically.

"Yer a good match I think. I know a good match when I see one." Diana leaned back into Rudy and smiled up at him.

"Tell me more about your kids," Jewel said, smiling at seeing them together. "Rudy won't talk about them much. He gets too sad I think."

"He's a softy!" Diana said, reaching up to put her hand on Rudy's cheek. "Well, there's Alisha, she's sixteen and is completely in-love with her boyfriend, which changes weekly. Then Paxton, he's fifteen and wants ta be a vet. Then there's the last of the Irish twins, Melanie, who's fourteen, and she, thankfully, is still in love with her daddy, and thinks that all other boys pale in comparison."

"That's fortunate," Jewel chimed in.

"Then we had a little break until Tina came along, she's ten, and then Thomas who's eight, and Joseph who's seven, and looks exactly like his uncle. I swear it's like I'm rockin' ya on my knee all over again," Diana said exasperated.

"That's it? Just six?" Jewel joked. "Are you having anymore?"

"No! We're done! I swear if this man even comes near me when I'm ovulatin', I beat him with a stick!" she said, wagging an accusing finger at Rudy.

"There's a price ta be payin' for bein such a good Irish Catholic," Rudy said, slipping back in a heavy Irish accent, squeezing Diana affectionately.

"Are you all Catholic then?" Jewel asked looking at Grady.

She didn't know why it suddenly seemed important to her. She had struggled with her faith for a long time, and had only attended mass when she absolutely had to. She never doubted that God existed, but she couldn't understand it. She'd sit in church, all the while wondering how it was possible that God could ever let her parents die. They were so perfect. She'd never seen parents like hers. Troy's mom and dad were always bickering at each other, and she had friends whose parents were divorced, or who fought all the time, but not her parents. They hugged each other all the time, holding hands, laughing, and stealing kisses every chance they got. They reminded her of them, Rudy and Diana, and she remembered the feeling her dad left her with by the river.

"We are," Diana chimed in, "though Grady here is a bit of a sinner. Not much of an altar boy either I might add," she said eyeing Grady sternly.

"I feel another story coming. Let's hear it!" Jewel said excitedly.

"Well, it's just that a growin' boy needs a little nourishment while he's servin' the altar," Diana said sarcastically. "He and his friend Jeremy ate enough wafers, and drank enough wine ta feed half the town."

"Well it hadn't been blessed. I'm not a complete ingrate," Grady added in his defense.

"They were so drunk, mom and dad had ta lay in the basement with them ta make sure they didn't choke on their own vomit, and get poor Jeremy sobered up before his mom could come get him. Jeremy's mom always thought Grady was an instigator, even though it was really the other way around, and they knew she was goin' ta hit the roof if she saw him drunk."

"He was the instigator! Drinkin' wine in our household was no big deal, but for Jeremy it was rare access, and he wasn't about ta let it slip through his fingers. He'd come up with this game ya see, and I couldn't back down, because I would have looked like a big chicken, which is pretty important when yer a young man. So we'd toss wafers in the air, and if ya didn't catch it in yer mouth on the way down, ya'd have ta take two big gulps. I don't know if ya've ever tried ta toss a wafer and catch it in yer mouth Jewel, but it's a little harder than it sounds, and before long, we were both smashed," he said with the memory of too much wine written on his face.

"I've never tossed wafers and tried to catch them in my mouth. I'll try it next time during communion," Jewel said laughing. "It'll spice things up a bit on Sundays."

"Ahhh. Ya found ya a good Catholic girl then," Diana said patting Grady affectionately. "Mom and Dad will be so happy."

"Well, *good* might be a bit of a stretch," Jewel replied, with the memory of the night before flushing into her cheeks.

"There's nothin' about ya that's not good Jewel," Grady said with his heart beating harder at the memory.

Diana could see the look between them, and eyed Rudy knowingly. She'd never seen Grady like that before. He was always giving Rudy a hard time about calling her all the time, and missing her. Now he'd met his match, and she couldn't be happier.

"I need ta find a bathroom before we head out," Diana said standing up suddenly, ready to have her time alone with her husband.

"Come with me and I'll show you," Jewel said, getting up off the ground, stretching out.

"He loves ya Jewel, I can see it plainly," Diana said after they'd made their way across the field a ways.

"I know he does. I love him back."

"I can't wait 'til ya come ta meet Mom and Dad. I've been dreamin' about a sister since before I could walk. Rudy has a sister, but we're not close. I'm lookin' forward ta knowin' ya better. You'll come ta Thanksgivin' then I hope. Grady always comes for Thanksgivin' when he can," Diana said, talking so excitedly she didn't stop long enough to give Jewel time to respond to her questions.

"I'd love to," Jewel finally replied, fighting back tears, putting an arm around her. *When did I become such a crybaby?* she thought to herself.

"Did Rudy tell ya he was born in Wyomin'?" Diana asked, making conversation.

"No. He never told me. Is that where he's from?"

"Well, he was born in Wyomin'. He's adopted. He doesn't really like ta talk about it, but I thought he'd probably tell ya since yer from there. I shouldn't have said anything,"

"All he told me was that he was from the Faqaiwi tribe," Jewel said, laughing at the memory, trying to lighten the tone.

"Oh my gosh! He's told that so many times. Makes me laugh every time!" Diana said throwing her head back as she laughed.

They made their way to and from the bathroom talking non-stop, laughing, and joking lightheartedly the whole time. She and Jewel hit it off immediately. Grady and Diana were exactly the same, and they had the exact same sense of humor, which completely cracked her up. Jewel was wishing she had more time to spend with her and Rudy before they headed off, but they were eager to leave and spend some time alone, and so they said their goodbyes. She knew she wouldn't be seeing her before she left, and she wondered when she might see her again. *Thanksgiving perhaps?* Jewel thought to herself, smiling as they watched them make their escape.

CHAPTER 18

A DAY TOGETHER

Jewel and Grady spent the rest of the day together, lounging in the tent, hiking around the lake that was nearby, both of them enjoying the freedom to touch each other and kiss when they felt like it, without worrying about making Rudy feel uncomfortable. The sun was up, and they enjoyed its warmth, both of them peeling off as many clothes as they dared, letting it soak up in their skin. They avoided the common areas around the base camp as much as possible, wanting to stay away from the other team members, and just spend this rare time they had alone.

They fished some, wanting to restock their supply of dried salmon for the next leg of the journey, but they also knew they didn't need to worry about it as much since Diana had brought them plenty of jerky, and other stores of food from home. At first, they felt like it was cheating, but they also knew that compared to the other teams, they were mostly surviving off the land. Gary had snuck in all sorts of dried foods that he wasn't supposed to have, and they all knew that bribing crewmembers to bring them snacks from town was easy enough. Base camp was a place where they relaxed, broke the rules, and enjoyed themselves, but when it came to the competition itself, they were all business.

Toward evening, Jewel and Grady decided they should make their way over to the winner's tent to congratulate them, and spend a little time with them celebrating.

"There's the love birds!" Angela cried out as Grady and Jewel made their way over to their campsite. "Rudy said you'd gone off in search of a little privacy," she said giving the two of them a salacious look.

The woman had a larger than life personality that Jewel found to be magnetic, and she was completely lit up the moment she saw her. She was a beautiful woman, and Jewel imagined that as a young woman, she had probably been chased by plenty of young men.

"Angela, you're the devil," Jewel said leaning in to give her a hug. "Are you jealous? Wishing you could sneak off for a little privacy of your own?" she whispered to her, nodding toward Joe.

"Sneaking off and finding privacy is a near nightly routine little lady. You two are amateurs," Angela said leading Jewel out away from the group. "I'm in my prime and the man's sex drive is unquenchable," she said throwing her head back in thanks.

"We're heading to the bathrooms. Be back in a minute," Jewel called out to Grady as they made their way in that direction.

They walked arm and arm to the bathrooms, laughing and talking excitedly, glad to have a little time in the company of another woman. They talked to each other as if they'd known each other for a long time. The bond they started from the first time they met was growing stronger each time they were together. It was a rare bond for Jewel. She was close to some of the girls where she grew up, and of course, she had been very close to Troy, but the previous several years she'd lived a guarded life. She'd never really let anyone get close to her, and never wanted to let them get close to her, for fear that maybe anyone who got close to her would die. Of course, logically speaking, she knew that it wasn't her that caused the death of people around her, but it gave her a good excuse to seclude herself until she was ready to open her heart back up again.

"Can I ask you a question Angela?" she asked hesitantly as they reached the bathrooms.

"Ask away pretty lady."

"Do you think it's really possible to fall in love with someone after knowing them for just a few weeks?" she asked, afraid to hear the answer. There was a part of her that wondered if she was being foolish. Nobody ever talked to her about dating or boys. Nobody ever talked to her about falling in love or having sex. Her grandpa did his best, but the subject of boys and sex was clearly not something that he felt comfortable discussing with her, and she definitely wasn't going to ask him about it, but she needed to hear someone speak aloud the things she felt in her heart.

"Of course! There's no logic in love. There's no secret recipe or formula that you follow. There's no road map or equation. There's no guideline to follow. There's no time limit. There's nothing except the future. Suddenly, you start to see a future. You start making plans you've never even dreamed of before, and you don't even realize it. It just creeps in, and fills you up. Does that sound familiar?" Angela asked.

"Yes, it does," Jewel said smiling. "I guess I just needed to hear it from another woman."

"I see the way you two look at each other. You remind me of my Jimmy and me. We fell in love the instant we met in college. The second day I was there, my mom jokingly asked me if I was in love yet, and I said... *yes I am*! She was quite surprised, asking me a hundred questions about him. I finally had to confess that I hadn't actually met him yet, but he was in my statistics class, and we immediately locked eyes until my heart jumped, and twisted, and warmed up to a temperature I'd never felt before. Within a couple weeks we were dating, and making lifelong plans with each other."

"So what happened?" Jewel asked.

"We married shortly after we graduated. We had three beautiful baby boys in five years, and lived a pretty good life for over thirty years," Angela said, trying to avoid a part of the story she didn't like. "One day, the summer before last, I was at home waiting for Jimmy to get back from a business trip, when I get a knock on the door. It was a police officer. As soon as I saw him, my knees buckled. My heart started racing a million miles an hour, and he had to grab onto me to keep me from falling down. I just knew he was gone. He had been hit by a drunk driver on his way from the airport and was killed instantly."

"Oh Angela, I'm so sorry," Jewel said grabbing her and hugging her hard, understanding the feeling of that kind of loss.

"I cried for a long time. My boys mourned the loss of their father, but I saw them move on. I saw that life went on, and that's why I'm here. Then I met Joe. It was an instant connection. It's much different from when Jimmy and I fell in love, but it's wonderful Jewel. With all the unanswered, puzzling questions life leaves us with, you have to take certainties where you can. Sometimes you just know. Love is what happens when you finally open up your heart a little and let it in. Didn't your mom ever tell you that honey?" Angela asked.

"My parents died when I was little. You sort of remind me of my mother. I guess that's why I was asking you. I didn't really realize that until just now. I hope you don't mind," she said, feeling a little unsure of how Angela would react to being compared to her mother.

"Oh honey. Come here," Angela said hugging her again more tightly. "I always wanted a daughter."

"I suppose we should go join them then. They're probably wondering what happened to us." Jewel finally said after a long hug. "Thanks Angela."

"Anytime you need to talk honey, you just don't hesitate. Unless, of course, we're running for the finish line, in which case you better just keep your head down and go for it. Don't underestimate the power of an old woman Jewel," Angela laughed.

The realization of why Jewel had felt an instant connection to Angela had taken Jewel by surprise. She remembered her mom laughing all the time, and she remembered her mom calling her *pretty lady*. Those were memories she'd tried never to think about. Whenever she did think about them, she would busy her mind to try to think about something else before it drowned her in sadness. Now, she remembered the laugh, and the way her mom smiled. She remembered it all, and she smiled in remembrance for the first time. It was a happy memory, as if it had been magically transformed before her eyes. She imagined it like a prison door that had suddenly been unlatched, freeing her from the solitary confinement that had kept her alone and afraid. Another building block was going up. Jewel could feel the warmth in her heart. She could feel love again.

"We were starting to worry about you," Joe said as they made their way back to the campfire where everyone was sitting, giving Angela a warm smile.

"We were bonding. We love you men, but sometimes we need a little girl time," Angela said, flashing Jewel a big smile.

Jewel remembered her mom saying the same thing to dad and grandpa, and off they would go to Billings or Casper to have their hair and nails done, or just go shopping. It was girl time, which meant that whatever it is they ended up doing or saying, was stuff that was only meant for the female variety of the species, as if it were a matter of duty. They went and did the things that society deemed a requirement for all girls, and made them normal. Girl time was a break from hunting, and trailing sheep, and all the other ranch duties they normally did. Girl time meant that they talked about things that were never discussed in mixed company, and it meant giggling and being silly. Jewel couldn't remember the last time she had girl time, and she smiled thinking about it. *It's amazing what can happen when you open your heart a little,* Jewel thought as she settled in among the competitors that had become her friends, and the man who filled her heart up again.

"What is it that girls talk about when they leave the company of men?" Grady asked. "Ya always go ta the bathroom tagether, and ya always come back laughin'."

"Well, we talk about clowns, and funny pictures, and other things that make you laugh, of course," Jewel said coyly.

"Clowns?" Grady asked hesitantly.

"Well, that's what we call you behind your backs," she laughed.

"Is it then?" Grady said, grabbing her and pulling her to him with a tickle. Grady looked forward to the times they all relaxed around the campfire together, and he could touch her without feeling like he was making Rudy the third wheel. There were many times when the three of them were sitting around their fire during one of the legs, when it was all he could do to keep from touching her. Not touching her was like trying to defy gravity, or trying to hold back the tides. It was impossible.

"Ok, I've got to know. What was the prize you won?" Jewel asked the members of The Adventure Team, leaning back into the warmth and comfort of Grady.

"I was waiting for Rudy. Is he coming?" Joe asked.

"No. He's busy tonight," Grady said shrugging. "Don't ask."

"Well, it's his loss then," Joe said as he dug into his bag for the stash. "I spent some time in Idaho several years ago, and enjoyed the wine the Basques had. I thought you might enjoy it Jewel, so I put in a special request to the crewmembers, and asked that the prize be Paisano. I hope you like it! Of course, I never thought in a million years we'd win that leg," he said laughing, pulling out several large bottles of the wine.

"I love Paisano!" Jewel said looking delighted. "I'm not too sure that anybody else will really like it. It's kind of an acquired taste, but I love it!"

"What is it?" Grady asked, eyeing the twist off caps dubiously.

"It's wine that probably would make a Frenchman turn up his nose, but it's wonderful! Thank you Joe!" Jewel said going over to hug him.

"I just enjoyed the songs and the company we all shared last time, and I thought that maybe I would try and pull a few strings to see if we could pry some more music from you," Joe shrugged.

"That's so thoughtful!" Jewel said giving him another hug. "Let's crack these bottles open then, and I'll find the guitar."

"I've got a special request," Daryl said, seemingly pulling it out of thin air, having retrieved it from Rudy earlier. "I haven't heard you sing before, but Mark and Todd said you were pretty good, and it's my birthday so...," Daryl trailed off, shrugging his shoulders.

"It's your birthday! Happy birthday then!" Jewel said with everyone chiming in to wish him a happy birthday. "What's your special request?" Jewel asked, positioning the guitar on her lap comfortably.

"Do you know Georgia on My Mind?" Daryl asked sheepishly. "My mom used to take me there to visit her family every year around my birthday, and I've been singing that song in my head for a week."

"I love that song! It was one of my grandpa's favorites," she said before starting in.

Georgia, Georgia,
The whole day through...

She crooned slowly and with as much soul as she could muster, always eager to deliver the feel of each song she sang. Everyone sat and listened intently, as word after word, and verse after verse, she carefully gave tribute to the song before making everyone cheer out.

"Topa!" Grady said enthusiastically, handing Jewel a cup full of Paisano when she finished the song.

"This stuff is terrible!" Mark said, "but it's the best terrible wine I've ever had."

"Topa!" they all chimed in, by now this being the standard toast for the group.

With the wine flowing and songs being sung by everyone, they all enjoyed each other's company until the small hours of the night, leaving only when they were certain they had sung every song they could remember, trying their hardest to come up with a song that Jewel didn't know, but finding none.

They had all been gathered around the winner's tent near the fire. The stars in the Alaskan sky were twinkling down on them as the cool summer night allowed them to comfortably sit out and enjoy the feel of the fresh air on their skin. They cooked various items of food that they all shared, and finished every last drop of wine.

Grady and Jewel took their leave and started making their way to their tent. "I missed Rudy tonight, but I'm looking forward to having a tent to ourselves," Jewel said, looking up at Grady as they walked arm-in-arm.

"Oh? That completely slipped my mind," he said sarcastically.

"It did?" she asked, not catching the inflection.

"Well, I almost forgot for about half a second in between the Happy Birthday song and the fourth rendition of Bohemian Rhapsody, but that was only ta keep myself from goin' completely mad," he said scooping her up in his arms, carrying her toward the tent.

"You should have said something. We could have left hours ago."

"No. Ya looked so happy singin' and laughin'. Ya looked carefree. It was nice ta see ya like that Jewel," he said smiling at her. "Ya always look like yer about ta be crushed by the weight of the world. It was nice ta see ya so relaxed."

"What do you mean? You make it sound like I'm walking around scowling all the time."

"No. I just mean that sometimes, even when yer happy, yer a million miles away. Yer somewhere I can't reach ya. Yer somewhere that scares ya maybe, and I guess… maybe it scares me a little too. I just liked seein' ya so happy. Ya were just right there with me, and I liked it," he said stopping to kiss her before setting her down, pulling her into the tent.

"I do feel like I'm being crushed by the weight of the world sometimes. I guess that's what you get when you run away. You don't really run away at all, because it follows you around like a cloudy day. I didn't realize it was so visible."

"Whatever it is that burdens ya Jewel, ya don't have ta face it alone." He reached up to stroke her cheek and draw her in for a kiss.

"Will you come back with me maybe? I mean, if you want to. I need to go back when I leave here, and I was hoping you would come with me, if you can," she said stumbling, feeling unsure of how to ask him, but wanting to make plans with him beyond the next few weeks of the competition.

"I'll come back with ya Jewel, and I'll take what burdens from ya that I can if you'll let me," he said hugging her to him.

Jewel could feel some of the tension release from her shoulders. She had been worried about what would happen between her and Grady once the competition was over, and was happy to know there was something to look forward to beyond Alaska. She knew she would have to go home, but she didn't want to go anywhere without him. For the first time in her life, she could see a future. She could see her future, and that included Grady. Somehow, beyond reason and logic, it just seemed to make sense.

"I don't want ta be another burden though Jewel. I'll go back with ya ta be with ya, and ta work with ya, but I'm not a charity case," he added, feeling his own burdens.

"Have you ever lived on a ranch Grady?" she asked without waiting for an answer. "There's always plenty to do. There's no such thing as charity on a ranch. Everyone works!"

"I've heard the first order of business on a ranch is keepin' the lady of the house satisfied," he said leaning down to kiss her more thoroughly.

"You're going to make a terrific rancher," she said stepping back and pulling her shirt off in invitation.

"You'll have to show me the way."

"Start here," she whispered, guiding his hands down to her until she could feel him cup her breasts.

She could feel her heart racing the moment she felt his warm hands on her. She never imagined feeling so out of control, all the while wanting more of it. She slid her hands up the front of him, and could feel his heart racing as fast as her own as he bent to kiss her again, taking as much of her in as he could in one kiss. They grabbed at each other's clothes, pulling, and yanking, barely able to get them off and tossed aside quick enough.

"I'm taken ya all the way and then some Jewel, 'til ya cry for more and beg me to stop all in the same breath. God I want ya!" he whispered breathlessly, easing her down to the bed of sleeping bags they had laid out.

Jewel could feel the urgency in him. It was different than the night before. At the cabin, he had held back, trying to be gentle and patient with her, but this was more intense. She could feel his hands pulling her, rough against her skin, her body rising up to meet his in answer, wanting more. Her own hands were less gentle, pulling him deeper and harder, never able to get him close enough to her.

"Do it then!" she cried out, feeling the need within her nearly explode. Each thrust sending waves of ecstasy through her body. The rhythm of him matched her own as he rose up higher above her going deeper.

"I can't... Grady...," she gasped not sure what she was saying, wanting more but going mad from it all at once, pushing him with one hand, and pulling him with the other, wrapping her legs tighter around him even as she begged him to stop.

He took her there, stopping only when they both reached exhaustion, collapsing into each other, gasping for air, both of them lost in their own desires.

"Yer wearin' me down ta a frazzle woman," he finally said as the two laid side by side, catching their breaths.

"If I'd have known that's what I was missing, I would have never waited so long," she said lying back with a sigh. "That's therapeutic. Talk about relaxing and releasing tension."

"Well, it can be a tension release, but it's not always like this Jewel," he said eyeing her sideways.

"I think I know that, but what do you mean?"

"I mean, the love, and just the way it is between us, is rare I think. I've been with other women, and it's never like this. What we have is... different," he said holding her hand tightly within his own as he collapsed next to her.

"I know Grady. I mean... I think I know. I didn't mean that it would be like this with just anyone. I knew the first time I met you that something between us was different. I don't need to sleep with other men to know that," she said turning to look him in the eyes.

"Well, the thought of ya bein' with another man makes me want ta hurt someone," he said turning to face her. "I have no right ta feel possessive of ya. I'm a jealous man as it turns out. I've never been jealous before, but suddenly I'm feeling things I've never felt before. Bear with me," he said stroking her face, tucking her hair behind her ear.

"I understand how you feel. I have no right to be jealous that you dated women before me. I would hardly expect less from a twenty-nine year old man, but still... it makes me feel jealous to think of it."

"Yer my first love... you'll always have that Jewel," he said kissing her hand, "and you'll be my last. Somehow, I just know it."

"That does take the sting out of it a little," she said running her free hand through his hair, trying to contain her smile.

They both fell asleep that night dreaming of their future together. They were dreaming of the days to come, both of them finally finding an answer to where their life was heading, and with whom.

CHAPTER 19

THE THIRD LEG

The three of them started out on the third leg, each lost in their own thoughts. Rudy came back from visiting Diana looking surprisingly upset. He hadn't been ready to say goodbye to her yet, and he was missing his kids terribly. He was starting to feel guilty for being on this trip, and he was looking forward to it ending. He also knew that it was going to be a month before he saw them again, and it wasn't setting well with him. During his military career, he was accustomed to being away from them for long periods of time, but it had grown increasingly difficult, and since he wasn't in the military anymore, he found it unbearable.

He remembered one time when he was in Afghanistan when he was separated from her and the kids for nearly eight months without ever getting to see them. He was afforded some privileges that allowed him to call home or even Skype on a near daily basis, and they all seemed to be able to make the best of it. He wrote to his kids daily, still wanting to be able to offer fatherly advice, and tell them how much he loved and cared for them.

They wrote to him quite a bit, especially Melanie, who was the quintessential daddy's girl, and could hardly go a day without sitting down and writing something on paper that she wanted to be able to share with him. Sometimes she would catch snippets of the news that talked about American soldiers being killed in Afghanistan, and she would frantically sit down and write to him, wanting to tell him how much she loved him before it was too late. When Rudy was home, Melanie was usually wherever he was, or at least not far behind.

He thought of his sons growing up, needing their dad at home to show them the way, and teach them how to be men. He knew they looked up to him because of his military career, but he also knew that it was time that he was there for them. He needed to be able to go to their school activities, and be there to tell them how to treat women, and how to find the right path in life. Paxton, Thomas, and Joseph… he rolled their names around in his head remembering them as babies, and how they had transformed as they grew up. He knew he already missed so much of their young lives, and he didn't want to miss anymore.

He thought of his daughters, and how they each had a way of nearly breaking his heart every time he looked at them. They were so fine and fragile looking to him sometimes, but then they would surprise him by taking off on their dirt bikes and jumping over a dirt pile in the hills behind their house, laughing and screaming with delight the whole time. He knew how important it was for a girl to have the right male role model, and prayed that he had given enough, even as he vowed to make up for every last second he missed with them. He cringed thinking of Alisha who was sixteen, and sometimes she already seemed lost to him. She looked exactly like Diana. She was tall, blond, and she had a look about her that kept one boy after another constantly fighting for her affection. Sometimes she looked all grown up, and it would stop his heart, but then the next day she would skip down the stairs in her pajamas and pigtails looking like a little kid again, and it would stop his heart again, albeit for a different reason.

Melanie looked exactly like him, as did Thomas and Tina, but the others were pure Diana. If he didn't know with complete certainty that his wife valued the sanctity of their marriage, he could have some serious doubts as to his involvement with the other three.

Melanie looked like him and she acted like him. Essentially, she was his exact female clone, and she even talked about going into the military the way Rudy had. He was close with all his children, but he and Melanie shared a special bond from the instant she was born. Melanie had been the only one of the six kids that was born by caesarian section, and when she had come out, Rudy was right there, never once letting her out of his sight. After cutting her cord and helping to get her all cleaned up, he sat with her alone as Diana was in the recovery room. Melanie immediately wrapped her little hand around one of his fingers, and she wouldn't let go. When Rudy would leave to go to the bathroom or take a shower, Melanie would start crying, and the only thing that would stop her from crying when she got really upset, was for Rudy to put his finger down near her and let her grab onto it. The first few nights of her life he spent each night lying beside her on the reclining chair with his hand dangling over the little baby bed in the hospital so that Melanie would stay asleep. To this day, if they are all sitting around watching a movie or something, Melanie is usually right there beside Rudy, holding his hand or sitting on his lap.

Then there was Joseph. Joseph and Grady were cut from the same cloth. Grady was seven when Rudy started dating Diana, and watching Joseph grow up was a lot like watching Grady grow up all over again. He was a large boy, and at age seven, he was already taller than his older brother Thomas was at age eight. Joseph was full of life, and said exactly what he wanted to say the moment he thought it. He wasn't shy or unsure of himself in the least, and he seemed to be completely oblivious to just how cute he was, and the effect he had on other people. He systematically planned everything out in his mind, getting a look on his face that he had seen on Grady's face a thousand times.

Tina was the one he worried about the most. She was shy, and he would often catch her off by herself, lost in thought, as if the weight of the world were on her shoulders. He would go over to her and ask her what she was thinking about, and she would often surprise him with her answers. One time she told him she was thinking about cancer, and why some people had to die from cancer and other people got to live, and how unfair it was. One time she told him that she was thinking about the astronauts that were at the space station, and how they must miss their families even more than everyone else, because they were light years away, and that had to be even harder than being in a different country. She was a worrier, and he was hoping that being home would help her, so she wouldn't have as many things to worry about.

Paxton was going to be sixteen pretty soon, and Rudy was looking forward to going home to teach him how to drive. He talked to Diana about it a little while she was there, and she agreed to wait until he got home before teaching him, which would be about the right time anyway. He looked forward to the experience so much, that a part of him wanted to throw his pack off immediately, to run home as fast as he could. They had saved a little money so that he would be able to put his money together with theirs to buy him a little car or truck to get him all the way through college. He couldn't wait to take him to pick something out. Paxton wasn't expecting their contribution, and he knew he was going to be excited.

Then there was Thomas. At age eight, he was already a year ahead in school, and even that seemed to be boring him. He was incredibly smart, and Rudy thought that if any of his children were going to be a brain surgeon or a rocket scientist, it was going to be Thomas. His mind worked so fast that most grown-ups couldn't keep up with him. They thought about buying him some science kits so he could explore the world of science better, but then one day they found him in his grandpa's garage, having built a complete go-cart out of an old lawn mower and some other items that he had gathered from neighbors and friends. He was looking forward to spending more time with him to help guide him in the direction to make the most out of the gift he had been given.

He thought of Diana. He was dazzled by her the instant he first saw her. She was this tall, beautiful blond that oozed sophistication. She had been invited to the Military Ball by a friend that she went to high school with, and Rudy was there as a service member in full uniform. He couldn't believe his eyes when he saw her date leave her at the table to go dance with someone else. He took it as his cue, not wasting any time before going over and asking her for a dance. "Your date is clearly insane to leave you sitting here to go dance with someone else. I promise I would never make the same mistake," he'd said to her, motioning toward the dance floor. He was thrilled when she explained that they were just friends, and she had only agreed to come in order to help him get a date with the girl he was dancing with. They danced together, laughing and talking non-stop until it was time to go. He got her phone number, and didn't waste any time calling her. His friends urged him to play it cool and wait a few days, but he thought these were foolish games, and he called her the next day, never once regretting his decision. He knew he was going to spend the rest of his life with her the first time he saw her in a full belly laugh. He asked her to marry him exactly two months after they first met, and she immediately said yes. He smiled thinking of her. She never wanted to leave her family in South Dakota, but she never hesitated when they were sent from one military post to another. He was eager to give her the life she wanted, which was to be settled and near her family. He was definitely ready to be done with the competition, and go home to his family.

Jewel was lost in her own thoughts. She surprised herself when she asked Grady if he would go home with her. It wasn't something she would have normally ever done. She had been closed off and alone for so long, she never imagined she would be able to suddenly be so open. She hadn't thought about asking him. It just came out without her ever thinking about it, and she was thrilled by his response. She imagined what their life might be like. She thought about all the things she wanted to show him, and all the places on the ranch that she liked to go. She wanted to take him up the sheep trail and to the creek that she loved tubing down. She wanted to show him the house where she grew up, and show him pictures of her mom and dad. She didn't know how it would go with Troy, but she prayed they would somehow end up as friends. She longed for it.

Jewel even thought about her family in Colorado. She wasn't exactly sure why. She never really knew them, but she felt differently all the sudden. Her heart was opening up, and with that, came a desire to let more love in. She hadn't ever been close to them, and there was part of her that resented them because of how they treated her father, but they were the only family she had, and she was feeling a need to get to know them.

She imagined Grady's family. Diana was wonderful, and they hit it off immediately, which excited Jewel. She was surprising herself lately. Normally she would have clammed up and made an excuse to go off by herself, practically barricading herself in her room. That's how the last several years had gone. For a long while, she didn't want to get close to anyone. She didn't want to share her life, or try to explain why she was alone, and why she didn't have a family. She didn't want to tell another person that her parents were dead. She didn't want to have to say it aloud again for a very long time. She didn't want to tell them about her grandma dying, or see the look of pity on their faces when she told them about her grandpa. She hated it when people would feel sorry for her. It was easier to just be alone. It was a vacation from having to explain who she was, summing up her life by tragic stories of death. She knew that people meant well, but she hadn't been able to pretend anymore. They would make their apologies when she would tell them, and she would politely say thank you and tell them it was okay, except it wasn't okay, and she didn't have the ability to say it was. She had lost the ability to fake it one more time, and so she just didn't get close to people for a long while.

It wasn't until she met Grady that things started to change. It was as if someone flipped a switch. She wanted to give love, and feel love again. She wanted to share her life suddenly. It wasn't that it didn't still make her sad exactly, it was that the sadness had become manageable. The sadness of her parent's death became a part of what made her who she was, but was no longer the whole of her. Grady seemed to be the key that unlocked her heart and let her accept love again. She smiled at him, watching his back as he hiked ahead of her, his own thoughts running wild as he made his way up the hill they were climbing.

Grady was thinking about the changes in his life. He never thought he would go to Alaska and fall in love. He was lost after he was discharged from the Army, and he wasn't happy to be at home staying with his parents. He could have stayed in the military, pushing papers, but that wasn't really an option for him, and he didn't know what he wanted to do with his life. He was paralyzed, not wanting to stay, and not wanting to leave. Every decision seemed to be a roll of the dice, and about as accurate as throwing a dart at a dartboard blindfolded.

He was surprised when Jewel asked him to go home with her. He wasn't expecting it, but it had been on his mind. He hadn't been able to think of his future without her in it from the moment he first met her. She was everything he ever wanted in a woman, but he never knew what that was exactly until he met her.

He never thought he would be going to a ranch in Wyoming, but the idea of it was exciting to him. He loved being outdoors, and had fond memories of spending time on one of his best friend's ranches when he was growing up, and he longed to have time alone with Jewel. Not just a few stolen moments here and there, but time... real time together... the kind of time where you could build a life together.

There was a part of him that wanted to grab Jewel that moment and run off with her, not wanting to wait another minute before starting their new life together. He was absolutely certain she was the right woman for him, but he was holding back, not wanting to scare her off. He knew she was wading into unfamiliar territory when it came to opening up to people. He could see it written all over her face when she would start to open up a little. It was like watching a small kitten cautiously dip a paw into the water for the first time.

The three of them mechanically spent the days and nights of their third leg on their journey doing all the things they needed to get through it, but the thunder and excitement of the competition had faded into something that would better be described as simply enduring it. In Rudy's case, he had gone from the excitement of going on an adventure, to realizing that he was missing the greatest adventure of his life at home. To Jewel and Grady, it had gone from being a great adventure, to being a small adventure in comparison to the excitement and anticipation they had found in each other.

They had pushed on through rain and cold weather this leg, endured chilly nights, and a low supply of food. They hiked through a boggy marshland that took them almost an entire day to cross, though it was only a few miles long. They spent a sleepless night huddled together under inadequate shelter and blowing wind and sleet, only to get up the next morning and hike through the same conditions they had spent all night trying to survive. Not only did the third leg start with less enthusiasm, and dwindling motivation, it came at them with a ferociousness that promised to take what little excitement they had left, and grind it into the ground.

They arrived at the finish line bedraggled and completely exhausted. They immediately spotted the prize, but even winning didn't inspire them to feel celebratory. They had been wet and freezing cold for five long days, and they were ready to go back to base camp. They hadn't seen the others since they were dropped off on the first day, but they were still a little surprised when they realized they'd won. They thought they were way behind; having gotten late starts, and long delays because of the weather. They thought for sure, The Alaska Team would be far ahead of them.

They huddled in together and snacked on the candy bars that had been their prize for winning this leg of the journey, each one of them sitting there eating silently as if to preserve what little energy they had left. They were surprised when they saw the helicopter arrive without seeing any sign of the other two teams. They knew that if the other teams didn't make it in time before the five o'clock deadline, they would be disqualified, and they would win the competition by default. Even that didn't do much to lift their spirits. The other team members had become friends of theirs and they were getting worried about them, especially considering how hard the last few days had been for them, knowing they were far more prepared than the others were.

"Have you seen any of the others?" the crewmember yelled through the spitting rain and the blowing wind, as he approached the three of them huddled together.

"No. We haven't seen them. It looks like they have another few hours. Can we wait inside?" Grady yelled back.

"We'll take you back to base camp and come back for them. You guys look miserable," he yelled, offering them a hand with their packs.

"Oh, thank you!" Jewel said getting up, finally showing a little enthusiasm. She hated being cold, and the last five days had been nothing but cold and misery. She fantasized about a hot shower, imagining herself standing there soaking up every hot drop of water until her skin looked red and inflamed.

They climbed into the helicopter, smiling for the first time in days, as they took off over the landscape toward a relatively warm shelter, and a comfortable place to sleep. Despite the warmth and shelter of the helicopter, the three of them still huddled together shivering, trying to keep each other warm, and continue their support of each other. They made plans, telling each other exactly what they wanted to do the minute they got to base camp. Jewel and Grady talked of a warm shower and dry clothes, and both of them were surprised when Rudy said he was going to drop his pack by the tent before quickly heading out to call Diana. They knew that he had been withdrawn since saying goodbye to her, but they figured he would at least want to get warm before heading out to go call her.

They got back to the winners tent, and as promised, Rudy grabbed a few things and headed toward town to call his wife. Jewel immediately started to peel off her rain gear, and readied herself for a hot shower.

"If I have this right, we are the only two people at this camp, and we seem to have the tent to ourselves for a couple hours," Grady said smiling at her.

"Then come take a hot shower with me," she said, unzipping another layer of wet clothing.

They didn't waste any time getting to the shower before stripping down and hopping in together. After enduring the miserable cold, and only being able to hold each other through several layers of clothing and rain gear for several days, they were eager to touch each other, feeling the warmth of skin on skin again. They helped wash each other, both of them taking their time luring the other one in. Jewel shaved her legs slowly, one at a time, watching him as he watched her, trying to see hidden crevices she had strategically kept just out of his sight.

"Let's go back to the tent before Rudy gets back," he whispered to her, trying hard to resist the urge to take her right there in the bathroom as she finished shaving.

"Okay, let's go," she said, turning off the water and wrapping a towel around her. Grady wrapped a towel around himself as well, and they ran back to the tent, dodging the cold raindrops that were still falling.

They barely made it to the tent before grabbing a hold of each other, completely lost in a desire they had yearned for nearly every second of every day. They kissed each other, and pulled each other closer, desperately wanting to feel each other's skin on their own. The gentleness they had the days before were replaced with primal need. Grady picked her up and laid her on his cot, quickly climbing on top of her. She reached down between his legs, eager to guide him to her. They came together all at once, both of them giving in to the desire they had fought off the last few days, getting lost in one another, one long thrust after another until they both cried out, finding the release they needed.

They laid there for several minutes, neither one of them wanting to move. They were finally warm, naked, and together, which is exactly what they both had been thinking about over the last few grueling days.

"I would love nothing more than ta lay here with ya all night," Grady finally said, "but I'm not wantin' Rudy ta come back and find us here like this," he said looking down at their naked bodies, eyeing Jewel appreciatively.

"You know I love Rudy, but I can't wait to have some time with you to lay around naked all day and night if we want to, and not have to worry about being interrupted," she said as they got up to get dressed.

"Me too Jewel. I've been dreamin' about the future, which is just another way of sayin' that I've been dreamin' about us," he said pulling his clothes on, leaning over to kiss her again.

Rudy had come back sometime later looking slightly happier than he had before he left. He took a quick shower, and the three of them didn't wait long before crawling into their beds. They heard muffled voices, which they assumed to be the other teams, but they didn't know or even seem to care if they had made it in time. After enduring several cold sleepless nights, the only thing they really cared about was a dry, warm, good night's sleep. They closed the tent up as much as possible to keep the evening sun out, and didn't wake up until morning.

PART TWO

An Alaskan
Misadventure

CHAPTER 20

MY (NOT SO) FAVORITE MEMORY

"I'm going to run to the bathrooms. I'll be back in a while," Jewel said, getting dressed and kissing Grady on the forehead before heading out the door in the early morning.

The morning was a little cool still, and as Jewel walked over to the bathrooms, she was grateful she had grabbed her coat and her wool cap and gloves the way Grady always insisted. He was extra cautious, and as the team captain, he insisted that they each be prepared at all times against the elements, and against wild animals, even when running to the bathroom. "The weather changes every five minutes," he had said. Jewel thought it was a little over the top, but that morning she was glad for his practicality, and on more than one occasion, she had been thankful to have her pistol with her that she always carried strapped to her side. You never knew when a bear was going to make his way through camp, and during one such visit to the bathroom, Jewel found herself face to face with a wolverine. As it turned out, a high-pitched shriek was enough to send the wolverine running, but still, it was nice to know that she had some way to protect herself. She was so lost in the thought of Grady preaching to her about keeping safe, that she never noticed the large man standing in the shadows of the trees near the bathrooms.

She was still smiling to herself thinking of Grady. She washed her hands and face, and was startled when she heard a man speak. She recognized the voice immediately, and it made the hair on the back of her neck stand on end, sending shivers down her spine.

"I knew you would come looking for me eventually," he said coming up behind her.

"Aaron! What are you doing here? I thought... didn't you... weren't you arrested?" Jewel stuttered, trying to regain her composure.

"They made all that up. They just wanted me out of the competition, because they knew I would win everything myself. They couldn't hold me. I'm a free man," Aaron said, spreading out his arms, pleased with himself.

"You're in the women's bathroom. I would appreciate it if you would leave," she said feeling alarmed. "I'll be out to talk to you when I'm done." Her voice was softer now, afraid to anger him.

"I don't think so. I came here for you Jewel. We belong together. I could see the way you felt about me from the beginning... singing to me, caring for me so softly and all."

"I'm a nurse Aaron. I was caring for you the way nurses care for their patients. I'm sorry if you thought it was more..." He cut her off, grabbing her and kissing her painfully, forcing his tongue between her lips.

"Stop it!" she yelled trying to push him away. He was a big man, nearly as big as Grady, and she couldn't budge from his grip, even as he used one hand to put it over her mouth to keep her quiet.

"You're just a little whore. You tease a man, practically begging me to fuck you one minute, and then you think you can just brush me off, and I'll just go quietly? Is that what you think?" he said through gritted teeth, pinning her between the wall and the bathroom counter.

"What was it you sang to me? My favorite memory was it? You think that's nothing!" he hissed at her as he took her down to the floor, straddling her and pinning her arms with his knees, trying to keep her from screaming out. "The first time we met is your favorite memory? I knew what you were trying to tell me!"

"I've got a nice place for the two of us Jewel. You'll see. You'll like it there, and it will keep you from whoring yourself to everyone! God women are such fucking whores!" he hissed at her more angrily, placing duct-tape over her mouth before she was able to scream out again. Inside she was screaming. What was happening to her was so unimaginable that she was struggling to process it in her mind.

He tightly wrapped her wrists together with duct-tape, and it was clear to Jewel, that this had been thought out and planned well ahead of time. He had been waiting for her, and had probably timed his ambush accordingly, knowing that she generally headed out to the bathroom early. He knew that Grady and her tended to be early risers.

"Let's go!" he said smiling at her, stopping to run his hand down between her legs with a peculiar look of seduction and lust as he met her eyes. He lingered between her legs, rubbing her harder, daring for a moment to shove his hand down the front of her pants and feel her warmth. He unzipped her pants and then his own, pulling on them both, before getting control of himself, thinking better of it.

"We'll save that for later. Won't we?" he said seductively, as if they were both enjoying themselves. It sent chills down Jewels spine. It was a look that didn't fit with what was happening. It was a look that was meant for a willing partner, and the fact that he didn't seem to recognize the difference, scared her. To Jewel it seemed that he thought he was rescuing her from other men, and from herself. He thought he was doing her a favor.

He pulled her up and tied a rope around her duct-taped wrists so he could easily pull her behind him, stopping only long enough to zip up both their pants.

A hundred thoughts were racing through her mind. She was trying to figure out what she could do to make sure he didn't take her to a different location. She remembered reading somewhere that if you're attacked, you should fight and kick, and do whatever you can to make sure they don't take you to a second location. She looked up at the massive man in front of her, his back now turned to her as he led her out of the bathroom door, and she decided to try to make a break for it as soon as they got outside. She knew she was going to have to pull hard to yank the rope out of his hand, but he must have considered this, she thought, as she watched him wrap the end of the rope around his hand several times, getting a firmer grip on it as he led her out the door.

She watched him, and could see that he knew exactly which directions to look to make sure nobody was coming from their tents beyond the direct site of the bathrooms. *How long has he been here?* she wondered, *and why didn't any of the crewmembers tell them he was no longer in custody?*

Jewel saw his hand release slightly, and she pulled as hard as she could while simultaneously running in the opposite direction. She was surprised when she actually got away, and nearly went tumbling over, as she broke free from him. She tried screaming as she went, but the duct tape muffled her voice. She ran as fast as she could, but he was able to catch up to her quickly, tackling her down to the ground in the tall grass. He crawled on top of her, finding the pistol immediately, and tossing it into the grass. Jewel had been expecting him to be angry with her, but he started kissing her neck and grabbing her breasts, and she could feel his excitement swell hard against her leg. This was exciting him, and the fear of it gripped her. *This man is crazy!* she thought, and a thought flashed through her mind, remembering the story she had read about Uday Hussein, and how he would become aroused by extreme violence toward women.

"If you're running toward Grady thinking he's going to save you, then you may as well forget about it Jewel. I already took care of that bitch!"

A shiver ran through her. *Oh my God, what happened to you Grady?* she thought, feeling her heart stop in her chest, and tears well up in her eyes.

"Oh God Jewel! I want you so bad right now!" Aaron said breathing hard against her, "we're going to have to wait though. Let's get out of here. I have a nice place for us," he said pulling her up and moving her toward an S.U.V. that he hid earlier, so it would be out of sight.

She remembered studying narcissistic sociopathic behavior in her psychology classes in college, and she wondered if this was what she was dealing with. Aaron saw himself as grandiose, always overestimating his appeal and his abilities, and she suspected that he was a chronic pathological liar. Every rebuff or attempt to remove herself from him, he translated as a personal weakness of hers, which allowed her to be coerced away from him unwillingly. He saw himself as an irresistible, attractive man that every woman wanted whether they knew it or not, and any rejection of him was a sign of their weakness to know and understand just how irresistible he was. He saw himself as saving her from throwing herself at other men, and making a whore out of herself. It was clear to her, that he somehow saw himself as her savior, and that once he got her away, she would be thankful to him.

"You're going to like this," Aaron said excitedly, as he slid behind the wheel, having secured her in the backseat out of view. "We're going on a nice little drive, and then we're going to have to hike a ways. It's pretty remote. I remember you saying how you liked to be out in the country away from everything," he said talking, as if they were on an exciting romantic getaway.

Jewel was lying down on the backseat where she was tied, and was trying to look out of the window as much as possible, but from her angle, all she could see was the sky. *Where is he taking me?*" she wondered. She was determined to remember as much as she possibly could. She was trying to judge how long the car ride was taking, and remember every tree and turn of the road. She thought of Grady, wondering what had happened to him.

"As soon as we get up here a ways, I'll pull over and get the tape off of you. I'm sorry I had to do that to you Jewel. I was afraid someone would hear us," he said smiling, as if they'd been in on this together. "Grady is such a little pussy! You don't want to be stuck with a little bitch like that Jewel," he said to her, clearly convinced that he had just done her the biggest favor of her life.

She kept thinking of Grady. What had Aaron done to him? Nobody would even come looking for her for another hour or more. She often lingered as she made her way to and from the bathroom, collecting leaves, and just studying the flora and fauna, always looking for the items that her guide had taught her about.

She judged that they were probably going forty-five to fifty miles-per-hour, which meant that she would be at least forty-five miles away before anyone even knew she was gone. Judging by the morning sun, and the way he was steering the car, it seemed like they were heading in a half circle, and may only end up by direct line, thirty miles from base camp.

"We're going to have a good life Jewel. This is a nice cabin. I was able to secure it for us on that first leg, though we may have a bit of cleaning up to do from the previous owners," he said smiling when he recalled how he had tied them to the trees out back, leaving them behind to feed the bears. They had invited him, Mark, and Todd over for some fresh water, but the old man got a little testy with him when he started asking too many questions. As a boy that had grown up in the Alaskan wilderness off the grid, he knew that asking questions would get them riled up, but he took pleasure in watching them squirm.

He purposefully left behind his empty rifle, making sure they had gone far enough away, before telling Mark and Todd he would have to run back to get it before catching back up with them. The two brothers were a lot smaller and a lot slower than he was, and so he sent them heading further away as he ran back to get his rifle. The old man never knew what hit him when Aaron snuck up on him, knocking him out with one swift blow to the head with a hatchet left near the woodpile. At least the woman put up a little fight, which Aaron likely hoped she would do. She had gotten him so excited, he wasn't able to take his time. He had her down on the ground fast, and took her right there as quick and as hard as he could.

"Let's stop here a minute. You're going to love this!" he said excitedly, pulling the car over and getting out, joining her in the backseat.

"Let me just get this off you," he said smiling warmly at her as he tried to gently pull the duct tape off her mouth, cutting it off her wrist before pulling her to him for a hug.

"Come on. Let me show you something." He yanked Jewel out of the car as she glanced around to try to figure out where she was.

"Where are you taking me?" she asked quietly, trying to convey a neutral tone, not wanting to excite him or make him angry.

"We'll turn off over there at the base of those foothills, driving along for a ways just beyond where it turns, and then we'll hike up from there," he said as if confiding in his best friend. "Don't worry. I've got everything we need. I'll take good care of you Jewel," he said leaning down to kiss her lightly on the cheek.

"First, I just need to check you Jewel," he said patting her down, running his hands over her breasts and between her legs salaciously. She remembered that Aaron found her gun earlier and had thrown it into the bushes. She prayed that someone would find it before a child got a hold of it. She hoped Grady or Rudy found it and would come looking for her. *I pray you're okay Grady,* she thought. Thinking of him gave her hope, and hope was something she desperately needed, so she said another silent prayer, ignoring Aaron completely.

"If Grady cared about you he would have made sure you didn't go walking around Alaska without protecting you," he said looking at her, as if he had just proven to her that Grady didn't care for her as he did.

Jewel decided right then that the less she said, the better off she was going to be. He clearly had some fantasy in his head, and she didn't think he needed her participation in whatever it was he felt was between them. One thing was for sure, she didn't want to make him angry, as this seemed to arouse him. She stiffened a little, remembering how excited he got when she tried to fight him off in the bathroom.

"You'll see. It may not seem like it right now, but you're going to thank me for this later. Grady is nothing compared to me. You'll see. Just wait," he said happier than she had ever seen him.

They both got back in the car, with Aaron opening the passenger door for her as if they were on a date. Jewels eyes immediately went to the ignition to see if the keys were there, but they weren't. She looked up at him an instant later, and he was looking at her as he came around the front of the car. Both of them knew what she had been thinking, and she could see a flare of anger surge through him.

"If you could just quit being a fucking little cunt, we might actually be happy!" he said angrily, getting in the car and slamming the door behind him.

Jewel said nothing. She sat in the passenger seat looking at everything around her, trying to memorize every detail of everything, knowing it would be futile to try to run for it. He would catch up to her immediately, and there was no place for her to go out there. She looked at the gravel road they had been driving on, trying to remember every turn, every bush, anything that might lead her back to where she had come from. *Where was Grady? Did he beat him or maybe even kill him?* Her heart ached, feeling uncertain of everything again, feeling life spinning out of control.

Aaron drove quite a ways along the base of the foothills, before finally reaching a spot where he could hide the car out of view, and start hiking toward the cabin. He had a pack and everything prepared for her, complete with a sleeping bag, and she was surprised to see that some of her personal belongings were in there. She remembered that she wasn't able to find them where she thought she had put them before heading out to the bathroom that morning, and she remembered thinking she would look for them later. *He must have snuck into our tent,* she thought to herself, shivering when she realized the only time he would have been able to was when she and Grady were in the shower the night before, which meant that Aaron must have been watching them the whole time.

I wasn't in the bathroom but a minute before Aaron came in. How could he have confronted Grady in that time? Jewel thought hopefully, piecing the last couple of hours together, trying to push out of her mind Grady's warm touch that woke her up that morning.

"I grew up in the backwoods of Alaska Jewel. Don't think you can run away or outsmart me. You'll never make it. Nobody is better at this than I am. I promise you that," he warned her sternly before starting up toward the cabin, leading her by a chain that he wrapped around her middle.

Again, Jewel said nothing. He didn't need any encouragement from her. He clearly thought quite a lot of himself, she thought as they made their way up the side of the mountain. He always talked about himself, and how he was better than everyone else was. She suspected that the people he always claimed to be better than were probably the one's that he felt the most threatened by, and she found this reassuring since he mostly talked about being better than Grady.

Jewel followed him, breaking off branches as she went, and stepping in spots she knew would leave prints, trying to leave some traceable sign, all the while memorizing everything around her. She pulled lint out of her pocket when she could, and dropped it in their trail, trying to think of every little thing she could do to make them traceable. She shivered when she thought of what he might do to her once they got to the cabin. She remembered the rage that had fueled his arousal earlier, and it terrified her.

They hiked for about six straight hours before finally stopping to rest for a little while. She was still exhausted from the last leg of their competition, and she was feeling drained and hungry. She thought of the night before when she and Grady made love in the tent, and she wondered just how much Aaron had seen or heard.

She thought he must have snuck into the tent while they showered, which meant he must have seen them run back to the tent in their towels, and he must have at least heard them as they made love, but she had a terrible feeling there was more to it than that. They were so caught-up in the moment with each other that someone could have been standing right there in the room watching them the whole time, and neither one of them would have ever noticed.

"I need to eat something. I'm starving. I don't think I can go any further unless I have something to eat," she said not looking at Aaron.

"Here, eat this," he said handing her a candy bar. As soon as she saw the candy bar, she knew it was from the cache of candy they had won. She wondered what else Aaron had gone through and taken from their tent. She imagined him going through their packs, taking things that he wanted, shuffling through their personal belongings. More than that, the candy bar was an indication that he wasn't all that prepared. She didn't know if his lack of preparedness was a good sign, or a bad sign. She contemplated both scenarios in her mind, trying to decide if his actions gave her any indication as to his long-term, or short-term plans for her. She thought about asking him directly, but she was scared to alarm him, or get him excited again. She knew she was going to have to tread lightly with him. He seemed to be one person one minute, and another person the next.

She watched him as he gathered wood and put some rocks together to make a little campfire. *Clearly, we're staying here for the night,* she thought, thinking this might be a good thing. She was still looking for every opportunity to leave signs behind, and she thought a small campfire would be another way that someone would be able to track them. Also, she thought that the fire might be visible from far away as it got dark, and she hoped that Grady and Rudy were looking for her. She imagined them, and wondered what they must be thinking. She hadn't planned it that way, but she knew the struggle in the grass was probably the best sign she had left behind that told someone something wasn't quite right. It was right outside the bathroom, and she tried hard to remember what it must look like. It was very tall grass, and she imagined that having it all matted down would send up red flags.

"I have to go to the bathroom," she said without emotion.

"Go ahead," he said smiling at her, knowing she wouldn't be able to go privately because of the short chain he had her on.

"Where am I going to go Aaron? Just let me go right over there," she said pointing to a nearby bush.

Aaron got up without saying a word, and led her by the chain near the bush she had pointed toward a moment earlier. He eyed her carefully with a smug look on his face, guiding the chain as if he were guiding a dog on a leash, clearly enjoying the degrading nature of it. She could see that he was enjoying the feeling of superiority it gave him, but she quietly squatted down out of his view. She knew she had no other choice but to appease him. She didn't want to excite him, and she removed any emotion from her face, not wanting to give him the pleasure of seeing any reaction from her. *I need to be smart about this,* she thought as they walked back over to the campfire when she was finished.

He spread out their sleeping bags, using his foot to scrape away rocks before laying the bags out side by side, preparing the area where they would sleep that night. Jewel knew she would never be able to sleep. He chained both her hands together and attached it to a short chain that he kept buckled to his belt. He was afraid she would run away, and he chained her ankles together before making her get in her sleeping bag, cuddling up next to her. She laid there completely disgusted with him, his arm resting over the front of her. She was full of so much anger as she laid there, she imagined ways she might be able to strangle him with her chains, or suffocate him somehow, but she knew he would be able to fight her off easily, and she was terrified of what he might do to her at that point.

She laid there with her eyes wide open all night, contemplating every little thing, thinking about Grady, and her heart ached as she thought of maybe never being able to take him home with her. It pierced her, nearly sending her into fits of crying, but then she decided it wasn't time for crying. It was time for strength, and she knew that it wasn't the time to think about what may be their lost future.

She listened to Aaron sleep, measuring his breaths, trying to determine how deep of a sleeper he was, making loud and large movements, testing the water to see if he was a light sleeper or not. She could tell that he was obviously a deep sleeper after making several large yanking movements, realizing that he hadn't stirred.

She was glad when the morning came. The night seemed to last forever with her in a constant battle in her mind, wanting to think of Grady, but fighting it off at the same time, not wanting to become emotional. She imagined he was out searching for her, but then, she wasn't sure he would even be able to, or maybe he would think she just got scared and ran off.

Her heart sank when she realized that Grady might not be looking for her at all. They both knew she had run away from everything. They probably thought she had simply gotten spooked, and decided to leave, running away once again. If a girl can leave her best friend hanging, then leaving a couple guys she had just met a few weeks earlier, would be no great feat.

CHAPTER 21

I Take Thee, Jewel Millet...

The morning finally arrived, and Jewel breathed easier when he got up and moved away from her. Lying next to him all night had seemed like a cruel form of torture. She had laid there and looked him over, studying every inch of him, thinking of ways she might be able to free herself. The smell of him was suffocating.

He was angry from the moment he woke up, throwing things around, and stomping around like a spoiled little child who wasn't getting his way. Jewel just sat there with her head down, afraid to rile him further.

"Let's go!" he barked at her after getting all their things packed back up in their bags.

She followed behind him as he led her through the bushes. They were off the beaten path, and she started feeling afraid that nobody would ever be able to track them through there. It was so thick and rugged, breaking off small branches here and there wasn't making any difference. For every branch she broke off, there were ten more to fill the space, but as the hours passed and they hiked on and on, she broke off as many branches as she could, feeling like she needed to do something.

She was famished, but she didn't want to ask for a piece of the jerky he was chewing. She hated being at his mercy, but then she finally decided that she needed to make sure she did everything she could to stay strong and healthy, and if that meant asking for food, then that was what she needed to do.

"Can I have some jerky please?" she finally asked.

"Ugh... yeah, if you want," he said shrugging, handing her a chunk. She realized that it had never even occurred to him that she might also need to eat something, and she thought hard about that. She wondered what that said about him. He wasn't able to feel empathy, which Jewel felt left him at a disadvantage, but it terrified her. Her ability to read people, and feel what they feel, was central to who she was as a person, and she thought that someone without that ability would be easy to deceive, but they were also quite dangerous. She thought that he must be so incredibly self-consumed that if something wasn't happening within three feet of his face, then it likely didn't exist in his world. She considered how she would be able to use that to her advantage.

She was still contemplating the numerous ways she might be able to exploit Aaron's weaknesses when they finally reached a small clearing, and she could see a cabin tucked into the trees. It was breathtakingly beautiful, and as they made their way to the cabin, Jewel was able to orient herself, remembering when they had crossed over the ridge several hundred yards further up the hill on their first leg of the competition. She thought hard, trying to remember how they had made it to the finish line, and trying to remember anything along the way that would help her to escape.

They walked up to the cabin, which was just a large open room with a kitchen in one corner, a bed in another corner, and a table and other storage items in the other corners. Over the door hung a branding iron that looked like a long S shape laid on it's side, and a sign that said, *The Lazy Snake.*

"Your castle madam," Aaron said as they reached the cabin door.

The year of the snake, she thought, remembering the time she had gone to Denver with Troy and his family. His mom had taken them to a fair where there were palm readers, tarot card readers, and psychics. A woman they met told her she had been born in the year of the snake. The lady said she was a charmer of human beings, and the snake would often bring her great joy, but would sometimes bring her extreme pain. She pushed it out of her mind as she walked through the door.

She could feel evil lurking in every corner of the cabin as she entered. The anger hanging in the air was so thick and palpable, she felt like she could nearly reach out and touch it, and she wondered how Aaron had come to acquire the place. There were items strewn about and knocked on the floor, and there was a stench in the air that nearly made her throw up. It was the smell of blood. *A struggle had taken place here,* she thought. *There may have been many struggles… years of struggles that lingered like thick smoke in the air.*

"Make yourself at home Jewel. This place belongs to you now. Make it yours honey," he said with an awkward attempt at a wink. The way Aaron called her honey made her shiver. One minute he was treating her like he wanted to kill her, and the next minute he was acting sweet and calling her honey. She knew she was dealing with someone who was living in his own fantasy world, and it terrified her. She studied everything around her, determined to find a way to get away from him.

She wandered around the little cabin, wondering how long she would be there. She knew that he would underestimate her abilities, just as most people did, and she also knew that he overestimated his own. He saw himself as more than what he was. She sensed that from the very beginning. He was somewhat attractive, but not overly. His eyes were rather close together and he was without any kind of jawline or chin, which gave his face a pinched look, and yet he saw himself as irresistible to women. He was rather large, but with more fat than muscle, and yet he didn't seem to know the difference, and he apparently didn't think other people did either.

I will get out of this place! she thought guarding her face, not wanting him to see the contempt she felt for him. *He's big, but he's dumb. He thinks he's smarter than everyone, and in the end, that will cost him.*

"I have something for you, and I want you to wear it," he said taking her left hand and slipping a ring on her ring finger. It was a simple gold band, and Jewel almost felt sorry for him, as he looked down at her pleadingly, trying to make her love him. Somehow, he thought what he was doing, was the right way to be doing things.

"Jewel Millet… it has a certain ring to it," he said smiling down at her lovingly, as if the two had just entered into a mutual union.

With that, Jewel could no longer keep her composure. She stepped back from him, looking up at him with disgust, took the ring from her finger, and threw it as hard as she could out the front door without ever saying a word. She looked back at him with such hatred that he had to stop himself from backing away from her. Her steady poise as she stood toe to toe with him was something that he wasn't used to seeing. At six foot two, and nearly three hundred pounds, he didn't find many people who were willing to defy him, but he finally decided to break the stare with a condescending smile, and turned his back to her to regain himself.

"I'm laying down the law right here and now," he started, "hear me now, because I won't repeat it," he turned to face her using his full height and weight in an attempt to scare her, "you now belong to me. You will do what I say, when I say it. If you try running away from me, I will chain you outside like a little dog, which will at least keep you on your hands and knees in the right position," he said reaching out to fondle her breast.

"You listen to me you pathetic loser!" she said stepping closer to him, "you'll keep your hands to yourself. If you don't, I'll cut your penis off and shove it down your throat!" she said never losing control of her voice, turning her back to him, and walking out the door as far as she could go with the chain still wrapped around her.

Jewel was shaking so hard, she thought her knees would buckle, and she would fall down to the ground. She knew if she tried to run, she wouldn't make it five steps before she collapsed, even if she hadn't been chained, and she knew he would easily catch up to her, so she sat down on the ground and waited for him. She needed to show him that she wasn't going to be a pushover, but she also needed to be smart and not push him too far. She had something he clearly lacked, and that was smarts, and a discipline of self-control she learned in the military.

"I'll go find it. It must have gone straight out there. That was my fault. I sprung it on you a little too early," he said apologetically, coming out of the door several minutes later.

Jewel never said a word, but smiled inside a little knowing she had scored a point in the battlefield of mind warfare. Psychological warfare was often more powerful than actual warfare. Fear, intimidation, self-control, and a strong, steady, and patient game of cat and mouse, could go a long ways toward winning a war, and clearly this was a battle between the two of them that began in this man's mind long before. He may have had the element of surprise, but she had the element of training and education, could see within the man's mind, and knew how to navigate through it.

"I'm going in to clean up, and I'm getting pretty hungry. I'm going to need something to eat pretty soon. I assume you'll be taking care of that then?" she said standing up and addressing him like a child, asking the question as more of an order than an actual question, before turning and heading into the cabin.

Inside Jewel could see that whoever lived there before had few possessions. She found several books on the shelves, and volumes of journals that she found hidden under the bed in an old knapsack. She found some clothes, and Jewel could see that the woman who had lived there was much larger than she was, and the man was much smaller than Aaron was. She imagined them, and looked everywhere around the room, through cabinets and drawers, and boxes, looking for pictures, but finding none. She also looked for weapons, and other items that might aid in her escape, but quickly surmised that Aaron had spent time cleaning out the personal items that belonged to the previous residents, leaving behind only a few items that he missed, or thought might be useful to them.

She could see that there was a small shed outside that had a brand new padlock on it, and she guessed that there were things in the shed that were meant to be kept from her. There were probably weapons in there, and maybe a few items that had belonged to the previous owners that he didn't want her to see for some reason or another. *How in the hell did he get this place?* she thought, a chill running down her spine, knowing that something nefarious had likely occurred at the hands of Aaron. A sudden fear ran through her thinking of the mind game she was playing with him, knowing he was a dangerous man that may kill her. *Still,* Jewel thought, *in his own twisted little mind, I think he might actually love me.* She vowed to use that to her advantage, all the while compiling recon items in the back of her mind that would allow her to escape.

She looked at the bed. Part of her wanted to lay down on it and fall asleep, but she was scared to go near it. It terrified her to know that Aaron was likely going to rape her, and she wanted to stay as far away from the bed as possible, not wanting to encourage him. It was starting to get late though, and she didn't know how much longer she was going to be able to stay awake. She hadn't eaten more than a couple candy bars and a little jerky in two days, and she had done quite a bit of hiking. She hadn't slept at all the night before, and the adrenaline that had been keeping her going was starting to diminish. She knew that she was going to have to close her eyes eventually.

"Come here Jewel," he said motioning toward the bed.

She stood there not able to move her feet. She was completely paralyzed, not able to imagine having sex with someone other than Grady. Her mind raced, trying to think of something she might be able to say, or think of something she might be able to do to delay the inevitable, but she couldn't think of anything.

"I said, come here! If it's one thing I can't tolerate, its disobedience! When I tell you to do something, you need to listen!" he said impatiently, as if he were scolding a disobedient child.

Jewel shuffled her feet toward the bed, shaking uncontrollably, but determined not to cry. He impatiently reached out to her and pulled her to the bed, taking her and chaining her to the headboard. Fear was surging through her so erratically that she thought she was going to throw up. He surprised her when he turned and went outside, leaving her there by herself, calling out as he shut the door. "Get some sleep Jewel!"

She laid there saying one prayer after another, asking God to help her, and she remembered her dad by the river. "Please look after me!" she pleaded with him aloud as if he were sitting there next to her. She laid there for a long time wondering what was going to happen, but she couldn't fight it anymore and she finally fell asleep.

She woke up still thinking of the prayer, asking her dad to take care of her, when she rolled over and saw Aaron lying on the bed next to her. She was a little startled when she realized that she hadn't ever heard him come in. He was sleeping soundly, and she looked at him, wondering how such a man could become so twisted and violent. What was it that made someone so evil? There were those who had survived abuse, only to grow up and become abusers themselves, and then there were those that grew up abused, who were determined not to repeat the sins of their parents, completely stopping the vicious cycle.

She laid there looking around, studying everything she could, wanting to be able to take every advantage she could. She looked at the lump in his pocket, and wondered if the lump was the keys that would unlock her chains. She looked around the room for anything she might be able to use to free herself, but found nothing. She was lying on her back with her eyes wide open, staring at the ceiling, when he started to wake up.

"Did you sleep well honey?" he asked her sweetly.

"I slept as well as I could chained to a bed," she said emotionless, "but I need to go to the bathroom. I need to get up!"

"Alright," he said getting up and unlocking the chain that tethered her to the bed. She still had a chain around one of her wrists that connected her to a longer chain that he used to lead her out to the outhouse, but he took it off her before she went inside. She noted that the lump in his pants pocket was indeed the keys to her chains when he unlocked her from the bed, and that was the first thing that gave her a shred of hope.

She was in the outhouse trying to make a mental note of how long it had been since she went missing. It had been exactly two days, and that realization completely sunk her spirits. She wondered how it was possible that there weren't any signs of anyone looking for her. They hadn't seen any signs of any people, and she wondered how long it would be before she would ever see another person.

She made her way out of the outhouse finding him waiting right there for her, but she knew he was too consumed with himself to catch the disappointment that was written all over her face. She was trying to hide it, but she was finding it increasingly more difficult to keep her emotions under wraps. He was in quiet contemplation when he opened up the cabin door and pushed her inside, leaving her standing there by herself without anything chained to her. *He's letting his guard down a little,* she thought as she went over and sat down in the chair, watching him out the windows.

"I'm going hunting. Come here!" he said coming back into the cabin moments later. He had a wad of chains and padlocks in his hand, and Jewel started bolting out the door before she could think straight. He caught her before she took more than a few steps, easily wrestling her to the ground, chaining her hands and legs. After he got her arms and legs secured, he reached up and hooked the chain, connecting the two to a new hook that he recently installed on the beam near the ceiling. *He really planned this out,* she thought to herself, realizing she was stuck there, and she was trying to keep the fear from engulfing her, closing her eyes to stifle her emotions.

She laid there in the middle of the floor where he had left her, trying to remember every detail of the trip up there. She was certain he had hidden the keys to the car in the front driver's side wheel well. She remembered seeing the lump in his pants pockets from the car keys, but then after he came around to where she was, there was nothing left in his pocket.

"Dear God, please look after Grady, and help me get away from this cabin and from Aaron. Lord, I pray that you will not forsake me. Our Father who art in heaven...," Jewel prayed quietly The Lord's Prayer, over and over, feeling it was the only thing in that moment that would stop her from completely losing it. There was a part of her that wanted to break down crying, but she knew there was no time for that. She knew that crying would hurt her. She needed to stuff the tears as deep as she could and feed off their energy. That's the way she always remembered it after the death of her parents. Somehow, not shedding the tears gave her the power and the energy she needed to endure pain, and she dug deep within her, determined to build on the energy to help her survive.

She remembered the journals she saw when she first looked around the cabin, and managed to stretch herself as far as she could, barely reaching the knapsack. She looked through them and could see that they were dated. She found the first one and opened it.

May 30, 1990
   We arrived at the cabin to start our new life. This isn't exactly what I imagined in my life, but I suppose it's about as good as I

can ask for now that I went and messed everything up. Ping seems surprisingly happy at least by Ping standards, and I'm just happy to see the light of day. Prison was hell, and this feels like a resurrection.

June 3, 1990

I swear to God if Ping wasn't a good hunter I would stick him like a pig and eat him for breakfast. My dad always said I'd end up with some no good for nothing bum, but even he failed to see what a miserable bastard I'd actually end up with.

June 7, 1990

I had a dream about my little Bobbie last night. I woke up and could still feel him in my arms. He was the sweetest little boy in the world and smelled like everything good in the world. He was the one good thing I did in the world. Well I suppose giving him up to a good family was the other good thing. He won't have to grow up all messed up like us.

She couldn't read anymore. It was page after page of one horrible life event after another. Their names were Jan and Ping, and they'd been running from something. Both of them had spent some time in prison, and were living there because they had either escaped prison, or escaped parole. They had obviously failed in society, and had been enjoying a relatively peaceful life in the backwoods of Alaska before Aaron came along.

Jewel had fallen asleep at some point, waking up with hunger pangs several hours later, hearing Aaron milling around outside. She was starving, having barely eaten in two and a half days, and she peeked out to see him putting a rifle and other items in the shed, locking it behind him. She watched as much as she dared, and then ducked down as quickly as she could, not wanting him to know that she knew where the guns were. She was completely irked, having seen that the rifle he had hidden in the shed was hers, but then pushed it out of her mind and immediately started remembering the details of the shed. How sturdy was the wood? Were there any windows, or weak and rotted boards? She remembered seeing that the door itself was newer against the rotten boards of the remainder of the doorframe, and she guessed that everything but the door itself was old and weak.

"I got us a rabbit," he said coming in like a proud warrior, dropping it at her feet.

Good grief, she thought, *the man grew up here and doesn't know the difference between a rabbit and a hare.*

"I would be happy to cook it up if you would like to unchain me," she said completely monotone, not wanting to give him the pleasure of any of her emotions, or any piece of her whatsoever.

"Maybe you could sing me a little song while you're cooking. That would be the perfect ending to this day, don't you think Jewel," he said sweetly, as if they had just spent a lovely day enjoying each other's company. He sat down in the chair and kicked back tiredly, apparently having gone to much effort to hunt the hare.

"I only sing when I'm happy, and when I'm helping people. I don't sing when I'm being held prisoner against my will," she said searing into his eyes, unable to stop herself.

"You'll do what I say! Now sing!" he barked at her angrily, making her tremble despite her best efforts to stand her ground.

She had been humming the song Mockingbird in her head since he gagged her and put her in the car. She remembered her mom singing it to her. It was something that always gave her comfort and peace. No matter what happened in her life, that song always brought her back to a quiet center that defined her, and allowed her to draw on that inner strength she always managed to find within her. It did that for everyone, not just her. She remembered in Iraq when she could sing most anything and it usually calmed people and put them at ease, but there were a few who had come in so distraught, it seemed like there was nothing she could ever do to comfort them. Often, she found that familiar song would manage to bring even the worst cases back to a place of peace they could draw strength from. It was a song of hope and unconditional love, and Jewel could see that it was having the same effect on Aaron. The menacing man without emotion or fear, or any sense of normal feeling whatsoever, was peacefully sitting in the corner nonchalantly wiping a tear from the corner of his eye, as he listened intently.

"Sing it again," he said more quietly.

She sang it slowly and quietly, over and over, while preparing the hare for their dinner, until she could see that Aaron had fallen asleep. She could see his jacket hanging there with the chest pocket gaping open, full of ammunition for her rifle. She casually walked by it, reaching in and grabbing a couple, startling him slightly. *He's sleeping lightly. I'll have to be careful,* she thought slipping the bullets into her boot as she leaned over pretending to scratch when he awoke.

The two ate their meager dinner in silence, and Jewel could see that there was something on his mind. She could see that whatever was on his mind was eating at him, but she didn't dare ask him. *Let it fester for all I care,* she thought, as she looked at the scratches from the chains that had bound her earlier.

"I'll give you a few days Jewel," he finally said angrily, "but after that, I'm fucking you whether you're ready or not. Got it!" he said before getting up and gathering the chains, moving them over to get ready to chain her to the bed.

"Wait! I need to go to the bathroom," she cried, choking on the knot that caught in her throat.

She had known from the moment he put her in the car, that she was likely going to be raped. She was glad she had been with Grady first. *I'll always have that, and nobody can take that away from me,* she thought as they walked out toward the outhouse.

Once inside the outhouse, she nearly lost it altogether. She was resolved not to show any kind of emotion in front of Aaron, but nearly broke down when he talked about raping her. She knew that a narcissistic sociopath thrived on strong emotion, and she had made a pact with herself never to give him any excuse to lose control. That's how they justified it. They would lose control of themselves and then blame their victim for pushing their buttons, or causing them to lose control, as if they themselves were just victims of the strong emotion that other people invoked in them. She wasn't going to give him the satisfaction, and she hoped that the part she had read about sociopath's being unable to get aroused without getting an emotional rise out of their victims, was actually true. She remembered reading about a case where the man broke into the woman's house. The woman just laid there like a dead fish, never screaming out or anything, and the man couldn't get aroused, and ended up leaving without raping her.

There was some hope, and she said a quiet prayer, crossing herself before stepping out of the outhouse. It was then that she realized that the crucifix she always wore around her neck, was missing.

CHAPTER 22

MILITARY ACTION

"What the fuck!" Grady shouted, slamming his hand down on the counter, "ya should have told us the minute ya knew he was no longer in custody!" he said, walking out of the police station in complete frustration and disbelief.

"This is bullshit man! I'm not goin' ta sit around here another day while Sheriff Taylor and Barney Fife bumble this," Grady said as he and Rudy made their way back to their tent at the base camp. The police had cordoned off the base camp after Grady and Rudy discovered Jewel missing, and they had determined there had been some sort of struggle that had taken place in the grass. Grady had found her crucifix on the bathroom floor, and there were several large handprints on the floor. They knew the prints were far too large to be Jewels, and Grady had run into town to notify the police immediately. It was then that the police notified them that Aaron had escaped custody the day he was supposed to be transferred back to Homer. They spent the night before pacing the floor at the police station, thinking that they must be getting ready to start a search, but in fact, nothing seemed to be happening at all.

"Let's go find her. Nobody here is more qualified than us to find her. We'll sneak back to our tents, get our stuff, and then head out," Rudy said, putting into words what he knew Grady was already thinking.

"Hey, we've been looking for you," Todd said as he and Mark ran up to them as they walked back to camp, "we were talking about some of the things Aaron said about Jewel. He said he was gonna take her to some cabin he owned, which was kinda weird, because earlier in the trip, he said he didn't own anything, and didn't even have a place to live anymore. I don't know... it's a long shot but... on the first leg we all came across this cabin and met this old couple. He said he wanted to live there, and then after we left, he said he had forgotten his rifle there and had to run back by himself to go get it, which we thought was really weird. That was the day before we met up with you guys."

"When he caught up to us, he was filthy and had blood on the front of his pants. He said he had killed a squirrel, but then had accidently left it on a rock when he stopped to take a dump, but I don't know. His story never made much sense to me," Mark said. "I tried to tell this to the police, but they seemed completely uninterested in the story, and kinda brushed us off saying they would come interview us in the next day or so, and here it is a day later, and they haven't asked us a single question."

"Daryl said his cousins Explorer is missing too, and he thinks they may have headed up this old back road toward the foothills. They were gonna head in that direction to go look for it if you want to hitch a ride with them," Todd added. "It sounds like it's kinda like the Wild West around here. People are used to taking matters into their own hands."

"Will ya help us a minute?" Grady asked. "We need ta sneak back ta our tents and get our gear. We're going after her, but we need ya ta create a distraction ta keep everyone lookin' in the opposite direction... give us time ta get our things."

"Yeah man! You got it! We'll go over there and throw a fit demanding our stuff. We'll try to buy five, maybe ten minutes. You'll have to move quickly though, and if you want to hitch a ride with Daryl, he said he would wait for you for a little while near the bridge. He'll probably want to leave within the hour," Mark said.

"Great! Thanks man. Give us two minutes and we'll be ready. As soon as we hear some commotion, we'll make a move toward our tents," Grady said.

"Wait! Let me go in by myself," Rudy said, "it's our best chance. All eyes are on you right now brother. There's no way you're sneaking in there. Go with them and make some commotion, and I'll meet you by the bridge at eleven hundred. That's less than thirty minutes from now."

"Alright, that sounds like a good plan. See you soon," Grady said as Rudy disappeared into the woods toward their tent.

Grady, Mark, and Todd made their way over to the other side of the camp toward Mark and Todd's tent, making sure they were far enough away from Grady's tent before Mark and Todd went under the cordon, starting the firestorm of commotion they needed to cause a distraction. Grady kept walking, acting as if he had no clue what the two were doing, before stopping to talk to Angela.

"What the hell is going on Grady?" Angela asked a little frantically.

"Rudy and I are going to go find her. These dumbasses around here are still trying to find their procedure manual. Just walk and talk with me a little ways. Rudy is getting our gear, and he'll be meeting me near the bridge at the old dirt road in about twenty minutes," Grady answered, putting an arm around her. "Mark and Todd thought they may be up near this old cabin. I don't know... it a long shot, but I don't know what else to do, I can't sit here and wait, and it seems logical."

"We're praying for her Grady. You find her," Angela wept, before breaking into a full sob.

"We will. I've spent a lot of years tracking people," Grady replied, feeling less certain than he sounded. Alaska was vast. Jewel had been missing for more than twenty-four hours. Had anyone told them from the beginning that Aaron had escaped custody, they would have left immediately to go find her, but the police didn't tell them until their second visit to the police station.

He hugged Angela, and then left her standing there. He disappeared into the woods, and made his way to the bridge in no time. Daryl and his cousins were waiting there for him, but there was still no sign of Rudy. He knew that even Rudy was going to have a tough time making it that far with both of their packs, and so he started heading in the direction he thought Rudy would be coming from. He found him heading toward him in true military fashion, his own pack on his back, and Grady's pack balanced on his head, with Rudy huffing it as fast as he could.

"Yer a beast man!" Grady said, coming up to relieve him as quickly as he could.

"I was going to grab Jewels medicine bag and a few of her things, but they were gone Grady. Someone had gone through her pack. Everything was poured out and then stuffed inside, completely messed up. Jewel wouldn't have left it like that. Aaron must have grabbed her stuff when we were all away from our tents," Rudy said breathlessly, with a chill going through him.

"Daryl said his cousin's Explorer leaks like a sieve, and they could see traces of it at the bridge. He thinks that may have been where Aaron left it when he grabbed Jewel," Grady said hopefully. "Dammit Rudy! I should have acted sooner, but ya know how the woman is. She likes ta go off on her own sometimes lookin' at plants and such," Grady said, shaking his head, feeling infuriated with himself. "I thought the police would be doin' more by now! I can't believe this!"

"You couldn't have known man," Rudy said, grabbing his shoulder. "Aaron's not too smart Grady... he wouldn't have taken her far. He thinks he's so much smarter than anyone else is, and that makes him easy and predictable. If he had an inkling of just how dumb he really is, that would actually raise his IQ slightly."

"I say we see if we can find that cabin first," Grady said. "If she's not there, we'll make other plans from there, but the cabin seems like the most logical place, and I don't know where else ta start."

"Hop in the back with us," Daryl said, helping Grady and Rudy with their packs as they walked up to the truck. "We'll head out to the foothills, and from there we'll have to hoof it. This old truck won't make it out in the brush, but I'll help you track her," he added, sitting down and leaning against his pack.

"Ya might get in trouble Daryl. Rudy and I talked about it, and we are both willin' ta take the risk, but we hardly expect ya ta take that risk. Ya hardly knew her, and we might even be implicated in her disappearance if we aren't able ta find her," Grady said, his voice breaking just a little toward the end. The thought of not finding her was enough to drive Grady near breaking. He had been frantic since finding her crucifix in the corner of the bathroom. He knew she never took it off, and he became alarmed when he realized the chain was broke. He could see that some kind of struggle had occurred in the grass, and he hoped Jewel hadn't been hurt by it too much.

"I know this place like the back of my hand. I'm going!" Daryl said absolutely. "I haven't known her very long, but I've known her long enough. I don't want anything bad to happen to her, and I know this place better than most. If we don't find her at that cabin, I know some other places we might look. Pull up over here a minute," he yelled to the guys in the front cab after they had driven a ways.

They pulled up in the same location Aaron had stopped to cut Jewel's duct tape off her. There were fresh oil stains on the gravel from the leaky Explorer, and Grady found some duct tape that had been thrown aside. He picked it up with his gloved hand, and examined it a little before placing it in a bag Rudy handed him.

"That's her hair stuck in here," Grady said, feeling both angry and excited, knowing he was on the right path. "I would know it anywhere!"

"That's encouraging man," Rudy said, trying to give Grady hope, his own heart aching at the thought of Jewel being duct taped, "we're on the right path!"

"See over there," Daryl said, pointing at the base of the foothills urging Grady to take a look through his scope, "there's not a road there, but you can see that a car drove through there recently, because the grass looks flattened down. I'd lay odds there's a patch of fresh oil drippings along there." They could see that the wheels of a car had tamped the grass down, and they suspected that it was the path Aaron had taken. The area they were in was not a heavily traveled or populated area, and the tracks looked pretty well defined, which meant they'd been made recently.

"Let's get after it then," Grady said, feeling anxious to get moving, trying to shove the image of her being duct taped out of his mind.

"Wait a minute Grady," Daryl said, "let's check it out, and we'll make sure it's the Explorer that went through there, but then we'll head in another way. If it's the cabin I'm thinking of, he'll be able to see us coming miles away if we go up from that direction. The old man who lives there is a fugitive, they say, and he's completely paranoid. He has a bunch of lookouts, and I'm sure the man who took her is probably smart enough to find them. There's also a bunch of underground hideouts all around that place. The old man had been in Vietnam, and was not dealing with a full deck of cards, always feeling the government was out to get him and take over his mind and such. If Aaron took her into one of those underground bunkers, we may never find her," he said, regretting the last few words the moment he said them.

"If we come in around from the other side, we can lay eyes on him long before he ever realizes we're there. Mark and Todd say he's a real dumbass, and he talks a good game, but doesn't know a damn thing," Daryl said, adding to their basic profile of who they thought Aaron was. "It'll take us a little longer to get there, but it's the right way to go in."

Grady knew from his sniper training that the man's logic was right on. Daryl was a hunter, and he knew how to surround his prey. It was much the same as being a sniper. Hunting man, or hunting animal, took much of the same skill. He didn't like the idea that it would take longer, but he knew they needed to get the advantage of sneaking up on him if they were going to find her.

"That sounds like the right way ta go. How much longer will it take do ya think?" Grady asked.

"It'll probably take an extra half day or more. I'd say we could be there by the day after tomorrow Grady, but that's only if we go all night tonight. We should stop at a little clearing around on the other side, and make camp for a few hours. It'll be dark by then. We're no good to her if we're all worn out," Daryl said. "I say we get close tomorrow night, and then make for an early morning ambush if she's there. We can't go traipsing around there in the dark. I'd bet anything the old man has a bunch of animal traps set around there."

"I'm glad yer here man. Ya'd make a hell of a sniper," Grady said. "That sounds like a good plan."

The crew headed out, reaching the base of the foothills within an hour, and it didn't take long before they confirmed that the missing Explorer had likely made the tracks. They had walked up a ways, and found fresh oil on some grass reeds, which made it likely they were tracking the right car.

"We'll take you around to the other side where you'll need to start hiking up, and we'll wait before coming back for the Explorer. If we head in now to get it, we'll blow your cover, and he'll likely get spooked and take off with her," the driver of the pickup said.

"That's great man! Thank you!" Rudy replied as they all climbed back in the pickup.

Grady tried his hardest not to imagine the worst, but remembered all too clearly the anger coming from Aaron as they got off the helicopter after that first leg, and he couldn't help but think about all the things he had told Mark and Todd that he wanted to do to Jewel. He didn't know what he was going to do to the man, but it was going to take all that he had in him not to take the law into his own hands. The police hadn't even managed to organize a search yet, and didn't necessarily believe that she was even missing. "This place should be swarming with police," Grady said aloud to everyone and no one, "and yet there's absolutely no trace of them."

"God let me find her," Grady prayed aloud, kissing her crucifix he had barely let go of since finding it, as they drove toward the backside where they would start hiking up the mountain.

He knew that he needed to get his mind straight. Somehow, he needed to take the personal emotion out of it, and look at it as just another mission. He needed to steady himself, and not let his racing pulse dictate how he proceeded. He thought about all the dangerous missions he had been on when he was in the military. He remembered some of the other soldiers getting anxious and riled up, but he never seemed to. He thought only of the mission itself, taking all the emotion out of it, thinking only of the systematic plan he had laid out in his head, going from one-step to the other, steadily executing his plan.

He stored the thought of her in the back of his mind, thinking of everything he needed to do to track them, compartmentalizing the mission as a search to find a dangerous man, rather than a search to find the woman he loved. He evaluated Aaron, trying to remember every detail about him, trying to see things through his eyes in an attempt to predict what steps he may be taking, and how prepared he was. Mark and Todd said Aaron was all talk. They said he talked a big game, but in reality, he wasn't very capable. He summed Aaron up in his mind, carefully calculating his competence and the mistakes he was likely to make. The military trained him to find mistakes and exploit them. He was certain he would be able to outsmart Aaron, but what gave him the most comfort, was knowing Jewel would be able to outsmart him. What she lacked in physical strength, she would be able to make up for in wit and determination. He just hoped she would be able to outwit him until he was able to get there.

CHAPTER 23

THE YEAR OF THE SNAKE

"Get off me!" Jewel screamed, trying to fight Aaron as he yanked off her clothes. He had chained her to the bed earlier, and she somehow managed to fall asleep, feeling somewhat comforted, at least for the night, that she had a few days before he would rape her. Apparently, he changed his mind, and she found herself fighting against a man more than twice her size, and against chains that weighed heavily against her arms and legs. He was sweaty and vile, and the smell of him made her gag. She was flailing wildly, determined to kick him off her, screaming as loud as she could.

"Fuck you! You little cunt! You teased me enough! You belong to me now, and that's that! You better just get used to it!" he shouted, as he pulled her pants down, getting angrier when he realized the chains were working against him.

He grabbed his hunting knife, and the sheen on the blade caught in the moonlight, flashing a blinding ray of light in her eyes. She screamed loud, startling him enough to make him stop for a second.

"God that excites me! You look so beautiful right now! You're like riding a wild and crazy mustang," he said kissing her, pulling wildly at her clothes. He took the knife and cut her pants away, not wanting to stop long enough to let her out of her chains. He pulled his shirt off, and Jewel could see just how large he was. Even if it was mostly fat, she knew she would never be able to fight him off, but she was determined to try.

She knew fighting him was causing his excitement, but she couldn't stop herself. The man on top of her was so terrifying and disgusting, it was pure instinct and survival that caused her to fight back. She felt like an animal trapped in a snare, and even though she knew pulling against it would cause more pain, she couldn't stop herself from trying to free herself from what was happening.

"You're such a pathetic loser," she finally said through gritted teeth. "Go ahead then Aaron. I'm sure the only way you would ever be able to have sex with a girl is to force her. Nobody would ever want to have sex with you willingly," she added. "Pull out that pathetic little penis you tried so hard to impress me with." She didn't care if he decided to cut her throat. She was so revolted by him. The thought of death seemed more appealing than enduring rape.

"Shut the fuck up bitch!" he yelled, slapping her hard across the face several times with a full swing, trying to escalate it to keep up his level of excitement. He was straddling her as she laid flat on her back, pinned to the bed by the weight of his body, and pinned by the chains tethering her to the bed.

"Is that all you've got?" she said gritting her teeth, acting unimpressed. "This may just be the most pathetic rape in the history of rapes. How bad do you have to be to fuck this up?" she laughed, trying to belittle him, exercising what little power she had, knowing it might cost her, but in that moment, she hoped he would just reach over and slit her throat.

"You fucking little cunt! I oughta cut your fucking throat!"

"That would be preferable over having your disgusting little penis inside me," she said boldly, egging him on even more, feeling him go limp above her.

With that, he smacked her across the face as hard as he could with a full swing, several times, before rolling off her, stomping around the room throwing things, slamming doors and drawers, and hurling objects toward her as hard as he could. Several rocks and books hit her hard, and she could feel welts rising up on her face and body. One rock hit her square in the cheek, and she could feel the welt throbbing beneath her hand as she reached up to protect her head from more flying objects. Finally, he had enough, and went outside kicking things, slamming the door as he left. She could still hear him kicking and throwing things outside, and she prayed he wouldn't come back in for another assault.

She laid there feeling bumps and bruises pulsating all over her body and face. Her head was pounding from him hitting her, and from the stones and other items he'd thrown at her. Her pants had been cut open, leaving her exposed from the waist down, and her shirt had been torn open, leaving her breasts bare. She laid there trying to slow her breathing, but she could feel her heartbeat thumping in every sore on her body. She could feel the weight of the chains more than ever, pinning her limbs to the bed, as she laid there completely helpless, trapped like an animal. She listened as closely as she could, trying to predict what would happen next, her mind frantically searching for refuge, but finding none. She could hear him out near the shed, and she suddenly feared he would come back with a rifle and shoot her altogether. *Damn my arrogance!* she cried to herself, certain he was going to kill her.

He suddenly came through the door, throwing it open still fueled by rage, but smiling wickedly, carrying a bottle of rum, duct tape, and the branding iron from over the door. She recognized the object in his hand immediately, and she screamed wildly, straining against the chains that held her. Fear ran through her. He needed to make her scream to get excited, and he was going to take her to her limit. Nobody would be able to stay calm in the face of a branding iron, and she knew it.

"Where's your mouth now bitch?" he said more calmly, setting the branding iron down in the fireplace, sitting back casually to take a long pull off the bottle of rum he held in his hand.

"I'm sorry Aaron. I... I was just scared... that's all...," she said stuttering. "You have me shackled to a bed, slapping me, cutting my clothes off me. How do you think I should behave? Please just let me go. I want to go home," she cried, pleading with him, fighting back panic.

"This is home baby," he said lovingly, going over to stroke her cheek softly where he had just moments before slapped her so hard she thought she would lose consciousness. "This is our home now. You just have to accept that, and the sooner you do, the easier it's going to be for us."

"Please don't hurt me anymore," she begged him as he turned to look at the branding iron he had laid in the fire. She followed his eyes to the iron, and saw it lit up red from the heat.

"You'll feel better after it's over honey. You'll see," he said talking sweetly, stumbling a little as he walked over to take another long pull off the rum.

He readied himself better this time, cutting the rest of her clothes from her body, and stripping off his own before getting the branding iron out of the fire. She yanked and screamed, but it was no use, as soon as he saw the fear in her eyes, she could see that it started to excite him. He stood in front of her stroking himself with his free hand, smiling crudely at her with the branding iron in his other hand. He watched her with excitement as fear tore through her. She knew she would scream uncontrollably as soon as he got near her with it.

"No! Please no! Oh god no!" she screamed as he moved closer to her, touching the iron to her leg with a look of pleasure on his face. She screamed as loud as she could, nearly passing out from the pain that radiated from her thigh when he pressed the red-hot iron against her skin.

"Oh god Jewel! You fucking little whore!" he yelled smiling, fully excited, positioning himself between her legs violently, digging his hand into the seared skin to make her scream louder. He grabbed at her breasts and violently pushed one hand down between her legs, grabbing at her as rough as possible.

She could feel him push himself inside her, but the pain from the branding iron was so intense it was all she could think of. In and out, he went as hard as he could. She could smell his breath on her as he screamed at her and hit her, calling her vile names as he did. The stench of him infiltrated her head until she thought she would puke.

Somehow, she felt like she had moved outside her own body, fighting the pain radiating from her leg and her face, and fighting the stink of him. Just when she thought he'd had enough, he would come at her again, causing her to scream out, getting more and more excited. One hard thrust after another tore through her, over and over, tearing at her flesh, ripping at her insides. The pain and the stench finally overwhelmed her enough she could no longer hold back, she turned her head and started puking violently, which only slowed him down long enough to turn her on her stomach, entering her again from behind, harder than he had before.

"I'm going to fuck you all night you little bitch," he roared, pleased with himself, stopping occasionally to drink more rum and dig his hand into her burn again, eliciting more screams from her, and repositioning the chains that kept her spread eagle on the bed. Finally, it had caused too much pain, and she could feel herself slip into unconsciousness, drifting away into a place within herself.

Somewhere in her dreamlike state, she could still smell him, but his physical assault on her faded away. She dreamed of being on the ranch. She could feel herself running through the field, the sun on her face, with her mom smiling at her. She found a place of peace she could escape to, and it lifted her up and held her there, keeping her shielded from the physical world for a brief moment.

Horrific smells and loud noises interrupted her dreams, but she tucked herself into some sort of cocoon, wrapped inside memories that seemed to be shielding her from pain, until it finally stopped, and she was able to fall into a fitful sleep. The nightmares took her through more horror, chained outside like a dog, broken and beaten until she begged for death, but then she awoke.

She awoke early in the morning as she always did, finding him sleeping naked beside her. She nearly vomited again at the sight and smell of him. The scent of him, and her vomit from the night before, hung stagnant in the air. *I could choke him to death with my chains,* she thought, but she knew he could easily wrestle her away from him.

"Get up!" she said angrily, elbowing him to wake up, not able to lay there next to him for another second, "I need to go to the bathroom."

He eyed her for a second, trying to find his bearings, and remember where he was. He had drank nearly the entire bottle of rum he brought out the night before, and was feeling the effects of it like a vice bearing down on his head. He managed to make it up several minutes later with a little extra prodding by Jewel, but he couldn't look at her.

"Let me out of these chains so I can get cleaned up and go to the bathroom," she said as Aaron slowly pulled on his own clothes, avoiding her eyes.

He let her out of the chains, and she was able to get up, her body feeling like it had been hit by a freight train. She ached from head to toe. Her insides felt like they'd been torn out, and she could feel the searing pain deep within her, radiating up and piercing her heart. She made it to her pack, and found more clothes before heading out to the outhouse, never saying another word to him.

Her whole body ached. Every step she took sent pain shooting through her that threatened to knock her over. She could feel blood and other fluids trickle down her thigh as she limped out to the outhouse, but she was determined to fight the pain, and walk with her head up. She could feel his eyes on her, and she knew he was feeling ashamed of himself. She suspected he was going to be especially nice to her all day to try to make up for the pain he caused. Such is the way of a sociopath.

She remembered reading about such people, studying them in her psychology class, never feeling completely convinced that people like him actually existed. One moment he was filled with rage, and the next moment he was speaking to her sweetly. She shook her head thinking about how he called her honey and baby, trembling when she thought of it. Somewhere inside that crazy head of his, he was convinced they were a couple in love, and on some kind of romantic getaway.

She could barely endure the pain of the burn on her thigh as she pulled on her jeans, but there was no way she was going back out there without them covering her. She would have to wash it later and get it bandaged up when she could find a moment alone in the cabin, chained or not. She felt the side of her cheek, and knew it was swollen and getting bigger. She could feel the pressure of the swelling pushing one of her eyes closed. Her entire body ached as she felt welt after welt, remembering the violent temper tantrum he threw. She felt between her legs briefly, but the pain was too great, and the blood was too fresh.

I have to find a way out of here, she cried inside. She knew he was capable of anything, and she knew he could kill her anytime he wanted, which seemed preferable to going through another night like the one she'd just endured. She was certain she wouldn't be able to bear such an ordeal again. Her heart ached for Grady. *Was anybody looking for me? Was Grady okay?* she thought nearly breaking down. *There's nobody else.*

She knew she had been gone for about three days, but she hoped they hadn't waited to go looking for her. Surely, they would have found my necklace, and realized something happened to me. "Please dear God, please let me get out of here," she prayed, trying to steady herself. She wanted to break down and cry. She wanted to scream, and kick, and hit things. She wanted to let out all the anger and hurt she felt boiling inside her, but she knew she needed to stay level headed. *I have to stay in control of what I can,* she thought. *I can outsmart him. I know I can if I can just stay calm and keep my head. I can win.*

She separated her mind from her body as much as possible. She needed to ignore the smell of him on her that was threatening to consume her. She needed to go beyond the pain from her wounds, and let it feed her resolve to find a way to escape from him. *I will win! I will find a way out of this!* she thought to herself, stuffing away the desire to breakdown and cry, grabbing a hold of the anger that would fuel her to find her freedom.

He will not win!

CHAPTER 24

THE PURSUIT

Grady tried to sleep once they made it to the clearing, but he was too restless, so they decided to pack up again and hike through the rest of the night. It was slow going at first, as they carefully crept through the dark night, always watchful for traps or cliffs, but at least they were moving. Grady couldn't sleep knowing that Jewel was in the hands of that man, remembering him eyeing her the way he did, and remembering the uneasy feeling he had about him from the very beginning. He remembered seeing the evil that hung like darkness behind the wickedness in his eyes, and it sent a chill down his spine. With each step he took, he vowed never to let her out of his site again. He thought of her skin and her hair, and he cringed when he thought about her rare innocence. He wondered if that would all be lost. He understood what Aaron's intentions were with her, and the thought of it cut deep in his heart.

He wondered for a second if he would feel the same about her, but then cursed himself for thinking such a thing. He knew that nothing could change how he felt. He knew they belonged together. He briefly wondered how he would live without her, which made him move faster. He knew Rudy and Daryl were trying their best to keep up even as he pushed on harder, and he knew they probably needed a rest, but the need to move closer to her was fueling him to go faster and farther.

"Let's stop up here before reaching that ridge Grady," Daryl said breathlessly, pointing toward the ridgeline they were approaching as the morning sun started to illuminate the mountain. "We need to glass the valley below to make sure nobody's down there. The cabin will be just over the next ridgeline beyond the next valley. "There's really good hunting down on the other side, and I wouldn't be surprised if someone were down there hunting or checking traps."

Grady readied himself, moving up the ridgeline with catlike stealth. People often wondered how such a large man could move about so quietly, seemingly invisible, until they saw him in action. He seemed to float above the ground, never making a sound, placing every foot ever so gently in all the right places. He got his binoculars out and studied the valley, searching for anything out of the ordinary, any movements or unnatural colors that sprung out. The Army had trained him to look for certain colors, and unnatural movements, and he had a knack for always finding his target. He hoped he would see her and be able to run down immediately to rescue her, but he knew that the hunt was only beginning. He had tracked the enemy. He had the skill and the patience it took to find his prey, and he vowed not to rest until Aaron was dead or behind bars.

They knew they had to stop and rest for just a few hours, or they wouldn't be any good to Jewel. They didn't make a camp or even a campfire; they just laid down where they were in order to rest a few hours as much as they could. That was a typical military tactic that Rudy and Grady had employed many times throughout their careers. They knew that just lying down and resting for a couple hours, could do much to fuel a body that was running mostly on adrenaline.

"I could move faster by myself guys," Grady said, knowing Rudy and Daryl weren't ready when they woke up a couple hours later. "You said the cabin would be straight on this heading Daryl?"

"Yep. If you really hoof it you could be there by the next day, but you'll need to watch your step. Word is the old man has traps set all over that valley Grady," Daryl said.

"I'll head straight, and the two of you circle around toward the back. Either way we'll meet back up near that cabin sometime tomorrow," Grady said, searching Rudy's eyes for approval.

"You know I don't like it," Rudy finally said, "but I know you need to keep moving. It might not be a bad idea to split up anyway. We'll draw less attention if the bastard is out hunting, and we'll have a better shot of reaching the cabin unseen."

"Alright then, I'm heading out. I need to keep moving. Two shots means we found her or we need help," Grady said shaking hands with the two men.

"Be safe brother," Rudy said as Grady took off at a quick pace. He knew that Grady put himself in lots of dangerous situations before, and he knew that he had an unwavering way about him that allowed him to keep his head, but this was different. He had already seen him lose his cool at the police station, which had surprised him a little, but he wasn't in fear for himself. He was in fear for a woman he had fallen in love with, and love usually causes people to make costly mistakes.

Grady knew that as well. He knew he was making decisions, and doing things he may not be doing if he were only thinking about himself, but he wasn't. He needed to be safe, but he needed to do this at a greater speed than he was used to. Careful, calculating, patient, logical; these were his greatest tools when it came to being an Army sniper. He had always been very successful, and he knew they were the right tools to do the job, but this was different. Time was not on his side, and his emotions were running wild. He knew the extra risks he was taking, and he accepted them, carefully running all the possible scenarios through his head as he always did when he was on the hunt.

The valley below was enormous, but Grady never stopped to consider the enormity of it. He fell into a comfortable, steady pace that would have been a fast jog for most people, and he was covering ground far quicker than most people would be able to do. He headed straight on the exact heading he had discussed with Daryl, marking targets on the horizon to aim for, stopping only long enough to glass the ridge and take a quick sip of water. He was determined to get there as fast as he could. He ate small bits of jerky as he went, running everything through his mind over and over, carefully calculating how he would handle every possible situation.

His back was killing him, but he pushed it out of his mind. The hard nodules of damaged muscle tissue were eating away at him like battery acid, but the memory of war fueled him even more. He knew the evil that some people were capable of inflicting on others, and women and children were most often the targets. He had witnessed it on many occasions. Young girls in villages in Iraq and Afghanistan who were treated like slaves, of little value. Men in his own Army unit who were capable of things that made his stomach sick just thinking of it. He thought of the pleasure that some men got when they would take out a target, relishing the blood spatter as the bullet tore through flesh, and it was that look that always turned his stomach.

He knew the consequences that came with his job as an Army sniper, but it was the high value he put on human life that made him good at it. He took the responsibility of it seriously. His respect for life allowed him to advance on a target carefully, without the bloodlust he saw in other men, always causing them to make mistakes. Hitting the target was always the last resort, and he was happiest when he could advance on a target to get information, rather than ending life, but he knew that the targets he did hit were necessary. His beliefs conflicted with his religion, but he truly believed that some life needed to end, for the greater good. There were targets he hit who were so evil it made his stomach knot when he thought of the atrocities they were capable of committing.

His dad was upset with him when he decided to become a sniper. He had breezed through all his engineering classes, and he could have gone far with it, in or out of the military, but he wanted to be a sniper. He had a natural knack for hitting his targets from impossible distances, in unimaginable conditions, plus, he enjoyed the adrenaline rush of sneaking in and out of places without being detected. His careful planning, and his systematic calculations that were always taking place in the back of his mind, gave him the ability to practically see around corners, predicting what would happen next through an intricate process of elimination, of various sequences. Beyond that, he felt it was important.

He had always found world leaders interesting, always wanting to read about them, studying the men whose main desire was to control others, regardless of how much damage it caused in the world. Through it all, he felt that good men had a duty to fight against it all. He never wanted to be someone who sat on the sidelines and complained about it, without ever doing anything to help. He wanted to be someone who could give freedom to those who needed it. He needed to ease suffering. He felt it was a duty he was capable of, and therefore, he felt it was his responsibility.

One shooting pain after another, he moved closer to the cabin, and hopefully, closer to Jewel.

CHAPTER 25

LEAD ME LORD, LEAD ME BY THE HAND

Jewel got herself dressed and cleaned up as much as possible, longing to take a scalding hot shower to wash the stink of him off her. Her body ached from head to toe, and the burn on her thigh had blistered and popped when she pulled her jeans on, making her worry about infection. She knew she would have to give herself some antibiotics, and she tried her hardest to shake the thought of having Aaron's sperm inside her. The thought of disease and pregnancy made her pulse quicken, as horrible thoughts of him chaining her outside like a dog infected her mind.

She had experienced unusually bad periods from the time she first started when she was fourteen, and had gone on birth control to help ease the pain. She didn't need to worry about pregnancy when she and Grady had been together, but she didn't have her pills anymore. The risk of pregnancy was great, and the thought of it terrified her more than the rape itself. She counted the days in her head, wondering how close to ovulation she was. She knew it was close, probably day twelve or thirteen of her cycle, which meant that ovulation would occur in the next day or two, and for the first time, she cursed herself for being like clockwork on her twenty-eight day cycle, ovulating almost exactly every time on day fourteen. She could feel ovulation coming usually, getting period-like cramps, and she searched her mind for any of those familiar signs, but she couldn't think straight. Her body ached too much, and trying to focus in on one little pain was too difficult.

She was thankful Aaron had grabbed some of her items, including her medical bag. While he was outside, she found a quiet place where she could tend to her wounds, and give herself an antibiotic shot. She managed to see a reflection of herself in a kitchen pan, and could clearly see the swelling and bruising deforming her face. She took ibuprofen, drinking it down with the remainder of the rum still left in the bottle Aaron had brought in the night before. It took the edge off her a little, but left her wanting more, enough to erase the memory of his brutality.

She cleaned the cabin as much as possible, trying to get the stench out of the air from the night before, but it was no use. It wasn't the smell of the puke that was overwhelming her, it was the smell of him. He sweated out vinegar and garlic, and the thought of it curled her stomach all over again. Every time she breathed in too deeply, the smell made her start heaving all over again, but there was nothing left in her. It was just dry heaves sapping her energy with every involuntary reaction.

The rape was just a vague memory compared to the branding iron, and the smell itself. It was a crude, handmade iron, and Jewel imagined her thigh forever marked with the sign of the snake, and she remembered the smell of burnt flesh.

The bastard clearly underestimates me if he thinks I will just give in and accept this, she thought to herself angrily. *I'll find a way out, and there's not a damn thing he can do about it!*

She prayed silently, asking for the saints and angels to pray for her, to help her get through it just as she had gotten through the deaths of her parents and grandparents. The power of prayer was all she had, and it was giving her strength. *I may just die here,* she thought, *but I will be saved. To live is Christ, to die is gain,* she tried telling herself.

She shook her head thinking of death. *I am not going to die here! I will get out of here!* she thought, suddenly feeling resolute. She longed for Grady. The thought of seeing him, and letting him hold her again, gave her both strength and weakness. It was a vulnerability she hadn't allowed herself since she was a child, and yet, the power of such a strong emotion was driving her to dig within herself to find a way to get free from Aaron. She wondered if Grady would want her anymore, but she pushed the thought out of her mind as quickly as it seeped in. She couldn't lose hope. She had to think of everything good, so she could find her freedom again.

He stayed outside all day while she cleaned as much as possible, moving slowly as she did, each step shooting pain through her. She was exhausted from the constant lack of sleep over the last several days, and she was famished from having barely eaten anything. She was bruised, and she ached from head to toe, but the work gave her something to do. There was no way she could have just sat there doing nothing. She felt anxious, tired, and angry, with a cocktail of emotions that seemed to be boiling just below the surface, about to burst at any moment. She had to occupy her hands and her mind as much as possible, resisting the urge to crawl in a corner to cry herself to sleep.

She would look out at him occasionally to see where he was, wanting to monitor him. She saw him several times snacking on one thing or another, as she sat inside with her stomach growling. He hadn't been hunting again, and she was wondering how it was he thought they were going to be able to survive. She suspected that he hadn't had to do much for himself as a child, and was finding this survival situation a little more challenging than he thought it was going to be. The only thing she had inside was some water. She drank it down sparingly, not knowing where it had come from, but needing it to settle her stomach and keep herself hydrated.

"I'll bet you were a little whore in high school," he said storming in the cabin suddenly, interrupting her thoughts. "I'll bet you spread your legs for half the football team, all the while teasing and taunting, and acting all innocent. Girls like you make me sick! My mom was a little whore too. She gave it up for everyone, 'til my dad came along and took her in outta pity. I saw you and Grady. You couldn't spread your legs fast enough, and now here you are spreading them for me."

He had been there, she thought, remembering the night before her abduction. She sat listening to his ranting, knowing there was nothing she could say that would make him change his mind about what he perceived to be reality, and so she said nothing, concentrating, not wanting to show any emotion on her face. He was hot and cold, and she thought that if she waited a few minutes, his mood would change again, and he would go back to pretending they were in love.

She imagined he had grown up in horrible conditions, and was determined to make everyone pay for it. Todd and Mark told her a few things about what he had said about his parents, and it wasn't good. There was a part of her that felt sorry for the little boy that endured so much, but people overcome battles every day, and most of them do it without raping and hurting people. She didn't feel sorry for him. She thought he was a loser, and that he would get what he deserved one day. She did the only thing she knew to calm him.

Lead me Lord, lead me by the hand
And help me face the rising sun
Comfort me through all the pain
That life may bring...

She sang on, soft and low. She could feel the tension in the room ease. She saw his shoulders drop, and the anger in his face soften. He seemed to consider every word she sang, grasping at every meaning, perhaps saying a silent prayer for his own salvation. He didn't look at her as he usually did when she sang. He sat down and closed his eyes, and Jewel could see his lip quiver just a touch. Pain was everywhere, and she sang on, quietly erasing the evil that lurked in that room, if only for a moment. The melodic words she sang, pierced the ugliness in the room. She could feel the good sweep in through the windows, and she slipped into that quiet place within her that allowed her to find peace and solace.

The two sat in silence for a while until Jewel could see that Aaron had fallen asleep. He had quite a lot to drink the night before, and she wasn't surprised to see him so sluggish. He saw himself as a strong and powerful man, but in reality, he was overweight, lazy, and he wasn't nearly as smart as he thought he was.

She waited in silence, hoping he would sleep hard, and she immediately started looking for ways she might be able to make an escape. She tested the water, making a little noise without getting up, to see if he would stir, but there was no movement. She had packed little things she had from her medical bag in the pockets of her pants and shirt, with the hopes of having something to help her if the opportunity to escape presented itself. Thoughts quickly raced through her mind. Since they had spent the day milling about, him outside, and her inside, he had allowed her to be unchained, once she admitted to him that she wouldn't be able to outrun him.

Her mind was racing. *Should I try to run down the mountain to the car to make my escape, or should I try to bust through the shed and grab my rifle I saw him put in there. He set it right inside the door,* she remembered, thinking of every detail, trying to map it all out in her mind. She knew he hid the ammunition in a different spot, but she still had the two bullets from earlier, and she knew he wouldn't be expecting that.

She thought that one, or maybe two firm hits with the hatchet would allow her to knock the hinges off the latch that was holding the padlock on the shed. She had looked at the latch several times from a distance, and she could see that it was old and rusty, and thought it might break off from the rotted wood doorframe easily enough. She remembered her and Troy breaking into an old shed near his house looking for hidden Christmas presents. They hadn't been more than nine then, and they were able to break the latch without much effort.

She quickly decided that would be her best chance of escaping, provided she was able to find the hatchet without spending too much time. It would be dark in a few hours, and she knew she wouldn't be able to make it down off the mountain that fast with all her bumps and bruises. She closed her eyes and thought for a moment, trying to trace in her mind the movements Aaron had made earlier when he was out chopping wood. She remembered hearing a thud before he gave up chopping and moved on to something else, and she decided he had probably left the hatchet in a log near the woodpile.

He hadn't worked at chopping very long, and she wondered how he thought he would ever be able to provide enough for them to survive out there. He worked slowly, and he didn't use his head. He would work for a minute, and then sit down or get easily frustrated with something and then move on to something else. The fact that he had done as much as he did to plan it out, and prepare for keeping her at the cabin, was remarkable in itself, and she wondered how much of the chains and padlocks had been retrieved from the previous owners of the cabin. She also wondered if perhaps he had only meant to keep her for a short while, before getting rid of her all together. She swallowed hard as the thought of death loomed for a second, strengthening her resolve for a possible escape.

She heard the deep heavy snore, and she could see he was sleeping hard. She quietly got up to sneak out of the cabin, not daring to grab her coat or anything else as she made her way out, for fear that the sound of it would wake him. She slipped through the door that he left slightly open when he came in earlier, making sure not to move it, remembering how the hinges had squeaked earlier. She glanced back, not seeing any movement, and made her way over to the hatchet, carefully placing each foot down on the ground the way she had been taught to do when she was hunting, not wanting to make a sound. She pushed the pain in her leg out of her mind, knowing she had to fight through it; the adrenaline was helping to numb all her aches and pains as it surged through her.

The hatchet was right where she thought it would be, but it took everything she had to get it out of the log it was dug into. *The man's strong. There's no doubt about that,* she thought, fully understanding the danger she was in. She knew if he caught her, he would never let her off the chains again. She knew this would be her only chance to escape, and she was going to take it.

She finally got the hatchet out, her heart racing so fast it was nearly jumping out of her chest. She thought that would have been the easy part, and started to wonder if she was making a terrible mistake. She pushed the doubt out of her mind, and quietly crept back toward the shed, examining the hinges carefully, deciding where to hit it, knowing that she wouldn't have much time to grab the rifle and make a break for it before Aaron made it out of the house. Her heart started pounding faster when she heard a rustle inside the cabin, making her feel like she was going to pass out, but then she heard the snore deeper and louder, and tried to steady herself. *Come on Jewel! Get a grip!* she scolded herself, trying to stop the shaking in her hands and legs.

She found the bullets she had managed to keep hidden in her boot, and put them in her right pocket, wanting to make sure they were in a place she could access easily. She readied herself, imagining every step she would need to take to secure the rifle, and take off running in the right direction. She would need to grab the rifle and make a break for it, knowing she wouldn't have enough time to load and shoot before he made it out of the cabin. She realized her initial thought to head straight down the mountain wasn't going to work, as she saw there was a cliff just a few yards away.

She quickly changed plans, deciding to bolt across the valley as fast as she could, which was going to be a bit riskier since it was uphill. She was going to have to run toward the cabin itself, along one side, but she thought Aaron would run out of the door on the opposite side since it was a more natural way to exit from the cabin, given the landscape, and that would buy her time. If he ran in the direction she was planning to go, he would be able to catch her immediately, but it was a chance she had to take. There was no other choice, she shook her head, convinced it would be the direction he would least expect her to go, and she set her sights on an outcropping of rocks, deciding to head in that direction once she had the rifle.

She thought again of the two bullets in her pocket. There would be no warning shot, and she remembered her dad telling her never to aim a gun at a person unless she meant to kill them. She was going to have to shoot to kill if she was going to save herself, and she knew it, but it went against everything that was natural for her. Hunting had been a part of her life, and she did it thoughtfully, making sure she only killed what they would eat, but this was going to be different. This was a man's life she would be taking. The nurse in her screamed no, but the memory of his brutality from the night before strengthened her resolve to survive.

She knew he was unusually fast for a man his size, and she examined every log and rock that would be in her path to the rock outcropping she set her sights on. *He may be fast, but I have the advantage. He's not expecting this, and I am,* she told herself, crossing herself before deciding on the weakest spot on the hinge, keeping an ear out for the snores that were still coming from the cabin.

She looked back at the cabin one last time before taking careful aim with the hatchet. She knew she would only have one chance to hit it hard… maybe two. *If I don't get the rifle, I'll head east and try to run toward the car and hold onto the hatchet. It's the only chance I'll have,* she thought, knowing he would quickly catch up to her if that should happen, but she took a determined swing giving it everything she had.

To her horror, she realized the latch didn't come off, and she quickly hit it two more times, freeing it from the side of the shed. She didn't dare look back. She fumbled with the latch, pulling it the rest of the way off the side of the shed, screws and all, and she finally swung the door open, grabbing the rifle. It was right where she saw him put it, and the minute her hand touched it, she grabbed hold of it and took off in the direction up the valley, never once looking back. She ran as fast as she could, her heart pounding wildly before she dared to glance back. She saw him, and realized she had been right about him not expecting her to run in that direction, which gave her valuable seconds to get further away from him.

He had run out of the door toward the downhill side, causing him to circle back around the house. She knew this gave her extra time, but she never let up. She could see the outcropping of rocks getting closer as she ran as fast as she could, quickly gaining on them, but she felt like everything was happening in slow motion.

She could hear him running after her, each of his footsteps sounding like thunder in her ears, and then she heard a rustling sound that startled her, causing her to glance back to see that he had fallen, buying her more valuable time. He had tripped over the log she had noted in her mind when she decided on a path moments before.

He was yelling at her, as he struggled to get back up. She turned and saw him yelling, but she couldn't hear it anymore. His voice sounded muffled and drowned out by the thrumming in her ears. Time seemed to be moving slowly, as if she were watching a movie in half speed. The only thing that was moving quickly was the pounding in her heart, and the quickness of Aaron running toward her, screaming at her as he did.

She made it to the outcropping of rocks, and quickly dug into her pocket while positioning herself to take aim at him. He was moving slower, having taken a heavy fall, but she wasted no time.

She loaded the two bullets in the gun as she had done hundreds of times before, her hands trembling out of control until the song from earlier steadied her, the words running through her mind, *lead me Lord, lead me by the hand.* She crouched down on one knee to take aim at the giant man running toward her. She zoned in on him as she would zone in on an antelope sprinting across the plains, waiting patiently for the right shot. She could see the coy look on his face, clearly thinking she was aiming at him with an unloaded gun. Of course, he wouldn't be expecting her to have it loaded, and a part of her looked forward to the surprise on his face when he heard the shot.

She waited for the right moment, aiming for his head, never once letting him get out of her crosshairs. Boom! The shot rang out, and she quickly cocked the gun again readying herself for the next shot should she need it, but he was down, and she could see him splayed out on the ground, arms and legs going in every direction. She had shot him right in the head, and the realization of it rang out nearly as loud as the ringing in her ears. She had to resist the urge to shoot him again, trying to steady herself, patiently watching for any movements from him before satisfying herself that he was down.

She collapsed on the ground, every tear she had been holding back releasing all at once, stopping only long enough to glance at the body lying on the ground, reassuring herself that he wasn't moving. Her shoulder ached from the recoil, adding to the many aches and pains throbbing through her body. Everything stopped. She could hear nothing. She could feel no pain in her body. She could only feel the turmoil that was raging within her. It was screaming at her and she cried out, swimming in the realization of everything that had occurred over the last few days, and the precious few minutes that had just passed, seemingly in slow motion.

CHAPTER 26

A SHOT RANG OUT

Grady jolted his head up hearing the gunshot. It wasn't far off from where he was at, but at the pace he was going, it would take him another hour or more to get there. He threw off his pack, stopping only long enough to get a few things he would need, and then took off running, more than doubling his pace, his rifle in his hands ready for anything. His heart was pounding in his chest, more from the thought of Jewel being hurt than the physical exertion itself. *It could have been the man hunting.* He told himself, trying to calm himself. It was a single shot, which could have meant any number of things. He knew that Rudy and Daryl would have likely heard it as well, and were probably going to start heading straight in that direction. A single shot was never a signal shot, and Grady knew that it wasn't likely to be Rudy and Daryl.

He ran hard, looking around to scan the woods around him as he went, but throwing a certain amount of caution to the wind. If it was Aaron or Jewel, he had a pretty good idea what their position was from the direction of the gunshot. He covered a pretty good distance in a short amount of time, slowing slightly as he started up the hill toward the ridgeline. He could feel the pain radiating through him as the wounds from war rang out through his body, but he shrugged it off, and ignored it in order to keep going.

As he reached the ridgeline, he stopped himself short, not wanting to give away his position if someone was down on the other side hunting. He crept up the bank slowly, soundlessly glassing the valley below carefully. He could see the cabin immediately. There was smoke coming out from the chimney, but it was dwindling, and he suspected the fire was nearly out, indicating that nobody had tended to it for a while. He scanned the cabin, and the surrounding area, seeing nothing to indicate anybody was in or around it.

There were areas in the valley he couldn't see because of the thick vegetation, but he saw something that caught his eye. From his angle, he could see something that looked like the bottom of a small boot, but the rest of the figure was hidden behind trees and bushes. He searched his mind, trying to recall what the boots

169

looked like that Jewel had worn, but he couldn't remember. His heart was racing. He carefully looked around at the surrounding area, but it was thick with brush, and he found nothing. He started cautiously making his way down the side of the hill. He went slow and steady. He knew that he couldn't get sloppy, even though it took every ounce of control he had not to go racing down the hill frantically in search of her.

He employed all his military training, creeping along soundlessly, noticing every detail of the area around him. He could feel something in the air. There was a presence, and he could smell blood, causing the hair on his neck to stand up.

~~~~~~~~

Jewel let out her last tear, knowing that she needed to get herself together and get moving if she was going to make it down off the mountain. She had seen animal traps as her and Aaron made their way up the mountain, and she suspected there would be several more placed around. She didn't want to encounter them; the thought of the iron jaws clamping down on her sent a chill down her spine. Getting herself off the mountain was going to be nearly impossible, but she never even once considered staying in the cabin and waiting until morning. Just looking at it gripped her heart, making her nearly breakdown crying again.

She made her way cautiously toward Aaron, rifle positioned on him at all times ready to fire her last shot, not ready to trust that the threat of him was truly gone. She watched him closely for a minute, looking for any signs of life, like the rise and fall of his chest, but there was nothing, and she could see she had hit him right in the center of his face. She lowered the rifle, moving toward him, not wanting to touch him or smell him ever again, but she felt for a pulse, and found nothing. The man was dead, and she sighed, crossing herself without thinking. *It was still life,* she thought, *and I took it.*

She patted his pockets, double checking to make sure she didn't feel the car keys or anything she might need to help her get off the mountain. He had a bracelet around his wrist, and Jewel could see there were keys on it. *Probably for the padlocks,* she thought, and unhooked it from his wrist, thinking she might be able to find the rest of the ammunition before heading down toward the car.

She eyed the distance she had covered, and could hardly believe she had made it that far, but she knew adrenaline could fuel someone beyond their natural abilities. She had seen it in Iraq, and she had just experienced it firsthand. She had used everything and more to get to the outcropping in the time she had. Aaron had been quick, and she realized just how lucky she had been to make it as far as she did without him catching her. Had it been a normal day, she would have never considered that such a thing would have been possible. She wouldn't have placed good odds on someone being able to accomplish what she had just accomplished, in as little time as she had to get it done.

Grady quietly made his way down into the valley not knowing what he was going to find, never once losing sight of the place where he thought he saw the bottom of a small boot. There were a thousand thoughts racing through his mind all at once, but never once did he imagine he would come up to the site that he saw before him, seeing Jewel on her knees leaning over a man's body, patting down his pockets.

"Jewel! My god is that you?" he said running toward her, stopping dead in his tracks when she turned to look at him. Her face was so badly swollen and bruised, for an instant he wasn't sure it was her. Her hair was matted and flying around her wildly, and she was filthy from head to toe, but he could see in the one eye that wasn't swollen shut, that it was definitely her. He hurried to her as fast as he could.

"Grady! You came for me!" she said pulling herself up, using every last drop of energy she had to go to him. Her leg was throbbing, nearly making her drop back to the ground with every step she took toward him. The sprint she made to the rock outcropping had used up every last drop of determination and energy she had in her, and the adrenaline that had fueled her earlier was leaving her empty and weak.

"Of course I came for you Jewel!" he said scooping her up, holding onto her tightly as he dropped down to his knees with her securely in his arms.

She hugged him close, not caring about the bumps and the bruises, or the pain. Everything washed away from her, and she once again broke into an uncontrollable sob. She buried her face in his chest, holding him as tight as she could.

"It's okay darlin'. I'm here. I've got ya, and I'm goin' ta take care of ya," he said quietly, comforting her until he felt her go limp beneath him. "I only regret I can't kill the man myself," he said quietly, more to himself than to her as he glanced at him lying on the ground with blood pooling around him. "What happened Jewel? How did ya...?" he asked gesturing toward Aaron's body, not sure how to finish the sentence.

"I got away, and I shot him. I had to, or he would have killed me," she said trailing off crying.

"Rudy and Daryl are up here searchin' for ya, and Todd and Mark helped us too. Joe and Gary were in town tryin' ta get the police organized ta create a volunteer search party. We're all here for ya Jewel. We all love ya," he said squeezing her more tightly, "and I wouldn't be half surprised if Angela managed ta call in the National Guard."

"Ouch, that hurts Grady!" she squealed as he stroked her leg.

"Are ya alright Jewel?" he asked carefully touching her face, "did he...," he stuttered, the words caught in his throat.

"Do you think you'll ever be able to touch me again?" she cried, unable to look at him.

"Nothin' could ever keep me from touchin' ya darlin'. Do ya understand that! Not one thing! Do ya hear?" he said forcing her to look up at him.

She just stared at him, unable to grasp what he was saying.

"What I was goin' ta ask is… did he die right away?" he asked.

Again, she just looked up at him and stared. A million thoughts were running through her mind, making the words that were coming out of Grady sound like they were being spoken in another language. She couldn't make sense of any of it. It was like she was caught in a strange dream, where nothing made sense anymore, and she was trying desperately to wake herself up.

"There's a car at the base of the foothills. I need to get my things in the cabin. I want to get out of here Grady," she said moving away from him suddenly, wanting more than anything to wash herself.

"Shhh, let's wait for Rudy and Daryl to catch up with us. I'll get ya out of here as fast as I can Jewel," he said keeping a steady tone, not wanting her to see the reaction he felt in his heart. She was badly bruised, and he could make out the outline of a man's hand that had been left on her cheek. He could only imagine what she had been through the last couple of days. Her other cheek had been hit with a blunt object, and she was favoring her right leg. "Let me take care of ya Jewel. Ya don't have ta face this alone. I'll never leave ya."

"I can only imagine what I must look like," she said wiping her face, attempting to tidy up her hair as more tears escaped down her cheek.

"That doesn't matter. It's what's on the inside of ya that makes me love ya," he said touching his hand gently to his heart. "Ya couldn't look bad ta me darlin'."

"He drank too much last night, and when he fell asleep today, I made a break for it. I got the rifle and I shot him. I ran as fast as I could," she said crying again, rattling on again frantically, as if she had to convince herself that it was real.

"Shhh. Ya did good. Ya did what ya had ta do ta survive. I'm proud of ya darlin'," he was talking calmly to her, whispering to her like a trainer would talk to a skittish horse to keep them from running off or going crazy.

"Are the police coming? Do you think we should just leave him here? I don't want to touch him again," she sobbed.

"Don't think about any of that right now. The most important thing is ta get ya down off this mountain, and get ya takin care of. Ya let me worry about everything else. Will ya let me take care of ya Jewel?" he asked quietly, trying to calm her.

He carefully took her hand to coax her back to him, wanting to hold her and comfort her. He held her there quietly for a long time until he could feel her heart beating normally again. He could see that everything that had taken place was breaking her down. He had seen it in war. He remembered seeing men and women who looked practically invincible on the battlefield, completely breakdown once they were finally out of immediate danger. It was the natural instinct of human survival that allowed a person to do unthinkable things to save themselves, only to collapse into the weakest form possible to heal their wounded souls.

They sat quietly for a while until a motion caught Grady's attention from the corner of his eye. They both crouched down, not wanting to make a sound. Both of them zoned in on the direction from where they had heard the noise. Jewel looked at her rifle lying just out of reach from her, and she longed to have it on her once again, but Grady was way ahead of her as he had his own rifle at the ready, and was scanning the terrain through his scope.

"Pizza!" Grady called out, and Jewel couldn't have been more surprised, looking at Grady as if he had lost his mind. He just shrugged at her.

"Enchilada!" a voice rang out, seemingly from nowhere. Jewels eyes were focused on Grady, thinking he was losing it, having been on such high alert for so long, but was relieved to finally see his shoulders relax as he laid his gun down.

"Come out then," Grady said moving to stand up, "it's just Jewel and I. We're safe."

"We're coming brother," Rudy said coming out of a heavy thicket some hundred or more yards away.

"Pizza?" Jewel asked.

"I wasn't sure he would remember, but it was a game we used ta play when I was little. It was an alternative ta Marco Polo. I figured it was probably him, and I really didn't like havin' my gun pointed at the man."

"Jewel! Honey! Is that you?" Rudy said running up to her to grab her gently, hugging her to him. "We were so worried about you. We've been hiking for more than two days straight. There was no stopping this man right here," he said nodding toward Grady.

"Thank you Rudy. Thank you for coming for me," she said hugging him harder, tears welling up again.

"Thank you too Daryl" she said going up to hug him as he made his way out of the bush.

She was relieved that Rudy didn't seem to react to her bruised face, but the extent of just how bad it must have looked was written all over Daryl's face. He looked at her in horror before turning to cover his reaction.

"I... I... sorta knew about this cabin, and Mark and Todd thought this might be where you were headed... ugh... I was glad to help," Daryl said stuttering, trying to steady himself.

"You shot the man?" Rudy asked Grady accusingly, worried for a moment that he had shot him out of revenge.

"I shot him!" Jewel said with a little satisfaction, looking Rudy square in the eyes. "Now I need to get out of here. I can't stand it anymore," she said nearly breaking down again.

"I left my pack about two miles back. I need ta go back and get it," Grady said.

"You take my pack, and I'll go get it and catch up with you," Daryl said.

"That's kind of ya Daryl. I'll take ya up on it," Grady said thankfully. "We need ta head ta the cabin and retrieve some of Jewels things before headin' down toward the base of the foothills. Jewel said there's a car parked at the bottom, probably yer cousins. Jewel's leg is hurt, and she's movin' a little slow. It should be easy ta catch up with us. Are ya sure ya can hike that far Jewel?" he asked. "Maybe we should hike a little ways and then camp for the night."

"No. I need to bathe. I don't care what it takes. I have to get down tonight. Please. Please help me get down tonight. I need to get away from here," she was pleading, frantically motioning for them to get moving.

"Alright Jewel. If that's what ya need, then that's what we'll do. Come on then," Grady said wanting to get her away from there.

"There's a cell phone in my pack, and a booster. You can call when you get down off the mountain, or maybe even near the bottom. You should have service by then," Daryl said as he started heading toward the location where Grady had left his pack.

"Thanks man!" Rudy said as the three made their way toward the cabin. What had taken her less than a minute sprinting from the cabin to the rock outcropping, now took nearly ten minutes. Her entire body was screaming at her with every step she took, but she was determined to keep going. She knew it was more logical to camp for the night, and then hike down the next day, but she didn't care. Her skin was crawling with the stench from Aaron to such an extreme, that it took everything she had not to completely breakdown.

"I don't want to go in there again," she said as they approached the cabin.

"Ya don't have ta," Grady said helping her down to sit in a grassy area. "Sit here and I'll go in ta get yer things. Rudy will sit with ya," he said exchanging a knowing look with Rudy.

"You're one tough lady Jewel," Rudy finally said as they both watched Grady make his way into the cabin.

"I don't feel very tough right at the moment. I feel broken and bruised. I've cried more in the last few weeks than I have in a lifetime. I don't think I'll ever be okay again," she said confiding in Rudy, tears rolling down her face uncontrollably.

"It takes a mighty strong person to cry Jewel," Rudy said sitting with her in the grass, taking one of her hands in his own. "What's harder? Keeping your guard up and never letting yourself feel anything, or risking it all by completely opening yourself up, letting yourself be vulnerable, and letting people care for you and help you?"

"I guess I've never really thought about it like that before," she said thoughtfully, eyeing Rudy sideways, wiping away another tear. "It's really hard to let yourself feel things sometimes." She squeezed Rudy's hand affectionately, crying again, unable to stop herself.

"It might not seem like it now Jewel, but you'll heal, and Grady will help you, and I'll help you too. You may as well accept it sweetheart," he said hugging her close to him, kissing her on the forehead.

"He raped me Rudy. Don't you think that changes things between Grady and I?" she asked hesitantly.

"No. I don't think it changes anything Jewel. It creates a challenge that you'll both have to work through, but it doesn't change anything," he answered matter of fact. "Aaron didn't take your heart and soul Jewel. He took forced sex, and nothing more... not unless you let him. Don't let him Jewel. Put it into perspective, and Grady will too. I know that's easier to say than it is to do. I'm not trying to sound cold, or belittle what you've been through, I just want you to understand that for Grady, the sexual part of it... well... it just won't matter. He loves you."

"Thank you. I really needed to hear something like that right now. Hope is all I have right now," she said very softly, feeling drained.

"You have a lot more than hope Jewel. You have Grady, and you have me, and I promise you Jewel, and I've known Grady a long time... about twenty two years or so, and I feel like I can say this with absolute certainty, he'll follow you to the ends of the earth... rape or no rape. It won't matter."

He hugged her and let her cry for a while, sitting there on the grass with her, holding her as tightly as he dared. He thought about what he would have done, and how he would feel if it were Diana instead of Jewel, and though unimaginable, he knew it wouldn't change how he felt about his wife, and he knew Grady well enough to know that he would put it into perspective, and not let it change their relationship.

CHAPTER 27

DOWN THE MOUNTAIN

Grady knew there was nothing in the cabin they absolutely had to have, but he needed to see it for himself. He needed to understand some of what she must have felt. He knew they would need to investigate everything, and he didn't really want to disturb anything, but he had to see it.

The scene inside the cabin was almost more than he could take. He gasped when he saw the chains, remembering the bruises on Jewels wrists. He clenched his jaw, trying to maintain control of his anger. She needed him to stay strong and calm.

The stench in the air hung like a heavy cloak that would hang on anyone who entered. He could feel it seeping into his pores as he made his way around the room scanning every detail, wanting to understand some of what she had endured. It reeked of vomit, and there was a strong scent in the air that he knew was the scent that lingered after sex. Anger flared though him as he took it all in, and his heart ached thinking of what had suffered. He was suddenly very thankful he had insisted on pushing on, rather than sleeping at camp the night before. He wondered how he could have lived with himself if he had been peacefully sleeping while she was being tortured. As it was, it was going to be very hard to forgive himself for not being able to protect her from Aaron.

He went through the cabin carefully, only wanting to touch the items that belonged to Jewel. He caught sight of Jewels torn clothes left in the corner near the bed, and he wasn't able to stop himself from choking up. He grabbed her medical bag and walked out, resisting the urge to burn the place to the ground. It was an evil place. He could feel it all around him. He was eager to get her away from there.

"Let's go then," Grady said going over to help Jewel to her feet. "All I got was yer medical bag. I didn't want ta disturb anything. The police will need ta investigate. I figured that's what ya wanted when ya said ya needed yer things," he said trying to keep his voice steady, avoiding her eyes.

"That's... ugh... all I really... wanted. My grandpa gave me this bag," she said eyeing Grady carefully. Something inside the cabin had spooked him, and she climbed into a shell within her as she remembered the chains, and the torn clothes lying in the corner. It was then that she remembered the bracelet with the padlock keys she had taken off Aaron's body, and she searched into her pocket to retrieve them. She stared at it for what seemed like several minutes, not sure what she should do with them. Her mind was going blank. All her emotions were raw, and her head was throbbing and spinning so fast, she thought she might start puking again. The need to lie down and sleep was nearly as strong as her desire to go wash herself, but not quite.

Grady looked down at her hand and quietly went over to take it from her, tossing the bracelet toward the house once he realized what the keys were for. After seeing the chains on the bed, he knew that what she was looking at were the keys to those chains. "It's goin' ta be alright Jewel," he said softly touching her face and hair, leaning down to kiss her gently on the forehead. "Everything's goin' ta be okay."

Rudy had to brush tears out of his eyes as he sat and watched the two of them. He saw the horror on Grady's face as he walked out of the cabin, and couldn't recall a single time he had ever seen him looking so distraught. He knew that Grady needed to see for himself, but he didn't think it would be appropriate for him to go look, as if it were a sideshow at the circus. Whatever it was inside that cabin would be revealed to him if they chose to talk to him about it. He wasn't going to embarrass Jewel by walking over there to see for himself. When he looked over at her, he could see the relief on her face when she realized they would be leaving without him going in.

"I just need to take some ibuprofen real quick," she said trying to kneel down to fish through her bag.

"Here's some water, and here's some jerky I brought for ya," Grady said fishing through his pockets to retrieve the items for her.

"Let me get that for you," Rudy said coming up to stop her from kneeling after seeing how much pain she was in. "You're just going to have to let us help you. Stop being so tough for a while alright?" he said softly as he fished through her bag to retrieve the medicine.

"I would happily let you carry me down the mountain if you want."

"If needs be Jewel, I will gladly carry ya down. Rudy's right. Let us help ya darlin'. Tell us what ya need, and we'll do everything we can ta help ya," Grady said trying to reassure her.

"Okay, but don't make me cry again. I promise to ask for help when I need it, just please don't make me cry anymore," she said taking Grady's hand as the three of them headed off to make their way down the mountain.

It was slow going. Jewel was weak, and Grady could see the pain written on her face with every step she took. He hoped the painkillers she had taken would kick in so they would be able to get her down the mountain more easily. He made her stop several times to drink some water and eat some jerky.

"I have a candy bar," Grady finally said remembering the candy bar he had stuffed in one of his pockets. They stopped, and Grady helped Jewel sit down while he found the candy bar. "Eat this Jewel. The sugar will give ya some energy. We have a long way ta go darlin'. I wish there was an easier way ta get ya down."

"Thanks Grady, but I'm okay. I'm bruised... I'm not broken, and I can't take this awkwardness between the three of us," she said feeling annoyed. "Women are raped every day!"

Rudy and Grady sat motionless, not wanting to interrupt her, and not wanting to say something wrong. They didn't know what to say or do. She had gone from sobbing to angry, and they had never seen her mad like that before.

"It was a branding iron!" she said angrily, pointing toward the pain in her leg, "and I thank God for it, because it was so damn painful I barely remember the rape at all, most of which occurred long after I had slipped into unconsciousness."

"Jewel...," Grady started after watching her carefully for several minutes, "there's nothin' ya can say that will push me away," he said barely whispering, meeting her eyes.

Grady knew what she was trying to do. He knew she had a tendency to run and push people away. He thought she was probably terrified, not knowing how he would react if he knew everything that happened to her. She was trying to scare him away, giving him the ugly truth of it as harshly as she could, laying it all out on the table, giving him an easy out. He knew her emotions were all over the place, and she was exhausted and weak.

"That goes for me too Jewel. You can't push us out. Tell us as much or as little as you want, and I know I speak for Diana when I say that as well. She'd be up here in a heartbeat tending to your every need if you gave her half a chance," Rudy added.

"I'm sorry. I know... I think... bear with me okay? I'm a wreck!" she said reassured, as a tear ran down her cheek once again. Her mind was erratic. One minute she felt like breaking down and bawling, and the next moment she felt like she was going to fly into a rage that she had never quite experienced before.

"We know Jewel. It's okay. Do ya feel okay ta get movin'?" Grady said standing up, helping her to her feet once again.

"I feel better. The painkillers kicked in, and the candy bar has given me some energy," she answered, looking up at Grady, trying to give him a smile. She could feel the love coming from him, and she thanked God that he didn't seem to have a reaction to how her face must have looked. She suspected that Grady and Rudy had learned to conceal their reactions to wounds during their time spent in war, though she knew it must have looked bad. Had he looked at her any differently than he had before, it may have been the one thing that would have made her fall apart completely.

The three of them slowly made their way down the mountain. Rudy and Grady were helping her, lifting her down areas that were too painful for her to climb down, the three of them falling into a steady pace, albeit a slow one. It was dark, and Grady was starting to get worried about Daryl when he suddenly caught up to them.

"I was gettin' worried man," Grady said, greeting him with a handshake.

"You left that pack quite a ways back Grady. I don't know how you made it as fast as you did to where Jewel was. You said maybe two miles, but I say it was closer to four or five. You must have been booking it. I think Rudy and I were closer to Jewel than you were. Did you start running when you heard the shot?" he asked.

"Yeah, as soon as I heard the shot, I ditched my pack and started runnin' in that direction. I didn't think it was that far back man. Sorry. I was runnin' on pure adrenaline!"

"No problem. It just took a little longer, that's all," Daryl said.

"Geez man! We were only about three miles away when we heard the shot. You must have been flying. I thought we were moving at a pretty fast clip," Rudy said shaking his head.

Jewel hadn't really stopped to think of what Grady and the others had been through since the morning Aaron took her. She knew they must have been scared for her. She looked up at Grady, and could see the stress and the strain in his face, and she impulsively reached out to grab a hold of his arm, suddenly needing to touch him. The two of them locked eyes, and he instinctively pulled her in close to him, holding her as tight as he dared.

"We should be getting close," Daryl said, taking the lead as Grady and Rudy held back to help Jewel.

It was dark by then, and they were moving at a snail's pace. Jewel was exhausted, and she didn't know how much more she could take. Her legs were shaking, and she could feel every muscle in her body throbbing. Each welt that had taken the brunt of the assault Aaron had bombarded her with, was pulsing like a heartbeat with every step she took.

"Do I need ta carry ya Jewel?" Grady said looking at her weakened form, feeling his own exhaustion.

"No. I just need a minute."

"One of us could run up ahead. Once we get to the bottom, we should have cell phone service, and we could call for an ambulance," Daryl said.

"Daryl, ya've been a lifesaver man. If ya don't mind runnin' up ahead then and callin', Rudy and I will take turns carryin' Jewel down. How much longer do ya think?"

"I would say I could be down in maybe a couple hours if I book it, but it's probably more like four hours at the pace you're going," he replied. "I'll book it man, and see if I can have them waiting for you when you make it down."

"I think the keys to the car may be in the driver's side wheel well in the front," Jewel called out after Daryl started running.

"Got it!" They heard him call back.

"I have to go to the bathroom," Jewel said meekly, looking at Grady awkwardly.

"Ummm… okay. Do ya need me ta help ya?" he asked her.

"Well… can you just come over there with me, and I'll go behind that bush," she answered.

Rudy sat down to wait as Grady and Jewel walked out of sight so she could go to the bathroom. Jewel walked behind a small bush, but Grady could see she was trembling.

"Don't go anywhere," she said in a near panic as she fumbled with the buttons on her jeans, looking around frantically, just barely far enough away so she could squat behind a small bush out of sight.

"I'm right here. I'm not goin' anywhere darlin'," he said turning to look at her, catching site of the burn on her leg and remnants of blood on her inner thighs. The sight of it caused the breath to catch in his lungs, making him feel like he was going to suffocate. He turned his head as she squatted down, and he closed his eyes trying to get control of the emotions that the sight of her wounds elicited. He wondered about the blood on her inner thighs. Based on a previous conversation they'd had, he knew it wasn't blood from her period, because he knew it wasn't the right time. He took a deep breath to calm himself as she finished up. He knew that a strong reaction from him wouldn't help her.

They made their way back to Rudy, and they each sat down for a minute to rest before getting back up and hiking some more. Grady carried Jewel as much as he could, but sometimes thought that made it worse. She cried out in pain no matter where he touched her, and his heart ached each time she did. She was trying her hardest to walk on her own, but her body was weak, and she felt like a rag doll. She didn't have anything left in her.

"Do ya want ta stop and sleep for a while Jewel?" Grady asked her, seeing her nearly stumble and fall down the mountain.

"No. I can't Grady. I need to be away from here," she was pleading with him tearfully, strengthening his resolve to get her down off the mountain, "I need to get washed."

Grady thought of the blood on her legs. He understood her need to wash herself, and he was determined to give her what she needed.

Rudy and Grady took turns carrying her, or helping her as she took one painful step after another. They could see she was completely drained, but they also knew there was nothing they could do to make her want to stop and rest for the night. She kept talking about the smell of him that was stuck to her. She needed to wash it off her as soon as she could. Sometimes it would overwhelm her, and she would wretch as they sat by her helplessly watching, knowing that the best thing they could do to help her was to get her down safely, where she could be taken care of.

"Daryl must have made the call. I see flashing lights," Rudy called out from up ahead. He had been walking up ahead of them with a stick, checking the area for animal traps as they went.

"We're almost there darlin'," Grady said as much to himself as to her. He was feeling the fatigue from the last several days catch up to him. He hadn't even closed his eyes in the last few nights, and he had hardly eaten since he realized Jewel was gone. His body was starting to shut down, and carrying Jewel was getting harder and harder. Each step became a task in itself, but he insisted on carrying her himself as much as possible. He needed to feel like her savior. The woman had saved herself, killing her own attacker, and he needed to help her. All things being equal, he knew that a woman could pull a trigger as easily as a man could, but there was that part of him that wished he could have killed Aaron himself.

"I would have never made it down by myself," she said as if reading his mind. "I was going to head out immediately and try to make it down by myself. That was my plan. God knows what would have happened to me if you hadn't found me."

CHAPTER 28

HOTEL HOSPITAL

The ambulance was waiting for them at the bottom of the mountain, and Grady laid her out on the stretcher as gently as he could, not wanting to wake her. She had fallen asleep several minutes before as he carried her, and he savored the peaceful look she had on her face.

"Only family can go with her to the hospital. Are you her husband or something?" the medic asked Grady, urging him to say yes.

"I am," he answered, climbing in the back of the ambulance with her.

"What hospital are you taking her to?" Rudy asked the medic.

"Here," the medic said handing him a card, "you can call this number and ask for her room. They'll get you in touch with her."

He closed the doors, and the ambulance started toward the hospital, leaving Rudy and Daryl standing there with the missing Explorer that belonged to Daryl's cousin. The police were there asking them questions, and cordoning stuff off, making everything look very official.

"Your husband said you have quite a few bumps and bruises all over you. We're not going to remove your clothing until you get to the hospital. I'm just going to put in an IV to get you hydrated," the medic said to Jewel with a soothing voice, as they drove along the bumpy road.

"My... husband..." she said looking over at Grady who could only shrug in response.

"He said you have a fairly bad burn on your thigh, and he told us a little bit about your injuries. We'll need to get some fluid samples, but it won't take long to get to the hospital, so we'll wait to get you someplace more comfortable," he said trying to make her comfortable. "Would you like some water?"

"Will I need to make a statement or something? There's a man lying dead at the top of that mountain," she said with the magnitude of the situation threatening to overwhelm her again.

"We know. That's all being taken care of. You don't need to worry about any of that right now. Let's just get you feeling better. Someone will be by to talk to both of you after we get to the hospital."

Jewel quickly fell asleep again with the warmth of Grady's hand holding her own. When she awoke, a nurse was wheeling her into the hospital, and she was in a complete daze trying to remember what had led her there. It all came rushing back to her, and she immediately regretted making the effort. The only thing that gave her comfort was seeing Grady near her. She tried to smile up at him with her bruised and swollen lips, feeling comforted when he smiled back before they took her where they wouldn't allow him to go.

Grady paced around the waiting room anxiously, occasionally glancing toward the door where they had taken her. He sipped coffee and attempted to eat a cookie that the nurses offered him, but his stomach was in knots, and he couldn't get it down. He wanted to be there for her. He wanted to know every detail of what happened to her, and yet at the same time, he didn't want to know any of it. His mind was racing, and he could barely sit down, but he felt like he was going to collapse in a heap on the floor if he didn't rest soon.

Suddenly a doctor came out to talk to him. "We're going to perform an exam on your wife. It's called a rape kit. They'll need to take samples to confirm that she acted in self-defense. It's all procedure. Nobody doubts her story. It's clear that the man brutally attacked her. She has a deep burn mark on her right thigh, she has bruises and cuts from the shackles he had her chained in, and she said he pelted her with rocks and other objects causing the welts. She's lucky to be alive," the doctor said without emotion. "After we're done, you can go back with her. It'll take at the most about twenty minutes. I'll send a nurse out to get you as soon as we're done."

Grady stood there in a complete daze when the doctor left. He considered all that he'd said to him, so unemotionally, about Jewel being pelted with rocks and them performing a rape kit on her. It all suddenly hit him, and made his head spin. He ran outside finding relief when the chill of night hit his sweaty skin. He dropped to his knees on the grass, not able to stand a minute longer. He was exhausted, and had been riding a roller coaster of emotions over the last few days. His body and mind were reeling, and he was feeling confused by the lack of food and sleep. He suddenly just broke down, and let it all out.

He had no doubts that he loved her. He hadn't ever felt that way before, but he wondered how they would ever get through it. He wondered if she would ever want him to touch her again. There were too many thoughts, and too many unanswered questions running through his mind. He was suddenly not sure of anything anymore, and his mind was racing wildly despite his best efforts to calm himself. He let it all hit him right in the heart, until he remembered that the thought of living without her was unbearable. It was the one thing he couldn't imagine. He held onto that thought. It was the only thing he could hold onto to calm himself.

He sat in the grass for a few more minutes, calmness coming back to him again before he made his way back in the hospital, heading straight for the bathroom. He washed water all over his face and neck, wanting to look more together when they took him back to see her. He looked tired, and he longed to take a hot shower and climb into a bed next to Jewel. He was filthy from head to toe, having slept and hiked several days wearing the same clothes.

He went back out to the lobby and sat quietly for the first time in days. His brain was firing strange thoughts at him, fueled by the lack of sleep and food, urging him to lie down and fall asleep, but he sat and waited until he could go see Jewel. He pushed away any doubts he had in his mind. He knew the time wasn't right for serious thought. He knew he was too tired to think of anything too deeply. The only thing he was sure of, was that he wasn't going anywhere without Jewel.

An officer came and talked to him, and he answered all her questions, offering a few comments that she hadn't thought to ask about. She was a polite woman, with a sympathetic demeanor, and Grady was pleased to know that she was the person who had been with Jewel conducting the investigation. The last thing Jewel needed was someone with a cold demeanor questioning her story.

"Are you Grady?" a nurse asked coming out to find him sometime later.

Grady looked at the officer questioning. "It's okay, we're done here. I'll probably be talking to you and Jewel again later."

He nodded at her and shook her hand hurriedly, "Yes, I'm Grady. Can I go back now?"

"She's really tired, but she refuses to go to sleep until she sees you. We're going to be taking her up to a private room to let her sleep for a while. You're welcome to go up with her. We could release her now, but the doc decided to let her get a little more hydrated first, and give her some time to rest," the nurse said, filling him in as she walked him back where she was.

"Jewel, are ya all right darlin'?" Grady asked going in to sit beside her, stroking her hair.

"They just patched Rudy through to my room. He's going to come get us tomorrow," she said taking his hand. "They're going to let me take a shower as soon as I get up to the room. You can take one too if you want," she added, suddenly alarmed that he may want to shower with her.

"A shower sounds good. As soon as ya get yer fill of it, I'll gladly jump in ta get washed," he said seeing the alarm on her face. "Did ya get anything ta eat?" he asked her, not sure what to say.

"My stomach's in knots. What about you? Did you eat anything?"

"My stomach's in knots too," he said awkwardly.

"Jewel," he said after several minutes of them sitting together silently, "you'll need ta drive the car here. Ya've been through a lot. I want ta grab ya and hold ya, but I'm afraid ta. I don't want ta push ya or hurt ya. I want ta crawl beside ya in yer bed, and never let ya go. You'll have ta tell me when and how much. I'm sorry ta put that on ya, but I can't bear the thought of addin' ta the pain ya've been through. Tell me what ta do," he said putting his head down on her hand that he'd been holding, choking back tears.

"Oh Grady, if it's too much for you…"

"Too much?" he said cutting her off, "dammit Jewel! I told ya yer not pushin' me away, and I'm not runnin! The only thing in the world that scares me darlin', is livin' without ya."

"I'm sorry. I'm neurotic as it turns out. You may need to remind me again over the next few weeks. I'm scared Grady," she said breaking the man's heart in two, tears running down her cheeks again.

"It's okay ta be scared, but ya don't have ta do it alone. Lean on me Jewel."

"Excuse me… ummm… Ms. Etchemendy… I'm Melissa. I'm here to take you up to your room," the nurse said coming in. "We'll get you some towels, soap, and shampoo and such, and you can get all washed up. We'll get you some things too so you can get showered," the nurse said looking at Grady's disheveled appearance. They both looked like they hadn't bathed in weeks, and lord only knew how they smelled.

The nurse pushed Jewel up to the hospital room where they'd be staying, and Grady followed behind. It was nice of them to let them stay there. They could have discharged her, but since the hospital was near empty, and the staff knew they didn't have any of their money or identification with them because of the competition, they decided to let them sleep in one of the hospital rooms under the guise of making sure Jewel was being rehydrated.

Once in the shower, she found that no matter how hard she scrubbed, the pain of what she endured was not going to wash away so easily. The nurse had given her three douches, and she used all three of them, wanting to rid him from inside her as thoroughly as possible, despite the burning that they caused against her torn skin. She was sore, but she was starting to feel much better since she had completely washed the stench of him off her. *Down the drain with you forever!* she thought watching the dirt circle the drain. Even the bruises on her face seemed less grotesque. They had given her some painkillers and anti-inflammatory pills. She wondered if they were working that quickly, or if it was just her hopeful imagination, and the psychological healing powers of being clean.

"I feel much better," she said coming out of the shower, "it's all yours."

"Ya look like ya feel better. I'll be just a minute," Grady said stepping into the bathroom.

She was wrapped in a hospital gown they had given her, and she climbed into bed, finally feeling like she could rest. She was exhausted and her stomach was growling, but she couldn't have eaten anything.

Grady didn't have any clean clothes to put on, so the only thing he had on when he walked out of the bathroom was a towel wrapped around him, and Jewel was surprised to feel the heat in her rise when she saw him.

"Is this going to be alright Jewel? I don't have anything to put on," he said feeling unsure of how to handle the situation.

She shook her head yes. "Will you sleep next to me Grady?" she asked sympathetically, feeling unsure herself.

"Of course Jewel. Let me hold ya and keep ya comforted while ya sleep."

The two of them snuggled up to each other, and fell asleep within minutes. They were exhausted and both of them slipped easily into dreams, never once letting go of each other.

~~~~~~~~

"Shhh, wake up Jewel. It's okay. I'm here," Grady said waking Jewel as she cried and flailed wildly in her sleep.

"Grady?" she cried turning toward him, throwing her arms around him.

"I've got ya. Ya were just havin' a bad dream darlin'."

"My thigh… it hurts. As soon as I felt the pain again, I thought I was back… ugh… back with Aaron and…," she cried without finishing the sentence, not wanting to explain.

"It's alright Jewel. Let me call the nurse and get ya some more painkillers," he said sitting up.

"No, it's all right. I'll just take ibuprofen. I don't want anything stronger. Can you just hand them to me?"

"Here ya go," he said handing them to her, "and here's some water. Anything else I can do Jewel?"

"Just stay with me. That's what I need the most."

"Ya can tell me about it if it helps ya," he said lying back down beside her, holding her close.

"He needed for me to scream and be afraid in order to get excited. I sensed that early on, and did too good of a job staying calm I guess. He got so excited when he touched the iron to my thigh, I couldn't help myself. I screamed so loud… it was terrifying, and the more terrified I became, the more excited he got. Every time I quit screaming he would dig his fingers into the burn, and I would cry out even louder," she whispered as they laid side-by-side in the dark.

"Nobody could stop themselves from screamin' in that situation. He was sick Jewel. Ya outsmarted him though. Ya should be proud of yerself. Yer damn tough woman."

"I am… a little… proud of myself that is. I mean… I haven't really thought of it much yet. Once I get caught up on sleep, eat again, and think things through… I'll probably feel differently."

"We'll get through it together Jewel. It'll take some time, but we'll work through it."

"Tell me what happened that morning. When did you know I was missing?" she asked, turning to look at him in the dark.

"I knew right away. I woke up earlier that mornin' with an uneasy feelin'," like when yer skin kind of crawls and alerts ya ta somethin' without the rest of ya knowin' exactly what the matter is. I got up and walked around a bit, finally shruggin' it off as old ghosts from Iraq or Afghanistan, convincin' myself that's all it was, despite my best judgment," he said quietly, stroking Jewel's arm as he quietly recounted that morning. "When ya left for the bathroom I had ta resist the urge ta go with ya. Then ya didn't come back right away, and I still had ta stop myself, because I know how ya liked ta take yer time ta look at the plants and such. Finally, after about twenty or thirty minutes, I just decided ta go look for ya, all the while tryin' ta come up with a good excuse ta tell ya about why I was bein' so overprotective, but then when I saw the grass outside the bathroom all tamped down and found yer pistol, I knew somethin' happened. I ran around screamin' for ya, and when ya didn't answer back, I got scared. I took off runnin as fast as I could ta the police station in town. I thought the police would start lookin' for ya right away. I should've left right then ta look for ya," he said leaning toward her kissing her forehead.

"Let's not blame ourselves Grady. If we do, we're going to make it harder. The only person to blame is Aaron. If we both start thinking about what we should have done, or what we think we could have done differently, then we're just going to prolong the suffering. It's not your fault, and it's not my fault, but I know it doesn't feel like that right now, because for some strange reason, it's somehow easier for me to blame myself, and for you to blame yourself. It's Aaron's fault, and he paid the ultimate price for it," she said with a sudden burst of logic, surprising them both.

"Yer right Jewel. I'm glad ta hear ya say it though. It sounds reasonable. I think with another hour or two of sleep, and a tic tac, ya might be able ta cure cancer," he joked, squeezing her playfully.

"I know it sounds reasonable. As a nurse, I said something similar to men and women at the hospital every day, trying to get them to see the reality of it. It was true. It was always true, but convincing someone who feels responsible for something that they couldn't possibly be responsible for, is tough. It really has to do with forgiveness. Everyone has to forgive themselves for those things that they blame themselves for, whether they're to blame or not."

"I just wish I'd have started lookin' for ya earlier."

"It's not your fault Grady. Just know that. We live in a society that relies on professional services like police officers and detectives. We don't live in the Wild West where everyone has to fend for themselves, and take the law into their own hands. You went to the police to get help as anyone would and should do. You risked everything, and you came and found me. There aren't very many people who would do that," she scolded him, cupping his face in her hands.

"I know Jewel. I know yer right. It's not my fault, and it's not yer fault. I went against my better judgment though, and I'm not ready ta forgive myself just yet."

"Alright, well… we'll work through it together then," she said hugging him close to her.

They laid there rolling their conversation around in their heads a while before falling back to sleep. They had already been asleep for six hours before the nightmare woke them, but they went on to sleep another six hours when they finally started to stir.

"I can't believe I'm awake before the two of you," Rudy said walking into the room as they started to wipe the sleep from their eyes and stretch out. It was late in the morning, hours past when they would both normally be awake.

"Rudy, we're starving! Please tell me ya have a steak or somethin' in yer pocket," Grady said sleepily.

"No, but I have my wallet, and all our stuff that we had stored. The competition is obviously over. Come on and get ready. I'll buy breakfast," Rudy said throwing some extra clothes down on the bed for them that he brought.

"Wow, you even brought me a bra and panties," Jewel said, eyeing Rudy curiously.

"Well, Angela helped me. She picked out your clothes too, and she said she put a note in there for you. She was flying out this morning, but made me promise to give you this kiss," he said leaning down to kiss her on the forehead, lingering to stroke her hair affectionately.

"You look much better Jewel."

"Thanks Rudy, and thank you… for everything…," she said choking up.

"Shhh… it was my pleasure sweetheart. I'd do it again in a heartbeat."

She just smiled up at him, and climbed out of bed carefully when he offered a helping hand. Every ache and pain shot through her like a lightning bolt, but she felt remarkably better than she had the night before. She reached to the side table grabbing the bottle of ibuprofen the nurse left for her, and popped four of them in her mouth, taking a long drink of water as she did. She made her way into the bathroom to get dressed, leaving Grady and Rudy in the room where Grady was already getting dressed.

The nurse had bandaged the burn on her thigh, but the pain was strong. She was hesitant to pull on her pants, but she was surprised when they slid on easily, and she realized for the first time, just how much weight she'd lost in the last few days. Her stomach was rumbling, and she felt weak, but she was glad to be up and going. She found the note from Angela, and unfolded it carefully.

> Dear Jewel
>
> I'm so glad I was able to meet you. You're a very special lady, and I know that whatever the details are of everything that monster put you through will not define you. You are greater than him and his ugliness. You are fine and beautiful inside and out, and I hope you never forget that. If I had a daughter, I would want you to be her, and please feel free to think of me if the day should come when you need some motherly advice. I'm not well practiced with girls, but I've

learned a few things along the way, and I have a soft shoulder to cry on if you should need it.

Take care of that man of yours. He loves you sweetheart. Don't question it. Just let it take you to the end of the earth, and never look back. That kind of love doesn't come around very often.

I love you pretty lady! Keep in touch!

Angel-a

Jewel sat there for a moment thinking about the letter. She knew that Angela was right about not letting what happened define her. She needed to focus on what lay ahead of her, instead of what was in the past. She knew she needed to heal, but she was determined to rise above it. She smiled thinking of Angela.

"So now what?" Jewel said coming out of the bathroom a while later while Grady brushed his teeth. "Where are you going Rudy... now that the competition is over?"

"I'll be heading back to South Dakota, probably working for my father-in-law for a while," he said with a heavy sigh. "He wants me or Grady to take over his construction company. It wouldn't be a bad gig if the man wasn't such a control freak."

"I'm sorry Rudy. I know you were hoping to start your own business with the winnings from the competition," she said going over to give him a hug.

"It's not your fault Jewel," he said giving her a stern look. "You're safe. I'm going home to see my wife and kids. My brother here is hopelessly in love. The world seems to be in perfect order," he smiled and then hugged her in return.

"I'm about ta starve ta death!" Grady said looking refreshed.

"Oh by the way Grady, the nurse wanted me to tell you that she has your *wife's* belongings downstairs for you," Rudy said raising an eyebrow at him. "Is there something you need to tell me?"

"Well, we didn't get married if that's what yer askin', but there is somethin' I need ta tell ya brother," he said returning Rudy's glare. "I'm goin' ta Wyomin' with Jewel when we leave here, so you'll have ta face Dad alone."

"I figured. You'd be a fool not to. I'm happy for you man," Rudy said patting Grady on the back as they made their way toward the car Rudy had borrowed.

Jewel couldn't help but smile a little. She was finally excited to be going home. She couldn't wait to show Grady everything. Hearing him tell Rudy he was going to Wyoming, without her having to ask again, reassured her that things between them were going to be okay. She thought of all the places she wanted to show him, and she was even excited to introduce him to Troy, even though she was a little nervous about how everything would go down. She knew Troy though. He was forgiving, kind, and she knew they would hit it off immediately if given half a chance.

CHAPTER 29

THE GIRL WHO WENT MISSING

"I have a plan," Grady finally said, breaking the silence after they ordered their breakfast.

"No way!" Rudy said sarcastically, winking at Jewel.

"I haven't even talked ta Jewel about this," Grady said smiling at her, "but I was thinkin' that since we don't know when the police are goin' ta release us ta leave the state, we should all bunk up together ta save money, then we can rent a car ta drive back ta South Dakota. That way I can get my things, and introduce Jewel ta the family," he said grabbing her hand, "and then Jewel and I can drive my truck ta Wyomin'."

Jewel wasn't the least bit surprised that Grady had completely planned out the near future. She had always wanted to drive through Canada, and she was excited to be able to meet Grady's family, including Rudy's kids. Plus, she had been a little worried about having to stay behind in Alaska until the police released them, and she was glad to know that Grady had been thinking about that.

"One of the crewmembers said we could stay at the base camp for a few days if we wanted. They aren't scheduled to tear it down until next week, but they were removing the police barricades this morning," Rudy added. "I don't know if you would want to stay there or not Jewel," he said as he suddenly remembered seeing the signs of struggle that had taken place in and around the bathroom.

"I think that sounds like a good plan," she said smiling at them both. "I would like to meet your family. The officer that came in to talk to me before the exam said we would probably have to stick around for at least a few days, and no, I wouldn't mind staying at the base camp," she added squeezing Rudy's arm. "I have far more good memories there than bad ones."

"I'm just a little surprised you haven't charted it out yet, and given us each a daily itinerary. You're getting sloppy man. I don't know if I can travel with you anymore," Rudy said smiling, leaning back in his chair, shaking his head at Grady.

"Excuse me. I don't mean to pry, but are you the girl that went missing?" the waitress asked, coming up to their table to fill their coffee cups.

Jewel just stared at her in complete disbelief. She was caught off-guard, completely unaware that anyone else knew what happened. It never occurred to her that it was probably big news around there, and it wasn't something she could hide. Her face was badly bruised and swollen, she had limped all the way from the car, and overall she was moving like someone who was in a lot of pain.

"I'm sorry honey. I shouldn't have said anything. I'm just happy you're okay. I prayed and prayed for you, and that boy got what was coming to him. His dad was a horrible man too. You're every woman's hero around here."

"Thank you for praying for me," Jewel finally said. She squeezed the woman's arm affectionately, and tried to give her a little smile.

"You're welcome honey. I'll pray for you to get better too, but first, I better just get your breakfast," she said warmly.

"That's really sweet, but still, I hope they let us go soon. I don't want to walk around here with everyone staring and pointing at me all the time," Jewel said a little deflated.

"I guess Aaron's dad was notorious around here. He roughed up a few women, and nobody ever did anything to him. Everyone was scared to death of him. Daryl and some of his cousins were telling me about it. They didn't even know the man had a family, but the local media pieced it all together pretty quickly," Rudy said. "I'm sorry Jewel, but it's kind of big news."

"Ya stick out a little Jewel... with the bruises and all. We can go if ya'd like," Grady said sympathetically.

"It's alright. I'm not leaving this restaurant without food," she said making light of it. "I might hide out for a while after that though. I hope they let us go pretty soon."

"You might be the only person in the civilized world without a cell phone Jewel, so I gave the investigator Grady's number. They're supposed to be calling pretty soon to give us a heads up of when we'll be able to go... assuming everything goes the way it should," Rudy said shrugging.

The three of them each slipped into their own thoughts. Clearly, Jewel did what she needed to do to defend herself, but she did kill a man, and there were going to be questions and procedures that the police needed to follow. The other issue they were worried about is whether Grady and Rudy would face charges for breaching police lines to retrieve their packs before going after Jewel, especially since the police had specifically warned them not to. The police hadn't even organized a search party by the time they had found Jewel and got her off the mountain, and there was a certain amount of embarrassment and some finger-pointing going on. Authorities led them to believe that the police were going to go easy on them, but having to wait to get the official word, was making them all a little anxious.

"If they start delaying and making one excuse after another, I say we hire a lawyer. It's a free country. If we want to go find our missing loved one, we should be able to do it," Rudy said breaking the silence, "and lord knows you did what you had to do Jewel."

"Let's not worry about it right now. We have a few more days in Alaska. Let's make the best of it," Grady said taking Jewel's hand. Rudy had a tendency to get worked up about these things, and he didn't want to add to Jewel's stress. She had enough to deal with. Plus, he realized early on that Rudy and Jewel were cut from the same cloth. Even Diana had commented about that. They were passionate people who had a tendency to take the world's burdens and carry them all on their shoulders, and he didn't want them both to get worked up.

They ate in silence, each of them lost in their own thoughts. The last few days had taken a toll on them, and brought about changes in each of their lives they couldn't have imagined.

Grady had been lost after leaving the Army. Since he was a small boy, he imagined his life as a career soldier, much like Rudy had been. He had gone home to South Dakota after he was discharged, and immediately started helping his dad in his construction business. He started spending time with Debbie, an old flame from high school that had recently separated from her husband. It was a life that part of him really wanted to settle for, but there was something missing, and he never knew what it was until he met Jewel.

Debbie had been his first girlfriend, and they dated all throughout high school, but Grady was never in love with her. They had a lot in common, and were good friends, but there was always something missing, which didn't stop him from trying to do what he thought his mom and dad wanted for him. He decided to ask her to marry him after high school graduation. He thought his mom and dad wanted him to get married, live down the street from them, have a couple kids, and take over the family business, which was a logical conclusion. They had certainly hinted about it enough times, but the morning of his high school graduation, he was standing in his room looking at the ring when his mom came in and saw him frowning at it.

"Someone who's gettin' ready ta propose shouldn't look that sad an' lost," his mom said.

"It'll be fine," he replied.

"Fine? Is that what ya dream of? A life that's just *fine*? Ya need bigger dreams son."

"That's not what I meant exactly. It's just that...," he started, not sure how to say what he was feeling.

"Don't live *our* life Grady! Go out an' get yer own! This isn't you. This isn't what ya want. It couldn't be clearer if it were written out and stapled ta yer forehead," his mom had said, grabbing him by the shoulders, making him look at her.

"Isn't this what I'm supposed ta do? Get married and take over the family business. Isn't that what Dad wants? Isn't that what good sons do? It's a successful business. Who wouldn't want ta have that handed ta them?" he said exasperated with himself.

"First of all, yer dad's not handin' ya nothin'! Ya'd have ta work yer ballocks off son, and even then, yer dad will only retire when they pry the last hammer out of his cold dead hands. Come back in twenty years and run it if ya want. You'll still have ta run him off, because he'll still be out there thinkin' he can do it all himself."

"Ya don't think Dad will be mad if I leave ta join the Army?"

"He'll be mad as a hatter for about five seconds, and then he'll wish ya well, like he always does. He wants ya ta be happy son."

"What about Debbie?"

"Ya can't marry a girl ya don't love, just because ya think ya ought ta."

"I do love her I think," he said shrugging.

"No ya don't. If ya did, ya'd be scoldin' me for suggestin' such a thing, and fumin' at the gills. *I love her I think* are not exactly the words of Shakespeare. Is that what ya plan ta say when the priest asks ya if you'll take her to be yer lawfully wedded wife?"

"I know you're right Mom. I knew it in my heart, I guess," he finally said after considering for a minute. "I needed ta hear ya say it. Ya always know just what ta say."

He walked down the aisle to graduate thinking of Debbie the whole time. They had grown up together, and Grady wasn't looking forward to telling her that he was breaking up with her. He had already been talking to an Army recruiter long before that day, and Debbie knew it, but she was thinking that wherever he went, she would be going.

As it turned out, she took it pretty well, and they stayed in touch through the years and remained friends. As soon as the Army discharged him, and he arrived at his parent's house, Debbie hadn't taken very long to make it over there, and they had spent some time together. She was going through a divorce, and she had two small children. She said she wasn't looking to get involved with anyone, but Grady suspected there was more to it than that, but then here he was, getting ready to bring a woman home, and he was going to have to face Debbie. There hadn't been anything but friendship between them since high school, but still, she had been a good friend, and he wasn't sure how she was going to take it.

CHAPTER 30

A TRIP TO THE BATHROOM

"Grady, are you awake?" Jewel asked carefully, shaking him awake.

"What is it Jewel? Are ya okay?" he replied a little alarmed.

"I'm sorry to wake you, but I have to go to the bathroom, and I... well... I mean... would you mind going with me?" she stuttered. She hated to admit she was afraid of anything, but it was early in the morning, still dark outside, and she had avoided the bathroom at base camp as long as she could. Nature was going to force her to face her fears, but she wasn't quite ready to face them alone.

"It's okay. I'll go with ya. Just let me get my shoes," he said, forcing himself to a sitting position.

"Is everything okay?" Rudy asked sleepily.

"Everything's fine. Go back ta sleep," Grady said.

Base camp reminded Jewel more of a ghost camp at this point. The police and investigators, such as they were, trampled on everything, and it had a used up, empty feeling about it. The place where she had enjoyed herself so much, and made so many good friends, had become a sad and lonely place. She was looking forward to leaving. She didn't want to remember it that way. She wanted to remember it full of friends and laughter, and full of love.

"We don't have ta stay here again Jewel. Ya've got enough things ta deal with right now. I want ta get ya somewhere ya feel safe and comfortable. I'll not have ya struggle through like this. It's breakin' my heart darlin'," he said, hugging her to him as they made their way across the field toward the bathroom.

"I didn't think it would bother me so much. It's a place. It had nothing to do with what happened. Why would a place bother me?"

"I don't know. It's best we leave it though, so ya can have yer good memories, and leave the bad ones behind as best ya can."

"My favorite one is that first kiss we had in our tent," she said smiling up at him.

"Mine too. I think about it every five minutes," he said smiling back at her. "I'll go in and check it out with ya, and then let ya have yer privacy," he said taking her hand and leading her into the bathroom.

Going in sent a chill through both of them. Jewel remembered the fear that tore through her when she heard Aaron's voice, and Grady remembered the fear he felt when he found her crucifix, and realized that something terrible had happened to her. Neither one of them had been in there since that day, but no reminders were present. Everything had been swept out and cleaned. It was just a regular bathroom.

"All clear. I'll be right outside the door," he said, leaning down to kiss her forehead.

Jewel was happy that Grady mentioned leaving there. She knew they all needed to save money, and she didn't want to be the cause of them having to spend more than they had, but she was ready to go. She was looking forward to moving on to the rest of her life. What happened with Aaron was not going to define her. It was a horrible thing that terrified her to think of, but she was also very proud of herself. She defended herself. She took everything she had been taught and saved herself, and that meant a lot to her. She knew she wasn't going to be able to just forget about it and move on, but she was at least ready to start moving in that direction. The thought of moving in that direction, knowing Grady was going with her, sent excitement through her. She was ready to start the rest of her life.

"Okay. I'm ready. Thanks for coming with me," she said sheepishly, coming out of the bathroom.

"I'm proud of ya for askin'. There's hope for ya yet," he said smiling at her, wrapping an arm around her as they walked toward their tent.

"What do you mean?" she asked, crossing her arms in front of her.

"I think sometimes ya feel like ya have ta do everything on yer own, and not let anyone help ya," he said stopping to stand face to face with her. "Ya've tried ta push me away, and do it all on yer own, but yer startin' ta learn that I'm here for ya, and ya can lean on me, and I like that. I like it a lot."

"So I'm not completely hopeless then?"

"Yer nothin' but hope Jewel… yer my hope and my heart. Do ya know how much I love ya?"

"I hope it's as much as I love you."

"It's more. It has ta be. There are no words for how I feel about ya. I'm guessin' it's the kind of love that made someone invent poetry."

"You say the sweetest things Grady," she said, stretching up to wrap her arms around his neck to hug him.

"I'm sayin' things that would have made me roll my eyes had I heard someone else say them just a month ago. Ya do somethin' ta me Jewel. I can't explain it," he said to her, grabbing her hand, leading her past the tent toward the lake.

"You don't have to. I feel it too."

"I can't wait ta introduce ya ta my mom and dad, and take ya around home a little before we head ta Wyomin'. Do ya think we might stay a couple days when we get there, or are ya eager ta get home?"

"I would love to spend some time with you where you grew up. Of course we can stay," she said, feeling like she needed to say something but wasn't sure how to.

"You know Grady… I'm going to be all right. I know you're trying to cater to me right now and make things easy for me. I really appreciate it too, but I'm really pretty okay. I obviously have bruises and bumps that are healing, but inside my heart, I'm feeling relatively okay. I knew he was going to rape me," she said stopping to sit down on some rocks by the lake. "I knew he was going to rape me, and I thanked God I had been with you first. I prayed I would get through it, even though the thought of him touching me made me want him to kill me instead, and I egged him on, hoping he would. Then he got the branding iron, and the pain was so horrific I thought I wasn't going to be able to handle it, but Grady, in a way it was a blessing for me. It took the pain of the rape away, and replaced it with something that would heal more easily. I don't know, it seems crazy, but I barely remember the rape at all. I remember the pain in my thigh mostly, and I'm thankful for that. I just hope that you'll be able to live with it too."

"I'm angry Jewel, but not for me. I'll love ya no matter what he did ta ya. There's nothin' that can change that. I'm angry, because the thought of ya havin' ta go through somethin' like that is unthinkable ta me. We'll get through it tagether. Ya can cry about it if ya'd like, but don't tell me yer okay for my sake. I think maybe ya have some things you'll have ta work through, and that's okay. I'll work through it with ya."

"I feel okay! Don't you think I know how I feel?" she replied angrily.

"I'm just sayin' that yer goin' ta need time to heal Jewel, and I'm not talkin' about yer bumps and bruises. I don't think the magnitude of what happened has hit ya just yet, and I think yer tryin' ta push it ta make everything okay too fast, maybe ta make it easy on Rudy and I, or maybe because ya don't want ta face it just yet. I know how it feels ta kill a man, and no matter the circumstance, no matter that ya did it ta save yer own life, it's goin' ta hit ya hard at some point, and when it does, I'll be there ta catch ya," he said standing there shaking his head. "I don't know, maybe I'm wrong. Maybe I'm sayin' it wrong. I just mean ta tell ya that I'm hopin' ta have a lifetime with ya darlin'. We have time. We don't have ta rush anything," he said, sitting down beside her, cradling her face between his hands.

"I just want everything to be the way it was before. I guess I'm afraid of losing you," she finally said after considering what he said for several quiet minutes.

"Ya don't have to worry about losin' me. It's not possible. I think I know ya because I've seen ya in action. Ya have no patience for the future, and ya remind me of sleepin' beauty in there," he said motioning toward the tent where Rudy was still sleeping. "The two of ya are so much alike. Ya want to fix the whole world in a day, and if ya can't, ya carry the weight of it around on both shoulders."

"You think I'm like Rudy?"

"Ya are, and I'm just like my sister, which is probably why we hit it off from the start, and if ya want ta get real crazy, I can tell ya that yer a lot like my dad and I'm *exactly* like my mom, and those two are a perfect match. They met when they were in preschool, and they've been inseparable ever since. They never dated anyone else, and they're each other's best friend. There's not a doubt in my mind that we belong tagether Jewel."

"Thank you. Thank you for telling me that. That means a lot to me. I can't wait to meet the rest of your family," she said smiling at him. She knew that Rudy and her were a lot alike. If she didn't know better, she would have thought he was her long lost brother, but of course, she knew that wasn't possible. They were a lot alike though, and remembering him and Diana together made her smile. They had been together for over twenty years and they still acted like high school sweethearts. They reminded her of her own parents.

"Besides Jewel... just lookin' at ya, or just ta have ya brush up against me or touch my hand. Listenin' ta ya sing and care for people the way ya do. Nothin' could keep me from ya, and I'm a very patient man. I'll wait as long as it takes 'til yer ready. Just let me hold ya 'til ya heal. That's all I'm askin'."

"Sometimes I feel like you've been inside my head doing a complete survey. You always seem to know just what I'm thinking and feeling, even before I do. You package things up so easily, and make the most complicated things seem so simple," she said quietly. "Maybe you're right Grady. Maybe it hasn't hit me yet, but I hope you're wrong. I never used to cry, and lately I just seem to cry all the time. You must think I'm a big crybaby."

"I'd be worried if ya didn't cry, because ya'd be closed off from me, and I don't think I could take that. I can take anything but that."

She was afraid of closing herself off again. She'd been emotionally shut down for a long time, and she didn't want to go back to being alone. She had come out of her shell since meeting Grady and Rudy, and she was enjoying life more than she had in a long time. She didn't want to face what happened to her at Aaron's hand. She was holding onto the happiness she'd felt over the previous few weeks with everything she had, but she knew that Grady was probably right. She hadn't allowed herself to feel it too deeply. She pushed the abuse and the shooting out of her mind, brushing it off like it was just a small annoyance, but part of her knew the flood was coming, she just hoped it wouldn't drown her in the process.

"After my parents died, a certain part of me shut down, and never opened back up again until I met you. That part of me had been missing for so long, I guess I forgot it ever existed to begin with. I sort of got used to it not being there," she said shrugging. "I'm afraid of going back to that. I'm sorry if I try to push you away sometimes. It's not what I want."

"It must have been hard for ya. I can't imagine growin' up without my mom and dad, an only child without Diana in my life. I'd probably shut down pretty hard if somethin' ever happened ta them," he said sympathetically, "yer a damn tough woman Jewel."

"If it hadn't been for Troy, I probably would have crawled in a hole and died.

He and I were best friends from the time we were born. After Mom and Dad died, he just kept coming over, and he would just sit with me. I hardly said a word for about the first six months, but he'd just stay with me and walk with me whether I said anything or not. Sometimes he'd get me laughing so hard I thought I was never going to catch my breath again. He made me go to prom, and to football games, and tricked me into joining the track team with him," she laughed.

"Tricked you? How does that happen exactly?" he asked.

"He really wanted to join the track team, but he swore up and down that he wouldn't do it unless I joined too. I finally gave in. I didn't want to be the reason he didn't join. It was fun though. Some of my favorite high school memories were in track."

"Sounds like Troy was a good friend ta ya?"

"He was... *is*... a good friend. I hope he'll forgive me for running off. He's a really good person. He didn't deserve that. I don't know what happened exactly. We were just sitting there laughing and hanging out like we always were, when all of the sudden, he came over to me, got down on one knee all serious, and then asked me to marry him. I acted as though he just smacked me in the face," she said shaking her head. "I told him he had to leave, but that I would think about it. Then I avoided him until I left for college, and then ignored him, and didn't return phone calls or emails."

"Why didn't ya just tell him that ya didn't want ta marry him?"

"I don't know. I was afraid to do anything. There was no right answer, and so I gave him no answer. I just retreated inside myself. It was selfish. Everyone expected us to get married. Most everyone thought we were boyfriend and girlfriend. I don't know; it was as if our predetermined path was suddenly at the starting line, and I wasn't ready for it. I kept hoping I would have a change of heart, and then I could call him and say yes. I love Troy, but I don't love him in that way. Do you know what I mean?"

"I think I do. When people ya love expect somethin' out of ya, it's hard ta let them down. Ya just want ta please them and do somethin' ta make them happy. I almost asked a girl ta marry me, and I almost settled for a life I didn't want, just ta please my dad. I thought it was what he wanted for me, and I longed ta make him proud of me," he said shaking his head in remembrance. "Before comin' here, I had a glimpse of what my life would have been like had I gone through with it, and I would have been miserable. Ya can't marry someone ya don't love Jewel."

"So what happened?"

"Well, she was a girl I dated in high school. I thought we would get married, live next ta mom and dad, and have the grandkids nearby while I ran the family business, but that's not what I wanted. It was what I thought Dad wanted, but I was wrong about that as it turned out. I joined the Army instead, but after I was discharged, I went back home and spent a little time with her before coming here," he said as he gingerly brought up a subject that he thought might get sticky.

"So you have a girlfriend?" she asked, pulling back from him a little, suddenly alarmed.

"No Jewel," he said grabbing her hand, pulling her back to him. "She wasn't my girlfriend. She was getting divorced and needed a friend. My dad would kick my ass if I dated a married woman, but I wouldn't have dated her anyway. She hadn't been a faithful wife, which is why she was getting divorced, and Mom and Dad didn't really like her, but she had been a good friend in high school. I didn't see any reason we couldn't hang out and be friends, but there was nothing more to it than that."

"So why are you telling me about her?" she asked with her heart beating faster.

"Well, she wants there ta be more. She asked me ta think about things while I was away, hopin' we might get back together when I get home, which is when her divorce will be finalized. I just wanted ya ta know about her. She might be a bit surprised that I'm bringin' a woman home with me, that's all."

"So there's a woman in your home town who's getting divorced right now, expecting you to come back and be with her, but instead you're bringing home another woman?" she asked summing things up.

"I can't change what she wants and expects Jewel. I thought I made it clear there was no chance between us, but she kept pushin'. She asked me ta think about it, and ta tell ya the truth, I never gave her a second thought from the time I first laid eyes on ya. Ya have nothin' ta worry about darlin'. I just didn't want it ta be a surprise for ya in case she showed up at the house or somethin'. She does that," he said exasperated.

"Well, I suppose I can hardly blame her," she said smiling, "I would be chasing after you too if I were her."

"That would require that I run, and I don't think I have it in me ta run from ya. I want ya too much," he said, carefully pulling her onto his lap as they sat by the lake.

"I hope I don't have to challenge her to a duel or something," she said attempting to make light of it.

"She's a very aggressive woman Jewel. She'll probably show up at the house. She knows Mom and Dad can't stand her, but that doesn't stop her one little bit. She married a man that works for my dad, they had a couple kids, and then Debbie started foolin' around with other men. Ya can handle her Jewel. She's no match for ya."

"Is she the only woman I'm going to have to fight off, or are there more?"

"There's an old barfly down at the local pub that said she wants ta ride me like a wild stallion, but she can be bought off with liquor. I wouldn't worry about her," he teased. "Ya hardly have room ta talk woman. I'm goin' ta spend the rest of my life fightin'. I see the affect ya have on men."

"The rest of your life is it?" she asked, raising an eyebrow at him.

"I'm sorry. I presume a lot, don't I? I would ask ya ta marry me right now, but it wouldn't be fair. Ya have too many things ta think about right now, and it wouldn't be right ta ask," he said grabbing her face, forcing her to look in his eyes so she'll be able to see what he was trying to say. Grady had no doubt in his mind that he wanted to spend the rest of his life with her, but he didn't think it would be right to add to the many things that she needed to think about and work through. He also didn't want the prospect of getting married to distract her from working through the emotions she was sure to be experiencing from the shooting, and the abuse she had just gone through. He wanted to ask her when things had settled down a little.

"Will you ask me one day though, if I promise not to run away?" she asked wrapping her arms around his neck, kissing him lightly with her bruised lips.

"I'll ask ya a million times until ya say yes."

CHAPTER 31

LEAVING ALASKA

"We're free!" Grady said hanging up the phone. "We have ta go sign some paperwork, and then we're free ta go!"

They had all been anxiously awaiting that call. They'd been at the hotel for nearly two weeks with all three of them in one hotel room, Jewel and Grady in one bed, and Rudy in the other. They tried to spend most of their time out hiking and fishing, but the walls were starting to close in on them, and they had already thoroughly explored the small town they were in.

Rudy had been on the phone several times a day talking with his wife and kids, and missing them more and more. He'd also made plans with his father-in-law to run a project he had recently been awarded. It was going to be a bit of a challenge for him, but he had a natural ability to build things, and he was looking forward to it. It was the business end that seemed daunting to him, but his father-in-law was determined to teach him after hearing the news that Grady wouldn't be staying.

"That's good news!" Rudy said excitedly. "Daryl said he'd give us a ride to Anchorage where we can rent a car. I hope he can do it today. Let's call him."

Rudy was excited to be going home to see his wife and kids. He was starting to look forward to a more settled life where he could spend more time with them. Having Jewel snatched out of his life as she was had them all a little shook up, and he was realizing just how precious time really was. He'd grown very close to Jewel through the competition, and after hearing the bits and pieces of what she went through, he was aching to go home and hold his wife and kids close to him. Even working with his father-in-law didn't sound too bad.

"I think Rudy's a little anxious to get home," Jewel said to Grady, gathering up her things as Rudy made his way outside to call Daryl where he had better reception.

"Rudy was nearly as crazy as I was when ya went missin'. It shook him up a bit. I've never seen him so rattled, and he's a career soldier, so that's sayin' somethin'. I think he wants ta hold his family close right now," Grady said, helping her get everything packed up.

"He's been so calm and cool about everything. I guess I didn't realize it was affecting him so much."

"I'm tellin' ya woman. The two of ya are the same. Bottle it up and shrug it off like it's nothin', and let it eat ya from the inside out, all the while makin' jokes and bein' sarcastic as hell."

"What's that?" Rudy said, walking back in the room.

"Nothing, just that Grady thinks you and I are hopeless. I'll explain later. What did Daryl say?" she asked grinning at Grady.

"He's picking us up in about half an hour. The secretary at the police department is his cousin, so he already knew we were being released. Let's get rolling people! I have a lovely wife waiting for me at home," Rudy said grabbing his things and getting them packed. "Now what's this about us being hopeless?"

"He thinks we bottle things up and make jokes, and that we don't deal with our feelings," Jewel said.

"Feelings? I've heard of those. Isn't that the lint and stuff that gets stuck between your toes?" Rudy joked, smiling at Jewel. "What feelings are we talking about exactly?"

"The ones we're bottling up and making fun of! Duh! Try to keep up, will you?" she laughed.

"Oh! Don't remind me! I'm trying to ignore them. Sheesh! No consideration whatsoever."

"Hopeless! Completely hopeless!" Grady said, rolling his eyes at them as he started packing things outside.

The last several days had been an emotional roller coaster for Jewel. She would be happy one minute, angry the next, and then nearly falling apart a moment later. The bruises on her face and body had turned from black to purple and yellow, and the burn was scabbed over and healing nicely, but inside she was in turmoil. She dreaded the nights when it was time to fall asleep. She would snuggle up next to Grady feeling safe and happy, and even excited by him, her body responding despite her fears, but she fought sleep as hard as she could, knowing the nightmares would pull her into a deep vat of terror.

In the nightmare, she doesn't get away. He catches her, and she falls apart, becomes beaten and broken, lying out on the hard ground outside, chained like a dog. She could feel him pulling at her, and tearing her clothes off, raping her and beating her over and over until she can't take it anymore, and then she wakes up screaming. Grady and Rudy would jump up trying to comfort her, but they were all exhausted and on edge a little, and Jewel refused to tell them much about the dream. She would just shrug it off and tell them she couldn't remember; knowing they didn't believe her, but the thought of telling them about it was nearly as terrifying as the dream itself. It was almost as if saying it aloud would make it come true, and it was humiliating, and horrible. The only time she rested comfortably was during the day, when they would hike out near the river and nap.

With a more serious look on her face, Jewel went over and wrapped her arms around Rudy, hugging him close. "I'm sorry Rudy. I didn't know how hard this whole thing had been on you. Thanks for worrying about me, and caring for me. It means a lot that you do."

"You know I love you kid. You're like a sister to me. I couldn't bear the thought of never seeing you again, or think about having that beast hurt you," he said hugging her to him as hard as he dared. "I'm proud of you though, and… you'll heal Jewel. It'll take some time though. Don't rush it. I think you're going to the most healing place in the world. Grady's family is full of some of the best people I've ever known. They'll wrap you up in so much love you'll be gasping for air. It's just what you need I think. It's what we all need right now."

"And what about you?" she asked.

"You don't worry about me Jewel, or Grady. You let us do the worrying. That's what will help us feel better. We both feel like we failed you a little, whether we did or not doesn't really matter… it's just how we feel. We just need to take care of you right now. Let us," he said earnestly. "You said it yourself Jewel. Men always feel like they have to take care of the women in their lives. It's especially true for two military men who have been trained to protect. We can't help it. Just let us take care of you for a while sweetheart."

"Well, I'm not really used to being taken care of, but I admit, I couldn't have managed these last few days without you two," she said, wiping away a tear.

Jewel's grandpa had always been there for her, and she had been thankful to have him, but she never just allowed herself to be taken care of by him. She took on as much of the responsibilities of the household and the ranch, as she could. He had been very sick and was pretty old, but even more than that; there were things that an eleven-year-old girl in the grips of puberty just can't share with her grandfather. She had to learn on her own how to handle her monthly cycles, and hair growing in places that she wasn't expecting, and then there was the issue of what to do with the hair after it had grown in. It was her junior high coach that had finally taken her aside and told her she might want to start shaving her legs and armpits, long after the other girls had it figured out. She never did learn about wearing makeup, other than the few times they had gone to Denver and she had a makeover.

Troy took care of her, in that he kept her from isolating herself in high school, and provided her with a friendship that kept her emotional state above water, but having someone there to actually step in and do things for her, was something she wasn't quite used to.

"I stand corrected. There may be hope for you two after all," Grady said coming in to see the two embracing and wiping away tears.

"Jewel! You're looking much better," Daryl said following Grady in.

"Daryl!" Jewel said excitedly, grabbing him and hugging him. "I'm feeling much better. Thank you for everything Daryl. You've literally been a lifesaver, and now you're driving us to Anchorage. Promise me you'll come visit us one day."

"I will for sure. It's not a problem Jewel. I need to get some things in Anchorage anyway, and your timing couldn't have been more perfect. It's the nearest place for shopping and such, and I have some friends there I'll be visiting too," he said grabbing some of their things to help get it packed outside to the car.

The four of them got everything packed in the car, and they headed down to the police station where they could finalize paperwork, and then head out to Anchorage. It was at the police station when they heard the rest of the story about them finding the remains of the couple that had once lived in the cabin. *Jan and Ping,* Jewel thought, remembering the journals she had read, crossing herself briefly when she thought of them meeting a horrible end at the hands of Aaron... her former captor. It would be sometime before they could conclusively determine that Aaron was the one who killed them, but it seemed likely. The news sent a chill through them when they realized just how dangerous Aaron really was, and how close Jewel had come to meeting a horrible end herself.

They were more eager than ever to get out of there. They had been worried about everything going smoothly since it had been one delay after another, and there was always a chance that the police could file charges in the future. It went surprisingly well though, and they were ready to get out of Alaska before the police chief changed his mind. They were all a little upset that defending oneself could result in having possible criminal charges hanging over their heads for an extended period of time. They were ready to move on.

The car ride to Anchorage was full of some serious talk, then laughter, and finally some music. Todd and Mark ended up cutting a deal, so they could buy the guitar they had borrowed for Jewel, and had left it with Daryl to give to her. He brought it with him on the car ride after having it cleaned and repaired for her. Jewel was so excited to have it. She nearly broke down crying once again when he gave it to her. It seemed that tears were never far from filling her eyes. One minute it was from happiness, and the next minute it was from grief.

"This is the sweetest thing. Didn't Mark and Todd leave before they knew I was safe?" she asked.

"Yeah, but they wanted to do something for you, and they were hopeful. It was inconceivable to them, or any of us, to think that you wouldn't be able to play that guitar again," Daryl said.

"I'm glad they left their contact information. I think I know how to get a hold of everyone except Gary, though Angela probably has his information. We should plan a reunion. Wouldn't that be fun?" Jewel said smiling. "We could have everyone come to the ranch."

"That would be fun," they all agreed, and with that, Jewel sang, longing for the feel of the ranch she had left behind so many years earlier.

I draw a mental picture of the way of life for me,
A pasture full of horses that only spirits see.

An angel there among them I'm ridin' for the brand,
Working clouded pastures in the ever after land.

My heard of broncs are legends, rodeo was their fate,
Now their hooves are pounding thunder as St. Peter pulls his gate.

Outlaws here in Heaven, they dodged the Devils tack,
They won't be bucked down below to fill o'l Satins slack.

I pushed my wild remuda away from Hells front door,
Into a grand arena constructed by the Lord.

Rounded up one last time for their biggest rodeo,
To meet old cowboys head to head for a sold out Friday show.

I draw this mental picture that some won't understand,
But a show like this in Heaven was all the masters' plan.

By: Sam M. Kiefer

Jewel sang one song after another, letting Grady and Rudy get lost in their own thoughts. She had agreed to leave the worrying of the trip to them. They had originally planned to take their time to get back to South Dakota, camping and sightseeing along the way, but they had become increasingly more anxious to get there, and decided they would drive through as much as possible. Each of them would take their turn at the wheel while the others slept, stopping only to get a room when they couldn't stand it any longer. What they thought was going to be a fun adventure, had turned into a long and arduous car ride that none of them were looking forward to.

Normally, Jewel would have wanted to be in on every detail of the trip, wanting to help plan and make sure she was contributing her fair share, but at the moment, she just sang, enjoying the weight they were lifting from her shoulders, finally feeling okay to let someone else do the worrying for her. The fact that she had finally let go enough, and trusted someone enough to let them carry the burden of the trip for her, was freeing, and it gave her something she hadn't known in a long time. It was a feeling of togetherness. It wasn't just her anymore, and she could finally feel it, and trust it. She slipped into its warmth and security, smiling inside in a way she hadn't done for over a decade. It was the feeling that a young child takes for granted, wrapped in the love and security of their parents, not having to worry about the details, being able to just wake up in the morning and have breakfast without ever worrying about why or how it got there.

"Here we are. This is the rental place we called earlier. They're supposed to have a car ready for you," Daryl said, finally pulling into Anchorage and the rental car business.

Grady went in and got everything taken care of while Rudy and Jewel thanked Daryl profusely, making him promise over and over to keep in touch, and come visit them. Daryl was a down to earth guy that valued hard work and honesty. He was cut from the same cloth as they were, and they had all become close friends. They were going to miss him.

"We're all set. We have that lovely mini-van over there, which as far as I can see, will be our home for at least the next week," Grady said pointing to a dilapidated old mini-van that looked like it had its fair share of use over the years. It was faded blue and had rust over all the wheel wells, but they had been assured that it would get them where they needed to go.

"Well, there weren't too many places around here that were going to let you rent a car going one-way to Belle Fourche, South Dakota. I think you might be driving it toward its retirement home. It should get you there at least," Daryl said shrugging, feeling a little alarmed at the looks of the car.

"It'll be fine. No worries," Rudy said patting Daryl on the back.

"We appreciate everything ya've done for us. Anything we could ever do ta repay ya, don't hesitate ta ask. Ya know how ta reach us," Grady said. "As for the mini-van, I'll give it a good look over before we head out."

Grady was nothing if not handy. He knew the mechanics of a car like the back of his hand, and what he didn't know, he could usually figure out pretty quickly. Aside from being a mechanical engineer, his dad bought him an old pickup when he was fourteen, and they had completely restored every inch of it together. It was a great learning experience for him, and it was the thing that made him decide to become a mechanical engineer, though his military career had taken him down an entirely different path. Prior to that, from the time he was a small child, he was always fixing things or tearing apart lawnmowers, or chainsaw engines, always trying to figure out how everything worked, before putting it all back together, usually making it run better in the process. The mini-van looked a little haggard, but they weren't too worried about it. They were just happy to have found a way to get on the road.

They all said their goodbyes to Daryl, and they eagerly made their way out of Anchorage, wanting to put miles behind them while they were still anxious. They were certain the desire to get there fast was going to dwindle as the hours, and the miles wore on. At the moment, it was fun and exciting, and they were enjoying the prospect of their new beginnings. Jewel sprawled out in the backseat with her legs stretched out in front of her, guitar comfortably perched on her lap, and she picked the first song that came to her mind.

Old cowboys they will tell you
how their cattle they will graze,
Face to the wind nose to the ground
through the Kansas windy days.

A PRECIOUS STONE

Strange but true to nature,
the cattle face the wrath,
of the wind that Kansas serves them
along the seasons path.

A Cowboy's not that different,
head strong to the wind,
stand to face the fury
and broken fences he can mend.

The path of least resistance
is not always our best choice,
in times of hard decisions
we hear our inner voice.

This voice that lies within us,
our conscience God will send,
that's built from hard decisions,
and battles with the wind.

From our past learned life's hard lessons,
that guide us on our way,
like how to do it wrong just once,
and get the most out of this day.

Once I saw a Cowboy
to his back the wind blew South,
his pony raised his tail
and blowed the bit right out his mouth.

So the Cowboy turned to face the wind
a harder path you'd say,
with the bit secure in his pony's mouth,
he guided him on his way.

To get to where your' going
the easy path you can defend,
but to get to where you want to go
you must ride into the wind.

By: Sam M. Kiefer

CHAPTER 32

ROAD TRIP

They drove for over thirty straight hours, with each of them taking turns to drive or make sandwiches, stopping only long enough to make quick bathroom and fuel stops, and to stretch for a minute. They sang or played trivia, and took turns sleeping, talking incessantly at times, and then sitting in complete silence at other times. The old mini-van was holding up well, but was burning oil about as fast as it was burning gas, and they had to add a quart of oil every time they stopped.

"I need to get out of this car for a while," Rudy finally said. "Do you guys want to stop in Edmonton and walk around a little, and then maybe have an actual meal somewhere?"

"I wouldn't even mind gettin' a room. I need ta get out of the car. We're only about halfway there... maybe not quite, but still...," Grady said.

"I think the muscles in my legs have completely given up hope of ever moving again. Just drop me off here and I'll catch up with you later," Jewel moaned.

"Alright, well it seems we are in agreement then," Rudy confirmed.

They decided to drive through Edmonton and find a hotel on the other end. None of them were used to driving through a city, and they were swept up in the traffic and the sites, exiting off the Yellowhead Highway only when they felt like they had survived the brunt of all the hustle and bustle. They quickly found a hotel near the highway, checked in, and decided on a long walk before stopping for a meal.

"I think my face will be just about healed up before we get to your house Grady," Jewel said when she came back from the bathroom at the restaurant.

She was getting used to the stares she got when people looked at the bruises on her face, but she was ready for them to be gone. It irritated her to know that people likely assumed either Grady or Rudy were the ones who put them there. She would watch as people startled when they saw her face, and then looked at Grady and Rudy like they were monsters. She was certain that it bothered them too, but they would never say anything.

"Well, truth be told, we thought ya'd want it that way darlin', which is why we insisted on drivin' instead of flyin'. We thought ya'd want ta get healed up first," Grady confessed.

"You didn't want to bring me home battered and bruised?" she asked. "Do they know...," she trailed off, clearing her throat, "do they know what happened to me?"

"They don't know the details, but they know the gist of it. Rudy called Diana right away before we came lookin' for ya, and then of course he's talked ta her a hundred times since then," Grady said, rolling his eyes at Rudy.

"It's your story to tell Jewel. She knew you were missing and that we were going to find you. She was worried sick and asked about how you were doing, and if you were all right. I didn't tell her any details, but she knows the gist. I hope you're not upset with me," Rudy added.

"No. Of course I'm not upset with you. I just don't want to walk in your parent's home and have everyone look at me with pity," she said looking at Grady. "I don't like when people feel sorry for me. I saw that same look on everyone's face every time I walked in a store, or a restaurant, or the office at school, for years after my parents died. I was so happy to leave home, just so I wouldn't have to see that pitiful look on everyone's face anymore."

"They're going to look at you in awe sweetheart!" Rudy said. "They're in complete disbelief that Grady is head over heels in love, and they can't wait to meet the woman who's making him all googly-eyed."

"Besides, Mom said Diana has done nothin' but talk about ya since she visited. They're all just excited ta meet ya. She told Mom I was bringin' home Rudy's clone," Grady added.

"I do have one confession, and I may as well just tell you right now Jewel. Diana said Maggie, Grady's mom, had a little prayer service for you at the house. Father O'Malley came over and all the nuns, and of course the rosary club. All Maggie told them was they were praying for a young woman who was missing and needed their prayers. She didn't even tell them your name, but it might come up, and people might put the pieces together, and they may have even seen some of it on the news," Rudy said shrugging.

"That is so sweet!" Jewel said feeling touched, tears threatening her once again.

"Oh... okay... that wasn't the response I was expecting," Rudy said, exchanging a puzzled look with Grady.

"There's nothing more touching then when complete strangers pray for each other, is there?" she asked looking at them both. "Can you imagine anything kinder?" she said wiping away a tear. "I'm so sorry. I'm crying again."

"It's all right darlin'," Grady said hugging her to him, motioning with his eyes at Rudy to give them a minute.

"I'm going to the bathroom. I'll be back in a minute," Rudy said excusing himself.

"All I do is cry anymore. There's a slow leak that feels like it's going to burst at any minute. I'm not ready to meet your parents Grady. They're going to think I'm a mess," she said trying to stop herself from crying.

"They won't judge ya at all Jewel. That's not who they are. Ya could walk in the front door cryin' yer eyes out, and they would go out of their way ta make ya feel better. Ya don't have ta worry about anything, but if yer really feelin' worried about it, we can change plans and head straight ta Wyomin'. Rudy would understand. We could make a trip ta South Dakota some other time," he said hugging her to him.

"I haven't been worried about it at all. I'm just tired. My emotional state is outside of my control right now. I've never felt this out of control before Grady. I've always managed. I've always been able to put on a front and make people think that everything is perfect, even when it's not," she said looking at Grady, as she wiped away more tears, trying to stop herself from losing it altogether.

"I think this is progress Jewel. It's harder ta let it out and cry a little, than it is ta put on a front. I think there's hope for ya yet," he said squeezing her, running his hand through her hair to soothe her.

"I want to go meet your family Grady. I'll feel better tomorrow after a good night's rest, and I think I need about an hour in a hot shower."

"Why don't I take ya ta the room and ya can take a long hot shower. We'll go have a beer and give ya a little privacy," he said kissing her lightly. "Do ya think you'll feel okay by yerself in the room for a while?

"The bar in the hotel? The one that's like thirty feet from our room?" she asked feeling foolish.

"Yep. We won't be far away."

"Alright, I think I can handle that," she said smiling up at him.

They got to the room and Jewel wasted no time spending as long as she possibly could in the shower, letting the last thirty plus hours of a stagnant car ride wash off her, checking all the areas on her body that had been bruised and welted. She was healing slowly but surely, and she dared to feel between her legs for the first time since the exam. She explored in and around, checking everything, and finding none of the painful tears or bruises that she felt that first day, the last time she dared to touch herself. *His remains have all vanished. There's nothing left but his rotting corpse inside a low budget pine box,* she thought crossing herself.

She knew she didn't have a choice. She knew she had to kill or be killed, but she took the responsibility of it very seriously. She was meant to heal others, not hurt them. She wished she had never been placed in that situation, where she was forced to make that kind of choice, but at the same time, she was glad that she knew how to handle a gun, and was able to defend herself. She was through thinking of it all when she finally laid down and immediately fell asleep, barely stirring when Grady and Rudy came back in the room, each of them crashing the second they hit their beds, and for the first time since it all began, she slept peacefully, dreaming of family and friends.

~~~~~~~~

"Ya had a good sleep then Jewel?" Grady asked as they began to wake up the next morning. Grady realized the second he woke up that Jewel hadn't woken up in the middle of the night with nightmares.

"I had a really good dream last night," she said smiling. "It's going to be a good day."

The three got up early and tried to get going, but after getting everything packed back into the minivan, they realized it wasn't going to start. Grady tried turning the key several times, closing his eyes as he turned it the last few times, listening for the sounds from the car, giving him clues as to what may be wrong with it.

"Dead battery?" Rudy asked.

"I think it's the starter. Let me check it out," Grady said getting out of the car.

He popped the hood and checked things out as best as he could without having all the proper tools. Jewel got out and watched him going over the entire engine, looking for anything that might be out of place, but found nothing.

"I definitely think the starter's out. We should call the rental place and see if we can get a replacement car or something," Grady said, turning to lean up against the car.

Rudy was already on the phone trying to get through to them, but he kept getting put on hold, and his patience was starting to run out. They were all sitting out on the sidewalk, basking in the morning sun as Rudy waited on hold. Jewel and Grady sat looking at Rudy when he was finally able to talk to someone, trying to piece together the one side of the conversation they were able to hear, and it wasn't sounding very promising.

"Well, they're willing to get it fixed for us, but they can't give us a replacement vehicle. They're going to call around to see if we can get it towed and repaired, and then they'll call me back," Rudy said after hanging up. "I imagine it's going to take them a while to get back to us."

"Let's walk down ta that parts store ta see if they have the parts and tools we need, and see if we can just get it taken care of ta get movin'," Grady said standing up, pulling Jewel up as he did.

"Well, we may as well check it out," Rudy agreed.

Grady got all the information he needed on the car, and the three of them started walking down to the repair store they had passed the night before when they were driving back from dinner. It was about a mile away, but it felt good to get out and walk around a little. It was a beautiful, sunny day, and they weren't disappointed about not being in the car. After that last thirty-hour stretch, practically non-stop, they weren't looking forward to riding again, and the car problem was a welcome delay.

"Those starters in those damn things go out all the time. We have several in stock. You can borrow these tools if you want... maybe you could leave a driver's license or something for a deposit," the clerk said to Grady as they discussed all the possibilities of what could be wrong with the car.

They decided to borrow the tools and buy the starter, getting a ride from the clerk back down to the hotel where their rental car was sitting. Grady didn't waste any time digging into the car, and Jewel loved watching him and helping him as he worked on it. Since long before she could remember, she loved hanging out with her dad in his shop, helping him work on cars, or tractors, or one thing after the other that broke down or needed maintenance.

Jewel made herself useful by handing Grady tools as he asked for them, and she lent her hand a few times to help in places where his hands were too large to reach. They made a good team working together when they needed to, and making idle chit chat when they could.

"Ya have a grease smear on yer face Jewel," Grady said smiling at her when they finished up. "Do ya have any idea how beautiful ya look right now?"

"Grease? Is that what does it for you?" she said smiling back at him.

"I don't know. I just... well... ya just always look that way ta me, but what really blows me away sometimes is ta see ya all messed up and dirty without a care in the world of how ya look, not even knowin' that ya look breathtakin'. Ya just get in and get yer hands dirty, grease smeared on ya, dirt on the front of yer shirt... I don't know Jewel... I can't explain it," he said carefully wiping the grease away that was smeared on her face, kissing her softly on the lips as he did.

"Thank you," she whispered kissing him softly in return.

Rudy had decided to make himself useful by heading over to the grocery store that wasn't far away, getting snacks and sandwich items they would need for the next leg of the journey. He found Jewel and Grady still kissing as he rounded the corner, making his way toward the car.

"You two are really going to miss me interrupting your privacy all the time, aren't you?" Rudy said, walking up to them carrying bags of groceries.

"You're not interruptin'. The car should be ready ta go. We were just comfortin' each other, because we missed ya so much," Grady said winking at Jewel. "Besides, I owe ya brother. How many days and nights did I spend watchin' you and Diana kissin' and huggin' all the time, not ta mention the loudness of yer... nocturnal activities, and that's my sister, which is twice as bad!"

"That's true, and I owe you a few thousand more interruptions come to think of it," Rudy replied.

"I'm going to miss you Rudy... with or without interruptions," Jewel added, getting the tools wiped off and placed neatly back in the toolbox.

"I actually don't want to even think about you two leaving. I... I just can't even think about it right now," Rudy said, shaking his head as he loaded the groceries in the car.

"Ugh! Your whole family is going to hate me for taking you away Grady," Jewel said exasperated.

"No, they won't Jewel," Rudy replied. "They would be mad if he stayed and settled for a life that he didn't want. They're thrilled that he fell in love, and is going off to live a life he's excited about. Trust me Jewel! There's a very aggressive… ummm… lady… I guess you could call her that, for mercies sake, ready to snare him in her iron jaws the second we roll into town. They may petition the Pope to canonize you after saving Grady from her."

"Is this Debbie you're talking about?" she asked, catching the dirty look Grady was giving Rudy.

"Yes," Grady said irritably. "I told her about Debbie."

"Oh good, that will make it easier to explain the cloves of garlic Maggie has hanging on the door in case the evil spirit shows up," Rudy joked.

Grady got the car started back up without any problems, and the three of them piled in, stopping to exchange the tool box for Grady's driver's license back at the parts store. Jewel thought about Debbie, wondering about the extent of hers and Grady's relationship. She sounded like a terrible woman, and it puzzled Jewel that Grady would date someone like that, but she understood the majority of their relationship had been in high school, which would have been more than ten years ago for Grady. Still, she couldn't help feel a little jealousy, which was something she had never felt before, at least not when it came to romantic relationships.

"You got awfully quiet back there," Rudy said to Jewel as they waited for Grady to go get his driver's license and return the toolbox. "I shouldn't have brought up Debbie. You don't need to worry about her Jewel. She is… evil. That's really the only word I can think to describe her. She lies all the time, she's really loud, and she thinks she's better than everyone. She's an awful mother, she was never faithful to her husband, and there were many rumors about her when Grady and her were dating in high school. She likely wasn't faithful to him either."

"Why did he date her? It doesn't seem to fit with who he is," she asked.

"Because she's really aggressive, and she just kind of forces herself into people's lives. She probably threatened to cast evil spirits against any other girl who came near him," he replied jokingly. "Mostly, I think he kind of just went along with it. He wasn't ever out chasing girls. He was mostly interested in sports, and she was just… well… she was just always there. She was like a vulture circling the house when Grady came back from the Army. He never loved her. He's never been in love with anyone before. You have nothing to worry about," he said turning to look at her sprawled out in the backseat.

"Well, I'm not really worried about it. I know Grady loves me. I was just curious why he would date someone that everyone dislikes so much. She must have some good qualities," she said.

"She might have had possibilities in high school, but Grady wasn't interested in dating her when he got back. He just sort of hung out with her because she would never go away," he laughed as Grady got back in the car.

Jewel had herself comfortably laid out in the back where she could easily pick up her guitar and sing a few songs. "Any song requests?"

"Sing us a song that's uniquely Wyoming Jewel," Rudy said.

"Uniquely Wyoming?" she asked, puzzled for the first time. They had tried to stump her, but she always managed to come up with the words and music to every song they threw out there, but this one had her puzzled for a moment. "Alright then, you asked for it. A Wyoming man made this song famous, and if this doesn't encapsulate the spirit of the people of Wyoming, then I don't know what does."

…We've got a five dollar fine for whining
We'll tell you before you come in
If it ain't on your mind to have a good time
Ya'll come back and see us again

"I don't know if that counts. Chris LeDoux was a national star. We may have stumped her Grady. What do you think?" Rudy said when she finished the song.

"It counts! Chris LeDoux was from a town not far from my family's ranch. I actually met him once," she said smiling, "though I have no memory of it, because I was only four, but Grandpa told me about it. My mom and dad loved him! He was uniquely Wyoming, and therefore, so are his songs."

"Maybe ya should have been a lawyer Jewel," Grady joked, pulling out on the highway. "I think she wins this one Rudy."

"I'm not sure you're an unbiased jury," Rudy said eyeing him narrowly. "Alright then, let's hear one from the Faqaiwe tribe," he said laughing.

"Oh! I have one!" she said surprising them both. "Now let's see if I can remember it. It's pretty complicated. You know how messed up those Faqaiwe's are?" she said laughing. "Here we go. Listen carefully."

Jewel went on to sing a very complicated song about a man who ends up becoming his own grandpa through strange and unique marriages, and odd twists and turns that could, however unlikely, take place in a modern nuclear family.

…My wife is now my mother's mother
And it makes me blue
Because, she is my wife
She's my grandmother too

"Ha! You'll pay for that young lady!" Rudy said laughing as Jewel finished the song, laughing hard as she did.

"That was pretty good Jewel," Grady chimed in laughing. "How is it that ya know the words and music ta every song? It's amazin'."

"Well… I was a twenty two year old virgin when you met me. What else would I have to do?" she joked.

They rode like that laughing and talking, alternating sleep, making each other sandwiches, and taking turns driving as they had on the first half of their drive, stopping only long enough to fuel up and take bathroom breaks. Jewel couldn't remember a time when she felt more of a belonging. She felt like she had known Grady and Rudy her whole life. Laughing and joking, and even crying with them started to feel like the most natural thing in the world.

She didn't think it was possible to feel closer to anybody. Of course, she had felt close to Troy, but this was different. It was different because she was different. She had opened herself up to them in a way she never did with Troy. With Troy, she was guarding her heart with everything she had. Her heart was tender and raw, and she wasn't willing to be vulnerable or cry ever. Troy treated her like she was tender and raw. He coddled her and kept her away from anything that might hurt her. He did everything he could to protect her and she appreciated all of it. It was exactly what she needed at that time in her life. This was different because she was with people who thought she was tough and could handle anything, and that was allowing her to move on and grow. She was exactly where she needed to be, and she knew it and felt it.

PART THREE

SOUTH DAKOTA

CHAPTER 33

BELLE FOURCHE

"Here we are in Belle Fourche, South Dakota Jewel," Rudy said smiling. "Don't blink or you'll miss half the town."

"I look like five miles of bad road, and I need to brush my teeth," Jewel said looking at herself in the rearview mirror, trying to smooth her hair that was going in all directions. "At least give me some gum. I don't want to meet your family with dragon breath."

"Ya look better than most people look after they've slept peacefully in a warm bed, but I'll concede on the gum part," Grady said handing her a pack of gum, carefully dodging a swat from her.

"Oh my gosh! Just get there and get me out of this car," she moaned. "I can no longer feel my legs or my butt!"

They pulled up in front of Grady's family home, and Jewel soaked it all in looking at it. It was beautiful and obviously well taken care of. Somehow, it was just as she imagined. It was a two-story, traditional colonial house, white with black shutters. Perfectly manicured flowerbeds lined the front of the house and the cobbled walkway leading up to the door. There was a trellis on the front of the house on each side of the doorway where white and lavender floral vines had climbed, complementing the vines that grew up and around the white picket fence that surrounded the lawn and the decorative hedges. Large maple trees had grown tall and stood high above the house, shading the cobbled driveway on one side of the house that led to the hidden garage in the back. It was a house that invited everyone inside. It screamed love and family, and Jewel smiled as Grady opened the car door and helped her out.

"Leave yer stuff. I'll get it later," he said smiling at her.

Diana was running down the walk with a trail of kids running behind her, surrounding Rudy in hugs and kisses. Grady's mom, Maggie, and dad, Patrick, were following close behind. They all took their turn to meet Jewel, giving her hugs and grabbing Grady for a multitude of hugs and kisses. Jewel could easily see that Grady got his looks from his mom, and his build from his dad. Maggie was tall and blond, and she had the same ice blue eyes that Grady and Diana shared. Jewel knew that Grady's parents were well into their sixties, but Maggie looked younger than her age, and she imagined that she must have been quite stunning when she was a young woman.

His dad on the other hand, looked much different. He had dark hair and olive skin, with hazel-green eyes. Patrick was a large man, standing well over six feet, and slightly taller than Grady was at six-four. He was thick with muscle, and had large rugged hands. Maggie was quite tall herself, several inches taller than Jewel, and she was thin, and had soft, gentle hands. Surrounded by Maggie, Patrick, Grady, Diana, and Rudy, at five foot eight inches tall, Jewel felt a little on the short side.

"Oh my gosh! You're even more beautiful than Diana said, which is pretty hard ta imagine. She gushed about ya fer hours," Maggie said, grabbing Jewel by the arm and leading her inside after hugging her several times.

"Ya got ya a pretty lass," Patrick said, nodding toward Jewel with an arm around Grady. "Say goodbye ta her son. Yer mammies got her now. You'll not see her again fer awhile."

They made their way inside where Maggie and Diana had been preparing a family meal for them. There was a pot on every burner, and there was something cooking on the grill that immediately reminded Jewel of barbeques they used to have on sheep trail. She took a deep breath, smiling as she did. They had gone all out anticipating their arrival, and Jewel couldn't have felt happier. The hustle and bustle in the house was so completely alive that it felt like an entity all its own, and suddenly, it seemed like the magic of a carnival had been bestowed on her, giving her that feeling that a child gets when they see the bright lights of a Ferris Wheel, and the carnies selling cotton candy.

"Aren't you glad I talked you out of that Big Mac Jewel?" Rudy said making his way in the kitchen, lifting the lids off the cooking pots.

"Get ya out ya bugger," Maggie said, slapping Rudy's hand before pulling him in for another hug. "Now out of the kitchen with ya. It'll be ready in a bit. Take everyone out ta the back patio where we'll be havin' dinner," she ordered with a smile.

There were kids running around, and there was chatter coming from every direction. It was a little overwhelming for Jewel, but she looked at all the chaos and smiled. She finally understood what Rudy was talking about, feeling so much love that she would be gasping for air. The house was full of it, and it was so thick she could feel it. There was happiness and laughter surrounding her so completely it was nearly tangible. There were aromas coming from food that had been lovingly prepared. There were pictures on the walls full of growing children and aging parents. It was practically like a Hallmark card, and Jewel looked around in awe. It was a stark contrast to the old, crooked pictures that still hung on the walls at home, stopping shortly before her eleventh birthday, as if the world had quit spinning after that one fateful day.

"How was the drive then?" Diana asked, putting an arm around Jewel.

"It was long, but it was kind of fun too," she said remembering the bond she shared with Grady and Rudy. She was pleased to see Diana, and returned the gesture by wrapping a friendly arm around her. She knew that Rudy missed her terribly, and she was happy to see them together, but she had shared a connection with her when she visited them in Alaska, and she was delighted to see that hadn't changed.

"Are you gonna marry Uncle Grady?" came a small voice. It was Rudy and Diana's youngest son, and she remembered Diana telling her that his name was Joseph, and he looked and acted just as Grady did when he was little. She could clearly see that was the case. Looking at the little seven-year-old boy was like looking at a mini version of Grady.

"Ha. Well, I don't know," Jewel said laughing. "You must be Joseph. You look just like your Uncle Grady."

"I'm Joseph, and I think that you're really pretty. Do you want to see my tree house?"

"I would love to see your tree house," Jewel said smiling. "Is it here?"

"No, it's at my house, which is like maybe a hundred hours from here I think, but can you come to my house and see it?" Joseph asked, flashing baby blue eyes at her that melted her heart.

"Our house is actually just a few blocks away, which apparently is the equivalent of a hundred hours away ta a seven year old," Diana said laughing. "They'll come by maybe tomorrow Joseph."

"Will you come outside to the back yard with me? Grampy has a trampoline he put out there for us. Do you want to jump on the trampoline with me?" Joseph asked grabbing her hand.

"Give her a little time Joseph. Why don't ya take Jewel here outside where Grady is, and let her relax fer a while," Diana said while she stirred pots, and chopped vegetables, preparing their food.

"I've been sitting and relaxing for about forty hours. A jump on the trampoline might be just what I need," Jewel said taking Joseph's hand more firmly. "Unless you need help with dinner?" she asked as Joseph pulled her toward the back door.

"We got it, but don't let him pester ya too much," Diana said smiling. "I did say he was just like his uncle, which means that he won't give ya a moments rest."

"Ya go outside. We got plenty a help with dinner," Maggie added, squeezing her arm and smiling at her warmly.

Joseph led Jewel outside and they each jumped on the trampoline. Her own grandpa bought her a trampoline when she was little, and jumping on it was a favorite pastime of hers. She was fearless. She could do flips and turns, and she amazed Joseph with all the things she could do on it. They all watched her as she took turns with all the kids, making Joseph squeal in delight with every flip she did. It felt good to burn off some of the energy she had built up sitting in the car the last forty hours. All the other kids had come out to the yard and were watching her as Grady, Rudy, and Grady's dad sat up on the porch talking and grilling.

"You're awesome!" Joseph squealed as Jewel made her way off the trampoline. "Will you teach me how to do that? I will be your very best friend!"

"Only after you learn all the safety rules, and promise to never ever break any of them," she replied, just as her grandfather had said to her before he let her jump on her trampoline.

"Okay! What are the rules?" Joseph asked with so much excitement that she could hardly stop laughing. He was jumping around and talking non-stop as he introduced her to his siblings, stopping to tell her a little story about each of them, or adding some small tidbit about their favorite food, or favorite thing to do. She loved watching him hug each one, or grab their hand affectionately.

"Well okay," she said after all the formal introductions were made. "First you have to make sure it's okay with your mom and dad. That's always the first rule," she said before explaining the rest of the safety rules to Joseph and the other kids. The trampoline had only been set up for a couple days, so this was all new to them. Prior to Jewel getting there, the trampoline had been little more than a possibility that they were all too afraid to push the limits on. She instructed them all to take off their shoes, and she explained the geometry that would bounce them in the opposite direction from what they would be expecting. She was still talking to the older kids, when Joseph ran back with more energy than he had just moments before.

"Okay! Okay! Mom and Dad said yes!" Joseph screamed, running around in circles with a broad smile.

Jewel patiently taught them all a few small tricks, going over the rules of safety repetitively, just as carefully as her grandpa had done with her. She knew the trampoline could be dangerous, and she didn't want anyone to get hurt. Before too long, they were getting the feel for it, and starting to do small tricks, with everyone on the porch cheering for them as they did one trick after another. It felt good to Jewel to be outside jumping and moving around. Paxton, Melanie, and Thomas were naturals. They caught on quickly and had no fears about it whatsoever. Alisha was sixteen, and a little more reserved, as she teetered between still being a child, and wanting to be a grown-up, but once she let down her guard a little, she started having fun and did a few successful flips. Tina was glued to her side. She was a beautiful ten-year old girl who looked much like herself.

"I think we look alike," she said smoothing Jewels hair. "We have the same hair and almost the same eyes."

"I think you're right. We do look a lot alike," Jewel said, pushing the hair out of Tina's eyes, staring at her more closely as she realized just how much they did actually look alike.

"Mommy said you're a nurse. I want to be a nurse when I grow up. Just like you."

"Do you like taking care of people?" Jewel asked her.

"I want to help people who need help, and then make them feel better."

"You'll be a wonderful nurse then, because that's exactly what nurses do!"

Jewel sat with Tina as the other kids took turns jumping on the trampoline. It was a gorgeous summer evening, and she inhaled it all in, basking in it. The laughing kids, the talk and laughter coming from the deck, the smell of the barbeque grill, and the fresh cut grass was more than she ever dreamed of. She looked up smiling and laughing as she watched Joseph squeal delightfully, as he flew higher up in the air.

"Time ta eat," Diana yelled. "Come in and get washed up."

The timing couldn't have been better. Jewel was starting to get worried about the trampoline. She didn't want anyone to get hurt doing something she taught them to do. Plus, they had spent over seventy hours in a small mini-van, and it was all starting to catch up with her, and the wonderful smells coming from the kitchen reminded her that she was starving.

"Will you sit by me?" Joseph asked, grabbing Jewel by the hand as they headed toward the deck.

"Are ya tryin' ta steal my girl?" Grady asked, grabbing Joseph and picking him up tickling him as he did.

"He's my best friend. Isn't that right Joseph?" Jewel said, trying to save Joseph from Grady.

"Yep!" Joseph said matter of fact between squeals.

"Ya've been here for an hour, and ya already have a best friend?" Grady asked smiling at Jewel.

"Yep!" she answered just as adamantly as Joseph, giving the enamored boy a wink.

"We'll be on our way after a bit Jewel, and you can have some peace," Rudy said.

"Don't hurry off on my account. You have wonderful kids Rudy," Jewel said squeezing his arm.

"It's my beautiful bride here. She's the reason they're so wonderful. She's a good momma," he said hugging his wife again. The two were practically attached at the hip, and seeing the look between them, it was obvious they were anxious to get home and have some time alone.

"I'm sorry. I should have helped," Jewel said seeing the food spread out on the table.

"No. I wouldn't have it. Ya can help later. Tonight yer a guest. Tomorrow ya won't be a guest anymore and ya can help," Maggie said gruffly, but always with a smile.

"Don't worry lass, she won't be kickin' ya out. Tomorrow is Sunday services, and after ya've gone ta Sunday services with us, you'll be good as family," Patrick said, winking at her in a way that reminded her of Grady.

"Oh, I would love to go to Sunday services," Jewel said sincerely. She thought about going to church on the drive there. It was something she felt like she needed.

She was never particularly fond of it before, but it suddenly seemed more important than ever. She wanted to give thanks, and she wanted to be able to speak to a priest at some point. There was a part of her that would never be able to heal until she spoke to a priest.

"Diana said ya might," Maggie said taking Jewels hand, leading her to a place at the table with the most comfortable chair.

"Tomorrow ya have ta sit in a lawn chair. That chairs fer guests," Rudy said with a heavy Irish accent, poking fun at his in-laws. "Ouch!" Rudy squealed after receiving a friendly jab from his mother-in-law.

The dinner was wonderful. It was full of talk and laughter, everyone smiling and poking fun at each other. Jewel felt like if she smiled any wider, her face was going to break. She looked at each one of them carefully, taking them all in. They all asked her questions about her life, and about growing up in Wyoming, and she equally liked hearing about their life in Belle Fourche. They all enjoyed a long and wonderful dinner that Jewel took in as slowly as possible, relishing the food and drink nearly as much as the laughter.

"Is Maggie short for Margaret then?" Jewel asked as things quieted down a little, and children scattered.

"Yep, named after Saint Margaret herself," Maggie answered.

"My confirmation name is Margaret. The priest back in my hometown calls me Maggie. I like that name," Jewel said smiling at her. There was a little tension Jewel sensed when it came to Grady's mom that Jewel wasn't quite certain of, plus she had never been invited to a man's house to meet his parents before. She was feeling desperate to make a connection with her.

"Don't pay her no mind lass," Patrick said as Maggie made her way in the kitchen, insisting that Jewel take it easy and not help clear the dishes. "She's feelin' a bit crabby since she found out ya'd be headin' off ta Wyomin' so soon. She'll come 'round."

"I don't think we're in a big hurry. We'll be here a few days or more… maybe a week," Jewel said making eye contact with Grady, sensing some of the same angst from Patrick.

"She can only stay mad fer about five minutes. It'll pass an' you'll be like two peas in a pod before ya know it," Grady said reaching out to grab her hand.

"Can we call you Auntie Jewel?" Joseph asked, going up to Jewel, helping himself to her lap.

"Don't you think you should save that for your actual Aunt?" Jewel asked looking at Grady pleadingly, not sure how to answer.

"Not yet Joseph, I haven't even asked her ta marry me… yet," Grady said stroking her cheek.

"Why not? Mommy said you were in love with each other and were meant to be together," Joseph asked innocently.

"Run along Joseph!" Rudy said grabbing the boy, coming to the rescue. "I think you found a lifelong friend here. Does he remind you of anyone?" Rudy said pointing at Grady behind his back.

"He does seem to be just like you Grady," she said smiling at him.

"I don't know. He's not nearly as attached ta ya as I am," he joked, knowing the boy had barely left her side since she got there.

Jewel was yawning uncontrollably, but trying her hardest to hide it. The last several days of traveling, combined with a huge meal, was wearing her down. Everyone was talking all at once, and the kids wanted her to jump on the trampoline some more. Jewel's head was starting to spin, and she was finding it hard to keep up with everything around her.

"Ya have the whole basement ta yerselves," Maggie said coming back out to sit with them after getting the kitchen cleaned back up. "We're not so auld fashioned as ya might think," she said winking at Jewel.

"We're heading out!" Rudy said, patting Grady on the back and squeezing Jewels shoulder. "We'll see you tomorrow probably."

The eight of them said their goodbyes, making their way out to the car. Jewel could feel the energy in the house decrease monumentally, and she let out a long sigh without thinking about it.

"It's a lot ta take in isn't it?" Maggie said, smiling at Jewel more warmly than she had earlier. Maggie had gotten used to Grady being back, and she knew she had to say goodbye to him again, which Jewel imagined was going to be difficult. She couldn't imagine what it was like to have a son who had gone off to fight a war in Afghanistan and Iraq, especially after leaving their own country to get away from such strife.

"They're wonderful. I love every one of them," Jewel said. She couldn't stop smiling. The kids were amazing, and she loved seeing Rudy and Diana together again.

"Those kids were gushin' over ya Jewel. Ya've a way with the babes," Maggie said.

"That's a relief. I've never really spent much time around kids. Are they always so easy?"

"They're good kids, but they might have been on their best behavior, and Joseph might be experiencin' his first crush," Grady said getting up. Jewel was yawning so much he thought that he needed to get her to a bed as soon as he could. She hadn't really slept that much in the car, and Grady suspected that she was afraid of having more nightmares.

"Let's get ya ta bed then woman," Grady said pulling her to her feet. "I'll just get her settled and come up and have a drink with ya Dad."

Jewel could see there was tension between Grady and his dad, and maybe even his mom too, which may have been part of the tension between Jewel and Maggie at dinner. She suspected that it had to do with Grady leaving, instead of staying behind to run the family business. There was a part of her that wanted to stay amidst all this family. It could get lonely on the ranch. Sometimes the most exciting part of the day was when the UPS guy stopped to deliver a package. She remembered Grandpa enjoying that so much, that every time the UPS guy showed up, he ended up inviting him in for drinks and dinner with the two of them, and she suspected that the UPS guy actually planned it that way. The UPS guy was, after all, one of his son's oldest friends, and it was fun to catch up.

She knew she had to go back though. She had been gone too long and it was time that she faced Troy and his family. It was her family's ranch, and she had walked away from it without thinking about it, leaving the burden of it to Troy and his parents.

"We should invite your family to come stay with us at the ranch. Maybe you could mention Thanksgiving to them or something. That might help soften the blow a little. I know they probably want you to stay," Jewel said when they get downstairs.

"Bribery! I like it!" Grady said cradling her face in his hands. "Now get ta bed woman. Ya need a good night's rest and I'll be right upstairs. Do ya think you'll feel safe down here by yerself?"

"I love it here Grady. I'll probably be asleep before you reach the top stair," she said kissing him more thoroughly than she had since the abduction. "I was looking forward to cuddling up with you though, but I'll manage," she shrugged smiling up at him.

"I know Jewel. Me too. I can't wait 'til we can just be tagether for a while. We haven't had much time with just the two of us, and I've been dreamin' of cuddlin' up next ta ya and holdin' ya for some three thousand miles. Do ya want me ta stay with ya then?"

Jewel wrapped her arms around his neck and looked up at him. "Go have a drink with your dad. We're going to have plenty of time together. You're never going to be able to get rid of me. I love you and your family too much."

"They loved ya as I knew they would," he said wrapping his arms around her tightly.

This was the most intimate moment they'd had since the abduction, and Grady was enjoying the feeling of holding her so closely again. He had been hesitant to grab her when he wanted to grab her, or kiss her when he wanted to kiss her. He knew she needed time to heal, and he didn't want her to feel like he was pushing her, plus, keeping his distance was the only way he knew to resist the desire he felt for her.

"Will you cuddle up with me when you come to bed… even if I'm asleep… the way you did the other night at the hotel?" Jewel smiled up at him. "I loved lying there with you like that the other morning. I had actually woken up earlier, but I didn't want to move. It felt so nice, and you're so warm."

"I'm glad ta hear ya say that Jewel. I was afraid ya might have a hard time with it. I don't know how much space ta give ya, and all I want ta do is just grab ya up and hold ya close ta me."

"Grady," she whispered, "there's never been a single second I didn't want you to hold me or touch me. I… I could never confuse your touch with… well… with what happened. Does what happened to me… does it make you feel differently… about touching me?"

"No. Nothin' could make me feel differently. Ya don't have ta worry about that darlin'," he said leaning down, kissing her softly. "Do ya want me ta stay with ya 'til ya fall asleep?"

"I'm okay. Go have a drink with your dad. I'll be here when you get back," she said kissing him in return.

CHAPTER 34

AN UNEXPECTED PROPOSAL

Jewel woke up smiling. It had been another night without a nightmare, and she could feel the warmth coming from Grady as he slept next to her. It was rare that she woke up before him, and she enjoyed looking at him, as he laid there naked from the waist up. It was a stolen moment where she could just look at him without feeling like she needed to look away. She traced the outline of him in the dark with her eyes. He was covered by nothing more than a thin sheet. She could see the finely chiseled curves where muscles protruded out through his sun-kissed skin. She had to resist the urge not to trace him with her fingers. She looked at his face so quiet, peaceful, and completely relaxed… a state it was rarely in for this man that always seemed to be planning everyone's next move, carefully considering every detail, and it's many possible consequences.

She studied each blond eyelash, some of which were reddish orange, and matched the colors of his eyebrows, and the stubble on his face. She loved the curls in his hair, and longed to run her fingers through it every time she saw it. It was always carefree and effortless, and Jewel doubted that he had any idea how attractive it made him. To Grady, his hair was just something that kept his head warm, but aside from drying it off with a towel after he got out of the shower, he seemed to forget that it was even there.

She stretched out, feeling rested and completely happy for the first time since before the abduction. She had a couple nightmares when she tried to nap on the long car ride, and hadn't gotten much sleep, so she was happy she had finally been able to get a good rest. She couldn't remember the last time she had slept so deeply.

She could see that it was still dark out, but for her, it was time to get up. She tiptoed into the bathroom to brush her teeth before making her way quietly up the stairs, hoping to sneak outside to watch the sunrise.

"An early riser then?" Patrick said, meeting her at the top of the stairs, nearly making her scream out. "I'm sorry child. I didn't mean ta scare ya," he said, wrapping an arm around her when she jumped.

"It's okay. I'm a little jumpy. I wasn't expecting anyone to be awake. Do I smell coffee?"

"Let's get ya a cup, and go watch the sunrise then," he said, guiding her by the arm toward the kitchen.

Jewel could see how it was that she, Rudy, and Patrick were alike. The three of them had dark hair and olive skin, in contrast to the blond hair and paler skin of Grady, Diana, and Maggie. It was more than just appearances though. Patrick had the same sarcasm and reservation about him that she had. He was holding back telling her something, just the way she herself was doing. Grady, Diana, and Maggie had no such reservations. If they needed to say something, they said it, though not with total abandon. They said it after careful consideration, and they said it gingerly, but at least they said it. She admired that ability, but failed to employ it herself on most occasions.

"Grady has never brought a lass home before," Patrick finally said after they sat quietly together for a long time, both of them having been caught up in the beauty of the morning sunrise. "He never brought Debbie home. She would just show up whether ya wanted her ta or not," he said rolling his eyes, indicating it was the latter part of that he subscribed to.

"Well, I'm glad to be here. I've never been invited home to meet a man's family before. I guess this is a first for both of us."

"We're glad ta have ya Jewel," Patrick said, reaching out and squeezing her hand. "I've always trusted my instincts. They've never steered me wrong, an' my instinct tells me yer a fine woman, and I can tell that my boy is crazy for ya. I wondered if I'd ever see the day."

"Well, I'm crazy for him too. I hope you'll forgive me for taking him away," she said hopefully. "I can see how close you all are, and I love it."

"Yer not ta worry. We knew he wouldn't stay. I'd be a bit disappointed if he did. He's a man who needs ta find his own way. I'm proud of him," he said nodding, and Jewel sensed that whatever angst had been between them, had been resolved over drinks.

They sat comfortably together, chatting and watching the sunrise, before Grady and Maggie made their way out to join them, bringing with them some fresh coffee and scones for breakfast. Jewel watched them as they carried everything out and poured more coffee for all of them. Maggie was at least five foot ten, and she had the same skin tone and hair colors as Grady. She could see the similar features they shared, and she wondered for the millionth time who she would have looked like more, her mom, or her dad.

She knew she had the same dark hair and darker skin tone like her father, but she got her blue eyes and her thin build from her mom. It was more than that though; it was mannerisms, and expressions. She could look at Grady's mom and dad, and find the same features and expressions on Grady's face... a similar smile, or a similar raise of the eyebrow. She had a box full of pictures at home of her mom and dad, but she never dared to look at them before for fear that she would finally breakdown once and for all. She suddenly felt a desire to pour through them, and she made a mental note to go look for the box as soon as she got home.

"Ya must have slept well last night Jewel," Grady said, leaning down to kiss her on the top of her head as he found a seat next to her.

"I can't remember the last time I slept so deeply. I don't think I moved a muscle all night."

"I'm glad ya were comfortable. I want ya ta feel at home while yer here." Maggie smiled at her.

It was a beautiful morning, and Jewel was looking forward to getting out and exploring the town. She was anxious to meet people Grady had grown up with, and to see where he had gone to school, and hung out as a boy. She was also looking forward to going to church.

"Will I need to schedule an appointment to make my confessions?" Jewel asked, breaking a silence that hung in the air. She had been thinking about it, and she surprised herself when she asked it aloud. She and Grady had talked about it several times before, and he knew that talking to a priest was something she felt she needed to do. In part, it had made him angry that she felt she needed to be absolved for defending her own life, but such is the way of Catholics. Guilt is a part of life, and it was certainly part of the religion, though it wasn't necessarily a bad thing. "I suppose without guilt, evil would just run amuck," he had finally said relenting, knowing there was nothing he would ever be able to say to make her think or feel any differently.

"Grady said ya wanted ta talk ta Father. Ya just tell me when, and I'll call him an' tell him," Maggie said, reaching out to take Jewel's hand. "Ya have nothin' ta feel guilty for though. Grady said as ya'd no choice but ta save yer own life. Yer an inspiration ta women, and Tina felt so empowered by it that she went ta school the day after she heard the basics of the story, and punched the little boy who had been buggin' her, right in the nose!"

"She did?" Jewel asked alarmed. "What happened?"

"Well, we didn't really know about it before the principal called an' suspended her from school for three days. We knew this little boy liked her, but we didn't know that he was tryin' ta stick his hand down her shirt, an' had cornered her a few times at school. It had frightened her a little, but after she heard what ya did Jewel, she went ta school the next day, punched that little scoundrel right in the nose, an' told him he better not ever touch her again!" Maggie said slapping her hand down on her leg. "Well, Diana went down there, an' at first the boy's ma was upset with Tina, but after he confessed ta harassin' her, well, I hate ta think what the woman did ta punish him. I suspect gettin' flattened by a girl two years younger than him was just about all the punishment he needed, but then Paxton and Thomas, an' even little Joseph, made sure ta let him know there would be no more funny business or he'd get what was comin' ta him."

"That explains why she's been so glued to me. Thank you for telling me that. That means a lot to me. I'm glad something good has come from it! Maybe there are a few others out there who decided to stand up for themselves because of it. That makes it seem... I don't know... worth it maybe?" Jewel said shrugging and smiling a little.

"You'll go ta confession. Give it ta God and you'll feel whole again. It's just the way it is," Maggie said, nodding to Jewel as if it were simply an obvious fact that was common knowledge.

After casually talking and drinking coffee half the morning, they all finally got ready and headed out to church. Jewel was surprised to see Rudy and his family there. It wasn't surprising to see them at church exactly; it just seemed like a monumental task to get a family of eight anywhere, and so early. Jewel wondered how they managed, but before she had much time to think of it, she ended up with Tina and Joseph grabbing her hand, and taking turns cuddling up next to her throughout the services. She sat with Tina on one side of her, and Joseph on the other, with Grady sitting next to Joseph daring to put a hand on Jewel's knee occasionally, only to have it quickly removed by the boy.

It was a small town, so having a stranger at Sunday services was something that had many people looking her way. She met a few of their eyes as they looked at her, and she was surprised when she was met with a smile instead of the pity she had grown accustomed to back home. She wondered how many of the people in there had heard her story, and she smiled remembering the story Maggie told her about Tina feeling empowered enough to stand up for herself. She smiled down at the girl, hugging her close to her, which brought a huge smile to the girls face.

Jewel listened closely as Father started his homily. "Sometimes we get to see miracles happen before our very eyes. Beyond all odds, we find we can survive, even thrive, because of the Grace of God," he said making eye contact with her. "God doesn't have you on puppet strings, controlling your life. You don't pray to have God intervene and act on your behalf. You pray, and through Christ, you have strength. *We can do all things through Christ who gives us strength.* Now, does that mean that I can go play in the NFL?" he asked looking out in the crowd, waiting for their response. "No. It doesn't, does it? It means that if you bring Christ into your life, then whatever it is that you are doing... whatever it is that you need to do, you can do that much better... much easier... more gracefully, and more thoroughly, if you do it with Christ in your heart, and in your life."

Jewel listened to every word, remembering how she felt when she had pushed faith out of her life. After her parents died, she tried to convince herself that there was no God, but she always knew it wasn't true. Faith was part of who she was, and she knew that everything Father said was meant for her, and she wondered how many of those sitting there felt the same way. She enjoyed the services more than she had ever enjoyed them. She never liked it as a kid, and she liked it even less after the death of her parents, but it had become something she felt completely drawn to suddenly.

She remembered the feeling she had after being washed down the river. It was real to her, as if her dad had been there in flesh and blood, and she couldn't get it out of her mind. She had never quit believing in God, but she had certainly felt angry and betrayed. It was confusing to her, but everything started to make sense to her after that day by the river, without her ever really knowing or understanding why. It just was.

After services they had all gone out to breakfast, and Jewel not only got to meet the infamous Mrs. Pinker, who was indeed a very beautiful woman who had stolen Grady's heart as a child, she got to meet Debbie as well.

"You're an ass Grady!" Debbie yelled at him, standing there with her two kids, yelling at him on the sidewalk as they left the restaurant.

"I never made any promises ta ya Debbie."

"No! You didn't, but you're still an ass! You should have told me so I didn't have to find out in the middle of the sidewalk in broad daylight," she said, yelling more loudly, making as big a scene as she possibly could.

"I don't owe ya a damn thing! Not one damn thing! I told ya how I felt before I left. Nothin' was ever goin' ta happen between us Debbie. If ya didn't want ta believe it, that's yer own damn fault," he said, walking away from her as she followed behind him, screaming.

Patrick and Maggie were standing with Jewel, while Grady tried to get away from Debbie, but Debbie just kept following him and yelling at him, dragging her kids behind her as she did, and Jewel had to resist the urge to go over there and comfort the kids who looked terrified.

"For Christ's sake Debbie, think of what yer doin' ta yer kids right now. Yer scarin' them. Don't ya ever think of anyone but yerself? Get a grip of yerself, and don't ya dare come by the house either!"

"Don't you tell me what to do!" she yelled after him, never once even glancing at the two kids she was dragging behind her. "Christ Grady, couldn't you have at least picked a girl your own age? Did you have to go to the grade school to find some young tart? Is that it?"

"Now that's enough! I'll not have ya callin' her names Debbie. She's one of the best people I've ever known, and you'll not disrespect her. Do ya understand!"

"You'll just use her like you used me!" she yelled.

"Ya used me Debbie, and ya damn well know it! Just as ya used yer husband, and all the men ya cheated on him with. If ya had half a brain, ya'd beg him ta take ya back, and do good by him. He's a good man Debbie, and he's the father of yer children. Do the right thing, and leave me alone!"

They all piled in Patrick and Maggie's car, and Grady was fuming. He hadn't really expected to make a public scene on his first day back home, but there was no helping it when it came to Debbie. She was completely without any kind of filter. She lacked any type of consideration for consequences. She was a person who was constantly just right there in your face, and she never once seemed to notice that the people around her were always fighting to free themselves from her presence.

"How did I ever put up with her in high school?" Grady asked rhetorically.

"Ya were so busy in high school. If she hadn't been pursuin' ya night and day, ya likely wouldn't have dated anyone," Patrick said shaking his head. "Man but she's an aggressive woman."

"She came by the house at least once a week, askin' about ya, and gushin' about missin' ya an' such. The woman makes me nuts!" Maggie added, swatting in the air as if she were trying to swat a pesky fly.

"I'm sorry Jewel," Grady said grabbing her hand. "I didn't know how that was goin' ta go. Ya never know with that woman. She's predictably unpredictable, like a hurricane."

"Well she's lovely. I can certainly see why you dated her," Jewel said sarcastically, thinking of the two sad little faces that had been looking up at their mom the whole time.

Grady was still fuming, and Jewel could sense that he wasn't really appreciating the sarcasm, but she was feeling a little miffed herself. She knew that it wasn't Grady's fault. He had obviously made it clear to her that there was no chance of there being anything between them, but it had turned into an awkward and embarrassing moment, and she didn't like that kind of confrontation. It was only then that she remembered Troy. The scene between her and Troy might make this one look like a cakewalk. She hadn't ever heard Troy raise his voice, but if there was anyone who deserved it, it was her.

"It's alright Grady," Jewel finally said, squeezing his hand in return and smiling up at him. "It's not your fault, and I can hardly blame her. You're a good catch. I wouldn't be too happy either if you didn't want me. I think I would be crying and yelling in the streets too."

Grady and Jewel were sitting in the backseat of Patrick's car, with Grady's dad and mom in the front as they drove toward home. Grady was so taken with Jewel in that moment that it all came flooding out of him without him having any ability to stop it.

"Will ya marry me Jewel? I can't wait another minute ta hear ya say yes. I can't live my life without knowin' you'll be with me all the days of my life," he said pleadingly. "Marry me."

Jewels heart was beating fast hearing him speak the words she herself felt every moment she was with him, and his dad nearly drove into a fence when his mom squealed with excitement.

"Oh my Lord in Heaven!" Maggie said loudly, slapping her knee.

"Oh Grady! Of course, I'll marry you. I love you," she said, throwing her arms around his neck. "You know I can't live without you."

"We're goin' ta have a weddin'!" Maggie said excitely. "Pull this car over Paddy. I've got ta jump up an' down an' hug these two."

Grady knew that asking Jewel to marry him in the backseat of his parent's car as they drove home from a horrible scene on the sidewalk, was probably not the most romantic way to propose to a woman, but he couldn't help himself. He suddenly had perfect clarity. He knew that the ability to think of life without Jewel in it had ceased to exist from the moment he met her, and it had come flooding out of him with absolute certainty. They were so wrapped up in each other they could barely contain themselves, and they didn't even notice when they pulled up in front of someone else's house.

"We have ta stop and tell Diana an' Rudy," Patrick said excitedly.

"They're gettin' married! They're gettin' married!" Maggie was yelling as she ran up to the door that Rudy and his family were making their way out of.

"What?" Rudy said, coming up to Grady and Jewel smiling.

"I couldn't see waitin' another second," Grady said shrugging as Maggie and Patrick filled them in on the details.

"Now can I call ya Auntie Jewel?" Joseph asked excitedly.

"Of course ya can!" Diana said, wrapping her arms around Jewel excitedly.

They were all hugging and congratulating them, right there in the front yard of Rudy's house, as the scene with Debbie was completely forgotten.

"We'll ask Father if he can do the services," Maggie said hugging Grady again.

"Wait! Time out! This is Jewel's wedding too. Don't ya think she ought ta have a say?" Grady said mouthing the words, *I'm sorry* at Jewel.

"I would love to get married here. What do you think Grady?" Jewel asked smiling up at him. "I mean… I don't have any family back home. This seems like the perfect place… unless you were hoping for a long engagement?"

"I want ta marry ya this second. We belong ta each other Jewel," Grady said cradling her face in his hands, kissing her firmly.

Before Jewel and Grady even knew what hit them, there was a whirlwind of plans being made, and it wasn't long after that when Father O'Malley himself showed up at the door, and proceeded with the hugging and plan making that had taken place since the announcement was made. There was a flurry of ideas swirling around so quickly, that nobody even noticed when Grady pulled Jewel out the front door to escape the frenzy.

"I'm sorry Jewel. Somethin' just came over me. I couldn't hold it in another minute," he said when he finally got her somewhere quiet.

"Don't be sorry. That was amazing Grady. Your family loves you, and you're going to be leaving soon, and now they're so happy," she said hugging him again.

"But what about you Jewel?"

"I've never been happier. Don't you know that?" she said searching his eyes.

"Well, do ya want ta get married here? I mean, I know things like this are different for women. Ya might have an idea of what ya want fer a weddin'."

"Until now, I haven't ever been able to imagine getting married, and now, it all seems perfectly clear. Right here with your family and everyone around us. I can't think of anything that would be better. I can't imagine going anywhere else."

"Ya've got lots of family now Jewel. Probably more than ya bargained for," he said grinning at her.

"What was it that made you suddenly want to ask me after seeing Debbie?" she asked a little curious.

"It wasn't sudden Jewel. I've been tryin' ta slow down and wait, tryin' ta give ya time ta heal, and get things sorted out with yer ranch, and with Troy. Everythin' between us has happened so fast, but then seein' Debbie, and seein' how ya handled that ugly scene… the sad look ya had on yer face when ya looked at her little kids, so scared and confused. I don't know Jewel. I just couldn't wait another second. I hope ya don't feel like yer bein' pushed inta somethin'."

"I feel like we've been trying to stop something that can't be stopped. It kind of seems fast, but then again, it seems like I've known you my whole life. I can't see my life without you in it. I don't feel like I'm being pushed into anything. I'm happy," she said wrapping her arms around him.

"I just had ta get ya away for a minute. It all happened so fast, but we should probably head back if yer up for it," he said after hugging and kissing her right there on the sidewalk for a long time.

"Let's go then."

They made their way back to Rudy and Diana's house, and it seemed that they were hardly missed, though the frenzy had died down a little. They seemed to have made as many of the plans as possible, and everyone was laughing and talking excitedly. The hugging continued once again as they walked through the door. There was going to be a celebration!

"There's a little paperwork to take care of, but I don't see why there's no reason we can't get this done. How does next Saturday sound to you?" Father O'Malley said to Grady and Jewel.

"That sounds wonderful," Jewel said excitedly. "Do you really think we can get everything done by then? That's just six days from now."

"I used ta be a weddin' coordinator, an' I still do it on occasion. Ya just tell me what ya like, an' we'll make it beautiful!" Maggie said, grabbing her and hugging her once again. "We can call Mrs. Mowry an' get ya a beautiful cake made, an' we can get flowers from Mabel's Flower Shop, an' we can go ta Rapid City an' get dresses an' decorations…"

Jewel smiled at Maggie and Diana as they talked about all the things they could get, and all the ideas they had to make the wedding special, and ideas on where they could go for the reception. Her head was swimming. She never imagined that a wedding required so much planning and preparation, and she was glad that the two of them seemed to have everything under control.

"Hold onto your hat sister! These two are going to take you on the ride of your life. You thought the Alaskan Wilderness was tough, let's just see how you fair after a few shopping trips with these two. You might want to pack your pistol just in case," Rudy joked, coming up to wrap an arm around Jewel, as Diana and Maggie talked about all the different possibilities for the wedding.

"Do you think that will be enough? It only has five shots," Jewel joked in return, throwing an arm comfortably around Rudy.

"Something tells me you'll be just fine," he said winking at her.

CHAPTER 35

CONFESSION

Nobody had gotten much sleep Sunday night. The adults were celebrating with too much Irish whiskey, and everyone was so excited making plans, that sleeping had gone out the window. Grady and his dad headed out early. Patrick wanted to take him around and show him the construction jobs he was working on, and spend a little father and son time together, while Jewel stayed behind in the able hands of her future mother-in-law.

"I arranged for ya ta meet with Father O'Malley taday Jewel. I'll drop ya by an' ya can call me when yer ready," Maggie said, hugging Jewel once again.

"Thank you. That's so thoughtful of you," Jewel said. She was eager to go talk to the priest. She needed to talk to him about everything that happened with Aaron, and about the shooting specifically. She hadn't told anyone the whole story, and she was starting to feel a little anxious about it. She told Grady bits and pieces, but the fine details were like little bits of cancer that were eating away at her, and she felt like she needed to tell someone. She knew she didn't have to tell a priest to be forgiven, but she liked the tradition of talking to a priest to confess her sins. She couldn't imagine any therapy that could be more uplifting and freeing than that. It's something she had done since her first communion in the second grade, and it had usually proven to be the best medicine when something was bothering her, as long as it didn't include talking about the death of her parents.

They had gotten ready, and Maggie and her drove down to the church where Father O'Malley was waiting for her. The church was the centerpiece of the town, and Jewel smiled looking at it, remembering how good she'd felt after Sunday services. It was a beautiful church with its large columns in front holding up the gable where a statue of St. Paul stood like a beacon. The large dome behind St. Paul stood high like a lighthouse signaling the believers, helping them find their way home. She stepped inside walking through the ambulatory, pausing to say a prayer before heading toward the offices to look for Father O'Malley, since she didn't find him near any of the confessionals.

"Hello again Father," Jewel said, finally finding him in his office, "will we be going to the confessional?"

"There's nobody here but the two of us. If you would feel more comfortable there then we certainly can, but it's my understanding that you're in need of more than a confession," Father said.

"That's true," she said, not sure where to start, trying to mask the nervousness she felt. "It might seem like more of an exorcism by the time I tell you everything I need to tell you."

"Tell me as much as you like, and don't worry about embarrassing me or yourself. Nothing you say will leave this room. Speak freely. Open up your heart and just let it out," he said to her warmly. "You would be amazed at what can happen when you open your heart to God."

They talked a little about her background, and about his, and they got to know each other a little with some small talk. Jewel immediately felt comfortable, and started from the very beginning, which is to say that she started from the minute she first met Aaron. There had been a part of her that worried that she had led Aaron on, just as she had with the doctor in Iraq, and she wondered if she had invited his attention somehow. She told him every lurid detail, stopping only long enough to sob and gather herself back together enough to continue. She told him about the rape and the shooting, and finished with all the nightmares that had been haunting her. They talked about everything over several hours, until Jewel had completely run out of anything to say about it. She leaned back in her chair feeling lightened, and they sat together in silence for several minutes.

"To sin or not to sin seems so simple doesn't it?" he finally asked her, but without waiting for an answer. "People have a way of making it sound simple when they're casting judgment, but it's more of a challenge in practice. It's not all black and white either, though it looks like it should be, but I think intention is what defines sin. It wasn't your intention to go out and kill a man. You intended to help him. You're a nurse. You used your skill to heal him, and he threatened your life in return," Father O'Malley said, leaning back, looking at her intently. "We're supposed to turn the other cheek like Jesus did, is what most obedient Christians would say, but there's one big problem with that… you're not Jesus. We can try to be like Him, and follow his example, but we are human. We're mere humans with a God-given need to survive."

"You're equating what you did with someone who intentionally goes out and commits murder," he said locking eyes with her. "*Thou Shalt Not Kill* is what the commandment says. For most people that is black and white and very simple, because they will never be faced with a situation where they will need to consider it, but you have, and you know what your decision was. Your decision was to live. You made a decision to value the life *you* were given. It was a choice you were forced to make," Father said, leaning back and smiling. "You made the decision to live Jewel, and I think it was the best decision for you, and I'm glad you chose life."

"You intended to keep yourself from being a victim, and you had no choice but to follow your human instinct to keep yourself alive. In doing so, you were faced with an impossible decision that is neither right nor wrong… it just is. However, you have accepted Jesus as your savior, and if you ask Him to forgive you, He will. The trick is to find forgiveness for yourself. Once you do, you will be free. The bruises have healed, but I can see that the heart hasn't healed just yet. Pray about it Jewel. Ask God to forgive you, and He will, and then ask God to help you forgive yourself, and you will. It may take time, but you will see the power of God if you pray about it."

They talked like that for a long while, and when Jewel left, she felt like the weight of the world lifted off her shoulders. It was a beautiful day, and she hadn't been able to get a hold of Maggie so she decided to walk back to the house. It was several miles, but it felt good, and she loved breathing the country air as she walked away from town toward the house. It was the first time since the abduction she had been anywhere on her own, and she felt surprisingly well.

"You look like you did the first day we met you Jewel," Rudy said, catching up with her on the sidewalk.

"I do? What do you mean?" she asked, smiling at him, wrapping an arm around him as he came up beside her.

"You just seem happy and content, and you're just out here walking by yourself, not afraid of anything. It's good to see," he replied, putting an arm around her in return.

"I just came from meeting with Father O'Malley. He's a good man. I like him, and I feel better than I have in a while."

"And you're going to be my sister-in-law, so you're probably pretty excited about that as well."

"Of course! You know I only said yes for that reason right?" she joked.

"Yep! I knew it! It was obvious," he laughed.

"Why didn't you ever tell me you were born in Wyoming Rudy?" She comfortably rested her hands in the crook of his arm as they slowly walked down the street.

He had a surprised look on his face, but then finally answered. "I don't know. It would be a short story," he answered, tensing up.

"Have you ever thought about finding out who they are?"

He hesitated, but then proceeded. "A couple times I thought about it. There was a guy I knew who had to have a bone marrow transplant, and the most likely people who would be donors were his family members. I wondered what I would do. That was before my kids were born. I suppose now it doesn't matter."

"I'm sorry if it feels like I'm prying. You don't meet very many people from Wyoming when you're out in the world," she explained.

"You're not prying. Maybe now that I'm retired from the military, I'll have more time to think of things like that. I don't really like talking about it much, but

I probably should. That's the thing about Diana… and Grady too… they don't let people like us keep things too bottled up. They yank it out of us whether we like it or not, and that's usually the thing we need the most," he confided, skillfully changing the subject.

"I assume you'll be Grady's best man. Do you think Diana would stand up for me?" she asked a little hesitantly.

"Oh geez Jewel. I thought that maybe you two already had it arranged. She's been going on and on about it. She might have made an assumption. She's just so excited."

"Well, I don't really have anyone. I mean, I have friends that I grew up with, but I haven't been very good about staying in touch. It would be awkward if I called one of them unexpectedly and asked them. Besides, I love Diana. I think it would be perfect to have you and Diana standing up for us."

"I just have one little favor to ask," he said, eyeing her with some amusement.

"What is it?"

"Joseph wants to give you away. He said that since your dad wasn't here, and since you two are best friends…," he said, trailing off with a chuckle.

"Ha! That is so cute," she laughed. "Well we are best friends, so I can't see where I could possibly go wrong with that. I would love that Rudy. I was wondering about who would give me away. That would be great."

Jewel was smiling so much she could hardly contain herself. From the moment she said yes, she had been worried about not having anyone to stand up for her or give her away, and now everything seemed to be falling into place. It wasn't the fairytale wedding that girls dream of, without her mom and dad there, but from where Jewel was standing, it was better than she could have imagined. Something inside her felt changed. It was as if a switch flipped on that allowed her to accept what is, making the best of it, and that's exactly what was happening before her eyes. She felt like running through the streets laughing and cheering, and after saying a quick goodbye to Rudy, that's practically what she did, never stopping until she made it back to the house.

~~~~~~~~

"Hello?" Jewel said, creeping into the house. She walked around in every room, and to the backyard, and was disappointed not to find anyone there to share in her excitement. She headed down the stairs, to the back bedroom in the basement, to find Grady asleep on their bed.

She stood there in the doorway watching him for a while. He was lying flat on his back with his hands neatly folded over the top of him, one bare foot resting over the other. It was one of those moments when she could trace with her eyes over every square inch of him, indulging herself, and taking him all in, stealing her breath away as she did. She traced his jawline, making her way down to the muscles that she could see defined through his white t-shirt he always wore. She made her way down the full length admiring the nice way he filled out his faded blue jeans, until she could no longer stand there without touching him. She walked in and quietly shut the door, locking it as she did.

"What are ya doin' Jewel?" he asked without ever opening his eyes or moving.

Jewel smiled, quickly slipping off her shoes, and crawled on top of him. "I was going to start by kissing you passionately until you felt like you were going to go completely mad," she whispered, kissing him softly at first, but then deeper and more urgently.

"If this is what confession does for ya, then I'm a big fan," he said, kissing her in return, carefully pulling her closer to him, but holding back, not wanting to push her into anything she wasn't ready for.

Everything that Jewel had been afraid of, and had been holding back, was gone, and she ran her hands up his shirt, urging him to take it off, slipping her own off as she straddled him.

"Are ya sure about this Jewel? Are ya ready?" he gasped. He had been waiting patiently for this moment, taking cold showers, and willing himself not to become aroused by her as he sat by her or slept next to her night after night. He hadn't expected her to want any type of sexual contact so soon. He figured it would be several more weeks… or even months.

"I want you Grady. I want to feel you on me," she urged him in between kisses.

Without being able to control himself any longer, he grabbed her and rolled her onto her back, kissing her deeply, skillfully unhooking her bra as he did. She gasped as she felt his warm tongue on her breasts, first one, and then the other, teasing her as he did. She knew he was trying to hold back a little, wanting to be gentle with her, but she was feeling no such reservation. She suddenly needed to feel him all over her. It was as if every touch, and every kiss, was erasing Aaron from her once and for all. The fear of never being intimate with Grady again was gone, and his touch became the cure that was now releasing her from all that she had been afraid of, and she completely let go of everything outside of that moment.

Grady lifted himself up, pulling off her bottoms before taking off his own, both of them lost in the desire of the other. He crawled on top of her, and she arched up to meet him, wanting to feel his skin on hers, parting her legs in answer to the urgency they both felt.

He slowly ran his fingers down between her legs, wanting to see her react to his touch, looking for any sign that she wasn't ready, but he found none. He watched her as she closed her eyes and tipped her head back, lifting her body to meet his, pushing his touch into her even deeper, until he could no longer hold back anymore.

They joined together, instantly finding the slow rhythmic motion they needed, both of them wrapped up in the other, until finding the release that overcame them both, leaving them breathless and euphoric. They laid like that for a long time, neither one of them wanting to move, holding onto the moment as long as they could, touching each other in a way they had been afraid of since the abduction.

"I was just lyin' here thinkin' of ya, wantin' ta hold ya and touch ya," he finally said breaking the silence, "and then all the sudden, ya come in, and my prayers are answered."

"I'm pretty sure that wasn't God's doing," she said smiling.

"Ya surprise me Jewel. I was expectin' ya ta be teary-eyed after tellin' yer story ta Father."

"I feel like I was just released from prison. The kind of prison where they torture you with mind-controlling propaganda, making you believe something that's beyond reason and logic. Father O'Malley has a way with words, and... I don't know... I guess it was just the telling of it that helped a little," she said lying back. "I needed to tell someone that was neutral. I mean... I didn't want to tell you everything, because you would have pictured it in your mind, and I didn't want you to. That would have hurt you, which would hurt me even more."

"I'm glad ya feel better, and not just so I could take ya ta bed, though that's a nice perk," he said smiling at her, "and I'm definitely not goin' ta ever be a monk. I would have waited as long as it takes Jewel, but keepin' my hands off ya is no easy task."

"It's not easy for me either," she said, reaching up to kiss him again. "Even that night in the hospital, as badly bruised, and tired, and afraid as I was, I still felt desire Grady. That never went away."

"Thank ya for that Jewel. I needed ta hear that," he whispered, stroking her face.

"Why are you here anyway?" she asked, suddenly remembering that he was supposed to be with his dad, and his mom was supposed to be there waiting for her.

"Dad collapsed, and I rushed him ta the hospital, but he's okay. He gets himself worked up and excited, and he has seizures sometimes. He always has. The only thing that calms him down is Mom. They're runnin' the usual tests on him. They'll probably be back tonight or maybe in the mornin'," he answered casually.

"Grady! Oh my gosh! Why did he get so worked up?" she asked anxiously.

"He's fine, and don't ya dare try leavin' this bed woman," he said eyeing her narrowly. "This happens once every two or three months when he doesn't get enough sleep, and then he thinks he can go out, and climb on a roof, and show up a bunch of twenty year olds. He can't climb on roofs anymore, because he gets vertigo, and that's what causes it."

"So why does he do it?"

"Because he's stubborn, and he thinks nobody can do anything right except him," he said tensing up a little shaking his head.

"What does he do for his vertigo?"

"Not one thing! He comes home and pretends like it doesn't exist until the next time it happens."

"Massage therapy is very effective in treating vertigo that causes seizures. I studied this, and I actually interned with a physical therapist one summer while I was in school. I saw the benefits of it. Has he ever tried anything like that?"

"Probably not… everyone just wants him ta take drugs, but he doesn't like the drugs, because it turns him inta a zombie. As far as I know, nobody has ever offered anything except the medication."

"Would you like me to talk to him? It'll give us something more to talk about while we're sipping our morning coffee," she said, stroking the worry lines on Grady's forehead.

"He's a reasonable man. He might consider somethin' like that. If ya wouldn't mind talkin' to him about it…," he shrugged.

"I wouldn't mind at all. I love your family Grady. You're blessed."

"I'm glad ya think so Jewel, because they're goin' ta be yer family too pretty soon," he said smiling at her, reaching to pull her in for another kiss.

"Jewel McDonald," she said rolling it off her tongue several times.

"What's yer middle name Jewel?" he asked awkwardly, feeling like he should already know it.

"I'm not telling! I seriously don't know what my parents were thinking!"

"Tell me woman!" he said tickling her.

"What's your middle name? Tell me yours, and then I'll tell you mine," she said grabbing his hands.

"It's Ryan, now spill it!"

"Ryan? I like it. If we have a son, I think we should name him Ryan. Ryan McDonald. That sounds nice."

"Yer stallin', now spill it woman!"

"I change my mind! I'm not telling you," she screamed as he took her down and started tickling her harder.

"Tell me or I'm goin' ta tickle ya 'til the neighbors call the cops, because you'll be screamin' so loud!"

"Okay okay okay!" she yelled, laughing and trying to catch her breath.

"It's Esther! Esther! Can you believe they named me Esther?" she laughed as she pulled a pillow down over her head.

"Come now… it's not so bad. Esther was my grandmother's name," he said pulling the pillow off her head.

"Really?" she asked feeling hopeful.

"No! Not really. That's a hideous name Jewel! Nobody in my family has ever had such a hideous name!" he said wrinkling his nose, pretending to be offended.

"Oh you!" she said grabbing the pillow, hitting him with it repeatedly.

"I'm just kiddin' Jewel," he said laughing. "Esther is a fine name… for a goat maybe, or a…" he trailed off in fits of laughter.

"You're officially on my list!" she said laughing along with him.

"I love that yer middle name is Esther. It's perfect. It's absolutely perfect," he said smiling at her a little more seriously. "I'm serious Jewel! Yer just this perfect woman… yer beautiful and smart. Yer an amazin' singer, and yer this exceptionally lovin' and carin' woman," he said cradling her face, kissing her gently, "and yer middle name is Esther, and I love it. Jewel *Esther* McDonald. It's perfect."

"So you like it, because it makes me flawed?"

"No, it doesn't make ya flawed. It's a bible name. Esther is the name of one of the most amazin' women in the history of the world. I think it's perfect, because it's not perfect," he said shrugging. "I don't know… sometimes I just look at ya, and wonder how somethin' so perfect would want ta spend her life with me. I'm unemployed. I've been discharged from the Army. I don't know what I'm doin'. Why do ya want me Jewel?" he asked, looking down at his hands with a more serious tone.

"How can you ask me that?" she asked incredulously. "Don't you know that I fell in love with you the first time I saw you?"

"Ya don't need me. Ya can take care of yerself. Ya have a ranch. Ya have a good aim. There's nothin' ya can't do," he said throwing his hands up in exasperation.

"Except love… I couldn't give love. I couldn't accept love. I didn't know anything about love until I met you, and it was the one thing that I needed the most. Without it, nothing else matters," she said, locking her eyes with his, wanting to make him see the love she felt and how important it was to her.

"Ya don't need me for love Jewel. There'd be a thousand men linin' up ta love ya if ya gave them half a chance."

"I didn't know how to give anyone a chance until I met you. Do you think I didn't have men who were interested in me? You took something that was broken, and you brought it back to life. Can't you see that? You've given me everything I need. Having a good aim doesn't matter without you. When I was in Iraq, I would see the bodies of the soldiers that had died, and it always seemed like such a shame to me, because they had families that were going to grieve them. I always felt that it should have been me. I should have gone home in a body bag, because I had nobody. There was nobody waiting at home to grieve me. You gave me a reason to *not* want to go home in a body bag. Do you have any idea how good that feels?" she said fighting back tears.

They both sat in silence for a moment, afraid to say another word, both of them considering the things said by the other.

"Does your dad want you to stay and run the business Grady?"

"No, but I feel like I should. I would be able ta do it really well, and I could give ya a life. I could provide for ya, and give ya things that ya need."

"I don't need *things* Grady! and I don't need you to settle for a life you don't want just so you can provide for me. How shallow do you think I am?" she asked angrily.

"I don't mean it like that. I just want ta take care of ya, and give ya somethin'… hell I don't know Jewel!"

"Then come to Wyoming with me and help me. I can't manage my ranch on my own. How many twenty two year old women do you know that have a twenty-eight thousand acre ranch to run Grady? I can't run all the equipment or fix things. I don't know anything about engines or repairing roofs or plumbing. I inherited a huge ranch I can't manage on my own. Do you have any idea what I'm faced with?" she said getting up, starting to get dressed and feeling overwhelmed, which always prompted her to want to run away.

"I'm sorry Jewel… stop… come here," he said, taking the clothes from her hands and leading her back to the bed. "I don't know what I'm sayin'. I wish I could have saved ya. I think I would feel better had I shot that bastard for ya. I feel like I let ya down. I didn't get there fast enough. I didn't hear ya yellin' for me at the bathrooms. I should have got there faster."

"You found me Grady. You got there before the police managed to make it out the front door. You came because you knew something was wrong right away. You carried me down off the mountain. You know I would have never made it down by myself. Can you imagine what would have happened to me that night if I would have made it halfway down, and you know I would have tried. I would have frozen to death Grady, and you know it, but there's nothing I can say that's going to make you feel better. You have to forgive yourself. You have to reconcile it in your own mind just as I have. You know that everything I've said is right, but you have to deal with it, and you have to do it without pushing me toward a line of a thousand men who would never be able to give me what it is I really need."

"Yer right Jewel. I know yer right."

"Are you having second thoughts about getting married?" she asked feeling suddenly scared.

"God no! Don't ever think that Jewel. I've no doubts about it."

"Maybe you need to talk to Father O'Malley. Maybe it would help. We've been through a lot," she said shrugging her shoulder.

"I already did Jewel. I guess I just needed ta hear it from ya. Nothin' seems real anymore unless I hear ya say it. I love ya that much," he said hugging her close to him.

"Don't ever scare me like that again. I can't imagine my life without you," she said cradling his face, kissing him thoroughly.

"You won't ever have ta Jewel," he said rolling her on her back, wanting to take in every ounce of her, kissing her softly and soundly, and taking his time with her as she pulled him in harder and deeper.

This time they lingered. They savored every moment as if in slow motion.

CHAPTER 36

THE PERFECT DAY

"What are ya doin' here so early man?" Grady asked as Rudy awoke him the next morning.

"Your dad's still in the hospital. They're running some more tests this morning, and I'm going to run some crews for him, but I need your help. I can't find his keys for the shop, and I could use some help on some other things."

"Alright, give me a minute. I'll be right up," Grady said, snuggling up to Jewel's naked body one last time, and crawling out of bed reluctantly.

They had both been stirring before Rudy came in, and Grady was longing to climb back in bed with her and share another moment like the ones they shared the night before, but he knew he needed to get up to help Rudy. He was being primed to take over as the General Manager for the company, but hadn't planned to start until he had settled in for a few days. Grady was hoping the transition would go well, in part, to make his own leaving a little easier. He got up and pulled on some clothes before climbing back on the bed to talk to Jewel.

"I'm goin' ta help Rudy taday. Mom and Diana are plannin' on takin' ya ta Rapid City for some bridal shoppin', but I need ya ta do me one favor," he said rolling her on her back to make sure she heard him, "when Mom offers ta buy ya yer bridal gown and things, just say okay. Can ya do that for me?"

"What? Why would she buy me things? That would be awkward," she said forcing her eyes open.

"Because she wants ta. She knows yer own mom isn't here, and she wants ta do it for ya. She has officially adopted ya whether ya marry me or not. She lost her own mom when she was a young girl. She knows what it's like Jewel. Just let her give ya what she herself needed when she was a young bride."

"Okay. I will, but of course I'll have to put up at least a small protest at first, just so I won't look like a complete beggar."

"Of course," he said smiling at her, kissing her forehead. "God I love ta look at ya in the mornin'," he said crawling on top of her for one last lingering hug and kiss before heading out, "with yer hair all messed up, and yer naked body beneath this thin sheet... do ya have any idea how hard yer makin' it ta leave?"

"You completely wore me out yesterday anyway. I need rest and rehydration. Now go!" she said smiling up at him.

She laid there for a long while, languishing in the peacefulness she felt. She could hear the muffled voices of the two men upstairs, and smiled at the familiarity of them. Her whole life was changing fast. It wasn't long ago that she had found herself completely alone, having pushed away the last few remaining friends and family she had, never letting anyone get close to her. What was it about these two men that finally allowed her to come out of her shell? They wouldn't let her push them away no matter how hard she tried, it was exactly what she needed, and it was at exactly the right time.

There she was, lying naked in the man's house, getting ready to go shopping for a wedding dress with his mom, and she couldn't be happier. She couldn't wait to try on dresses, to pick out just the right one, and she realized for the first time that it wasn't shopping for dresses that she had hated when she was younger; it was doing it without her mom. She was looking forward to going shopping with her future sister and mother-in-law. She was going with family. She belonged to something again. She was a part of something bigger than a single being again, and it felt amazing.

By the time Jewel got dressed and ready for the day, she could hear someone walking around, and she made her way upstairs.

"Good morning," she called out as she came up the stairs. She was dressed casually in khaki shorts and a blue tank top, wearing a pair of sandals she'd bought at a gas station during their road trip, and she couldn't wait to get out in the summer heat and spend the day shopping.

"There's my new daughter," Maggie said hugging her, also dressed casually for summer. Maggie was a beautiful woman. She looked much younger than her age, her skin barely showing signs of wrinkling, and her hair was still a light blond, all pinned up neatly.

"How's Patrick?" Jewel asked.

"He's mad as hell! They insist on keepin' him an' runnin' a few more tests, but the technician won't be available until this afternoon. He hit his head pretty hard when he collapsed. He needs a good rest, and their forcin' him ta stay in the hospital... with a little extra proddin' on my part," she said winking at Jewel, "and it's just what the man needs!"

"Good mornin'!" Diana said walking through the front door excitedly. "Are we ready for some shoppin'?"

"We thought we'd take ya to the mall in Rapid City ta do some bridal shoppin'. What do ya think Jewel?" Maggie asked. "I want ta buy ya a fine gown."

"I... I would absolutely love that!" Jewel said, remembering what Grady had told her that morning, "but you really don't have to buy it, I can pay for it."

"I insist. Will ya let me do it for ya? I really want ta," Maggie pleaded.

"Ummm… yeah… of course… I mean… if you just really want to then… yes… thank you," she said, stumbling through the feigned protest.

"Let's get a move on then! Times a wastin', and it's a little over an hour's drive. We got dresses ta buy, an' shoes, an' accessories. Got ta have accessories! Ya can't be walkin' down the aisle wearin' old shoes an' a borrowed dress like I did. We'll get ya fixed up right," Maggie said, gathering up her purse, pushing Diana and Jewel toward the door.

Jewel could feel her stomach rumbling with hunger, and she longed for some coffee, but she couldn't resist getting caught up in the excitement coming from Maggie. "Let me just grab my purse," Jewel said running down the stairs, not wanting to keep them waiting. She knew they were excited to go, but she also knew that nobody was as excited as she was. She couldn't remember a single time in her life when she had been excited to go shopping. Of course, before her parents died, she had taken it all for granted, but she intended to squeeze every ounce out of the day. She quickly grabbed an apple off the counter, and ran out to the car where they were waiting for her.

"Where are the kids?" Jewel asked, thinking of little Joseph wanting to give her away as she climbed in the car where they were already waiting for her.

"Alisha is takin' them ta the pool taday. I know their sizes better than they do anyways," Diana answered.

They talked non-stop on the car ride, with Maggie and Diana sharing stories of Grady and Rudy, and the kids, and them asking Jewel questions about living on a ranch. Maggie and Diana were careful not to ask too many questions, not wanting to stir up painful memories, but still wanting to get to know her better.

There were only a few stores in Rapid City where they could shop for bridal gowns, but the problem wasn't that they had too few options; the problem was they couldn't decide which of the many gowns to choose from. Jewel had never tried on so many dresses in her life. She remembered the prom dresses. She would grab a couple to try on in the right color and then make a choice, deciding everything within a few minutes. It was a ritual that had been lost to her back then, because she was just going through the motions. It wasn't real. She had been on autopilot trying to do all the things she was supposed to do, and say all the things she was supposed to say, but doing it and saying it without any emotional attachment.

This day was different though. She was completely swept up in the emotions she was supposed to be swept up in. She smiled, and laughed, and modeled every dress for Diana and Maggie with an excitement she forgot existed. She tried on shoes. She tried on jewelry, and helped pick out dresses for the rest of them. The ritual of picking out a wedding gown had quickly turned into one of the happiest days of her life.

"I like this one the best!" Jewel finally said walking out of the dressing room, wearing the dress they all liked the best. It was a strapless, A-line princess cut dress, adorned with lavish amounts of beadwork, and crystals dotted the length of the satin, making it look full and flowing, with a long train. Jewel stood on the step in the middle of all the mirrors to model it one last time for them; this time with the shoes she liked the best, which were the most attractive, because they had the lowest heel. She could actually walk in them, compared to the higher one's Diana had picked out that made her walk like a duck, and made them all laugh hysterically as she tried unsuccessfully to make her way to and from the dressing room. They were a simple, satin shoe with a two-inch heel, and they were perfect.

"Yer stunnin'! Absolutely stunnin'!" Maggie cried wiping away a tear.

"That's the one for sure Jewel," Diana said wiping away tears of her own. "Grady is goin' ta die when he sees ya! How do ya think you'll wear yer hair… up like this… or long with curls and such?"

"I don't know. What do you think? I've never really thought about things like that much before," she said, having never given thought to her hair, beyond deciding between a braid and a ponytail.

They tried on different jewelry, and Jewel tried things for her hair. Diana and Maggie each picked out dresses they would wear for the wedding. They also decided that it would be fitting to have Alisha, Melanie, and Tina wear bridesmaid dresses. Diana's dress was a full-length gown made up of darker lavender, while the girl's dresses were lighter in the same lavender tone that would hit the girls just above the ankles. Diana bought all the shoes for them, and Maggie arranged for all the tuxedo rentals for the boys. Jewel sat back and watched them in action. She was thankful they were there to make all these arrangements, or she would have been clueless as to where to begin.

"Thank you for this day," Jewel said, smiling at Maggie and taking her hand when they stopped for dinner. "You have no idea what today has meant to me."

"I think I've an idea. I know what it's like ta grow up without yer ma', though I had my da' still," she said thankfully.

"This is the first time in my life I've enjoyed shopping for dresses. I didn't know it could be fun."

"Ya took ta it real well!" Diana joked, making them all laugh as they remembered the many dresses she tried on.

They laughed and talked all through dinner and on the drive home, squeezing every last drop out of the day just as Jewel hoped. It had been wonderful, but Jewel was also excited to get back and see Grady. She thought about his lingering hug and kiss that morning, and her heart raced a little as she remembered the day before. *In just four days I'm going to be married*, she thought smiling to herself, *there's just one thing missing.*

~~~~~~~~

"I need to call Troy," Jewel said quietly to Grady after they arrived back at the house. "I just feel like I need to at least tell him, instead of just showing up at home married."

"Of course Jewel. Do what ya need ta do darlin'. Come use the phone downstairs where you'll have some privacy," he said, taking her hand and leading her to the phone.

"I'm nervous," she said holding the phone in her hands.

"I'm sure he'll forgive ya Jewel if ya give him half a chance. He sounds like a good man. Just tell him yer sorry, and leave the details for another day. It's a good first step," he said standing in front of her with her face cupped in his hand, kissing her lightly before taking his leave.

Jewel's knees were shaking as she heard the phone ring, but she was too anxious to sit down.

"Hello?"

"Hi... ugh... Jolene. It's Jewel. Can I please talk to Troy?"

"Ummm... yeah... it's Jewel..." Jolene said trailing off, handing the phone to Troy.

"Jewel?"

"Yeah... Troy... it's me...," she said choking up.

"Are you alright Jewel? Is everything okay?" he asked alarmed, having lived in fear of a tragic phone call for the last several years.

"Troy. I'm perfect. Everything's fine. I have so much to tell you, and I have a thousand apologies to make to you, but for right now, I just have to tell you something."

"What is it Jewel?" he asked confused, and a little annoyed.

"I'm going to be coming home, but Troy... I'm getting married on Saturday," she blurted out excitedly.

"Married? You? You let someone get within a hundred yards of you? Ugh... I'm sorry. I shouldn't have said that."

"No. It's okay Troy. You have every right to be mad at me. I've been horrible, and I wouldn't blame you if you never wanted to speak to me again, but things are different now. I'm... well, I'm okay again... finally, and I just wanted you to know. I know it's unfair of me to say this, but none of it would have been possible without you. You were the best friend I could have ever asked for, and I just wanted to tell you."

"I don't know what to say Jewel. You left me here to pick up all the pieces for you. You never even asked, you just assumed. You never even answered me, or sent a card or anything when I said I was getting married, and then you call me and tell me I was the best friend you could have asked for. Wow! I don't know what to say."

"I know Troy. I don't expect anything from you. I'll be coming home, and I'll take care of my own responsibilities. You won't have to worry about them anymore. I just hope you'll let me talk to you and try to explain. I just pray that you'll forgive me one day. You deserved better than that."

"I'm a little floored right now Jewel. I didn't know if you were dead or alive. I just need to take a little while to think about things. I don't know what to say right now."

"I understand. I just wanted to tell you I was getting married, and that I was coming home. I didn't want to just show up married. You can reach me at this number if you decide you want to talk to me. I'm sorry Troy. I'm really very sorry," she said hanging up the phone.

When she hung up, she took a long deep breath. She couldn't believe how calm and cool Troy had been. She was almost disappointed. She felt like she deserved to be yelled at and scolded for hours, but as usual, Troy was kind and levelheaded. She smiled a little thinking about the sound of his voice, hearing him say Jewel the way only he does, pronouncing it almost with a *Ch* at the beginning the way he did when they were little kids.

She didn't know if Troy would ever forgive her, but she laid back and smiled at the day, sighing heavily. It had been a perfect day, laughing and talking with Grady's mom and sister, picking out her wedding dress in anticipation of marrying Grady, and she smiled thinking of Troy. *It was good to hear his voice again. I don't deserve forgiveness, but I'm not running anymore, and that's really something.*

She made her way back up the stairs, and smiled as Grady caught her eye. She watched him trying to keep up with the chatter as Diana and Maggie described the bridesmaid dresses, and talked about the tuxedo rentals, giving them a list of when each of them needed to go down for their fittings, and then pick up their rental.

"I'm makin' ya responsible for this Rudy!" Maggie said waving a finger at him. "Ya make sure all the men get their fittins', pick up their rentals, an' get their shoes."

She watched as the kids ran screaming through the house, playing tag, and hide-and-go-seek. All of it made her smile, but she noticed that Patrick was missing, and decided to make her way out to the back deck where he liked to sit. Grady had brought him home from the hospital earlier while they had been out shopping, and he was feeling a little upset by the whole event.

"Are you feeling better?" she asked, finding him sitting quietly on the deck with a frown on his face.

"I feel alright. I've been poked an' prodded, an' nobody in those places ever listens. They just talk, an' they're nothin' more than drug dealers." Patrick was a large man, and Jewel imagined his pride was hurt more than anything, having been brought down by something inside him that he couldn't control.

"Grady said you had vertigo. Would you ever consider massage therapy instead of drugs? I've seen it work, and it can be very effective for some people. I interned one summer for a physical therapist, and I was amazed at some of the results."

"Grady mentioned that ya said somethin' about that. Yer the first person in the medical profession ta offer an alternative ta medication. I'd be willin' ta try anything that doesn't make me feel like a zombie," he said softening a little.

"Let's try it then. Is there anywhere in this house that's quiet?" she asked with little hope, chuckling a little as the noise flowed out of every room.

"That's a very good question young lady. There's one place an' it has a decent table in it that may serve as a massage table if yer offerin'. Let me tell Maggie, so she can keep the kids upstairs."

They made their way down into the basement to a room that was on the opposite end of where Grady and Jewel slept. There was a long, skinny folding table in there that had been used previously as a makeshift bar, and it was the perfect height for giving someone a massage. Jewel laid some blankets down to make him comfortable, and started with the massage.

"Now just lay still and be quiet. Close your eyes, and try not to think of anything. If you have to think of something, then think of something quiet and peaceful."

She started on his head, positioning her thumbs and fingers in the pressure points the way she had been taught, slowly releasing tension and built up pressure. She closed her eyes, trying to remember every pressure point, and what each one meant, slipping into a slow, quiet song as she usually did when she worked with people.

> *Friend of the home: as when in Galilee*
> *The mothers brought their little ones to Thee,*
> *So we, dear Lord, would now the children bring,*
> *And seek for them the shelter of Thy wing.*

She moved down his back, finding the relevant pressure points, and the hard nodules of tension that she felt, slowly releasing it, her hands working gently, quietly singing her song as she worked.

> *Lord, may Thy Church, as with a mother's care,*
> *For Thee the lambs within her bosom bear;*
> *And grant, as morning grows to noon, that they*
> *Still in her love and holy service stay.*

She made her way down to his feet, remembering the importance of each pressure point. This was the area most massage therapists missed, and she knew that for vertigo, it was usually the most important. She knew that the feet carried the most tension, and the pressure points in the feet could affect all the organs in the body. She continued the therapy, and she continued her singing.

> *Draw through the child the parents nearer Thee,*
> *Endue their home with growing sanctity;*
> *And gather all, by earthly homes made one,*
> *In Heaven, O Christ, when earthly days are done.*

"How does that feel?" she asked finally finishing an hour and several songs later.

"My new daughter-in-law has a lovely voice, and healin' hands," he said getting up off the table. "I do feel better. I don't feel like I'm goin' ta tip over. Ya might be onta somethin' lass!"

"If you already feel better after one treatment, then you'll probably respond very well to regular treatments. I prescribe one to two massages weekly," she said wrapping an arm around him as they made their way back upstairs.

"You'll have ta stay then little lady. I doubt there's anyone in this town that would know how ta do that."

"Ya feel better then Dad?" Grady asked as they made it back upstairs.

"I do. I'm a believer. I don't feel like I'm walkin' sideways, an' I don't feel like I need ta hold onta the walls ta keep me steady," he said coming to sit down outside where everyone was gathered.

"I can go talk to some therapists in town to find the right one for you. It sounds like you'll respond very nicely to this type of treatment," Jewel said snuggling in next to Grady.

"I doubt you'll be able ta find one that has the voice of an angel," Patrick said winking at Jewel.

"She does have a voice of an angel, doesn't she?" Grady said squeezing her, kissing her on the forehead.

"We heard ya had a lovely voice Jewel. Would ya mind singin' us somethin'? I saw ya had yer guitar with ya downstairs. Go get it would ya Joseph?" Maggie asked, not waiting for her response.

"Sure. I love to sing. That would be the perfect ending to a perfect day. Any requests?" she asked.

"Go ahead! Try to stump her! I dare you!" Rudy said, challenging anyone to come up with a song Jewel didn't know.

"I'll bet ya don't know the Irish Weddin' Song. That 'twas the song we first danced ta when we were married," Patrick said, taking Maggie's hand.

"I do actually know that one," she said surprising them all. "I had to sing it at a school play once, but my accent isn't very good. Maybe you could help me with that Rudy," she said winking at him. "I think it goes like this."

In good times and in bad times
In sickness and health
May they know that riches are no need for wealth
Help them face problems they'll meet on their way...

She was more or less singing directly to Grady as she thought of the day spent picking out her wedding gown with Maggie and Diana, and looking forward to their upcoming wedding. Everyone sat quietly, listening to her as she sang, and she could see Patrick and Maggie wipe away a tear or two as they remembered their own wedding day.

CHAPTER 37

BEST FRIENDS

The next couple of days they spent in hurried preparation, picking out cake, flowers, music, and getting all the licensing and paperwork in order through the church. "Getting married is hard work," Jewel said after making her way upstairs where everyone was gathering for a relaxing barbeque. It was the eve of her wedding day, and everything was finally ready. She was looking forward to sitting out on the deck to have a cold beer, and relax for a while.

"Hello Bestie," Joseph said grabbing her hand, leading her out back where everyone was gathered.

"Joseph, are you ready to give me away tomorrow?"

"Only since you're marrying my uncle. If it were anybody else, I would have to say no," he said as if the weight of giving his blessing for her to marry had been a difficult decision.

"Did I hear the doorbell?" Maggie yelled from the back porch, poking her head around the corner.

"I got it Mom," Grady said heading for the front door, patting Jewel on the butt as he passed her.

"Hi," the stranger said as Grady opened the door. "My name's Troy Landas. This is my wife Jolene Landas. We were looking for Jewel… ummm… Etchemendy. I'm hoping this…" Troy said before being interrupted.

"Oh god Troy! Holy crap, you made it. Jewel is goin' ta be so excited yer here. Come in man," Grady said, shaking his hand and welcoming them inside. "Go get Jewel will ya Tina?"

"Auntie Jewel! Auntie Jewel! It's for you! Someone's here for you!" Tina yelled as she ran to the back porch excitedly.

"Troy, I'm Grady," he said reaching out to shake his hand. "I'm glad ya came man. I thank ya. Jewel said ya were a good friend ta her growin' up, and I can see why."

"Troy! Jolene! How did you know to find me here?" Jewel said in complete disbelief when she saw them standing at the door. She wanted to go hug them both, but held off, not sure how to approach them.

"Caller I.D. Jewel. Google Maps... you never were good with technology," Troy said nervously, smiling at her, giving her a warm hug and a quick peck on the cheek.

"Jolene you're pregnant. You look beautiful," Jewel said choking up, giving her a friendly hug. Jewel always thought Jolene was one of the most beautiful girls in school, and seeing her pregnant and glowing, confirmed that belief. She was tall and slender with long blond hair, and big brown and gold eyes. There was no mistaking that she was pregnant, because she was just as tall and slender, but with just a baby bump sticking out in front, and she looked amazing.

"I'm seven and a half months along. Anyone who doesn't think nine months is a long time has never been pregnant," she said smiling nervously.

"This is Grady. We're getting married tomorrow," Jewel said excitedly, grabbing Grady's arm.

"We met," Troy said smiling, looking at Grady more closely with Jewel standing beside him, scrutinizing him with more interest.

"Would ya come in for a bite and meet everyone? We have burgers and hot dogs on the grill, and about ten different side dishes. Ya won't go hungry," Grady said, welcoming them out to the back porch. "We have beer, and soda or tea for the expectant mom."

"Ummm... yeah... sure. Thank you," Troy agreed as they followed Grady out to the porch where Grady immediately started making all the introductions. Everyone was gathered around a large picnic table that sat on the back deck, as they usually were. Food was cooking on the grill, and kids were running in every direction, either jumping on the trampoline or playing basketball.

Jewel was completely stunned, but smiling, aside from being a little nervous. She never expected Troy to show up. The fact that he never called back had been eating away at her, but she had been trying to push it out of her mind to concentrate on the wedding, not wanting it to spoil their day. Even Jolene seemed pleased to see her, and Jewel couldn't wait to get them alone so she could talk to them, especially Troy.

Her eyes were glued to them, looking at all the ways they had changed, and just seeing them together as a couple for the first time. Troy stood right at six feet tall with dark hair and steel grey eyes. He had a medium build and had rough, calloused hands full of scars. His legs were bowed, and he always looked like he'd be a lot more comfortable if he were sitting on the back of a horse. Jewel used to tease him that he'd be six inches taller if he could somehow straighten out his legs. He was always dressed in pressed Wranglers, a button down shirt, cowboy boots and a cowboy hat, and this day was no exception. Jolene was wearing a faded denim sundress, and for the first time, Jewel could see how perfect they were for each other. She thought of them together many times after getting their wedding invitation, but she could never quite picture it. She could see that special language they shared with each other and her heart warmed seeing them together. It all seemed to make perfect sense.

She watched them as they got their dinners, and engaged in casual conversation with everyone. Troy smiled at her, and she could tell that he was just as happy to see her. She kept having to wipe away a tear here and there, feeling so overjoyed to see him.

"So tell us somethin' about Jewel. Tell us a funny story or somethin' from when she was little," Diana said to Troy and Jolene.

"Okay... let's see... my favorite Jewel story is when she decided to do her dad a huge favor, and painted his old truck for him. She was about seven or eight I think, and Mr. E was always talking about it being old, rusty, and no good for anything. So, Mr. E was away for about a week, and Jewel decided she'd surprise him while he was gone, and Mrs. E didn't have any idea what she was up to. She never went out to that old shop anyways, and Jewel practically lived out there and had full run of the place. Well she painted it all right. Every square inch of it was hand painted with a huge paint brush, and about ten variations of barn red paint," Troy said laughing. "She painted the wheels, the tires, the bed, and just for good measure, she painted the inside of the doors too, because she thought they needed to match."

"Ya painted the man's truck!" Grady said incredulously. "Remind me ta hide the keys."

"That old truck is just still right there. Runs too, but its ugly. It's just about the ugliest truck I've ever seen. I have to drive it into town once in a while, and I just about die of embarrassment every time I do, but it makes me laugh every time I get in it."

"Sounds like it needs a new paint job. Good thing you'll be heading back huh Jewel?" Rudy said joking with her.

"It really was a lot of work. I thought he'd be so proud of me. The whole time I was painting, I was just thinking my dad was going to come home and be so happy, he was probably going to want to take me to Billings to celebrate, or maybe buy me a new horse."

"So what did he have ta say about it then lass?" Patrick asked.

"He said, *Jewel, what happened to my blue truck? Why for the love of god did you choose red?*" she said laughing.

"He wasn't mad or anything?" Thomas and Joseph ask simultaneously.

"Now don't you get any ideas," Rudy said eyeing them both narrowly.

"He was mad, but I didn't realize it until I was older. He knew I'd worked hard on it, and he didn't want to hurt my feelings, but when I got older, and remembered him going off to the woodshed yelling and cursing, I realized that it wasn't because of raccoons like he'd claimed, it was because he was mad about the truck."

"She drove it all through high school though. Every day she drove that thing, and proudly. Some of the red paint has chipped off, and you can see some of the blue paint coming through, but it runs great," Troy said smiling.

"Tell us another one," Alisha and Thomas both called out.

"Alright, here's one. One time I picked Jewel up to go to the prom. She was all dressed up in some frilly red dress, high-heeled shoes and everything, which was a rare occasion for Jewel. She even sort of had her hair done up. I had just broke my arm, and so when we were heading into town and got a flat tire, Jewel had to get out to change the tire in her dress and heels. I tried helping her as much as I could, but of course, she wasn't having any part of that. She was determined to do it all on her own, not wanting me to hurt my arm any worse," he said smiling, his eyes nearly filling with tears as he chuckled, remembering the moment fondly.

"Well, when she got back in the truck, she was covered in mud and grease from head to toe. Her hair was all messed up, and one of the straps on her shoe was busted. God we laughed so damn hard. Here I was all dressed up in my white suit without a spot on me, and Jewel looked like she had just wrestled a herd of wild pigs," Troy was laughing so hard he had to wipe away tears, and so was everyone else.

"Well, she just walked into the dance like she didn't have a care in the world, no shoes, covered in grease and mud, and we danced non-stop. We had a blast, and anytime anyone said anything about her being dirty, or mentioned the little tear she had in her dress, she would pretend like she didn't have one clue what they were talking about. It was classic Jewel."

"Yep! That sounds like Jewel," Rudy said in agreement with Grady as they both shook their heads, remembering her covered in dirt throughout the competition, seemingly without a care in the world.

"Jewel makes grease look good," Grady said wrapping his arm around her.

"I remember that," Jolene chimed in. "You even had Jill Averson out there dancing with you. She was a disabled girl that went to school with us," she explained. "She would usually just stand in the background and watch, but with Jewel out there dancing in a ragged, dirty dress, everyone's inhibitions went out the door. That's the way all proms should be come to think of it."

They told one story after another, both Troy and Jewel sharing childhood stories, and laughing together comfortably as if it had only been a matter of days since they'd last seen each other. Even Jolene chipped in, telling about a time when they had played volleyball together, and nearly won the state championship, which was no easy feat for a community as small as theirs. Despite their lack of friendship in high school, they had actually made a pretty good match, set, and spike duo on the volleyball team.

"Tell us another one!" Joseph said.

"Well, the truth is that Jewel here is my oldest and dearest friend. We did everything together from the time we were babies in the crib until about four years ago, and this is the first time I've seen her since then. I could tell you a million stories, but if it would be alright, I'd really like to talk to Jewel alone for a while," Troy said looking at Grady and Jewel questioning.

"Of course! Please. Jolene could stay and have another plate of food for the babe?" Grady said looking at Jolene.

"Yeah, I'm fine honey. Go," Jolene said smiling at Jewel and Troy.

"Okay, well do you want to go for a walk or something?" Jewel asked Troy, eager to talk to him alone.

"That sounds good," Troy said shaking Grady's hand thankfully, kissing Jolene before following Jewel outside.

Troy and Jewel made their way out the front door, and walked a ways down the street together, not sure where to begin. Jewel didn't know how to start. How do you apologize for four years of the silent treatment? How do you tell someone you love and care for how sorry you are for treating them so poorly? She was thankful when Troy finally broke the silence.

"Those are good people Jewel. I like them, and I like Grady. He seems like a really good guy," he said as they continued their slow stroll down the block.

"They're wonderful, and Grady's amazing. I'm really happy Troy," she said sincerely. "I didn't know if I would ever feel this happy again."

"I had to come see for myself, and I had to come here to apologize Jewel."

"What? What do you have to apologize for?" she said a little stunned. "I'm the one that has to apologize Troy!"

"You did already, and you'll explain the details later, but I had a hand in this too Jewel. It's not just you that made mistakes, but you think it is, and that breaks my heart. The truth is… well… the truth is Jewel… I never wanted to marry you, and I obviously figured out that you didn't ever want to marry me either," he said shaking his head. "Christ! The thought of you and I getting married is ridiculous! It'd be like marrying my sister… my own flesh and blood practically. Did you ever even feel like you had a choice in the matter?" he asked incredulously. "It's like it was all prearranged, like we were living in some culture where the parents decide who their kids marry. I was just a young kid doing what I thought I was supposed to do," he added, hanging his head afraid to look at her.

"Oh Troy. Why didn't you tell me that? You said you loved me, and you wanted to spend the rest of your life with me. I just freaked out! I didn't know what to do! How could I tell you no, but then how could I ever tell you yes? There wasn't any right answer."

"I get it. I really do, and I do love you, and I do want to spend the rest of my life with you Jewel, but like it's always been… not as a married couple. You're my best friend, but I don't want to be married to you. I just want my friend back, and I'm sorry, but the thought of ever kissing you again is just weird."

"You asked me to marry you because you wanted to take care of me the way you always did," she said summarizing everything he had just said.

"I'm sorry Jewel. The truth is that I was always sweet on Jolene. Remember in our senior year when you refused to go to the Sadie Hawkins dance, and I had the stomach flu?" he asked her.

"Yeah, I remember."

"Well, I didn't have the flu, and I swear to God it's the only time I've ever lied to you, but Jolene and I took off and went to spend the night together at the lake."

"Oh my... why didn't you tell me?" she asked shaking her head.

"I don't know Jewel. I wanted to. Keeping anything from you was like holding back the tides. You were just so fragile ... you know... you always looked like you were about to finally breakdown once and for all. I just wanted to take care of you. I couldn't risk telling you anything that could make you more sad. It was just too heartbreaking to watch. One minute you would be laughing and joking, and the next minute you were broken and sad."

They walked in silence for a moment, both of them knowing that what he said was the truth. She finally stopped to look up at him, breaking the silence.

"Thank you for telling me that you didn't want to marry me, and that you don't ever want to kiss me again," she said suddenly laughing and crying at the same time. "That's the best thing you could have ever told me Troy. I mean... you're right. I never felt like we had a choice. I always thought we would just grow up and have to get married, and that would be that, but then the time came, and I wasn't ready for it. I realized that's not what I wanted, but then you seemed to want it, and I just didn't know what to do. I just kept hoping I would have a change of heart, but I never did."

"You're crying Jewel. I never thought I'd see the day," he said pulling her close to him, hugging her tight, "you must be doing all right. I can tell that things are different... just the way you are with Grady and his family, laughing and showing affection."

"That must be why Jolene always hated me," she said suddenly, a light bulb going off in her head as she choked back more tears.

"That's exactly why Jewel, but she understands, and she regrets it. She's a good person Jewel. You two probably would have been best friends in high school if it hadn't been for that. You're so much alike, and you have the same sense of humor. I don't know if you knew this or not... I sure didn't, but when their house burned down, it was your mom and dad that donated most of the lumber so they could rebuild."

"I didn't know. I had no idea, but I do sort of remember when that happened. Wow, I'm completely blown away right now Troy, but you know, I think running away might have been for the best," she said eyeing him sideways as they made their way down the street.

"What do you mean Jewel?"

"I mean that you always coddled me, and it was exactly what I needed at the time. I'm afraid to imagine what my life would've been like without you. You were my crutch, but I needed to learn to walk without a crutch. I laughed when you made me laugh. I ate when you made me eat. I went to dances because you made me go to dances, and I played sports because you made me play sports. I'm so grateful for it, but I think that maybe I needed to go out and learn to live on my own. I was too dependent on you for everything. My mood was your mood. My laughter was your laughter. I was just going through the motions, but you kept me from isolating myself, and I'm thankful, and I'm sorry."

"I just don't understand why you wouldn't respond when we sent you the invitation to our wedding," he said broaching the final unanswered question, the one that had angered him the most.

"I thought you would be pining away for me, and that it wouldn't be fair to Jolene!" she said laughing hysterically.

They were both standing in the street laughing so hard they had to wipe tears out of their eyes and off their faces. They both knew how ridiculous it was that they could ever be romantically involved with each other, and it became so perfectly clear that it was laughable.

"We were fools Jewel. Just kids. I will never tell my kids who I think they should marry. I mean, I know they meant well, but hell! They sure made it tough!" he said shaking his head.

"I have so many things I want to tell you Troy. Like… I'm a nurse, and I went to Iraq, and I want to tell you about Grady, and his family, and how we met, and just a million things. Every time something has happened in my life, I always thought of telling you about them, but I couldn't."

"I know what you mean Jewel. Truth is, I look for any excuse I can find to drive that old truck. I've missed you," he said hugging her tightly again.

"I'd like to give you away Jewel. I mean, I know it's kind of an old-fashioned notion, but Dad was your Godfather, and I…"

"Wait! What do you mean *was*?"

"I'm sorry Jewel. I don't want to give you bad news the night before your wedding. Dad died about a year ago. He had a heart attack."

"Oh Troy, I'm so sorry. I should have been there for you!" she said regretfully, remembering how Troy had been there for her when her parents died.

"It's okay Jewel. It's really okay. Jolene was there, and we got through it. There's a big difference between having both of your parents die when you're eleven, and having one parent die when you're twenty-one, so don't feel bad about it. I got through it," he said kicking himself for slipping up.

"Where's your mom?"

"She moved into town a few months ago, and is teaching classes at the college in Sheridan. She's doing pretty good. It's okay."

"Life does go on doesn't it?" she asked hanging her head.

"It does Jewel, and I'm really glad, because you look really good. You look happy. Sitting out on the porch, telling stories and laughing… it was like you were yourself again… before…," he said not needing to finish.

"I would like you to give me away Troy. I might have to do some smooth talking, but it would be perfect. Having you here is the greatest wedding present I could have ever asked for," she said hugging him tightly.

"Well, you can thank Grady for that. Don't be mad at him, but he called me and asked me to come," Troy confessed, holding her tight to him so she couldn't pull away. "It didn't take much asking though. I wanted to come. Don't be mad at him for interfering. I know how you hate that. He's a good guy, and he loves you."

"I'm not mad. I'm grateful! This couldn't be more perfect."

The two of them walked back to the house arm and arm, walking and talking incessantly all the way, just as they had always done. They both knew there were many things left to discuss, like the running of the ranch, and details about the last four years, but for the moment they were just happy to be together. When they reached the front door, they found Joseph sitting there waiting for them

"So if me and Auntie Jewel are best friends, and you and Auntie Jewel are best friends, does that mean that you and I are best friends too?" Joseph asked Troy as they all walked back in the house.

"I think that's how it works alright!" Troy replied, smiling down at the doe-eyed boy.

"Okay well, Dad said that I'm supposed to give Auntie Jewel to you, and then you're going to give her away. Is that right?" Joseph said looking for confirmation. Jewel could clearly see that Grady and Troy probably worked this out ahead of time, and she smiled watching the plan reach its final stages.

"Well, if you wouldn't mind too much, I think that would be a pretty good way of doing it," Troy agreed.

"Okay, but promise me you won't give her to anyone else!" Joseph said pointing his finger at him, scolding him.

"Okay! Okay! I promise!" Troy said playing along as they all erupted in laughter.

"And I didn't really think it was possible to love you anymore than I did this morning," Jewel said whispering to Grady as they watched the exchange between Joseph and Troy.

"You know I'd do anything for ya darlin'," Grady said, smiling down at her.

"Okay! The party is over! Time for all the boys ta go!" Diana said loudly. "All the boys are going ta our house, and all the girls are stayin' here, and we'll meet at the church sharply at two! Got it?"

"Are ya up for it man?" Grady asked Troy.

"I'd really love it if you stayed," Jewel said taking Jolene's hand.

Jolene and Troy smiled at each other just as Grady and Jewel made eye contact, exchanging the same unspoken understanding. Jewel suspected this had been worked out ahead of time as well, given the ease at which everything was happening.

"I think we're in. Let me just go get your bag honey," Troy said running out to the car.

"Thank you Jewel. This means so much to Troy. He's really missed you," Jolene said putting an arm around her.

"It means a lot to me too," she said putting her arm around Jolene, her eyes filling up with tears again, "and not just because of Troy. I'm really glad you're here."

"Me too Jewel."

The boys finally left, but not before Grady and Jewel stole away for a few quiet moments before both sides overran them. The excitement in the air was so thick and contagious that Troy and Jolene managed to just fall in with the group to enjoy the beginnings of the celebration as if they had been there all along. Jewel was sure that all the muscles in her jaw and face were going to be stuck in a permanent look of laughter.

Maggie, Diana, Jewel, Jolene, Alisha, Melanie, and Tina were at the girl's house, and Patrick, Rudy, Grady, Troy, Paxton, Thomas, and Joseph were at the boy's house. Jewel had no idea what to expect, but the idea of having Grady and Troy together was an answered prayer. It all happened so fast she could hardly believe it, and having Jolene with her made her just as happy.

She had worried that even if Troy and her patched things up, they would always be separated to some extent because of Jolene, but she didn't have to worry about that anymore. This was confirmed to her that night as they all played games, told stories, talked and laughed, and Jewel even played a couple songs for them until they all decided that it was time for bed around midnight.

Jewel could hardly sleep she was so excited, but she finally managed to fall asleep lying next to Jolene somewhere around one in the morning. She smiled watching her sleep, remembering all the angst that had been between them in high school. Never in a million years would she have ever imagined it would be possible to have Jolene sleeping in a bed right next to her while Troy and Grady bonded.

CHAPTER 38

FOREVER

"Oh my gosh! You're getting married today Jewel!" Jolene said excitedly as Jewel slipped into her wedding gown. They had all been up and around since the early morning, making breakfast, and drinking coffee before the mass rush to fix hair and makeup began. Curling irons were out making their rounds, and Maggie was getting everything pressed and cinched, making her way from one room to another.

"I've never really worn makeup before, but I read that it's smart to wear a little just so your face stands out more in the pictures. What do you think?" Jewel asked Jolene.

"Well, lord knows you don't need it… you've always been so pretty, but I agree. We'll just put a little on so the white gown doesn't wash out your face in the pictures. I'll help you. Come sit back down again," Jolene said motioning to the toilet seat where Jewel sat while Jolene fixed her hair earlier. She had fixed her hair, meticulously curling her hair, pinning each curl up neatly. She looked amazing with just a few strands sticking out, wrapping playfully around her chin.

"You've been great Jolene. Thank you. I'm really glad you're here."

"Me too Jewel," she said sincerely, "everything seems like it worked out just right didn't it, and Troy was so happy to hear from you."

"It did. It actually worked out. It seemed completely hopeless not that long ago, and I thought you hated me."

"I never hated you, but I was mad. I always had a huge crush on Troy. We always seemed to like each other in that way, but he was always so protective of you, wanting to take you to prom so you wouldn't sit at home by yourself, and of course, that just made me love him even more. For a while there, I thought the two of you were actually going to get married, and it was so confusing, because I knew Troy loved me, but then he loved you too… just not in the way I thought as it turns out."

"I'm sorry it was so hard on you. It's really too bad. We could have been good friends in high school. We were an unbeatable duo in volleyball," Jewel said smiling at her as she concentrated on putting makeup on her face.

"Wow! That looks great Jolene. You should do makeovers. You've got skill,"

Jewel said studying herself in the mirror. She thought of a picture she had seen of Audrey Hepburn once, and couldn't help but think of it as she looked at herself in the mirror.

"Well, that is what I do. I only do it a few days a week, and then I do it on special occasions for proms and weddings. I do hair and makeup, and then I go to school a couple days a week, but I'm going to take time off when the baby comes."

"How lucky for me that a professional hair and makeup artist came to do my hair and makeup for my wedding day. Do you know whether you're having a boy or a girl?" Jewel asked eyeing her bump.

"We don't know. We didn't want to find out. We want the surprise of finding out that day."

"We've got about five minutes before we need ta leave!" Diana yelled through the house excitedly.

Jolene finished up, and everyone piled into the car to get to the church where Troy would be waiting for them outside. Everyone was to go inside except Troy, and then when they heard the music, Troy and Jewel would make their way down the aisle. Troy's first job was to make sure the bride and groom didn't see each other before she walked down the aisle.

"Here you go Auntie!" Melanie said handing her a small blue handkerchief from the backseat. "It's something blue!"

"And I have this for ya." Maggie said placing a beautiful strand of small white pearls around her wrist. "It's something old, an' I'd like ya ta have them deary."

"I gave her something borrowed!" Alisha called out. "Can you believe that she didn't have a single pair of white panties?" They all laughed, and were still laughing when they pulled up to the church to find Troy standing there giving them the all clear, and since Grady had secretly planned this out to have Troy there, he had also made sure to have a tuxedo ready for him, and Troy was looking especially handsome.

They all got out of the car, and Jewel was suddenly terrified as she saw the number of cars that were parked in the parking lot. She knew that his mom had been busy on the phone, but she had no idea that half the town was going to be there, most of whom she didn't know.

"You look beautiful Jewel," Troy said after kissing his wife, giving her directions on where to go sit.

"Thank you. How's Grady? Was he nervous?"

"He's excited. He knows he's damn lucky. You did good Jewel," he said taking Jewels hands. "We got to talk quite a bit last night, and I'm looking forward to having him come help on the ranch."

They stood together face to face, holding hands until they finally heard the music start and could make their way down the aisle. "It's going to be alright Jewel. Just breathe."

She took his arm, giving it an affectionate squeeze as they walked into the church and started down the aisle. Jewel locked eyes with Grady the minute she entered the church, and she could hardly believe her good fortune. Everything she didn't know she ever wanted was standing there at the end of the aisle waiting for her, and smiling, and he looked very handsome. She knew he was outside of his comfort zone dressed up in a tuxedo, but she also knew that he looked better in it than most of the male models she had seen in the bridal magazines, and the look on his face when he saw her told her everything she needed to know.

She felt beautiful all done up in her wedding dress and the meticulously pinned up hair and makeup that Jolene did for her, but she wasn't convinced that it was enough until she saw his eyes light up. His eyes were fixed on her, and she on him. She was just praying she would be able to get through the service without breaking out in tears again.

The church had been meticulously decorated, and Jewel wondered how her mother-in-law had managed to pull off all the flower arrangements, and the decorations that made it look like it had been carefully planned out for months. The arrangements were a beautiful mixture of various kinds of white flowers, with just a hint of purple lavender mixed in. She was breathless as she looked around seeing all the unfamiliar faces, and the few familiar ones, nearly losing it all together seeing Angela and Joe sitting there. She blew kisses at them, resisting the urge to go up and hug them. She had no idea they were going to be there.

She crossed herself and genuflected as she and Troy reached the front of the church, meeting Grady's eyes as they stood facing each other.

"Ya look beautiful Jewel. I'm the luckiest man alive," Grady said with his eyes still fixed on her.

Father smiled at them as they turned their attention to him when the music stopped, and a quiet anticipation enveloped the church. The priest started beautifully, talking about his long relationship with Grady and his family, and about how lucky they were to have such a fine addition to their family. "Who gives this woman to be married to this man?" he finally asked.

"I do," Troy said locking eyes with Jewel, hugging her affectionately before shaking Grady's hand. "Take good care of her," he said choking up.

"I will brother. Thank you," Grady said sincerely, giving Troy a knowing look that told Jewel that they had indeed had a very long talk the night before.

The ceremony continued on as most Catholic weddings do, which is to say that it was long, and there was lots of standing, and sitting, and kneeling, but Jewel listened to every word of it. She took every word that was spoken, and considered it completely, wanting to remember every moment, and wanting to keep every promise she was making. It wasn't until the priest asked for the symbolic exchange of rings that Jewel had even considered rings, and she had a moment of panic before seeing Joseph step up and hold them out for them to take. She gave Grady a curious look, and he gave her a coy look in response. She recognized the small gold band immediately as her moms. The tears pooled over and rolled down her face, and she was grateful for the blue hankie Melanie had given her earlier.

She managed to get through the rest of the ceremony without completely losing it, but every time she looked at the wedding ring on her finger, she nearly broke down crying again. The band had three small diamonds in it, but she remembered that one had always been missing, and wondered where it had come from. She couldn't have been happier and more excited, and she knew that her parents would be thrilled with her wearing the ring. She also thought about the black and white picture of her great grandmother wearing it.

"Ladies and gentlemen, may I present to you Mr. and Mrs. McDonald."

Grady was so excited, he scooped her up and carried her from the church, and continued carrying her down the street where they would be having their wedding reception. Everyone followed behind them, throwing birdseed and yelling words of congratulations to them. The day was beautiful. It was a warm summer day, and Jewel reveled in every moment of it waving to everyone in the family as Grady cradled her in his arms as if she weighed no more than a small child.

"How did you get my mother's wedding ring?" she asked looking at her hand adoringly.

"It was an idea I had, and when I talked ta Troy on the phone he thought he might be able ta go in yer house and see if he could find it. I hope ya don't mind. I didn't actually know if he had it or not until last night. Ya were really close ta havin' a plastic ring from the dollar store darlin'," he said winking at her. "I hope its ok. My Mom wears her mother's weddin' ring, and I know how much it's meant ta her."

"It's wonderful. That was so thoughtful Grady. Thank you. It's very special. Mom and Dad would like that I'm wearing it, and I love it, but it used to have a missing diamond. How did you manage to get it replaced so quickly?"

"I called in a huge favor, but yer not ta worry darlin', and I did give ya fair warnin' of the barfly that wants ta ride me like a wild stallion," he said with a smirk.

"Really? We've been married for five seconds and you're already trading sexual favors to keep me dripping in diamonds?" she said playing along.

"Not quite, and I would hardly call it drippin'. I said she could be bought off with liquor, and so that's what it took. She is a jeweler, aside from bein' a terrible drunk, so I plied her with liquor this mornin' ta get her up bright and early ta set the diamond for me. It cost me a bottle of fine Irish Whiskey, but yer worth every drop darlin'," he said smiling at her.

"What a relief. I was starting to think the bed might get a little crowded tonight," she said kissing his neck.

"Not a chance. I have ya all ta myself tonight. I have a surprise for ya, but I'm not goin' ta tell ya about it right now," he said as they reached the hall where they would be having their wedding reception.

The hall was full of dishes and plates of food, and everything had been beautifully decorated. There was a band inside that was all set up, and looked to be waiting for them to arrive. It was as close to a fairy tale wedding as reality gets, but Grady walked straight through the hall to a room in the back before finally setting her down, taking both her hands in his.

"I just need a minute with ya Jewel," he said before grabbing her and kissing her more passionately, away from the crowd of people who were starting to fill up the hall. "I meant it ya know… every word of it. I listened ta every word Father said, and I just want ya ta know it wasn't just ceremony for me. I mean… ya know… people take these vows every day, and every day people get divorced, betraying those same vows. Ya don't ever have ta worry about that Jewel. I know there will be hard times, and that it's not all a big fairy tale where we ride off and live happily ever after. We'll have good and bad days, but I'll always fight for ya… I'll always fight for us."

"Me too Grady. I won't ever be the one that turns and runs. I've tried that, and I'll never do that to you. I promise," she whispered faintly, getting lost in his eyes, making an even deeper promise, completely unspoken.

"I have this for ya darlin'," he said, taking her hand and slipping a diamond accent ring on her ring finger next to her mother's wedding ring. It was a beautiful band of small diamonds that matched her mother's wedding band perfectly. "I didn't want ya ta think I was bein' cheap by given ya yer own ring, but I thought ya'd want ta wear yer mother's ring, and I thought this went nicely with it."

"Oh Grady! It's beautiful, but you really didn't have to do this," she said looking at the two rings together adoringly. "I don't need lavish diamonds and things like that."

"I wanted ta get it for ya, and I wanted ya ta have a ring from me. I don't want ya ta see yer weddin' ring, and think of only yer mom. I want ya ta think of me. Do ya know what I mean?" he asked.

"I understand, and I will look at both of them and think of you… always. Thank you," she said reaching up to kiss him.

They finally made their way back out to the hall where they were greeted by family and friends, everyone going up to meet Jewel and offer hugs and congratulations to the couple. Jewel found Angela and Joe, and went up to them hugging them thoroughly. The entire family, which included Troy and Jolene, sat at a big long table at the head of the room that was neatly decorated with the same floral arrangements, and was nearly overflowing with bottles of champagne.

"Ladies and gentlemen, can I have your attention please?" Rudy yelled out, clinking his champagne glass in an effort to get everyone's attention. "I would like to make a toast to the bride and groom."

The room slowly grew quiet with everyone settling in to listen to the speeches that were about to ensue. Rudy gave a raucous toast, telling the story of their first meeting in the bar not long ago, though it seemed like it had been quite a while since they had all been through so much together.

"I couldn't believe my eyes that first day when Grady managed to have this beautiful woman sitting at our table within just a few minutes of meeting her. It was like a raging forest fire between them from that moment on. It was like being caught between the sun and a volcano, and it was obvious from the very beginning that Jewel was a perfect match for Grady. From that first day, Jewel became like a sister to me. My wife said we're clones of each other, and that we have the same exact sense of humor, which explains why Grady fell madly in love with her." He had them all laughing as he told a few funny stories about Grady when he was younger, before finally giving a heartfelt wish of eternal happiness, nearly bringing everyone to tears.

"I would like to make a toast," Joseph said standing up on his chair, trying to keep everyone's attention. "I want to thank my Uncle for marrying my best friend, because if you think about it, that's pretty smart of him, because we already like her and everything." The room clapped and laughed as Joseph took a bow.

"Well that's a pretty hard act to follow," Troy said standing up to make another toast. "Jewel is my oldest and dearest friend. She's almost exactly three months younger than I am, and I don't think it's a coincidence that the first three months were the most troubled months of my life. I wasn't gaining weight or making any of the progress that a baby is supposed to make in their first three months. The doctors called it *failure to thrive*," Troy said clearing his throat. "Then Jewel came along, and our moms were together all the time, so they naturally put us together when we'd nap. That's when my life changed. I started gaining weight, and making strides in all the motor skills that were expected of a three-month-old baby, and well... I started thriving."

"My mom likes to tell the story about finding us in our crib with Jewels arms wrapped around me protectively," he stopped, smiling at Jewel before continuing. "We've pretty much been taking care of each other ever since, and I wasn't a bit surprised when Jewel went to school to be a nurse. It's clear she was born to take care of people, and make them feel better, and I couldn't be more proud of her. It is an honor that me and my lovely wife could be here to celebrate this with you Jewel... and Grady," Troy said choking up, raising his glass to signal the end of his speech, leaving few dry eyes left in the room.

Diana made a speech, and then his dad told a few stories to welcome Jewel to the family. Everyone danced, laughed, and ate until the sun was starting to set, and Grady finally decided it was time to whisk Jewel away for the evening. Jewel's head was spinning, and he had caught that special signal that couple's share, letting the other one know they'd had enough, and it was time to go. He was ready to go as well, and had arranged to take her to a quaint little cabin that at first he worried about, thinking it might remind her of her most recent cabin experience.

The cabin he was taking her to was very luxurious, and he planned to spoil and pamper her without her having to pretend like she was living like the rich and famous. They were going to have three nights, and two and a half days, which would be the most time they'd had with just the two of them since they met, and Grady could hardly think of anything else. The only thing Jewel knew for sure was that they wouldn't be leaving for Wyoming until the end of the week. She had no idea he had arranged for the cabin, and the time alone.

"Are ya ready ta make an escape darlin'?" Grady asked, finally pulling her away from all the people that had come to the wedding. She had been catching up with Angela and Joe, and in a small town like Belle Fourche, everyone knew everybody, and many of the people that had come to the wedding were people that Grady had grown up with, and knew quite well, but Jewel had a magnetic personality, and once people met her, they wanted more of her. She had been dancing and socializing non-stop since they walked out into the hall, and Grady had barely been able to catch up with her all night.

"I'm ready to have some time alone with my husband," she said wrapping her arms around him, kissing him.

Grady started making goodbyes and announcements to leave in an effort to get Jewel out the door, but not before throwing the bouquet into a group of young, screaming girls, which nearly caused an all-out brawl when it was about to land in the arms of one young girl, only to be snatched by someone nearby. He took that as an opportunity to make a break for it, grabbing Jewel by the hand, the two of them running to his truck that he had parked on a nearby side street.

"I only just learned to walk in high heels Grady, and now you have me sprinting," she said panting as they made their way to the truck.

"Yer chariot madam," he said holding the door open for her. His truck was a blue and white, fully restored nineteen sixty-eight Ford that she hadn't been able to see until then, and she was very impressed. It had been in storage, and he hadn't been able to get it out until the day before when he and his dad unburied it from a storage place where it was being kept.

"This is beautiful Grady!" she said sliding into the passenger seat. "You really did all this?"

"Yep, I bought this when I was about fourteen, and me and my dad fixed it up tagether. By the time I was ready ta drive, I had a pretty decent pickup, but it didn't look this nice until I was discharged. That's when I got the interior fixed up, and got the new paint job. Just in time for a beautiful bride," he said pulling her closer to him, kissing her thoroughly as they drove out of town toward the cabin he had arranged for them.

"Where are we going?" she asked.

"I have a surprise for ya. How would ya like to have a few days with just the two of us?"

"I would love that. Are you serious? We get time with just the two of us?" she asked wrapping her arms around him, kissing him passionately, and nearly making him drive off the road. "Wait a minute! I need my things."

"All yer stuff is at the cabin. Alisha went and got yer stuff all packed, and she took it to the cabin earlier, along with some groceries and stuff for us," he said gasping as Jewel kissed her way down the front of him. "Careful Jewel, I don't want ta make love ta ya on our weddin' night in the front seat of my truck, but I'm just a man. I can only resist ya in that dress for so long."

"Well, how long of a drive is it? Because, I'm only a woman ya know," she said teasing him with an Irish accent, "and I can only resist ya in that tuxedo for so long ya know."

"It's not too far. If ya mind yer manners, and keep yer hands ta yerself woman, we might make it," he said winking at her. "Then, I'm goin' ta take ya ta bed darlin', softly and gently at first, but then, I'm goin' ta do that thing that makes ya squeal out so much."

"Ohhh… I do like it when you do that," she teased, running her hand up his thigh, kissing his neck.

"Yer not followin' the rules darlin'… do ya know what yer doin' ta me? Are ya tryin' ta make me crash?" he said nearly driving off the road again.

"Do you really want me to stop?" she said untying the bow around his neck, unbuttoning his shirt.

"I don't ever want ya ta stop, but we have about a half hour more 'til we get ta where we're headin'. Sing me a song or somethin'. Will ya?" he asked stroking her leg.

"I don't have my guitar, but I have been thinking of a song that makes me think of us. Do you want me to sing it?"

"Sing ta me darlin'. I love ta hear ya sing."

And so she sang a song of promise, and he listened to her slip into a peaceful place she seemed to always go to when she sang. It was still somewhat bright out, as the setting sun shined through the window, illuminating her like a spotlight on a stage. He drove faster, wanting to get to the cabin as quickly as he could. He was ready to have her all alone.

~~~~~~~~

"Ya've a lovely voice darlin'. The first time I heard it ya blew me away. I couldn't have been more surprised."

"I hope you like it, because you'll have to listen to it for the rest of your life," she said twisting the rings around on her finger, unable to stop herself from smiling. "You really arranged all this Grady? You got my bags, groceries, and everything taken care of?"

"I wanted ya ta have a special day darlin'."

She smiled over at him, and he smiled back. Finally, they pulled off the main road, turning off on a well-manicured gravel road toward a distant cabin they could see because of the lights coming from it. It was a beautiful, upscale cabin overlooking a small pond that glimmered in the moonlight that was just starting to emerge. The structure was a log cabin that looked like a picture from a postcard. They pulled up next to it excitedly.

"What do ya think Jewel?"

"It's beautiful! We really have three nights here with just the two of us?"

"Well, I asked Rudy ta stop by an' interrupt us periodically just for old-time's sake," he said pulling her out of the pickup. "I have ta carry ya over the threshold or its bad luck. Come here woman."

"Really? I thought you were supposed to carry me over the threshold of *our* home… not a rental cabin."

"I don't really know darlin' so I'll just carry ya over a bunch a threshold's between here and yer ranch, just ta be on the safe side," he said as he carried her to the front door of the cabin.

"Wow, this is beautiful Grady. We won't have to *pretend* we are on a luxury vacation for the rich and famous. This is amazing, but how… I mean… you didn't have to spend this much money… I mean…," she trailed off not knowing how to say what she was trying to say. She knew that Grady wasn't exactly rolling in money, even before leaving the military, and she wondered how he was able to afford the place, but she didn't want to hurt his pride. She knew his lack of money and employment had been weighing heavily on his mind. She knew he had been worried about giving her things that he felt like he needed to give her.

"Not ta worry darlin'. Truth is, I built this place, and the man I built it for let me borrow it. He owed me a few favors 'cause I helped him out quite a bit with permittin' and a few other things when he was tryin' ta get the approval."

"You built this place? It's beautiful Grady. I didn't know you knew how to build like this," she said looking in awe around her as Grady put her down. "I've always admired people who could build things… and I didn't think it was possible to be more turned on by you than I had been five minutes ago."

"Confession and carpentry? That's what does it for ya?" he said smiling at her sideways, "ah but yer a strange woman Jewel."

"And what is it that does it for you then?" she asked wrapping her arms around his waist.

"You," he said cupping her face in his hands, "and now I get ta call ya my wife, and that is probably the thing that does it the most." He leaned down and kissed her reaching up to stroke her hair, only to find his fingers stuck in hair-sprayed hair and hairpins.

"Ya must have about ten pounds of hairpins in there darlin'. It's a wonder ya can hold yer head up," he said inspecting the top of her head more closely.

"I know. Jolene spent more than an hour curling every strand of hair, and pinning it up neatly. I was thinking it might be easier to just shave my head and start over, rather than try and get all the pins and hairspray out," she said jokingly.

"Let me help ya," he said as they made their way in the bathroom where they both started extracting pins, letting her curls fall down her back, one by one. Jewel watched him in the mirror as he concentrated on each pin, trying to get them out without pulling her hair. He brushed out each newly freed strand, softly running his fingers through it, stopping only long enough to kiss her on the cheek or the back of her neck.

Every inch of her body was alert, responding to his every touch with a heightened sense she had never felt before. After he was satisfied that he had found every pin, he stood behind her, both of them looking at each other as they stood in front of the mirror, her black, silky hair falling carelessly around her bare shoulders, toppling over her strapless wedding gown. He ran his fingers through her hair; each movement was slow and methodical, neither of them wanted to rush a single moment.

"Yer stunnin' Jewel. I've never seen someone so beautiful."

She slowly turned to face him, reaching her hands up around his neck, pulling him down to kiss her. She loved running her hands through his hair, and loved when he reached his hands around her pulling her closer to him. She wrapped her arms more tightly around his neck, gasping as he lifted her off her feet, carrying her into the bedroom. He set her down, and she could feel her heart beating harder, her pulse racing through her body as he unclasped the hook on her gown and started sliding the zipper down until the dress fell down around her, leaving her standing there in a white strapless bra, panties, and a garter belt with stockings. She kicked off her shoes as he scooped her up, laying her down on the bed. He never once took his eyes off her as he went over and flicked off the light. The moonlight was shining brightly through the skylights, and through the large windows that were overlooking the pond.

She watched him as he threw off his jacket and kicked off his shoes, making his way back to the bed where she waited for him. She reached up and started unbuttoning his shirt as he climbed on the bed hovering over her, kissing her softly with each kiss going deeper. She ran her hands up the front of his chest, peeling his shirt off before reaching down to unbutton the slacks of his tuxedo. He unhooked her bra, and threw it on the floor, reaching down with his lips, tenderly kissing each breast as he ran his hands down the length of her.

He pushed one leg between her legs, parting them as she bent her knee, wanting to feel him push closer to her. He grabbed her leg, reaching behind and unsnapping the garter, sitting up and slowly pulling off each stocking, never taking his eyes off the deep blue eyes looking up at him. She watched him pull each one off her. She loved looking at the silhouette of him in the moonlit room, the curvature of a muscular frame urging her to reach up and touch him as he slid off her panties. She sat up, reaching out to him as he slid out of his trousers. She loved watching his pulse quicken as the warmth of her hands wrapped gently around him. He leaned down, easily pulling her further up the bed as he positioned himself between her legs, running his hands from her ankle, all the way up her leg, careful not to touch the scar from the branding iron, not wanting to remind her of that night.

She felt her head swimming, as much from his touch as from the glasses of champagne she drank earlier. She kissed him harder, pulling him into her as she wrapped her legs around him. She could feel him starting to lose control, pushing deeper into her, each thrust more urgent than the last one until they both lost control, each of them lost in their own pleasure.

"Grady... promise me you'll always make love to me like that," she said sometime later, still languishing in the tingling she felt through her whole body.

"Jewel," he started, "wild horses couldn't keep me from ya."

"I'm just glad ya like it," he said after several minutes. "Some girls don't... or so I've heard."

"Well, surely none of the girls you've been with would object to it," she said feeling a stab of jealousy, thinking of him with Debbie.

"What was that look for?" he asked seeing stress in her face.

"Am I really that easy to read?"

"Ya wear worry on yer face like a neon sign Jewel."

"Well, I've never been with anyone else... well... except... well you know... anyway, it's just hard to think of you with other girls, which is crazy... I mean... it's not like I would have expected you to be a virgin or anything," she stuttered, looking away from him, trying to conceal what was probably written all over her face.

"Well, I haven't always been a good boy... I can't lie about it," he said lifting her face up to meet his eyes. "There were girls here and there that I had sex with, but I've never made love ta anyone but you Jewel, and that's the truth of it."

She smiled, feeling the flush in her face as she looked up at him. "What makes me any different than any other girl? I mean... we all have the same parts, right?"

"The fact that ya think that, and that ya'd have ta ask, is exactly why I love ya darlin'. Ya really just have no idea, do ya?"

She shook her head, not sure how to answer. "Well, I'm glad you think so anyway."

"Do ya think that all men are alike then? One's as good as the next is it?" he asked her more seriously.

"No, of course not. What do you mean?"

"I just mean that I think maybe we're made for each other," he said kissing her hand gently. "When we kneeled at the church and said a silent prayer, I just thanked God that I'd found ya. I couldn't understand other men when they'd get all wrapped up in a woman, wonderin' if there was somethin' wrong with me for never feelin' like that. Turns out, there *was* something wrong with me," he smiled at her, reaching down to kiss her gently on the lips, "I hadn't met ya yet."

"I love the way you put things Grady. We are meant for each other," she said cuddling up next to him.

CHAPTER 39

HONEYMOON

"What are ya doin' darlin'?" Grady asked, propping himself up on one elbow rubbing sleep from his eyes as he awoke the next morning.

"I'm just looking at your handy-work," she said walking around the room in Grady's button-down shirt, looking at the detail in the carpentry of the log cabin he built, imagining him carefully smoothing each log, and patiently fitting everything together.

"Yer a strange woman... If yer really that interested in carpentry, I could probably get ya a job with my dad," he said smiling coyly.

"I have no carpentry skill," she said seriously. "Really... I have none, believe me, when it comes to carpentry, I have absolutely no skill aside from being a decent assistant. I mean... I can paint and sand, and do stuff like that, I just don't have skill in actually building anything. I was just thinking about something...," she said eyeing him carefully.

"What is it Jewel?" he said sitting up more interested, still stretching and waking up.

"Well, my parent's house... my house I guess... it's on the edge of the land, right next to the land my grandfather gave to the Landas Family... Troy's family. It's a stone's throw from where Troy and Jolene live. It's an old house, completely falling down. My dad tried making it into a home, but it's always been a losing battle. My great-grandparents built it too close to the creek, and it's flooded a dozen or more times. After mom and dad died, grandpa and I lived in a portion of the house, and we sort of closed off the rest. It was a lot like living in an empty hotel, I think. I could see them and smell them everywhere, and the rooms we had closed off haunted me every day," she said going over to hand him a cup of coffee, sitting down on the bed beside him.

"I would stare up the staircase at the closed doors, and think of them in there, remembering how it used to be. Sometimes I would pretend that my mom was in there getting dressed, or maybe taking a long hot bath. Anyway, the thought of going back to live there is part of what's kept me away so long. I was just thinking

272

that… well… maybe we could build a house," she said shrugging. "I mean, there's this area on the ranch a little closer to the mountains with the creek running nearby, but not too close, it's got all these big beautiful trees all around where Troy and I built a treehouse, and… well… it's my favorite place on the ranch. I always thought it would have been the best place to build a house."

"So ya want me ta build ya a house ta live in?" he asked reaching up to tuck a long strand of her hair behind her ear.

"Well, once you see the old ranch house you'll understand. It's just an idea," she said turning away, still finding it difficult to ask for help. "Not just see it… but feel it. There's something sad and lonely about it that I can't explain."

"I would love ta build ya a house darlin'. I was wonderin' what I could give ya that ya don't have, and if it's a house that ya want and need, then buildin' it for ya would give me more pleasure than ya could possibly know," he said reaching up to stroke her face, making her look at him again. He was happy to feel like he had something that he could offer her. He had been worried about his role on the ranch, not wanting to interfere with Troy, but wanting to be able to contribute in a meaningful way.

Jewel let out a breath she'd been holding, and she sighed happily. "Oh Grady, if I could live at the ranch, but not have to live in my parent's house, do you know how happy that would make me?" she said hugging him.

"It costs a bit ta build a house Jewel. I don't know how soon it could happen, but I do have some savin's ta get a pretty good start," he said considering the possibility more thoughtfully, his mind already making plans.

"Well, Troy wants to buy a two hundred and fifty acre area that is kind of carved out of their land. It would make their land more valuable, because they don't really have their own egress the way it is now. Troy's made a decent living off my ranch since I've been gone, but I still want to make it up to him for taking on the huge responsibility. I was thinking that maybe I could sell him the acreage he wants; taking off a reasonable amount to pay him back, and that would give us enough money to start building a house. Troy said he's been saving for it. He'd still have to take out a loan, but he wants it, and I think we could all make it work. Also…," she said looking him in the eye, "my grandpa owned some acreage in town. My grandma lived there with my dad when they closed the old school house out near the ranch. It's about twelve acres I think… anyway, I was thinking…," she said smiling at him, "with your experience that you have building and selling houses, maybe we could develop it… turn it into a subdivision, ya know, there's always a need for reasonably priced homes in town."

"Wow. How long have ya been up darlin'?" he said a little surprised.

"I'm sorry Grady. It was just a thought. I know you don't want to do construction, and I don't want you to feel like I'm pushing you into anything. It's just… when I saw how beautiful this cabin is, my mind started reeling… you're so talented," she said barely looking at him. "If I could have one talent, it would be to build things like this. It's so well done."

"I'm glad ya think so," he said smiling at her. "I like ta build things Jewel. I just don't like doin' it fer my father. He's a good man, but he like's things done his way, and that can be a bit of a challenge at times. Different people have different ideas... ya know how it is. It's just that ya have me at a bit of a disadvantage. I'd like ta help ya make plans, but I haven't been there, and I can't be much help until I get there ta see for myself."

"Be careful what you ask for Grady. I'm going to go home to run my family's ranch because I have to... because it was chosen for me. I suppose I could sell it all and leave, but I just can't do that, so I have no choice," she said shrugging. "I'm a nurse. That's what I love. Taking care of people who need me, people that I know I can help and make feel better, is what I like to do. I mean... not doing it is like surviving on junk food... you can live off it, but it's not good for you. Do you know what I mean?" she said searching his face for understanding. "I mean... in order to live a healthy life you need steak, veggies, and fruit... not just junk food."

"That's an interestin' metaphor Jewel. Are ya tryin' ta tell me ya want me ta run the ranch so ya can go be a nurse?" he asked.

"I'm just trying to tell you that... well... I don't know exactly... only that if you weren't coming back with me, I may still be on the run. I mean... I need you to help me. I can't run that ranch without you, and then seeing that you're a mechanic, and that you can build things... well... it just seems like it's perfect kind of," she shrugged. "I guess I'm trying to warn you a little, because you're worried about not having enough to contribute to the ranch, and I'm worried that I may be asking too much from you. The truth is that you're probably more qualified to run the ranch than I am, and I may need to lean on you more than you want."

"So... ya need me? Is that what I'm hearin'?" he said grinning at her.

"Yes. I need you more than you bargained for probably," she said with a nervous laugh and a little smile.

"Ya know how ta warm a man's heart Jewel," he said stroking her cheek. "I have been worried, thinkin' that ya'd be out there wantin' ta do it all on yer own, and me at home sweepin' floors and cookin' dinner for ya like a good little wife," he winked. "If ya've need of me ta help ya that would make me happy. I don't want ya ta have ta survive on junk food. The thought of learnin' ta run a ranch is excitin' ta me, and bein' able ta build my wife a home... well... that's a dream come true."

"Really?" she asked smiling at him excitedly.

"I'm lookin' forward ta our future tagether, and we both must've been worried... you thinkin' ya need me too much, and me thinkin' ya don't need me much at all. Maybe we should just try talkin' ta each other in the future when we have worries... what do ya think darlin'?"

"That sounds like a good idea," she said hugging him as he leaned to kiss her on the forehead. "Talking things through? What a revolutionary idea Grady. It's no wonder that I love you so much," she said getting up to pour them both more coffee.

"It's radical, but I think we should give it try," he said making his way to the bathroom.

"Meanwhile, let me cook you breakfast. How do you like your eggs?" she asked

"Scrambled."

"Oh good, that's actually the only way I know how to make them."

Jewel made her way to the kitchen looking out at the pond as she did. The cabin was on the edge of a hill, with the back part sitting on the bank, while the front stood on stilts. It was one large room, with only the bathroom completely separated. The bedroom area was in the back of the cabin, and from the bed you could see the sky through the skylights, and that area was separated by a long bar that was the backside of the kitchen area. The kitchen itself was beautifully done with oak cabinets and granite countertops, and you could look down at the living room area that stepped down several steps, and had a ceiling that was more than sixteen feet high. There was a long walkout deck off the living room, and the wall was glass from ceiling to floor, showing off a spectacular view from anywhere you stood in the cabin.

"Did ya not learn ta cook Jewel?" Grady asked walking out of the bathroom in just his underwear. She looked up to see him standing there with his blond locks going in every direction, and his very fit physique, and she nearly dropped the eggs on the floor.

"Ummm… what were you saying?" she asked turning away from him, trying to hide the blush on her face.

"Do ya know how happy it makes me ta know that I have that effect on ya?" he said coming up behind her, wrapping his arms around her. "Now ya know how I feel every time I look at ya. I can hardly think straight."

She set the eggs down on the counter and turned around, wrapping her arms around his neck, kissing him deeply. That's all it took before they found themselves sprawled out on the kitchen floor grabbing at each other, feverishly lost in the passion they felt for each other. Jewel pulled him to her as hard as she could, rising up every time to meet him, getting lost in the rhythm they danced to in perfect unison, until they both cried out.

"Damn Jewel. I didn't know it could be like this. Ya have me right where ya want me. Ya could lead me ta slaughter right now, and I'd have no choice but ta follow ya blindly 'til my death."

"Well, I won't lead you to slaughter so long as you free my hair from the cabinet door where it seems to be stuck," she said catching her breath, and laughing as she finds herself tethered to the cabinet.

"How did that happen?" he asked laughing and smiling at her as he worked her hair free, still laying on top of her, trying not to crush her.

"Don't move," she said giggling, "the eggs are teetering on the counter. Move slowly off of me and I'll push them with my foot," she said trying to control her laughter.

"I don't care if we break a thousand eggs Jewel. That was amazin'," he said reaching up and pushing the eggs further up on the counter before getting up, pulling her up with him.

She was still wearing his button down shirt, but he could see her nipples beneath it, and he couldn't help but reach for them as she tried straightening her hair, looking around for her underwear.

"Even after I have ya, I want ya. How do ya do that ta me woman?" he said kissing her as she stood on tip toes kissing him back.

"I think you were dazzled that I knew how to cook scrambled eggs," she teased, getting back to the task of cooking.

"I was sticking my foot in my mouth, stupidly asking you why you never learned to cook. I think that's where we left off," he said pulling on his underwear and finding a t-shirt to throw on.

"It's okay. My grandpa taught me how to cook a few things, but he had never really cooked much either until grandma died. We learned the basics together, and Mrs. Landas taught me a few things too. She helped me make homemade chocolate chip cookies once. I had to cook ten dozen of them for a fundraiser, so I know how to cook those. Plus, I know how to cook roasts, and well... basically just meat and potato type meals ...nothing too fancy. I like fried eggs, but I've never figured out how to get them cooked without them ending up at least partially scrambled."

"Alright then... ya make scrambled eggs taday, and tomorrow I'll make us fried eggs," he said pouring them each a fresh cup of coffee.

"Do you cook a lot?" she asked him as she cooked the scrambled eggs in one pan and bacon in another.

"My mom and dad both taught me ta cook. They wanted ta make sure I was well rounded. Not wantin' me ta be one of those guys that laid around and drank beer while my wife took care of everything."

"Remind me to thank them later," she said smiling over at him as he pulled plates out for their breakfast, and poured them each a glass of orange juice.

They ate their breakfast and cleaned up together, before getting dressed and starting out on a hike. The day was beautiful. The sun was shining, and there was just a light breeze as they made their way down the hill to walk around the pond. They headed out in the foothills toward a lake they had marked on the map, strolling hand and hand as they went. Jewel had her hair pulled back in a braid, and wore a white tank top, khaki shorts, and her hiking boots. Grady was wearing the same t-shirt he had thrown on earlier, shorts and his hiking boots. They were dressed for the warm summer weather.

They were glued to each other, each of them caught up in the words and music of the other, both of them taking every opportunity to touch the other, or lean in for a soft kiss. Grady had thrown a few things in a small pack to take to the lake. It was early afternoon by the time they decided to stop at the lake, and they were both sweating profusely. It was over ninety degrees outside and they were starting to feel the effects of the summer sun.

"Let's take a swim!" Jewel said sitting down to unlace her boots. "Come on. We haven't seen another soul all day. Let's take a little swim."

"A skinny dip? Is that what yer askin' of me?" Grady asked sitting down to pull off his boots. "The cold water is goin' ta ruin my whole image."

"I'll help you with that later," she said winking at him.

"Well, I can't turn that down. Besides, I think there's some hot springs that bubble up around here somewhere. Maybe we can find them."

"Alright then," she said pulling off her tank top and shimmying off her shorts, barely taking her eyes off his as she stripped off her last few remaining items.

"Wow. Yer beautiful Jewel," he said catching up to her by quickly pulling his clothes off and taking her hand.

They both made it into the water up past their knees before finally agreeing to dive in to swim out where it was deeper. The cool water felt good on their skin, washing away the sweat from their hike, and the sweat from their night and morning together. Jewel scrubbed at her hair feeling the stickiness from the hairspray as she freed it from her braid, and ran her fingers through it. They swam further out lying back enjoying the coolness from the lake and the warmth from the sun at the same time.

"You're getting sunburned," she said swimming up to him, wrapping her arms around his neck as they both treaded water.

"And yer gettin' more tan," he replied, pulling her close to him kissing her thoroughly.

"I think your image is intact," she said smiling at him as she felt the hardness against her leg.

"Sorry Jewel. I can't hide it. It's what ya do ta me."

"Don't apologize for that," she said kissing him harder, wrapping her legs around him and pushing herself closer to him as he pulled her in. She could feel the warmth of him slide inside her, both of them teasing the other, knowing they would never find the satisfaction they both craved treading water in the middle of a cool lake. Still, she felt herself arching and responding to his touch, with no more control over it than the moon and stars.

"Jewel, I have ta have ya. Let's move ta more shallow water," he whispered, kissing her neck and stroking her nipples playfully.

They made their way to a little cove where there were some large rocks sticking out of the water. He found a place where he could reach; gently pressing her up against one of the boulders where she wrapped her legs around him once again, pulling him to her, wanting to feel him inside her again.

"Grady," she cried out feeling his need like never before. His hands were all over her, and for the first time she felt him lose total control, not holding back at all. Usually he carefully kept control of himself, wanting to be gentle with her, wanting to satisfy her need before feeling his own, but he was wrapped up in his own desire, which allowed her to lose control right along with him, until they both found their release.

"Jewel, oh god are ya alright?" he asked coming to his senses once again several moments later.

"I've never seen you let go like that before," she said stroking his hair as he kissed her more gently.

"Did I hurt ya Jewel?" he asked sheepishly.

"No, and I'm not complaining if you did," she said meeting his eyes. "I've never felt anything like that before. I didn't know making love could hurt and feel good, and feel hot and cold, all at the same time," she said smiling at him. "I'm not broken Grady. You don't have to treat me like I'm fragile."

"Yer just so fine and delicate lookin'. Ya surprise me sometimes when I take yer tiny little hand in mine and ya don't break in two," he said interlinking his fingers with hers watching carefully as he does. He could see that his hands were more than twice the size of hers, and he found the softness of her skin, and the small fine bones mesmerizing. Whenever he held her hands in his, he couldn't resist the urge to kiss them with as much gentleness as he could muster, feeling like they may break if he kissed them any harder.

"You should have seen me and Troy. We climbed trees, jumped from rooftops, crossed raging rivers, and shot every kind of gun imaginable, no matter how hard it kicked."

"Are ya sayin' ya like it when I lose control of myself?"

"I like that you trust me enough to let go. Maybe some moments are for tenderness and others aren't."

"I think maybe right now ya need more tenderness," he whispered stroking her face. "Ya've been through a lot. I'm sorry if I hurt ya darlin'. I just want ya so much sometimes I can hardly control myself, but I don't want ta remind ya of somethin' ya don't want ta remember. I mean… I don't want anything I do ta ever make ya think of…"

"Shhh… don't say that Grady. That's not even possible. I feel safer with you than I've felt since I was a child."

"Ya think yer not good at talkin' about yer feelins', but yer better than ya think Jewel."

"Speaking of feelings… I think I'm losing feeling in my feet," she said as a chill rushed through her body.

"Let's lay in the sun a minute ta dry off. I brought us a blanket," he said as they made their way toward the shore.

"How is it that nobody's here?" she asked, remembering her nakedness as they came out of the water.

"Well, it's Monday so I guess most people are at work. Also, this isn't a very populated area, and there's not any RV campin' nearby. I think the cabin owners around here mostly use the lake on the weekends. They're either glued to their binoculars watchin' the show, or they're not here," he said as they walked naked toward their clothes.

"It's Sunday silly. Try again."

"It's Sunday," he said suddenly remembering. "Oh crap! See that bare ridge over there?" he asked pointing at a spot across the lake where Jewel could just barely see the top of a building.

"I see it," she said pulling her clothes on feeling suddenly alarmed.

"That's an Apostolic Lutheran Church. They spend all day there."

"Well that's good news right? They're inside the church and not outside watching people mate," she said joking with him.

"Yer not a bit worried that someone could have seen us?" he asked smiling at her as he got dressed.

"There's nothing we can do about it now. I wouldn't want to make a habit of it though," she said suddenly feeling shy, imagining what they would have looked like.

"Ya can still blush after makin love ta me like ya did out here in front of the whole world? Do ya know how much that makes me love ya darlin'?" he said smiling at her, and going over to kiss her, grabbing handfuls of her hair as he did. "I love when yer hairs all crazy like it is now. Ya look like... well... I don't know exactly... yer just so damn beautiful, with those deep blue eyes and that black hair all messed up, falling down in all directions."

"Well, I'm glad you like it when my hair's messed up, because I've never been one to spend much time fixing it. You didn't say anything about me wearing make-up yesterday though. Did you like that?" she asked as they walked back toward the cabin hand in hand.

"Ya looked amazin' Jewel. Ya took my breath away when I saw ya walkin' down the aisle ta me. I had ta steady myself, all the while thankin' God that he let me find ya," he said dodging the question.

"That was smooth. Maybe you should run for office," she said sarcastically, giving him a coy smile.

"Ha! Well, I like ya better without make-up, but ya did look amazin' yesterday. Diana said ya wanted the pictures ta come out better, and I remembered readin' about when Nixon and Kennedy debated each other on live television. Kennedy wore the make-up, but Nixon refused, and even though Nixon did better in the debate, Kennedy got more favorable reviews because of his appearance. I figured it was somethin' like that."

"Yes, exactly... I didn't want to look like a tired old man!"

They both laughed for a minute before Grady finally spoke more seriously. "It's yer face darlin'. If ya want ta wear make-up, it's up ta you. Ya don't need it, but I can see that ya might want ta wear it on special occasions and such."

"Well, I'm glad you didn't say that I looked much better, and I should wear it all the time, because I don't really like messing with it. I wore it at prom, and occasionally I wear a tinted lip balm, but that's about it," she said shrugging. "Jolene helped me. That's what she does… hair and make-up."

"Ya had a good visit then?" he asked her.

"Yes, thank you Grady. Thank you for calling Troy. That was the best wedding present ever," she said beaming. "It all worked out better than I could have imagined. Troy never wanted to marry me, he was just doing it because he felt like he had to, and Jolene was mad at me because she knew it, and they were sweet on each other."

"Why would he feel like he had ta marry ya?"

"Our parents always said it. They always said we would grow up and get married. It was something we both always felt we would do when we grew up, and then with my parents dying, and Troy always being there to take care of me… I think he just felt like he had to keep taking care of me… fulfill what he thought was expected of him."

"That's a good friend!" Grady said. "I can see why he's so important ta ya. He's a good man. I'm lookin' forward ta gettin' ta know him and hangin' out with him more. He invited me ta go huntin' with him this fall and help him do some guidin'."

"I'm so glad you two hit it off, and I'm so glad I figured out why Jolene hated me so much. It always bothered me. She didn't seem to have a reason to hate me, and yet I knew she did. I was so wrapped up in my own grief; I couldn't see what's so obvious now."

"Nobody can blame ya Jewel. I've tried ta imagine my own life if my parents had died when I was eleven. It would have been much different. I can't even wrap my brain around it," he said looking at her in awe.

She smiled over at him. "I love that you never have that look on your face that people force when they're trying to show sympathy that they don't necessarily feel. Instead, you look at me like I'm strong… not weak. That first time, by the river when I told you about my parents… I was surprised to see you look at me the way you did. I wish I could tell you exactly what that meant to me."

"Yer just about the toughest person I know… well… mentally anyways, but ya still look like ya might break in two sometimes with yer tiny little bones, and yer skinny little arms."

"Do you think I'm too skinny?" she said looking at her arms more closely.

"How much weight did ya lose do ya think?" he asked her carefully. He thought she was way too skinny after losing so much weight because of the abduction, but it wasn't something he wanted to bring up to her. She was still amazing looking, but she did look like she needed to gain some weight.

"I'm not really sure, but I did lose some weight… maybe ten pounds or so. I'll put it back on," she said looking down remembering why she had lost weight to begin with. At five feet eight inches, Jewel was a little on the skinny side at her normal weight of one hundred and twenty pounds. After losing weight, she knew she was way below where she needed to be, but she was hoping Grady hadn't noticed that much, even though it had nearly taken her own breath away when she caught herself in the mirror one day.

"Ya couldn't look bad ta me Jewel, but ya are a bit on the thin side. Ya seem ta be gettin' yer appetite back though. What's yer weakness when it comes ta food? What's yer favorite?"

"Popcorn and licorice. I love movie popcorn. It's really the biggest reason I like to go to the movies," she said shrugging. "I get a medium popcorn with extra butter, a bag of licorice, and a large diet of some kind. I eat this all on my own without sharing a single kernel. It would be a little embarrassing if it weren't so completely dark in the movies where we can all gorge ourselves under the cover of darkness."

"Well then... would ya like ta go on a date with me tonight Jewel? I'll take ya ta dinner in town and then we'll go ta the movies."

"And then a walk in the moonlight and things like that?" she teased, remembering his first attempt at explaining the first date he would take her on when they were still in Alaska.

"If ya play yer cards right woman," he said grabbing her and tickling her.

"Where would we go? I mean... back to Belle Fourche?" she asked not wanting to go somewhere where she might have to share Grady.

"No. There's a little town about twenty minutes from here. If we're lucky we might be able ta find a small café fer dinner, and see whatever movie they happen ta be playin'."

"I would love to go on a date with you Grady," she said wrapping her hands around his arm and smiling up at him as they reached the cabin.

"Alright then, let's get showered and head in that direction. We can walk around a little and check out the town, but there are only a few hundred people there so don't get yer hopes up."

CHAPTER 40

IT'S A DATE

They both got showered and ready to go, and Jewel was looking forward to being out in the world as a married couple. She twirled the bands around on her finger smiling happily to herself. The band of gold that she put on Grady's finger was borrowed for the sake of ceremony, and she frowned looking over to see his bare ring finger as his hand dangled across the steering wheel on their drive.

"What is it Jewel? What's with the sad face?"

"Well… I'll never be good at poker, which kind of bums me out a little, but aside from that, I was thinking about you not having a wedding ring. I'm sorry I never thought of getting you one. I never even thought of rings until Father asked for them, and then I was so surprised to see my mom's ring I…"

"Jewel, it's really okay. I'm not sure me wearing a ring is a good idea anyway."

"Oh, well… what if I bought you a ring? Would you wear it?"

"If it's important ta ya I would," he trailed off trying to think of what he wanted to say. "Ya don't have anything ta worry about ya know? I wouldn't ever… ummm… stray. I wouldn't ever violate the sanctity of marriage. I'm not exactly the most devout Catholic, but I'm not a heathen either. When I make a promise, I keep it."

"I didn't mean it like that Grady. I trust you completely. I just mean that I like looking at my wedding bands… it makes me happy, and I liked looking at yours too… well… before I knew it was borrowed. Didn't you?"

"I must admit that I like seein' yer little hand with a weddin' band on yer finger. It's a statement that says, *she's mine… back off…* but I thought maybe it was just a guy thing… kind of like peein' on bushes ta mark my territory or somethin'."

"Oh my! Evolution seems to be taking its own sweet time, doesn't it?" she joked. "Why would you think you wouldn't want to wear a ring?"

"I work with my hands a lot… machinery, tools, climbin' up and down ladders, and around on roofs… I had a friend, Albert, when I was in first grade. We were out playin'. We decided ta climb up the side of this girls house ta scare her, but when we went ta jump off, Al sort of hung there for a second, and then all the sudden he dropped. At first I was glad because I was anxious to run away, but Al screamed, and it took me a second ta realize that his finger had been severed. The ring got caught on a nail, and when he jumped, it yanked his finger off at the joint. I guess I have a fear of that."

"That's terrible! No wonder you don't want to wear a ring. Now I don't want to wear one," she said looking at her wedding bands unable to stop herself from smiling. "Well, I guess I still do, but I can see why you don't."

"I would hate it if ya didn't wear a ring. I would be crazy jealous, I'll admit. As it is, I'm probably goin' ta have ta fight off a few brazen men over the next fifty or sixty years."

"Don't you trust me?" she asked putting her hands to her hips even as she rode shotgun in his pickup.

"I trust ya darlin', but I don't trust a large majority of the male population, especially when there's a beautiful woman about, and I think I've good reason."

"Well, you don't have to worry. I'm never taking them off. I love them. Maybe I could buy you a ring that you could wear once in a while when you're not working," she suggested.

"I would like that," he said taking her hand and squeezing it affectionately.

They arrived in town, and Jewel could see why Grady thought they would be lucky to find a small café for dinner. It was a very small town, but it was clean and well taken care of. She jumped out of the truck excitedly when Grady pulled into a parking spot along the main road in front of a building in town.

"Let's walk through town, which I'm guessin' should take us about five minutes, and then we'll figure out what time we need ta be at the movies," he said unable to stop himself from making plans while Jewel was content to just go where the wind took her.

"It's right here. It's *Best of the West Week*. They're showing Tombstone! My favorite movie!" she said excitedly, turning around to face Grady.

"Never saw it. Must be good then?" he asked casually.

"You never saw it? How is that even possible? It's the best movie ever!"

"I've never really watched much TV or movies since I joined the Army. I don't know, it kind of seemed silly for some reason, especially seein' how Hollywood portrays reality. It's too dramatic, and yet, it always fails ta capture the real drama... ya know, like when someone is just alone, and all the bombs have quit fallin', and yer just alone with yer thoughts. It's the scariest, most dramatic part."

"Do you mean after you came home... after you were released?"

"Yeah, I do. Runnin' around and doin' what yer trained ta do is easy compared ta findin' yerself alone an' doin' everything but what ya were trained ta do," he said a little sadly.

"Still... running around doing everything but what we're trained to do, can bring about unexpected gifts," she said smiling up at him.

"Yer right darlin', I wouldn't trade ya for anything in the world."

"Not even for another year of dodging bullets in the desert?"

"Not even for ten," he said wrapping an arm around her.

"What is it that you liked about being in the Army? I mean... war is so... awful, and people are hurting each other and killing, and it's usually because of a bunch of egotistical, narcissistic men who want more power and control over people that just want to be free," she asked looking up at him as they walked down the street.

"Well... the key word is *free* I guess. Here we are walkin' around doin' whatever we want, free ta live like we want, free ta go ta school or drop out, and free ta go as far in life as we can. Contrast that with the young girls who aren't allowed ta be educated, or ta choose their own mate, or ta even think fer themselves. They have less value than livestock. I just always imagine that they're sittin' there in all their misery, wonderin' if someone is goin' ta save them, askin' God why He has forsaken them, and prayin' just fer common decency... and for love maybe. I don't know... it's just somethin' I think about. I don't know if I made a difference, but I like ta think I may have helped someone see and feel what it's like ta be free," he said shrugging. "What about you? What did ya like?"

"I liked being able to comfort people. I was a surgical nurse, but that's not what I liked the most. I liked sitting with people and talking to them. Taking someone who was rattled and broken inside, and letting them say what they needed to say, or to just sit with them a while holding their hand, letting them feel peace and quiet. I think it healed me as much as it healed them. We needed each other."

"I'll bet there's many a soldier that tells the story of the beautiful nurse that listened ta them and helped them in Iraq," he said stopping to read a sign. "Let's go in here Jewel. Do ya want ta?" he asked pointing at the front of a bar that claimed to have the *World's Greatest Cheeseburger*.

"Well, I am a cheeseburger connoisseur. It wouldn't be right if I didn't try out the World's Great Cheeseburger," she said as they made their way inside.

"This is a once in a lifetime opportunity Jewel. We can't pass it up!"

They made their way inside and sat down at a little table near the bar. Grady was making idle talk with the bartender who was clearly flirting with him, despite the fact that she was sitting right next to him. She couldn't help but follow the bartender's eyes to the empty spot on his left hand, looking for a wedding band, and Grady apparently caught it too, quickly making it a point to bring up the fact that they were on their honeymoon. I tidal wave of happiness filled her up when he introduced her as his wife for the first time.

"What?" Grady asked taking her hand across the table.

"That's the first time you introduced me as your wife. I like it... that's all," she said smiling broadly, neither one of them taking their eyes off each other as the bartender set their beers down on the table in front of them.

They sat at the bar and ate their cheeseburgers, drinking a few more beers while chatting with the locals that were sitting at the bar. Everyone was friendly, asking them about their recent wedding and how they met. A few of them even bought them some drinks in celebration. They were a little reluctant to mention the fact that they hadn't known each other for very long, but it came out anyway, and they were reassured when an older couple who sat at the bar told their story about getting married after only knowing each other for two weeks. The couple then happily described their subsequent thirty years of trials and tribulations, before smiling warmly at each other.

They were relieved when it was finally time to head to the movies so they would have time to sober up before driving back to the cabin. By the time the movie was over, they were sobered up and ready for bed. The excitement of the last several days, and the excessive amount of alcohol at dinner, was wearing them down. They made their way back to the car, chatting about the movie and sharing their lives with each other non-stop.

Jewel had never been so open about everything with anybody before, but with Grady, it seemed to always just flow out of her with ease, never once hesitating or feeling like she needed to hide the difficulty of her childhood. Grady just listened. He didn't judge her or take pity on her the way she was used to people doing, which always made her avoid the conversation altogether. Instead, he complimented her on being strong, and looked at her with admiration and gratitude for not letting it break her.

She listened to him talk more about his time in Iraq and Afghanistan, and his apparent love for children. His stories of freedom always seemed to involve smiling children, or the happy faces of girls who were able to attend school once again. She could see there was a part of him that would always be missing if he didn't feel like he was helping people be free, and find opportunities to go as far in life as they could. She wondered if he would be able to feel complete on the ranch, living a simple life that didn't involve freeing people from enslavement.

They talked well into the early morning, deciding to have a few glasses of wine after they made it back to the cabin. They were completely focused in on each other, enjoying the luxury of their solitude… no interruptions, no phones, no television. It was just the two of them holding on to every minute before finally having to let sleep take them.

CHAPTER 41

MADISON GEARY

"That's a great way to wake up in the morning," Jewel said, still languishing in their morning lovemaking session. "Are we complete freaks or something? I mean… is this normal to want each other so much?"

"Well… we're newlyweds, and we wanted each other from the moment we first laid eyes on each other, but we had ta wait, and we weren't able ta have much time alone, and so forth. I hadn't been with a woman in more than a year and you… ya waited yer whole life so… I guess we're probably normal."

"Well, I appreciate the full analysis, but how did you manage to keep women away from you for more than a year? That doesn't seem possible," she said as her hands traced the lines on his chest as they laid there in bed cuddled up.

"There were opportunities, but I had a bit of a transformation when I left the Army. It was life altering. All the sudden I didn't know who I was, or who I wanted ta be anymore, and then there was Debbie," he said meeting Jewels eyes as she looked up hearing the name, "she was circlin' the house like a vulture circles a dyin' animal. If there were any interested women nearby, she would have scared them off. She was willin', but I wasn't interested in gettin' wrapped back up in that. I knew she'd been unfaithful ta her husband and I knew who she was… aside from the fact that my dad would've castrated me if I'd been sleepin' with a married woman… separated or not," he added emphatically, "and how in the world did ya manage ta keep the men off ya Jewel?"

"I think I was just cut-off by my own choice. I may as well have been walking around with a big sign on me that said LEAVE ME ALONE! I always had Troy in high school. Everyone thought we were a couple, and I guess looking back, I used that to hide behind. In college, I took way too many credit hours each semester, including summer. All I had time to do was study and work my internships. What took me two years, should've taken me three. Then there was the doctor in Iraq. I was just really infatuated with him… or… maybe my picture perfect fantasy of who I thought he was. There were other opportunities, but I always managed to

seclude myself, and avoid them. I just wasn't ready," she said shrugging. "I mean…
it wasn't that I didn't have desires, it just required too much… intimacy I guess."

"I was worried ya might never want me ta touch ya again," he said, lifting her
chin to meet his eyes.

"I was worried you might not ever want to touch me again, but… I don't
know… the worst of it wasn't the rape. I didn't really figure it out until last night,
thinking about what you were talking about, being free… or *not* being free. That
was the worst of it… not being free. Having someone take away your freedom is
devastating."

"It makes me boil inside ta even think of it. Yer tougher than me Jewel. Ya seem
ta be able ta put it aside easier than I can. I don't know what's wrong with me!" he
said as Jewel felt his body tense up.

"I can tell. You'll run your hand up my leg… always skipping over the scar on
my thigh. Why do you do that?" she asked calmly, hoping he'll relax and open up
about it.

Grady hesitated for a second, but decided to just throw it out there. "It's
because I don't want ta be in the middle of makin' love ta ya, and remind ya of him.
I remember ya said that he would dig his fingers in ta hurt ya more. I'm afraid if I
touch it ya might think of that night."

"There's nothing you could ever do that would make me think of him. He was
a monster, and you're… the opposite of that. If it had been something that had
gone on and on for days or weeks, then it would probably be very different for me at
this point, but it didn't. It happened one time, and I was able to free myself, and…
well… I don't know, but that heals me in a way that is difficult to explain," she said
sitting up to face him, covering herself with the sheet. "Then you came for me…
and Rudy… and Daryl. It's hard for me to describe what happened to me when I
saw that you came for me, but… well… something changed inside me. There's no
way for me to tell you what's it's like to feel like you could disappear off the face
of the earth without anyone noticing, only to find yourself suddenly surrounded
with people who would risk everything to save you. It's unexplainable… especially
for someone as emotionally handicapped as I am," she said, making fun of herself.

"Yer better at explainin' things than ya think Jewel." He reached up to softly
rub his hand over the scar on her leg, looking her in the eyes the whole time.
"Thanks for tellin' me that."

They sat there a second staring at each other, contemplating the magnitude of
their conversation. Having him finally touch her scar seemed to bridge a gap that
still laid between them, and she released tension she'd felt because of it. Every time
she thought she couldn't feel closer to him, something would happen to inch them
together more closely than before. They were still sitting there swimming in all the
feelings they were caught up in, when they heard a car pull up in the driveway with
the horn-honking non-stop.

"What the hell!" Grady said, jumping up to pull on his pants.

He was still looking for a t-shirt to pull on when the apparent horn blower started pounding on the door. Jewel grabbed a few things and ran into the bathroom, still wrapped up in the sheet she pulled off the bed.

"Grady! Ryan! McDonald! You son-of-a-bitch! What the fuck are you doing in my house?" Debbie yelled as Grady opened up the door and she stormed in angrily. "You better not have brought your little whore here!"

"Debbie! This isn't yer house now get out!" Grady yelled at her pointing at the door.

Debbie stood her ground looking around the cabin frantically. "This is my house! We're not divorced yet, and if Greg said you could use this place without talking to me first then there's going to be hell..." Debbie yelled, but then stopped mid-sentence as Jewel calmly walked out of the bathroom.

She had gotten dressed, threw her hair up in a quick ponytail, and she was looking breathtaking. "What's with all the yelling out here?" Jewel asked loudly, coming out of the bathroom, sweeping calmness over the room like a soft blanket as Debbie stopped dead in her tracks and just stared at her.

"Oh! This is rich! You brought a... a... woman to my house?" Debbie stuttered, a little unnerved by Jewel, despite her best efforts to maintain her composure.

"My name's Jewel. I'm Grady's wife. What is this all about?" she said crossing her arms in front of her, giving Debbie a stern look, much like a parent would have when they were scolding a child.

"I... uhhh... this is my house," she stuttered. "I heard... uhhh. I heard Grady brought you here, and I don't think that's right. I think you should leave," she said straightening herself, trying to regain the nerve she lost when she saw Jewel.

"So Greg is your estranged husband, and you're upset that he said Grady could bring me here, because you still have feelings for Grady? Is that it?" Jewel asked in that innocent way that always endeared people to her, and clearly, Debbie was no exception.

Grady couldn't help but stand back and watch this unfold. He hadn't ever seen Debbie so unsettled before. She usually filled up a room by her very presence, much like a strong gust of wind that whips through the house unexpectedly, scattering papers about, and littering the floor with dried crusty leaves from outside, making the people around her take cover.

"Uhhh... I guess... I shouldn't have come. I just got so mad when I heard you were here," she said apologetically, glancing at Grady bewildered, but focusing mostly on Jewel.

"It's okay," Jewel said, cautiously reaching out to wrap an arm around Debbie. "Grady said you two were good friends. I understand it could be difficult for you. Would you like to have some coffee with us?"

"Ummm... I don't... I should go... probably," Debbie stumbled, looking at Grady confused.

"It's alright Debbie. Have some coffee with us," Grady said, feeling a need to come to Debbie's rescue despite himself. She suddenly seemed like a small, broken woman, and it startled him to see her that way.

"Please. Go sit on the deck and I'll make a fresh pot of coffee, and then we can sit and talk for a while," Jewel said, motioning to Debbie and Grady to go sit on the deck while she made her way to the kitchen.

Jewel hated confrontation, but fortunately, she had an ability to bring a calm feeling to most situations. There were several fights that broke out in the hospital, but she could always diffuse it before things got completely out of control. Escalating confrontation never rattled her unless it involved her directly, which was part of what made her such a good nurse. In reality, part of her calming effect was because of her looks, with her black hair and olive skin, contrasted with the deep blue of her eyes with sparkling violet flecks; it usually startled most people when they first looked at her. She was literally stunning to most people when they first met her, and she had a softness about her that made people want to reach out to her and take shelter under the blanket of tranquility she offered.

When she was in the bathroom getting dressed, she never thought twice about going out to try to bring peace back into the cabin that had felt like a sanctuary only moments before. There was a part of her that felt sympathetic to Debbie, especially when she heard her yelling, sensing the pain of regret, and years of hurt. Plus, she thought Debbie couldn't be all-bad. Grady had spent quite a bit of time with her, so she knew that she must have some redeeming qualities.

"Here we are," Jewel said, bringing a tray with everything they would need for coffee, complete with a basket full of muffins. She could feel the tension when she walked outside, with Debbie sitting at the table uncomfortably, while Grady stood leaning against the rail with his arms crossed in front of him, showing his contempt for her.

"Thank you. That's so nice of you after I stormed in here first thing in the morning screaming and yelling," Debbie said looking down, taking her coffee black while Jewel poured a cup for her and Grady.

Jewel smiled at her sympathetically. "Emotions can cause us to do things we wouldn't normally do," she offered sympathetically.

"We wouldn't have come here if I'd known ya had a fondness for the place Debbie. Greg said ya'd agreed ta give him this place while ya keep the house in town. I wasn't tryin' ta rub yer face in it," Grady said relaxing a little.

"I hate this damn place! He only had you build it to get away from me. He's taking the kids. He's taking the house. He's taking this place, and what does that leave me with?" she barked bitterly.

Grady relaxed a little uncrossing his arms. "I'm sorry yer goin' through all that, but I'm not ta blame. I never led ya on. Ya knew we weren't gettin' back together."

Jewel sat there quietly sipping her coffee, careful not to interfere with the conversation that was transpiring between them. She sensed that her presence there was allowing the conversation to proceed without yelling and screaming.

"You're right Grady," Debbie said after several quiet moments, standing up and reaching into her purse, and for a moment, Jewel startled, thinking she was going to bring out a gun and shoot him. She hadn't known until a moment later that what she threw out on the table would hit him in the heart, almost as hard as a cold steel bullet. "I found her. She's yours. I delivered her five months after you left for the Army, and then gave her up for adoption," she threw the picture on the table, stopping for a moment to watch the array of emotions unfold on Grady's face before storming out, leaving an air of wreckage in her wake that made a chill run down Jewel's spine.

It wasn't until they heard the gravel flying in the driveway that they both started to grasp the magnitude of the situation. Grady slowly, very hesitantly, walked over to the table and picked up the picture, trying to digest everything that had just transpired. He searched the girls face in the picture, looking for signs of his paternity, a million thoughts racing through his mind wondering what her name was, and where she was, even as doubt and distrust of Debbie gave him pause.

Jewel sat there staring at him completely frozen, watching him as he scanned the picture, and she tried to make sense of everything that had just taken place.

"How can this be?" he said looking up at Jewel for the first time.

"Could it be true Grady? I mean... did you know she was pregnant? Would she lie about this just to hurt you?" she finally asked, swallowing hard, struggling with her emotions.

"I don't know anymore. I knew Debbie was... mean... I guess... for lack of a better word right now, but I'm stunned," he said shaking his head. "She never told me she was pregnant. She didn't look pregnant or...," he said trailing off, searching his mind for memories he had long forgotten.

"There's something written on the back," Jewel said, standing up to look at the picture with Grady.

Madison Geary, Age 10
1409 Barker St
Casper, WY

"Casper Wyoming?" Grady was staring at Jewel as if in a trance. "She said she had the flu. She was sick for a while the month before we graduated."

"Casper's not far from the ranch. Just a little over an hour. We'll find out. We'll go talk to Debbie, and we'll just find out. It's not your fault Grady. She didn't tell you. How could you have known? You were just a kid," Jewel said talking nervously, feeling the tension rise in Grady as he considered the possibility that it could be true.

"I don't know what to say right now Jewel. I mean... look at this picture," he said handing her the picture of the girl that undeniably resembled him in a way that made his knees shake. "It's like I'm starin' at a picture of Diana."

Jewel looked at it for the first time. There was a smiling, blond-haired, blue-eyed lanky girl standing in the seat of a swing on the playground. It was just close-up enough for her to pick out the features that were the same one's she'd seen on Grady and Diana's faces. Debbie was tall, and had light brown hair and hazel eyes. The girl in the photo had the face of Grady, and they both knew it.

"Well… like I said earlier Grady. There's no point in thinking of *what if* or *should*. We just have to look at what *is* and move forward. We'll figure it out together," she said, sensing a need to calm him down, reaching out to rub her hand along his forearm.

"Yer something else Jewel. Ya just found out yer husband may have a half grown child, and yer calm as a cucumber," he said touching her face; torn between the agitations he felt over the recent development, and the love and happiness he felt for his new bride.

Inside Jewel was feeling overwhelmed thinking of Debbie, and she was running the math around in her head. Grady would have graduated in May at the age of eighteen, which would mean that Madison would have been born in October, around the same time her parents died, only to end up living in a place that's just over an hour away from her home. She had considered the seven-year age difference between her and Grady, but it never seemed like much of a difference until she realized she was eleven when the child was born. She stared at Grady's face, not taking anything in, just getting completely lost in her own thoughts.

"I'm… a little… overwhelmed right at the moment, but… as soon as that passes and we can sit down and think this through, I think we'll be able to figure things out. What's going through your mind right now?" she asked, suddenly feeling scared that Grady was reconsidering the direction of his life.

"Jewel! How can ya even think that?" he asked incredulously, in answer to the look of fear he saw on her face, knowing how distrustful she was of anything that was labeled with the word *forever*. "I just vowed ta have ya and hold ya 'til death do us part. Do ya doubt that I meant it?"

Jewel immediately let out a breath. "No Grady. I don't doubt it at all. I'm sorry… I'm completely hopeless, but I'll keep trying. How the hell do you do that anyway?"

"Yer not hopeless at all," he said ignoring the question, wrapping his arms around her, pulling her into his chest. He felt in tune to her in a way that he never thought possible, and in a way that he knew he would never be able to explain to her without sounding creepy. Sometimes when he answered her un-verbalized thoughts and fears, he spoke out without ever realizing that she hadn't actually said it aloud, surprising even himself at times. "Come on Jewel. Let's go for a hike. As much as I'd like ta drive home and ring Debbie's neck this instant, its better we let the dust settle and figure out where ta go from here."

Jewel wasn't surprised by how calm Grady was. He wasn't the kind of person to react emotionally without thinking things through, which was one of the things she loved about him. He needed to consider all his options, and she figured that he already had about ten different paths he was contemplating, methodically narrowing down his options for one logical reason or another.

They finished getting dressed, and packed a lunch while snacking on muffins for their breakfast. They were both unusually quiet, digesting the magnitude of what Debbie told them, considering everything it meant, not just for them, but for the little girl, and maybe even for Debbie.

Since the moment they got in Grady's truck after leaving their wedding reception, they had been constantly chatting with each other, wanting to take advantage of every moment they had with just the two of them, but now there was silence. It was a comfortable silence that reminded Jewel of being with her grandpa. He seemed to know when to leave her alone to her thoughts, and although she knew Grady was knee deep in his own thoughts, she sensed that he was purposefully letting her think things through.

They left the cabin and walked in the opposite direction of where they had gone the day before. Jewel wondered where they were going, but decided not to ask. He seemed to know where they were going, and she knew that he never did things without having a plan. She followed quietly behind him, easily keeping up with a slow, casual pace that they enjoyed outside of being in the competition.

They walked for an hour or so, and after a steep, steady climb, they finally reached the top, which overlooked a big, green, beautiful valley below that went as far as the eye could see. At the top, there was an outcropping of rocks, and Jewel could smell the sulfur long before she saw it. There was a natural hot spring that pooled in the rocks, with the most crystal-clear water she had ever seen.

"It's beautiful," she said breaking their silence.

"I knew ya'd like it," he said turning to look at her, both of them smiling as their eyes met. "If I'd known ya liked ta skinny dip so much, I'd have brought ya here first."

"Can we swim in it? Isn't it too hot?" she said, remembering the steaming hot pools she had seen at Yellowstone, with scalding hot water.

"It's like bath water. It'll feel good in a while when we cool off a bit. Come here... quietly," he said grabbing her hand, creeping a few hundred yards away where they could look out over a ledge at a protected area where he previously saw a herd of elk. "Well they aren't here, but a couple times when I came up here they were bedded down right there. It's a little late in the morning. Its best ta come up in the early mornin' or in the evenin'. It's interestin' ta see."

"You're going to love the Big Horn Mountains. I have so many places I want to take you, and I'm sure Troy does too."

"I can hardly wait darlin'," he said tucking a rogue hair back behind her ear the way he always did. "I suppose we'll have ta stay a couple days in Belle Fourche, but I'm ready ta get goin'."

"You are? That wasn't what I expected," she said.

"What were ya expectin'?" he asked surprised.

"I don't know exactly. I figured we would need to stay so you could get more information from Debbie... maybe discuss it with your parents. I don't know. I thought that maybe you would want to ask around town to see if anyone else knew about it. Things like that," she said shrugging.

He shook his head calmly and unemotionally. "I don't ever want ta talk ta Debbie again, and I've no intention of talkin' ta the gossipers in town. I always defended her when people called her the devil, or teased her about castin' evil spells and such. I would make excuses for her, truly believin' that everyone had their good side. Her good side was more of a sliver that got smaller and smaller, and apparently disappeared altogether," he said, sitting down on the rocks, settling in for a long explanation that Jewel sensed he needed to let out.

"Someone once told me that someone who's nice ta ya, but mean ta the waitress... is not a nice person. It wasn't until I heard that when I truly figured her out. She's not a nice person, despite how she was ta me. She made a choice for the both of us. I don't know why she didn't tell me. She would have been four or five months along when I broke up with her. She had ta know that I would have stayed with her had I known she was pregnant. Why didn't she tell me? What the hell was she plannin' ta do? I mean... it seems ta me that she would have made the same decision whether I'd stayed with her or not. Then... lookin' at how she is with the two kids she has... it makes me think that she probably never wanted kids. The thought of that woman bein' anywhere near a child of mine makes me cringe. Maybe it was for the best... I don't know, but what I do know is that the only thing that matters is what's best for this little girl. I mean... I guess I'm assumin' she is actually mine given the fact that she looks exactly like me. I'll find the truth... *we'll* find the truth, and then we'll do whatever is best for her. If she wants ta meet me then that's what we'll do."

"Do you think we should get as much information from Debbie as we can?" she asked.

"I'll talk ta Greg and then we can decide from there. He's a good man, and I don't think Debbie is capable of tellin' the truth. I don't want this ta be tainted by her, and I don't want any relationship I may potentially have with the girl ta involve her. It has ta be separate," he said looking at her. "Ya have ta understand Jewel... before the competition; I spent nearly a year at home seein' Debbie on a regular basis, offerin' her a shoulder ta cry on and... friendship. She never once mentioned anything about this. She must have been searchin' for the girl all along, and then did ya see the evil look on her face when she saw how hard it hit me?"

In fact, Jewel couldn't get that evil look out of her mind. She wondered what her motivation in searching for the girl, and then telling Grady about her, was all about. It certainly didn't appear to be an act of love. "I saw it. It gave me chills. Why do you think she told you now?"

"My guess… well… maybe ta convince me ta get back together, but then when she saw that was definitely not goin' ta happen, she decided ta use it as a weapon instead… hopin' ta cause a problem between me and you maybe," he said taking her hand and kissing it. "Maybe ta take somethin' perfect and strain it a bit."

Jewel sat completely still for a moment looking at Grady, lost in her own thoughts, feeling a little scared. The sky was blue and the sun was touching their skin lightly, warming them, and glistening off the pool of water beneath them. There were green rolling hills stretched out as far as the eye could see, lightly dotted with purple and yellow flowers, scattered about in a beautiful disarray.

"I think it was impulsive. I don't think she planned it like that. She came in high and mighty, but on the deck, she looked broken and sad. I think she played her only hand," she said not without some sympathy. "She couldn't have known that we can't be splintered."

Grady swung his head around at her, relieved to hear her confirm what he himself believed. "How is it yer not the least bit upset, or hesitant, or… I don't know… somethin'?" he asked incredulously.

"Well… I mean… I knew you weren't a virgin. You said you had been with other women that… that you hadn't been a good boy. I suppose that with men… I mean… how do you know you don't have ten children out there somewhere?" she asked, not in an accusatory way, but with an innocence that Grady couldn't help but smile at when he looked at her.

"Well, I've taken matters inta my own hands ta make sure that wouldn't happen in most cases," he said not going into details. "Debbie was on birth control… or at least that's what she told me. I trusted Debbie in high school… probably because I was too young ta consider the possibility that someone would lie about that. Then there's you Jewel," he said smiling at her automatically as he met her eyes, unable to stop himself. "I trusted ya since the moment I met ya… probably because I'm older and wiser."

"Do you think I should quit taking it? Should we let nature take its course?" she asked suddenly, surprising herself. "It's not something we've ever really talked about."

Jewel hadn't planned on bringing it up, but things just seemed to flow out of her in an easy way when she was with Grady. It had been that way since they first met, which was something that drew them together so closely… neither one of them able to hold back and hide their feelings from one another, which made it easy for Jewel to see the answer long before Grady ever answered her.

"Do ya think you'll feel okay without it?" he asked excitedly, pulling her to him instinctively.

"I've been on it since I was fourteen. I suppose it'll be a transition, but I…

well... I think that maybe we should just let nature take its course. It's served us well so far."

They sat there on top of the hill, quietly contemplating their future together. Everything was before them. They talked about Madison Geary, each of them remembering the ice blue eyes that stared back at them from the photo, the same ones they both knew were Grady's. They talked about their marriage and their new life together on the ranch in Wyoming, and the possibility of children in their future.

They enjoyed the hot spring pool and ate their lunch they had packed, laughing at times, and then talking seriously at other times. They snuggled together for a nap, lounging in the warmth of the summer sun before they decided to make their way back down to the cabin. When they got closer, they could see a car parked at the cabin, and Grady recognized it as Greg's.

"Let's hope it's actually Greg, and not Cruella Devil," he said smiling down at Jewel, but a moment later, they could see Greg sitting up on the deck as they made it closer.

"Grady... Jewel... I'm sorry to bother you. Debbie left a note, and said she was coming up here. Have you seen her?" Greg asked as they stepped up on the deck.

"She came by here this mornin', but then left in a hurry. I figured she was headed home, but I don't know... she could have been headed anywhere," Grady replied.

"She cleaned out all our accounts, and her apartment is empty. Surely she wouldn't walk away from her kids," Greg said hopelessly. Greg was shorter, only slightly taller than Debbie was at five foot, five-inches, and he had a slight build. His head was clean-shaven, and he had a goatee that was dark auburn in color. Grady had said he was a very hard working man, who was completely devoted to his children, and Jewel frowned a little when she saw the sadness in his soft brown eyes.

They stood there looking at Greg sympathetically, wondering how Greg's information fit in with everything that happened that morning. "Let's sit and have a drink," Grady finally said, motioning Greg back to where he had been sitting on the deck as Jewel took the cue to go bring out glasses, and something stiff to drink.

"Ummm... do you mind telling me... ummm... what she said to you?" Greg asked carefully, not wanting to pry, but trying to get some clues as to where she might have gone.

Grady reached in his shirt pocket and pulled the picture of Madison Geary out, briefly looking at the face again before laying it on the table in front of Greg. "Do ya know who this is?"

"She told you then," he said lifting his head slightly, eyeing Grady over the rims of his glasses. "Yeah, I know Grady. I had to lock her in the closet at her apartment to keep her from showing up at your wedding to tell you there in front of half the town... making as big a scene as she possibly could!"

Grady tensed up, automatically sitting up straight and looking at him menacingly, Jewel thought, as she made her way to the table where they sat. "Well… I suppose I should say thank you for that, but how long have ya known man?" he asked exasperated.

"A little over a year, but she told me she was going to tell you. I can see by the look on your face that you've only just recently found out," he answered, looking like a frightened child that just got caught doing something naughty, never taking his eyes off Grady.

Jewel could see Grady's body relax a little as he looked Greg over, finally deciding to trust him, and she let out a breath as he did. She poured them each a glass of cabernet, which was the only thing they had, and all three of them drank it down a little more quickly than would have been socially acceptable in any other situation.

"She barged in here this mornin', screamin' an' yellin'. Jewel had her calmed down ta the point that I thought we might actually be able ta have a conversation, but then she pulled out that picture," he said, nodding toward the picture of Madison, still sitting on the table in front of Greg. "She told me she gave her up for adoption five month after I left fer the Army. How did she do that without everyone in town not findin' out about it?" Grady asked Greg, crossing his arms in front of him and shaking his head.

"Didn't she go with you?" Greg asked, sitting back in his chair puzzled, throwing his hands in the air. "When she left… ugh… the two of you left together, right?"

"No. Debbie and I broke up after graduation, and aside from emails and a few phone calls, I never talked to her or saw her again until I was discharged," Grady said, throwing his hands up in the air along with Greg. "I had no idea she was pregnant!"

"Grady. Let's back up here. Debbie said she left with you after graduation. You had the baby together, and then you both decided to give the baby up for adoption when she decided that she didn't want to marry you. She said she was searching for the girl, and found her against your wishes. How much of that is true?" Greg asked exasperated.

Jewel sat quietly curled up in one of the chairs at the table, sipping her wine as the saga continued to unfold before her eyes. There was a part of her that felt like she was an intruder in the conversation, but she knew that Grady would want her to stay, which he reassured her by looking at her briefly, communicating in that unspoken way that couple's often do.

"I broke up with Debbie after graduation, and I never saw her again until I was discharged, at which time I made perfectly clear ta her that I wouldn't get involved with her again. I didn't ever know she was pregnant. I didn't know anything until she barged in here this mornin' and told me that she found her, that she was mine, and that she had given her up for adoption five months after I left fer the Army," Grady said leaning back in finality. "How did ya find out about it?"

"Before she had her appendix out last year... right before we split up... they sent her all the paperwork. Under number of pregnancies, she wrote three. I thought there had to be some kind of mistake, so I asked her about it. Of course, she told me it was a mistake, but then, when I was sitting in the doctor's office waiting for her and the nurse to come back as they got her height and weight, I glanced through her file and saw it again... this time in two different places. Apparently she had made that mistake three times," Greg said, remembering the pain from his marriage. "She finally came clean when I found some letters from the adoptive dad. That's when she told me her version of the truth."

"Greg. Ya know me man. Do ya think I'd give up my own flesh and blood?" Grady asked, leaning on the table, looking at Greg intently.

"I found it hard to believe Grady. It never made sense to me, but she was my wife, and I wanted to believe her. You know Grady, I knew from your dad that you wouldn't get involved with her again, despite what she was telling me." Greg said, giving Grady a look to make sure he knew that he understood this. "How much do you know about the girl?"

"I know what's written on the back here," Grady said nodding at the picture. "Do ya know anything about her?"

"I have all the files that were saved on our computer. I'll get you everything I have," Greg said, standing up to walk over and lean against the rail, staring out absently.

"Where do ya think she's gone?" Grady asked sympathetically, seeing the grief on Greg's face as he turned away.

"I don't know. Despite it all, my kids love her. She's so damn selfish though. I hope she never comes back," he said, turning to look at them with a look of anger on his face. "I'm so sick of her bullshit! Is there one damn thing she ever told me that was the truth?" he asked rhetorically. "If I'm lucky she'll be gone for good, and I never have to deal with her again. Is that terrible?"

"Ya've had a time with her man. I don't blame ya one bit, but why did ya come out here lookin' for her?" Grady inquired. "What were ya expectin'?"

"I thought she might burn the place down... maybe shoot the two of you... I don't know. She's so damn... unpredictable! I loved her and hated her for the same reason. Also, I just wanted to know what she told you. I was hoping you were going to tell me she was taking the money and moving to another country or something," he said forcing a smile, trying to make a joke of it, but failing miserably. "I'm sorry! You two are on your honeymoon. I should leave you."

"Not at all!" Jewel said as Greg looked at her apologetically. "Have another glass of wine."

Greg stayed a while as Grady skillfully turned the conversation away from Debbie, and brought up fonder memories of their childhood together. It was clear they had been close once, and Jewel sat back enjoying the stories, listening to them laugh, all the while navigating around any stories that might have involved Debbie.

They started in comparing stories of Grady's dad as Jewel opened up their second bottle of wine. Greg worked for him, and clearly had an admiration for him, never having had much of a relationship with his own father; Patrick had become a father figure to him.

"I'm glad yer doin' it man. Ya have the patience of a saint," Grady said toasting Greg as Greg expressed his appreciation for getting to work for his dad.

"Alright, I'm going to leave you two before I'm unable to drive home. The last thing you need on your honeymoon is a drunk sleeping on the floor next to you," Greg said laughing, getting up to take his leave as Grady and Jewel stood up to tell him goodbye.

They said their goodbye's, with Jewel and Grady standing on the deck waving to Greg as he pulled out of the driveway. Greg had managed to answer many of the questions they had about Debbie and Madison, and they were happy that Greg offered to give them all the information he had about the adoption. There were still many unanswered questions, but for the moment, they were happy to have their time alone again, deciding to shower first and then make themselves dinner. They talked non-stop considering all the possibilities, both of them feeling more at ease with the situation now that the idea of it had completely sank in, and some of the truth of what happened was more clear to them.

They knew this was the last night of their honeymoon, taking every opportunity to touch each other, or steal another kiss. They talked and drank and made love until the small hours of the night left them tired and worn out, lingering as long as they could on every moment, before finally closing their eyes and drifting off toward a new day.

PART FOUR

THE RANCH

CHAPTER 42

CAMPING

"I've got it laid out so the length of the house is perfectly parallel ta the mountains," Grady said excitedly as he carefully explained the layout of the house he was getting ready to build. He was walking along the length of the future house explaining things as he went from one stake to another. He had already taken a motor grader and created a solid pad to build on, clearing away the vegetation, and getting everything graded with strict precision, so it was easy to see the outline of where the house would be. He was dressed in a tight white t-shirt, faded Levis, and work boots, and Jewel was watching him describe everything in detail. He was using his hands, and pacing everything off, but she was finding it hard to concentrate on what he was saying, distracted by the emotion he stirred in her.

She was happy to be out in the summer air in the country, in the part of the ranch that was her most favorite. It was a place near the base of the foothills, looking down at the creek running just a few hundred yards away. From where the house would sit, they would be able to see the snow-capped mountains out of the Southwest windows, or look down at the creek to the Northeast. In front of the creek, on the side they were on, there was a clearing where she and Troy had played non-stop when they were kids. Her dad had helped them build a small foot bridge, and just across from there was a tree house they had built and played in for thousands upon thousands of hours.

When she had arrived back at the ranch, one of the first things she wanted to do was go find the tree house. These were some of the best memories from her childhood, and she sat in there recalling her and Troy's dad carefully planning to build this somewhat elaborate structure for them to play in. It was up in the cottonwood trees, and it spanned from one tree to another, and then another. It had an escape route where they could slide down a pole to make a quick getaway, which was an important factor in all their childhood games. They had carried up discarded household items that they used to decorate the inside, and the faded outline of the words they had written on the front of the treehouse could still just barely be read. It said: KEEP OUT! NO PARENTS ALLOWED!

They had only been at the ranch for a few weeks, but it didn't take Grady long to realize how haunted Jewel was by being in her parent's old house, aside from the fact that it was clear the house was falling down around them. He had already been up on the roof twice to make repairs, and the smell of previous floods lingered almost as thick in the air as the sadness that was present in Jewel's eyes whenever she was inside. It was an old stick house that was beautifully built, but built in the wrong spot, though it was easy to see how the original homesteaders could have made the mistake, because it looked like they were a ways from the creek, but it came up faster and higher than anyone had realized before it was built.

It was a medium sized, white, two-story house with a big layout on the main level with the living room, the kitchen and the dining room taking up one large open area in the front of the house, and then two small bedrooms and a large bathroom that took up the back of the house. The upstairs area had another three bedrooms and a bathroom, and was accessible by a long staircase in the center of the house, and since the death of her parents, the upstairs had been completely abandoned. Grady would see Jewel look up the stairs every time she would walk by them as if she expected a ghost to come down each and every time and steal her soul once and for all. He'd watch her as she sat in the chair with her back to it, watching out the window, and every now and then, she would turn around and look toward the stairs with emotion that was both fear and anguish.

She had lived in one of the bedrooms downstairs even before her parents died, and her grandpa had lived in the other bedroom, and then they shared the large bathroom that sat between them. Her bedroom was in the back right portion of the house and it had two large windows, both of which gave her a view of the creek that had always seemed like a constant threat, as they battled to keep the spring runoff out of their house. One of the windows gave her a view of Troy's window, and they would often use flashlights to signal each other late at night. Her grandpa's bedroom had been the room her grandparents had always lived in, since her grandma had been sick for so long, and hadn't been able to make the stairs for as long as Jewel could remember.

When they arrived in the house, everything in her room, and the whole house for the most part, had been exactly as she left it. Her room had a full sized bed with a princess headboard that her dad made her when she moved from the nursery room upstairs, to the room downstairs when she was about nine. The room was painted a light lavender color, which had always been her favorite color, and her mom had stenciled tiny little sunflowers all over the walls in random spots, which matched the quilt on her bed, and the throw rug that sat on the hard wood floors that ran throughout the whole house.

The one extra bedroom upstairs had long since been abandoned, since it represented her mom's failure to have another baby, and had brought tears to her mom's eyes every time she dared open the doors, which made Jewel equally as sad. It had been beautifully decorated at one time with everything a little boy would have dreamed of, with hand-made quilts and handcrafted wood furniture. The other bedroom upstairs had been hers from the time she was born until she moved downstairs. It had been closed off because of a crack that had occurred from settling after they had a particularly wet spring one year.

The other bedroom was her parent's room, and the mere thought of ever going in there again sent chills down her spine. After the accident, she had gone up there and laid in the bed, hardly ever leaving for several weeks. She could feel them there, she had said, and she didn't want to ever leave. Then one day, Troy came over and insisted she leave with him just for a little while, and so she went reluctantly, and within a few minutes of being outside, she felt like her soul had been restored to some degree. She hadn't realized until that moment that she was slowly, and painfully, being suffocated by the grief that consumed her as she laid in that room and cried, and she never went back in there again, afraid that if she did go back, she might never find her way out again.

Jewel had told Grady these things, but he hadn't realized the magnitude of how much it ate at her until he saw it steal her happiness every time she walked through the front door. Having her out away from the house was his favorite times of the day. She was the Jewel he had met in Alaska and had grown to love and care for, but each time they entered the house, darkness fell over her and she would retreat into a place inside her that scared him. He would look over at her sitting in her mom's rocking chair by the fireplace, lost in a memory that took her so far away from him that he felt like he may never be able to reach her again.

"What is it Jewel?" Grady had asked one night as Jewel laid in bed beside him, so far away from him that she may as well have been on another planet.

"This place is haunted Grady. My grandma had several miscarriages here, and then so did my mom," she started, continuing the story only after he prodded a little. "One time, my dad and grandpa had taken grandma to the hospital. There was a terrible snowstorm, and so mom and I stayed behind. Mom was just over twenty weeks pregnant, which was the safe zone, and we were all resting easy thinking that she was home free. She hadn't ever made it that far before, except with me, and the doctors told her that if she made it that far, she would probably get through the whole pregnancy," she explained before continuing.

"Since it was just mom and I, I got to sleep in bed with her. It was pure bliss. I loved cuddling up next to mom in a warm bed!" she said with her voice cracking at the memory. "Sometime in the middle of the night, I woke up feeling something wet. The moon was full that night and when I brought my wet hand up to look, I screamed seeing that it was covered in blood. Mom had just been lying there sleeping peacefully until I started screaming, at which point she bolted out of bed, immediately clutching her hand to her stomach. We were both covered in blood, and the look on moms face was complete panic and terror. She started doubling over in pain, making her way to the bathroom, deciding to get in the tub to try to contain the blood that was coming out of her. It was just so bright red, and I thought she was going to bleed to death right there before my eyes. I took off running as fast as I could to Troy's house. There was about a foot of fresh snow, and I left this awful red trail as I ran barefoot across the field to their house, with my nightgown soaked in blood. When I got back, I peeked my head in, and I could see it. It was this tiny little baby all wrapped up in a little wash cloth, and for a brief moment, I thought it was okay... but then, I looked at moms face and the pain there told me all I needed to know. I just hate this place Grady. I don't want to be in this house," she shuddered.

"How old were ya Jewel?" Grady had asked her, choking back the emotion he felt after hearing her story.

"Seven I think...," she whispered, staring off into that world that took her away from him.

It was the next morning that Grady set out with renewed determination to build a new home, pulling Jewel out the door with him, wanting to keep her with him and away from the house as much as possible. They hadn't finalized everything with Troy yet to get all the money, but Grady had some savings, and so did Jewel, and they both decided that building the house would be a priority over anything else, wanting to get it built before the winter that was quickly approaching.

"You're amazing!" she said, impressed with the layout, smiling in that way he had grown accustomed to, and that she was completely incapable of when she entered her parent's old house.

"Anything for you darlin'," he said pleased with himself.

"Here's the plan," he said walking up to her trying to keep a serious look on his face despite the fact that all he wanted to do was grab her and take her behind a tree. She looked absolutely stunning standing there with her long black hair down for once, being teased by a slight breeze. Her skin was tanned, and she was dressed casually in a white cotton tank top and a pair of denim shorts, "and I'm not askin'... I'm tellin'," he said composing himself with his eyes boring into hers, making her step back instinctively. "We're movin' in with Troy and Jolene. All the stuff in the house will be stored in the shop, and I'll be takin' the house down ta salvage some of the wood and such ta use for the new house."

Jewel stood there never saying a word, listening to him word for word, as he took control of her life in a way that they both knew would be difficult for her. Their eyes never left each other's, and Grady squared himself preparing for the onslaught of resistance that was sure to come from her, boring into her with those icy blue eyes that she had often found herself completely lost in. She was still distracted by the look of him with his sandy blond curls carelessly going in various directions.

"Okay," she said looking down, shrugging without emotion, leaving Grady standing in front of her looking confused and a little stunned.

"Just okay?" he replied. "Will ya feel okay usin' the old wood?" he stumbled, going straight to the part of his rehearsed speech about salvaging wood and appliances from the old house to cut their expenses.

"No. I don't have anything against the wood. I mean… I probably wouldn't even recognize it right?" she asked looking back up, considering all the possibilities.

"Ya might, but it will be… different. It'll be renewed and beautiful… like a restored car or a refinished chair," he answered. "I'd like ta use the farmhouse sink and the old gas stove too, but that's up ta you darlin'."

"When did you and Troy make these plans?" she asked crossing her arms. "This seems like his doing somehow, because this is what he does. He tries saving me from it all. He's like a vampire slayer or something."

"It was Jolene. I was talkin' ta her about how hard it was for ya, and the next day she came and told me she'd gotten the spare room made up for us an' insisted we come stay. She said her and Troy had been talkin' about it, plus she was hopin' ta have ya close when the babe comes."

"Are you taking care of me then?" she asked quietly, looking up at him with a look of sadness, breaking his heart. "Are you my new vampire slayer?"

"We all need ta be taken care of sometimes Jewel. Even if yer parents hadn't died, ya'd still need someone," he said searching her face for understanding. "I can see it. I can see yer face change as ya walk through the door of that house, and it scares me darlin'," he said grabbing her face with both of his hands. "I've never seen such sadness, and it breaks my heart wantin' ta protect ya from it."

"I guess I never really thought of that before… *everyone needs to be cared for.* I mean… logically speaking," she laughed nervously, "of course I knew that, but I guess I always thought that *I* wouldn't need help if my parents hadn't died. I always imagined things in my life would be perfect, and all the imperfections were a direct result of them not being here anymore. I mean… of course I didn't *think* that… I guess somewhere in me I just always *felt it* without ever realizing it before," she said smiling at him finally. "You just have a way of putting things, making a light bulb go off in my head sometimes."

He wrapped his arms around her pulling her as close and as hard to him as he dared. "I'm glad for it," he whispered.

They stood like that for a while with their arms around the other. Jewels head rested on his chest, and his chin rested comfortably on the top of her head. They seemed to mold together perfectly, and sometimes when they were wrapped in this embrace they found it difficult to let the moment pass without taking an extra minute to pause and savor it.

"Is that all?" she asked as they reluctantly stepped back from each other, remembering the large bags he had thrown in the truck before bringing her out there. "What were the bags for?"

"Well, Troy loaned us his huntin' tent. I thought we could camp here some days and then stay with Troy and Jolene some days. What do ya think?" he asked excitedly. "At least until winter comes."

Jewel had often lain in bed in the old house thinking about how much happier she would feel if she were camped outside. Grady and her hadn't had a single night of intimacy since they had been sleeping in the house, and aside from a romantic afternoon they had spent stuck in the mud in Grady's truck during a torrential downpour, they hadn't had any intimacy at all since leaving South Dakota. Jewel knew it had been getting increasingly more difficult for Grady, the two of them having been completely incapable of keeping their hands off each other for longer than a few hours at a time before then, only to have it abruptly end. It had been difficult for Jewel too, but she found that her mood changed dramatically every time she entered the house, and she was completely incapable of bringing herself to feel romantic in her childhood bedroom where they decided to sleep at night.

"Thank you for taking care of me," she finally said reaching up and wrapping her arms around his neck, kissing him more passionately than she had in weeks. "I've tried doing everything on my own, shutting everyone out, and it doesn't really work very well. I guess I'll just be thankful for the people in my life who want to help… just don't ever feel sorry for me. That's the one thing I couldn't take."

"I won't, because I don't," he said smiling at her. "Yer the toughest person I've ever known."

"Let's set up camp then. I've set this tent up a million times, and I assume you've probably brought my toothbrush and everything else that I need."

"I did. I don't want ya ta go back in that house," he said enjoying the closeness they'd been missing. "I'll get everything packed up and moved out, and ya can just tell me if there's anything special ya want in the house before I start takin' it apart."

"Thank you. How would I ever live here if you weren't here to build us a home?" she asked, reaching out to hold his hand as they made their way toward the truck to unpack their things.

He wrapped his fingers around hers and smiled down at her. "Well… I guess I can see why ya ran so fast and so far, not wantin' ta come back. I never knew a place that could bring about so much feelin', but it seems ta hit ya like a ton a bricks, and no matter how hard I try, I can't stop it from happenin'," he said scooping her up and kissing her soundly, fueled by weeks of longing. "Are ya sayin' ya can't imagine life without me then?"

"No. I can't imagine life without you," she said smiling at him, kissing him fiercely.

They worked together getting the tent and camp set up, and were doing a fairly decent job of it, but Jewel was happy when Troy and Jolene showed up to help. It had been a long time since Jewel had set up the tent and she was feeling the strain of having lost too much weight, which apparently had been mostly muscle.

"Jewel! I never knew you to be such a wimp! You've always been so freakishly strong. We need to get you fattened up again and working the ranch… build those spaghetti arms up a bit," Troy joked, not knowing what had happened to her at the hands of Aaron. She had been reluctant to tell him, mostly for Grady's sake. She knew that Grady blamed himself still, and she didn't want to put added pressure on him. She knew Troy would react angrily, and would want to blame someone, and she assumed that it would be natural for him to want to blame Grady since he was so protective of her. Besides, it was something she didn't want to discuss and she didn't want to burden Troy with her troubles the way she once had. He had Jolene, and he had a baby on the way. He didn't need to worry about her, and she didn't want him to. She could see that it was natural for him to want to care for her, but she could also see that he was relieved that he didn't need to anymore. It was still too fresh and she decided it could wait... maybe forever... or maybe when it no longer mattered.

Grady and her shared a knowing look. They both knew she was weaker than she had been because of her weight loss, but they also knew that she was gaining some, and had come a long ways since her drastic weight loss that occurred seemingly overnight. Grady could see that stress killed her appetite, and he struggled to make her eat enough with the haunting of the ranch house looming over her constantly. He had taken her to a movie several times a week, wanting to feed her as many calories as he could, but also enjoying the time they had together. She didn't want to spend the money, but he knew that it was good for her, and he loved being in town with her, having her introduce him to people she had known her whole life.

"Jolene, I hope I look half as pretty as you when I'm pregnant," Jewel said going over to sit on the tailgate with her as the boys set up the tent. She was radiant with her long blond hair blowing in the breeze, wearing a yellow cotton summer dress that made her look like a beautiful sunflower.

"Oh you're so sweet Jewel. I feel like a whale sitting here. I'm so ready to be done, and I still have another month to go, and my feet hurt so bad," Jolene moaned, looking at her tiredly.

"Slip your shoes off and put your feet up here," Jewel said patting her legs. "Let me massage them for you."

"Ewww! No Jewel. Feet are gross," she said shaking her head.

"I insist! Put them up here. I'm a nurse! These hands have touched far more disgusting things. Let me be a nurse. I miss it," she said pleading with her, jumping at an opportunity to lend comfort to someone in need.

"Alright, if you insist," she said, lifting her legs and resting her feet on Jewel's lap, leaning back comfortably on the bags that were sitting there.

Jewel reached over and was able to grab some hand lotion out of her purse that had been sitting there, and started massaging Jolene's feet. She dug into the tense muscles that caused Jolene to moan loudly with pleasure as the tension eased, eliciting strange looks from the boys as they set up the tent. Jewel closed her eyes trying to remember all the names of all the bones and muscles in her feet, and found she was a little alarmed at how swollen her feet were and asked, "Have they checked you for preeclampsia?"

"Ummm... I'm not sure. What's that?" Jolene asked relishing the foot massage.

"It's high blood pressure. It's very common in late pregnancy. I'm sure they've checked you for it, but you should ask them about it tomorrow when you go in just to be sure," Jewel said casually, not wanting to alarm her, but feeling a little more swelling than edema that she thought would be typical at this stage.

"Will you go with me Jewel? I really don't like my doctor that much. I mean... I like him, it's just that I think he's a little overworked, and he doesn't really have time to spend with his patients. There's always a waiting room full of pregnant women being herded through there like we're part of an assembly line or something. Oh that feels good!" she said leaning back relaxed, causing the boys to look over at them again.

"Of course I will. I've never been pregnant obviously, but I've heard the last month is rough. Don't be afraid to ask me to do things for you," Jewel said comfortably. She and Jolene had fallen into a comfortable friendship.

"I'm so glad you're here. I get kind of lonely out here. Having you guys here has been wonderful. Plus... having a nurse here while I'm pregnant makes me feel better."

"I'm glad you're here Jo, and I love you and Troy together. It all makes perfect sense now," Jewel said laughing. "I remember that time we all went to the lake. You were so mad at me and I couldn't figure out why. It's so obvious now. I was just so self-consumed with my own loss; I couldn't see what was happening around me."

"It's okay Jewel. I know it was hard for you. I remember when your mom and dad brought us all out here for your tenth birthday party. They were so damn... I don't know... just so kind and sweet, and just so in love with each other, and I thought your dad was the most handsome man I had ever seen in my life. I cried when I heard about their accident. I cried for a really long time," she said opening one eye, smiling at Jewel.

"You did? That's so sweet. Thank you for telling me that. That means a lot to me."

"Is this how it is then? The women lounge about while we work our tails off," Grady joked as Troy and him made their way to stand with them by the truck where they sat.

"I was starting to think maybe we needed to give you guys some privacy with all the moaning and groaning going on over here," Troy said, going over to stand behind his wife, squeezing her shoulders as he did.

"Jewel is spoiling me. I'm never moving," Jolene said, still lying back comfortably, barely opening one eye as they joined them.

"I'm working on Jo's feet. They're swollen and they hurt," Jewel said, smiling at Grady who had come up and tucked a loose strand of hair behind her ear.

The four of them talked easily, laughing and enjoying the company of each other until Jolene decided she finally had enough. Being pregnant was taking its toll on her, and they left with Jolene promising to come pick Jewel up before her prenatal appointment the next day. Jewel smiled thinking about the way things worked out. They were all becoming good friends, and Jewel couldn't believe that after all the worrying that had haunted her over the last several years, that this was how it had all worked out.

"What is it darlin'?" Grady said positioning himself between her legs as she sat there on the tailgate, still smiling to herself.

"I'm just blissfully happy. I love being out here… seeing you and Troy together, building a friendship… sitting here with Jo… all of us laughing and talking. I just love it," she said smiling. "Do you like it here Grady?"

"I do. I'm excited ta get started on the house. I like Troy and Jo, and Troy's showin' me the ropes," he said cupping her face in his hands, kissing her softly. "Mostly I like havin' ya ta myself."

"I'm sorry… I… haven't been a very good wife lately… I mean… I don't know. I can't feel romantic in the house where I grew up, laying in my princess bed. It's not that I haven't thought about it though. I still want you like crazy," she said wrapping her legs around him.

"Ya don't have ta apologize Jewel. I can see what it's like for ya in the house."

"No. I do have to apologize Grady. I've been letting something come between us, and that's not fair. I swore I wouldn't let it, but it overwhelms me. I don't want to be that quiet, withdrawn person, but I can't help it sometimes… I mean… I kind of let myself wallow in it a little and… I'm not really sure why."

"Ahhh. I understand the need ta wallow sometimes. I did a bit of it when I was first discharged. It does overwhelm ya a bit doesn't it?" he said. "Still… I think maybe seein' what it does ta ya helped me understand a little, but I'm glad ta have ya out of there smilin' again."

"Why do you want to lose your accent Grady? You make everything sound fantastic," she said still feeling easily distracted by his presence, pulling him in closer, remembering when they first met and he told her he was trying to lose his accent.

"Ya like it then do ya? 'Cause I can lay it on a bit thicker ya know," he said in a thicker accent than she had ever heard from him before.

She tipped her head back laughing. "Oh brother! Let's make a fire and set up our sleeping bags."

They both laughed as they grabbed the bags and carried them toward the tent. Grady was saying everything in a thick accent making her laugh even harder.

"So why? I mean really? Why do you want to lose your accent?" she asked again after they quit laughing, as they started to set up camp and prepare a fire as dusk neared.

"Because I don't want ta be mistaken as a foreigner. I'm proud ta be American. My parents are proud ta be American, ta have the opportunities that we have here that so many take for granted. Everyone always thinkin' the grass is greener on the other side. I've seen too much of the rest of the world not ta be thankful for what we have here, despite all our imperfections. Did ya think I was a foreigner when ya first met me?" he asked looking over at her as she zipped their sleeping bags together.

"Ummm… yeah. I guess I did… not that it mattered. Well… not to me anyways. You could have been from Mars for all I cared. I still would have followed you to the ends of the earth," she said seductively, coming up to wrap her arms around him, feeling like her old self again.

"It wouldn't have mattered if I had been from Ireland?" he said stroking her face.

"I… I don't know. The fact that you served in the military is something that I really loved about you from the very start. I can't answer that question. Who you are is what I love. That's all I know," she said exasperated by the hypothetical question.

"Well… I guess it doesn't matter then. I can talk without an accent if I concentrate, but it's not how I would normally talk. It feels awkward, and I tend ta start soundin' like John Wayne, draggin' everything out with some effort. I've spent too much time with mom and dad, and ya've heard the two of them."

"I miss them. I think we should invite everyone here for Thanksgiving. Do you think the house will be ready? Where would we put everyone? How many rooms will we have?" she asked trying to recall what he had been telling her earlier when he was explaining it, and she was imagining him without a shirt on.

"Slow down Jewel. Yer makin my head spin," he said getting the fire started. "I'm plannin' the house so that buildin' on will be easy and make sense. Ta start it will have three rooms, two baths, a nice big livin' room, and a huge kitchen since that's where most people gather. One of the rooms will actually be the laundry room until we do the addition next spring. The addition will include a dinin' room, a laundry room, plus a half bath and a garage."

"Wow! You've thought this through, but what if we have six kids?" she asked surprising him.

"There will be plenty of room ta build more off the back, or build a second floor if ya have yer heart set on a half dozen kids or so," he said smiling at her. "Is that what ya want then? That's somethin' we've never talked about before."

"Ummm… I don't know. I've never thought about having kids until we decided I would quit taking birth control."

"And how is that goin' for ya?"

"Fine so far. I haven't really noticed a difference. I guess I'm a little scared. My grandma had several miscarriages, and so did my mom. I seem to have a bad history on both sides. What if we couldn't have kids?" she asked, finally bringing up the question that had been lingering in the back of her mind.

Grady thought quietly for a moment, taking her hand, studying the fine bones of her fingers as he always liked to do, before finally responding. "I don't know Jewel. All I know for sure is we're made for each other. If that does or doesn't include havin' babies, then we'll figure it out together."

"We're pretty good at trying," she said smiling up at him coyly, "and I've missed you. Would you like to take me to bed?"

Grady grabbed her immediately, throwing her over his shoulder and standing up all in one fell swoop, making Jewel scream as he did, both of them laughing at his immediate response. "Ya don't have ta ask me twice woman. I'm just a man. Besides, I have ta carry ya over the threshold."

"You've carried me over every threshold this side of the Mississippi," she laughed.

Grady walked inside and set her down taking her face in both his hands before kissing her wholly, stopping only long enough to lift her shirt over her head, whispering in between kisses. "I've missed ya Jewel... kissin' ya... touchin' ya. Will ya forgive me if I lose all control?"

"I won't forgive you if you don't," she whispered back seductively, urging him on.

The tent was set up comfortably in the clearing by the creek, just below the treehouse, with a blow-up camping mattress for a bed, complete with blankets and sleeping bags, but it wouldn't have mattered even if it had been nothing but a dirt floor. The weeks without intimacy caught up to them, and they both completely let go, forgetting everything but the feel and touch of the other... kissing, touching, and pulling the other closer in a frenzied passion.

Jewel ran her hands over the parts of him she had just hours before imagined touching as she tried to listen to him explain his plans for the house. He was over the top of her, both of them having stripped everything off in their frenzy, each seemingly lost in their own desire until they both found the release from all the longing that had been threatening to consume them only moments before.

He shuddered as the release engulfed him, kissing her with a passion that she hadn't felt from him in several weeks, and they lingered in it for as long as they could. It was a kiss that could be felt from head to toe, bringing a closeness that was beyond the physical world. She could still feel him inside of her and they paused like that joined together as long as they could, wrapped up in each other, savoring the sensation they had just shared.

"I've never felt anything like that before Jewel. I know I say that every time, but ya do somethin' ta me that I can't explain," he whispered, still lingering above her, kissing her more softly.

"You don't have to explain. I feel it too," she whispered back, still running her hands across the muscular frame above her.

After several minutes, he finally rolled to lie beside her, pulling her close to him as he did, both of them feeling the fatigue from that sudden release of energy.

"How do you figure out how to build a house Grady? I mean... where do you start?"

"I don't know. I just see it in my mind. I envision it as I draw it on the paper and see it come ta life. This one was easy, because I look at ya, and I see the walls around ya, and see what it is that ya might like, and it just comes together. You're my building muse Jewel," he said with his eyes closed, a flicker of an upturned smile on his face.

"Well, how do you know what I might like? We've never really talked about it."

"Because I watch ya. I see what catches yer eye, and what makes ya happy. The little comments about things ya liked about Mom and Dad's house, or Troy and Jo's, or when yer lookin' at magazines, or describin' somethin' ya read in a book."

"Wow. You really listen to all my mumbling?" she asked surprised.

"Not all of it I'll admit. The bit about yer weddin' dress ya were explainin', or the outfits the ladies were wearin' in the magazine ya were talkin' about tends ta make me drift off in space a bit, but some things I can't help but listen ta an' take note."

"So you've designed this whole house around things you think will make me happy?" she asked.

"No. I designed the house around things I *know* will make ya happy."

"So what if I hate it?" she teased.

"Then I'll put a nice roof on the tree house for ya, and wave ta ya now and then from my new front porch," he teased back with his eyes still closed, the smile still lingering on his mouth.

"Grady?" she said leaning over him within inches of his face as he laid facing upward.

"What is it darlin'?"

"I would love anything you built for me," she said kissing him softly on the lips and then nuzzling down beside him, wrapped up in the crook of his arm.

"I hope so Jewel. I hope so," he whispered as they both drifted off for a nap.

CHAPTER 43

LITTLE GIRLS

"You open it! Read it to me. I'm nervous as hell!" Grady said, handing the unopened letter to Jewel as he paced the floor in front of her. They were in the living room at Troy and Jolene's. Jewel had been cleaning up a bit while Grady repaired the plumbing under the sink. Troy was still out fixing a section of fence that had fallen down, and Jolene had been napping upstairs. They had just been finishing up for the day when Jolene yelled down the stairs to remind them that she had some mail for them that was sitting on the front seat of her car.

"Okay, but come here. Sit down! Let me pour you a little something to take the edge off," Jewel said, pulling him into a chair. "Geez! I've never seen you like this! Well… not since you plowed me over in the street in Alaska."

Grady cocked an eyebrow at her, watching her as she poured him out a glass of whiskey and water. "Okay, here goes…," Jewel said handing him the drink before sitting down in front of him to read the letter. He was seated in a big comfortable chair with his feet up on the ottoman while she sat on the ottoman facing him. They had been waiting for a response from Madison's adopted parents after Grady had sat down and meticulously wrote a letter to them before they left South Dakota, explaining what happened, and explaining his intentions to do whatever is in the best interest of the child. Every day since then, he had checked the mail to see if there was a response, but now that he had one, he could hardly bring himself to read it.

After they went back to Belle Fourche, they were able to get all the files and everything from Greg, and they quickly determined that Grady was most definitely the father of the girl. It had been a roller coaster of emotions that seemed to engulf the whole family, as Grady sat his parents down, along with Rudy and Diana, and explained the entire situation. They were all in complete disbelief, except for Grady's dad. Jewel had yet to hear him say one good thing about Debbie, and that day had been no exception. He said he wasn't the least bit surprised, and that in all honesty, he had been shocked that Debbie hadn't tried something nefarious before Grady left for the Army.

Maggie wavered between excitement of having another grandchild that looked like her son, and rage that Debbie had made this decision on her own, without discussing it with anyone. "Our own flesh and blood is out there in the world, and we have never even met her," she cried shaking her head.

Rudy and Diana were in complete disbelief, immediately jumping to the conclusion that it was some sort of scam that Debbie was trying to pull, but it was difficult to stick to that theory once they saw the picture of the little girl standing on the swing. There was a moment when Diana swore that it must have been a picture of herself from her own childhood that Debbie had somehow managed to get a hold of, which later turned out to be what convinced her that the girl must be Grady's after all. "My gosh! She could be my twin!" Diana finally said, sitting down quietly, shaking her head in disbelief.

"Well… you have to make contact with her. She's family," Rudy said with certainty.

"Interestin' ta hear ya say that brother," Grady said, eyeing Rudy knowingly since he had all but refused to discuss his own adoption. "I'll write ta her parents. They'll have ta decide. It's not about what's best for me or anyone else here. It's about what's best for the girl."

And that's exactly what he did. Writing letters wasn't his strong point, but he carefully sat down and hand wrote several rough drafts, scratching out things and adding others, wanting to make his intentions known, but also wanting to convey his genuine interest in meeting her. He wasn't exactly sure how he felt about it all, but the image of her, and the outline of her face with the same features he saw when he looked in the mirror, was sticking with him, and he couldn't help but think about her.

Jewel never faltered. For the first time in her life, she just accepted that whatever happens is meant to happen, and that as long as she was with Grady, everything would simply work out. She knew there was nothing she could do to change it, and she knew that it didn't change how she felt about Grady, and so she just supported him, helping him write and re-write the letter.

"Okay. Here we go," Jewel said clearing her throat.

> *Dear Grady,*
>
> *Thank you for the letter and thank you for being so frank with us. Your letter touched us deeply. We can't imagine how difficult it must be to find out that you have a child out in the world that you never knew about. The picture of you and your lovely wife is wonderful to have, and the resemblance is staggering. Madison looks at it constantly, carrying it around as a bookmark in the book that she's reading.*
>
> *We decided long before we ever adopted a child that we would be open about it from the very beginning. We didn't want to raise her as*

our own only to later devastate her with such news. Besides, she looks absolutely nothing like us. I imagine we wouldn't have been able to keep it a secret much past the age of five even if we had wanted to. I'm 5'2" and my husband Jay is 5'7", and at the age of eleven, Madison is already as tall as I am. Also, Jay and I both have brown eyes and dark hair, and as you must already know from the picture, Madison is fair skinned with blond hair and blue eyes.

I appreciate your concern for her in wanting to do whatever is best for her, and leaving the decision to us and to her. We are so deeply grateful for that, because we knew the day would come when she would start wondering, and we would want to start searching for her biological parents. You hope the biological parents will be great, but you never really know.

We sat down with Madison and read your letter as a family. We felt it was important that she understood that you did not give her up for adoption, nor would you have chosen to. I feel she is very fortunate to be able to learn something that important. How must it be to wonder about such things, asking yourself why, or possibly questioning yourself, only to find out that very important fact?

Madison is very excited to meet you, but she's also a little nervous. She is torn between wanting to meet you, and not wanting to feel like she is betraying us. We all have a very close relationship, and she needs a little more time to come to terms with everything. Madison is a very thoughtful and logical person... a trait she has because of how we raised her, but also one that she must simply have in her genes, judging by your thoughtful letter.

She is writing and re-writing a letter to you, but I'm not sure when she'll finally perfect it and decide to send it. Meanwhile, I thought I would drop you this note to let you know that we received your letter, and how we feel about it. We know you must be wondering.

Madison would love to hear from you more, but for now, we would appreciate if the letters were addressed to Jay or I. We feel that we need to guide her through this process. She is only eleven, and although she seems so grown up at times, she is still very young... I'm sure you must understand that. Please keep in touch. Jay and I look forward to meeting you as well.

Sincerely,

Mandi and Jay Geary

"Wow!" Grady said leaning back in the chair, "this is really happenin'. They seem really nice."

Jewel could see the relief wash through Grady, as he sank back in his chair and closed his eyes.

"Are you happy now?" she asked rubbing his leg. "You look like you just had the weight of the world lifted off your shoulders."

"I'm relieved. I was half expectin' a letter tellin' me ta leave her alone and go away. That would have been hard ta do."

"You wrote her a very nice letter Grady. I never had a doubt they would want to meet you."

"Come here Jewel," he said pulling her onto his lap. "I can't imagine goin' through all this without ya. Ya've been my rock… my voice of reason, even though I know it must be hard for ya a little."

"I'm fine Grady. My life is easier, happier, and more certain than I've ever known it to be in my adult life. Whatever obstacles I'm faced with right now… *we're* faced with now… seem… manageable. It's a little scary, but… I'm okay with it."

They could hear Jolene upstairs milling around, and were anticipating a quiet evening with the four of them having dinner together, but they were suddenly interrupted from their moment when the quiet upstairs erupted. "Jewel! Jewel! Come quick!" Jolene yelled from upstairs.

"Oh my gosh! I'm coming!" Jewel yelled back suddenly terrified, sprinting up the stairs two at a time toward the voice, with Grady not far behind. Her heart was thumping, imagining the worst. When it came to pregnancies, and things that can go wrong, she was a little fearful given her family history.

"I either lost complete control of my bladder, or my water broke," Jolene said standing immobilized in the bathroom as a pool of fluid gathered around her feet.

Jewel stopped dead in her tracks for a second when she saw Jolene standing there near the sink with her long blond hair flowing down her back, wearing a white cotton summer dress. She was completely taken by the loveliness of seeing this pregnant woman standing there looking sublime. The sun was peeking through the small bathroom window, casting a light that made her look all the more majestic, as if God Himself was shedding this brilliant white light on her, signaling the arrival of her beautiful baby, and washing a calm over them.

"Your water broke Jo. We should probably get you to the hospital. You should have plenty of time, but it's a long drive. Grady!" Jewel yelled as she turned, running into him, nearly knocking herself down in the process. "Ouch! Will you go find Troy? I'm going to get Jo in the car and head toward town, just to be on the safe side, and you guys can catch up to us."

"No! I'm not leaving without Troy!" Jolene said adamantly.

"You're an hour from the hospital, and your water just broke. You could go quickly, or you could go slowly. Do you want to chance it, because I've never delivered a baby before Jo," Jewel said reasoning with her.

"Ummm… alright, let's go then. Get my bag… and my purse, and oh… I have dinner cooking in the crock-pot, and…"

"Okay Jo. Relax alright," Jewel said, taking both her hands in hers to calm her. "We'll get it all taken care of. Come on. Let's get you in the car, and I'll get everything we need and we'll start in that direction. Grady will find Troy, and it'll all be fine. I'll just put this towel down for you on the front seat," Jewel said, grabbing a towel off the rack as she calmly led Jolene toward the downstairs to get her in the car.

"Oh god!" Jolene screamed, nearly falling to her knees but for Jewel's hand she was still holding. "Owww!"

"You were having a contraction. Are you alright to continue now?" Jewel asked her, as the pain seemed to lessen. Jewel was holding both her hands again, having tucked the towel under her arm as Jolene doubled over, feeling the pains of early labor.

"Okay. Let's go. Oh no. Where's Troy?" Jolene said waddling toward the car. "Oh no! Owwww!" she screamed again just a few seconds later, nearly falling to the ground again as they came down the stairs.

"Your contractions are really close," Jewel said, thinking that they may not make it to the hospital in time. "Ummm... Jo... let's just take a minute here. Let's have you come lay down in the spare bedroom," Jewel said, leading Jolene toward the bed in the guest bedroom downstairs that was near the back door.

"Shouldn't we get going?" Jolene asked worriedly.

"I want to just check you before we get in the car. Your contractions are really close together. What do you think?" Jewel asked trying to calm her.

"They seem close, but shouldn't we be hurrying? You said yourself you've never delivered a baby Jewel! Owww!" she screamed again, with more pain than previously. She was doubled over and Jewel was afraid she was going to drop to the floor.

She waited for the contraction to pass, holding Jolene's hands to keep her from falling down, giving her something to squeeze through the pain.

"No, but I am a nurse Jo," Jewel finally said as the contraction passed, "and my gut tells me we should just make sure we don't do anything hasty, like jump in the car and race toward town frantically. Let me just check you out and assess the situation, and we'll go from there. Let's be smart about this, okay? Do you trust me?" Jewel asked, exuding calm she didn't feel inside.

"Lord knows I do Jewel."

"Alright then, let me just take care of things. Okay?"

"Alright," Jolene said, feeling somewhat calmer. "Owww! Oh no! Jewel!" she howled again, feeling the muscles constrict, this time with more intensity. She had made it to the bed, and instinctually pulled her knees up toward her chest, getting into a birthing position.

Jewel couldn't believe her eyes when she was finally able to assess how far along in the delivery she was. She could see the top of the baby's head, and although she had never delivered a baby before, she knew it wasn't going to be long.

"Okay Jo. We're in good shape. You're going to have this baby quick, and everything's going to be just fine," Jewel said reassuring Jolene, delivering the news as if it was exactly what she wanted to hear. "I'm going to take care of everything okay?"

"I'm scared Jewel," Jolene quipped.

"I know honey," Jewel said stroking her hair. "This is all perfectly natural though. Troy was born at home, and look at how good he turned out. In fact, he was born in this home."

Jewel got pillows and blankets situated in between the contractions as best she could, though they were coming quickly. She was trying to keep a calmness in the room that Jolene desperately needed. Each contraction came harder than the next, and she could see more and more of the baby's head with each push. She washed Jolene with soap and water, wanting to make everything as sterile as possible. Her insides were turned and twisted with worry, but not wanting to alarm Jolene, she did the one thing she knew would bring peace and calm, and she started humming and singing in a soft, quiet voice. She knew it was the only thing that allowed her to hide the feelings that were usually written all over her face.

Mary, did you know
That your baby boy will one day walk on water...

She wasn't sure what made her choose that particular song, other than the fact that she regarded every birth as a miracle from God, and she had no doubt in her mind that she was witnessing the hand of God right there before her eyes. Still, singing about delivering Jesus Himself seemed overzealous, but it had the intended effect, which was to ease the fear she saw on Jolene's face, and have her push through the contractions with relative calm.

...and when you kiss your little boy
You've kissed the face of God

"You're doing good Jo," Jewel said, smiling down at her as she placed some more towels under her, and got a large bowl to catch some of the afterbirth. She also grabbed a plastic tablecloth she'd found when she was cleaning the kitchen earlier, and decided to put that down under Jolene to protect the mattress. "We're just about there. It won't be long."

"I wish Troy was here," Jolene cried out.

"I hear Grady's truck. I'll bet he found Troy," Jewel said, trying to maintain her calm while placing a blanket over Jolene in case Grady walked in.

"Jo! Jo! Where are you?" Troy yelled running through the house.

Jewel walked over to the door, not wanting to shout in the room where she was trying to maintain a sense of calm. "We're in the spare room Troy," Jewel called out as monotone as she could. Troy had automatically headed up the stairs, but Grady was standing there, and the two of them exchanged a look that held within it an entire conversation that need not ever be spoken.

"She's in here. She's having the baby. Get Troy and tell him to calm down please," Jewel said to Grady, gesturing in that way that universally tells people to calm down.

"Troy's here," Jewel said unnecessarily as Troy walked in the room, having been somewhat slowed down and calmed by Grady.

"Troy! You're here. We're having this baby right now!" Jolene said breaking into tears.

"You're in good hands Jo. There's nobody I would trust to take care of you more than Jewel," Troy said meeting Jewel's eyes, feeling Jolene's hand relax beneath his as he reassured her.

"Let's get some water boiled shall we?" Jewel said turning to Grady as he cautiously poked his head in. "Just in case we have to sterilize something, we'll be ready."

"You can come in Grady," Jolene said motioning to him.

"Right, let me just put some water on," he said awkwardly, trying to keep from looking anywhere that he didn't feel he should be looking.

"I think we're close Troy," Jewel said as Jolene closed her eyes and pushed through another contraction. "I think we need to get to it though. Next contraction, I want you to push through it a little longer, but not too hard. Just breath through it and push steadily?" Jewel said stroking Jolene's leg. Although she had never delivered a baby before, she understood the body, and felt that a more gradual delivery would allow the birth canal to open up without tearing.

"Tell Grady to come in. We should all be here. He can be up by my head," Jolene said quietly, feeling a sudden calm wash over her as she readied her mind for what was about to happen.

Jewel was surprised by how calm Jolene had become. She smiled watching the situation unfold, seeing Jo and Troy together, the sun shining through like a halo illuminating the small white room, a gentle breeze lifting the curtain just slightly, allowing the scent of summer flowers to waft through the room. Her heart skipped a beat as Grady made his way in, and sat near Jolene's head opposite Troy, taking her other hand, and giving Jewel a reassuring look that warmed the fullness she felt in her heart. She crossed herself, feeling the presence of God, thinking of the blessings that were filling the room this child was being born into.

"Push through it a little longer Jo." Jewel said, knowing it was time to get the baby out. She could see the top of the head clearly, and knew that the next big push was going to bring this baby into the world. She steadied herself, running through her mind all the things she would need to do once the baby was finally out, thinking of all the vitals she would need to check to reassure them everything was okay. She was used to working mostly on grown men, and a few female soldiers that came in, but mostly men. She tried to miniaturize everything in her mind, imagining every limb and organ on a smaller scale.

She had been reading Jolene's baby book, and took special care on the section that highlighted the important factors of what would need to be done in case there was a home delivery, knowing that being so far out in the country made that a possibility, however unlikely.

"Okay Jo. Next push is the final one. Are you ready? I want you to push a little longer now okay?" she said as she positioned herself to catch the baby for the final push.

"Owww!" Jolene screamed loud as she pushed a little harder. Her legs were bent, opening herself up as much as possible to make the delivery easier.

"Keep pushing. Keep pushing. Don't bear down, just push steadily," Jewel said excitedly, knowing it was just a matter of seconds before the baby was finally out. Jolene was squeezing Troy's hand on one side and Grady's hand on the other while Jewel positioned herself holding onto the baby ready to grab it when it came out, helping Jolene keep her legs bent.

"It's a girl!" Jewel yelled as the baby slid out in the towel she had readied. "It's a girl Jo!"

Jewel used the aspirator she had found in the plethora of baby items that Jolene had readied over the last nine months, and used it to suck out the fluids in the baby's nose and mouth. She could feel a collective sigh in the room as they all heard the baby cry, followed by the cries of the four of them as they witnessed the beginning of this new life on earth. Her owns tears were streaming down her face as the miracle of life overwhelmed her, and she saw the emotion coming from Jo, Troy, and Grady. She cleared the fluid from the baby's face, and then laid her on Jolene's chest, just as she had seen done in the movies.

"We have a baby girl," Troy said with his voice cracking. "She's so tiny! Is she okay do you think Jewel?"

"She's perfect. We'll call the doctor here in a bit. I'm sure they'll want you to head into town and get everyone checked out at some point," Jewel said wiping away tears as Grady met her eyes. "I think we'll want to make sure Jo is stable, and make sure everything is okay before we jump into a car and start bouncing down the road."

"She is perfect!" Jolene sobbed. She's so beautiful!"

Jewel choked again at the emotion that enveloped the room, thanking God that she was allowed to witness something so perfect and so complete. She cleaned away the wet towels full of all the fluids, busying herself as she completed all the tasks that were necessary to make her patient feel more relaxed and comfortable.

"I'm going to wipe you off Jo," Jewel said, warning Jo before she touched her again, a task that would have seemed unthinkable a few hours ago, but now seemed perfectly natural. "I need to make sure you're not bleeding where you're not supposed to be bleeding, and just make sure everything's okay."

"This seems like it should be weird, but it's not," Jolene said as Jewel examined her, and got her cleaned up using a warm washcloth.

"Don't be silly Jo. I once had to sew up a man's scrotum after draining pus out of it. Believe me... this is nothing!" Jewel said, basking in the satisfaction she always felt when she was within her element as a nurse. "Everything looks like you would expect it to look at this juncture. I think you're fine Jo."

Jewel continued cleaning up, putting fresh towels under Jolene, and then motioned to Grady so they could give the new parents a little time to themselves. "We'll give you a few minutes, and in a while, I can help you get her cleaned up if you want. Just call me if you need me."

Jewel made her way into the kitchen where she immediately went to the sink and washed her hands thoroughly, before wrapping her arms around Grady. The two of them stood in the kitchen for a long while, never once speaking, just standing there hugging each other, running the miracle of birth back through their minds over and over again, thinking of their own wants and desires, and imagining the years to come as they watch the little baby grow up through the years.

"That was incredible Jewel. Didn't they tell her just yesterday that it would probably be another week at least, and that it would probably go slow since it was her first baby?" he asked breaking the silence.

"Yes, but that baby had its own plans. That was certainly one of the most remarkable nursing experiences I've ever had... that's for sure. I think I'll go ask them if they want me to call the doctor. It's kind of quiet in there," she said taking Grady's hand, anxious to be near them again to make sure everyone is okay.

"We decided to name her after the woman who delivered her," Troy said as Jewel and Grady poked their heads through the door. Troy had her wrapped up in a little blanket stroking her little cheek before handing her back to Jolene to get her latched on so she could nurse. "We decided to name her Esther!"

"What? No! You can't name her that!" Jewel responded with a horrified look on her face. She felt like the perfection of the moment was being scarred by the sound of the middle name that she always hated.

"Oh, he's joking Jewel. He was just trying to get a rise out of you, though I really don't know what's wrong with the name Esther. It's not that bad," Jolene said helpfully as Troy excused himself for a moment to get Jo a drink of water.

Jewel forced a chuckle, relieved that they were just joking. "Okay, so have you picked a name?"

"No. Not yet. We can't decide," Jolene shrugged, still smiling about the joke.

"Do you want me to call the doctor for you?" Jewel asked, checking on the baby as she nursed healthily, peeking under the sheet for any signs of unusual bleeding coming from Jolene.

"I suppose. I don't really want to go anywhere though," Jolene replied contently.

"Well you look fine and so does the baby, but I need to prepare and cut the umbilical cord and..."

"Owww!" Jolene cried out suddenly, feeling the contractions hit her again. "Oh gosh! I feel like I'm having another baby Jewel!"

Jewel pulled back the covers to check her, putting the bowl near her to catch the afterbirth. "Sorry. I should have warned you. It's the placenta, which is normal and necessary. Did you read any of the books I gave you?" Jewel asked teasing her.

"I couldn't read that part without freaking out. I really wish I had now, but thank God you were here Jewel."

"I'm thankful too Jo," she said smiling warmly at her as she got everything cleaned up again. "How about Mandy? I always thought Mandy Landas would be a beautiful name," she said with a half-smile, recalling the unhappiness she felt when she thought about being married to Troy.

"Grady said Anna because he thinks she looks Italian like Mom... with the black hair... Anna Landas. What do you think babe? I really like it," Troy said as he and Grady came back in to sit with Jolene.

"I like it. What would the middle name be though?" Jolene asked hopefully.

"Belle! It should be Belle!" Troy added excitedly.

"Anna Belle Landas... I love it," Jolene choked up happily.

"That's cute. I like it," Jewel added.

They all sat around together, each taking turns holding Anna, delaying the inevitable trip that Troy and Jolene were going to have to make to the hospital to get everyone checked out. They would need all the proper shots, and examinations, and all the other mandatory things that humans somehow managed to survive without for thousands of years until the last seventy years or so. They were all wrapped up together in a moment that could never be replicated, and they all knew it. It was a day that seemed to be etched out of the heavens, ceremoniously delivering new life, as further evidence of God's amazing grace. They took pictures with all of them holding Anna, and even managed to get in a few group shots after finally figuring out the timer on Troy's new camera. It was only after Jolene started to feel overly exhausted that they finally gave in to the inevitable continuation of life beyond that one precious moment they shared.

They all pitched in, getting everything and everyone loaded into the car so Troy could drive Jo and Anna to the doctor's office. Jewel had helped Jolene get changed into something more comfortable, and had wrapped the baby up with all of them taking turns to figure out the very complicated car seat contraption they all jokingly referred to as the baby limo. They hugged each other, and wiped tears from their eyes as they waved goodbye. The emotions of the moment had left them all ripe and exposed.

Grady and Jewel stood out in the driveway, and watched the car drive away until they could no longer see it anymore. It seemed as if all the electricity that had been making all their senses stand alert just under the surface of their skin, had suddenly contracted, leaving them both with a sudden fatigue as they shuffled inside and sat down together in the big comfy chair.

"You just delivered a baby Jewel," he said, turning to her, running his hand under her shirt as his excitement grew.

"And that turns you on?" she asked with some amusement.

"You turn me on Jewel. You turn me on," he said pulling her down beneath him where he could explore her more easily.

CHAPTER 44

A TANGLED MASS

Grady's head swirled as he looked at the boy in the picture he held in his hands. It was a face he had seen a thousand times. The face of a man he loved. A man that has been like a brother to him, that he knew well, and trusted with life and limb. He stood there in complete disbelief, and his mind raced as he wondered how it was even possible to find a picture of him where he did. He was feeling confused and overwhelmed by the possibilities. He looked at the familiar eyes staring back at him from the picture, and irrational thoughts flashed through his mind.

While he was dismantling the old house, Grady had come across a strange box hidden in the floorboards under the bed where Jewel's grandfather had slept. It was wrapped inside of multiple layers of plastic, presumably to keep it safe from flooding. He opened it without even thinking about it, expecting to find a lost treasure from olden times, perhaps something to surprise Jewel with later. What he actually found was something that could change the course of everyone's life, as he imagined all the scenarios of what finding that picture would mean in his life, and his future with Jewel.

His mind was racing out of control. For a moment, he didn't know whether to break down crying in the middle of the floor, or run yelling and screaming from this house, and maybe even this ranch, and perhaps even Jewel herself. He frantically considered the possibility that it could have all been a big set up; in the few seconds he had, as his mind raged out of control. He had to sit down right there in the middle of the floor to steady himself. Everything he seemed to be working toward suddenly seemed tainted by something ugly and wicked. The possibility of a spontaneous meeting in an unlikely town in Alaska may have actually been planned out, and that flooded his mind irrationally. A meeting by chance, now appeared to have been contrived. The thoughts surged uncontrollably through his mind, rising and falling almost as fast and as hard as the blood pumping through his veins, as his heart rate sped up. The fatigue of working long days trying to get the house built, combined with the impossibility of what he held in his hand was making his head spin.

"Having a little rest are you?" Jewel said coming into the room, but then stopped abruptly when she saw the look on Grady's face. "What is it?"

"I'm goin' ta ask ya once, and I need ya ta think carefully before ya answer, because I'll only give ya the one chance ta tell me the truth," Grady said eyeing her carefully, like an interrogator would eye his prisoner, still operating under the influence of the irrational thoughts that had seized him moments before.

"Grady you're scaring me. What is it?" she asked with her heart pounding fast as she stood completely still, afraid to make any movement at all, never having witnessed anger like that on Grady's face before.

Grady hung his head trying to gather his thoughts amidst the onslaught of irrational emotions wreaking havoc on his brain, attempting to make sure he asked the right question, before finally just blurting it out, "Did ya know that Rudy was yer uncle Jewel? Did ya know it before we met?"

"What? What are you talking about Grady?" she asked loudly. "Rudy? As in... Rudy? What the hell are you talking about?" she said kneeling in front of Grady, focusing in on the box in front of him, looking for clues to this puzzle he had just flattened her with. Her face went white as she started reading some of the documents in front of her, the same one's Grady had apparently read only moments before, looking quickly through all the pictures of the man that had become her friend and family. "What does this mean Grady?"

"So yer sayin' ya didn't know?" he asked with a confused rush of emotion.

"Know what? What does any of this mean Grady? I can't think," she said feeling overwhelmed by all the papers she was holding in her hand. She stood up suddenly, threw the papers down, and then ran out of the house as fast as she could. She didn't know where she was running, but the effort of running was cushioning the blow she felt from the implications of what she had learned moments before.

Grady knew the truth as soon as he saw it written on her face. She didn't know, and he got up to run after her, realizing how accusatory he came off only moments before. "How could I have even doubted her?" he kicked himself, quickly chasing after her, having regained control over his mind once again.

"Jewel! Wait! I'm sorry darlin'!" he yelled as she ran further and further toward their new house. He cursed himself, knowing the realization of what she had just learned must have hit her like a ton of bricks. "What an asshole!" he yelled aloud, cursing himself, and shaking his head as he ran after her. "Jewel, please stop!" but she kept running, and he had to stop as the pains from his war injury shot through his back. He walked toward the direction where she ran, hoping to find her near their house, which at the pace he was walking would give him a little time to consider what it all meant. He knew that Rudy had been adopted, and now that he was feeling more level headed, he nearly laughed when he thought of the unlikely coincidence that he was married to the granddaughter of Rudy's biological father.

Grady finally made it to their unfinished house, finding Jewel sitting quietly on the floor inside, hugging her knees to her chest. "How could you Grady? How could you accuse me of lying to you like that?"

"Forgive me Jewel. I don't know. I'm sure if I would have had a few more minutes ta think about it, I would have managed ta come up with a more reasonable response. I found out just a second before ya, and my head swirled, and I was dazed, and everything seemed so twisted and confused all the sudden," he said standing in the doorway, careful not to approach her just yet. "I found a box in the floor boards. It suddenly seemed like a secret that everyone must've known about but me. I couldn't imagine a scenario in those few seconds of confusion, where ya couldn't have known, and everything seemed contrived and engineered all the sudden. I'm sorry Jewel."

"I have... an uncle... I guess. Someone I love who shares the same blood as me. There's someone in the world that looks kind of like me and shares... I don't know... DNA I guess. I don't know what it all means yet, but... do you really think I could have hidden that from you?" she asked looking up at him angrily.

"I can't... I mean... I don't know how I could understand the magnitude of what it means in yer life Jewel. I'm so sorry. I wish ya hadn't come in when ya did. I probably would have regained my senses if I'd had a bit more time ta think it through."

"That's not what I asked Grady! Do you think I could keep something like this from you? Do you not read me like a freakin' book! You seem to know what I'm thinking before I do! Do you really think I'm so manipulative and conniving that I could arrange us meeting, and maybe even arrange us falling in love and getting married? While I'm at it Grady, I thought I would arrange getting kidnapped and raped, just so you could come after me, and then arrange for you to take me home with you and manipulate you into spontaneously asking me to marry you," Jewel yelled standing up to continue her diatribe. "You must think I'm a freakin' social mastermind Grady! I was going to use my genius for world peace, but I decided to do this instead!"

"Alright, I deserve all of that, and probably a bit more. I don't usually fly off the handle like that Jewel. You know that. I deserve like... I don't know... thirty lashes... maybe with a blunt object of some sort," he said shrugging apologetically.

"Forty. I think forty lashes would probably be more appropriate," she said trying to keep the smile from her lips.

"Will ya forgive me then Jewel?" he asked, reaching out to her cautiously.

"I have to forgive you. I love you too much not to, but I'm mad at you right now... don't touch me!" she said even as she grabbed the hand he was offering.

"If I could start over I'd sit ya down and tell ya softly, takin ya on my lap and holdin' ya as the truth of it hits ya in the heart, and then I'd let ya cry a bit if that's what ya needed," he said cupping her face with his free hand.

"Well, I don't think it's hit me yet, so you might get your chance later," she said trying not to smile up at him just yet.

"Meetin' ya the way I did, and havin' us fall so hard for each other so fast… it all seems too good ta be true sometimes. Things that seem too good ta be true scare me. Why do ya think that is?" he asked quietly.

"Because things that are too good to be true, usually are, and we haven't really known each other that long. I guess we'll just have to learn to trust it," she said reaching out to wrap her arms around his middle, pushing herself into the warmth as she felt him hug her back.

"I feel like I've known ya my whole life Jewel. The fact that I questioned ya is a reflection on me, and my own insecurities."

"Thanks for saying that Grady. You know I would never lie to you, or keep things from you. Even if I tried, you would read the writing on my face like you always do."

"I know Jewel… now that I've regained my senses… I know it. There's no question."

"In that case… I guess I'll reduce your sentence to a spanking instead of forty lashes," she said looking up at him playfully.

"From punishment ta reward just like that," he said leaning down to kiss her, grabbing her and holding her even tighter.

"Do you think Rudy knows?" she asked suddenly, pulling back, considering this possibility for the first time, realizing that she essentially just accused Rudy of the same thing Grady had just accused her of moments before.

"No. He would have told me. He's always been tight-lipped about his adoption, but… I think he would have said somethin'," he said with less and less certainty. "Come on Jewel. Let's walk back ta the house and get the pickup, and the… box of stuff… and we'll talk it through a bit."

"Why would Grandma and Grandpa give a child up for adoption? They tried to have more kids, but couldn't," she asked rhetorically, a little puzzled.

"I had only looked at it for a minute before ya came in Jewel, but the mother listed on the birth certificate had a different last name than Etchemendy. I'm treadin' lightly here Jewel. I know ya were close ta yer grandpa, but I'm guessin' yer grandma wasn't his biological mother."

"You think my grandpa had an affair?" she asked angrily.

"I'm sorry Jewel. First, I insult ya, and then I insult the memory of yer grandpa. Maybe it would be best if I just let ya read through the papers, and come ta yer own conclusions," he said apologetically.

"No. I can't go through this without you Grady. It's just shocking! The man I knew would never do such a thing."

"This must be very overwhelmin' for ya Jewel. Just promise me not ta go runnin off again if I step over the line. Yer too damn fast woman, an' runnin' is my weak spot. I'm just glad ya've taken ta runnin toward home, instead of away from it."

"Well, it's good to know where a man's weak spot is," she said unable to resist the flirtatiousness she always felt when her and Grady were alone. "At least that's what my dad always said."

"Yer my weak spot Jewel," he said wrapping an arm around her, pulling her close to him.

"You must have been shocked when you opened that box, and saw Rudy's face staring back at you. I can only imagine the confusion you must have felt. I guess I can see why you would jump to all sorts of crazy conclusions. When something crazy and unexplainable is presented to you, the only logical explanation is something crazy and unexplainable."

"Stop it Jewel. Yer tryin' ta excuse what I said, and there's no excusin' it."

"I'm just imagining what it must have been like for you. It's called empathy. I know you wouldn't have jumped to the conclusions you did without something that elicited strong emotions. I know you Grady."

"Thanks Jewel. Yer the most gracious person I've ever known."

They walked in silence for the remainder of their walk, eager to get back to the box to read the documents that were in there. There were also several letters in there they had yet to read, and they wondered about the secrets they held. Jewel tried to digest what it meant to her to know that Rudy was her uncle. She remembered feeling an instant connection to him, but never in a romantic way the way she did with Grady. It was an instant bond she felt with him that she had seldom felt before in her life. She remembered all their similarities, and smiled at their shared sense of humor. She thought of his looks, remembering when she asked him about his heritage. She thought of little Tina, and how much they looked alike.

She remembered thinking that Rudy looked Basque since the first time they all met. They both had the dark hair and the olive skin, though she had her mother's blue eyes, and he clearly had the brown eyes that were more typical of the Basques. She was thinking how she felt about him being her uncle, though not totally convinced just yet since she was unable to trust the truth amidst the onslaught of emotions they had both been bombarded with earlier when they were frantically scanning the documents, unable to process the evidence that was being presented to them.

"How do ya feel?" Grady asked, stopping Jewel and taking both her hands in his before they went back in what was left of the old house. Grady had torn down most of the outer walls, and used the majority of the wood, but had started tearing into the wood that was used on the inside walls and the floors. From above it likely looked like a maze you would find through a cornfield at Halloween. They had reused the old farmhouse sink in the kitchen, and a couple of the toilets and fixtures, though Grady had completely restored everything, giving it all a new luster and a feeling of renewal.

Some of the old vanities and old furniture they had managed to sell in a community garage sale they were having in town, which allowed them to buy some of the other appliances they needed. The old gas stove would be used in the new house, but Grady had plans to restore that before he brought it in. It never ceased to amaze Jewel at just how creative Grady was and how capable he was of taking something old and broken down, and turning it into something so beautiful. Their new house was coming along just fine, and they had started to sleep in the master bedroom using their new box spring and mattress on the floor until Grady could build the bed frame and headboard he was planning.

"I feel… fine… I guess… now that I got you back in my camp… so to speak," she said laughing at the expression that happened to describe their actual living conditions when they weren't at Troy and Jolene's.

They walked in, and Jewel gathered up all the documents and pictures she had thrown down before running off earlier, while Grady checked the floorboards, finding another hidden box. "Oh no!" Jewel said feeling exasperated, trying to make light of the situation. "There are probably documents in their telling me I'm your long lost cousin from Ireland and everything else was a big joke. Would you still love me if I was your first cousin?" she asked grinning at Grady as she took the box from him.

"Yer gettin' punchy darlin'. Let's take these back ta the house and open a bottle of vino. We could both use a little toppin' off at this point."

"Alright. Do you think we could stop by Troy and Jo's first? I want to let Jo know I'll be there tomorrow night to get up with Anna so she can get a full night's sleep."

They had been staying in their new house more and more since they had actual walls and a roof, but Jewel made sure to spend a few nights a week at their house, so Jo could sleep through the night while she cared for the baby. Getting up in the middle of the night for Troy was not an option since he woke up early in the morning, and worked all day… sometimes until late at night. Grady was helping Troy as much as possible, but had also been under the gun trying to get the house built before the winter set in. The four of them had all become good friends, but they were all eager to have their own living space again, so they made the house building a priority, with all of them pitching in on weekends to get as much done as possible.

"Yep. We'll stop by and… oh! I forgot ta tell ya that Rudy, Diana, Mom, Dad and the kids are comin' this weekend… ironically. They have gifts, and some things for the house, plus the kids are excited ta camp out and do ranchy things."

"Ranchy things?" she asked mockingly.

"Yep. Joseph has big plans for doin' ranchy things."

"That's exciting! I'm so excited to see everyone. We'll have to decide how we're going to handle this whole situation, but I'm excited."

"Me too Jewel. They're driving two separate vehicles though so… I'm not exactly sure what to expect. They're rentin' two RV's and bringin' tents and all sorts of things Mom and Dad got for us.

"We're going to have to tell Rudy. It wouldn't be fair to keep it from him," Jewel said feeling a little overwhelmed suddenly.

"First Madison... now this? Mom and Dad are probably goin' ta have ta up their blood pressure medicine."

"Let's just take all this back to the house and figure things out. My head is spinning. I'm pretty sure I'm sleep walking right now and just having a weird dream," she said quietly.

After a brief stop at Troy and Jo's, the two spent the rest of the night carefully reading through all the documents, studying pictures, reading and rereading letters, including a carefully constructed letter written to Jewel by her grandfather's own hand.

> *My Jewel*
>
> *If you are reading this, then you know my secret and probably have many questions. I'm sorry I never could find the courage to tell you about all this myself and that you had to find out like this. I always loved your grandma Jewel. I loved her from the first day I met her and her memory continues to fill my heart even as I write this letter to you. She was my one true love. It's no excuse, but after she had several miscarriages and two stillborns, she completely lost interest in me. I briefly found comfort in the arms of a woman in Kaycee who worked at the gas station. When she got pregnant, considering the fact that we were both married to other people and we were both in our forties, we decided the best thing we could do is put the child up for adoption. It was a difficult time and such an enormous decision that I had no choice but to tell your grandma. She was hurt and angry, and not just because I had the affair. She was heartbroken that it was so easy for other's to have babies and so difficult for her. She always had her heart set on having an even dozen. She immediately pushed for the adoption, though we both always regretted it. All we knew was that a baby boy was born and was adopted out to a good family. We imagined him, and what he must look like, running the possibilities of how he must have resembled his brother through our heads over and over. It was especially difficult after the accident.*
>
> *You'll remember that I subdivided the property and sold off two thousand acres after your grandma died. Of course, we officially gave the Landas family their land, and the rest was for the boy. It was something grandma and I talked about, both of us deciding that we wanted to leave the boy something, feeling like we owed him a piece of his heritage. The land was put in a trust for him, and all we can do is hope that his adoptive parents did the right thing and passed it*

on to him. We pray he's a good neighbor to you and hope that maybe you'll find each other.

    I'm sorry I couldn't tell you. I just didn't know how. Your life was already so sad and confusing for you. I just didn't have the heart to drop this bombshell on you. I pray you're in a better state of mind. One night I was thinking about it all, trying to decide if I should put it in a safe deposit box that you would somehow get access to when you reached a certain age when maybe you were in a better place in life. Then one night it hit me. I thought surely if you reached a point where you could tear this old house down then you must be healthy and happy again. I pray that's where you're at now, and I hope that wherever you're living is further from the creek and smells better.

Jewel and Grady met each other's eyes smiling, both of them knowing that's exactly where they both were, and laughed at the fact that the house was further from the creek, both of them instinctively breathing in the fresh clean smell of the new house.

    I will be looking over you granddaughter, who will forever be the light of my life. Please forgive me for my weakness.

                                    Grandpa

"Sooo... Rudy's adoptive parents must not have told him?" Grady questioned, confused.

Jewel was still digesting the letter, imagining the motions her grandma and grandpa must have gone through. She was imagining them sitting on the porch together, half facing each other, and holding hands like they always did, while he made his confession to her and begged her for forgiveness. She thought of her grandma, remembering the sadness in her eyes when she talked about all the children she was never able to have, and the loss she felt when the one she was able to have was tragically killed in a car accident. She tried to imagine her grandpa standing in the gas station flirting with another woman, but she couldn't go there. It was impossible to think about. She wondered if her mom and dad knew.

She did the math in her head, subtracting Rudy's age to come up with the year when the affair took place, and what it must have been like at that time. She wondered about Rudy's adoptive parents, imagining their feelings of joy in adopting a baby boy, just like the images she remembered seeing on the commercials promoting adoption as a choice. She thought of Rudy, wondering what it would have been like to have him as her uncle growing up, and how everything in her life would likely be much different, which caused her to jerk her head suddenly to stare at the man beside her.

"All I know for sure is that everything that's happening right now is all meant to be. I'm so thankful to be right here, right now, with you, in this beautiful house you're building for us. Everything else... well... we'll just figure it out," she said climbing into Grady's lap as they sat together on their bed.

"Okay, but you surprise me sometimes Jewel. Sometimes you just surprise me with a reaction I'm not expecting."

"Sometimes I surprise myself. Who I am right now isn't who I've always been. I mean... this is all new to me, but where I'm at, and who I am right now, is exactly where I want to be," she said shrugging.

They sat there in silence for a while holding each other, both of them feeling thankful for all the events that had led them to that moment. It was interrupted by the sound of Troy's pickup as he pulled up in the space where their future garage would be next spring.

They made their way out to see him, feeling a little alarmed at what could have brought him out there, especially since they had just seen them a couple hours ago when they stopped by their house.

"What is it man?" Grady asked as Troy exited his truck.

"Sorry to alarm you. I forgot to give this to you earlier. I think it's from Madison, and I know you're anxious to hear from her," he said handing Grady a letter.

"Thanks man!" Grady said taking the letter excitedly.

"Thanks Troy! That was sweet of you to bring it out, or were you trying to get out of a diaper change?" Jewel asked jokingly.

"You're on to me. We flipped a coin. The winner got to bring you the letter, and the loser had to take care of the toxic waste coming out of Anna. Man the child can cause a stink," Troy laughed, smiling with pride as he talked about his baby girl.

"Well... come and have a glass of wine then," Jewel said motioning him toward the house to get out of the light drizzle that was starting to fall.

"Thanks, but I better get back. Surely, it's all cleaned up by now," he laughed as he anxiously made his way back to his truck.

"Thanks again!" they both said simultaneously as they watched him drive off.

"Another letter calls for another bottle of wine," Grady said as they both eyed the letter dubiously. They were excited to hear from her, but they had been on an emotional roller coaster for most of the day, and were feeling a little exasperated by the day's drama. With another glass of wine in hand, and the both of them sitting comfortably on the bed, they opened the letter and read.

Dear Grady

I'm sorry it took so long to write. I had to think things through a little. The news that you didn't know I even existed and that you would have never agreed to give me up is something I've never thought about before. Boys always get a bad rap! The movies always make boys out to be the ones who don't want the kids, leaving the mom to make the decisions about kids. It looks like that is usually what happens, but sometimes I guess there's an exception, which I guess makes me kind of lucky to find out that my biological dad is exceptional. Anyways mom and dad and me have been talking about it and that's kind of how we see it.

I have a volleyball game in three weeks in Sheridan and I was wondering if you and Jewel would like to come watch me. My mom said she would put a copy of the schedule in here before she mails this showing the dates and times and stuff like that so hopefully you have that. Maybe afterwards we could just meet and hang out a little and see if we want to be friends. Well that's usually what I do when I meet new people. I just hang out with them and then if we like some of the same things and listen to some of the same music and end up laughing and talking then we decide we like each other and then hang out some more. Do you think you would like to do that? You can invite other people to. I'm not the best player on the team but I'm pretty good. You'll be able to find me right away because I'm the tallest girl on the team and well my dad said that you and me look a lot alike and so if you really are my dad then you won't have any problem finding me. It will kind of be like a test I think because I think that if you are related to someone then you'll just recognize them right away. Well that's how it is with my friends who aren't adopted anyway so I think maybe it should sort of be the same except this might be just a little different since you've never seen me before. Do you know what I mean?

I think I will like your wife. She is really pretty and she looks sort of like my friends sister and she's really nice so maybe Jewel will sort of be like her. That's what I think. My mom thinks Jewel must be a model or something. My dad said you look like a nice couple and that he is relieved which he said makes him feel less stress which I think is good.

Can you send more pictures? I love your picture but I kept it in my book and it sort of got ruined just a little but I can still see your faces but that's about all. Can you send some more and I will make sure I don't keep it in my book this time. I would really like that.

Please write soon. I think we are already becoming good friends. What do you think?

Yours truly,
Madison

Jewel and Grady were both wiping away tears after reading the letter. They figured it would be a long time before they would get a chance to meet her, and were relieved and excited that it was going to be so soon. They quickly checked the schedule, with both of them knowing that even if they had other plans, they would change everything to make sure they could be at her game.

"The game is actually in just over two weeks. Too bad it's not while your family is here, but then again, that might be a little overwhelming for Madison. We have a lot to do, and a lot to talk about, and a lot to think about, but right now…," Jewel said drinking the last of her wine. "I'm a little drunk."

"Ya can hold yer own when it comes ta wine Jewel. Would ya like another glass… maybe another bottle or two?" he said jokingly as he looked at the empty bottle they had just opened, tipping it up as if to inspect the bottom for holes.

"I'm in complete and utter disbelief right now. Rudy is my uncle, and you have an eleven-year-old daughter that we are meeting in a couple weeks. Diana is my sister in-law, and my aunt!" she said tipping her head back and laughing hysterically.

They both started laughing, with Jewel trying to squeak out verses from the *I'm My Own Grandpa* song that she had sung to Rudy mockingly, as she recalled the Faqaiwi Indian joke he played on her. They cracked open their third bottle of wine as they went from laughing and joking about it all to crying, before winding back around and laughing and joking again. They were both on a roller coaster of emotions, with the ups and downs fueled by more wine, before finally crawling into bed and crashing. They both slept fitfully as they continued to wake throughout the night, realizing that the dreams were less bazaar than their reality.

CHAPTER 45

COMPANY

The new house was hardly ready for company. All the outer walls were up, it had a roof, all the plumbing and electrical, and even a heater, but most of the inside walls were mostly studs still, and although they did have a shower and a bathroom, it hardly allowed for much privacy. They decided there was nothing they could do about it, and agreed not to worry. Grady had warned them ahead of time, and that was after all, why they rented the RV's, but still, Jewel wanted to make their stay as comfortable as possible. They were only going to be staying with them a few days over a long weekend, not wanting to take the kids out of school more than a couple days, and that was the only thing that gave Jewel comfort. While she was excited to have them visit, they had been living kind of rough, and they had been so warm and welcoming to her, she was eager to be able to show them the same kindness.

They had talked at length about how and when to tell Rudy, and had decided it would be best if Jewel took him aside by herself, away from everyone, and then presented him with all the documents. Jewel was feeling a little nervous about it, but not as much as she would have thought. She felt very close to Rudy, and she needed to meet him face-to-face to present him with everything she knew, and let him know that the news was a welcome surprise to her. She didn't know how he would take it exactly, but something told her that coming from her, it might soften the hardness he felt about his adoption. They already felt such a kinship with each other that finding out they were bound by blood, seemed like a gift to Jewel, and she prayed Rudy would feel the same gratitude.

"Here they come!" Grady yelled to Jewel from outside, as she made their bed, in a final attempt to make something look presentable.

"What are they hauling?" she asked, running outside to watch them drive down the long road toward their house. They had two rented RV's and one of them was pulling a small, enclosed trailer.

"Well, I told you they were bringing stuff for us. Some of it is the rest of what I had in storage that I asked them ta bring, and who knows what else," Grady said shaking his head, but smiling.

They had cleared a space for their future garage, and directed them as they backed their RV's in to the clearing, having already decided that it would be the best place for them to camp out.

"Joseph! Come here Bestie!" Jewel said, hugging him as he bounded out of the RV excitedly.

"Auntie!" he yelled, hugging her tightly.

They all hugged each other excitedly, with all the kids surrounding Jewel, barely giving her a moment of breathing room. She had formed a strong bond with them in the short time she had spent with them in Belle Fourche, which started the moment she first jumped with them on the trampoline, and continued through phone calls and emails.

"Jewel, you look great. You look... better. I mean... it's probably not a compliment to tell a woman that she looks good because she gained weight, but... you do," Rudy said, hugging her tightly.

"Rudy, I am so excited to see you," she said nearly crying, hugging him to her with a flood of emotion he had yet to come to know or understand.

"Come here Sis!" Diana said, grabbing Jewel and hugging her tightly after breaking free from the big bear hug from her brother.

Maggie and Patrick both hugged her and Grady, and the kids quickly ran around the property curiously examining their surroundings, burning off some of their pent up energy from the long drive. Everyone toured the house, with Grady displaying his handiwork with nearly as much pride as Jewel felt watching him, remembering how hard he had worked on it so far. It was beautifully built, with Grady meticulously making sure everything was fitted together with perfection.

The wood used from the old house had been stained and reused, and reminded Jewel of the fairy godmother who had turned Cinderella's ragged dress into a beautiful gown. He had taken something damaged and soiled, and turned it into something that was magnificent. It took her breath away every time she looked at it, which she often did, when they would lay in the hammock she had strung up in the clearing near the creek, so they could admire it at the end of each day. They had both been working very hard. Grady was the builder while Jewel sanded and painted, and did any number of duties to help, both of them working long hours every day.

The area where the hammock hung was the place where they still had the tent set up, and where they often hung out in the evening near the campfire. It also happened to be the place where they hung out when Troy and Jo came over, and where the kids were now gathered ready for camping.

After the tour was over, it was only a matter of time before they gathered around the camp, and everyone was delighted when Troy, Jo and the new baby showed up. Jewel was overjoyed by all the love and laughter she felt, and she knew not to take a moment of it for granted. She reveled in it, wanting to soak up every ounce of it, and remember all the smiles and life brought back into the land that had once felt like her own personal tomb.

They grilled burgers and hot dogs for dinner, and the kids made s'mores over the campfire, after quickly deciding that the six of them were going to camp in the tent, while their parents and grandparents would sleep in the RV's. Grady offered to stay with them, but was relieved when they insisted they wanted to sleep in the tent without an adult. He and Jewel hadn't spent a single night apart since the abduction, aside from the night before their wedding, and he liked it that way. Every day as they worked on the house, he looked forward to the time of night when he could crawl into bed next to his wife, enjoying the warmth that he always found there, sometimes to make love, other times to just talk or listen.

Their relationship had grown secure and solid, and with every step he took during the day, or any little thing he did or saw, he immediately thought of telling Jewel, even though she was usually right there with him working alongside him, doing everything she could to do her part. Seeing her laughing with his parents, or playing with the kids, stirred something in him that was already so deep he wondered if he would ever reach the limit of the amount of love he could feel. He was happy when everyone started getting everything ready to turn in for the night.

"I love ya Jewel," he said softly, cupping her face between his hands as they finally climbed into bed next to each other later that night.

"I love you too," she said, a little taken by the surge of emotion that was coming from him. "Are you happy to have your family here Grady?"

"I am, and I love seein' ya with them. The kids adore ya, and Mom and Dad just smile every second yer around. Ya have a way with people. People respond ta ya in a way I've never seen before," he said between kisses.

"I wish they lived closer," she said, gasping as he kissed her neck.

"I'd have ta fight every day ta have just one moment alone with ya," he said, taking one of her nipples in his mouth, smiling as she cried out and pulled him closer to her.

She lost the ability to respond verbally beyond anything other than a gasp or a stifled moan, and he worked his way down the length of her, skillfully pulling off their last remaining clothes as he did, seemingly lost in his own need. She loved these moments when he would let go of the carefully managed control he always tried to maintain. He usually saw her as something fragile he needed to handle with tenderness, always mindful of her small frame compared to his own rugged mass, but occasionally he would just let go. His primal need to simply take what he needed, would lead him down a path that was beyond control, and she reveled in it, allowing herself to be taken beyond the limits of restraint.

She was lost in her own pleasure when she heard him and felt him give in to his need, released from the desire that had taken control of him. She simply tilted her head back, savoring the moment before his mind would bring him back around toward self-awareness.

"Damn Jewel," he gasped, kissing her deeply as he regained himself.

"I love it when you let go like that Grady. You have no idea what it does to me," she whispered, still languishing in the pleasure that radiated through her body.

"I can't help myself sometimes. I'm like a sailor on the sea, tryin' ta harness the power of the wind, yet always knowing that I'm just a man that's completely at its mercy," he said, falling on the bed next to her.

"Sooo... I'm the wind?" she asked confused.

"No. The desire I feel for you is like the wind."

"I see. So you're at the mercy of your desire for me then?" she asked, clarifying the analogy.

"I'm guessin' poetry wasn't yer best subject," he said laughing.

"That would be a good guess. I'm so literal that reading between the lines, or finding meaning beyond what's actually said, is sometimes lost on me, but I love the way you put things. If you had been teaching poetry, I probably would have done better."

"You are very literal Jewel, but I love that about you. You always say things exactly the way it forms in your brain. I never have to read between the lines."

"And you say things in this prolific way that makes me think about things in a way I never thought of before, making me realize that everything's not as black and white as I thought it was. You're kind of like music."

"An analogy? Okay. Here we go. How am I like music?" he said smiling, enjoying the unusual conversations they often had when they were lying in bed together.

"Well... music *is* poetry, but... I don't know... when I'm singing it, I just get it. You're like music. The way you put things... I just get it."

"Maybe yer not as literal as I thought," he said stroking her hair.

"Were you good at poetry? I mean... you're an engineer. It seems like you would be better at science and math."

"I was always good at science and math, but I liked reading, poetry, creative writing... classes like that. I had to work at them harder, but they were my favorite classes. Math was a breeze. I never had to work at it very hard."

"Math was a breeze? Are you mad?" she said, looking at him as if he had horns sticking out of his head.

"Well... it was easy for me. I always just got it, and I was lucky to have a couple of really good teachers in high school that got me off on the right track," he said shrugging. "What about you? What were your favorite classes?"

"They were all my favorite. I loved anything that gave me an excuse to seclude myself. I loved it so much, I started taking college classes when I was a junior in high school, even though I already had a full schedule. Anytime I would start to think or feel, I would throw myself into something else, diving in head first until it consumed me, but it wasn't exactly a breeze. I had to work hard at everything except music."

"So how did you learn music?"

"I just listened to it, and then I could play. We always had a piano, I don't ever remember not being able to play it, and my mom said that from the time I was just a toddler, I started playing with a little mandolin that I picked up when we were at a garage sale. I refused to leave without it. It just happened from there."

"So where's the piano?" he asked, wondering why he never saw a piano in the old house.

"Well, when Grandpa died, I wanted to sing a song at his services, but was surprised to learn that the church no longer had a piano that worked. I hadn't been there in a while, and Grandpa never said anything, even though he never missed church. It was his piano. I just thought he would like them to have it. He was very... devout," she said with less certainty, since she learned his secret. "I kind of wish I had it now."

"Are ya angry with him then?" he asked, thinking about their recent findings about Rudy.

"No. My Grandpa has surely faced his judgment. I just mean that I wish I could put it in the front room, on that East wall, next to that big giant window. It seems like a good place for a piano."

"Ahhh... Here I thought ya were gettin' all sentimental about yer grandpa, but yer really just decoratin' the house."

"I've decorated every room in this house in my mind. You have no idea what this place means to me," she said, pushing herself up on one elbow to look at him. "I haven't had a real home in a long time."

"I'm glad darlin'," he said smiling at her, brushing the hair out of her face the way he always did, "and I'm glad ya like decoratin'. That's the part I don't like doin'. We make a good team, which sort of reminds me of somethin' ya mentioned before," he said cocking an eyebrow at her.

What's that?"

"Well, the property in town. I thought we could develop it like ya said. Troy is happy here. He wants ta run the ranch, and I'll help him as needs be, but meanwhile, I need ta make a livin'. I was thinkin' we could develop it, sell off a portion, reinvest it, and then develop some more. The portion we keep, we can rent ta get a steady income comin' in."

"You've talked to Troy about running the ranch?"

"A little, just small talk, but I'm makin' presumptions. I think he's worried he's goin' ta be out of a job pretty soon. It's up ta you Jewel. I don't mean ta step on yer toes, but I'm a planner, and I have ta think of our future. What do ya want ta do Jewel?"

"I'm actually a little relieved to hear you say that. I've been worried about the whole situation, because I assumed that things weren't going to work out the way they have. I figured Troy and Jo would want to leave, and I... or we... would have to run the ranch, but now that we're here, I realize that they're pretty content...

especially since we made that deal with them about the land. I think Troy wants to keep running the ranch, and I guess I'm happy to hear that you weren't counting on it… I mean… I can't just kick Troy out, and I've been a little worried."

"Alright then… if ya could choose how it would all work out then, what would ya choose?" he asked trying to figure out what she wanted. He knew she was up in the air when it came to the ranch. She understood the overall picture of what happened on the ranch, but the fine details were completely lost to her, and making decisions about it overwhelmed her to the point that he could see the panic written all over her face every time she was forced to make a decision. She knew she was woefully unprepared to make any decisions about the ranch.

"I think the running of the ranch needs more structure, in that we should create a board, so that we can learn the process and make decisions together. Officially, Troy will be Ranch Manager, and will continue to do… well… just everything he does, which you and I should learn about so we could step in if we need to. I've been asked to work in the ER a few days a week, which I would like to do," she said eyeing him carefully, "and you could do something fantastic that you love to do, like build houses, or restore old cars, or… I don't know… takeover the world, or whatever you think you would like to do… developing that land is probably a good idea."

"Do you really think I want ta takeover the world?" he asked, smiling at her.

"I'm sure you probably have a plan about it somewhere in that head of yours," she said, leaning down to kiss him on the forehead.

"Sounds like I'm not the only one who's been makin' plans."

"I've been selfish and immature, and I left everything to Troy to figure out. Playtime is over. I need to step up," she said with new determination. "Do you want to develop the land in town? I mean… is that something you would be happy doing?"

"I'm kind of excited about it ta be honest," he shrugged. "We could start our own construction company ta get all the work done, with me runnin' all the crews. I've spent plenty of time workin' with engineers and city officials ta get all the permits and approvals, plus I've checked in town, and there seems ta be a demand for housin' that's not bein' met. Half the land could be for pre-sold houses, and the other half we could plan on rentin' ta keep a steady income comin' in, and ownin' our own business would give us some flexibility ta still be involved in the runnin' of the ranch as we need ta be."

"We should sit down with Troy and Jo then, and tell them what we think. It all sounds good, but you didn't say anything about me working at the hospital."

"We could certainly use the income, and if it's what ya want ta do, then ya should," he said frowning a little.

"What's with the frown then?" she asked with a puzzled look.

"It's just that I like our days right now. I like workin' with ya out here with just the two of us. I mean, I knew it was goin' ta change, but I'm not ready for it ta change just yet."

"Do you want me to put on a hard hat, and come be one of your crew members?" she asked teasing him.

"No! I'd have ta fight off all the men every second of every day. I'd never get a damn thing done," he said pulling her down to kiss him, before swiftly rolling her onto her back, pinning her beneath him once again. "Ya'd look damn fine in a hard hat though."

"Well, we'll both be working in town a few days a week. We can eat lunch together, and we still have our nights together," she said wrapping her legs around him, pulling him in again.

CHAPTER 46

UNCLE RUDY

"What's up Sis?" Rudy asked, as he and Jewel caught their breath, reaching the top of the hill they were climbing.

"That obvious am I?" Jewel asked hopelessly, feeling confused as to how she could be such an open book.

"Let me give you a little hint. When you're trying to think of what to say, you mouth the words. Did you know that?" he asked turning to her.

"I have caught myself doing that before. You're very observant," she said stalling.

"Well?" he asked again.

"Well… yes. I do have something to tell you. Come here," she said motioning toward the flat rock where she had been leading them. The flat rock was a place she had often come to when she was growing up. It overlooked the valley below, and if she sat right in the middle she could look out and see nothing but the mountains on one side, and rolling hills on the other. From that one spot, nothing man-made was visible. There were no phone lines, no fences, houses, or stalls. There was nothing but vast amounts of land, hand-carved by Mother Nature herself.

As a child, she would often go there and pretend that she was a young Native American girl, hundreds of years before civilization brought forth the progress of *things* that now threatened to drown them. It was so quiet and peaceful there, she sometimes felt she could see and feel beyond what could normally be seen and felt in the physical world. When she thought of how she might tell Rudy about her grandfather, she had immediately thought of taking him there, hoping the spiritual magnificence of the place would somehow lend comfort to him as she dropped a bombshell on him.

"My gosh Jewel. Am I dying or something?"

"No! Of course not. I'm sorry Rudy. Bear with me. I've only just come to terms with this myself."

He was momentarily confused, but then became caught up in seeing her struggle with the news. He thought about rescuing her, but he sat motionless, unable to help her. He knew what was coming, but he wanted to hear what she had to say… imagining how she might put it. It was only a matter of time, and the look on her face, and her constant nervousness and fidgeting, told him that the time had finally arrived.

He remembered how he had struggled with his own emotions shortly after she told him her name was Jewel Etchemendy from Johnson County, Wyoming. He knew immediately who she was. He remembered the lines of the family tree that had been so carefully severed just above his name, leaving him dangling out there on the page like an ugly smudge that couldn't be erased. He traced the lines of the tree in his mind, extending down from the man who was his half-brother, and saw her name hanging there proudly for the entire world to see, the heir to the Etchemendy throne as he saw it, choking back the sorrow that always slithered down the back of his throat when he thought of it.

"Well, when Grady and I were tearing down the house, we found a box in the floor boards. Grady found it actually, and then I walked in a moment later. He was so stunned by what he found that he accused me of hiding it from him. I didn't know what he was talking about at the time, but we finally calmed down and read through everything together, and what we found Rudy, is your biological father," she said clearing her throat, never once taking her eyes from his as she delivered the news. "Rudy, my grandfather is your biological father."

"What? Are you saying that you didn't know?" he asked confused. "Are you really telling me you didn't know?"

"Rudy? I'm… what are you saying? I'm… ugh… did you know all along?" she asked, her head spinning as she looked at Rudy, feeling a sense of alarm.

"I knew who you were the minute you told me your name," he said matter of fact.

"How did you know? Why didn't you say anything to me?" she asked stuttering, the ugly web of deceit tangling her mind.

"Why didn't I tell you what? What was I to say? Hi Jewel Etchemendy, I'm the discarded half uncle nobody wanted," he said mockingly.

"If I had known about you Rudy, I would have wanted you."

"Did you really not know about me?" he asked a little heatedly, the broken record of assumptions playing over and over in his head, ignoring the obvious look of innocence written on her face, but knowing without a doubt, that she was telling the truth.

"I swear to God Rudy. Until Grady showed me this box," she said holding out the box for him that she held in her hand, "I didn't know anything about this. I've known about this for less than one week."

His head was swimming with the news, shattering all his carefully held beliefs that lived in his mind up to that point. His mom and dad decided to wait until he was an already confused adolescent boy, in the midst of puberty, to tell him they adopted him, and it crushed him. When he found out about the land, and traced his biological father back to the ranch, he imagined the Etchemendy family in a certain way. He imagined them all sitting around at the dinner table laughing and talking, hugging each other, and thanking God that they had rid themselves of that one mistake.

He imagined his half-brother, greedily wanting to keep all the land for himself, and his biological father, reluctantly carving off a small piece of his land to ease the guilt he had, perhaps making one last attempt to get into heaven as he neared death and paid for his sins. He knew his own pain fueled the negative light he saw them in, but at times, it comforted him, wanting to see them in such a way so that it might lessen the pain of abandonment he felt. He needed to make them into villains so that he could pretend to feel thankful to be rid of them.

Despite himself, he liked Jewel the instant he met her. She was everything he had never imagined her to be. He was taken aback when she talked about the death of her parents and her sad childhood, the news of his brother's demise reaching him for the first time, challenging all the ideas he had as to why they never stayed in touch.

"Rudy. I love you. You know me," she said, taking his hands, forcing him to meet her eyes. "Do you trust me?"

"I do trust you Jewel," he admitted, nodding his head.

"If I had known I had an uncle like you, I would have run to you and forced my way into your life," she said firmly. "The question is, if you knew who I was, why didn't you tell me, and why didn't you tell Grady when we were in Alaska?"

"I was going to, but then everything just snowballed. We went from being out of the competition to being back in, and then to see the way Grady was falling for you, and how well you two fit together... I don't know Jewel... I just decided to leave it alone. I didn't want it to influence the relationship between you and Grady, and I was a little shocked. I didn't know my brother died, and I didn't know my biological father died. I figured it would all come out in due time, and it looks like it has."

"I'm in complete shock right now! Did you know my dad? Did you know Grandpa? Why did you assume that I knew about you?" she asked nervously, never waiting long enough between questions for any answers to come forth.

"Did you really not know about me Jewel?" he asked searching her face for answers.

"No Rudy. Grandpa was... I don't know... I would have never thought it possible that he would have been capable of cheating or keeping secrets. That's not the man I knew, and my parents never said anything. My dad always talked about the loneliness of growing up an only child. He wished they could have given me a brother or a sister. I mean... I was only eleven when they died. Maybe they would have told me...," she said choking up a little before clearing her throat. "Maybe they would have told me eventually."

Rudy shook his head as he struggled to piece it all together outside his own thoughts. "When I was on leave one summer, I followed a lead I had and found my father... your grandpa. Your dad and your grandpa came and met with me one afternoon, and we sat and talked for hours, hitting it off right away. I could tell that your dad was still wrestling with the news, but he seemed genuinely happy to meet me. He had tears in his eyes as he shook my hand, and we both cried a little as we hugged each other and said goodbye, promising to keep in touch. It was the first time in my life I felt like a whole person. I never understood why he didn't keep that promise. I was so angry Jewel!" he said shaking his head. "I struggled with it for a lot of years. I wrote them a few times, but never got a single response. It wasn't until I met you, and you told me about your parents dying, that I realized that it must have been shortly after that meeting when your dad died."

"Oh Rudy," she said hugging him, imagining how he must have felt the abandonment all over again when the response to his letters never came. "Did Dad tell you about me?"

"Yes, and he showed me pictures. He even gave me one that he had in his wallet. As soon as you told me your name, with that dark hair and those deep blue eyes staring at me, I thought of that picture safely tucked away with my adoption records. There was no doubt in my mind who I was looking at Jewel."

"You must have been... well... maybe a little... relieved I guess, when I told you my parents died," she asked feeling a little defensive, peering up at him reluctantly.

"Maybe just for half a second, and I'm sorry for that. I never understood why I was given up for adoption in the first place, and then after they didn't keep in touch, I was devastated. You question yourself... your own worthiness. It's... it's not something I can describe Jewel," he said shaking his head. "I guess I was glad to have an explanation finally, but my relief to finding the answer, was immediately overshadowed by the grief that I felt when you described the pain of losing your parents."

"I wonder why Grandpa didn't keep in touch with you," she wondered aloud. "He should have."

"I don't know Jewel, but as a dad, I shudder to think how broken I would be if one of my children died, but then... on the other hand... as a dad, I couldn't imagine handing one of my sons over to be raised by another family. Believe me... if there was an answer that made sense, I would have already found it. I've thought about it a million times."

The two sat silent on the flat rock for a while, both of them contemplating the past and the present, wondering how things happened the way they did, searching their minds for logical explanations. The majesty of the rock was doing its job, wrapping them in comfort as their emotions surged through them like whiskey coursing through the blood stream. Jewel imagined the meeting that had taken place, thinking of her dad with tears in his eyes, overjoyed at having a brother at last.

"You're my uncle Rudy," she finally said with a half-smile as she lifted her eyes with her head still facing down.

"Come here Jewel," he said wrapping an arm around her, as much for affection as to conceal the tears that were forming in his eyes. "It's a good feeling to know you have blood in this world."

Jewel started crying the minute the words came out of his mouth. The years of feeling like the last Mohican since the death of her grandfather, flooded out of her with the realization that there was someone in this world, someone like her, that she could love and care for, and someone that would love her back. "We're orphans no more Jewel. We've got each other."

"My dad always talked about how he hated being an only child. It's so unfair Rudy. I'm so mad at Grandpa right now."

"After you told me about your parents dying, and how devastated you were, I guess I started to understand why your grandpa never kept in touch with me. He had his hands full taking care of you. It sounds like you were pretty fragile. It probably scared him. He did the right thing by trying to protect you from any more pain."

"Did you ever meet your biological mother?" Jewel asked reluctantly, the heat rising up and flooding her face, still upset with the notion that her grandpa could be with another woman.

"Yes. We exchange cards and emails mostly. She lives in New Mexico with my half-sister. She said your grandpa was a good man. She said they were both just lonely. She was married to a man that didn't love her and hadn't touched her in years, and he was married to the love of his life who hadn't touched him in years. I guess physical needs win over sometimes no matter what the circumstance."

"What about your parents that adopted you?" Jewel asked.

"Well, I've told you a little about them. They're mom and dad. They love me. They're good people, but they couldn't have kids, ironically, until shortly after they adopted me. I was three months old when Mom got pregnant with my sister."

"They must be good people Rudy, because you're one of the best people I've ever known."

"Ahhh. You're just saying that because we're family," he said giving her a friendly squeeze.

"My dad would have loved you so much," she said catching herself before the flood of tears overwhelmed her again. "You're so much like he was. I think that somehow, deep inside me, I must have known. I opened up when I met Grady and you, and it wasn't just Grady either and the way I feel for him. It was you Rudy. You cracked the shell I had been hiding in. I became a different person when I met you guys. I just put myself in your hands. If you had known me the second before you met me, you would have never thought that was possible. I went from being so dependent on Troy, to leaving here and never letting anyone in, to immediately putting myself in yours and Grady's hands. It's kind of crazy to think about looking back."

"It's funny how life works out sometimes isn't it? Maybe it was just the right time. I mean, think about how you might have handled it if you would have found out about this when you were say... I don't know... sixteen," he said picking a random number. "Think about that time in your life. How would this have looked to you then? How might that affect how you and Grady ended up together?"

"I know Rudy," she agreed, "I've thought about that. Anything that would have landed me somewhere that doesn't include Grady at this stage in my life, is unthinkable to me. I guess things worked out the way they were supposed to, but I haven't come to terms with it yet. I'm still mad at Grandpa. I thought you might like to read through all this though," she said handing him the box. "Does Diana know?"

"Of course. I can hardly tie my shoes without sharing it with her," he said taking the box in both his hands eagerly, hoping it may hold some answers for him. She had included everything in the box, including the letter her grandfather had written to her. She wanted him to know everything she knew.

"What about the kids?" she asked.

"They know I'm adopted, but I've yet to explain to them that my sister-in-law is my niece," he said smiling at her.

"Do you want me to sing *I'm My Own Grandpa* to you again?" she joked, both of them breaking out in laughter at the relative truth of the twisted family structure of the song she had once sang to him as a joke.

"I hummed that damn song in my head the whole day after you and Grady got married," he said still chuckling.

"So what does Diana have to say about all this?" she asked after they stopped laughing at the absurdity of it all.

"Well... she and I both thought that you might've known," he said shrugging, "I mean... we thought you probably had an idea, but we weren't sure, so we didn't want to say anything to Grady or anything. Diana was sure there was some logical explanation, and of course she was right," he said rolling his eyes, knowing he was going to have to eat a little crow.

"Oh! I almost forgot. I have this for you," she said, placing a very small pocketknife in one of his hands that she'd had in her pocket. It was actually a key chain, and had a folding blade, wooden handle, and a carving of a large elk on the side.

"What's this for Jewel?"

"It was Dads. One night I found it when I was in his shop helping him. I asked him if I could have it and he came over, took it from me as if it were made of glass, put it back where he had it stashed, and then gave me a sad face. When I asked him about it, he told me about the day he bought it. Grandma was due any day, and everyone was talking about the little brother he was going to have. So... he went out and bought this for him, wanting to make sure that he had a good present for him when he finally came. He was really excited to have a baby brother, but then just before the baby was due it died. Dad said he was so sad that he would just lay in bed for a whole week rolling this little pocket knife over and over in his hands," she said wiping away a tear. "Anyway... I knew my Dad. He would have wanted you to have it. He would have liked that very much."

Rudy took the knife, examining it more closely, as if it held the hidden secrets of a life he had once imagined. It was so small that it made him smile as he considered the logic of a boy picking out a small enough pocketknife for a baby, never once considering that a pocketknife in general would not be an appropriate gift for a newborn. He suddenly felt he had been handed the key to all the many treasures that he had never known. He clasped his hand around it tightly, feeling the weight of the knife as he remembered the heartfelt hug and the strong handshake from the man who once longed for a little brother. "Thank you Jewel," he said fighting back tears, fully understanding and accepting the enormity of the gift.

"What about Patrick and Maggie? What do they know?" Jewel asked, breaking the silence as thoughts reeled through her mind.

"They know everything Diana knows. That woman tells her Momma everything. She can't help it, and I guess I should be glad that my wife's best friend is her mom, and not some meddling Nancy gossiping around town."

"Meddling Nancy?" she said cocking an eyebrow at him.

"Well, you know" he shrugged. "It doesn't matter Jewel. Those people love you to death. You could probably stab someone with an ice pick just for looking at you cross-eyed, and they would complement you on your technique."

"But I didn't stab anyone with an ice pick, and I didn't do anything wrong. Why would you say it like that?"

"I didn't mean anything. It's just that I guess they aren't thinking too kindly of your grandfather. I've known them for a long time Jewel. They're just being protective."

"I don't know exactly what to think Rudy, but I am who I am in large part because of Grandpa. He did everything for me. He had arthritis and heart disease, and he was sick with a broken heart from losing his wife and my dad, but he never missed a single game I ever played in, driving all over Wyoming. He took me to Wal-Mart so I could get my first bra and buy tampons. He took me dress shopping, and took me to Disney Land, and rafting, and camping, and hunting. He learned to cook, making sure I had everything from the food pyramid every single day. He stayed up all night with me holding my hair as I puked when I had the flu. When my parents died, he gave up everything so that he could take care of me. He quit golfing and hanging out at the bar with his buddies. He gave up cigars and chewing tobacco. I can't defend what he did Rudy, but he wasn't a bad person. He was a good person who did something bad," she said in defense of the man she knew.

"He must have been good Jewel, because I see the woman he raised, and I know her to be good!"

"It must be really hard for you. It would probably be easier for you if he had been a horrible person, because the puzzle would fit together so much better. I don't understand why he did it exactly. I just know that Grandma had so many miscarriages, and was so broken by it, it must have been devastating for her to realize it really was just her, and that Grandpa could have easily had more children," she shrugged. "I don't know Rudy. It was the wrong decision. I could have had you for my uncle all along, but then you might not have met Diana, and I might have never met Grady. I'm just so thankful to be sitting with you right here and now, in all the mess and muck that's been left behind, so long as I get to go back home to Grady. What about you?"

"Well, Grady's not exactly my cup of tea, but I get your meaning," he said smiling at her.

"You know Rudy, for a couple of emotional invalids, we didn't do half bad. We discussed feelings, and we even cried a little," she said, recalling the exasperation Grady often expressed with them when it came to serious discussions that involved feelings.

"Feelings? Those are those little microbes that get in between your toes and make them stink, right?" he joked.

"Exactly!" she responded, smiling as she looked up at her uncle.

They sat and looked out at the landscape for a while, each of them lost in their own thoughts, when Rudy finally broke the silence.

"I'm proud to have you for a niece Jewel. If you're the prize, then I'm more thankful than anyone could ever know."

She smiled up at him and nuzzled in closer as he kept his arm wrapped around her, both of them grateful for the blood and the friendship that bound them together.

CHAPTER 47

―――――

YOUNG LOVE

Being sixteen, nearly seventeen, is something that inherently demands independence, and a vacation that does not include your parents, but the fact that Jewel was there, made the pain of her continued adolescence, bearable.

Alisha had an instant connection with Jewel, taking comfort in the fact that she had this amazing woman to look up to that wasn't that much older than her, and the fact that Jewel was married to her uncle, made her that much more admirable. She always looked up to her uncle, seeing him as the perfect representation of everything a girl would want in a man, but not in an inappropriate way. She didn't think of him as anything other than an uncle, though she aspired to find a great man one day, knowing that men like him existed in the world. She saw him as a man of honor, who always thought of others first, always looking for ways to do what is right, and what is best for those around him. She aspired one day to not only find someone who was just like him, but to *be* someone just like him.

"How did you know that you loved Uncle Grady?" Alisha asked Jewel one afternoon as the two of them headed into town to do some grocery shopping.

"Well, from the first time I met him, I started to feel things I had never felt before. I would sit next to him, or just look up at him, and my pulse would start racing," she said smiling over at her as she steered her dad's old truck toward town.

"That's physical though. I mean, how did that make him any different from anyone else? How did you know it was actually love?" she asked with more determination.

"I didn't really have to ask myself if it was love… I just knew. It's like the sky… it's either sunny and blue, or it's not… you don't have to wonder about it. Why are you asking Alisha?" Jewel asked, wondering what the urgency was coming from her.

"Because I've been dating someone, and he's so cute, and so sweet, but he wants something a little more. I mean, he's a year older than I am, and will be going to college next year. He wants to… ugh… well have sex, and I'm not sure if I should," she said shrugging, a little unsure. "I'm sorry. Is it okay that I'm talking to you about this? I mean… it's just that I thought you would understand more than anyone since you're only like six years older than me."

"Of course it's okay to talk to me," she said searching her brain for the right answers, praying she can give her the right guidance.

"How old were you the first time? Do you mind me asking?" she asked, feeling reassured that going to Jewel was the right thing to do.

"Well… I was twenty-two. Grady was the first man I was with, and I'm glad about that. It was perfectly clear from the very beginning that our futures were headed in the same direction. He didn't pressure me; in fact, I wanted to, but he wouldn't until he felt it was the right time for both of us. I think that's how you know if you should sleep with someone or not."

"You waited until you were twenty-two!" she said incredulously, "but most of the girls I go to school with have already had sex, some of them with multiple guys. I'm like one of the only girls I know who hasn't had sex."

"So? You can't make decisions about what's best for you based on the choices that other people make. I think that you know it's not the right time for you, or you wouldn't be asking," Jewel said giving her a discerning look.

"I guess you're right, but I'll be seventeen in a few weeks, and everyone is going to think something's wrong with me if I'm still a virgin."

"So what! Who cares what anyone thinks, but I guess that's why they call it peer pressure," Jewel said shaking her head. "I sort of had it easy, because I had Troy, and I'm sure everyone assumed Troy and I were sleeping together, and so I didn't really have to be subjected to the peer pressure that much. I didn't realize how lucky I was to escape that until just now. What's this boy's name?"

"His name's Virgil, but everyone calls him Nico. He's the star of the football team, and every girl wants to be with him. He's going to South Dakota School of Mines next year just like Uncle Grady. I don't know… I mean… I guess he's just everything I thought I wanted in a man. I mean… why wouldn't I want to?"

"Well if you have to ask…," Jewel said shrugging, raising her eyebrows at her. "I think you already know it's not the right decision, or you wouldn't be questioning it."

"So if I have to ask, then it's probably not the right time, or the right guy?" Alisha asked clarifying it.

"Exactly, and I don't mean that you ask yourself in the heat of the moment. I mean you ask yourself before you ever leave your house. It doesn't really count if you change your mind suddenly, because your body starts making all the decisions when you're out with him, and you're suddenly all hot and bothered," Jewel said, shooting her a look as she pulled up in front of the grocery store.

Jewel threw an arm around her as they walked in the store, hugging her to her in a way that felt perfectly natural, as if she had done it her whole life. She was offering up affection like only an aunt who had known her, her whole life would do.

They wound their way through the grocery store, down one aisle and then the next, talking all the way, picking items out, and carefully deciding how much of each thing they should buy to feed so many people. She was thankful to have Alisha with her, who was clearly more used to buying large quantities of food to feed their large family of eight, than Jewel was.

"Jewel?" said a voice from behind her.

"Michael? Is that you?" she asked, turning to see the boy behind her, only to find that he was already distracted by her niece.

"Jewel... you remember me then?" he asked.

"Of course I remember you. How could I ever forget?" she said remembering the little boy she had mentored when she was in high school, going up to give him a hug. "Are you working here Michael?" she asked, seeing the apron he wore that was typical of those who worked in the produce section of a grocery store.

"Just through this semester, and then I'm starting at U.W. I'm going into the R.O.T.C. program. I'm graduating early," he said proudly, struggling to keep from staring at the blond-haired, blue-eyed girl standing beside Jewel.

"I'm sorry Michael... this is my niece, Alisha. Alisha, this is Michael. I was his tutor and his mentor when I was in high school."

"She helped me with writing. I was terrible at it, but she was a good teacher," he said shyly, unable to take his eyes off Alisha. "I heard you got married Jewel. I would love to meet your husband someday. I hope he's a good guy."

"He's great! Why don't you come out and have barbeque with us later tonight. Alisha and her family are here visiting, along with my mother and father-in-law, plus you could meet Grady."

"Ugh... okay... I would love to," he said. "I heard you tore down the old house and are building something else. I would love to see everything. Is Troy and Jolene going to be there?"

"Yep. You know where everything is. The gate codes haven't changed. If you just drive past where the old house was around that first hill along the creek a ways, then you'll find us. You remember where the treehouse is don't you?"

"I sure do. Couldn't forget it," he said smiling down at Alisha, unable to resist glancing at her every few seconds, despite his best efforts.

"I also used to babysit Michael, and so did Troy. He lives out on a nearby ranch and knows the land about as well as anyone. He rides his horse around there more than anyone, and pretty much comes and goes as he pleases. I'm actually surprised I haven't seen you around yet Michael."

"Ha. Well, this is only one of my jobs. I work at a construction job too, just trying to save as much as I can for college. I haven't had much time for anything else, but I'd love to come out tonight. Can I bring anything?"

"Nope. Just come out and relax for a while. You can meet Grady and his family, and say hello to Troy and Jolene. Have you met the baby?"

"No! I heard the baby was born, but I've been so busy," he said shaking his head.

"Good. We'll look forward to seeing you later then," Jewel said catching the look Alisha and Michael shared.

They said their goodbye's, and finished the rest of their shopping, with both of them waving to Michael one last time before leaving the store. Jewel could tell right away that Alisha and Michael had been eyeing each other the whole time they had been standing there talking in the produce section. She thought of their earlier conversation, wanting to somehow bring it up to turn it into a teaching moment, solidifying the idea that she wouldn't be so interested in this boy if the one back home were really the right guy, but she didn't want to make presumptions. She figured Alisha would bring it up if she hadn't already figured it out in her own mind, which she knew she likely had.

"He was cute," Alisha finally said after they drove in silence for several miles, and there was no doubt about it that he indeed was very cute. He was tall, had dirty blond hair with light green eyes, and Jewel could instantly see them together like some sort of Barbie and Ken look-a-like couple.

"He is cute. He was always a cute kid. Hard working... good family. He's about your age," Jewel said smiling over at her.

"I suppose you're going to tell me that this pretty much answers my own question. Do you still think other men are cute even though you're married to Uncle Grady?"

"Ummm... I suppose. I haven't really thought about it, but yes. Thinking someone is cute, and wanting to spend a lifetime with them are two different things though. I think when two people start seeing their future together, intertwined... not fantasy, but actually making real plans, making decisions to achieve that future... I think that's something you need to be on the lookout for when you're trying to decide if you've met the right guy or not," Jewel said, wanting to bring the point home. "When Nico talks about going to college, does he talk about you anywhere in that college scenario?"

The frown on Alisha's face answered the question without her having to verbalize it, and they both knew it.

Jewel was glad they'd had that talk when she saw them together later that evening. From the moment Michael showed up, she could see Alisha and him gravitate toward each other. Everyone could see they hit it off, and nobody was the least bit surprised when he offered to take Alisha and her sibling's horseback riding the next day.

"Is it safe?" Diana asked as they made plans for a long ride through the mountains, complete with a picnic.

"Of course," Jewel said nonchalantly, "I survived."

"Nobody is more qualified to take them than Michael here. He knows these mountains like the back of his hand, and he knows horses better than anyone I've ever known," Troy added, trying to ease a mothers natural worries.

"Well, I think it would be fine. The kids really want to go," Rudy said shrugging.

"I'll take good care of them," Michael said, locking eyes with Alisha as the other kids gathered around him united.

"Alright then," Diana said throwing her hands in the air. She knew it was already too late to try to change the kid's plans. They had talked of going horseback riding the entire drive from South Dakota to Wyoming, and now they seemed to have the perfect opportunity to go with a kid that was not only well versed in traversing the mountains, but had grown up on a horse ranch, and knew exactly which horse to put with each child. Besides, it was undeniable that Michael was a big hit with all the kids, and most especially with Alisha.

Michael looked each person in the eye, and shook their hand when he was introduced to them earlier, and Rudy was very impressed with the young man from the moment he met him. Rudy wasn't the least bit disappointed that Alisha had an interest that would perhaps make her think twice about the little scoundrel at home she was dating. He had heard stories about Nico, and he wasn't at all happy that he was dating his daughter.

"So what will you be studying at U.W.?" Rudy asked Michael.

"I'm going into their engineering program. I haven't really decided which exactly... probably mechanical, or maybe structural," Michael said humbly.

"Just like Grady here," Rudy said nodding with approval, smiling at his daughter as he did.

It was a fun evening with all of them gathered out near the camping area cooking on the grill, and roasting s'mores by the fire. Jewel sang a few songs, and they all laughed and talked for hours. Patrick and Maggie had brought steaks to grill, and side dishes to share with everyone. Kids ran in all directions, catching fireflies, and chasing each other around, up and down the treehouse non-stop. Jewel smiled, watching it all unfold. She hadn't asked Rudy and Diana yet what they had planned to do with their land, but she secretly hoped it would work out so they could at least maybe build a summer home, and plan to spend more time there. Having them there made everything feel like things were right in the world.

Her feelings were solidified when she saw Michael show up bright and early the next morning trailing six horses behind him, all saddled and ready for the day. The look that transpired between Alisha and Michael when their eyes met, reminded her of the look that often transpired when she looked at Grady, and it did not escape her notice that Alisha got up early to make sure she had everything packed for their picnic. It was the earliest she had seen her get up without complaint, in the time she had known her.

~~~~~~~~

Michael got Joseph, Tina, Melanie, Paxton, Thomas and then finally, Alisha, all set up with the horses he had hand selected for each one of them for the day. He knew each one of these horses, had broken each one of them, and trained them since he was a boy. The gentlest horse he reserved for Joseph, and it had been his horse when he was younger, and he knew it well. She was a beautiful roan that he had fallen in love with the moment he saw him at the horse sale when he was just about Joseph's age.

For Tina he chose a small paint that fit the description of the kind of horses she thought were the most beautiful, and would be easy and gentle with her for the ride. He knew he had chosen wisely when Tina let out a loud shrill in all her excitement, and the paint barely seemed to notice.

For Melanie, and the other two boys, he chose from his favorite quarter horses. They were gentle but strong, and he thought they would be thrilled to have the bigger horses with a little more power behind them. Their excitement was evident from the moment they laid eyes on them. The horses were often used during hunting season when him and his dad guided hunters through the mountains, and he knew the three of them would easily handle them.

For Alisha he had reserved a natural blond quarter horse that he thought of the moment he saw her, and imagined her out riding freely across the high plains, like some sort of dream that could only be cultivated in the mind of a young man. He smiled when she climbed up on her and rubbed her gently, showing her love and respect for the animal. She smiled back at him as he came up beside her on his own horse, a large gelding that he bought for himself when he turned sixteen, in lieu of a new car.

"You're a natural Ally... I mean... can I call you Ally?" Michael said blushing a little, realizing suddenly that he felt a little more comfortable with her than would have been expected at this stage. "I mean... it's just that I heard your dad call you that and, I don't know, it seems to fit you."

"I would like it if you called me Ally," she said smiling, knowing that the only other people in her life that called her that were her family.

"Well Ally, let's get these siblings of yours wrangled up and headed out, shall we?" he said smiling at her.

He led the way, with Alisha following close behind, and one by one, the rest followed. The others were used to following Alisha's lead. She was practically like a second mother to them, though her parents made sure not to lean on her too much. Paxton and Melanie were not far behind her in age, but they followed her lead nevertheless, and helped with the younger kids without a second thought. Above all else, they had been taught to band together and love each other, and the six of them were very close. They looked out for each other, and they gravitated toward each other when other kids sought independence.

"Stay up with me Joseph," Alisha called out, wanting to keep the youngest of them at her side, with Paxton flanking Thomas's side, and Melanie naturally falling in next to Tina to make sure that everyone was being looked after.

"So, you're a junior?" Michael asked as Alisha rode up beside him.

"Yes. I have a long ways to go," she said regretfully. "How is it that you're graduating a semester early?" she asked him as they rode toward the mountain, side by side in an easy walk.

"Truth be told, I'm actually a semester behind. That's why Jewel was my tutor. I was held back in grade school. They didn't figure out I was dyslexic until I was in the third grade, and by that time, I had a lot of catching up to do. I got caught back up in high school though, and was able to finish a half a year early. Jewel was a good teacher."

"I love her. She's so... I don't know... real. Do you know what I mean?" Alisha said thinking about her aunt.

"I do. I know exactly what you mean. There's nothing about Jewel that's not exactly the way you see it. She's always been that way."

"Look at all the antelope!" Joseph said excitedly as they came across a field where they were known to gather in large quantities.

They all fell in beside each other, and Michael laughed a little seeing them all. They were all so excited to be out riding, and it had turned out to be a beautiful day. It was a long ways from the guiding that he normally did, taking grown men out who had often times turned out to be anything but excited, despite having spent quite a bit of money to be on the adventure. Some of those he guided were regulars who came every year, and others were those who were simply checking an item off their bucket list, completely taken aback by the ruggedness of the country, and the harsh elements that could often be found in that part of the world.

They rode on for a couple hours until Tina finally put her foot down, demanding they stop alongside a creek they had come across. She was hungry, and when that happened, there wasn't any negotiating with her. She was much like her dad in that regard, and Alisha knew there was no use in arguing with her about it.

"We can stop here. If I can get a couple of the boys to help me with the horses, we'll get them settled, and then we can have some lunch," Michael said.

"Boys! Why can't I help with the horses?" Melanie said with her hands on her hips, giving him a stern look.

"Ugh... you'll do just fine. Come help me then," Michael said, handing her the reins to a couple of the horses, realizing for the first time that the girl was a natural when it came to the horses, as was Paxton.

"I think I want to be a large animal vet," Paxton said, leading a couple of the horses to the clearing where Michael was getting them settled after everyone was safely dismounted.

"Well, you're good with horses. I'll bet you'll be good at it," Michael said.

Alisha spread everything out for the picnic, handing them each a sandwich that she'd made, along with some fruit and chips that she brought. Joseph, Tina, and Thomas were off exploring up the creek, while Melanie and Paxton stayed near the horses, petting them and brushing them, unable to get enough of them, leaving Alisha and Michael sitting there on the blanket they had spread out for lunch.

"Jewel said you might be coming back for Thanksgiving?" Michael asked hopefully.

"I hope so. Uncle Grady said we could come stay with them anytime we wanted."

"Maybe we could go to the movies or something next time you come."

"Okay," she smiled shyly. "I wish we weren't leaving tomorrow, but we have school the next day, and Mom and Dad won't let us miss school very often."

They talked back and forth for a long time, the kind of small chatter you would expect from a couple of teenagers, though it was immediately clear they had formed a lasting friendship. Alisha seemed to let down her usual poise she always tried to maintain when she was around the boys at school, and comfortably relaxed and could just be herself in a way that she wasn't used to. Michael was relaxed, and they talked and laughed non-stop, before deciding to go play in the creek with the rest of the kids, and just have fun.

They spent the rest of the day riding further up the mountain, before deciding they should probably head back before their parents called out a search party for them. All the kids managed to make it back in one piece with just a few scrapes here and there that was typical of young kids exploring the country.

"Thanks Michael," Alisha finally said after they returned later that day. "I had a really good time, and so did the others."

"Me too. Promise me you'll call and write like you said?" he said reluctantly, getting ready to leave as he said his goodbye's to Alisha.

"Of course I will. You too?" she asked, fidgeting nervously with her hands, looking up at him.

"Every day," he said, suddenly deciding to lean down to kiss her softly on the lips before taking his leave.

CHAPTER 48

WINTER WORK

Saying goodbye was bittersweet. Grady and Jewel had been ready to get back to work to get their life assembled into some kind of order, but they were also sad to see everyone leave so soon. They made plans to have everyone come again for Thanksgiving, and Alisha was already dropping hints about staying with them over the long Christmas break, in hopes of getting to spend more time with Michael, whose kiss she could still feel on her lips every time she closed her eyes.

Their visit had been a welcome break from the constant work they had put into getting their house built, but as the cold months ahead closed in on them, they started to feel the pressure of getting as much of the house complete as could be managed, in order to make their winter as comfortable as possible. They were both used to the cold, but that never stopped the winter from harshly reminding them how cold they can feel, so deep in their bones, as October pulled them deeper into the frigid months ahead.

They fell into a daily pattern of getting up early, and working late into the night. They were getting ductwork completed, and windows sealed and trimmed. They sanded and painted, cleaned and put a finishing touch on everything that needed completion, until they thought they could finally do no more before winter. They would have to wait until spring could bring about renewed energy that would inspire them to continue with the never-ending projects that came with home ownership.

Jewel was so happy when the day finally came when she could open all the items that her in-laws had brought with them, combined with the items they had chosen for themselves. She had never decorated a home before, but it came easily to her as she selected each item, looking at every picture or every lamp, wondering where it might fit the best, often switching it from one place to another until it all came together. There were items she kept from her parent's old house as well, and in the new surroundings, she could feel the old and new meld together in a way that made everything feel like home. Items that had once brought painful memories, suddenly became cherished memories in their new surroundings. Occasionally she would show up with something she bought at a thrift store, and Grady would patiently move the furniture from one room to another as she decided where its final resting place would be.

On the wall where her new piano sat, the one Grady had found for her in an ad, was the focal point of their home. There was a picture of her, Grady, and Madison they had taken when they met her for the first time at her volleyball game in Sheridan. The picture had been taken nearly as an afterthought, but it turned out so well that Jewel surprised Grady with one she had enlarged, and had beautifully framed to match the décor of the rustic luxuriousness Jewel had cultivated through her careful selection of all the items that adorned their house.

"I've a surprise for ya darlin'," Grady said as Jewel came into the house one night after she had returned home from her job at the hospital.

"What is it?" she asked, shaking off the cold at the door as she shed her outer layers, hanging them up on the handcrafted coat rack Grady had made for them. The front entrance was tiled with slate that separated itself from the hardwood floors that were laid throughout the rest of the house, and it gave them a place to keep their outer clothes and boots.

"Come here," he said leading her by the hand toward the bedroom.

He led her in the back, never once saying a word, but she could see the bedframe the instant she walked in the door. It was a king sized, four-poster bed made of wood and iron, an exact representation of the one she had carefully described to him. He had set up an office in her dad's old shop, and had been working on it in between calls and meetings to get everything in place for the development he was starting in the spring.

"It's beautiful Grady," she said running her hand along the carefully crafted frame. "You never cease to amaze me."

She looked at it in awe, seeing the detail that went into the woodwork, intertwined with the inlaid wrought iron. He had carefully pegged together every joint, fitting everything together as if the two pieces of wood had been grown and cultivated together, for the express purpose of presenting itself as some magnificent piece of artwork. Etched by hand along the length of the headboard was an outline of the Alaskan Mountain Range, with a darker stain filling in the slight etchings, just enough to make it stand out to draw the eye toward the majestic skyline.

"I hope ya like it," he said proudly. "Is it close ta the one ya had in yer mind?"

"It's exactly the way I saw it in my mind. I swear, sometimes I think you're actually in my mind. It's fantastic Grady!"

"Now that would be interestin'."

"If you could read my mind right now, you would immediately take me to bed," she said reaching up to pull his lips down to meet hers.

"Really?" he said raising a seductive eyebrow at her. "I'd love ta, but I made ya some dinner."

"You made us a bed, and dinner?" she asked smiling up at him. "Are you going stir crazy?"

"A little, but everything will be set ta get started on the development early spring. Just another month maybe…"

"Thank you for finishing this Grady. Our room looks complete."

"Yer welcome darlin'," he said putting his hand around her face and neck, pulling her in for a long, warm kiss the way he always did. "First dinner, and then early ta bed," he whispered, leaving her wanting the latter before the former.

They had spent the winter with Jewel working at the hospital a few days a week, and both of them getting more up to speed with the running of the ranch, while Grady got everything set for the development that would start in the spring. Troy had been happy when they were finally able to sit down with him, and tell him what they hoped to do with organizing a board, and keeping him as the General Manager of the ranch. The four of them constituted the entire board since it was the four of them that had an interest in the success or failure of the ranch. Jo had been helping Troy with the books since before they were even married, and she knew the financial end of things better than anyone. Troy liked having the four of them together to talk things through, and bounce ideas off each other, rather than the pressure he had felt over the last year and a half since the death of his father, who had been the primary caretaker of the ranch since Jewel's grandpa died, and even before.

Everything was working out well, but with winter having set in and taken hold, they weren't able to break ground on the development in the fall as Grady had originally hoped. As it turned out, the timing was going to work out much better for them since they had finally settled everything with Troy and Jolene, and received the money for the land they had partitioned off. The money was going to give them everything they needed to finance the infrastructure for the development until they were able to pre-sell some of the lots, and build custom homes.

Already, Grady had several interested parties after advertising for the upcoming development, and he had drawn up rough plans for several homes. He was talking to many potential homeowners, most of whom were people who were living in rental homes, but were looking for something more permanent. The boom in the oil and gas business in Wyoming had brought a need for more housing, but the approval process was taking longer than he anticipated. The government offices were behind in getting everything approved in a timely manner, but he was working with them to get things going a little quicker, having cultivated some good relationships at the public works department. Legally, he didn't feel comfortable taking down payments until everything was officially stamped for approval, not wanting to have to go back later to explain things if it were delayed, or rejected altogether.

Grady had been able to get several workers lined up to form the construction company that he was starting in order to manage the entire build, managing subcontractors, and self-performing portions of the work themselves. He had taken all the required classes, and passed all the required exams to be able to self-perform some of the underground work, and get his license as a general contractor, an application process that was a feat in itself. His dad had to write several letters to the city, and to the state, certifying that he had worked for him, detailing the degree of his experience.

Over the Christmas holiday, when Alisha had come to stay with them and Michael was there on a regular basis, Grady was impressed by the hard-working nature of the young man. He arranged to have him work for him over the summer, while Alisha agreed to work with him in the office to get things straightened out a few days per week, while helping them around the house on other days. Alisha and Michael had kept in touch as promised, and had been inseparable during their short visits together over long weekends at the ranch, and other holidays that afforded them each enough time off school to make the trip feasible for both of them.

Meeting Michael made Alisha understand what Jewel had tried to convey to her. She had gone back home, letting her boyfriend know that she wasn't ready for sex, and she let nature take its course, as he found a more willing partner, leaving her to contemplate her growing relationship with Michael. Michael seemed to think taking things slow was the best course of action, considering they were so far away from each other, and Alisha had yet to even graduate from high school.

They talked on a daily basis, and even sent snail-mail, surprising each other with cards and letters, random pictures, and small gifts. They had talked about Alisha applying at U.W. to enter into their engineering program, rather than going to South Dakota, and both of them were excited about that, though Michael offered to consider a transfer to South Dakota if Alisha had her heart set on it. They seemed to be making plans together for the future.

When Grady and Jewel weren't busy working, they drove from one game after another, driving all over Wyoming to see Madison play volleyball, then basketball, then track, and she had even stayed with them a few times over some long weekends. Getting to know her had been a thrill for everyone. She was exactly like Grady. She looked like him, and the way she carried herself left no doubt that she was his daughter, answering many questions for all of them as to how many mannerisms were inherited biologically, and how many were habits that had been picked up by influence. Once, they had picked Madison up in Casper one long weekend to take her to Denver to help her celebrate her birthday, going to a football game, a play, and just enjoying all the things that were available to do in the big city. Grady and her had developed a relationship that Jewel watched with awe. Somehow Grady knew how far to take it, without ever really holding back on his duty as her biological father. It was complicated, because he knew that Madison had been torn between the parents that raised her, and the connection she felt with her own flesh and blood.

Grady had carefully cultivated a relationship with Madison's parents, inviting them over regularly, realizing how important this would be for Madison. Having Jay and Grady in the same room, two dads, both of them wanting and needing the love of their daughter, had been a terrifying proposition for everyone at the beginning. Grady understood how difficult it would be for Jay to see them together, knowing how much alike they were, especially knowing that Jay would never know that same feeling of having someone who was bone of your bone, and flesh of your flesh. There had been some tension, and perhaps there always would be, but they shared a common goal of wanting what's best for Madison, and they put their own feelings aside.

There had been some discussion of shared custody, but it was still too early. Nobody wanted to press the issue, and besides, Madison was getting to be old enough to make some of her own decisions on these issues. For the time being, Grady was careful to defer to Madison's adopted parents when it came to making decisions about what was best for her. Mandi was an exceptional person, and there was no doubt in Grady's mind that she loved her, and absolutely wanted what was best for her. There had been no contact from Debbie, and Grady was glad for that. The last thing they all needed was some loose cannon to swoop down and infect them all with mind games and selfish motives.

When she visited, Madison would help Grady in the shop, assisting him with whatever it was he was working on, and enjoying every moment of it, reminding Jewel of the time she had spent with her own dad in that very shop. She watched the girls face as it occurred to her multiple times, just how much alike the two of them were. She was watching someone who was seeing what it was like for the first time in her life to be with her own kind. They gravitated to each other, much like children and babies descend upon each other, wanting to be near someone relatable. They looked alike, and talked alike, both of them tall and blond with the same blue eyes, making it difficult for anyone to stop looking at them. They both had the high cheekbones, and a strong jaw line, one hard and rugged to define the lines of a man, and one soft and feminine that you would expect to see on a girl.

They had the same way of seeing the invisible paths that allowed them to envision all the various forks in the road, and their probable consequences, before carefully planning everything out in the future. When Jewel would bring up an idea of a vacation or trip they could all take together, she could see them both take on the same look that told her they were lost in the various pathways that would eventually lead them to respond in some way she never expected. Watching them was like watching twins, she often thought, seeing them laugh the same, and make all the same faces.

"Can I introduce ya as my daughter?" Grady had carefully asked her one day as they headed into town to go to the hardware store.

She sat quiet for a moment, which didn't surprise Grady a bit. He knew she never said anything without thinking it through, but the silence still scared him for a brief moment before she finally responded. "Well, it's not like we could ever hide it. If you told someone I wasn't your daughter, they would think you were lying," she said smiling over at him. "Should I call you Dad then?"

The question had taken him completely by surprise, and he was at a loss for words. It's something that he had thought of often enough, but he didn't think they were anywhere near that stage in their relationship. "I talked to my Dad... ugh... Jay about it. He said it would be okay with him if it's okay with you. It's okay if you don't want me to," she said suddenly afraid of his response.

"I'd love it if ya call me Dad," he said to her, reaching over and squeezing her leg affectionately, causing her to flash a smile that melted him, and introduce her as his daughter he would, to everyone they came into contact with, whether they asked or not.

He would proudly throw an arm around her and pull her close to him, introducing her as his daughter, both of them smiling so broad that Jewel sometimes felt a pang of jealousy watching the two of them together. She knew it was ridiculous to feel jealous, but they were still newlyweds, and she was used to having him all to herself, feeling the same broad smile spread across her face as he introduced her as his wife.

Jewel and Madison had finally been able to form a good relationship, despite the jealousy that they both sometimes felt, having to share the attention and affection from Grady. One morning when Grady was in the shop early, and Madison and her had both been sleeping in a little, Madison came to her meekly, waking her up.

"Jewel? Are you awake?" she had asked standing at the door. Jewel looked up at her, and could immediately see that something was different. The child that had gone to bed the night before in her Mickey Mouse pajamas with a milk stain on her upper lip, was now standing before her with a look that stole the face of the child, and brought forth the signs of impending womanhood.

"Yes. I was just lying here, willing myself to go back to sleep. What's up Maddie?"

"Jewel, I started my period I think. I'm... ugh... I woke up with blood in my underwear. Do you have anything I could use?" she'd asked.

"Oh. Of course Maddie, let me get something for you," she said getting up and getting some pads she had in the bathroom cabinet. "Do you know what you need to do? Are you crampy or anything? Need some Ibuprofen?"

It was a girl moment that had allowed them to take a step back from the struggle between them, and start enjoying each other as female companions. It started to change the course of their relationship, bringing forth something they could build on... something beyond just the extension of their individual relationships with Grady. They became friends finally, and an easiness between them started to develop that was endearing and sweet, making Grady smile every time he saw them together. It was as if the layers of childhood had to be peeled back so they could start enjoying each other as friends. They had no parental relationship, and had never been sure what they were to each other, but as two women, they could finally come together in a way that only women understand.

All winter, they had gotten into the habit of having dinner with Troy and Jolene at least once a week, but sometimes it was several times a week, and sometimes Jewel's Godmother, Troy's mom, would go out and have dinner with them too. Jewel and Jo had become practically inseparable, making trips to Billings to go shopping together, or just hanging out at the house with Anna. They were always talking about, and doing all the girl things that Jewel had passed up when she was a teenager, unable to see the joy in any of it at the time. It was something she started to relish, seeing everything good in it, wanting more of it, and not taking a single moment of it for granted.

Grady and Troy had formed a bond that often made Jewel stop and pinch herself, still astonished at how well things had worked out. Grady had gone with Troy on all his guiding and hunting expeditions, and they had even managed to sneak off by themselves a few times to do some hunting, and get both their freezers stocked up for the winter. They worked in the shop together, with Grady helping Troy work on the equipment they used on the ranch, and teaching him the finer details of building furniture, though he was no slouch when it came to carpentry himself, and Grady was able to pick up a few tips from him as well.

Jewel loved to listen to Grady and Troy as they went through the house, with Grady describing techniques that he used to fit the pieces together so exact. Their house was absolutely stunning. It combined a luxurious classic style, with a rustic feel of a cabin, making all who entered feel like they had just been transported into a high-end Scandinavian Ski Lodge, complete with the snow-capped mountains that were visible outside of the large windows facing southwest. The ceilings had been left open so the beams were visible, making everything feel open and clean. Grady had even found the elk antlers that had been mounted after Jewel got her elk one hunting season, and placed them up high on one of the walls. It had been the last hunt she had been on with her dad, and so her grandpa had them put on a special mount for her, and it meant a lot to her when she came home one day to find them hanging there, complimenting their décor.

As soon as you entered the front door of their house, its beauty, and the open feeling struck you. The entrance itself was an island that looked out over the open floor plan of the living room, and the large kitchen area separated by a kitchen island that was also a bar/dining area. To the left, was a hallway that took you to the side of the house where a large master bedroom and bathroom were, plus two small bedrooms and a smaller bathroom. If you went to the right, there was a door that would eventually lead out to the garage, and to a stairwell that would one-day lead to the second story. There were large picture windows taking up large spaces on the walls, one of which was a bay window where they could sit and stare up at the mountains. There was a wood burning stove in one corner, with big over-stuffed leather chairs facing it that provided a cozy place to snuggle up, and hide from the cold wintery outdoors.

One morning they were outside trying to get shoveled out after a two day spring storm that left them buried in snow drifts, when Jewel looked up to see Grady standing there staring at the house thoughtfully. She could practically see the synapses in his brain firing as various plans were considered, some discarded, while others were more carefully studied.

"What?" she asked, taking a break from her shoveling to stare over at him. "What are you planning now?"

"I guess I was just wondering if we might ever have a need for me to build that second floor," he said looking back at her. It had been a subject they had both avoided over the last several months. It had been about eight or nine months since she had stopped taking birth control, and they were both a little surprised that nothing had happened yet, especially since Troy and Jolene just told them Jo was pregnant again.

Jewel dropped her head feeling a pang that had been plaguing her for several months, making Grady regret saying anything. "I'm sorry Grady... I... ugh... I was afraid of this," she said taking the shovel and walking back to the house.

"Jewel, it's okay Jewel. I'm sorry. I didn't mean to say it like that," he said going in after her. "I didn't mean anything by it. I was just thinking that since we officially made one of the spare bedrooms Madison's... if we would have our own babies..."

"And what if we don't?" she said hanging up her coat and pulling off her boots at the door.

"If we don't then we don't... we'll figure it out," he said struggling with his own boots at the door as she made her way toward their bedroom.

She had gone straight into the bedroom and started to run a bath, a place that had become her sanctuary, giving her a place to run toward, instead of just running. He had been pleased with himself when he first realized the oversized bathtub he had splurged on for them, had become her safe haven. He knew her tendency to run away from pain, always trying to find a place that would comfort her, but rarely ever finding it. He came to understand that her leaving the ranch initially, and running away to everywhere, and nowhere, had a lot to do with the fact that she didn't have a safe place to run to on the ranch that didn't haunt her... until now.

"Jewel," he said going up behind her in the bathroom, as she concealed her face from him. "I'm sorry. I didn't think before I spoke. I know this is a scary subject for you."

"We should probably talk about it. I know you've been thinking about it, and so have I... especially since Troy and Jo's announcement."

"It's still early Jewel. Ya were on birth control for a long time. Doc said it'd be about a year probably before we should start worryin'."

"Doctor Yeager said he would give me a checkup and run some tests."

"Doctor Yeager? Ya mean the young, good-lookin', single doctor that just moved inta town?" he asked, wrapping his arms around her as she stood with her back turned to him.

She smiled a little despite herself. "He's a good doctor," she said turning around to face him.

"Maybe I should do my own examination... a little more closely," he said slipping her shirt off over her head as the bath filled.

"Grady... I'm serious. We need to talk about this."

"I know Jewel, but we've got a lifetime ta talk about it, and what I'm thinkin' about can't wait, and if I'm doin' the math correctly, it might not be bad timin' either."

"You're keeping track of my cycles?" she asked looking up at him.

"Ummm... not really. It's a twenty-eight day cycle Jewel... it's not hard ta do, especially since yer like clockwork. I could practically set a watch ta ya," he replied reaching up to cradle her face in his hands. "It was two weeks ago taday that ya came in here and closed the door behind ya, taken yer own sweet time, relaxin' in the bath the way ya like ta do when ya start. That means its day fourteen, and if I'm rememberin' right from health class... that's the day a young, single man should avoid at all costs," he said flashing her a smile, "but I'm not a young, single man now am I?"

"Is your biological clock ticking?" she asked looking up at him. "Are you ready to have kids?"

"I already have one. It's you I'm worried about. Ya'd be a good mom Jewel, and I want ya ta know what it feels like."

Two weeks later, instead of her slipping into the bath to soak away the pains of monthly cramping, absolutely nothing happened.

CHAPTER 49

EXPECTING

"Are ya all right Jewel?" Grady asked her as she made her way out of the bathroom after another bout of puking.

"Why do they call it morning sickness if I'm going to be puking at ten o'clock at night?" she asked lying down beside him.

Jewel was right at three months pregnant, and morning sickness had come on quite strong from the very beginning, leaving her feeling sick and weak most of the day. She and Grady had decided early on that she would leave her job at the hospital, both of them feeling afraid that she may struggle with maintaining her pregnancies as her mom and grandma had struggled. The development Grady was building had turned out to be so promising that they were able to rest easy as Grady pre-sold one lot after another, already looking for more properties to develop as the need for housing continued to rise.

"Do ya think this is normal?" he asked alarmed at how much she had actually been puking, especially since he knew that her pregnancy was high risk given her family history.

"They gave me an IV when I went in earlier today, because I was a little dehydrated. Everything else checked out just fine though," she said leaving him with a pang of jealousy, imagining the young Doctor Yeager examining his wife.

"I'll bet he checked ya out quite thoroughly," he said shooting her a look. "The man has an enviable job as far as yer concerned darlin'."

"I love it when you get a little jealous Grady. It's just so cute," she said. "He's the best doctor. You wouldn't want me to go to a less competent doctor just so he wouldn't be young and good-looking would you?"

"Ahhh... so ya do think he's good-lookin' then?"

"Well... I suppose he has a certain quality, but my standards are pretty high... I'm a bit spoiled," she said rolling on top of him, the feeling of nausea having passed, giving way to what he considered a more favorable side effect of being pregnant, which was her insatiable sexual appetite.

"I'm afraid ta touch ya darlin'. Are ya sure yer up for this?" he said barely waiting for her response before slipping the nightgown off over her head.

"Just don't stop touching me," she said pressing herself against him, suddenly aware of just how much her belly was sticking out.

"Yer more beautiful than ever Jewel," he said sitting up as she straddled him, feeling her hesitate after catching site of her protruding belly, reaching both his hands up to feel the fullness of her breasts, making her gasp.

"Do you really think so?" she barely whispered.

"If I could stop time, it would be taday... right now. Ta have ya just the way ya look right now."

She was beautiful, with her silky black hair falling down around her, all the more so given the glow from her pregnancy, and her full breasts readying themselves for their natural chore of motherhood. She had been out in the sun in the afternoons as July brought forth sunny, warm days that she basked in, giving her skin a golden hue.

She was on top of him taking her need from him as he completely surrendered beneath her. He loved looking up at her lost in her own desire, all inhibitions thrown out the window, completely lost in the sea they swam together. He reached up, and felt the round hardness of her nipples as they sprung forward, making her gasp even more. Just when he thought he might not be able to survive another moment without feeling the release, he sat up and pulled her down on him harder until they both clung to each other, pulling the feeling within them even deeper.

"Oh dear god. That was amazing," they both gasped moments later, their need for each other tampered for the moment.

"Did the doc say everything was okay then?" Grady said after several minutes. "When will we... be sure that everything will be okay?" he said cursing himself as he remembered the stories she told him of her mother's miscarriage, and her grandmother's stillborn.

"Everything was fine. I talked to Doctor Bowman. He was the doctor that treated my grandma and my mom. He's retired now, but he said that I don't have the same issues they had. I asked him to check it out, and he did, sitting down with Doctor Yeager and going through everything. He said mom and grandma both had cysts in their uterus, and as far as he could tell, it didn't sound like I had anything like that. I guess that's partly why they put me on birth control when I was so young. He said it was smart that Grandpa told them to do that, because it might have prevented the growth of cysts that could have caused me to have the same problems. They're going to do an ultra-sound the day after tomorrow. Do you want to come?"

"Of course I do. That's all good news Jewel," he said smiling at her. "Did ya have good check-ups when ya were in the Army then?"

"Well, the truth is that I was told I didn't need to have a pap smear until I started having sex, so I never had any check-ups as far as that end of things go."

"Well, if it's an issue of frequency Jewel, we might need ta get ya a personal physician," he joked. "By the time this pregnancy's over, I'm likely ta be dead from exhaustion."

"I might be able to feign sympathy if I had ever seen an ounce of resistance," she replied, smiling at him.

"And leave ya hangin' in yer time of need, with all these terrible side effects from pregnancy?" he said with a crooked smile, throwing up his hands in surrender. "I wouldn't dare. I'm here for ya darlin'."

"Oh well, your sacrifice will not go without reward, I promise you. You have it soooo rough."

"It's a sacrifice I'm willin' ta make," he said trailing off as they heard a car pull up finally. "I hope that's Alisha then. If she keeps makin' our young Michael get ta bed so late, I may have ta start puttin' my foot down."

"Production? You're worried about production? Do you think they're sleeping together?" she asked not hesitating, thinking of all the time they'd been spending together.

"I don't think so. No," Grady replied shaking his head. "Michaels wound up so damn tight, there's a part of me that wishes they were, but no… as it is, I'm likely ta have ta turn the hose on him pretty soon ta get him ta slow down a bit."

"Oh… well that's good then," she said contemplating Michael's apparent frustration as evidence that Alisha's virginity had not be compromised, finally shaking her head in realization that only a man would ever suggest that being wound tight was a sign of sexual purity.

She came in and called to them, letting them know she was headed to her sleeping quarters, which was actually Madison's bedroom where she slept even when Madison was visiting, sharing the double bed they had put in there that had been Jewel's. The two of them had grown very close, with Alisha picking her up and driving her home whenever she needed a ride, and spending a little time at the mall in Casper occasionally, hanging out and just getting to know each other.

The entire family had come to visit at the beginning of summer. They had a very large celebration inviting Madison and her parents, and just about everyone they knew. It had been a long, cold winter and the first sign of spring, and show of green grass, made them feel nearly as thankful as the day when Jewel first realized she was pregnant. They made the announcement of her pregnancy at the celebration, and just about everyone broke out crying and congratulating the young couple… everyone that is, except Madison. She had been worried about her place in the family, but after they sat down and reassured her that her place was secure, and that they were depending on her to be a loving and caring big sister, she relaxed about it, and started helping Jewel whenever she could.

Having Madison there to meet her cousins and grandparents, and of course her aunt and uncle, was one of the most emotional times of Grady's life. He and Madison had grown so close, and seeing everyone welcome her without any hesitation reminded him once again how lucky he was to come from such a loving and caring family. Madison had been quite nervous about meeting everyone, not having much family to speak of from either her mom or her dad since they had both been from Texas, and most of their extended family had been scattered throughout the state, growing more and more distant from each other as the years passed.

The cousins were so excited to meet her that it only took a few minutes before they were all running around the ranch dragging her with them as if she had always been there. Maggie and Patrick had brought her gifts, and Diana had put together a scrapbook that showed pictures of everyone in the family, but mostly pictures of Grady as he was growing up through the years. Madison was so excited to have it she nearly burst out crying, but decided instead to steal herself away for a few quiet moments by herself to pour over every picture. The other kids waited as long as they could, wanting to give her a few minutes, but before long, they had her by the hand again, dragging her along to play another game, and Madison couldn't have been happier about it.

One of the most interesting moments occurred when they tried explaining to her that Jewel and Rudy were not only in-laws, but they were also uncle and niece. She was pondering it as she pondered most everything before responding, when Tina finally spoke up saying, "Try not to think about it too much. Just go with it," making everyone burst out laughing, before finally agreeing that it was probably the best advice she could have had on the subject.

"Maybe ya could talk ta Alisha then?" Grady finally said, wondering how to handle the delicate situation as they lay there together, with Jewel snuggled up in the crook of his arm.

"Ummm… okay… what do you mean by that exactly? Are you worried about your nieces honor, or are you trying to get Michael to… ugh… get loosened up a little?"

"Jewel! Seriously. What do ya take me for?"

"Well, okay, so what do you want me to talk to her about then?"

"I don't know exactly. Just thinkin' she might need someone ta talk ta is all," he said shrugging. "I mean… she's seventeen. She'll be eighteen in a couple months. It wouldn't be unheard of that she would want ta start havin' sex. Debbie and I started havin' sex when she was sev… well… never mind," he said after catching Jewel's eye, "sorry Jewel."

"Oh no, please… go ahead. I love to hear about you and Debbie," she replied sarcastically rolling her eyes. "I'll talk to her though."

"Thanks Jewel. Yer a good aunt… and a lovely wife," he said wrapping his arms around her as they snuggled up under the covers together, both of them quickly falling asleep, if only for a short time.

CHAPTER 50

HISTORY REPEATS

"Jewel! Oh my god Jewel! What's happenin'?" Grady cried out after finding her in the bathroom kneeling on the floor, crying in pain. He had awoke out of a deep sleep to find her gone from their bed, but then immediately saw the light from the bathroom and heard faint cries.

He could see blood on the floor, and he knew without having to think about it, exactly where it had come from. He immediately scooped her up and started heading for the door, despite the fact that he was wearing nothing but his underwear, and she was wearing nothing but a little nightgown.

"I'm takin' ya ta the hospital," he said as he carried her to the car.

"It's happening Grady. I'm losing the baby," she sobbed. "Just like my mom did."

Hearing the commotion, Alisha ran into the room. "Is everything alright?" she shouted following them outside.

"I'm takin' Jewel ta the hospital. Somethin's wrong," he said quickly strapping Jewel in the car, making his way around to the driver's side.

"Wait! Uncle Grady! You're in your underwear. Let me just grab you a shirt and some pants, and get a blanket for Jewel. She's shivering!" Alisha yelled as she took off running back into the house.

She came back only moments later carrying Grady's shirt, pants, and some shoes, and she grabbed a blanket for Jewel, which she immediately started wrapping around her as Grady quickly slipped on his clothes.

"Call an ambulance and tell them we'll meet them somewhere along the old highway. I'll flash my headlights at them when I see their lights. She's lost a lot of blood," he yelled after her as he pulled out of the drive.

Alisha was crying, but she ran as quickly as she could back into the house calling the ambulance as soon as she got in the door. Immediately after that, she called Michael.

Grady was driving as fast as he could, cursing himself for not smoothing out the driveway last weekend as he had planned, having to drive more slowly than he wanted, to avoid all the potholes.

"Talk ta me darlin'," he said worriedly as Jewel laid there trembling, slumped over in her seat.

"It's my worst nightmare Grady. Just like my mom and grandma," she sobbed uncontrollably.

He drove with one hand, and placed the other one on top of her, wanting to comfort her as much as possible. It was clear that the baby was likely gone. There was just too much blood, but the loss of the baby was the least of his worries. He looked at the size of her and his mind flashed back to all the blood on the bathroom floor, and all the blood that was soaking through her nightgown and blanket, and he wondered how much blood she had actually lost. He had to find that place of separation that existed in the heart and soul of every soldier, to allow them to set aside fear and emotion, and concentrate on the main objective, which at the moment was getting Jewel to a place where they could take care of her.

His heart ached when he allowed himself one fraction of a second to consider the possibility that her life could be in jeopardy, and he quickly stopped himself. He realized that he needed to stay calm. He couldn't go flying down the old darkened highway too fast. He remembered all the deer he had just barely missed on several occasions, when he had been casually driving down that same road, and he knew that driving at night at excessive speeds was not the right thing to be doing. The last thing they needed was to end up in a car accident.

The moon was practically non-existent, and it was so incredibly dark out that Grady could feel a prickle on his skin when the eeriness made the hair on his arms and neck stand on end. Jewel had gone quiet again, and if he hadn't known any better, he might have actually thought she had peacefully fallen asleep. He kept talking to her, and he would be reassured briefly as she mumbled back to him, but as soon as she would go quiet again his heart would start pounding, and he was wishing he could grab her and hold her on his lap as he drove, if only to feel the beating of her heart.

Finally, after driving for what seemed like hours, though it was closer to half an hour, he saw the flashing lights, making him let out a long breath he hadn't realized he'd been holding. He immediately started flashing his lights at them, signaling to make them slow down. They seemed to be flying down the road a little too fast though, and he wondered if it was an ambulance that was coming for them. It wasn't until they got a lot closer that they slowed down, as he frantically flashed the lights over and over at them.

They pulled off on one side of the road, and he pulled off on the other. He could see them get out and get the stretcher, but he had already grabbed Jewel out of the car and started carrying her toward them. She felt cold, and she laid in his arms like a rag doll, causing Grady's heart to drop in his stomach.

"She's pregnant and maybe havin' a miscarriage. She's lost a lot of blood," he said nearly panicking as he placed her down on the stretcher, part of him wanting to get her to them so they could care for her, and the other part of him not wanting to let her go.

"We got her," the EMT said as they got her loaded in the ambulance. "Sit up there," he said pointing to a seat in the back of the ambulance as he climbed in with her.

The car had been immediately forgotten. He could care less that it was sitting on the side of the road with the keys still in it. At the moment, his only concern was for Jewel. His eyes were fixed on her, watching the rise and fall of her chest with each breath she took, as the EMT started checking all her vitals and quickly, and quite skillfully he thought, put an IV in her. He looked at her covered in blood from the waist down, his mind desperately trying to calculate the blood loss as he watched the EMT discard the blood-soaked blanket.

"Is she goin' ta be alright?" he asked, his voice cracking, in part because he was too afraid to hear the answer, still thinking of all the blood.

"A little blood goes a long ways," the EMT said peering up at Grady. "Especially on such a light colored blanket."

Grady's mind raced, and he let out a breath, instinctively bending down and kissing her on the forehead whispering to her. "It's goin' ta be alright darlin'," he said as much to himself as to her, flashing back to all the blood he remembered seeing from his days in the military.

He'd seen it all before, and in situations far more grotesque and evil. He remembered a friend of his that he watched die on the battlefield, holding him as hard as he could, his fingers pressed tightly against the wound that was spilling his blood. The pool of blood that surrounded them seemed to grow quickly despite his best efforts to stop it, until his friend drifted away beyond his reach, to a far better place, he hoped.

She opened her eyes for a moment as if to comfort him, her mouth and nose covered by the respirator, making the scene look all the more dire. He tried looking down at her reassuringly, but it was her that was comforting him in that moment as she reached her hand up in search of his, perhaps sensing his fears, and haunted memories. He grabbed a hold of it without hesitation, trying to stay out of the way, as the EMT continued to listen to sounds through his stethoscope, and monitor her blood pressure. He fought back the tears as her tiny little hand intertwined with his, making him feel like he still had something to hang onto.

The ambulance ride seemed to take forever, giving Grady ample time to contemplate his faith, though the inside dialogue didn't take long. He cursed himself for doubting, knowing that the presence of God was all around him, and always had been. It's only those who are blessed with the luxury of never having to call on a higher power, who are able to take it for granted, he had often said. He knew it all too well, crossing himself, and saying the Lord's Prayer over and over in his mind as the ambulance made the last few turns that would take them to the emergency room. Instinctively, he reached his free hand up, and made the sign of the cross on Jewel's forehead, causing her to open her eyes once again, as if to thank him before closing them again.

He stayed right by her side as they wheeled her from the ambulance into the hospital, answering questions as they were asked, as the nurses took over, transferring her from the stretcher onto one of their own, causing her to clutch her stomach and moan in pain again. He felt like it was all happening in segments, the euphoria of the moment that seemed to run in slow motion was making his head spin. He remembered only hours before seeing her leaning over him, her long black hair falling down all around them as they made love. He nearly fought back when they took her back to a trauma room where he wasn't allowed to follow, but stopped short, knowing he needed to let them take care of her.

Hours seemed to pass, though it had only been about twenty minutes when the doctor finally came out to talk to him. He was an older gentleman, but was impeccably dressed and obviously in very good shape for a man his age, though Grady was a bit surprised to see someone so old working at that hour.

"Jewel's stable, but she lost the baby, but not a lot of blood, though it looked like quite a lot I understand," the man said grabbing Grady's arm, leading him over to two chairs where they could sit down. "I'm Doctor Bowman. I was her mom's doctor. I'm retired for the most part, but I help out sometimes when they need me to fill in. Don't you worry about Jewel... she's tough. I ought to know because I delivered her. She came out fighting and never stopped, though she was a couple months early," he said smiling warmly at him.

Grady breathed easy when he recalled hearing about Doctor Bowman, and he felt immediately comforted to know that this was not just a doctor who was looking after a patient. This was a doctor who was looking after a girl with whom he had a very special relationship, and he knew that she was safe. He immediately trusted the man, as Jewel herself did.

"I'm glad you're here Doctor. I figured she probably lost the baby. As long as she's okay, that's all I care about."

"She'll be fine... physically that is, but I saw her mom and her grandma go through quite a lot emotionally. Women get attached in a way I don't think we'll ever be able to fully understand, and their hearts are so tender, I swear I don't know how something can be so tough and so fragile all at the same time," he said shaking his head. "All you can do is just give her time and... well... she's going to blame herself. Maybe you can help her so she won't do that."

"Can I see her?" he asked fighting back tears as he imagined Jewel quietly blaming herself, as she recalled her mom's miscarriage that she witnessed when she was a small child.

"They're just getting her cleaned up. They'll be out to get us when they're ready. I'm having them do some testing for chromosomal abnormalities, given her family history. Chromosomal abnormalities are the most common cause of miscarriages, and it would basically tell us whether or not there was a miscarriage because of an abnormality in the baby, if it's positive, or a probability that there was something abnormal in the uterus, if it's negative. We don't usually do this kind of testing if it's a woman's first miscarriage, but since she has a family history, I think its best."

"When will we know?" Grady asked with a little hope, thinking there could be an explanation that could absolve Jewel of the guilt she was likely to feel.

"It used to take some time, but given all the advanced testing we have available, we should be able to have some answers fairly soon. I'll track it down myself. Jewel is very special to me, and if there's any way I can take advancements in medicine, and help her in a way I was never able to help her mother, then I would love to be able to do it."

"Thank ya sir," Grady said shaking his hand, touched by his concern for his wife. "I appreciate it, and Jewel will too."

Just then, the nurse came out to get them. Grady and Doctor Bowman shook hands again as the doctor went to check on other patients, promising to stop by and see them after he made some rounds.

When Grady walked into the room his heart broke seeing her lying there with her eyes closed, looking so peaceful and angelic, though the tracks from tears were still visible on her face. He wondered how they would get through it. He knew how hard it was going to be on her. She had been terrified that she would be unable to have babies, going through one miscarriage after another, as her mom and grandma had done, having them one by one tear their hearts out and leave them feeling like an empty shell of a woman.

He walked over and sat down in the chair beside the bed, not wanting to wake her from this moment of peace. She still had an IV in her, but she looked clean, and less... bloody than she had when they were in the ambulance. He thought about calling Alisha to let her know that Jewel was okay, but he couldn't leave her. He needed to just sit there and watch her to assure himself for a moment that she was all right.

"This is the second time you've had to take me to the hospital," she said reaching her hand up and running it through his hair as he rested his head in his hands.

"Jewel. I thought ya were asleep darlin'."

"I think I was for a minute."

"I'm sorry darlin'," he said reaching up and putting his hand on her stomach, meeting her eyes as he did.

She shrugged, shaking her head as if it were nothing, even as she fought back tears. "I'm not surprised. I guess I was kind of expecting it. I don't stand a chance."

"As long as I have ya with me, that's all I care about," he said trying to reassure her, but not certain what to say to her.

"You might not think that in twenty years when we're old and childless," she said staring at the ceiling trying to hide her emotions, fighting back more tears.

"I can't say that I know how it is ya feel darlin', but I'll not have ya questionin' my love for ya. If I say I'll love ya forever, then I will," he said not looking at her.

"Besides, in twenty years, we'll still be young enough ta enjoy the life we build, no matter how the cards get dealt."

"My hormones are a little crazy right now Grady. Keep logic to yourself for a while, and just let me cry a little, okay?"

"Alright Jewel. I'll let ya cry a little, and I'll cry a little with ya, but then we move on and find the gratitude in all the blessings we've been given, and leave the heartache behind."

She couldn't help but laugh a little. "That seems fair," she chuckled.

"Fair, but funny, is it?" he asked a little surprised to hear her chuckle.

"You even have a grieving plan. It's not funny. I shouldn't be laughing, it's just that... I can't help it. You're not going to let me fall apart are you?"

"No. I'm not darlin'."

The doctor came in just then. "Jewel, you're looking lots better my dear," he said coming up beside her opposite Grady, grabbing her hand and smiling at her warmly. "Let me tell you something you may not know. Twenty-five percent of all women experience miscarriages. Let's not jump to conclusions. Also, medicine has come a long way in the last fifteen years. If your uterus has issues that we need to address, then we have options. Your chances of being able to successfully have a baby is much better than your parents and grandparents, and I wouldn't tell you that if I didn't believe it."

"Wow. Really?" she said as they both jerked their heads up and looked up at him hopefully.

"Yes. It's all true. Meanwhile, we're going to run some tests, keep our chins up, and take things as they come."

"Alright," they both agreed, looking at each other with surprise and reluctant hope.

"Right now, you're free to go, and there's a young man and a lovely young lady waiting out in the lobby for you. I believe she said she was your niece, and she brought this for you," he said smiling at them, handing her a bag of clothes he forgot he had been holding. "Call Doctor Yeager and make an appointment, and he'll examine you in a few days. Nature will take care of the rest."

The moment felt a little unreal. Jewel had just started getting used to the idea that she was pregnant, and suddenly she felt empty, and yet... the talk from Doctor Bowman made her feel a little better. She knew that miscarriages were more common than people realized, and she knew that modern medicine was able to help many women that were unable to be helped even ten years ago.

With nurses still coming and going, she had gone in the bathroom to put her clothes on remembering the last time she had been in a hospital bathroom getting dressed; thinking about how much her life had changed since then. She couldn't help but smile as she thought of it, despite the void she felt in the pit of her stomach.

She remembered when she was a child, and she used to think that maybe she was getting all the hurt and pain out of the way at a young age, and the rest of her life would be easier somehow, as if there was a limit on the amount of hurt a person would have to feel in a lifetime. She laughed at the idea, understanding as she grew older, that everyone faced pain and obstacles in life that they had to endure. She considered it all for a moment, realizing that the obstacles and pain aren't necessarily the problem, it's how we handle them that determines how good or bad we do. That was something she had come to know all too well after the abduction. Her attitude about it, and the love and support that she got from those around her, helped her understand that it would be easier to overcome if she simply focused on what she was grateful for, instead of the things that hurt her.

That was something she had failed at after her parents died. She had been saturated with the pain so much so that she often felt like she was treading water, barely able to keep her head above the pain that was drowning her. Of course, at the time, she had been on the verge of puberty, and more in need of a mother than a girl would have at any other time in her life, and everywhere around her had been sadness. At the time, it felt like the pain was the only thing that made her feel like she was still alive.

She considered for a moment all the things in her life that were good, and as she opened the door and saw Grady standing there waiting for her, she couldn't help but smile, and seeing him smile back at her was all that she needed to take the next steps toward the rest of their lives.

CHAPTER 51

THE NURSE AND THE SNIPER

"Are you happy Grady?" Jewel asked quietly as they laid in bed together one evening, each of them lost in their own thoughts. Their lives had become stuck in an anti-climactic rut after the letdown from the miscarriage, and Jewel had been worried about them both. They were busy enough, or at least Grady had been since he had the business he was running, building one custom home after another.

"Yeah, of course. Why are ya askin' me that Jewel?" he said staring at the ceiling unenthusiastically.

"Your enthusiasm is earth shattering. How could I ever doubt it?" she asked sarcastically.

"I'm sorry Jewel. Ya know I love ya darlin' and wherever ya are, is where I'll be happy," he replied staring at the ceiling still, casually tossing a ball from one hand to the other as he laid there lost in thought.

"Okay. So what if I were in Uganda? Would you be happy there?"

"Even if ya were on the moon," he said rolling toward her. "What's goin' on Jewel?"

"Well... hear me out okay?" she asked, rolling toward him, grabbing his hand.

"Alright," he said raising an eyebrow at her.

"Well... Major Johnson, the Chief Nursing Officer that I worked for in Iraq, contacted me. She retired from the Army. She's working at an orphanage in Uganda, and it was an interesting conversation," she said raising an eyebrow at him, equal to the one still raised on his face. "She needs nurses and security people, which... kind of fits us... I mean... they have a bunch of ex-military men and women that provide security, and help rescue some of the child soldiers. I couldn't help but think it might be something we could help with. Ummm... I mean, I'm a nurse and you're a sniper and...," she shrugged waiting for his response.

"Ya want ta go ta Uganda?" he asked incredulously.

"I just... I miss it and... we're so young and... I know you must miss it too Grady. You love helping kids be free and... I don't know... I kind of want to go, but only if we go together."

"What are ya talkin' about woman? We just settled here and started a life, and now ya want ta scrap it and go somewhere else? I'm stunned. Are ya not happy Jewel?"

"I don't want to scrap anything. I love it here, and I love this house," she said squeezing his hand reassuringly. "It would just be for a few months... maybe four or... five at the most."

"Four or five months?" he asked, searching her eyes for answers as if there was a complete explanation to be found deep within if he stared hard enough. "What about the construction company? What about Madison?"

"I've thought about this Grady. With Rudy, Diana, and the kids moving here, I thought maybe Rudy could fill in with the construction company, and they could even live here if they wanted to while we're gone. As for Madison, well... I mean... she might even be able to come for a week, or maybe you could come back for a week to see her."

"I think ya've gone mad!" he said, considering the possibility for a moment, even as he shook his head at her. He couldn't deny the fact that there was a big part of him that missed traveling into dangerous territory, and helping those in need.

"You can't tell me you don't miss it Grady, and that it doesn't excite you just a little," she said challenging him.

"What about Troy and Jo?"

"They don't need us. Do you have any doubt in your mind that we could step in if we needed to? I mean... it wouldn't be without some serious growing pains, but we could do it, and it's not going to happen anyway. They're perfectly content... especially with another baby on the way."

"Ya don't think they'd be mad that we leave for a while?"

"No. Not as long as I tell Troy this time, and don't leave him guessing," she shrugged.

"I have ta admit that it sounds excitin'. I'd like ta dig inta the details a little, and think it through... talk about it a bit more."

"So you're interested?" she asked excitedly.

"Yeah... I mean, it sounds interestin'. I've actually thought about doin' somethin' like this before. I was thinkin' about it after I was discharged. There's lots of shippin' companies, and other corporations that are always lookin' for hired soldiers... usually ex-military. It's probably what I would have done for a time if I hadn't met ya. I spent a bit of time researchin' it before I came ta Alaska."

"Really? So you're really interested! I'm really excited now," she said getting up excitedly, jumping up and down on the bed.

"Wow. Just ta see ya jumpin' up and down on the bed like that in yer shirt and underwear makes it all worthwhile," he said watching her more intently, still lying on their bed. They hadn't been intimate since before the miscarriage. The doctor said six weeks, but Grady was starting to think that five weeks was close enough, and apparently Jewel was too. She dropped to her knees on the bed, and climbed up on top of him, kissing him excitedly, and he lacked any resolve to feign resistance.

The next day they sat down together and researched the region in Uganda where they would be, and were able to arrange a phone call with Major Johnson to get more details on what would be expected of them. One of the first things that came up was a news story about four Christian orphanage workers who were kidnapped and beheaded. Another story that came up was about a group of armed rebels who came into a different orphanage, and took as many of the children as they could, wanting them for soldiers and prostitutes. They knew it wasn't going to be without risk, but they were both excited to be able to have the skills and the means to be able to do something that may lend aid to children who may otherwise not have anyone to help them. They looked at pictures of young girls and boys that were in need of some of the most basic supplies, and they both knew without a doubt they were being called to do this.

One of the first things they did after both of them decided they wanted to do this was to sit down to discuss it with Troy and Jo, and then Rudy and Diana. Troy and Jo were definitely disappointed, but understood their desire to go do something that would help those in need.

"I wondered if you were going to be able to just come here and settle down Jewel," Troy had said.

"What do you mean? Why would you think that?" she asked looking at him oddly.

"You only just started to live. You need to go out and do it for a while," he answered.

"What about you? You've been here your whole life. You've hardly ever left Johnson County."

He shrugged his shoulders, and raised his arms in surrender. "I know, but that's me. I'm right where I want to be. I hate leaving Johnson County!"

Both Troy and Jo hugged them and cried. They were happy for them, but they were going to miss them. The four of them had grown very close, and Jewel knew they were going to miss seeing Anna too. There was still the matter of getting things arranged with Rudy and Diana, but it was starting to look like this might actually happen, and they were getting more and more excited.

The phone call with them went surprisingly well. "That would sort of make the transition a little easier for us. That gives us a place to stay until we can decide where we want to build exactly, and I think I could step in and take-over the construction company fairly well... I mean, I assume you have it all set up like your dad's?" Rudy had said over the conference call they had with the four of them.

The construction company was set up exactly like his dad's, and even shared the same name of McDonald Building Company, LLC, though they were two completely separate businesses. Grady thought it would be a tribute to his dad to give it the same name, and Patrick had taken it exactly the way it was intended, honored that his only son would want to name his company the same as his own, linking them without actually linking them legally.

Plans were being made at lightning speed, but the most challenging part was yet to come. Sitting down and talking this through with Madison was difficult. The situation was difficult because they wanted to have Madison come and live with them all the time. Grady and Madison had become father and daughter in every way, and although she was still very close with her parents, Grady and her had formed a bond that was unbreakable. Still, Grady worried about telling her. The fact was that he was not her legal guardian, and he had no legal right to her, which left him in limbo. He had been completely at their mercy as to when he could see her, and when he couldn't, and he had to plan everything around their schedule, making himself available whenever they decided he could see her. He hoped they would work with him, and may even let her come visit them, and get the experience of visiting another country to see how other people lived.

They had decided they would only go for three months, leaving in September and then coming back just after Christmas. They hoped that Grady would be able to fly back and spend Thanksgiving break with Madison, and then maybe have her come stay with them over her Christmas break. It's what they hoped for, but this was going to be completely up to Madison's parents, though they thought Madison might have a say in it as well, and so she did.

Everything was settled. Rudy, Diana, and the kids would stay at the house temporarily until they could rent something bigger, and decide where to build their house. Troy and Jo would continue doing everything they normally did. Madison would be able to spend Thanksgiving with Grady when he came back to the states, and they would decide on Christmas break later on when Grady and Jewel were in Uganda, and had a little more time and experience to determine whether it was safe or not.

"Ya know, I'd like ta die before I put her somewhere I didn't think she'd be safe?" he'd said to her parents as he wrapped a protective arm around Madison, hugging her to him. Seeing them together was undeniable even for Madison's parents. They absolutely belonged together, and the gap in the years of being apart was quickly closing in, faster than anyone would have thought possible.

"I'm going to miss you, but I'm also very proud of you for wanting to take care of orphans. That's pretty cool!" Madison said beaming up at Grady. "Do you think I could still go spend weekends with Ally?" she asked, using Alisha's nickname as the rest of the family did.

"Of course ya can. Everyone asked the same thing of ya. Even Troy and Jo are hopin' ya can go spend weekends still. Our home *is* yer home Maddie. Yer welcome there whenever ya like. They'll be a few more kids around, but that's yer bedroom," Grady said emphatically, wanting to make sure she understood that.

"You can spend as much time with us as you can before we leave. Just call me anytime. I'll come pick you up whenever you want," Jewel said to her, wanting to show her support, always encouraging the relationship between Madison and the rest of the family.

The next month was filled with planning, making arrangements at home, getting Rudy on-board with everything he needed to manage the construction company until the rest of the family could come later, and spending as much time with Madison as possible. They were both excited to be going somewhere where they could do what they felt was their natural calling in life, though they knew there would be some risk.

Part Five

UGANDA AND WYOMING

CHAPTER 52

A NEW JOURNEY

They would be flying into the landlocked country of Uganda after a few days layover in Amsterdam, where they would arrange to pick up some items that Major Johnson needed for the makeshift orphanage where they would be staying. The orphanage was set up like a Mobile Army Surgical Hospital in that it was meant to be mobilized within a few hours' notice, was visible enough to notify anyone who saw it that they were there for humanitarian purposes, and was stable enough to house and care for those in need. The ability to move around was necessary so they could go where they were needed, caring for those in rural communities before transporting orphans off to more permanent facilities in the city. The mobile orphanage was necessary so they could embed themselves in an area, determine their needs, and then nurse them to a state where they could travel to a permanent facility. The idea was to get them somewhere where they could live in relative peace, be educated, and learn to help others and give back to their communities, hoping to foster a new culture of fellowship and community.

Uganda was a relatively young country, established in 1962 after gaining independence from Britain, while maintaining its membership as a commonwealth. Independence has been anything but peaceful, and Uganda is still suffering the consequences of several military coup's, including the corrupt dictatorship of Idi Amin who seized control in 1971 and created a reign of terror that spanned eight years, murdering at least 300,000 of his own people, and driving out thousands more. He turned many young children into child soldiers or prostitutes, fanning the flames of a culture that was constantly and perpetually at war, for the sake of corruption and power.

Idi Amin's reign of terror was followed by even more terror, and more corruption, when the neighboring country of Tanzania, aided by Ugandan exiles, invaded the country in 1979. The so-called "Bush War" by the National Resistance Army, operating under the leadership of the current Ugandan President Yoweri Museveni carried out mass killings of non-combatant Ugandan citizens, leaving many in need. Yoweri remains in power since 1986, and has been praised by the

West as bringing in a new kind of leadership in Africa, though little has changed in the country, and millions of people still suffer the consequences of generations of fighting.

Many were murdered and millions more were displaced as Yoweri led Uganda into a civil war with the neighboring country of the Democratic Republic of Congo, and corruption within the government is so rampant it has prompted many countries to consider cutting off aid after hundreds of millions of dollars were reported to have gone missing.

With Rwanda bordering on the Southeast of Uganda, and the atrocities of the Rwandan genocide still looming thick in the air, there were many in need, displaced, poor, broken, and orphaned. There were many mouths to feed, bodies to cloth, and souls that needed mending, as refugees fled into the country and took cover.

~~~~~~~~

Jewel sat on the quiet plane watching everyone sleep as one hour after another passed for the long flight over land and water. It had already been a long trip, and they hadn't even made it halfway yet. They had driven from the ranch to Denver, stopping in and spending a night with Madison in Casper before they left. That alone had been nearly enough to make them stop dead in their tracks and cancel the trip altogether, and even as they sat there on the plane, Jewel wondered if they were making the right decision to continue with their three months in Uganda.

When they arrived at the house to pick Madison up for the night, Mandi, Jay, and Madison had asked them to come in and sit with them around the dining room table. They were immediately alarmed, knowing that the dining room had been reserved for serious conversation. Madison had told them that she always knew when there was trouble, because they would be waiting for her around the dining room table with serious looks on their faces, or they would somberly ask to speak to her and head into the dining room. It had been so unnerving to Madison, that she swore she would never have a dining room when she grew up, which made Jewel change her plans from having a formal dining room area in the cabin, deciding instead to have a combination office and craft area.

Their anticipation for a very serious conversation would not disappoint, but had been more serious than either one of them could have imagined. They didn't stall or mince words. Mandi simply threw it out on the table that she was in stage-four breast cancer for the third time, and had decided not to go through chemotherapy or radiation again. Jewel sat there completely dumbfounded, knowing that without treatment, Mandi would not have long to live. Jewel could see that Grady was finding it difficult to see a situation where that could lead to a successful conclusion. He sat quietly waiting for them to finish the rest of the announcement, expecting them to tell him in detail about some wonderful new option they would be pursuing in lieu of chemotherapy and radiation, but it never came.

"What are ya sayin'?" he'd finally asked in disbelief when the realization of what she said set in.

"I just can't go through it again, and it's more aggressive this time. My chances aren't good and I don't want to spend what little life I have left fighting a losing battle, puking constantly, losing my hair and my bladder and what little dignity I have left," Maggie had said with a relative peace that Jewel found remarkable.

She knew that Mandi, Jay, and Madison were Episcopalian and she marveled at Mandi as she talked about her absolute, unwavering faith in a way that made Jewel envy her. She envied people with such unyielding faith. She had always been one to question her faith and contemplate it all, often wondering if everything she had been taught by the church was fact or fiction. She had been told that questioning her faith was a good thing... that it was a way of growing in her faith, but as she sat their listening to Mandi talk about the Kingdom of Heaven, and meeting the Holy Father, she felt a stab of pain as she stuffed away any doubts, and supported Mandi in her beliefs.

"You're very brave," they had both finally said after discussing it all at length, crying with her one moment, and then smiling with her as she forced her own smile.

"If we need to stay...," Jewel said looking over at Madison, grabbing her hand, realizing they were leaving her in her time of need.

"No. I want you to go. I mean... I don't want you *not* to go. I'm going to spend this time with Mom and Dad. We just wanted to tell you in case...," Madison had said choking up, not able to say what they already knew, which was that Mandi could die before they return from Uganda.

"But ya never even told us ya had been through this before," Grady had finally said, wondering why they had kept this from them.

"We were scared Grady. We're sorry. We didn't know you at first, and didn't know if you would want to try to take Madison. Of course, now that we know you...," Mandi said shrugging apologetically.

"I understand. Ya didn't know me," he said, deciding to accept this explanation for the time being before leaning forward and addressing his own concerns. "I wouldn't try ta take her from ya, but I think I've earned the right ta be involved. She's my own flesh and blood. I didn't give her away, and I would have never made that decision had I known," he said reaching for Madison's hand and squeezing it affectionately, taking his eyes from Jay only long enough to give Madison a warm smile. They had come to realize that Madison and Jay's relationship had not been as close as they had originally thought, and on one occasion, Mandi let it slip that Jay had been unfaithful in the relationship, and had some other troubles that made them worry about Jay's influence on Madison. Jay traveled extensively for his job, and was always gone on one business trip after another, plus, he had been arrested on a couple occasions, once for possession with intent to sell, and another time for assaulting a woman in a bar, charges he denied, but with evidence that was hard to ignore, though difficult to prove. Another thing that they learned about Jay was something they had both taken very seriously, which was a dishonorable discharge from the Marine's for possession of a large quantity of drugs when he was younger. Grady had been fuming when he first realized Diana and Maggie had started to do a background check on Jay and Mandi, but after learning about some of Jay's history, they realized that what they learned was very important information they needed in order to be able to protect Madison as best they could.

Through much discussion with Mandi, Jay, and Madison, Grady and Jewel had decided to continue with their plans to go to Uganda, but their minds were reeling, considering the possibility of everything that could possibly transpire over the next year in regards to Madison. If Mandi were to die, and that was likely to happen in the near future, Jewel and Grady knew without a doubt they would pursue having Madison come live with them full-time, and they even considered the possibility that Jay would hand over guardianship without a fight.

When they had been at the ranch during a family barbeque, and Mandi told the story of the adoption, it raised a few eyebrows when she talked about how Jay had absolutely refused to consider the option of adopting, before suddenly relenting and then making most of the arrangements to appease his wife. They hadn't been in the car headed for Denver for even five minutes when Grady voiced his suspicion that Mandi had likely been trying to tell him something with that story, without outright betraying Jay, but telling it in a large enough crowd to leave no doubts if it ever came down to a fight. She was protecting Madison. They both agreed that Mandi was trying to tell them she wanted Madison to be with them.

"I'm stayin' here. I can't leave ya with… well… if something happens ta yer mom, I want ta be here," he said as they sat with Madison later that evening.

"No Dad. You're only going to be gone for three months, and I want to spend that time with… well… with them as a family I guess," she said trying to explain something that she barely understood herself, and didn't have words to explain. "I know how to get a hold of Ally, Diana, Jo, and well… everyone," she said laughing when she realized just how many there were.

"I can be on a flight headed back if ya need me, and don't ya dare hesitate ta ask if ya feel it's necessary," he said wrapping a protective arm around her.

"Our first responsibility is to you Maddie. Promise you'll let us know if you need us to come back?" Jewel reiterated.

They spent the rest of the evening laughing and talking with Madison in the easy way they usually did, with Grady taking Madison for a long walk to get ice cream so they could have some father-daughter time together. Jewel knew that it was going to be hard for Grady to leave her, and there was a part of her that regretted waving this carrot in front of him. She'd known he would want to jump on it. She knew he loved adventure, and would be excited about stepping back into his role as a soldier, feeling like he was helping those in need, and maybe helping someone be free.

~~~~~~~~

"What are ya thinkin' Jewel?" Grady asked, feeling Jewel fidget in the seat beside him, reaching up to tuck some hair behind her ear so he could see her face more clearly.

"I thought you were asleep," she said turning to look at him.

"No. I was stuck in that place that's right on the edge of sleep. Ya can see the softness of sleep lingering in front of ya, but there's an invisible tether holdin' ya back that won't let ya fall no matter how hard ya try," he said managing to make insomnia sound like the beginnings of a Walt Whitman poem.

"Madison?" Jewel asked, knowing that the thought of her was likely the tether keeping him from sleep.

"Among other things, but I asked ya first. What are ya thinkin' about Jewel? Ya haven't slept a wink."

"It was selfish of me to ask you to do this. I knew you would say yes, and with Madison...," she trailed off shaking her head, unsure of what to say.

"Ya don't have a selfish bone in yer body darlin'. Madison is... well... I think Madison is saying goodbye. She needs this time," he said smiling and shaking his head as he thought of her. "She's really smart... smart beyond her years. She's saying goodbye to her life as it is. She loves her Mom. She loves Jay too, but not in the same way. She knows things are going to change, and she's smart enough to know that these next few months are the end of one thing and the beginning of another. She'll get a hold of us if she needs us, and we'll be getting reports from Ally and Diana. She'll be okay Jewel," he said wrapping an arm around her reassuringly.

"So what's keeping you from sleep?" she whispered, as they both tried not to disturb the other sleeping passengers.

"Well... I was thinking a little about Madison, but mostly about how the hell I'm goin' ta keep ya safe in Uganda. There's a part of me that's excited ta go, but then there's another part of me that's worried. I had ya tucked inta the relative safety of hearth and home, and now here we are traipsin' off ta one of the most dangerous countries in the world, where killin' an American would hail any number of rebels a hero."

"Well, as long as I have you looking out for me, I guess I'll be safe," she said smiling at him, touched by his constant concern for her safety.

They both managed to sleep a little for the rest of the flight, snuggled up together, having eased each other's minds enough to finally rest before making their descent into Amsterdam. In Amsterdam, there was a warehouse full of donated supplies. Some of the supplies had been acquired through coalitions and various governments and organizations, and some of the supplies had simply just managed to show up without anyone acknowledging that they may have come there through less than legal means, though the need for them was too high to question those means.

They would be heading from the airport straight to the warehouse to make all the arrangements, per the instructions and list of supplies that Major Johnson had sent them. They weren't going to have much downtime before they caught their flight within the next twenty-four hours to Mbarara, Uganda. After that, they would be heading out on a Red Cross truck that would take them to a checkpoint where they would meet a team of soldiers that would take them out to the mobile site where they would be working. They both knew that the next few months weren't likely to spare them much opportunity for restful sleep, but they were excited, and were both looking forward to helping in a meaningful way.

The warehouse in Amsterdam was shrouded in mystery, and everyone they encountered regarded them with masked suspicion until they pulled out the official documents, and the list that Major Johnson had sent them. After people saw the official documentation, they usually eased up a bit and explained that they had been scammed on many occasions by drug cartels and other organized crime groups that would try to take all their supplies and sell them to various militia groups on the black market.

Their instructions were to coordinate and supervise the operation to get all of the supplies on the delivery trucks, and then safely stored on the cargo plane that would take them to Mbarara. The armed men who stood on guard, as they loaded the trucks and took them to the secure area where the cargo plane was, were dressed in quasi-military garb and were all well-armed, but Grady and Jewel knew that they were likely not official in their duties. They wondered if they were actually armed illegally, though they suspected that the precaution was not without warrant after the cold treatment they got when they first arrived at the warehouse.

In all, there were four rather large storage trucks that were stuffed full of medical supplies, food, weapons, ammunition, and blankets. Jewel couldn't help but see the irony of loading medical supplies and weapons on the same trucks, and once they were all loaded and they had a minute to sit back and think about it, the full impact of everything they were about to embark on hit her so hard she finally had to take a moment to sit down.

"Are ya okay Jewel?" Grady asked, going to sit beside her.

"I guess I'm a little scared. We haven't even arrived in Uganda yet, and we're already in danger," she said shrugging at him.

"As long as there's breath in my body, I'll make sure yer safe darlin'," he said, wrapping an arm around her protectively.

"You not having breath in your body is what scares me the most," she said turning her head and looking up at him as they sat side-by-side.

"These men here are soldiers for hire," he motioned toward the armed men who had been on guard that he had been chatting with earlier. "Some of them have been where we're goin'. I'll be gettin' all my gear the minute we leave European airspace, and you'll also get some gear too. We'll be fine darlin'. I talked to them a little. It's all well organized, and most of the rebels will leave humanitarian organizations alone.

Some of those men were in Iraq and Afghanistan, and most of the soldiers we'll be with once we get there, all have active military experience. We'll be fine Jewel."

In reality, Jewel's concern was more for Grady than for herself. She was suddenly aware at just how much danger she may have placed her husband in. She imagined him in full military gear, out fighting against armed rebels. She spared a brief moment to remember the images from the movie Black Hawk Down, never realizing that it had been a true story until stumbling across the actual documentary one day when she had been flipping through channels. She tried to get the images out of her mind of seeing the soldiers bodies being dragged through the streets, but they forced their way in, her defenses being way down and taken advantage of due to lack of sleep, and creeping doubt.

They rode to the cargo plane and supervised the unloading. They said goodbye to the caravan of armed soldiers, and made their way to the hotel to get some sleep, which couldn't have come soon enough. They crashed hard, sleeping longer than they would have thought possible, and much longer than they had intended.

They had a few more items they needed to gather before they could set out to Uganda the next day. Little did they know how much their lives were about to change.

CHAPTER 53

IMMACULEE' ILIBAGIZA

The minute they landed in Mbarara, their lives changed forever. They touched down and taxied toward the trucks that were waiting for them per the instructions, but as they neared the trucks, something didn't look right, and there was nothing they could do to stop what was already in motion.

The airport seemed empty. There wasn't any hustle and bustle going on that would be expected at an airport. It was a small airport with one runway and one small building that looked like it had been there since biblical times, once painted turquoise, but was now faded and riddled with bullet holes from previous conflicts. At the end of the runway was a taxiway, and at the end of that, trucks waited and were covered with rebels armed with machine guns. There were at least a hundred of them, maybe more. They were sitting on top of the hood, and were standing out on top of the cargo hold where all their supplies would be loaded. It was a ragtag group of young men, dressed in ragged clothing and headbands, jumping up and down excitedly, shooting off their guns in the air.

They could see a couple bodies lying out on the pavement near the trucks, and their hearts stopped, realizing the rebels had taken over their operation. Grady, and some of the other volunteers that had been on the plane with them, yelled to the pilot to keep going or turn around, but even as they said so, they knew they were trapped. The rebels were all around them, had already shot out their tires, and besides, they would be in need of fuel before they would be able to go anywhere. Suddenly, Grady was glad he hadn't changed into the military garb they gave him, and they quickly made the decision that he and Jewel would portray themselves as missionaries, as they were instructed if anything like this were to happen.

The rebels surrounded them within seconds after stopping the cargo plane. They forced their way onto the plane and immediately grabbed Grady, Jewel and the other passengers, practically dragging them off the plane despite the fact that they had not resisted at all, and had made motions to cooperate, showing they had no weapons on them, and were not there to harm them. Grady and Jewel never took their eyes off each other, but had been forced to let go of their hands, as the rebels pushed them outside toward their apparent leader.

"Whachya do here in Uganda?" the leader of the rebels barked at them after they were brought toward him, forced to their knees, and holding their hands on their heads. He was a rather large man with a look of hatred on his face that couldn't be masked. This was a man who did not know the meaning of mercy, Jewel guessed, and a chill ran down her spine as his eyes met hers, and she caught site of the long scar that ran across the side of his head.

"We're missionaries. My wife is a nurse, and I'm an engineer. We came to help administer medicine and help build the orphanage run by Margaret Johnson," Grady answered per the instructions they had been given. It wasn't untrue. When they had applied for their visas, they registered as missionaries, and listed themselves as a nurse and an engineer. This was the instructions they were given, and it made sense. Although they weren't there officially as a representative of a Christian organization, they were there to volunteer their time and help others, and what is a missionary, if not to help others?

"Why you come here?" the rebel leader asked Jewel.

"I came to give medicine to anyone who needs it," she said indignantly, noticing that there were several men in his militia in need of medical care. "I came to be near my husband," she added, wanting to make them understand that her husband was the man kneeling beside her, in case there was any mistaking it.

"You will come then and do that," the rebel commanded before barking orders at the men who had dragged them off the plane. He then went off to survey the supplies that were quickly being taken off the cargo plane.

The men took Jewel and Grady over to another group of rebels, and conveyed whatever orders had been given to these men, who quickly took charge of them as instructed.

"You go to them," one rebel said, pointing to another group of rebels they were being passed off to. The other volunteers, the pilots, and crew that had been on the plane, were also being lined up in the same fashion, some of them being instructed to go with them, while others were sent off in a new direction. Grady couldn't help notice that one of the crewmembers walked off in a third direction, and he wondered if he had been their mole. He had noticed him as they got on the cargo plane, and hadn't found him to be overly friendly, but then again, this wasn't an entirely unusual reception for blond-haired, blue-eyed men in this part of the world. He watched the man as long as he dared, trying to memorize as much about him as he could before the length of time to look would become suspicious. Jewel followed Grady's eyes as he studied the man, and made mental notes after having observed the same suspicious parting as Grady.

They sat there until they had questioned everyone and partitioned them out. The rebels quickly prodded them to follow them toward an area where they were loaded into the back of a pickup truck, covered in tarps, and then driven away. The rebels climbed in the cab of the trucks, and some followed in other vehicles, all of them armed with machine guns. There were twelve of them, and ten prisoners, including Grady and Jewel. The rebels were all fierce looking men who had clearly seen their share of violence and horror, judging by their scars and battle wounds. They didn't smile or have any emotion on their faces, other than contempt.

Grady held onto Jewel the whole time as they laid under the tarps, both of them praying to God, afraid to make a move or to even whisper to each other. They had searched them both for weapons before making them kneel before the rebel leader, and Grady was seething at how they had lingered between Jewel's legs and spent a little too long checking her breasts for hidden weapons, and he was worried about her state of mind at the moment, and worried about their intentions with her. He knew that her striking beauty would not go unnoticed, and he just held onto her and prayed hard. His mind considered every possibility, wondering about escape, but he knew they wouldn't get far. There were too many of them, and he knew they wouldn't hesitate to kill them. They didn't value life the way they did, and they both knew it.

They had discussed this possibility. They had discussed the likelihood that Jewel would be raped, and they would both probably be killed if they were to fall into the wrong hands. Grady shook his head thinking about their conversation. He should have ended it there, but Jewel had been adamant. She needed to go. She felt they had to risk everything to help people who would otherwise have no hope, and Jewel felt that hope was necessary for all mankind. Hope could break down walls and tear apart barriers, and that's what kept people alive inside, making them work toward goals and strive for freedom.

He kicked himself knowing he could have talked her out of going if he'd tried. He hadn't tried very hard, because his heart started racing, and his excitement surged the moment she mentioned it, and he himself had wanted to go so badly that he hadn't tried to talk her out of it at all.

Jewel's mind raced. She had known this was a possibility and she knew that Grady was likely torturing himself, trying to shoulder all the blame as he always did, and always feeling like it was his responsibility to protect her. She squeezed the arm he had wrapped around her so hard he was nearly cutting off her ability to breathe deeply, and they spoke that language that couples often speak without ever saying a word.

I love you and it's not your fault, she said with a squeeze.

I love you and I'm sorry, he said squeezing her even tighter.

They drove for hours, and Grady wondered if they were still in Uganda after having stopped and gone through some kind of checkpoint during their covered ride. He listened for key words of rebel groups, but there was little he was able to pick out until he heard the word that sent chills down his spine. *Interahamwe.*

He had read a little about the group. They were a group of Hutu rebels that had formed after they fled from Rwanda after the genocide in 1994. They had taken refuge, and banded together in the Democratic Republic of the Congo, and the Ugandan mountains. They were known to take prisoners for ransom, and they were also known for having absolutely no mercy for their victims. The Hutus had been the tribe that had committed genocide in Rwanda in the mid-nineties; brutally killing an estimated eight hundred thousand Tutsi's in a hundred days with some estimates going as high as two million that were slain. The mass killings had pitted family members and neighbors against each other. The killings were carried out using machetes, and women and children were shown absolutely no mercy. They were hacked apart and thrown into the river with just as much callousness and cruelty as could be managed.

Grady felt Jewel tense, and he knew that she had heard it as well. She had just finished reading the story of Immaculee' Ilibagiza, a Tutsi who had hidden out in a bathroom for several months as former friends and neighbors hunted her down, wanting to kill her after brutally slaughtering most of her family. Grady knew that Jewel was likely thinking of that brutality as the realization occurred to her. She had been so impressed with the strength of the woman, and her unyielding faith, that Grady silently thanked God for giving her that inspiration right before she needed it. He knew that she would be calling on that faith and thinking of Immaculee' a lot during this time.

Jewel and Grady had talked about the Interahamwe, but had dismissed them entirely, never once considering them as a realistic threat. They had clearly underestimated their reach. With all the commotion of everyone finally moving around, Grady took the opportunity to reach down and kiss her on the cheek, whispering to her as they finally stopped and it appeared that they would be getting out of the pickup.

"Immaculee' Ilibagiza," he had whispered, making her heart jump, since that had been exactly the person she had been thinking about at that very moment, remembering her remarkable strength.

Jewel made eye contact with Grady for a brief moment before the rebels grabbed them by the arm and took them out of the pickup. They knew they had been heading uphill since they had been jarred into a heap toward the other prisoners who had been squished toward the tailgate, and they were not surprised to see they were in a mountainous region. The rebels prodded them to follow them further uphill, as the other rebels followed behind with their machine guns pointing at them, and Jewel thought they would not hesitate to pull the trigger. It seemed perfectly clear that several of the rebels were itching for someone to make just one wrong move, so they would get the opportunity to quench their lust for blood.

They hiked for hours, and Jewel and Grady stayed as close to each other as they dared, but had nearly caused an all-out massacre when Grady grabbed Jewel's hand, and they were told not to touch each other again. Still, they were glad to be near each other, frequently meeting each other's eyes, looking for, and receiving encouragement from one another. After several hours, the rebels told them to stop their upward march and sit down along the trail they had been following. One of the rebels came and told them they would be sleeping there, and told them to hold out their hands as he slopped beans into their bare hands to eat.

They all looked at each other questioning the safety of the food, but after Grady took a bite, everyone else decided to join in. Grady's thought had been that if they wanted to kill them, they would all be dead. He suspected they very much wanted to keep them alive, so they could use them for some purpose, which would be either for some political negotiation, or for the simple desire for money.

It didn't surprise Jewel that Grady somehow managed to become the one everyone looked upon as the leader of this group of prisoners. She never considered for a moment that he wouldn't. He was a natural leader. He was always thinking and studying everything around him. He didn't wear emotion on his face, and he towered over everyone, which logistically speaking always made people look up to him, though Jewel knew it was more than just that. She had seen large men before who couldn't have led a group of boy scouts, let alone a group of grown men. The constant movement behind Grady's eyes, the way he carried himself, and the stoicism that radiated from him, sent off an aura that compelled people to follow him, without them ever realizing they were doing so.

"We all have ta go ta the bathroom," Grady said to one of the rebels as they came near them again. Jewel couldn't help but notice that Grady had laid on the accent a little thicker than normal, and it didn't go unnoticed by the rebel either. Her mind raced, trying to figure out why he would have done that. She knew the rebels had their passports and knew exactly who they were, though she also knew that practically nothing Grady ever did was by accident. He had his reasons, and it gave her comfort to know that his logical military mind was at work.

"Okay, come!" the rebel said, motioning toward the prisoners to follow him, directing them one-by-one toward a bushy area that would give them each a little privacy.

Jewel saw the careful way Grady studied all the rebels, but she doubted that anyone else in that group would have noticed. He didn't do it in an obvious way, but she knew him well enough to know that there was a lot going on behind those blue eyes of his. He had motioned with his eyes for her to keep her own eyes down. She knew he wanted her not to stand out. He wanted her to fade away. He had told her often enough that her black hair, and contrasting blue eyes, would always bring attention to her, and so she looked down, if only to ease his mind, and take away some of the burden she knew he felt.

The rebels led them back to the trail where they had sat and eaten, and motioned for them to lie down in the grass. It was clear they would all be sleeping right there for the night, within a very close proximity of each other, but just as Jewel went to sit next to Grady, one of the rebels came over to her and grabbed her by the arm.

"You will come with me!" the rebel demanded in a heavy clipped accent that sounded part British and part Indian. He was a young man, probably in his late teens or early twenties. Grady sized the man up, trying to decide whether or not to attack the man and attempt to protect his wife, or wait and see how it played out. He knew they would all likely get machine gunned if he made a move.

Jewel saw the look in Grady's eyes and tried to calm the storm before it happened. "Do you need medical care?" she asked suddenly.

"You are a nurse, and you will help my brother Hassan," he said, yanking her arm, and giving Grady a long menacing stare as he tapped the side of the hard steel he kept at his side. The young man was cold and hardened. He wore faded camouflage clothing that probably hadn't been clean since the day he put them on, which appeared to have been many years earlier. He wore a red bandana around his head, covering his dirty hair beneath, with wild black hair jutting out from underneath in every direction. His arms and his face bore scars that pronounced his life as a rebel, telling the story of a young man who had likely already lived beyond his total life expectancy.

She turned to look over her shoulder at Grady, as the young rebel pulled her further down the trail. Most of the rebels were in another area away from them, but two had stayed to watch over the prisoners, apparently taking the first shift as the other rebels slept or ate. She watched him all the way, until she went around a corner and could no longer see him, and he never took his eyes from her as he stood watching her leave, guarded by the two rebels watching over them.

She kept her eyes down, and was suddenly thankful that Grady had talked her into wearing long khaki pants, instead of the shorts she had on earlier. She could feel all the eyes on her as they paraded her through the camp, and led her toward the man's brother who was in need of medical attention. She sensed that singing or humming, or bringing any kind of unnecessary excitement to this crew, or attention to herself, would not be a good idea, and made a mental note to herself to keep that in check.

The man who was hurt looked much like the one who had come to get her, but she could tell that he was quite a bit older, and Jewel sensed that he was likely the leader of this small group of men. This was likely because he was older, and he seemed to command a certain amount of leadership, even as he sat fighting his pain.

"He had hurt dis arm," the rebel explained, pointing towards the man's swollen arm. She looked at it carefully before ever touching it. Just on the inside above his thumb, nearly halfway toward the elbow, she could see a bone protruding abnormally from the inside out, piercing the skin. She knew the radius was broken, and her mind raced, wondering how in the world she would be able to do anything about it, out there in the jungle. She could see the man was in a lot of pain, despite being quite medicated. She wondered what substance it was that he had taken, and wondered how she would monitor how much more to give him if he expected her to reset it.

She put her mind straight, and decided to treat him like any other patient. "How did you hurt your arm?" she said kneeling on the ground in front of him.

"He fell to da ground from da truck" the young rebel answered for him.

"How long ago did this happen?" she asked looking up toward the young rebel that was still standing over her.

"It happens dis early morning," he answered.

"Do you have any medical supplies... bandages... alcohol... any pain medications... antibiotics?" she asked.

The young rebel yelled to one of the other men who was sitting there watching him, and he followed whatever orders he was given in response to Jewel's request for medical supplies.

"You can help him?" he asked.

"It's going to be extremely painful. It's already very swollen. If I'm going to reset his arm, I need my husband to help me," she said giving him a serious look.

The young rebel once again barked orders at another man, apparently to bring Grady up to help her. She could see him raising his hand up high as if to describe someone very tall, and her heart raced with anticipation that Grady would be there with her. She hadn't realized until that very moment just how scared she was, and how much she was shaking. She had to fight back tears at that moment, and she knew she would have to fight back the urge to run toward him the minute she saw him come around the corner.

The first man came back with a bag that was full of all sorts of medical supplies. Jewel opened it up and fished through it, deciding to take everything out and take complete stock of everything, laying it out on a clean cotton towel that had been on top. There was gauze, bandages, tape, sutures, needles and vials of medicine labeled in English, and Jewel wondered if the supplies she was searching through were the ones they had brought with them on the plane. They were all new, and the medical bag itself appeared to be unused and full of supplies that would have come as part of a field kit. Just as she was reading the labels on the vials, searching her tired brain for their medical purpose, she caught sight of Grady coming around the corner with his hands on his head. The man behind him was holding the machine gun to his back, and Jewel flared with anger the minute she saw it, which did not go unnoticed by the young rebel that was sitting near her, watching her go through the medical bag.

The young rebel yelled something to the man who had the gun on Grady, which caused an argument among the group for a brief minute. The language was completely lost on Grady and Jewel, but they locked eyes with each other and spoke a language of their own without ever saying a word. The man took his gun from Grady's back finally, and Grady carefully walked toward Jewel, afraid to make any sudden moves, slowly bringing his hands down from on top of his head as he did.

"Dis is you husband?" the young rebel asked.

"Yes," Jewel said, briefly taking her eyes from Grady to look the young man in the face.

Her heart was racing as Grady came over to her, kneeling down and putting a protective arm around her instinctively. "Are ya alright Jewel?"

"I'm okay," she assured him before turning her attention back to her patient.

"This is going to hurt your brother severely. He needs to understand that, and everyone in this camp needs to understand that, because I don't want anyone getting jumpy and shooting us when we go to set this, and he screams bloody murder," she said. "I'm going to take this medicine and this needle, and I'm going to give him an injection right here," she said pointing to the location of her own armpit, where she would attempt to block the nerve, so it would be less painful when she reset the bone.

"When I'm done resetting the bone, I'm going to clean the wound, stitch it up, give him another injection to stop him from getting an infection, and then I'm going to wrap it up so he can't move it," she said looking the young rebel in the face. "Do you understand all that?"

"Yes," he said simply.

"Okay, well… you need to explain that to him then," she said.

The young man sat and explained everything to his brother in their native language of Kinyarwanda, motioning toward his own armpit as Jewel had done. While the explanation ensued, Grady and Jewel took every opportunity to move closer to each other, sending electricity from one body to another, speaking a language that was all their own.

When he finished his explanation, Jewel reminded him that he also needed to explain everything to the other men who were standing nearby, so they wouldn't become too alarmed during the whole process. They waited until all the chatter stopped, and the young rebel came back over to them again, and nodded at Jewel to confirm that he had completed his task.

"Alright, what is your name?" she finally asked the young man.

"I am Kinyera" he said, "and what do I call you?

"I'm Jewel, and this is my husband Grady," she said emphasizing the husband part once again.

Jewel once again described the process of what was going to take place, making sure Kinyera relayed everything to his brother, so he would know what to expect, though she suspected that whatever drug he had taken was making his ability to follow along rather difficult. The other men started to gather around them as Jewel made preparations, carefully pulling away any loose clothing from the wound, and cutting the shirt just a little so she could find the place in his armpit where she would need to do the nerve block.

"Grady," she said turning to look at him, "I will need you to take his upper arm very firmly. Don't move it around or anything… just keep it as still as you possibly can and let me do all the work. Wait until I'm ready, and then take him like this," she said demonstrating on him how she wanted him to hold the man.

"Kinyera, can you get one more man to help us? I need one of you to hold his legs, and another to hold his other arm and keep his head still. If I don't get this in there in one move, it's going to be that much more difficult," Jewel said mentally preparing herself for the task. She knew that his arm needed more than she was going to be able to give him, but she also knew she needed to do everything she could. She would set the arm, and then place bracing around it as best she could, and still be able to care for the wound. If she were at an actual hospital, she would likely be assisting a doctor with this procedure, and the doctor would put pins in to ensure that it healed properly, but she knew that wasn't an option.

When everyone was in place and confirmed to her that they understood what their task was, she took one final breath and started the procedure. The man was lying there in a total daze, and to Jewel's surprise, he barely seemed to notice when she started the nerve block. She knew that for many people this could be quite painful, and she knew that people under the influence of narcotics were unpredictable, and could sometimes have unusual strength. "He must be more drugged than I realized," she said aloud to nobody in particular, as they sat for a minute to let the nerve block take effect.

She nodded to Grady, who carefully placed his hands around the man's upper arm the way Jewel had instructed, and the other two men held tight to the limbs that were their designated areas of responsibility. She could hear the man moan half-heartedly, before quickly forgetting his pain, and slipping back into his daze. She touched his arm carefully, feeling the muscles and the bones beneath her hands as best she could through the swollen tissue, deciding how best to proceed. When she was done checking all she could, and had decided on a path to take, she couldn't stop herself from humming a very slow rendition of Mockingbird, surprising everyone but Grady.

She pulled the two sides of the radius together as she hummed, making everyone around her feel like it was all happening in slow motion. It had been a clean break, and Jewel was able to make the two ends meet once again the way they were supposed to, immediately making his arm look less deformed, though it seemed to have finally been the one thing that would jolt the patient out of his drug induced state of indifference. She could feel him struggling beneath the three men that held onto him, rattling the trigger-happy men that surrounded them.

"Tell them to back off Kinyera!" Jewel demanded, immediately causing Kinyera to yell at the men to calm down.

"Whatever you do, don't let go of that arm, and keep it as steady as you can," Jewel said to Grady as she held the bones together with one hand, and attempted to wipe off some of the blood with the other, so she could place some bracing around his arm to keep it in place. She had quickly slipped on a pair of latex gloves before she started, and was glad she did as the blood started gushing the minute she started moving things. She was concentrating on the task of making sure she got the arm set correctly, but that didn't stop her from glancing up toward Grady, meeting his eyes every few minutes.

"Move your hands up slightly Grady. I don't want this blood getting on you," she said glancing up at him. She knew that many of the other men could have helped her do what she had Grady doing. She had originally told Kinyera she needed the help of her husband, simply because she wanted to see him, but she feared she could have placed him in danger if he were exposed to blood-borne pathogens. She had considered this before she started, but after looking through the other latex gloves that were in the medical bag, she knew that none of them would even come close to fitting on his rather large hands.

She finally got his arm properly braced and cleaned up after stitching up the wound, and the man seemed to be resting more peacefully because of it. He had slipped into such a deep sleep that Jewel worried for a second that he may have succumbed to an overdose of whatever drug he had taken, but after checking some of his vitals, she was reassured that he was just in a deep sleep. He barely stirred when she injected the needle full of antibiotics into his right hip, a feat made all the more easy by the torn pants that exposed the fleshy tissue that was an ideal location for the shot. She sat back and breathed easy for a second, looking at him, and wondering why she cared so much about whether he lived or died, when her mind prompted her to recall their current situation as hostages.

"Nobody should have to suffer," she finally said thinking aloud, catching all the rebels by surprise. Grady wasn't surprised though, and he couldn't help but feel a sense of pride at his wife's skill and compassion.

"Ya did good Jewel," he said to her straight-faced, not wanting to reveal his emotions to these men.

Kinyera led them back to lie down with the others prisoners, but his demeanor was more relaxed. Jewel and Grady laid down right next to each other face to face, and Jewel noticed there was one other couple who had done the same. There were also four men of various ages, Jewel guessed one was in his mid-twenties, another was in his early forties, and the other two were likely in their mid to late fifties. The other two prisoners were young women, who had apparently been traveling together along with the youngest man, and those were the two that Jewel was most worried about. They had already started to fall apart, and the young man had done nothing to help them or comfort them, as he was clearly struggling with his own fear. Apparently, the two older men had also seen the vulnerability of the two young women, and they attempted to take them in under their wings, and Jewel had no doubt their intentions were sincere.

Jewel looked in Grady's eyes, and he instinctively reached up to cradle her face in his hand, before quickly looking over to see if the two rebels were going to put a stop to it, but they didn't seem to care. He took this as a good sign, but didn't want to push his luck, only going so far as to take her hand in his own, and give her as much comfort as he could. He knew she was frightened. She wore her emotions on her face as clearly as if it were written in plain English. He closed his eyes, knowing that she would never close hers until he did. He laid there holding onto her tiny little hand as he always did, and considered all that he knew of this group of rebels.

He noted they hadn't been especially violent. They hadn't harmed anyone, and even as the rebels dragged them around, they seemed to take some care in making sure they weren't overly rough. He thought of each rebel that led them on their hike. There were twelve of them, and he quickly decided who among them the leaders were, and who the foot soldiers were. This was usually fairly easy to figure out with these types of groups. Many of the men associated with these groups die fairly young, which automatically made the older ones the leaders, for, if nothing else, having simply survived this harsh lifestyle.

The youngest men were always the most dangerous. They were eager to make a name for themselves, and they lacked the maturity to be patient and think things through beyond the near future. This was almost always true, even within his own very well disciplined unit in the Army. Some things couldn't be trained into a person, even when the most powerful military in the world was doing the training.

He considered the leniency of the two that were watching over them, compared to the one earlier who appeared to be on the verge of mowing the whole lot of them over with his machine gun when he grabbed his wife's hand. He knew that he was the most dangerous of the lot. He was young and little, and Grady had looked into his eyes, and found nothing beyond a dark wall of hatred that stood cold and unwelcoming like a prison fence.

He thought of the long trip, wondering how far they had gone. He thought they hadn't ever gone more than about fifty-five miles per hour, and some of that had been uphill. He searched his mind, trying to remember the mountains that surrounded Mbarara, and he considered all the possibilities of where they might be heading. He thought he had remembered the Interahamwe having taken hostages before into the Bwindi National Forest, but he couldn't be sure, and he finally decided to try to get as much sleep as he could, knowing he was going to need to stay strong, not only for himself, but for Jewel's sake.

"Immaculee' Ilibagiza," they both reminded themselves as they settled into sleep.

CHAPTER 54

HELLO MARY SHELTON

Rudy, Diana, and the kids were happy to finally be in Wyoming. They had fallen in love with the place the moment they arrived that very first time, and Rudy was glad to be able to have something to finally give his wife a settled life in the country like she had always dreamed of, albeit in a different state than they were originally planning on. This didn't seem to bother anyone too much though. They were all used to moving around, and they loved the idea of being so close to the mountains, and so close to Grady and Jewel.

Moving had been something Rudy wanted to do all along, but he never considered the possibility that Alisha would want to move in her senior year of high school, but then again, he never counted on Michael. The other kids had been eager to move. Diana was flatly against the idea at first, but had surprised him a couple weeks after he first broached the subject. She had come to him one day when he was working in the office, and simply said, "okay, let's do it."

She knew he was miserable working for his father-in-law, and she also knew that her dad wasn't entirely happy with the arrangement either. Patrick simply wasn't ready to be retired, and was finding it difficult to give up enough control of the company to make Rudy want to stay. The opportunity for them to move to Wyoming, and manage Grady's construction company while building a family home, had been a blessing. Rudy wasn't in the position yet to start his own company from the ground up, but he was in a position to be able to take the reins and pick up where Grady left off, and he knew that their partnership after they returned would be ideal. They worked together and respected each other enough to defer to the other in their areas of expertise, neither one of them having so much pride that they would risk their relationship over prideful decisions.

Michael was off to college, but Alisha was content to just be near his home that he visited often, and she knew he would likely increase the frequency since she was there, and that was enough for the time being. Michael had made a special trip home the day they arrived, and spent the next two days showing Alisha and her siblings around town, taking her to the high school to tour everything, and introducing them to some other kids that they would be going to school with, which thrilled Rudy and Diana to no end. School had started a couple weeks earlier, but it was still early enough in the year to make the transition smooth.

Grady and Jewel's house was quite small for the eight of them, and so they decided to rent a place in town instead of staying out at the ranch. The kids found this to be quite disappointing until they realized that this saved them each an hour long bus ride to and from school, and then they decided that maybe it wasn't such a bad idea after all, though they knew that once their own home was built, they would be taking the long bus ride.

Rudy and Diana loved the idea that Tina was going to have an opportunity to spend more time with Jewel. Tina had a tendency to be meek and introverted, and she carried worry around with her everywhere she went, but Jewel somehow managed to bring her out of her shell. Jewel had become her hero. Jewel's ability to stand up for herself empowered Tina to stand taller, and she laughed more, and spent fewer hours worrying about the scary possibilities life sometimes brought forth. On top of that, she had become very close with Madison, and it thrilled them to know that all of them were going to get to spend more time with her.

Melanie and Paxton both talked non-stop about the horses. They both wanted one, but in the meantime, they were excited to be able to go out and help Michael with his. Paxton dreamed of growing up one day to be a large animal vet, and Rudy was excited to be able to expose him to the lifestyle, so he could pursue it for real if he chose to one day. He had gotten his driver's license, and Rudy and Diana helped him buy a car, so the opportunity to be able to drive himself out to Michael's place, and take Michael up on his offer to teach him all he knew about horses, was exciting. Melanie loved the horses too, but for her it was more for pleasure. She wanted to ride them and brush them, but her interest in them pretty much ended there, though she was looking forward to hanging out with her big brother at the horse ranch.

Thomas and Joseph were excited to explore the mountains. Rudy promised to take them all hunting and fishing, and they couldn't wait to have the time to spend with their dad. On top of that, they had been able to meet a few boys their age they would be going to school with when Michael had taken them around town, and they were talking about how much fun they were going to have in their new school.

Their lives were finally starting to look settled, after having spent most of their lives moving around from one Navy base after another, never really knowing how long they would get to stay in one place. Their biggest obstacle would be getting their home built. Rudy was already so busy with the business, and they hadn't managed to save much for a down payment, but Grady had made them a very generous offer letting them keep all the profits on the last lot if he could get it sold and built. That alone would allow him to get started, though he wasn't entirely sure where to start. He had one thousand acres at his disposal and no idea what to do with them. When he had first learned about his biological father leaving him the acreage, he wanted no part of it. He had been so angry that he never kept in touch with him, that his initial thought was to take the land and sell it to some developer or something, and never worry about how that might affect the rest of the land, but things had worked out differently. He looked forward to keeping the land open, and he looked forward to putting the land to work for him. He loved that he was going to be close to Grady and Jewel. They had also gotten to know Troy and Jolene fairly well, and were looking forward to spending more time with them and their baby girl, Anna.

Rudy was smiling to himself thinking of their future as he went through Grady's house checking everything as he promised to do while they were away, when the phone suddenly rang nearly causing him to jump out of his skin.

"Hello?" he said picking up the receiver.

"Yes. Hi. I… ugh… well… my name is Mary Shelton. I'm Jewel's cousin from Denver. Well… her mom was actually my cousin. Jewel actually always called me Aunt Mary, but technically, we're second cousins… ugh… I'm sorry. Can I start over?" she said stumbling through.

"Well, hi Aunt Mary, I'm Uncle Rudy. Can I help you with something? Jewel's not here right now," he said laughing to himself.

"Yes. I know she's not there. That's why I'm calling actually. Has anybody with the State Department been in touch with you?" she asked.

"The State Department? Ugh… no. Why?" Rudy asked suddenly alarmed.

"Well, are you Rudy Gillespie?" she asked.

"Yes, I am. What's this all about?"

"Well Rudy, Jewel, and her husband are in some trouble. I guess they went to Africa, and the State Department has been trying to reach their next of kin, but…"

"Next of kin?" Rudy exclaimed, feeling his heart beat in his throat.

"Yes. Apparently, they landed in Uganda on a mission trip, and something went terribly wrong. They were taken hostage, and the State Department has been trying to reach the people that were on the list of contacts Jewel and her husband left behind, and so far, I'm the only one they've been able to reach."

"Taken hostage? Oh my god! Did they give you any details?"

"They don't know much. All they know is the group took them when they landed in Uganda a couple days ago, and they are demanding one million dollars for each hostage. The group that took them is called the Interahamwe," she said struggling with the pronunciation.

They discussed all Aunt Mary knew in detail, which wasn't much. She told him that the State Department had been trying to keep a lid on the story until their family was notified, but for some reason, they had been unable to reach anyone that was on the list of contacts they had left behind. Rudy thought that it was all the moving around, and nobody being where they were supposed to be, and numbers being changed, and on top of that, Patrick and Maggie had taken a trip to Ireland, and wouldn't be back for a couple more weeks.

"I wasn't aware that Jewel was in contact with any of her family in Colorado," Rudy finally said, trying to discern why Aunt Mary was listed as a contact on Jewel's sheet, still feeling skeptical of everything that was coming out of her mouth, unable to accept what he had just been told.

"I was actually really surprised to get her letter. She must have mailed it as she was leaving on her trip. I knew her when she was a little girl, and always tried to reach out to her, but she never wanted any part of it, but then unexpectedly, I got this letter. I was thrilled, but then I get this call from the State Department, and I didn't know what to think. I thought I was being scammed at first, but the rebels sent a proof of life photo, and the State Department officials came to my house, and showed it to me so I could make a positive identification. I haven't seen Jewel since she was a little girl, but there was no doubt in my mind it was her. There's no mistaking those eyes."

"I'm absolutely stunned right now. I'm speechless. What do we do now? Did the man at the State Department leave a number?" Rudy rambled, feeling overwhelmed.

"I'm actually in Casper right now. I didn't know what to do either, so I just got in my car and started driving north, hoping to make contact with the rest of her family. I'm at a loss. I've been calling this number non-stop, and I was a little caught off guard when someone finally answered," she explained.

"Well Aunt Mary. I'm Jewel's Uncle, and Grady's brother in-law... which is a long story, but anyways...," Rudy said throwing his hands up in the air, never sure how to explain that. "I live in Buffalo with my wife and our kids. Why don't you keep heading north and meet me at my house... I'll give you the address, and we'll come together and see if we can call the State Department and figure out what to do."

They hung up the phone and Rudy nearly dropped to his knees. His mind was reeling. She had said the Interahamwe had taken them several days ago. This was a group he was very familiar with, having done some routine reconnaissance missions to gather information on them during his time as a Navy Seal. It nearly shook him to his core to think of Grady and Jewel among them. The Interahamwe were brutal, and had no value for human life. He had gone in to some of their "secret" hideouts they have in the dense equatorial forest that borders the DR Congo in the Virunga Mountains, and a chill ran down his spine when he thought of the horrific conditions that Jewel and Grady might be in. The Virunga Mountains ran through Uganda, Rwanda, and the Democratic Republic of the Congo, and they were vast. It would be like trying to find a needle in a haystack.

During his time compiling data on the Interahamwe, he and his team determined that they were about thirty thousand strong, and were living like animals. They were a group mostly of older militiamen who had participated in the atrocities in Rwanda, but they had also done some recruiting of younger men. These younger men were recruited because they were vulnerable and had nowhere else to go. They were orphaned boys or young men that were wanted by authorities, and they were hiding among other wanted men. They were young boys that had been taken from their homes, and forced into the lifestyle through fear and intimidation, and had been removed from their families for so long they felt they could no longer return.

There were women and children among this ragtag group who had come by force, or had come willingly, only because they had been discarded by society. There were young girls, some younger than his own children, who had been forcibly raped, and had produced children as a result. The conditions were awful. These "families" were not unions by choice. The women and children were little more than slaves. They had become pawns in the larger picture of the group's overall agenda, which was becoming more and more blurred. The only purpose for this group seemed to be terror for the sake of terror, while they quietly waited for the tables to turn in Rwanda, hoping the Hutu's would take control over the Tutsi-led government.

They seemed content to simply terrorize communities along the border between Rwanda and the Congo. They make a living by raiding villages, stealing food from crops, and collecting taxes by controlling river crossings. They descend upon groups of local inhabitants, raping women, and attacking people for no other reason than to create terror and remind people of their threat. There is much speculation that the group survives due to funding that is funneled through to them by the Rwandan government, to protect Rwandan's interests in the mineral-rich Congo. There had also been speculation that the Interahamwe needed capital to build their coffers more quickly to buy arms, to plan their next major attack on Rwanda, and Rudy suspected this had something to do with why they were taking hostages for ransom.

He went through the house one more time and checked everything, imagining them both still there, laughing, and joking, as they always seemed to be doing. He could still feel their presence. It was thick in the air as if it were billowing from a smoke stack. It radiated from every room in the house, and as he looked up and saw the picture of them with Madison, he vowed to do everything he could to get them back.

CHAPTER 55

A PRECIOUS STONE

Grady and Jewel sat together in one corner of the hut where all the prisoners were being held. It was hot out, and the last two weeks since they had been captured left them drained and exhausted. After they were taken, they had been marched for days toward an encampment in the forest that appeared to have been set up expressly for the purpose of keeping prisoners. It was clear that it had been a calculated plan that the rebels prepared for in advance. The hut was small and cramped, and the floor was just dirt and straw. All ten of them were caged together, leaving little room to spread out comfortably. The roof was thatched, and it sat on top of walls that were made of small tree poles and mud, providing them little fresh air. Jewel and Grady were the only Americans. Among them, there were mostly Europeans, with the exception of the two older men, who were both French Canadians. All of them spoke at least some English, though there hadn't been much talk between any of them that involved verbal communication.

During the long trek up to the encampment, they had been given strict instructions not to speak to each other, and they were all terrified to tempt the young rebels, who seemed eager to make an example out of any one of them. The only time Jewel and Grady felt comfortable speaking at all, was when Kinyera would come get them, and take both of them to check on their patient, Hassan, whose arm they had set and stitched up. They would also administer treatment to some of the other rebels on occasion. They weren't really sure why they would come and get the both of them, but they were grateful for it, and Jewel always made a point of including Grady in everything she did, supporting the idea that they were a medical team.

Jewel and Grady traced letters on each other's forearms to communicate with each other when they were huddled together in the hut, and they watched as others followed suit. Within just a few days, the ten of them had started to create signals, and other ways of communicating with each other, using eye and hand signals that became a game of charades. With all the time they had to sit there and waste away, it was Grady that proposed the idea that they needed to stay strong mentally and physically, and do what they could to remain hopeful, and not allow their bodies to breakdown. They took turns doing a regimen of exercises in the center of the hut, as everyone else sat against the walls in a circle. Grady would start a floor exercise, and then they would all take turns doing that exercise. Once everyone finished he would switch to something else, and they all took turns again, all of them doing this for several hours each day to keep from going crazy.

The food they had been given provided them with protein and carbohydrates, but the amount of calories were inadequate, and they had all started losing a little weight, which made a couple of the prisoners decide not to do the exercises. It was the young man, and one of the young girls, who had decided not to burn the extra calories by participating in the exercises, and the toll it was taking on them mentally was evident, though they were too far-gone to recognize it. They simply sat together in a corner and started to deteriorate, and there was nothing anyone could do to bring them out of the protective walls they had climbed into mentally.

Grady asked Kinyera one day if they could all be allowed to bathe in the creek, which seemed to surprise Kinyera. The rebels apparently took no such interest in bathing in the creek, but he agreed to let the prisoners go wash out their clothes, and clean their bodies. Each time they went, they were allowed to stay a bit longer than the last time, and it did much to lift their spirits. They had no idea what was going on with their capture or release politically. The rebels mostly spoke in their own language, and they had been given no indication as to what their status was, though they had all posed for a proof of life photo. They assumed they were being held for ransom.

Grady and Jewel decided that the time wasn't right to ask Kinyera about their intentions with them. They were building trust with him, and were afraid to rock the boat just yet. They talked with Kinyera about other things, and were surprised to find themselves liking the man, despite his holding a gun to them. He was very curious about life in America, and he asked them many questions about things he had heard, or pictures he had seen. He was the acting leader among this group of rebels, since Hassan slipped off into a fantasy world that involved large doses of drugs he was taking. The pain from his arm had apparently given him an ample excuse to stay high all day. Though Kinyera was young, they could see why he would be the acting leader of this group, aside from being the leader's brother. He was calculating, smart, and they knew better than to underestimate him.

Kinyera told the story of the day he became brothers with Hassan, and Jewel and Grady were surprised to hear the story of his kidnapping. He had been out with a group of boys playing one day in his village, when a group of rebels came and took them all. Kinyera told the story as if the rebels had done them the favor of caring for them, after the tragic death of all their parents, but he was fishing, probably having long suspected that their saviors were actually their captors. Kinyera had been sad and crying, but then Hassan came to him and took him under his wing. They became blood brothers, and they vowed to be brothers forever, and always look after one another. Kinyera studied their reactions as he told the story, searching for clues to support the ideas that he had about the real truth. He told them he had been about seven when Hassan became his brother, saying it with a sadness that couldn't be hidden, for the heart would always shine through no matter how much the brain had been twisted.

"Kinyera, do you think your family may still be out there somewhere?" Grady asked as Kinyera finished his story.

"Nah!" he said angrily. "There is no family. There is only blood among brothers," Kinyera said, repeating the mantra that had been brainwashed into him since he was seven, seeming to regret it the instant it came out of his mouth.

That was the first time they dared to ask such a question, and they knew it had been risky, but they both felt that it had sent a message to Kinyera to let him know that they understood the truth as to why, and how, he became Hassan's brother. The question was a way of telling Kinyera that they understood that he was as much a prisoner as they were, and it joined them together in a way that became very human, which was foreign to Kinyera, as far as Jewel and Grady could see.

They judged that Kinyera was likely in his early twenties, which would have meant that he was taken several years after the Rwandan genocide, and had likely grown up his whole life in encampments like the one they were imprisoned in. They knew that he likely hadn't been educated or ever lived a life resembling anything stable or non-violent. They knew he was a wildcard, but they thought that his telling of his story was his way... human nature's way, of reaching out and grabbing hold of something that humans craved, which was hope and freedom.

The other rebels were less willing to interact with them outside the invisible lines that separated the captors from the prisoners. They were all young though, and Jewel and Grady wondered how many of them had been taken alongside Kinyera, and were themselves just prisoners of this organization that sought to make soldiers out of young children. They realized that aside from Hassan, none of the men that were holding them prisoner in the encampment, would have been old enough to participate in the Rwandan genocide that occurred in 1994. Just as their curiosity as to why the young men stayed and followed orders started to reach its peak, the arrival of Taban, and several of his soldiers, answered their question.

Taban came into the encampment much like a tornado would descend upon a small town on the high plains. His very presence seemed to have the force of a thousand winds, sending young rebels scattering about like scared little children. He was a large man, with jet-black hair that was only slightly darker than his soul, pulling you unwillingly into an abyss with magnetic tentacles of darkness and hatred. He had scars on every inch of his body that was visible, with the most prominent one running from just below his right eye, and ending at his jawline. Just to look at him caused a lightning bolt of fear to shoot through you, imagining all the evil deeds he was capable of, and had likely already committed on multiple occasions. He wore a highly decorated uniform, complete with a beret, and carried a sidearm, a machete, and a machine gun. He was made for war, and not the modern kind that involved blowing people up from a civilized distance. The kind of war he was used to was more personal, and involved looking people right in the eye, ending their lives, and the lives of their entire family, without ever thinking twice about it. When Taban spoke, the deep tones of his voice vibrated through the ears so completely, that it reached down and grabbed his listeners in the pits of their stomachs, shaking the very foundation they stood on.

One of the first things Taban did when he came into the encampment was to set up a makeshift court, in which to interview his prisoners. A table and chair were brought outside, and one-by-one, the prisoners were led out of the prisoners hut to speak to Taban. He sat at the table like a king with guards positioned behind him menacingly, instilling fear in those who came to face him. The young rebels seemed to fade into the distance, as Taban and his men took over the camp, except Kinyera. Kinyera was present, without being obvious. He would listen carefully to everything that was said, without bringing attention to himself. He was smart, as was Grady, who peered out from a little crevice he had created in the hut, and he watched and listened intently.

As the interviews were conducted, there was another man who took notes, writing down random information. Grady could hear all the questions and answers, and they thought that the main purpose of the interviews was to instill fear in them. None of the questions that were being asked were anything of real importance, but the toll that it took on the prisoners was evident as they were led back to the hut after their interview. It was mental warfare, and Taban knew it. He narrowed his eyes at each one of them, instilling the kind of fear that one might feel if they had come face to face with a hungry lion.

"What do they call you?" Taban asked Jewel, with his voice booming.

"My name's Jewel," she answered, as she sat at the table across from him, running the Lord's Prayer through her mind over and over again to steady herself.

"Jewel. A jewel is a precious stone, no? Why does a precious stone come to Uganda?"

"I'm a nurse. I came to give medical care to kids at the orphanage run by Margaret Johnson." She gave him the rehearsed answer she had memorized on the long plane ride.

"Do you not have kids in America dat need medical attention?"

"The need isn't as great there," she answered, keeping her answers short and to the point, the way Grady told her.

He asked her many questions, trying to rattle her, but she held her own, answering the questions simply without appearing to wither in his presence, and for the first time, she saw a faint smile.

"You will examine me," he said, standing up and pulling off his shirt, exposing a very broad, muscular chest with scars running in every direction, sending a shiver through Jewel.

"I... ugh... alright," she said stuttering as her fear exploded, piercing the air between them.

She sat there motionless, unable to move as he stripped off his shirt. She glanced over to the crevice where she knew Grady was sitting and watching the interview. One of the rebels had scrambled to find the medical bag she had been using, and he dropped it at her feet before scampering off again like a little mouse who had hoped to go unnoticed. She gathered her nerves together, took a deep breath, and made the decision to put fear aside and just do her job.

"Please sit then," she said as she got up and picked up the bag, setting it down on the table, motioning toward the chair he had been sitting in earlier.

She pulled on the last pair of latex gloves that were in the bag. She already knew that the man had some sort of liver disease. She could see the prominent yellow hue that covered the whites of his eyes like a veil, and she suspected that it was Hepatitis C. They had read about Hepatitis C being widespread in this area due to the sharing of needles for the use of intravenous drugs. The fact that rape was such a major epidemic was in part responsible for the disease spreading like wildfire, nearly as fast as the aids virus.

"Have you been more tired than usual?" she asked him as she adjusted her gloves, keeping her eyes down.

"I am very tired," he answered, ordering the other men to leave him so that he could have as much privacy as could be afforded.

She had noticed earlier that his belly was distended outward, and she suspected that it was fluid retention caused by the disease since the rest of him was quite lean. She also noticed that he had been scratching his arms and legs while trying to conduct his interviews, another indication of the disease.

"Have you lost much weight lately? Vomited any blood?" she asked as she looked more closely at the yellowing of his eyes.

"I have lost much weight," he answered without emotion.

Jewel was certain that the man sitting before her was in advanced stages of liver cirrhosis, but she listened to his heart, and checked his pulse as slowly as she could. She wondered how this man would react to the news that he had an incurable condition that would likely kill him, or at least severely debilitate him in the near future. She wondered how much she should tell him, but then decided that she had to simply be honest with him, and deliver the news as professionally as she could, as she considered the fact that it may have been a trick. Surely, he had to have known for some time that something was wrong with him, and considering how prevalent the disease was in this country, he must have seen others suffer and then die with similar symptoms.

"Have you been checked by a regular doctor... had blood work done?" she asked him.

"No," he said with finality, "not for a long time."

"Taban... ugh... is that your name?" she asked getting a nod. "I think you have

410

cirrhosis of the liver, probably caused by Hepatitis C, but the only way to know for sure is to go to a regular doctor, have them check your blood, and run some other tests."

"This I know. What of everything else?"

Jewel let out a breath, realizing this had been a test. "You have high blood pressure, and your body temperature is raised, indicating that you have an infection of some sort."

"What can you do for me?" he asked.

"I can give you an antibiotic shot to kill any underlying infection you have, but you need to go see a doctor. There's not much I can do to help you out here," she said throwing her hands up, as if to display their current conditions to him for the first time.

"Where is you husband?" he asked her as he got up to put his shirt back on.

"He's with the other prisoners. You haven't talked to him yet," she answered.

"Bring him here," he ordered Kinyera.

Kinyera scampered to the hut as Taban ordered him, solidifying the idea that Kinyera himself was little more than a prisoner. He wasn't a prisoner held by armed guards, or by other means that were more closely associated with captivity; he was a prisoner of fear ingrained in him since his abduction when he was seven years old, imprisoned by the atrocities that he knew they were capable of committing. He was a prisoner held by a belief that he had nowhere else to go, belonged nowhere else, and would not be welcome anywhere else. He may even be wanted by law enforcement, and may face prosecution if he were caught by authorities, having committed atrocities ordered by Taban and other men just like him. Kinyera's prison walls stood higher and stronger than concrete and razor wire. Jewel considered all this as she proceeded to give Taban the shot of antibiotics and waited for them to bring Grady out.

"Why do you bring a precious stone to Uganda?" Taban asked Grady as the guards brought him out, sitting him down at the table beside Jewel, indicating with his hand that Jewel was the precious stone he was referring to. "A precious stone will always be a desirable item to be taken."

Grady knew this all too well. "She likes ta help other people. She wanted ta come," he answered, trying not to smile as he usually did when he talked about his wife, still laying on the thick Irish accent as he talked.

"You are not American?" Taban cocked his head questioning.

"I am American, but my family is from Ireland," he answered, hoping to instill the idea that to a certain extent, he could understand their plight, since Ireland represented the same type of conflict that had been present in most all countries that had been colonized.

"You had to leave Ireland then?" he asked.

"My parents did," he answered.

"Den you must understand how it is to be driven away from you own country?" Taban asked.

Grady's anger flared inside him, but he kept it well hidden. For Taban to make the comparison that he made, as he knew he would, was maddening to him given all the atrocities he knew the Hutu had committed against the Tutsi in order to be driven from their own country. It was hardly a parallel comparison, but it seemed to have had the desired effect on Taban.

"I know what my parents told me."

Taban and Grady talked back and forth for some time, with Grady being careful not to delve too deep into the politics that didn't support Taban's ideas. Political discussion could get heated in the most civilized situations, but when one was a prisoner, and the other was an armed captor, then political discussion was most assuredly inadvisable, especially if an opinion happened to differ from the man with the gun. Jewel sat there quietly and listened, keeping her eyes down, trying to concentrate on keeping her emotions off her face, which was nearly impossible for her.

"Take dis man back to da hut," Taban said, motioning toward Grady dismissively. "This precious stone will come with me."

"No! I'm not leaving without my husband!" Jewel yelled, getting up to run toward Grady as three guards held onto him.

"Jewel! No! She needs to stay with me!" Grady yelled as he struggled against the men who were holding onto him, dragging him back to the prisoners hut.

"Why are you doing this? I can't! I can't leave without my husband!" Jewel screamed as two men grabbed a hold of her and dragged her away.

"I love you!" They both yelled to the other as they were dragged away in opposite directions.

CHAPTER 56

SOLDIERS OF FORTUNE

Mary Shelton had turned out to be one of the biggest surprises of Rudy's life. The way Jewel always spoke of her mother's family, and how they had always looked down on her father, left him to believe that they weren't the sort of people he would enjoy associating with, but meeting Mary changed his opinion. He imagined that having anyone look down on your dad would leave a bad taste in your mouth, but Jewel obviously found Mary to be the exception, or she wouldn't have sent her a letter before she left for Uganda.

Mary was kind, smart, and above all else, she had money, and it had been her idea from the moment she found out Rudy was a former Navy Seal, to launch their own covert operation to find Grady and Jewel, and get them out. It wasn't a thought that hadn't already occurred to Rudy, but she turned the idea into reality when she started talking. She was a very well educated woman who had a Doctorate in Political Science, was a professor at Colorado State University, and had been on the National Security Council of Ghana during the Clinton presidency. Her husband had been a tycoon in the oil and gas business, and had acquired a massive fortune, all of which was left to her upon his death

It had been nearly a month since they'd been taken, and they weren't getting any information from the State Department beyond pre-approved statements that left them with more questions than answers. They received proof of life photos every week, showing them getting thinner and thinner, their sunken eyes, and Grady's unshaven face, showing the evident hardship of their captivity. Another alarming fact was that the background in the picture was different between Grady and Jewel, and in fact, had been different between Jewel and all the other prisoners, according to the State Department.

The State Department indicated that the Interahamwe were asking for a ransom, but they had been slow to provide any information on how an exchange would take place, obviously being cautious, not wanting to fall into a trap, or were delaying for some other reason. They had also indicated that Congolese soldiers had been in the area near where they thought the prisoners were being held, and this was causing the Interahamwe to have to go deeper into the forest to hideout. There was too much uncertainty, and too few answers, and so they made plans to take matters into their own hands.

"How did you gather information on the Interahamwe without being detected?" Mary asked Rudy, referring to his previous missions during his military career.

"That's the life of a Navy Seal. We use their own guerilla warfare tactics against them, most of which I can't discuss. I need to gather six to eight men, which I think I can do. I know plenty of retirees like myself that I served with at various times," Rudy said as he mentally prepared to do what it was they were getting ready to embark on. He knew that what they were proposing was illegal. He knew if local officials caught them they'd be imprisoned in Uganda, or the Congo, or wherever it was they were. He also knew that he might be interfering with whatever it was, if anything, that the U.S. military was planning, or perhaps even the U.N., but he doubted they had anything in the works to do anything beyond diplomacy at that point.

At first, he thought they were maybe making a mistake, but after Madison had come to spend the weekend with them, he knew they had to try something. Madison's mom was deteriorating fast, her biological father was a hostage in a foreign country, and her dad, Jay, was already making plans for his life after Mandi died, that apparently didn't include Madison, despite the fact that Grady was obviously not there to step in. Madison was beside herself with emotion. She wanted to spend time with her mom, but her mom's condition was far more advanced than anyone knew, and she was quite sick, resolved to die fairly soon. One of the few times they had even seen Madison have a smile on her face that wasn't forced, was when Diana took her on her lap one day, and told her she would always have a home with them.

They had come to understand exactly who Jay was when they found the link between him and Debbie. Some of it was speculation, but most of their information came from Debbie's ex-husband, and they felt his information was reliable. It somewhat explained the mysterious circumstances that surrounded Debbie's pregnancy with Madison, and the subsequent adoption, and it also seemed to explain why Debbie dropped the bomb on Grady the way she did, telling him that Madison was his, perhaps to help Madison in her own little way.

Debbie had arranged the adoption with Jay for a profit. Diana was never able to figure out the relationship between Debbie and Jay, but she suspected that whatever it was, it wasn't good. When Diana and Rudy mentioned to Jay that Madison could live with them until Grady got back, they could see the smile in his eyes as he feigned concern and told them he would think about it, though they knew he would jump on it.

Patrick and Maggie had driven to Wyoming nearly every weekend, wanting to be close to them all. It was a difficult time for all of them with Grady and Jewel missing. They banded together, leaning on each other, and bringing Madison into their inner circle so tightly that it was as if she had always been there, and it was exactly what she needed.

Mary had practically been living in a nearby hotel as they all gathered together and made plans, and her and Maggie had hit it off so well that they were practically inseparable, talking nearly every day, whether in person or by phone.

"Yer nothin' like what we were expectin' of Jewel's family," Maggie said one day when they were all sitting around together discussing things.

"Well… in hindsight I would have to say that it was pretty foolhardy of us all to be so adamantly against Eleanor marrying Alex. Eleanor just had this way about her," she said as she looked out toward heaven to pull her memories back to her. "She had this gravitational pull and nobody could resist her. She was fantastic! Everyone wanted to be near her. She had these piercing blue eyes that you could look into for days… the same one's Jewel has. She graduated from high school when she was sixteen and immediately went to college to get a degree in history, but she could have been anything she wanted, and she could have had anyone she wanted. Unfortunately, the one she wanted wasn't who everyone thought she should want, and that caused a rift that was handled poorly. Her mom and dad told her every chance they got that Alex wasn't good enough for her, which just caused her to distance herself from them, and it sure didn't endear Jewel to them. Jewel adored her dad, and anyone who dared say anything bad about him was her immediate enemy, and she didn't want anything to do with them."

"Well, she must have thought ya were different then," Patrick had said.

"Eleanor was my best friend growing up. It never mattered to me who she married. I loved her all the same. I wish I had made a greater effort to visit her more often. I always planned to, but then one day… well… it was too late," she said shrugging sadly. "I tried reaching out to Jewel after the accident, but she didn't want any part of it. I think she was just too heartbroken. I guess this is my way of making up for not trying harder."

If Mary was trying to make up for it, she was doing a good job. Rudy and Mary both used everything they could think of to gain an advantage. Mary used her diplomatic connections, and Rudy called all the retired men he knew to get a team put together. They discussed the cost of the operation in detail, but Mary didn't seem to care about that. She was prepared to spend any amount of money, but Rudy made sure to be a good steward, and not take advantage of the seemingly bottomless pit of funds at his disposal.

Rudy knew the mission was going to be far more dangerous than anything he had ever done when he was in the military, mostly because he didn't have the force of the U.S. government behind him, and this operation wasn't sanctioned, though he suspected that some of the operations he had been on previously, weren't exactly sanctioned either.

The first person Rudy called was Grady's friend Jared. He was the man who was supposed to have been with them in the Alaskan Wilderness Competition before coming down with the flu, which led them to the bar where they met Jewel. Jared was a former Green Beret, and he remembered hearing that he had spent quite a bit of time in this part of Africa. Jared never hesitated. He had been following the news, and the idea of going in himself had occurred to him on several occasions already.

His next call was to Sam, who was a man he had served with throughout the whole second half of his career. They had spent so much time together, and worked together so well, they could practically read each other's minds. Sam was his counterpart, and he knew without a doubt, he could be counted on in the most difficult situations.

Mary had a man that she knew through means that were apparently secret, but he agreed to go in, and they needed him. Sam was able to get one other he knew who was retired, and Jared was able to find a man that was willing to go in for a price. They all agreed they needed him, and Mary agreed to pay him what he wanted. He was a soldier of fortune who had only spent six years in the military before heading off in his own direction, working in the Middle East to provide security for private American corporations. He had also spent quite a bit of time in Somalia and Rwanda, which was relatively close to Uganda, and they thought he would have some insight into local customs and geography.

A meeting was set up where they could all get together and finalize plans. They weren't ready to launch, but they were gaining ground.

CHAPTER 57

THE COMPOUND

Jewel's spirits plummeted. Taban had taken her to live at his house, though she preferred to think of it as a compound, or a prison. It was an enormous mansion, beautifully and ornately decorated with the finest furniture she had ever seen. The house itself was probably ten thousand square feet or more, and the grounds spread out for hundreds of acres. There were multiple outlying buildings, an Olympic sized pool, tennis courts, and even putting greens. It was not the home of a militiaman that was trying to stay low-key, and not bring attention to himself. It was the home of someone who worked for the government, because in that part of the world, Jewel knew, the only people who lived outside of poverty were the corrupt government officials who were keeping them there, living off foreign aid, courtesy of the American taxpayer.

She had her own very luxurious bedroom. She was able to bathe, eat, and was encouraged to wear the elegant clothes that were provided to her, though she preferred to wear her own torn and shabby clothing, keeping them washed out so she could. Practically anything she could ever want was at her disposal, everything that is, except Grady. She asked about him, but was given the same answer every time she did.

"He is well," Taban would say to her. Taban had apparently brought her there to be his personal nurse. She attended to him daily, administering his medications, monitoring his vitals, and caring for the men in his charge that stood guard at the compound. Taban lived there, and people treated him as if he were a king, leaving Jewel to wonder exactly who Taban was. Her first thought was that he was a military commander of some sort, and she suspected she was no longer in Uganda, but she couldn't be sure. Nobody would talk to her about such things, and she dared not attempt to ask again. One day, she asked a bunch of questions to one of the maids, but later on that evening when they were at dinner, Taban warned her that he had ears everywhere and loyalty was central to his command. When he spoke, he sent a message through the fierceness of his eyes that spoke a language of their own. It was a universal language that could not be mistaken, and Jewel heeded the warning.

Each night when Taban was at the compound, he would send for Jewel to eat dinner with him. They would sit together at a fairly long dining room table, formally set with fine china, crystal, and sterling silverware. She was expected to be dressed for the occasion, wearing one of the many long evening gowns that had been provided to her, complete with shoes and jewelry. She wasn't exactly up on fashion, but as she looked at herself in the full length mirror that was placed in her room, she suspected the complete ensemble she was wearing that evening likely cost more than her college tuition. Her first reaction had been to refuse dinner with Taban, but she knew that wouldn't be wise. She also knew that she needed the time with him if she were going to learn anything about Grady.

Taban made for interesting conversation as it turned out, though Jewel knew that nothing that came out of his mouth was by accident. He was always trying to get her into a political discussion where she would have to choose sides or support his ideas, but she skillfully managed to plead ignorance, despite being fairly well informed about local politics. She would simply brush it off, and tell him she didn't know anything about any of it. She even used a line she had heard in a movie once, when a woman was trying to stop a man from hounding her saying, "politics is such a messy business. I don't pay attention." It was a line only a woman could get away with, since it was largely expected in that part of the world that women weren't capable of following politics anyway, and so she chose to use the man's chauvinistic tendencies against him.

The rest of her days were spent in her room, or she spent them caring for the soldiers in the compound who needed medical treatment. There was a room at the compound that was set up much like an outpatient medical treatment center, complete with every kind of tool, gadget, and medical supply imaginable, and Jewel couldn't help but wonder why they would have raided their cargo plane, or held them for ransom, when they had all of that at their disposal. Surely, the compound alone was worth more than all the money they would get if all the ransoms were paid, but then it occurred to her that Taban was likely wearing two hats. She suspected that whatever position he held that allowed him to live there like a king, was in complete contrast to what he was trying to accomplish through his involvement with the Interahamwe. She guessed that his public position that was likely funded by whatever government he represented, was simply a front. His true loyalties were something different altogether, and he had to find other ways to fund those efforts.

She was given an array of swimsuits, and she was encouraged to spend time at the pool, but had so far managed to make enough excuses to keep from having to go down there half-naked to lie on a lounge chair next to her captor. The last thing she wanted was to bring attention to herself. She knew that he was attracted to her, occasionally making suggestive comments, but overall he was being respectful, and she didn't want to encourage anything beyond that.

One day, guards came to her room early in the morning. She was already up drinking coffee, praying over and over for Grady and the other prisoners. Her heart was aching thinking of the squalid conditions he was living in, wondering if he had kept up with the exercises to stay strong, as she had. She pleaded with Taban one night over dinner to make sure the prisoners were given more food, refusing to eat her own meal, and Taban said he would send word to make sure they were given more rations. Despite having all the food she wanted, she was still losing weight. Eating was laborious. Stress always caused her to eat less and lose weight. She tried to force one bite after another into her, but it was difficult to get it down.

"You need to come," the guard said.

She gathered herself together and followed him to the medical treatment room. The surprise of what she saw caused her near paralysis for a few seconds, until her brain could process the scenario without jumping to conclusions, assuming the worst. The young man, and one of the young girls who had been at the prison encampment, were lying on cots in the medical room. At first, they looked dead, but a quick check was able to confirm they each had a pulse, though they were faint. They had lost so much weight that their skeletons inside of them were outlined in their pale skin.

Jackie and Lukas, she thought, trying to remember their names.

They were conscious, but unresponsive. They were both severely dehydrated, and her heart sank wondering about Grady's condition. Jewel suspected they had been suffering from intestinal parasites that were causing them to have diarrhea and vomiting, which was making them dehydrated and emaciated. Her first thought was to start an IV drip on both of them. She fished through all the supplies that she had at her disposal, knowing exactly where everything was, as she had previously gone through everything and rearranged things, as she would have done in Balad.

Getting the IV's in took several tries each. They were so dehydrated their veins were small, and made it difficult to get anything started. She needed to get fluids into them before she attempted to inject any medicines in them. Their clothes were filthy, and they reeked of human feces. Jewel decided to cut their clothes away from them, and sponge them off as best she could. One of the women who worked in the house was there to assist her, and they both had to stop themselves from throwing up, because the stench was strong as they cut their clothes away. Once they had removed all the clothes, they were able to wash their bodies and get them wrapped in clean blankets. They even managed to wash their hair to a certain extent, and cut away a good portion of Lukas's beard, as it was full of dirt and debris, some of which was likely his own vomit.

Jackie and Lukas simply just laid there unable to move under their own power. They were weak, and their bodies had broken down, teetering on the edge between life and death. Jewel suspected that neither one of them would have lasted another day if they hadn't been brought there to be treated. At that point, it was a matter of rehydration that would save their lives, along with some anti-viral and anti-parasitic medicines that she wasn't completely up to speed with, but she knew she had to try everything she could to make them better.

Within a couple hours after she started the IV drip, they both started to come around enough to open their eyes or moan in pain, which was a good sign. Pain was a sign of life. She knew that just the simple matter of being clean, and lying in clean blankets without being suffocated by a horrendous stench, was medicinal. She stayed with them every second, all day, and all night, refusing to leave when the guards came to get her for dinner with Taban. She worried about that for a while, wondering if there would be repercussions, but she decided she could rest easy when one of the guards brought her dinner down to her, as ordered by Taban himself.

She carefully combed out their hair, getting rid of the lice they were infested with, and she knew that Grady was likely covered in lice, and was probably miserable. She shaved away the hair under both of their arms, applying medicine to kill the lice eggs that she may have missed. She also tended to the messy business of cutting and shaving away hair to remove the lice that had infested their private parts. It wasn't something that ever bothered her. She remembered some of the other nurses snickering or feeling embarrassed to have to tend to someone's private parts, but to her, it was just part of the job. She just hoped she didn't find herself infested with lice later on.

Several days after they were first brought to the compound, they started to come to life. They were rehydrated and the medications were doing their job, and before long, they were able to eat bland foods and drink chicken broth, slowly regaining their strength. Jewel went to ask about Grady, but Lukas said he was given strict instruction not to talk to Jewel about the other prisoners. He said he could only say that the rest of them were okay, and then he quickly diverted his eyes, which left Jewel in a lurch, as she suspected that that was not the case at all.

"That's it!" she said when she was brought into the dining room one evening to eat with Taban. "I need to know about the welfare of my husband."

"You husband is dead," he said angrily before getting up to leave the room, leaving her standing there in her long evening dress, not sure whether to run after him and ply him for more answers, or drop to her knees and crumble. She decided on the former, though the guards quickly stopped her. They dragged her away to her room, where she was piled into a heap on her bed feeling broken and hopeless.

"Be very careful ma'am," one of the guards cautiously warned her before leaving her room. "Da doctor dat ask too many questions is disappeared."

She broke down and cried uncontrollably, letting all the feelings she had carefully stuffed down below the surface, bubble up and overflow, threatening an all-out flood of emotions she was sure she would drown in. She cursed herself for coming up with the idea to leave their perfect life in Wyoming to go to Uganda, where there was any number of threats that could end their happiness, most of which they had already faced. She didn't want to believe it, but the feeling in the pit of her stomach told her it was true. The look in Lukas's eyes the second before he diverted them, and the way that Jackie refused to even look at her, told her everything she didn't want to believe.

CHAPTER 58

___

"I AM WANT TO BE FREE."

The first night without Jewel engulfed the group of prisoner's in a dark cloud of pessimism. She had been the one who was always looking out for each of them, checking them for signs of health problems, or offering them each comfort. She was always offering them words of hope through the written outline of letters that she traced on their forearms. Having one of them ripped from the group so abruptly, was a stark reminder of just how defenseless they were against these men. They knew the rebels could take them out and kill them at any time, and just knowing that, made it difficult to have any hope at all.

Bryer, one of the older men, was a Baptist minister that had been traveling to Uganda as part of a larger missionary group, but had needed to take a later flight, hoping to meet up with his group later on. He led them all in prayer each day, morning, and then evening, which was their one act of defiance. They would gather in a circle holding hands, the reverend leading them through prayer with a loud boisterous voice, breaking the no talking rule, and Grady was surprised to see some of the rebels gather around their hut and listen, and perhaps even to say a few silent prayers of their own. Reverend Bryer would ask God to forgive the rebels, and he would pray loudly for their safe release. At first, a couple of the non-religious prisoners would not participate, but they started to come around, grasping at possibilities. Human instinct dictated the need to do what they could to survive, and sometimes that meant putting your life in a higher power, grasping at anything that would give them hope.

They continued their daily exercise routines, wanting to keep their strength up, and the rebels started giving them more meal rations that helped slow their pace of weight loss. Grady watched as Jackie and Lukas continued to deteriorate, refusing to participate with the exercises, slowly breaking down before his eyes. At first, he thought it was pure hard-headedness, but he realized there was more to it. They were both sick with something, and he notified Kinyera of this one day after Lukas became so sick he was unable to even make it to the woods to relieve himself, having soiled in his own pants.

Grady became a liaison between the prisoners and the rebels, communicating with the rebels through Kinyera. Kinyera and Grady would often sit and talk for long periods of time, when one day after another, Kinyera would go get him to look after Hassan since Jewel was gone. He had kept up the illusion that he was somehow trained in medicine, fumbling one day to give Hassan his last shot of antibiotics, doing everything exactly the way he remembered Jewel doing them.

Grady and Kinyera had developed a certain amount of respect for each other. Grady could tell there was a lot more to Kinyera than just a young rebel soldier. He was very curious about America, asking him specific questions about day-to-day life, and constantly asking Grady to describe American things. His favorite things to hear about were the amusement parks where families would go to ride on scary roller coasters, and indulge themselves with ice cream and cotton candy. Grady couldn't help but think that Kinyera would be an American success story given half the chance. He was curious and eager to learn, and despite his current position as an armed rebel leader in one of the fiercest terrorist organizations in the world, he was not without compassion.

Grady watched him wrestle with his situation, and he knew without a doubt that Kinyera knew that what he was doing was wrong. Kinyera saw beyond his lack of education, into a world where there was hope and possibility. Grady suspected that whoever Kinyera's family had been before, had ingrained something in him that the Interahamwe could never take from him completely. There was goodness in Kinyera that ran deeper than the indoctrination imposed on him by his brother Hassan, and the other Interahamwe leaders.

One day though, Kinyera turned on him and took him to a nearby hut, away from the others, bound in chains. Mugabo, one of the rebels, beat him so severely that he was left there in a heap on the floor, covered in his own blood. They kept asking him questions about his military training, and before Grady could answer, another blow would come at him, and he could do nothing to fight back, having his hands tied behind him, and his legs bound together. The brutality of the beating sent a shockwave through the other hut where the prisoners were held. The man who had administered the beating was the same young man that had nearly gunned them all down that first day when Grady grabbed Jewel's hand. He seemed to relish the opportunity to inflict pain. Grady could see it in his eyes when he reveled in the anger that fueled him. It was only after Kinyera finally insisted on stopping, that the young man finally relented and backed off.

Kinyera came to the prisoners hut one day and announced to them that he, Mugabo, and one other rebel soldier named Simon, were going to take Jackie, Lukas, and Grady somewhere for medical treatment, leaving Hassan in charge, despite his obvious drug addiction that left him completely incapacitated most of the time. This announcement sent a chill through each of them. Kinyera was the only stable and reasonable person in that rebel group, and the prisoners knew it. Hassan was a wildcard that would get high and drink to excess, often using the prisoners for his own amusement. One such day, Hassan had taken one of the prisoners, and made him balance things on his head that Hassan could use for target practice. When the man finally broke down crying, falling to the ground, Hassan simply laughed and ordered the other rebels to take him back to the hut.

Jackie and Lukas were carried out of the hut, and practically poured into the back of a jeep. Grady thought they were both dead. Their bodies had deteriorated beyond recognition. They had lost a bunch of weight, and neither one of them were strong enough to even open their eyes. They smelled horrible, and Grady knew they had been lying there in their own filth and puke for several days. He thought it was just a matter of time before they were dead, if they weren't already. He had also been loaded into the back of the jeep, and it was all he could do to stop from puking as the stench from the two of them filled the air.

Grady had bled profusely from the lacerations on his lips and a bloodied nose, and he was limping from all the bruising inflicted by Mugabo as he laid on the ground defenseless, taking one blow after another. His ribs ached, and he hoped they weren't broken. He was determined not to show them how much pain he was in.

They drove for hours, going at a very slow pace before stopping for the night to set up camp. "Do not look so well or you will have no need of medical attention," Kinyera whispered to him as he led him to the woods the next morning to do his business.

It was then that Grady understood why it was Kinyera had suddenly turned on him. He was trying to get him to wherever it was they were holding Jewel. His heart started racing, sending a wave of hope through him that was electric. He suddenly felt stronger, even as he bent over and limped more, acting the part of someone who was in dire need of medical care, as he made his way in, and then out of the forest.

When he came back from the forest, he made his way to the jeep where Jackie and Lukas laid in a heap, unable to move. He scooped water out for each of them, putting it to their lips, knowing that what they needed was far beyond what he was able to offer, but still, he had to try. Jackie's lips parted instinctively, taking in some of the water, and that gave Grady hope, but Lukas made no movement at all. He used his fingers to pry his mouth open just a little, and he dribbled small amounts of water in his mouth, hoping some of it might reach his body, but he wasn't holding out much hope.

Grady was still dribbling water between Lukas's lips when a fight broke out among the rebels. Mugabo was screaming at Kinyera, and had him down on the ground hitting him in the face.

"You!" Mugabo yelled at Grady. "I know what you two are about, and you will both die!" Mugabo yelled something to Simon, the other rebel with them, who went over to watch over Jackie and Lukas, who needed no watching over, as they were unable to move on their own. Mugabo kicked at Kinyera, and then ordered Grady to come as he held a machine gun to them both. He led them to an abandoned mineshaft, and he ordered them to get on their knees as he came up behind them.

"Follow me," Kinyera whispered to Grady as he kneeled before the bottomless mineshaft that he presumed was his grave. "Do what I do."

A shot fired, and Grady saw Kinyera fall face first into the dirt, causing him a moment of confusion, as he could clearly see that Mugabo had not shot Kinyera. A second later, he heard another shot ring out, and he did as Kinyera told him, falling face first into the dirt despite the fact that he also had not been shot. A second later, he felt the sticky liquid run down his face and knew it at once to be blood. He peered through one eye as he watched Mugabo pour the substance on Kinyera, as he laid there as if dead and he closed his eyes, pretending to be dead and do as Kinyera told him.

Just then, Simon came running toward them having heard the shots. Grady couldn't understand them, but it appeared that Mugabo was explaining himself to Simon. Grady laid there as still as he could as the rebel kicked him in the side that was already sore from his beating several days earlier. Mugabo pointed toward the camp, directing Simon to go back to check on the other prisoners as he finished up.

A moment later, he felt Kinyera grab his arm. "Come!" he whispered, grabbing Grady's arm as they ran toward an embankment that was about thirty yards away. Grady saw Mugabo standing there, and he saw the quick exchange that occurred between Kinyera and Mugabo as they nodded to each other before they ran off.

They hid behind the embankment, and they watched as Mugabo kicked dirt around, screaming into the air, clearly putting on some kind of show. Simon ran back to where Mugabo was, still yelling and screaming angrily, and the two of them peered down into the mineshaft while Mugabo explained what he had done with the bodies. Grady peered sideways at Kinyera who just shrugged, putting his fingers to his lips to remain quiet.

It was later, as they made their way to a pre-arranged location to meet up with a few other men, when Kinyera explained what had just happened.

"Mugabo truly is my brother. We came to Hassan together. He is not so bad as he pretends. He will do as I say. My mother is his mother. My father is his father. Dis I know."

Mugabo was Kinyera's younger brother, and had only been five when Hassan and his men took them. Kinyera thought that his parents were moderate Hutu's, which is why the Hutu's had taken them, feeling that they belonged to them given their Hutu bloodline, and as punishment for being moderates.

"Kinyera. Won't it be suspicious that your little brother killed you? Don't you think that will make people question if we were really killed by Mugabo?" Grady asked.

"No. Mugabo will share dis killing with Simon. Simon will take full responsibility by tomorrow. This is Simon."

"Why are you helping me?" Grady finally asked.

"There had been a man asking about American's dat were taken hostage. Taban know dis, and he will not let you woman go. He will keep her. He has a weakness that make him crazy. Dat is the woman. I have seen dis."

"What are you saying? What man has been asking about hostages?" Grady asked trying to follow along with Kinyera's logic that he felt had skipped over much of the vital information.

"Dis man try to find da hostages. Dis is why you woman was taken. Taban will not let her go. He will kill the hostages if he must. I will help them, but I must get you to dis man. You must tell him to stop asking question. I will help you find you woman," Kinyera answered.

"But why? Why are you helping us?" Grady prodded once again.

"Taban he has two face. I am used. Mugabo is used. We soil our lives as he live like a king and den betray us for da woman. Taban is Congolese General. Taban is Interahamwe General. He live two lives. He will kill da hostages. He will kill me and Mugabo, and everyone to have what he want. He want da woman."

"So by helping me, you're also helping yourself?"

"I think maybe you can help me," he shrugged. "I am want to be free."

They made their way to a small hut where there were two other men waiting for them. Grady was still healing from his beating, but the adrenaline he was feeling was fueling him, and he fought through the pain, eyeing Kinyera as he went to sit down, favoring his ribs that were screaming at him.

"I am sorry for dat," Kinyera said seeing him wince. "Dis was da only way to get you out. When I say to Mugabo he must beat you, he say no. He say you are too big. When he came to do it, he say he must hit hard or you will beat him. He would only do if I tie you hands."

"It's alright," Grady said, nodding at him, grateful for the beating that led to the place where hope could still exist.

Grady watched as the men made plans, talking among themselves in their own language. He wanted to be included in the plans, or at least know what they were talking about, but he couldn't understand their language, so he simply had to try to follow along, and wait until Kinyera could explain further.

"I am dead. You are dead. I am black, and easy to hide. You are not," Kinyera explained. "I take dese men, and we find da man who look for the hostages to bring here. You will wait."

"Do you know where Jewel is?" Grady asked hopefully.

"Yes. She is at the General's Mansion where the two sick ones go," Kinyera answered. "If I had let you be taken there, Taban would have killed you. You would be dead."

"So ya had me beaten, so I would get taken somewhere for treatment, where I would certainly be killed, only ta fake my death, covering me in God only knows whose blood, and then you bring me to an abandoned hut where I am ta wait until ya bring a strange man ta meet me?" Grady said, summing it up with a hint of a smile on his face, looking at Kinyera seriously.

"Yes. Dis is true," Kinyera answered, shrugging with a little smile of his own, "and it is only the blood of a pig," he said, as if it were perfectly natural to be covered in pig's blood.

CHAPTER 59

THE MILITARY MEN

Rudy was making progress. He had decided that the best course of action was to send Sam into the Congo to meet with a man that was a connection Mary had in the region. There had been talk about the hostages taken in Uganda, which gave them an idea of what region they were in, but Mary's connection was unwilling to discuss anything over the phone. Sam was the most logical choice to go in, because he had spent the most time in that region, was an expert in African affairs, and had specific expertise on the Interahamwe. It also helped matters that Sam was black, making him less obvious walking around, and Rudy trusted him completely. Sam was probably the one person, outside his only family, that he trusted the most. He was smart, and he was one of the most capable people he had ever known. He had put his life in his hands on numerous occasions.

Sam was an expert when it came to gathering intelligence, and not, necessarily, because he had been well trained. He had the kind of personality that made people open up to him. He would question people without them ever realizing he was gathering information from them. Sam was small, and wiry. He had a tendency to blend in and go unnoticed, unless he wanted people to notice him. He came off as kind of goofy, never giving anyone cause to think he was anything other than just some fun, goofy little guy that you could pal around with, and have fun.

Rudy also decided to send two men into Uganda to go and meet with Margaret Johnson. They knew she had some information, but given the evasive nature of their conversation with her over the phone, they figured she was afraid to say what she wanted to say. Jared, and Mary's friend Terri, were chosen to go into Uganda. Rudy wanted to go, but he knew that it made the most sense for him to stay in Tanzania, where they had set up headquarters for planning the mission, so he could lead the operation.

Jared had been a Green Beret in the Marines, and he was one of Grady's good friends. He was a quiet man, but when he talked, people listened. What he did have to say was usually either very smart, or very funny, once you understood his dry sense of humor. He was about six foot six inches tall, had sandy blond hair, and hazel

426

eyes. He had worn a full beard since leaving the military, and looked like a man who had spent his life playing defense in the NFL. He had a thick, stocky build, and large muscular hands. The only time Rudy had ever seen Jared falter, was when he came down with the flu in Alaska, and he knew that Jared was looking forward to making it up to them, though he also knew that his sickness had led to one of the greatest adventures of their lives.

Terri was quite possibly the nerdiest person Rudy had ever laid eyes on. He was small and wore thick, square glasses that made his eyes look walleyed. He wore a white, button-down shirt with it buttoned up all the way to the top, complete with a pocket protector, and he wore pants that couldn't have been yanked up another inch without splitting him two. In his entire military career, Rudy had never met anybody who looked less able to be a member of the military. If he hadn't known better, he would have placed odds that the man wouldn't have been able to run across the street, let alone survive basic training. It didn't take long to figure out where his strengths were though. Terri was a walking encyclopedia. He knew everything he had ever read, and he had read everything extensively. He was a secret weapon that nobody would ever be expecting. He was a medical doctor, and also held two degrees in engineering with a minor in bioscience, and an honorary doctorate from Stanford University. He was an expert in counter-intelligence, was a weapons expert, spoke six different languages, and was working on seven as he sat studying the Kinyarwanda language while they planned their mission.

They had set-up a fairly extensive communication center in a hotel that was a tourist spot in Tanzania along Lake Victoria. Mary and Rudy were posing as newlyweds, so they could room together, and direct the operation from the comfort of their hotel room without having to go out much and draw attention to themselves. Pretending to be married wasn't difficult since Mary and Rudy had an instant connection from the first time they met. It wasn't a romantic connection. They simply shared an interest in each other, and Rudy enjoyed hearing about the rest of Jewel's family. The rest of the men were either posing as typical male tourists that came to Tanzania to partake in the guided hunting tours and the red light district, or were pretending to be there on some sort of official corporate business.

Rudy had employed a system of communication that would allow the men to be able to call each other, and provide information, without using any of the key words that would bring attention to their operation. As former military men that had been involved in many different secret operations, they all knew that there were ears everywhere. Someone was always listening. There were certain words that had certain meanings, and when used with another key word, it meant something entirely different. It was a system they were all familiar with using.

A corporation that didn't exist had leased the cell phones they were using, and they couldn't be traced back to any of them. They had all altered their appearances, and each wore clothes they wouldn't normally wear. They had all taken different paths to get there, arriving separately, and at different times. The fake passports and the identifications Mary was able to put together for them were ordinary, and would bring the attention of nobody. Rudy was grateful to have them. He knew that the sudden arrival of six ex-military men, who had retired with high security clearances in various branches of the United States military, would have raised some eyebrows.

Thames and Doug were the other two men who made up the team of six. Thames was someone Sam had known, and Doug was the soldier for hire that Jared had contacted. Overall, Rudy was pleased with the men he had been able to find for the insane mission they were about to embark on. They were all professional, well rounded, and had skills that could only be understood by those who had served in the military.

Thames was ordinary when you first looked at him. He had soft brown hair and brown eyes, a medium build, and stood just under six foot tall. He looked like a man who would have sold insurance or worked in a bank, never experiencing anything more exciting than an occasional traffic altercation on his way to his regular nine to five job. In reality, Thames was completely crazy. He never took anything seriously, until it was time to be serious. He had retired as a Lieutenant Colonial in the Marines, and that was only because he had been diagnosed with lung cancer and lymphoma, and had been given six months to live. He had gone into the doctor with a lump in his throat, and before he knew it, his whole life was turned upside down. He decided to live out the last months of his life doing the few things left on his bucket list. That was five years ago. The diagnosis had been a misdiagnosis. The lump was easily removed with surgery, followed up with some chemotherapy to kill anything they may have missed. The lung cancer had never existed, though the decision to retire had been one of the best decisions of his life. He was crossing things off his bucket list that he had forgotten was even on there.

Rudy sent Thames to Amsterdam with a backpack and a camera, wearing khaki shorts and a t-shirt. He couldn't have looked more like a typical American tourist if he had tried. His mission was to take a bike out, appearing to be lost as he surveyed the warehouse where Grady and Jewel had been before they left Amsterdam, looking for any signs of nefarious activity. It wasn't the warehouse itself that he was watching, it was the activity surrounding the warehouse they were most interested in. Thames was to become the man spying on those who were spying on the warehouse, hoping to gather clues that could lead them to the hostages.

Doug was sort of an anomaly in the group. He had only spent six years in the military, but had an extensive background all over the world as hired military grade security. He looked like a stereotypical person you would expect to see in the military, as portrayed by Hollywood. He had a thick neck, and his muscular arms were covered in tattoos. His hair was crew cut, and his chest was barreled. He walked with clenched fists, and always looked like he was getting ready to fight someone. He was about five foot ten inches tall, had light blue eyes that seemed to soften the rough exterior, and he often surprised people who first met him when he would pull off his dark glasses to expose them.

Rudy had no doubt that Doug was well qualified, but what he wasn't sure of was his loyalty. A man who only worked for money, could always be bought. He would go into the Congo separately from Sam, and watch from afar, essentially keeping eyes on Sam to make sure he wasn't being trailed. What Doug didn't know is that Terri was diverted from his trip to Uganda to watch over Doug. Rudy needed to know if he could trust him, and he quickly learned that Terri had the ability to change appearance so dramatically, that Doug would never be able to recognize him. Mary trusted Terri completely, despite the vagueness as to the extent of their relationship, and that told him everything he needed to know about him. If Mary trusted him, then Rudy trusted him.

It hadn't taken Sam long to come back with information after they sent him to the Congo. Everyone had been talking about the hostages that were being held by the Interahamwe, though everybody claimed to know nothing. Sam met with the connection Mary had set him up with, and Sam's immediate reaction was that the man couldn't be trusted, for the simple fact that he appeared to be operating under a cloud of fear. Fear, he knew, could make even the most loyal and trustworthy men, unpredictable, and unreliable.

He had also been able to find out some information about some encampments that the Interahamwe were said to hold, which gave them some leads on some locations that were consistent with what they had already believed. They had been getting a steady stream of information from Sam right up until he disappeared, and though Doug appeared to know nothing about Sam's disappearance, Terri knew everything.

Rudy immediately decided to use that to his advantage. He knew the only thing that was equal to having good intelligence, was feeding the enemy misinformation that allowed him to predict their next move. He suddenly felt like a puppet master, and he realized that having Doug working for the other side, couldn't have worked out more perfectly. He decided to play along and not let Doug know that he knew anything. He would treat Doug no differently, but he knew it was going to be the greatest acting of his entire life.

CHAPTER 60

HIDING IN GOMA

"Fuck me!" Sam exclaimed loudly when Kinyera and his men dragged him into the hut, and he was finally able to see his captors and speak. He had been gagged, had a bag placed over his head, and his hands and legs had been tied together. "Holy shit! You're Grady then?" he asked suddenly, seeing Grady standing before him.

"I am. It's all right," Grady said trying to calm Sam, who looked like he was planning his escape. "Who are you?"

"I'm Sam. Rudy and Mary organized a group of men to get you and Jewel out of here. I served with Rudy in the military. I must be losing my touch," he said studying his captors.

"You were not so easy. We had luck on our side," Kinyera said.

"I knew it!" Grady said smiling. "I knew that man would do something, but who's Mary?"

"Ugh… your wife's aunt I think?" Sam said shrugging. "I don't know, but the woman has more money than God."

"Who is da tattoo man who follow you?" Kinyera asked him.

"Doug. He's with us… but… well, I'm not too sure about him."

"You should not trust him. He had already betray you," Kinyera said shaking his head. "He is a very bad man."

"I figured. The bastard!" Sam said shaking his head. "Where's the other hostages? Where's your wife?"

Grady and Kinyera told him all they knew. He had heard many stories of Sam over the years. He knew Rudy trusted him beyond a doubt, and he knew that he could trust him as well. He could see why Rudy always talked so fondly of him. He liked him immediately, but for the life of him, he couldn't figure out how in the world this goofy guy was going to help them find Jewel, until he turned the switch and started getting serious.

Suddenly, Sam became calculating and analytical, dissecting every bit of information they gave him, as he questioned Kinyera and his men, filling in the pieces of the puzzle the team had speculated about. They discussed multiple options, with Kinyera and his men adding information about the region that would help them or hurt them, depending on the approach they took for a rescue attempt.

Kinyera's men were Joseph and Olivier who had previously fled the entrapment of the Interahamwe. They had been taken as child soldiers when they were relatively older... Joseph around the age of eleven, and Olivier around the age of thirteen. They had finally escaped over a year ago to make it back to their homes in Uganda, only to find that the Interahamwe had murdered their parents, and many of the other people from their town. They returned to find burned houses and buildings, and nothing left of their homes they had longed to return to for so long. It was Kinyera's relationship with these two that had led him to believe that it would be possible for him to leave one day as well, though he knew that his two friends were far from being free. As Interahamwe soldiers, they had carried out robberies, murders, kidnappings, and various other atrocities. Authorities in Uganda, Rwanda, and the Congo wanted them both. Their freedom consisted of living under the cover of darkness, hiding in one abandoned house after another, and living on a diet that consisted of sparse amounts of bread and water that they were able to steal, and small animals they hunted.

As Grady listened, his immediate thought was that they needed two teams. They needed one team to go in and rescue the hostages at the encampment, and they needed another team to go get Jewel, Jackie, and Lucas, and they needed both rescue attempts to happen simultaneously.

"Are you saying that Jewel is being held at General Taban Kayibanda's house in the Congo?" Sam asked incredulously. "This is bigger than any of us," he said shaking his head.

"How do you know who he is?" Grady asked, standing before Sam statuesque, showing his resolve and determination.

"Terri. He's one of the guys that's with our crew. He was talking about the General. He knew everything about him, saying he had links to the Interahamwe, though he publicly condemned them. Dammit! I should have listened more closely. We need to make contact with Rudy and tell him we found you, and then come up with a plan," Sam said emphatically.

The hut they were in wasn't in an area where they could make contact, and besides, since they knew Doug was not necessarily on their side, they thought the cell phone they had may be compromised. They knew that Doug would easily translate the code words they had come up with if he were to get that deep into his betrayal, and make meaningful contact with the enemy.

Kinyera and his men knew ways of getting ahold of secure cell phones that nobody could trace. They decided to make their way to a house they knew of that was on the outskirts of the city of Goma where they had snatched Sam from. The house was hidden among the congestion of the city, and it would be a good place for them to hideout. It was a place Mugabo and Kinyera had talked about taking Grady when they planned their escape. Nobody went there without Mugabo's consent.

They knew they'd be safe there, and Taban's compound was also just outside of the city. The hideout would bring them closer to one of their targets.

They headed out toward the city, and Sam and Grady rode in the back of the jeep with Grady covered up with a tarp so no attention would come to him. Grady's appearance could not be concealed until they got to the safe house, so for the time being, they simply had to keep him hidden. A rather large, blond-haired, blue-eyed man would stick out like a sore thumb. Kinyera shaved his head, and switched clothes with Sam to change his appearance, much to Sam's dismay since Kinyera's clothes smelled like they had never seen a bar of soap, but he was a team player, and they had to do what they could to stay under cover.

They made their way to the safe house, and Grady was relieved to get out from under the tarp. It was hot out, and he was getting anxious. The house was a small one-bedroom house that looked like it had been built a thousand years ago, but had likely only been standing there for fifty years or so. It was unpainted and falling down, and the inside was furnished with a mish-mash of couches and chairs that were all being held together by their last thread. There was no electricity or running water, but it was a huge step up from the hut Grady waited in earlier, and he was grateful to be there to start making plans, and get in touch with Rudy.

He needed to have Kinyera go out and find him some clothes and other items he would need to change his appearance, so that he could come out from the shadows, and find his wife. Kinyera agreed to find some clothes for him, get some food, and find the s_cure phones. The Interahamwe had many connections they used to scramble phones, and although Kinyera was thought to be dead to most of his connections, there were some out there that he knew would help him keep his cover.

"Sam. I think you should get on a plane and head back to Tanzania. Meet with Rudy and tell him everything that's going on, and then have him call me on one of the phones that Kinyera comes back with," Grady said as they sat back and waited for Kinyera to return. "That's the only way we'll be sure nobody's listening. If Taban is the General you say he is, then we're going to have to be extra careful."

Just then, a man came busting through the door, and Grady and Sam jumped back scrambling off the couch they were sitting on to take cover. "Where's the enchilada?" The man asked, surprising Grady as he searched around for a weapon, knowing instinctively that he was the enchilada.

"Terri! Damn man! What the hell are you doing here?" Sam said coming out from his hiding place. "I thought you were in Uganda."

"I'm here for the two of you. I wasn't sure about the other men, so I held back. When I saw them leave, I thought I'd make my move."

"How did you know where we were? We were just talking about me flying back to Tanzania to meet up with Rudy."

"Rudy thought Doug couldn't be trusted, so he sent me to watch him… watch you," Terri said to Sam. "I didn't know who grabbed you at first, so I made the call to follow you instead of him, but he's still checking in with Rudy, so Rudy knows where he's at, or at least he knows whatever it is that Doug's telling him," Terri said.

"Are you communicating with Rudy then?" Grady asked, shaking his hand as they were introduced.

"Yes. Rudy and I worked out our own code, and we have our own secure phones. Let's make a call, shall we?" he said grabbing what looked like a little medical bag, which held his phones and his scrambler. Clearly, the man's cover had been that of a medical doctor, which of course, he actually was a doctor, and could have likely performed brain surgery right then if it meant keeping his cover.

Grady watched as the strange little man made the call, and talked in some nonsensical code they had devised. The man smiled up at him when he mentioned having found some enchilada's for his dinner, and Grady could hear Rudy's voice on the phone, which gave him just enough hope to strengthen his resolve, despite what seemed like an impossibility. When Terri mentioned that he couldn't find any Paisano to complete his meal, Grady frowned. He knew they were talking about Jewel.

Sam and Grady both listened to the conversation with amusement. Terri and Rudy sounded like two men in love who were desperately missing each other. One was a doctor who was in the Congo to volunteer his time providing medical treatment to those less fortunate, and the other was at home patiently waiting for his lover to return. Grady wasn't sure it was the greatest cover, given the fact that most of these countries had a death penalty for homosexuality, but then again, it was a conversation that would certainly be disregarded by anyone who happened to be listening.

"Alright," Terri said preparing to translate the conversation as he hung up the phone. "Rudy and Mary are gathering information about General Taban's compound. It's... well... it's impenetrable. It doesn't look good," Terri said glancing up at Grady reluctantly. "We're going to need to concentrate our efforts on that operation. Do you think Kinyera and his men would help with the other hostages? Is he trustworthy?"

"He saved my life. He's solid, but I don't know about sending him back to the encampment. That would be a certain death sentence for him. Kinyera said he would do anything, but... I don't know. Is there any way we could get him out of here if he agrees to help us?" Grady asked, broadening the operation beyond anything Terri and Rudy had discussed.

"Ummm... maybe? Mary managed to secure all of us fake passports and identifications. There may be something she could do. We're supposed to call them back in the morning. For now we need to hang tight."

Terri continued to translate the coded conversation, and they discussed their options until Kinyera came back with some supplies.

"Black hair dye? Floral shirt? Elastic Waistband? What the hell did ya do

Kinyera, raid yer granny's closet?" Grady said holding up the Hawaiian looking shirt, and the hair dye he handed to him.

"We have to get rid of dat bright hair. You stand out like a giraffe with a sunbeam on da top of his head," Kinyera said dryly, which they suspected was his attempt at a sense of humor.

Grady stood tall among most of the men he had encountered in that part of the world. It surprised him at first, but he remembered reading that the relatively short stature of most of the rebels had to do with poor nutrition. He noticed that many of the men in higher positions, such as Taban, had been rather large, and probably had never suffered without adequate food. It reinforced his belief that many of the young rebels were little more than prisoners themselves… another layer of victims in the endless battle for power.

CHAPTER 61

TOP SECURITY

"Mom's not even dead yet, and you're going out on a date?" Madison said quietly through clenched teeth, her arms folded across her chest to show her contempt.

"It's not exactly a date Mads. You'll understand one day when you're older," Jay said as he hurried around the house getting ready to go out, both of them talking quietly so Mandi wouldn't hear them.

"Are you going out with another woman, or not?" she demanded.

"Technically... ugh... yeah, but... you wouldn't understand Mads. Look!" he said standing before her, squaring himself off in a stance that was meant to intimidate, "I rented you some movies, and I got you a pizza. Go hang out with Mom, and don't make any trouble. Just mind your own business."

"She can't die fast enough for you, can she?" she said immune to his attempt at intimidating her.

"Listen Mads! If you want things to work out, you better just change your tune," he said getting in her face.

"My dad will never let me go. He'll come for me no matter what. He told me so."

"He's dead! You're not going anywhere unless I say."

Madison's eyes grew big, and her heart started pounding in her chest. The look in Jay's eyes was one she was familiar with, and it terrified her. "You don't know anything!" she screamed loudly as she started sobbing uncontrollably.

"In fact, I know everything little girl. I have connections your tiny little brain could hardly even start to grasp, so don't mess with me. If you want to go with Diana when Mom's gone, then you better just keep your mouth shut and play your cards right. Do you hear me?"

"How... how do you know he's dead?" she cried more timidly.

"Because I didn't waste my time in the military taking orders. I spent my time making connections. Some of those connections fly cargo planes to Uganda, and others, well... others can be easily bought. Did you ever stop to wonder why Doug hasn't been around lately?" he said with a smile, knowing that simply saying the man's name was enough of a warning.

"I hate you!" she yelled.

As soon as she heard the name Doug, fear ran through her body. He was a scary man that showed up at the house occasionally. When he showed up, Jay would drop everything, and they would go off in secrecy together. They had served together in the military before they were both dishonorably discharged for using their military connections to run drugs, escaping prosecution on a technicality. They had lost touch for a long while after Jay and Mandi were first married, but had practically been inseparable after starting their business together.

Jay was the kind of guy who liked the idea of living a simple married life in a small town, but he could never stay out of trouble. Making an honest living had always been beyond his abilities. He was too hotheaded, and he would often storm off the job angrily, leaving him unemployed once again, and looking for the next job. He thought he should be able to walk into a company and be the boss. The idea of having to work his way up was unacceptable to him, because he thought he was smarter than everyone else was.

The only thing he ever did right was marrying Mandi. She was the kindest person he had ever met. She always had something nice to say, even when he knew he didn't deserve it. He was drawn to her. He had grown up his whole life being criticized and condemned by his own family, and having someone like Mandi around to point out everything that was good about him, was irresistible. Mandi did her best to get him away from his old haunts in Texas, but trouble was everywhere, and wherever there was trouble, Jay wasn't far behind.

One day, after impulsively walking off yet another job, Jay was sitting at a local rundown bar in Casper trying to come up with another excuse to tell Mandi, when in walked Doug. It was a meeting by chance that would change everything in Jay's life. He would go from scraping by, and constantly letting Mandi down, to being able to provide for her, and become the man she seemed to think he was.

Doug and Jay ended up pulling their resources together by setting up a seemingly legitimate security company in Casper, named Top Security, that offered specialized security services abroad. It was the perfect place for such a business, because Casper was practically nonexistent in the world, and nobody paid them any attention. Had they had the inclination to go around town and start bragging about all their worldwide business adventures, nobody would have believed a word of it. They could fly in and out of Casper in different directions, never leaving behind a consistent path that might draw suspicion. Both of them had contacts through their illegal dealings in the military that allowed them to get their foot in the door with legitimate businessmen, looking to supplement their income by dipping their foot in the very lucrative business of illegal drugs, and so the business began.

Through the years, they expanded their dealings to include kidnap for hire, which always included working both sides of the deal, and then going with the highest bidder. They dealt in small arms that were in demand by smaller guerilla type militias on nearly every continent, which was always profitable. In addition, they dabbled in the very lucrative business of stealing and reselling medical supplies, and humanitarian food stores. The types of activity they would be involved with had very little limitation, and although they had never been directly involved in murder for hire, it wasn't something they would have completely taken off the table, and they had certainly been indirectly involved in several murders already.

Mandi lived under the illusion that her husband had somehow managed to become the C.E.O. of a very profitable security company, and she never seemed to question it, but she did have concerns with some of his associations, and that led to a constant battle in their marriage. She hated Doug and didn't want him anywhere near Madison, but he would constantly show up, and sometimes it was at very odd hours, which gave her cause for alarm. Her long battle with cancer had taken up so much of her time the previous eight years, that she hadn't had time to watch the situation too closely, and this made things easier for Jay.

When Grady told them they were going to Uganda to volunteer at an orphanage, Jay knew from the very first moment, that he was going to find a way to profit from it. These were just the types of opportunities he looked for. Actually knowing someone's full traveling agenda was a rare treat, and it didn't take him long to exploit it, especially when he figured out they would be arranging to get supplies from a warehouse in Amsterdam where he already had people embedded. Doug had flown to the region to meet with some of his contacts, and before long, they made an arrangement that would allow them to keep the majority of all the supplies, and a rebel group would be able to keep the hostages for ransom. This was a much bigger deal than he had ever arranged before, for the simple matter that he would essentially be delivering some very unfortunate souls into the hands of one of the most brutal terrorist organizations in the world.

It was all set. Jay arranged for his men at the warehouse to make sure the most lucrative supplies were on board the plane, including some weapons that were worth millions of dollars. He arranged for the airport security in Mbarara to be absent during a very critical one hour period of time when the cargo plane would land, and he arranged for his buyer to be there at the airport, along with the rebels, to take the supplies in one direction, and the hostages in another. It had been so perfectly orchestrated, and had gone off so smoothly, that Jay couldn't pat himself on the back hard enough.

What he hadn't counted on was Doug's chance encounter with Jared several years earlier that would somehow manage to bring his carefully crafted plan full circle. Jared's understanding of Doug was that he was a soldier of fortune who provided security for oversees corporations and their representatives, and he knew he had first-hand experience in African countries. When Jared was contacted by Rudy to put a team together to go rescue the hostages, his first thought was to get a hold of Doug, and Jay could hardly believe his good fortune.

CHAPTER 62

GRIEF

Jewel had assumed that the absence of her period had been because of the stress of captivity and the harsh conditions of the prisoners hut, but she knew better. She tried to remember when her last period was, narrowing it down well enough to know that she was about three months pregnant. She'd lain in bed rubbing her stomach, praying for the most, but expecting the worst. She was too afraid to tell Taban. She didn't know what he would do if he found out, so she decided to wait.

Taban had subsequently elaborated on Grady's death, and the finality of it had paralyzed her so severely, that she didn't even make it downstairs to check on Lukas and Jackie, deciding instead to have her assistant check on them and report back to her. She had simply laid in bed crying, unable to bathe, unable to move, and had refused to eat, right up until the first bout of morning sickness hit her and she realized she was pregnant.

She thought of her last night with Grady before they were taken hostage, and all the love they shared. She wondered about the baby, praying that this one thing between them would survive. This baby would know that it was conceived from love, even if it would never know its father, she vowed absently, knowing that their future looked bleak. She wondered about her situation, thinking that surely there would be international outrage, and perhaps there could at least be hope for her to return home one day, which only caused her to breakdown once again. She would have emerged from one tomb into another, she realized, when she thought of the home that Grady had built.

She thought of Troy and Jo, and everything that would be lost. She cried for Grady's family, and cursed herself for coming up with the idea to go there. They had been so happy. It all seemed so tragic. She couldn't imagine how she would ever live a normal life again.

Since realizing she was pregnant, she forced herself to eat and look for hope. She was being allowed more and more freedom around the house beyond just her room and the medical room, and she started to look for opportunities to escape. Every part of her wanted to just climb in bed and cry forever... every part, that is, except for the little life growing inside her.

438

CHAPTER 63

ELISE PIERSON

"You look like Tom Selleck from that TV show he used to be on when he was a private investigator," Sam said as Grady made his way out to model his new look for them. He had used the black hair dye to dye the hair on his head, as well as his eyebrows and his very thick mustache that he left behind, shaving away the rest of his beard that had grown during his captivity. They brought in buckets of water so he could get washed and shaved, and he was practically unrecognizable. Grady could hardly believe how different he looked.

"Magnum P.I.," Terri said. "That was the name of the show... probably way before your time," he added, looking at Grady who had no idea what they were talking about.

They were all sitting around, waiting until it was time for them to make the call to Rudy. It had been a sleepless night in the cramped house that was already hot and muggy; add to that, six grown men sweating and snoring, and that left little room for good rest. They sat and snacked on some of the bread that Kinyera had brought them to eat, and drank coffee, watching the clock tick down. Terri was very insistent that they wait until the exact time before making the call, so Rudy would have the scrambler ready. He was mostly worried about Doug at this point.

Terri had gone out late the night before to find Doug and see what he was up to, and what he found was alarming. Doug was meeting with some high ranking officials in the Congolese military, and he worried that Doug may have ties to the General, in which case the General would know that they were there looking for the hostages, which would blow their cover. The two men he met with were fierce looking men dressed in official military uniforms full of patches and medals, and he had no doubt that these men would either have ties to the General, or would be in direct competition with him, which added an extra element of danger.

They finally made the call with Terri, speaking in his nonsensical code again, playing the part of a man who missed his lover. Grady sat as close as he could, excited just to hear Rudy's voice, trying to keep the seemingly romantic nature of the phone call out of his mind as he listened. He was beside himself. He had been pushing the thought of Jewel out of his mind as hard as he could, afraid he would fall into despair if he thought about all the possibilities of everything that could go wrong, but suddenly he felt hopeful. Hearing Rudy's voice gave him the strength that he needed to go find her.

This time when Terri and Rudy spoke, Terri was able to translate as they went, so Grady could interject and participate in the conversation. They learned that the men Doug had met with were plants sent by some connections that Mary had, and their meeting was all about providing Doug with erroneous information that coalition forces were going to be launching an attack on the Interahamwe encampment where the prisoners were being held. Their hope was that Doug would spread this news among his contacts, hoping the Interahamwe would make plans to abandon the hostages and flee the area. They assumed that General Taban already knew about them anyway, so they decided to try and use it to their advantage.

As an added bonus, and what they couldn't have possibly planned on, was that the fake meeting Doug was sent on hadn't gone unnoticed by General Taban's men who were arranging a meeting between Doug and General Taban at a remote location in Uganda. They were finding a way to use Doug to their advantage. Having the General away from the compound was paramount to their plans to go in and get Jewel, because the entourage the General traveled with was extensive, and having him gone from the compound, reduced the armed men they would come up against by half.

Grady assured them all that Jared wouldn't have known about Doug's true nature, or he wouldn't have gotten him involved, which confirmed Rudy's belief that Jared was caught unaware that Doug was just a crook. Rudy had already sent Thames to Uganda to be with Jared after they gathered all the information they needed from the warehouse in Amsterdam, so they would both be there to provide erroneous information to Doug.

Sam would go to Uganda and meet Jared and Thames, who had already confirmed the location of the hostages, arranged for transportation, and picked up all the gear they would need, thanks to the contacts Mary had helped them with. They were certain that once word got out that coalition forces were planning a large-scale raid on multiple Interahamwe encampments, the Interahamwe would release the hostages, not wanting to jeopardize their strongholds. There was also information that they were providing that would allude to a large scale, international task force that would come down heavy on them if the prisoners didn't get out alive. They needed to be there to raid the abandoned prisoner encampment, and get the hostages out as soon as they saw the rebels flee.

Rudy made sure Doug had sufficient information to leave no doubt in the General's mind that this was serious. They had already put together official maps pinpointing all the locations of the Interahamwe encampments, thanks to the input from Kinyera and his men, and Rudy forged some documents that he had seen often enough during his time as a Navy Seal, trying to make everything look official.

Rudy had already heard back from Thames about his meeting with Doug, and they were happy with his reaction after going through all of the official documents.

"So what do we do?" Doug asked as he looked through the documents in disbelief.

"Just sit tight. The raid could happen tomorrow, or it could happen a week or two weeks from now. We just have to wait and see what happens. Rudy doesn't want to leave until we know one way or another. He's still hoping that we'll be able to get Jewel out alive," Thames said, "and he's hoping we might be able to recover Grady's body," he threw in to support Doug's belief that Grady was dead.

The plan to get the hostages out of the encampment was taking shape, but getting the three out of General Taban's compound was going to take more planning. Kinyera was certain that Taban would never let Jewel leave. "He will say she died. He will say she run away. He is crazy like dat for da woman he want. I have seen dis before."

They discussed all that they knew about the compound, which was very little. Mary had been unable to secure any plans for the place. You can turn on the Discovery Channel and get a complete layout of the White House, but General Taban's compound was not so accessible. The drug cartel built it, and they used it as a distribution center for poppy until the Congolese government seized it during a civil war in 1998. The place was said to have multiple underground tunnels, hidden rooms, safes that were impenetrable, and enough food, water and ammunition to sustain five hundred people for up to two years.

It was surrounded by open space, which was the hardest obstacle to overcome, because lookouts could see people coming for miles, which meant that doing something at night was an absolute must. Satellite images showed armed men on guard twenty-four hours a day, seven days a week. It seemed hopeless. The only information they had was from the memory of Kinyera who had gone there several years earlier to clean up a mess after one of General Taban's infatuations came to a bloody end.

They arranged for another meeting time with Rudy, with the time that was given always meaning something other than what they said. After they hung up, Grady simply sat there and hung his head for a minute, not sure where to go from there. He had to find a way to get to Jewel, but the compound was like a prison, and there was no way in and no way out... well... except for the front door.

"Describe what ya know about the compound again Kinyera. Tell me everything. Don't leave out a single detail," Grady said as he found a pen and paper in an attempt to come up with his own drawing.

The next several hours were spent trying to reconstruct a drawing by retrieving small bits of information from Kinyera's memory, one sliver at a time. It was a memory that Kinyera wished he didn't have. When he left the General's house after cleaning up his mess one night, he hoped he would never have to think of it again.

It started with an elaborate plan to take a young diplomat hostage and then trade her for ransom to the Belgian government. The General talked to them about all the riches and glory they would have. He told them their people would write songs about them, and their names would go down in history as having finally righted some of the wrongs that had been committed against them.

Her name was Elise Pierson. She worked in the Belgian Embassy in the Republic of the Congo. She was known to venture out and volunteer her time to help children throughout the region. She was a beautiful girl in her late twenties, tall and fair-skinned. She had a smile that lit up a room, and everyone that met her liked her immediately. The moment General Taban met her, he knew that he had to have her. To the General, women were nothing more than possessions. If he wanted something, he simply took it, no matter whether it was a small material item, or a human being.

The rebels had carried out their mission and taken the young woman hostage, along with two of her companions that had the unfortunate luck to be there when they took her. They took her to the prisoner's encampment as they were instructed, and for several days, they carried on with all their plans, having her pose for proof of life photos, all of them feeling proud of themselves, and feeling one-step closer to all their glory. It was a few days later, when the General showed up to talk to the prisoners, and then left with Elise.

At first, the rebels simply trusted him, but as the days and weeks passed without any movement on the ransoms, they started to suspect that the General had betrayed them, and decided to keep the young woman for himself. He made excuses, telling them the Belgian government wouldn't pay any ransoms, but through their own channels, they learned that the General had never even given the Belgian government the option. None of the proof of life photos of Elise had been passed on. Everything they found out confirmed their belief that the General betrayed them, and used them to do his dirty work, and there was nothing they could do about it.

They were taken from their homes as small children and turned into bandits. They had become killers, and kidnappers. Their souls had been lost. They were all wanted men, feared by all, and they had nowhere else to turn. The General, on the other hand, was a high-ranking military official who was either, highly respected, or highly feared. How could they do anything but continue to do his dirty work?

The General made promises, saying he had something better coming around the corner, leaving them all to hideout in the countryside and live off what they could raid from nearby towns. They lived like animals in the bush, surviving only because of the promise of future glory, and they were so desperate to believe that glory was near, they found themselves willing to cling to anything. They clung to anything that would promise to spring them from their shadowy cocoon, back into a society where they could live outside these boundaries where they scraped by and lived in squalor.

They believed him, despite having cleaned up his mess with Elise when he went ballistic one night, and stabbed her to death. It had been such a brutal killing that many of the young rebels who had committed horrible atrocities themselves, found it too much to stomach. She had been stabbed hundreds of times over every square inch of her body. Her head had been scalped, and her fingernails had been ripped from her nail beds. Her face and genitals had been completely dismembered, making her unrecognizable. When Kinyera had gone in to clean up the mess and discard of the body, he had been taken aback by the site, nearly falling to his knees.

The room was large, with white walls and white furniture. There were beautiful paintings that hung on the walls that were splattered with blood. The Persian carpets that had once been nearly priceless, were stained red, and covered in human tissue. There wasn't a wall, or a piece of furniture, that hadn't been sprayed with blood. Even the ceiling that rose over eighteen feet high, would not be spared. Her body had been stabbed so many times in the chest and stomach, that it had been nearly severed in two. Kinyera had never seen anything so horrible. The memory, and every square inch of that room, and the part of the mansion where it sat, was unfortunately burned into his mind forever.

"Why would ya think he would put Jewel back in that same room?" Grady asked shuddering, as Kinyera finished his story, and his detailed description of the house.

"Dat is where he put da last ones," Kinyera said shrugging.

"You mean there's been more since Elise?" Terri asked.

"Yes. There have been many," Kinyera said.

"Where did they go? What happened to them?" Grady asked as he swallowed the lump in his throat.

"I cannot know dis," Kinyera answered.

The room sat quiet for a while. They were all exhausted and lost in their own thoughts. They came up with a pretty good drawing of the compound, and were certain they would know where to find Jewel, if only they could find a way in, but that seemed impossible. The prearranged call with Rudy had been uninformative, and they made arrangements to be in contact the next day. It seemed that everyone was in a standstill. Plans were in place, and they were all waiting for the clock to tick down. It seemed there was nothing left to do but wait and see. The problem was that the six men sitting in the hot, muggy room in the old abandoned house, were not the kind of men to wait and see.

"Kinyera, I need to get out to that compound. What can you get us by ways of dark clothing, binoculars, guns, night vision goggles…?" Grady added flippantly.

"You wait here. I will bring things for you," Kinyera said motioning to Joseph and Olivier.

Grady, Sam, and Terri discussed a plan to go out and at least gather some intelligence about the compound first hand, from what they would be able to see from a distance in the dark. Grady knew how to get in and out of places without leaving a trace, despite his size. He had the rare gift of agility and stealth, and he planned to use every bit of it to his advantage as he surveyed the compound, and learned what he could. He wasn't about to just sit there and feel hopeless. He remembered promising Jewel that he would protect her to his last dying breath, and he meant it. He would never stop trying. There had to be a way in.

They reviewed the drawing they had come up with, based mostly on information Kinyera had, and what Terri remembered from things he had read about previously. The mansion was in the shape of a capital tee, with all of the living quarters in the upper left side of the cross. There were three entrances into the mansion, one on each end of the tee. All the entrances were heavily guarded. A very high concrete wall surrounded the compound itself that had guards posted every fifty feet. There were two gates through the concrete walls that were made of wrought iron. Each gate had two armed men who stood there on high alert, monitoring anyone who was coming or going.

They knew that if they had the right equipment… the type of equipment they would have had if they had been on an official mission for the U.S. Government, they would have been able to penetrate the compound with relative ease. With that, Terri decided it was time for him to use his credentials as a C.I.A. operative, call some contacts he had at the UN offices in Kinshasha, and see what kind of weaponry he could come up with to give them half a chance.

"Don't wait up for me, and don't ask any questions. I'll be back tomorrow," Terri said hiking his pants up, grabbing his medical bag, and walking out the side-door of the house they came and went through.

Sam and Grady just looked at each other and shrugged. Mary had known Terri for quite some time, but even she didn't seem to know exactly what he did, or she was being evasive on purpose, but she had assured them that she had never met anyone who came even close to being as smart, or as resourceful, as Terri was. They didn't know what he was up to, but they couldn't wait to find out what he came back with.

They were still discussing all the possibilities when Kinyera came back with a bag full of items, including some food for them to eat.

"I'm goin' ta owe ya man," Grady said, fishing through the bag Kinyera handed him.

"No matter," Kinyera said dismissing it.

Grady started pulling everything out of the bag, finding dark pants and black shirts for both him and Sam, black shoe polish for Grady to rub on his face, a pair of binoculars with night vision, and an M24 sniper rifle with a scope.

"Holy shit Kinyera! I was kiddin' about the night vision. This is incredible man! I should have asked for a Blackhawk Helicopter," Grady joked, patting Kinyera on the back, vowing to do everything he could to help him one day.

"It is no matter. Get dressed and we go to da compound. Dere is a culvert we can follow. If we follow dat culvert we will be able to get very close. You will get to see what you need to see."

CHAPTER 64

DESPAIR

"Do not look so sad my dear. You will have a good life. I will take care of you. You will live like a princess with everything at your disposal," Taban said, lifting Jewel's chin to look up at his face as he offered her everything he thought should be enough to satisfy the heart and mind of a feeble minded woman.

"I'm a prisoner. No more… no less," Jewel responded sadly.

"I did not kill you husband. I brought you here to keep you safe. If I had left you there, you would be dead. You should be thankful," Taban said.

"Should I also be thankful that you took us hostage?" she asked defiantly.

Taban loved the feistiness of the woman who sat before him. She had a way of cutting into him that left him feeling like he had just been kissed. She was different from all the others. She was not someone he would simply have fun with. This was a woman he would marry. She herself claimed to have no family. Everything he had been able to find out about her confirmed this. With her husband out of the way, there was nothing keeping him from marrying her and keeping her with him for as long as he desired. He was certain that he would be able to convince her to think of all the good that could come out of the arrangement.

She would marry him and have all the resources to set up aid for children, feeling like she was making a difference. She was perfect, because he knew that this time he would have to make it legitimate. Some of his indiscretions in the past had come with a price, and none other than the president himself, warned him that this would no longer be tolerated.

Most of the women he kept came with complications, with parents, or husbands and children waiting for them. That got messy at times when the family members started making too much noise, and he started getting pressure from some of the government officials to put an end to things, but this woman had nothing and nobody. He could convince her to make it official to give her a purpose in life. She would sacrifice herself to help others. This he knew, and he counted on it. He could see that as she talked constantly about wanting to help the little children. He saw how it pained her to see people suffering. Her husband was gone, and she blamed herself. He knew she would accept his offer before too long, so she could free herself from the guilt that was eating away at her.

~~~~~~~~

Jewel had fallen into an abyss that was threatening to consume her. No matter how hard she tried, she couldn't pull it together. She would make herself go down twice a day to check on her patients, but each step toward them was heavier and more difficult than the last. She was certain she would probably lose the baby, just as her mother and her grandmother had, and then she would have nothing. She never wanted to go home again. She never wanted to have to face Grady's family, or look into Troy's face to see the pity he would have for her. She never wanted to have to look Rudy in the eye, knowing how close they had been, and how it had been her idea to bring Grady there. She resigned herself to living a life in the confines of Taban's home, and considering the alternative of going home to nothing, it didn't sound half-bad.

She didn't exactly know what Taban's intentions were for her. He hadn't tried to rape her. He hadn't even tried to kiss her. He never came into her room, or invaded her space. If he wanted to speak to her, he would simply send someone to her room and bring her to him. One time, she had been sleeping, and had been dressed in nothing but a summer nightgown, quickly wrapping herself in a satin bathrobe as the guard urged her to quickly go to the General's room. She was certain he had sent for her for sexual purposes, but when she went into his room, she found him sitting comfortably in a chair in front of an unlit fireplace. She sat in the chair facing him, and waited for him to speak.

"What religion are you my dear?" he asked her.

"I'm Christian... ugh... I'm Roman Catholic," she answered with relief, after having sat there for several minutes, getting more and more worried about any number of things that might come out of his mouth.

"I too am Roman Catholic. Did you know that more than half of da people in dis country are Catholic?" he asked.

"I think I remember reading that," she admitted.

"Would you like to attend mass with me in da morning?" he asked. "We have our own church."

"Umm... yes. Thank you," she answered, wondering about the validity of a church, or a priest, that would serve within the confines of these wicked walls.

Most of her interaction with Taban was at dinner. She was expected to attend whenever Taban was home, and other than a few nights after hearing about the death of her husband, or the one night she spent looking over her patients, he had not tolerated her refusal. He made it clear that he expected her to be properly dressed, and ready without complaint.

Their dinners were the finest meals Jewel had ever seen or eaten. She imagined the chef back in the kitchen, fearing for his life as he presented each night's dinner, praying that it would be acceptable to Taban. Each night, Taban would either throw his napkin down in disgust after sampling the meal, causing attendants to scamper around excitedly in a frenzy, or he would eat his meal and give a nod of approval, causing everyone, including Jewel, to let out a collective sigh of relief.

Sometimes she had to remind herself that he was a brutal, psychopathic terrorist. He could be funny and charming, and he had an elegance about him that was in complete defiance of the scar that ran down his cheek. Other times, she had to remind herself that he could be funny and charming, when she would see him fly into a rage, yelling and screaming through the house, causing everyone to run and hide in fear for their lives.

Everyone in his house lived in fear of him, which caused her to wonder why. What had they seen? She didn't dare ask. Nobody talked to anyone. Guards and maids, and people who worked in the offices surrounded her, and yet there was complete silence. Nobody spoke to one another. There wasn't a water cooler where co-workers gathered to tell stories about their weekend projects. There was quiet. There was barely a look, or even a nod. There were people who passed each other in the hallway as if they were invisible. There wasn't even eye contact. It was sub-human. The fear of connecting defied human nature.

She spent most of the time in her room. There was no television to watch, or radio to listen to. She would sometimes pick up a book and read a few chapters, before realizing she had just read the chapters while thinking of something else. She longed to sleep as much as she possibly could. Other times she would check on her patients, but they wouldn't talk either. They had been warned just as she had, and so she attended to them as if they were each just an empty box, void of anything that would make them human. She wondered when the day would come that she would check on them, and they would simply be gone. Their stomachs had recovered, they were eating normally, and they no longer had diarrhea. It was just a matter of time before they would be taken away.

At the end of each day, she would force herself to her knees and pray. She would beg for forgiveness until she cried so hard she would collapse in a heap, and fall into a deep sleep. She felt so guilty for coming up with the idea to go there. She forced herself to feel it. She needed to punish herself. She felt like she deserved the punishment for Grady's sake, for his family's sake, and certainly, for Madison's sake.

CHAPTER 65

A MIDNIGHT RENDEZVOUS

The trip out to the compound left Grady with a feeling of helplessness. It was fortified, and built to guard against attacks, both large and small. Whoever built it thought of everything, and of course, only the drug cartel would have enough money to buy all the security bells and whistles that it was endowed with. Grady had lain in bed awake nearly all night, wondering how in the world he was going to get to Jewel if she were still there. He had only been asleep a few hours when he heard someone sneaking around near the side entrance of the house where they were hiding.

Terri had come back, but didn't want to wake anyone, so he was hiding out near the shed until daylight, when Grady heard him. "I barely made a noise," Terri said.

"That's all it takes," Grady said. "Do ya have any good news man? I need some right now," he said, sitting down on the stoop next to him where he was sitting near the shed.

"I have something. General Taban's head of security, Evariste Mobutu, has an unquenchable thirst for manly men... ummm... ya know... the Tom Selleck types," he said clearing his throat, giving Grady a knowing smile.

"What are ya gettin' at?" Grady said taken aback.

"I'm saying we have a way in. I have a connection. We'll call him Joe. He's C.I.A., and he's been planting young men in Mobutu's quarters for over a year now. He prefers Belgian men... ummm... tall...," Terri said, sizing Grady up, "dark hair, mustache, not bad to look at...if you're into that sort of thing," he shrugged. "Now hear me out."

"Alright," Grady said reluctantly, crossing his arms in front of him.

"We will go on a drive today, and we'll meet with Joe. There, you'll get showered and changed. He'll have a U.N. uniform for you to wear. You're going to need a cover. You can't be American. We'll say you're an Irish U.N. Peacekeeper that's conducting inspections on the U.N. offices in this region. Joe is a frequent visitor of Mobutu, and they often share their men, or so Mobutu thinks. Joe is currently talking to Mobutu about you. If Mobutu agrees to meet with you, then he'll send his men to pick you up at Joe's living quarters. They'll take you to the compound where Mobutu will be waiting for you in his room. His room is in the same wing as the one where we believe Jewel is being held. I have a complete map of the house. You'll go get Jewel in her room, and then you'll continue down the long hallway. At the end of the hallway, there's a room on the left, and a room on the right. You'll go into the room on the right. In the back of the room on the floor, under a large floor rug, is a hatch door that will take you into a tunnel that will lead you out of the compound. Not very many people know about the tunnel. It's likely that none of the soldiers will know to look there, so you'll want to be sure to shut it, and then put the rug down so it's not obvious."

"And... how am I ta get away from Mobutu and get ta Jewel?" Grady asked, wondering just how far he would have to go with Mobutu before fleeing.

"You'll need to slip this into his drink," Terri said, holding up a small vial of liquid. "It's tasteless, and it works fast. He'll immediately pass out, and he won't remember anything that happened. It has an amnesia effect, so anything that happens within a half hour of him passing out, he will have no memory of, so you'll have to do it soon. Once he's out, you'll need to strip him down, and then put him in bed to give him the illusion that he had a fun night with someone."

"What about Taban? How can we be sure Jewel is in her room, and not with him?" Grady asked, cringing at the thought, even as he asked it. He knew that Taban was likely interested in Jewel for sexual purposes. He tried pushing it out of his mind, but the thought of it kept creeping back in, and it was necessary to say it aloud, even if it pained him to do so.

"Joe knows about Jewel. One of his men came back with information about her. He said the only time she's not in her room is when she's having dinner with Taban. Taban won't be available for dinner tonight. He'll be in Uganda meeting with Doug. The other two prisoners have already been taken back to the prisoner's encampment. Jewel won't be missed until Taban comes back the next day. Hopefully by then, we'll be ready to go in and get the other prisoners. Whether they decide to abandon the camp or not, we're going in."

"We?" Grady asked for clarification.

"Yes. Us. The good guys. That's all you need to know," Terri said, urging Grady not to ask any more questions.

"How will we get out of the country? Our passports and everything were taken."

"When you get out of the tunnel, you'll need to drive to Kinshasha to the American embassy. You'll tell them everything that happened...everything except me," Terri said, surprising Grady.

"What about Kinyera? I need to do something to help him. He wants out of here. He saved my life man."

"Mary's working on those arrangements. I can't be involved with that."

They spent the morning discussing everything in detail, and studying the map of the compound, which added some of the detail that Kinyera couldn't quite remember. The tunnel wasn't on the map. The only thing they knew about the tunnel, was where it started, and where it ended. It was apparently near the culvert they had been at the night before, but Grady hadn't seen it, and he knew it was likely well hidden. If it were a straight tunnel, it would be about two miles long, though they suspected that it took some turns, and would likely be around two and a half miles long. Grady knew that Jewel was afraid of small spaces, but he couldn't see any other way around it. This was the only way out.

They discussed their plan with Rudy, who decided to switch gears and bring the rest of the team back to Tanzania so none of them would be implicated in anything. This was a Congolese General's home they would be breaking into. This could land them all in prison for a very long time, and not the kind of prison in America where you get a bed with three meals. The prisons in the Congo were more terrifying than death.

All of Rudy's team would be out of the country except Doug, who would be meeting with Taban in Uganda. Nobody was certain exactly what to do with Doug yet, but Terri seemed to allude to the possibility that there were arrangements made, and they knew better than to ask questions.

"Why wouldn't we just go to the embassy, tell them General Taban has Jewel, and then get her back?" Mary asked during their phone call.

"Do you think he would really admit to that?" Sam asked her, knowing he wouldn't.

"He will kill her," Kinyera said, shaking his head. "The only way she live is to sneak her out. It is da only way. If she live, she will be da only one dat make it out of Taban house alive."

Kinyera had instructions of approximately what time he needed to be at the tunnel. He would be the one to take them to the embassy in Kinshasha, and they all expected the escape to happen quietly. Mobutu wouldn't wake until the next morning, and he would be too embarrassed to ask anyone to fill in the details, so the absence of his bed partner wouldn't be discussed, and with the other prisoners gone, it wouldn't be unusual for Jewel to stay in her room until Taban's returns. They would have a long lead to get safely away from the compound, and get a head start to make the long drive to Kinshasha.

Terri rode with Grady to the meeting place where Joe instructed them to meet him. Joe was the most uninteresting person Grady had ever met, and he suspected this was what made him such a good spy. His wasn't the kind of face or personality you would ever remember. He was detached from the human experience. He saw through people, rather than at them. He looked Grady over, deciding that he would be to Mobutu's liking, sizing him up as he would a car, or a breeding stud, never once recognizing him as a person.

Terri and Joe had a brief exchange as Grady waited in Joe's car, and Kinyera and his men waited for Terri. Grady's head was spinning. He couldn't believe the situation he was in. His whole life, his and Jewel's, hung in the balance, and they were in the hands of young rebels, a spy, and some mysterious man named Terri, who apparently never needed to sleep, and had connections he could hardly fathom.

Finally, Joe took Grady back to get him cleaned and ready. Grady stood in the shower as long as he dared, washing away all the dirt that had accumulated throughout his captivity. It had been months since the last time he bathed, but he was too anxious to linger too long. He scrubbed as best he could, and then got himself dressed.

Everything was set for the evening. With Taban gone, and Joe assuring Mobutu that Grady was only going to be available for the one night, it was easy to convince him to make a rash decision, and have Joe send over one of his men for a midnight rendezvous. Mobutu was excited for a male visitor, and apparently, Joe was quite pleased with Grady's ability to clean up.

"Oh yes! Mobutu is going to like you," Joe said with more animation than he had seen out of the man since meeting him, leaving him to wonder if he was being set up. He had to keep those thoughts out of his mind. He knew that he was going willingly into the lion's den, but he knew there was no other way. He was being set up to go have a romantic interlude with a man who was in charge of security for one of the biggest terrorists in the region. The idea of it seemed preposterous. Anytime he summarized it for himself, or thought about it too logically, his stomach would twist and turn. He dared not think of it as anything other than another military mission.

When the armed security guards came to pick Grady up, he did exactly what Joe instructed him to do, which was to ignore them, and appear to have an air of superiority over them. He acted indifferent to them, and rode in the back of the car alone, as a sheik would ride in a limousine, sipping champagne as he's chauffeured to his destination. He sat in the back feeling the vial of Propofol in his shorts, wedged neatly between a couple of his body parts, and he cringed when he imagined what would happen to them if the vial were to break. He thought of the map that he had memorized, imagining all the steps he would take. He thought of Jewel, and his heart started beating faster as the thought of holding her came into his mind once again, something he tried not to think of if he was going to stay calm.

He took a long deep breath as they drove in through the gates. He steadied his body and his mind. He armed his mind in the way that soldiers do when they have a job to do that scares them to death. He detached himself from emotion, and ran the plan through his mind over and over again, until the man opened the car door for him, and led him toward Mobutu's room. He walked through the house looking straight ahead, all the while running the map through his mind. It was a very accurate map, and this simple fact gave Grady the confidence he needed in this situation to square his shoulders and plow ahead with the plan, as if there was any other choice.

He was escorted to Mobutu's door, never once making eye contact with any of the guards. Mobutu was a smallish man of about five foot eight inches in height, with a slight frame. Grady had to resist the urge to just grab him right then and snap his neck, before running off to get Jewel. He knew it wouldn't take much, but he was also trying not to blow Joe's cover, and so he needed to make the plan go as smoothly as possible.

At first, Mobutu treated the encounter as a simple pre-arranged business meeting, asking Grady questions, with Grady giving him all the right answers per Joe's instructions. Once Mobutu was satisfied that Grady was there for pleasure, he relaxed, and quite suddenly, he became very flirtatious, coming to sit right next to where Grady sat on the sofa. He started running his fingers through Grady's hair with one hand, while rubbing his upper thigh with the other.

"I need ta loosen up a bit. Can I make us both a drink?" Grady said as Mobutu smiled at him seductively.

"I like Scotch on the rocks. You'll find it all right there," Mobutu said, motioning toward the sidebar where there was a small sink, refrigerator, glasses, and just about anything a bartender would need to make any number of drinks.

"I already need ta adjust myself," Grady said, reaching down his pants to grab the vial. "It's been awhile since I was with anyone, ya see," he said turning, flashing the man a smile before mixing his drink.

The act was about survival, and not just his survival. He couldn't blow this. He knew the danger he was in, and he knew that Jewel's life depended on the success of him accomplishing this. He didn't know if Jewel thought he was dead or not, and he didn't know what state of mind she would be in. He knew right then as he poured Mobutu and himself a drink, that he would have done anything to get to Jewel.

He handed Mobutu his cocktail, and then unbuttoned his jacket as he watched him sip his laced drink. He was stalling, wanting Mobutu to drink as much as possible before he served himself up on a platter to the man. He took off his jacket, exposing the broad shoulders and large frame, and then sauntered over to a chair where he carefully laid his coat, watching as Mobutu took another long pull off his drink.

He slipped into the seduction, remembering one night at home when Jewel talked about how turned on she was seeing him in his business suit. He had gone into a full act of seduction, slowly removing his coat, and carefully exposing little bits of flesh as she shrieked with delight. He loved seeing the anticipation in her eyes as he teased her. He saw that same look in Mobutu's eyes, and he was counting down the seconds before he passed out, stalling as long as he possibly could.

Finally, after drinking less than half his drink, Mobutu slumped over in his chair. Grady quickly went to him, checking his eyes to make sure he was really out, before taking on the dreadful task of having to strip the man down and get him tucked into bed. Grady carried him to the bed. He threw one shoe in one direction, and the other shoe in another direction. Items of clothing were discarded throughout the room so that he could make a show of it, hopefully convincing Mobutu that he had a wild night be couldn't remember. He messed up the bedding, and then poured half the scotch down the drain so Mobutu would think he had too much to drink.

He wiped down the glasses and everything else he had touched, including Mobutu, eliminating his fingerprints before quickly slipping his U.N. jacket back on, and putting the empty vial in his pocket. Grady fished through the chest of drawers, finding the extra keys to the mansion just as Joe instructed him. He listened at the door, and hearing nothing, peeked his head out. There was nobody in the halls, so he walked hurriedly toward the room where they thought Jewel was being held. He counted the doors as he walked by them to make sure that he had the right room, and paused to take a deep breath before slipping the key in the door. He quietly walked into the bedroom, closing the door behind him.

He counted on her already being asleep, as the time of his meeting with Mobutu had been scheduled for an hour when most people were already sleeping. He walked soundlessly to the bed, the outline of which he could pick out as the moonlight shown through one of the small windows. He was staring at the bed, looking for signs of a sleeping woman, but he saw nothing. His heart started pounding wildly, when suddenly something rather large hit him in the head, causing him to fall to the ground.

He didn't know what hit him, but he was dazed for a moment as he laid on the floor, his vision blurring for a second until he focused in on the familiar looking feet and ankles he was looking at on the hard floor.

"Jewel? Dammit! Jewel, it's me!" Grady said faintly, trying to block the blows he was taking from a crystal vase Jewel was using as a weapon. His ribs were killing him from the beating Mugabo gave him, and he tried to protect them.

She continued to hit him and kick him, flailing wildly until he could get up, grabbing her and tackling her on the bed, and straddling her as she squirmed beneath him. He quickly covered her mouth to stifle the screams that started to come from her, but she bit his hand and flailed her legs, managing to get a knee up to kick him right in the crotch.

"Jewel! Dammit! It's me darlin'. It's Grady!" he groaned as he laid on top of her, trying to keep control of her without hurting her, but feeling his own pain.

He felt her go limp beneath him, and he cautiously took his hand away from her mouth.

"What? Grady?" she cried, lying beneath him breathless as the shock of what she thought was an attack still surged through her. She tried to see the man, but all she saw was black hair. "No! It can't be! I'm going to scream bloody murder you coward. You better just get out of my room! Taban will kill you!"

"It's me. It's Grady. It's me darlin'," he said, cupping his hand over her mouth, afraid she might start screaming again.

He was holding her as she thrashed around and tried to break free, until he felt her go limp again. The realization of what he just told her was finally sinking in enough where he could take his hand away from her mouth again, and trust it.

"Grady?" she sobbed, still lying there pinned beneath him. "Is it really you?" she trailed off, her voice cracking. "I thought you were dead!"

"Shhh... I know darlin'. I'll explain later. Right now, we need ta get movin'." He kissed her soundly for a minute before climbing off her, his whole body aching. "You need to get dressed in pants, boots, long sleeves, maybe a coat or something if you have it," he said, pulling her up with him.

She turned on a little lamp and stared at him a moment, before hurriedly grabbing clothes that would work for their journey. Her hands were shaking, and her mind was wrecked. She went from thinking her husband was dead, to thinking she was going to be attacked, to finding her husband standing right there in front of her, urging her to get dressed, and she was doing all of this under the influence of raging pregnancy hormones.

Most all of the clothes she had been given were dresses and high heels, but she pulled out her old ragged clothes and hurried to get dressed, even as she fought back tears and frantic thoughts. Her whole body was trembling as she pulled on her clothes.

Grady sat and watched her, rubbing his head and his crotch that were both throbbing with pain. His heart was pounding from the adrenaline that was surging through him, and the excitement of seeing his wife, but he was feeling aches and pains from where Jewel hit him with the vase, and where he had been kicked in the ribs that were still badly bruised. He didn't care though, he wanted to grab her and kiss her, but he knew they were far from being out of danger, and he was anxious to get moving.

She glanced up at him, and the reaction she had was one he hadn't been expecting. She immediately turned green and started heading into the bathroom where she proceeded to throw up. He followed her in the bathroom, and helped her back to her feet as she finished.

"Are ya alright Jewel?" he said wrapping his arms around her, realizing that he needed to stop a minute to calm her down if they were going to make it down the hallway, calmly and quietly.

"I just have butterflies. I thought you were dead," she said choking up. Her voice cracked, and she decided not to tell him about her pregnancy.

"I know darlin'. I'm here now, but we have ta get movin'."

She finished getting dressed, and they readied themselves for their escape, listening at the door before opening it to make sure nobody was in the hallway. Grady cracked the door open, and looked around before grabbing Jewel's hand, pulling her behind him as they quietly tip-toed through the hollowness of the long hallway, each footstep sounding as if it were echoing through the whole house.

Just as they found the door that would lead them into the room with the hatch door, a man walked out of the door on the opposite side of the hall. He immediately flew into action jumping on Grady, grabbing him around the neck, and trying to choke him, but Grady was running on a surge of adrenaline. He managed to pull the man over the top of him, body-slamming him to the floor before hitting him several times in the face, knocking him out cold. They had made a lot of noise and there was blood coming from the man's nose that was spilling on the hallway floor.

Grady quickly grabbed the keys to unlock the door to the room. Jewel was standing there in complete shock, holding back waves of nausea. As soon as Grady got the door unlocked, he grabbed the man and pulled him into the room. He pulled a sock off the unconscious man to wipe up the blood in the hallway, before shutting and locking the door behind them.

"Look around for some rope or something." Grady whispered when they got in the room.

Jewel started searching through desk drawers while Grady looked around, but they didn't find anything, and Grady, feeling time pass too quickly, made an immediate decision. He went to the man lying on the ground, grabbed his head between both his hands, and twisted with massive force. Jewel cringed hearing all the cracking that occurred when the spinal cord detached, and she just stood there staring at her husband in complete disbelief as he broke the man's neck.

"Come on. Let's go," he said grabbing her hand.

She slowly reached out and grabbed his hand, still staring at the man on the floor, watching him gasp for his last breath. Her head was spinning. Everything that was happening seemed unreal, and the only thing she wanted to do was lay down, feeling the nausea hit her empty stomach once again.

They quickly located the hatch door, and Grady figured out a way to make the rug fall into place after having lowered Jewel into the tunnel, and then dropped the man's body down into the tunnel with them to leave no trace of where they had gone.

They were safely out of the house and into the tunnel that supposedly nobody knew about, but Grady didn't want to waste any time. They didn't know how long the tunnel was, and he didn't know how long they would be able to go through the cold, wet tunnel without needing warmth and rest.

He worried about the effect the confined space would have on Jewel, and he thought that he would have to knock her out or something after he saw her reaction when he flashed the little credit card flashlight through the tunnel. They could both see how small and dirty it was for the first time. They saw things moving all around them, and the stench was horrible.

"I can't Grady. I can't do this," she said with terror in her eyes; the kind of terror that defies logic, making a small space seem more terrifying than a house full of armed terrorists.

"Yes ya can! Now take my hand and follow me!" he ordered her not giving her an option. He saw the startled look on her face, and reached down to kiss her on the forehead. "Will ya trust me darlin'?"

"Yes, of course I will," she said meekly, because she did.

They trekked through the dark tunnel, through several inches of cold water, trudging through spider webs and countless other things that seemed to fall from the ceiling, all of which they tried not to think of. They knew that part of the world was full of deadly snakes, spiders, and any number of other poisonous creatures, all of which liked to hide out in damp, dark, confined spaces. Jewel held onto Grady's hand so tight it was practically cutting off his circulation, and he held back nearly as tight. They simply kept their heads down, and they kept walking through the tunnel with a tiny amount of light from the small flashlight.

"I'm thirsty," Jewel whispered. "How long is this tunnel Grady? I don't feel well."

"We guessed it's about two and a half miles. I'd say we've gone about half the distance."

"Who's we?" Jewel asked.

"Me, Kinyera, Terri, Sam, Oliver, Joseph, Rudy, Mary... just to name a few. I'll explain it all later, provided I don't have complete amnesia and forget my own damn name," he said rubbing a large bump on his head where Jewel had hit him. Another large knot was forming on his scalp, and it seemed to have its own heartbeat. He was also feeling the effects of being hit in the forearm as he was trying to protect himself from being beaten by his wife. "Ya have a hell of an aim darlin'."

"Sorry about that. I thought you were one of the soldiers coming to my room," she said quietly with her head down, causing him to lose his breath.

He stopped and turned to her. "I'm sorry Jewel. I hope they didn't hurt ya too bad darlin'," he said choking back emotion, making him soften up a little from the adrenaline he was running on.

"You just killed a man Grady," she whispered absently.

"I know darlin'. I had ta do it. He would have killed us if he'd had half a chance. I'd have killed a hundred men ta get ya out of there if I needed ta."

"When I thought you were one of the soldiers, I wanted to kill you. I would have done it too."

She stood there for a moment with all her crazy emotions surging through her, having cried herself to sleep only a few hours earlier, before getting woken up suddenly from morning sickness, wishing she were dead along with her husband. She knew Grady would do anything to protect her, and for the first time, she trusted it completely, making the last several weeks seem all the more painful when she thought he was dead.

"They told me you were dead," she said with tears streaming down her face, "which was worse than rape, but Taban wanted to marry me. He didn't rape me. He said he had to make it legitimate this time. He knew everything about me Grady. It's like we walked into a trap."

"He didn't... nobody...," he stuttered, afraid to ask the question, pulling her to him hugging her.

"Nobody raped me. He brought me here and treated me like a queen. I had resigned myself to being Mrs. Taban. I didn't want to go home ever again... not without you. I couldn't have ever gone home without you," she said choking back more tears, wiping a few off her cheek that had escaped.

"Shhh... it's alright darlin'. I'm here now. Come on. We have ta keep movin'," he said grabbing her hand, dragging her along. He knew he had to keep her focused, and he needed to get her somewhere safe. He could tell she was on the verge of completely breaking down, but they didn't have time for that.

"Kinyera helped you?" she asked after they walked in silence for a long time.

"He saved my life," Grady said as a matter of fact. "I hope I can repay him."

They walked for a while longer before reaching an opening. They were both freezing after walking for a long time in cold water through the underground tunnel. It was still night out, and they had several hours before daylight would break. They were both covered in dirt, and cobwebs clung to their clothes. They made their way out near the bridge where they had agreed to meet with Kinyera and his men, but nobody was there, and Grady instinctively knew that nobody was coming. He didn't think Kinyera would betray him, but he couldn't be sure of anything.

He had a sick feeling in the pit of his stomach as he considered their situation. They were somewhere along the rebel infested border of Uganda and the Democratic Republic of the Congo. They were a long ways from the city, and they needed to trek through a very dangerous countryside without so much as a pocketknife for protection. Somehow, they needed to get to Kinshasha to the American embassy without being taken by another opportunistic group who would see them as a means to getting a sizable ransom.

He knew that Rudy had pulled everyone back to Tanzania, and that there was no hope of any of them coming to their rescue. His first thought was to make it to the safe house in Goma, but then he thought better of it. Kinyera either had turned on him, or had been found out, so he knew that nothing associated with Kinyera would be safe.

"Somethin's wrong," Grady said, "Kinyera was supposed ta meet us. Let's get out of here as quickly as we can," Grady said, grabbing Jewel's hand, running off toward the cover of the forest.

"I'm so scared Grady," Jewel said as Grady stood at the edge of the forest making plans as she rested, catching her breath.

"I'd feel a little better if I had a rifle in my hands, but other than that, we're in decent shape," he lied. "Do what I do. Don't make sudden moves, and keep quiet. We'll go for a while, walking as long as we can in the dark, before finding a place to hide out during the day."

"Okay. I'll try, but I'm so tired," she said rubbing her eyes. "I haven't been able to sleep since I found out...," her voice cracked.

"Come here darlin'. Come and let's sit a minute. I need ta just sit and hold ya a minute," Grady said, leading her toward a tree where they could sit and rest for a minute.

He sat, and Jewel climbed up on his lap kissing him thoroughly. She ran her fingers through his hair, and she touched the little hollow space behind his ear that she was so familiar with. He stroked the long silky strands of hair that fell in her face, and gently kissed her fingers.

"What you did was so dangerous Grady. I can't believe you came into Taban's house. Is that why your hair is black?" she asked, looking up at him as they both studied each other after having been away from each other for so long.

"Well, he thought I was dead, and I don't exactly blend in around this place. I had ta change my appearance, but… we shouldn't be talkin' like this. Someone could be listenin'. This forest has ears, and I'm sure those ears are bought an' paid for by Taban himself," Grady said giving her one long lingering hug.

"What should we do?" she asked nervously. "I know you probably have a plan, right?"

"I don't see how we'll be able to make it ta the embassy in Kinshasha without a car. It's too far away. Let's get ta Goma. We'll figure out a way ta make a call. We have ta try and reach Rudy. He's in Tanzania. He's probably pacing the floor right now, expectin' a call any minute. He'll know somethin's wrong if he doesn't hear from us pretty soon. Come on Jewel," Grady said, getting up and pulling Jewel up with him.

"This is our only chance."

CHAPTER 66

MUGABO

The evening was overflowing with bloodshed. An undercover military team, made up of unknown soldiers, stormed the prisoner's encampment just about the time Grady and Jewel were finding their way into the tunnel. If they had waited even a few minutes longer, their escape would not have been possible. All hell broke loose at the prisoner's encampment, and news flies surprisingly fast in the seedy underworld of kidnapping for ransom. Taban's compound was under complete lockdown.

The prisoner's encampment had not been completely abandoned as the military team had been told, and several lone rebels that were left there as sacrificial lambs, took their last breaths shortly after the military team arrived. The prisoners were loaded into covered cargo trucks, and taken to an unknown location, with their captors left lying on the ground to die, awash in their own blood.

Mugabo laid there completely still until he heard everyone leave, and he listened until everything was perfectly still for a long time. His bunkmate had been shot in the head and fell right on top of him, leaving them both to die in a bloody heap on the floor of their hut. He had been suspicious when he saw some of the men leave the encampment earlier that evening, leaving behind just a few of them to guard the prisoners, and he was wishing he had listened to his instincts. He knew Taban had betrayed them, leaving behind just a few expendables so the rescuers of the prisoners could claim a respectable victory, putting the whole thing to rest in one fell swoop.

He finally believed what Kinyera, all along, had been telling him. He didn't want to believe that everything had been for nothing... that everything he had endured, everything he had been fighting for, was just a small blip in the bigger picture, and that corrupt politicians used them as pawns to do their dirty work. Up until just a few hours ago, he regarded himself as a rising star, and a future leader of this group of rebels, but now he saw the truth staring back at him as he washed the blood from his face, watching his reflection in the moonlit pond he knelt in front of, trying to figure out his next move.

He made his way through the encampment, picking out weapons and ammunition, stuffing a bag full of what food he could find, before heading deep into the forest. The sense of freedom he felt moving along through the forest by himself, was both frightening and liberating.

When he was five, the Interahamwe took him and Kinyera from their homes. As hard as he tried, he could hardly remember life before that, other than a memory that had become increasingly more faded, of him walking hand-in-hand through a similar forest, and looking up to see his dad smiling at him. The memory always made him smile, and then he'd frown and harden an instant later. The Interahamwe told them that their parents were all gone, and that they no longer wanted them. They had been convinced that the rebel leaders were their new family. It all defied reason, and yet he tried to believe it all, so that it would not be for nothing. He needed to believe that the rebels told the truth, because what else would he have if none of it had been true? Where would he go?

He floated soundlessly through the forest at a quick pace, his minds-eye filling in the dark shadows where his eyes couldn't focus, wanting to distance himself from the prisoner's encampment. He knew these forests so well, and he knew the vegetation underneath him to such a high degree, that he could make his way through bushes and trees without ever making a noise.

He suddenly felt dirty and wretched, fully admitting to himself for the first time that everything they had been doing was wrong. It suddenly seemed perfectly clear, as if it had been written in stone, and he with the education to read it. He walked toward Goma, knowing that he needed to find Kinyera as quickly as he could. He needed to find his brother and flee, just as Kinyera had wanted to do for so long. He walked as a free man for the first time in his life, and he made his own decisions, feeling the weight of the world on his shoulders.

He stopped suddenly, hearing an unusual sound that was not part of the forest. He followed the noise that sounded like someone puking, a noise he had heard just a few hours earlier after one of the men drank too much of the liquor they had been supplied with. He quietly made his way closer to the noise and poked his head over a bush, when someone from behind grabbed him. They wrestled for several minutes, both of the men fighting for their lives. Grady was much larger, but Mugabo had been fighting every day of his life for survival, and he was not about to be taken down easily. It wasn't until Jewel hit Mugabo with a branch and knocked him out cold, that Grady was able to get complete control over the man.

"It's Mugabo," Grady said kneeling before him, lightly shaking him to wake him up. "This is Kinyera's brother. He helped me get away."

"This is the one who almost shot us all that first day," Jewel said, sitting down a good distance away to lean against a tree trunk.

"I'm worried about ya darlin'. Ya haven't kept a thing down, and ya've not had any water. Yer goin' ta get dehydrated," Grady said looking up to see Jewel's pale face.

"I'll be fine Grady. I would say you're in far worse shape than I am. Your ribs are badly bruised, probably fractured, and the knots on your head are getting bigger."

"Let's not forget that we'll probably never have kids now either," he said reaching to feel the sore spot between his legs.

"I'm sorry Grady," she said reaching for his arm.

"It'll be alright darlin'," he said looking over and smiling at her as he shook Mugabo.

"Don't you think we should tie his hands or something before waking him up? He's pretty fierce. I've never seen someone so determined, despite the fact that he looked like a little twig with your arms wrapped around him."

"Well, if I had something that I thought might hold him then I would consider it, but…nah… I think we're alright. Kinyera trusted him, and I feel like I can too."

"You don't think Kinyera betrayed you then?"

"No, I don't. Somethin' must have happened. He wouldn't have risked as much as he did ta save me, only ta turn around and betray me."

"You are right. My brother would not betray you," Mugabo said still lying there without opening his eyes.

"Mugabo? You recognize me then?" Grady asked, urging him to open his eyes.

"Yes, but right now there are two of you," Mugabo said, barely opening one eye to peer at Grady before quickly closing it again.

"I know man! She gave me a hell of a blow to the head as well. The other me you're seeing is probably the giant knot on my head from a crystal vase," he said, giving Jewel a playful grin, realizing that Mugabo likely had no idea what a crystal vase was.

"I am so sorry Mugabo, but you were trying to take my husband down. I didn't know," she said shrugging innocently.

"And why then did you hit you husband in the head?" he said turning his head to look at her.

"Well, look at him. His hair is black, and he has bushy black eyebrows and a mustache. I didn't recognize him," she said in her defense. "He looks like an assassin or something."

"Dis is true. It was not until I heard him speak dat I recognize him. He look very different," Mugabo said, propping himself up on his elbows to look at Grady more closely. "How is it you are here with da woman?"

Grady summarized everything for Mugabo, leaving out some of the details about Rudy and the others as much as he could. He explained the plan, and how Kinyera, Olivier, and Joseph were supposed to pick them up, but when they got out of the tunnel, Kinyera wasn't there. Jewel told him about the compound and everything that occurred there, including taking care of the two prisoners.

"Joseph cannot be trusted. I wish my brother would know dis. I will look for him," Mugabo said, getting up and reaching for his bag.

"You are with baby?" Mugabo said, reaching in and pulling out some bread and a thermos of water for Jewel.

"Ummm… yes," she said meeting Grady's eyes.

"Jewel! Why didn't ya tell me?" Grady said, kneeling down in front of her, cradling her face in his hands when he does.

"Because… I… I'll probably just lose it. What difference does it make?" she said with tears spilling over and running down her face. "A few hours ago I thought you were dead, and I was going to live a life as a prisoner, married to a terrorist! I thought you were dead!" she sobbed uncontrollably as he pulled her to him.

"I'm sorry darlin'. It does matter though. It matters a lot," he said stroking her hair. "I came as fast as I could get ta ya. I would have done anything ta find ya. I would have never stopped."

"I'm a mess Grady. I haven't slept. I haven't eaten. I feel like I could just lay here and puke all day and night. Please get me out of here," she said laying her head on his chest, feeling the solidness she had longed for night after night.

"We go. I take you to a place I know. You will be able to rest and make a call. Come," Mugabo said urging them to get moving. "Eat the bread and water. You will feel better. I have seen dis."

The three of them walked through the forest for a long ways, before heading out in a clearing they would need to cross that led to the outskirts of Goma. They followed a well-beaten path where many souls had trekked before, as they crossed from Uganda into the Congo.

"Here. Put this over you head and keep you eyes down. You will not look up! You will walk behind you husband and watch his feet to walk where he walk! Do you understand?" Mugabo asked giving the instructions as he would if they were his prisoners.

"Yes," she said fearfully, looking at Grady for assurance.

"I will not hurt you. I am mean business. I do not want you to be seen. Will you trust in me?" Mugabo asked, helping Jewel with the scarf that he wrapped around her head like a Muslim woman.

"Yes, I will trust in you Mugabo," she replied, fighting back tears once again, not sure of the words that were coming out of her mouth.

The strain from the last months were piling up on Jewel. She was near her breaking point. Everything in her life had been taken from her, and then returned so suddenly that it left her feeling wrecked and emotional… add on top of that some crazy pregnancy hormones, and you had a ticking time bomb that was ready to go off any minute. She was walking with her head down as she had been told, and for once, she was glad for it. She was fighting back tears, not wanting to have to meet anyone's eyes.

She could feel the bustle of the city all around her. There were cars and people going in every direction that she could see out of her peripheral vision. She could feel the added heat of the city, made by car exhausts and extra body heat. She heard the city noises all around her... horns honking, people yelling, radios blaring with words she couldn't understand. She prayed as she walked, hoping nobody would recognize the men she was following. She considered the backwardness of a society where you could see a woman walking behind a man submissively, afraid to look up for fear of being beaten, and not think it appalling. She was caught up in all her thoughts, concentrating on keeping up with the two men she followed, when Grady abruptly stopped, and she almost ran into him.

"Here. We will go in here," Mugabo said, heading into an old hotel that looked like it was falling down. "Wait here and let me check something."

Mugabo disappeared, leaving Grady and Jewel in the area that might have been the hotel's lobby at some point in time. It appeared that the place had been abandoned long ago. The walls were riddled with bullets, and everything of value had been taken long ago. Paint was peeling from the walls, and doors and windows were missing or falling apart.

Mugabo finally came back, motioning for them to follow him. Jewel's heart started pounding in her chest as they made their way up the old rickety stairwell, with the boards creaking loudly beneath their feet. He led them past the second floor up another set of stairs that had been hidden, to a room that was surprisingly decent. There was an old bed, and a desk with a folding chair.

Mugabo went into the closet immediately, and came out with a black Samsonite suitcase that looked completely out of place. Inside the suitcase were parts and pieces of phones that he proceeded to fit together, and pulling something from his bag he carried, he miraculously came up with a working cell phone. Jewel shook her head considering the resourceful of this man. She thought of people at home who would have one small issue with their phones, before heading down to the local store to raise hell, for having to endure that inconvenience. She vowed to give more thanks for all the conveniences she had taken for granted.

"Come lay down Jewel," Grady said, motioning toward the bed as he took the cell phone Mugabo was handing him.

She didn't hesitate, despite the soiled conditions of the mattress, and the mugginess in the room, she was exhausted. Grady sat down next to her staring at the phone, thinking of a plan. He knew that he could possibly be blowing Rudy's cover by making the call, and so he paused for a long while trying to figure out a way to say what he needed to say, in as little time as he could, before whoever was listening picked up their conversation. He rehearsed the code words in his head several times before dialing the number he had memorized earlier. He decided to call and hang up twice, remembering how one time they had agreed to do this to signal one another when they were planning a surprise for Diana.

""It's D's brother. We're in the city we called from yesterday. We need more tequila. Bring some salt and lime when you come. The ones we had are gone. We'll be by the pool. I'll check back around six."

Grady hung up the phone and smiled a little as Jewel looked up at him as if he were crazy.

"Planning a little party are you?" she said raising an eyebrow at him.

"The pool is a pre-arranged meeting place we worked out a few days ago. I told them I would call at six, which means that I'll call back at 2:00… that's an hour from now," Grady said sitting beside her as Mugabo sat on the floor and pieced together another cell phone. "Let's see. I'm guessing someone will be on a plane within the next two hours. It's another two hours before they land. It'll be another hour before they reach the pool. That leaves five hours before I have to leave."

"Before *you* leave?" Jewel said accusingly, propping herself up on one elbow. "Do you think I'm just going to sit here while you go off without me? No! It's not going to happen!"

"We will just give you a big stick. You can hit them on the head if they try to hurt you," Mugabo said with a half-smile, never looking up from his project.

"That's amusing, but I'm not letting you out of my sight. I need some men's clothing, dark sunglasses, and some scissors to cut my hair off. Are these things you could get for me Mugabo? I'm not waiting here by myself. You two better just get that in your heads right now."

Mugabo looked up at her and waited for the blow that he was sure would come, but just stared at Grady in disbelief as he shrugged his shoulder and said okay.

"Why do you not beat dis woman?" he asked with innocence.

"Beat me? Is that how it is Mugabo? A woman speaks out and men just beat them into submission," Jewel said angrily, "you have a thing to learn about women."

Grady, seeing that Jewel was angry and Mugabo was confused, stepped in to bring peace. "Well, she would shoot me for one, but I like her pretty little face like it is. I wouldn't want to see it bruised or swollen," he said cradling her face in his hand, kissing her lightly on the forehead.

"You do not beat da woman?" Mugabo asked looking puzzled, speaking as if Jewel were not present.

"No Mugabo. We don't beat women where I come from. A man who picks a fight with a woman is no man at all. Men who do such things are a disgrace in our society. They're shunned. This woman can defend herself," he said smiling at her. "She's a better shot than most men I've ever known, and she's the smartest, kindest person you could ever hope to know. How could you beat a woman like that?"

"You let her have a gun?" Mugabo asked Grady, alarmed at this outrageous notion.

"Mugabo… in America, everyone is free… men and women. Women do what they want. They don't answer to men," Grady said, causing Mugabo to wrinkle his face at this oddity that he had clearly never considered before.

"I think I would like America. I did not like to beat my woman. She was pretty, and she would cry for a very long time," Mugabo said in memory.

"What happened to your woman then Mugabo?" Grady asked carefully.

"She is dead. She died when she was having da baby," Mugabo said shrugging.

"Where's the baby?" Jewel asked.

"Da baby is dead."

With that, they all fell silent before nodding off, unable to fight it any longer, all of them exhausted from their sleepless night trekking through the forest. The three of them were sprawled sideways on the bed, with Grady in the middle curled up next to Jewel. It was a site that couldn't have been more unlikely.

CHAPTER 67

IN COUNTRY

"I'm going in country. I'm the only one Kinyera hasn't seen. If he's compromised, whether it's willingly or not, he could point you guys out. Besides, these two people are my family. If something happens to them, and I'm not there to do everything I can, I'll never forgive myself," Rudy said as he readied himself for the flight into Goma.

He had passports to get Jewel and Grady out of the country, complete with fake visa's that showed their arrival in the Democratic Republic of the Congo just two weeks earlier. He tried going through the proper channels, but he found himself not trusting the situation. The further he dug into General Taban's background, the further up the chain of command he went, straight up to the president himself. Rudy feared the embarrassment of the entire situation could lead to some difficulty for Grady and Jewel. They had intercepted information that could implicate the two of them in drug trafficking, a favorite charge by leaders of third world countries who want to discredit the do-gooders who come to their country and run into trouble.

He had information that Mary was able to find out about Kinyera and Mugabo. She had read about a village in Burundi that had been wiped out one evening around the timeframe that Grady indicated. Many of the people were killed, and nearly all of the young children were taken into the forest and were never recovered. That was not an unusual occurrence in this part of the world, but one raid stood out, because it had been such a massive kidnapping that the town where it occurred, was completely abandoned. The ones who survived were scattered throughout the region to the Congo, Rwanda, Uganda, and some further yet. The children who were taken became soldiers or prostitutes, or very young child brides.

In Mary's search to learn all she could about the raid, she saw an interview with a man who said he had lost his two young sons, ages five and seven, which were the ages that Grady said the two brothers had been when they were taken. He lived in Kigali, Rwanda, and spent two weeks out of every year searching the countryside for his two sons, posting pleas for their safe return on the sides of the last few remaining buildings in the town they were taken from. Mary was able to meet with the man, and came to learn that his son's names were Kinyera and Mugabo. "I think I may have information about your son's sir," she said reaching for his disfigured hand to comfort him. "I will be in touch with you."

At first, Mary was met with staunch refusal to help the two brothers. It was a very difficult situation that nobody was sure how to handle, which is why nobody did anything. The two boys were no longer innocent children who had been taken against their will. They were grown men who had committed atrocities against mankind. They were uneducated and violent. They were trained to kill, and they were immune to the horrifying effects of bloodshed. They were both wanted men in Rwanda, the Congo, Uganda, Burundi, and maybe even a few other countries. The only way Mary could convince her connections to help the two men, was to promise them they would be under Grady's constant supervision, provide them with counseling, and provide them with proper education. Mary agreed, and was given passports for the two brothers, as well as their father. The only thing left to do was convince them all to leave together, and find Kinyera.

In addition to everything going on, Rudy knew that Doug and Jay were business partners, thanks to his wife who insisted that she know everything about Madison's family, having hired a private investigator after finding some questionable things out about Jay. He wasn't sure what to do about that situation just yet, but for the moment, everything seemed to be working, and so he had no other choice but to leave it alone until Grady got back. Mandi was still fighting the cancer, and Madison was still able to spend time with Diana and her cousins.

Doug was told to lay low before sending him to meet with a man who would never show up, and in fact, didn't exist, to discuss the possibility of getting Jewel out safely. They had audio recordings of Doug's conversations with Taban's men to lead them back to Jewel for a price, implicating him in a kidnapping for ransom scheme. Mary was getting ready to leak this information to the State Department, provide them with a picture of Doug, and provide any additional information she had so they could investigate him, and his business partner, Jay.

Eight prisoners were rescued, and the Congolese military was celebrating their internationally recognized fight against terrorism. Somehow, in all the excitement of defeating the terrorists, the release of eight prisoners was celebrated, and the fact that two were still missing was never questioned. The eight prisoners were being isolated, and had not been available to answer questions from the press. The politicians were in a frenzy, with all of them maneuvering and positioning themselves, trying to get their stories straight. The world needed a success story so badly that pundits who had been all over television a week earlier, demanding the release of ten prisoners, were now on the news insisting that earlier reports of ten prisoners was wrong, and there were really only eight.

~~~~~~~~

"We're going too. I'm tequila… he's lime, and the salt is bringing the car around as we speak," Thames said coming into the room with his travel bag.

"Alright," Rudy said nodding to Thames and Sam to follow him as he made his way out the door to leave for their flight, where Jared was waiting for them with the car. They had discussed Rudy going alone on their two o'clock phone call with Grady, but Rudy was glad to have back-up. They had arranged for a bush pilot to be on-call to fly them in and out of the country as needed, which allowed them some flexibility. Rudy just hoped that he'd have a few extra passengers for the ride back.

He was nervous about going back into the Democratic Republic of the Congo. He had spent some time there when he was a Navy Seal, and it was a country he always disliked. He knew the temperature regarding Americans in their country ran hot and cold. He also knew that it was a very violent country where the value of human life meant little. He thought of his own children, safe at home, as he always did before a mission, and set his mind on the task ahead of him.

They dared not discuss much on the plane ride over. They never knew who they could trust, and who they couldn't, so they trusted nobody. They also knew that even the most trustworthy person could be duped into allowing hidden cameras, or perhaps even had them installed on their plane without knowing it. They knew that everything they were doing was extremely dangerous. There had been whispers about two Americans fitting Grady and Jewel's description who had been in the Congo as part of a drug smuggling operation, and they knew that if they made one wrong move, they could easily find themselves on that same list. For all they knew, the plane they were flying on at that very moment, could have been loaded down with drugs, a violation that would mean the death penalty for all of them.

They landed at the airport without incident, and made their way to the pre-arranged meeting place, where they ordered a drink before making their way out to wait by a pool area, which was really little more than an oversized mud hole where children played. Rudy looked around and saw a man leaning up against the driver's side door of an old beat-up jeep, looking like he was simply whiling away his time with nothing better to do than take long drags off his cigarette and enjoy the early evening. He saw the man stomp out the cigarette, get into his car, and drive around into the alley, as was the plan. They made their way toward the alley, and got in the pickup, before it quickly drove off.

"Terri! What the fuck man! Where's Grady and Jewel? They're supposed to meet us here," Rudy said alarmed. They had lost touch with Terri after he dropped Grady off with his connection that helped him get into the compound. He was worried about him, wondering if maybe Terri had been working both sides of the coin.

"They've been arrested and charged with drug trafficking. They're in prison. Mugabo and Kinyera are in there too. Kinyera is a dead man if we don't get him out right away. He's been brutally beaten, and he's being held in solitary confinement where I've been told he's barely alive. I have a man on the inside, a security guard who's going to connect with Grady once he's run through, but I have nobody in the women's prison. Jewel was dressed like a young man, and taken to the men's prison originally, before they loaded her back up and took her to the women's prison."

"This is fucked up man! Now what?" Rudy said hearing alarm bells go off in his head.

"Jewel's the one I'm worried about. There's nothing from stopping Taban from going in there and taking her out today. If he gets her, we'll never see her again. The man's a fucking lunatic!" Terri said shaking his head.

"How do we get her out? Do you have connections to get her out? Give me something man," Rudy said.

"We have two choices. Either we go public, spread her face all over the news, and fight the charges, or we bust in and take her. If we bust in we need to go now, and worry about Grady later. If we go public, we need to also do it now before Taban walks out the front door with her."

"Well, they couldn't possibly have any evidence," Thames said, thinking like a typical American where people are used to having legal rights to defend themselves.

"That doesn't matter. They'll have enough evidence before you know it. Trust me on this," Terri said leaving them with just the one choice, which was to break her out.

"Here's what I think we should do, but before I tell you, I need to know where the fuck you were Terri," Rudy said letting him know he was serious.

"Well, you didn't really think the Congolese military got those people out did you?" he said shrugging.

Rudy eyed him sideways, matching the half-smile on Terri's face before continuing with his plan.

"Thames, you go meet with Doug, and come up with a plan to get Jewel out. Doug has connections here, and he may be useful. He'll jump on the idea, because he's looking for a big paycheck. He'll be thinking he will have a nice little package to deliver to Taban. Sam will follow you and be there to watch your back to get Doug out of your way after you're out, so you won't end up dead in a ditch. Got it?" Rudy said getting an affirmative nod in return from both men.

"Terri, you, me, and Jared will use your connection to get to Grady, and the other two. After they're out, we'll head to the last pool, and wait for Mary to get us out. She knows what to do if she doesn't hear from us in the morning. This is our last chance. I'm out of tricks, and Mary has used up the last of her favors," Rudy said feeling the adrenaline surge through him.

The team of five made their way through town, before dropping Thames off, with Sam trailing a good distance behind. Thames and Doug would meet up and make plans to get Jewel out. Thames stepped out of the car and made the call as he walked through the streets, giving a performance of a lifetime, convincing Doug that Jewel was in prison, and they needed to get her out right away before Taban showed up. The thought of that happening sent fear running through Doug. He needed to get to Jewel so he could get a rather large payment from Taban. It would be the largest one he had arranged for so far, including the original delivery in Uganda. He jumped on it immediately, seeing dollar signs, all the while conveying concern for Jewel.

Thames had to put his personal feelings for Doug aside, throwing him high-fives a few times, as Doug successfully managed to orchestrate an entire jailbreak. He had bought off some guards at the prison, as well as a few in the military, who agreed to call a late night meeting that would allow everyone to turn a blind eye, as Jewel was escorted outside and delivered to the front door. In that part of the world, everything had a price, and anyone could be bought. They would wait for the ten o'clock meeting to commence, before sneaking in and out of the prison with Jewel safely by their side. Doug had a car they would park near the prison to make their escape.

Thames pushed the thought of Sam out of his mind. He knew Rudy trusted him completely and he had been very reliable, so Thames simply had to trust the situation. He had no way of getting word to Sam, but he knew that he was close behind, and he knew he would know their next move almost as quickly as they made it.

"You're incredible man! I can see why Jared called you," Thames said, patting Doug on the back as they made their preparations to go in and get Jewel, watching the clock tick down.

CHAPTER 68

OPPORTUNITY KNOCKS

Rudy, Terri, and Jared had a task ahead of them that was going to be a little more difficult than the task of getting to Jewel. Getting Grady and the two boys out of prison wasn't going to be easy. They needed to put their feelers out there and hope that an opportunity would present itself so they could exploit it. Terri had been unable to reach his connection at the prison, and he had no other choice than to go to the front desk and ask to get a message to him, the consequences of which could be insurmountable if it ended up in the wrong hands. The message asked that Grady, Kinyera, and Mugabo be jailed in the same cell, and that the connection meet him at the fence within the next hour. They were sitting there waiting for the connection to show up at the fence, when Terri saw him leading the three men out to a prison van.

"This is it! We need to carjack that van. Lord only knows where they're being taken," Rudy said, making a split decision to pull up in front of the van to take the prisoners at gunpoint. "Back me up boys!"

Opportunity had knocked, and they needed to take advantage of the situation. They were on a filthy urban street without any street lights, looking up at a massive perimeter fence that stood over sixteen feet high, and that was topped with razor wire. They knew that they had to jump on this, because they all knew that if the three prisoners were being taken out of the prison under the cover of darkness, they weren't likely to ever be coming back.

"Oh fuck! Here we go!" Terri yelled.

Terri pulled up in front of the van, and the three men, all armed, jumped out simultaneously and got the security guards to their knees. The guards were completely stunned, clearly not expecting that they would have any type of trouble. Rudy handcuffed them all and locked them in the back of the van. Grady and Mugabo made it to the jeep, both of them carrying Kinyera. Kinyera was barely conscious, and the jeep they were in was barely big enough for all of them to fit in. They jumped in, squeezing in as best they could, throwing a tarp over the three prisoners whose hands and feet were still shackled. They cut the tires of the van so the security guards couldn't follow them when they got loose.

"Holy shit man! Drive the fucking car! Don't stop for anything!" Rudy said as Terri weaved his way in and out of traffic. "We need to get to the last pool A.S.A.P!"

The streets were full of cars, trucks, animals, and people walking in every direction. Traffic laws were optional. Nobody seemed to follow any sort of organized commute through the city. Terri drove at full speed weaving through cars and people, driving down random side streets and through alleys. They could see a truck behind them for a while, but Terri managed to lose it as he took the back way toward the direction where they needed to go.

"We can't go in this. We have to ditch this jeep, and find something else," Terri said on full alert, looking for an opportunity for them to commandeer a different vehicle.

"Go through a residential area. Any cars parked outside will likely not be missed until morning. With any luck, we'll be long gone by then," Jared said excitedly, his adrenaline pumping.

They made their way to a raggedy neighborhood until coming to a dark area where they saw an old rusty van parked outside. It looked like most of the vehicles, which was to say that it was broken down, and fitted together with parts from dozens of different makes and models from other cars. They turned off their lights and drove by slowly, parking nearby to look over the area before making their move.

"I'll go check it out," Jared said slipping out of the jeep, creeping slowly toward the van. The house and surrounding area was darker than most neighborhoods they were used to, for the simple fact that there weren't any streetlights or yard lights that would be typical of most American neighborhoods. It was pitch black out, but he skillfully reached underneath, closing his eyes as he felt around for the wires that he needed to get the van started. Once everything was set, he slipped back over to the jeep, and instructed Terri to idle the jeep near the van with the lights on so that anyone who heard an engine would assume that it was the jeep, and not the van. They got the van started, and everyone moved without disturbing the neighborhood. They abandoned the jeep a few blocks away near a burned out house, and rode off toward their meeting place, resting a little easier.

"Rudy, ya saved my life man. I don't know where they were taking us, but I guessed that it didn't have a return ticket attached ta it. Some of Taban's men showed up, and the next thing ya knew we were being released ta their custody," Grady said. "Now we have ta go get Jewel. If he gets her, that's it man. He's obsessed with her. Kinyera told me all about it."

"We're on it brother," Rudy said, explaining the plan.

"I need ta be there. Take me there. I need ta make sure Doug doesn't end up with her. Turn around. Find Sam. I need to be there," Grady said alarmed. "Here. Unlock me," he said pulling the keys from his pocket he had picked up when they were surprised outside the prison.

There was no stopping Grady. He refused to leave the city without Jewel. He was insisting that they go hide out near the prison, and be there when Doug walked out with her by his side. He thought they could have underestimated Doug and his ability to see when his teammates were playing him.

Mugabo sat in the backseat holding Kinyera's head in his lap, but the other three prepared to back Grady up. They left the van sitting a few blocks away, and they all crept toward the women's prison and waited, hiding out of view. They watched as the guards all abandoned their posts simultaneously, and closed in on the car that pulled up in front of the prison and turned off its lights.

They watched Doug get out of the car, walk toward the side of the prison, and pull Sam out of the window well where he was hiding. He held Sam at gunpoint and led him toward Thames, who was standing by the parked car. Thames tried to pull a look of surprise off, but he knew that his cover was blown, and he instinctively tried to shield himself as Doug pointed the gun at him and fired. The pistol had a silencer on the end, and it wasn't until they saw Thames hit the ground when they fully understood what happened.

He turned the gun on Sam, and was met with an angry fist a second later, dropping him to the ground, knocking him out cold. Grady was standing over him with an anger that had been unleashed that could have rendered an entire military unit impotent. Fueled by adrenaline, Grady quickly found out from Thames what the plan was as he laid on the dirty sidewalk bleeding to death. A moment later, he was taking the keys off Doug and heading into the prison to find Jewel, armed with little more than a second hand plan, and pure determination.

He was met in the corridor by a female guard who was standing there holding Jewel by the arm, apparently there to deliver her to Doug. Grady reached out, grabbed her by the arm, and started running out with her. She had her head down, and was being pulled along like someone who was drugged, or badly beaten. He could see that she had been hit in the face several times, and after dragging her a few more feet, decided to pick her up and carry her out to the van. Rudy and Sam had made it to the van with Thames who had been shot in the forearm, shattering the two bones. Jared and Terri carried Doug into the prison walls, and left him lying there still unconscious while they waited for Grady and Jewel. As soon as they saw them, they all started running the few blocks away toward the van.

"Are ya alright Jewel," Grady said breathlessly as he slid in the van with her on his lap.

"I'm okay," she said with a shaky voice at a near breaking point.

"I've got a couple a men here that are broken and beaten, and in need of some medical care. That should cheer you up," he said rocking her gently, letting out a long sigh when he saw the side of her mouth go up in an effort to form a tiny little smile.

"Who's hurt?" she said trying to sit up, letting Grady see her completely for the first time.

"Jesus God Jewel! What the hell happened?" he asked taken aback by the bruising on her face, and the large gash over her eyebrow. Her hair was cut short, and her face was badly bruised and covered in blood. Both her eyes were black, and her nose looked swollen and deformed. Her clothes were men's clothes that she had attempted to disguise herself in when they were going to go meet Rudy before their arrest. The clothes had started out filthy, but after being beaten and dragged along the floor in a dirty prison, she looked and smelled horrible.

Grady composed himself suddenly, "You need stitches darlin'," he said reaching up with a cloth to apply pressure after seeing the large gash on her forehead.

"I'm okay Grady. Who's hurt?" she said looking around the car assessing the men who were all staring at her in disbelief. "Kinyera. Are you okay?" she asked as she leaned over the chair she and Grady were sitting in, softly stroking his head.

"I am okay," Kinyera said getting a nod of approval from Mugabo.

"And you? I... I don't know you, but you're hurt," she said looking at Thames.

"I'm Thames," he said nodding at her. "Doug shot my fucking arm! The bones shattered probably. I'd rather you not look at it right now," he moaned, cradling his arm.

"There should be supplies at the last pool. We should be able to hold out there for a while if we need to," Rudy said turning toward the back from the passenger seat to look at Jewel.

"Rudy," she cried, breaking into a sob as she said his name, leaning forward to give him a hug.

"Jewel, I'm glad to see you sweetheart. I've been praying for you day and night," Rudy said hugging her back.

"Thank you for praying for me Rudy," she said weakly as she leaned back, closing her eyes.

Terri was driving with Rudy sitting in the passenger seat. Grady, Jewel and Thames were in the middle seat, and Mugabo sat in the backseat with Kinyera lying down with his head on Mugabo's lap. Sam and Jared were crammed in the very back, but with the van loaded down with all of them finally safe, they rode in silence for a while as the adrenaline left their bodies leaving them completely drained.

It seemed they could finally rest easy.

CHAPTER 69

THE LAST POOL

They arrived at the last pool early in the morning, just as the sun was rising, which couldn't have been planned out better. They didn't want to be driving during the day in a stolen vehicle, in a country where none of them were supposed to be legally. They had crossed over the border into Rwanda following an old smugglers trail Mary had instructed them to follow. Without Mugabo there to help them stay on the trail, they would have lost it on several occasions, and would have likely been driving in circles.

It had been a sleepless night as they bumped along the road, all of them getting out on several occasions to move logs out of the way, or walk ahead of the van to judge accurately the direction of the trail through the thicker vegetation. Jewel sat with Thames for a while, holding his arm up to give him some relief. She knew the pinch points where she could apply pressure to allow the pain to ease a little, giving him small breaks so he could rest.

Mugabo sat in the back with his brother holding him steady, giving him small sips of water per Jewel's instructions. Kinyera had been badly beaten. Jewel checked him over briefly, and she was convinced he had several broken ribs, possibly a fractured jaw, and most definitely a broken nose. He was suffering the effects of a concussion, mixed with a severe case of dehydration. Whoever beat him wanted him to die a slow painful death. They all suspected it happened at the hands of one of Taban's pawns.

The last pool was so well hidden, that several of them had to search around for half an hour to find the entrance. Not even Mugabo or Kinyera knew the place was there. This was a place that one of Mary's connections had told her about. It was a place where he and his family had hidden out during one of the many conflicts that occurred in the 1990's, and he assured them they would be safe. The last pool itself was a little more impressive than the previous one. It was a deep mountain lake with a silty bottom. They cleaned out the van of all their stuff, and put complete faith in Mary as they pushed the van off the cliff, and watched it sink to the bottom, leaving no sign of its existence.

The plan was that Mary would send someone to retrieve them when the climate had settled down, and it would be safe for them to travel. They had discussed the possibility that it could be several weeks, and so they all resigned themselves to the fact that they would have to wait a while longer before they would be completely out of danger. They quickly gathered together and made plans, with Rudy taking the lead. Rudy had been in the leadership role all along, and for once, Grady sat back and followed. These men were used to being in Rudy's charge, and Grady needed to tend to Jewel.

The hideout itself was an extremely large dugout that was accessible through a small hatch door hidden under thick vegetation. It was a large room sectioned off by large boulders, with several storage trunks and large rocks that had been left in place when the hideout was dug. The first thing Jewel saw when she opened the hatch door and poked her head in, was a lantern and several lighters. She moved toward them slowly, keeping her fear of small spaces in check as the darkness closed in around her. She glanced back at Grady who was standing beside her in case they weren't alone.

Once she got the lantern going, she could see just how small the space was, and she had to catch her breath. She closed her eyes for a moment and took a deep breath. She needed to search through the hideout to find some supplies that she would need to help Thames and Kinyera. The trunks were full of blankets, sleeping bags, medical supplies, and some canned foods. Grady and the other men started dragging everything out of the hideout to air things out, and assess their supplies.

The men were sprawled out in the clearing overlooking the lake. Thames and Kinyera simply laid there fighting their pain, and Jewel was relieved to find painkillers and antibiotic medicine, though she worried about the expired dates stamped on the front of the vials.

As soon as she found the painkillers and syringe, she went to the two men and immediately gave them each a shot, seeing their pain ease almost immediately. She carefully marked each needle so she could reuse them, with them never having to share the same one. They were sprawled out in the sun, finding some relief finally as she checked them both over. The bones in Thames' arm were shattered, and it was going to be impossible to do more than keep him stable and comfortable until they could get him to a surgical center.

She crawled over to look at Kinyera more closely. His face was badly beaten, and he had a concussion. His ribs were broken, and he had a broken nose, which Jewel immediately reached up and set without thinking about it. She knew it had to be done immediately. Mugabo was still sitting right there with him, and he gave Jewel an odd look as he saw the deformed looking nose take a relatively normal looking shape once again. She finally determined that Kinyera's biggest problem was that he was severely dehydrated, and he had likely been near death when he was carried to the van.

"It's your turn Jewel," Grady said coming up behind her where she checked

Kinyera and Thames over. "This is Terri. He's a doctor. He's going to stitch up your face."

"Oh. I didn't know we had a doctor here. Can you check his arm?" she said ignoring Grady while she continued to check the two men over. "I think we're just going to have to stabilize it for now, and then when we get back, he'll have to have surgery. Kinyera I think will just need time... well... time and water."

"Let them rest a bit while he stitches ya up Jewel," Grady urged, coming to kneel beside her.

Both of her eyes were black and swollen. Her nose had also been broken, but she had already reset it herself when they were on the ride through the forest. The gash on her forehead had bled profusely, and she was covered in blood, which matted her short hair to the side of her head. Her lips were swollen and bleeding from a few lacerations that occurred during the beating. She was covered in dirt, and any number of other things she dared not think about. She wore the same men's clothing she had been wearing when they dressed her up to look like a man before they were arrested, on their way to go meet up with Rudy.

"Alright, come with me to the lake first so I can wash up," she said looking up at Grady.

"Okay darlin'. Come on," he said taking her hand, leading her toward the lake. "I had a feeling you would say that."

They walked in silence for a ways, hand-in-hand, neither one of them knowing what to say to the other. They were both exhausted to the point that each step seemed like a monumental task, and they dared not think of the trek back up to the hideout. They looked at the lake water longingly. It looked clean and inviting, and anything clean looked good at that point.

"Who did this to you Jewel?" he finally asked.

"My cellmates... they thought I was a lesbian, I gathered, and they were pretty excited about that. Once I realized what they wanted me to do, I went crazy. Trust me when I tell you that it was worth the beating to get out of doing that!" she said forcing a little laugh. "I'm glad you like it, but it's definitely not for me."

"Christ Jewel! Ya were nearly raped by a pack of ladies?" he asked, throwing up his hands defeated. "Is there anyone I won't have ta fight off ya?"

"Well... I wouldn't call them ladies exactly," she said looking up at Grady with a crooked smile, "that's debatable."

They made it to the edge of the water, and though it was cold, they were both eager to jump in and clean off. It was hot and muggy, and the prisons they had been in were filthy.

"Let's dive in on three," he said as they waded up to their thighs with all their clothes on, including their shoes.

"Okay. One. Two. Three!" they counted before diving in.

She scrubbed at her hair as she dove under. The feeling of getting rinsed off was refreshing, and she could feel the ease of pressure on her face as the caked on blood started washing away.

"Here darlin', I grabbed this for ya," he said handing her a bar of soap.

"Oh how wonderful." She closed her eyes and smelled the scent of soap as if it was the best thing she had ever smelled in her life.

She scrubbed at her hair, and rubbed the bar of soap into her clothes, slipping them off under water so she could scrub the grime away, even as Grady adamantly protested.

"It's not the first time you've swam with me naked in a lake," she said trying to wink at him, feeling renewed in the coolness of the clean water, and the freshness of the soap.

"Even with yer face bruised and beaten, I still want ya, and I'm tryin' not ta think of it or I'll be in a hell of a bad way," he said coming up to help her put her wet clothes back on her, shielding her from anyone's view. "Do ya think the baby's okay?" he asked carefully.

"Yes I do. I dreamed about him Grady. His name's Ryan, and he looks just like you. I think...well... I think everything's going to be okay. I just feel it," she said wiping away a tear. "It just has to be." She was shaking her head, trying to convince herself as much as him.

He smiled and choked back his own tears, letting out the breath he had been holding. "I'm glad Jewel," he said stroking her hair.

He used the bar of soap to wash himself as well, and then they made their way out of the water to sit on the bank. The gash on her forehead started bleeding again, and they had to get up and walk back toward the hideout where the men sat in the sun overlooking the lake. They were both looking forward to sitting out and drying themselves in the sun, and perhaps nap a bit, but first Jewel needed to endure some stitches.

"I'll trade you this bar of soap for that bottle," Jewel said sitting down by Rudy, handing him a bar of soap.

"I'm alright sweetheart. I showered less than twelve hours ago," he said handing her the bottle of whiskey he had found in the hideout, wrapping an arm around her. "I would appreciate it if you could stop getting kidnapped," he said forcing a smile.

She attempted to take a swig before Grady came and took it from her, giving her a curious look. Since the morning sickness had finally subsided a little, she sometimes forgot she was pregnant. Rudy gave Grady an odd look, and there was no doubt that he knew what was up, but they would tell him in their own time. He understood how difficult it could be for them.

Jewel watched with reassurance as Terri checked the two patients over, glad to have a moment where she didn't have to jump into action to care for the two wounded men. She was exhausted. It had been three nights since she had been able to sleep more than a couple hours at a time, and combined with the stress and strain of everything they had endured since they were taken, she was near collapsing.

"It's been a while since I did this, but one time when we were on vacation, my oldest daughter slipped and cut herself on the cheek. I was able to make the stitches so small and so precise, that she barely has a scar," Terri said, preparing a spot where he could proceed with the stitching. "Now come here little lady," he said patting a place in the grass next to the flat rock where he had everything laid out.

Grady came and sat next to her to watch as Terri made the tiny little stitches as promised. Jared, Sam, and Mugabo had already set out toward a clearing to see what they could hunt, and Rudy started preparing some of the canned food they found in the hideout. Kinyera and Thames slept peacefully in the grassy area where they were able to have some relief from their pain. It looked like they had all been spewed from the earth's surface; all of them tired and dirty, sprawled out all over the place. Blankets and sleeping bags were laid out on bushes and trees to air out in the sun. Trunks and other gear were sprawled out in every direction, as they took stock of what they had. They didn't know how long they would need to be there, and so they had to know what they had, and make it last.

Jewel sat with her eyes closed, feeling Grady's solid hand wrapped around hers as Terri stitched her face. Her clothes were drying quickly as the sun beat down on them, and warmed their skin. She was starting to feel the effects of the stress and strain, and she could feel her head spinning. Terri had given her a local anesthetic so she wouldn't be able to feel the stitches, and she never remembered lying down. She woke up several hours later wrapped in Grady's arms, with the smell of cooked meat stirring her belly. Grady was still sleeping soundly until she moved to get up.

"I'm sorry I woke you," she said sitting up, running her hands through his hair. "I miss your blond locks, but I'll take you in any color," she whispered, smiling down at him, as he lay prone on the ground.

"I miss your long hair, but I'd take ya bald," he said reaching up to touch her face.

Rudy, Jared, and Terri were sitting around a campfire cooking whatever the men had caught on their hunting expedition, and the others were starting to stir and make their way to sit with them. Terri had given Thames and Kinyera some more painkillers, but they were rested and came to join the group. Mugabo, Jewel, and Grady came and sat down with everyone as they gathered in silence, watching the fire burn. Rudy finally spoke.

"I don't know how long we'll be here. It could be a day, or it could be weeks. We'll have to wait and see. Mary won't come until its safe, plus, she needs to get everyone the right paperwork in order to get us out of here quietly," Rudy said clearing his throat. "That includes the two of you," Rudy said looking at Kinyera and Mugabo. "Mary found your father."

"Our father? What father? How? Do not joke with me man," Mugabo said, completely taken by surprise, looking at Kinyera wide-eyed.

"Grady asked if there was something we could do to get you guys out of here, but there's a catch," he said, pausing to make sure he had their full attention. "The two of you, and your father, provided he'll go, will go to Wyoming with Grady and Jewel," he said meeting Grady and Jewel's eyes. "It's going to be hard for you. It's a different culture. It's non-violent... relatively speaking," he admitted. "You have to be under Grady's supervision, you have to go to counseling, you have to go to school, and you have to work hard. This was the only way Mary could make the deal. Her connection wants you to do this, and then return one day to help your own people."

"We will do it," Kinyera said without hesitation, meeting his brother's eyes.

"You said you thought you would like America Mugabo. Here's your chance," Jewel said smiling at him.

"What is dis Wyoming? Where will we live?" Mugabo asked angrily as he fidgeted, afraid of all the freedom that was suddenly within his reach. "How do you know you have found our father?"

"Well, Jewel's aunt has connections, and vast resources," Rudy said looking at Jewel. "She found him. He was on a television program where he talked about you. Every year he takes two weeks, he goes back to your old village, and he posts information about you, looking for you. He's never given up trying to find you. She went and met with him, and he said your names. He said you were taken when you were five and seven, just as you said. She researched the year that the village was raided, and it fits with your current ages. There's just too many coincidences for it not to be the right man."

"Does dis father have a hand with all his fingers?" Kinyera asked, lifting his right hand in demonstration.

"Mary did say that his hand had been cut deeply, and was missing the upper part of his fingers," Rudy said raising his eyebrows. "Why do you ask Kinyera?"

"Because, our father used dis hand to stop da machete from hitting Mugabo in da head. Dis is all I remember of him," Kinyera said thoughtfully.

Silence descended upon the camp. They all imagined the scene of a quiet little village that was suddenly set upon by violent men with machetes, killing people, and taking children. The men all sat and thought of their own children. Jewel sat quietly and considered the last months since they had been taken hostage, and realized that nothing they had endured during that relatively short time, would come anywhere close to being as difficult as what Mugabo and Kinyera had to endure for most of their lives. She and Grady had been taken temporarily, and it would affect them briefly, but they would move on. Kinyera and Mugabo had been taken for their entire childhood, it would define them, and they would never be able to completely move on.

She watched them as they considered the impossible scenario that seemed to be happening before their very eyes. They were excited and terrified. When she and Grady decided to go to Uganda, they bought books and researched it on the internet, but the two boys would have no such luxury. They couldn't read, and they were completely uneducated by ways of geography. Where they were going may as well have been a trip to outer space, where no man had ever traveled before. They couldn't know that they were going to a peaceful land where rebels didn't run around with machetes. They couldn't know that they would be able to walk down a street without seeing bloodshed, or sit in a quiet park and watch children play in water fountains. They couldn't imagine the snowstorms they never knew existed, or picture the Rocky Mountains they had never heard of. There was a part of her that worried about them being able to assimilate, but she also knew they had no choice. These men helped them because there was goodness in them, and that was all she needed to know.

CHAPTER 70

CHRISTMAS

Several weeks had passed, and Rudy was starting to get worried. He had just made another notch in the tree he used to keep track of their time at the hideout, marking twenty-two days. They had been living off the land, with all of them huddling up in the hideout each night to sleep. It was cramped with nine of them in there, and tensions were starting to run high. Several of them had attempted to sleep outside, but it had rained nearly every night, and so they had no choice but to sleep in the dugout. Every day they woke with the hope that someone would come for them, but every evening they had been disappointed as they watched the sun set, and prepared for another night in the cramped dugout where they slept on the cold, hard ground.

They spent their days hunting or just hiking around the countryside. They hadn't seen another living soul since they arrived, and they were all getting comfortable exploring their surroundings. They swam in the lake and caught fish, or spent the days sleeping out in the hot sun, thankful to be out of the cold, damp dugout.

Kinyera was healing nicely and getting around much better, aside from the sore ribs, which would take some time to mend. Thames had his arm stabilized in a cast Jewel had been able to make out of a newspaper and some glue that she'd found, and he was getting around easily enough. Jewel was healing, and the bruising on Grady's ribs was almost completely gone, though Jewel suspected that they had indeed been fractured and still had a ways to go before they were completely better. He would still wince in pain when she would forget and grab him too hard, or when he went to pick something up that touched the sore area.

They all sat and waited. They talked at times, and sat in compete silence at other times. Groups would go off to hunt, and others would stay behind to keep the fire going. They never saw another living soul, heard a radio, or even saw a plane flyover. It felt like they were the last people on earth.

One day they had all gotten scared thinking Kinyera and Mugabo had run off and decided not to come back. They had left early in the morning, and when they still weren't back at dusk, the consensus was that they decided to abandon ship. They were all disappointed, on top of which they were still worried that the brothers could return to their ways as rebels, and take them hostage again. They were making plans on what to do when the two finally showed up carrying as many plantains as they possibly could, as well as a small deer. The plantains and the deer were tied to a stick with one man on each side carrying the load into camp, providing them all with enough food to eat for several days.

Jewel's morning sickness had subsided, and her face had almost healed aside from the scar that she would have forever. It was barely visible though, and Jewel was impressed by Terri's skill at making the stitches so small. There wasn't a mirror anywhere, but she could feel the small stitching, and she looked at her reflection in the still lake. She cringed every time she saw her hair, never once remembering a time when she didn't have her long, straight hair. She didn't want to cut it, but at the time, it seemed like her only hope, and besides, it was a small price considering all the horrible things that could have happened to her over the last few months.

She and Grady had managed to slip off by themselves one day, but Mugabo, who had been afraid to let them out of his sight for very long, had immediately interrupted them. They were eager to get back to their home to have some privacy they hadn't experienced since the night before they were taken hostage months earlier. The sexual tension that hung in the air between them had left them both feeling frustrated, and increasingly more agitated. They didn't know how much longer they would be able to wait, and not just for sex, but for the rest of their lives.

Jewel and Grady talked to Mugabo and Kinyera about Wyoming constantly, and since they knew what to expect, and could taste the freedom, they were not about to risk anything. They protected Grady and Jewel at all costs, offered to go hunting for them, and they had started to treat them like superiors, which made Jewel and Grady feel awkward.

"Mugabo, Kinyera," Grady said getting their attention, letting them know he needed them to fully understand something, "in America, we are equal. You," he said pointing at them both, "me, and Jewel," he said, "we are all the same. Nobody belongs to another. You will work for a boss, and you will need to do as they say and work hard. In return, you will be paid, but that is all. We are friends who look out for each other... nothing more. Do you understand?" he asked, knowing that this concept was completely foreign to them.

"We belong to you?" Mugabo asked confused, feeling anxious.

"No Mugabo! You belong to you," he said pointing a finger at Mugabo's chest. "You belong to your family, and any other person you want to belong to, until you decide you don't want to belong anymore. In America, you are free man!"

The idea of not being controlled by another individual was as foreign to them as the land they were dreaming of. They didn't remember having ever lived a day when their lives didn't depend on following orders given by a glorified slave owner that the media sometimes called terrorists. They had been prisoners who were stolen from their lands, and used by the men who claimed to be their family. They were still discussing the idea of freedom, and the actual actions of a free man and a free society, when Rudy came and sat with them.

"I think today is Christmas," Rudy said with some sadness. "My kids are opening their presents without me again."

"I'm so sorry Rudy," Jewel said wrapping her hands around his arm, resting her head against him.

"It's not your fault Je…," he started, before stopping suddenly to listen for a repeat of the noise he just heard, turning to Grady knowing he heard the same sound.

The two men sat and listened carefully, hearing an outside noise for the first time since they arrived at the hideout three weeks earlier. They all froze in place, making eye contact with each other to communicate their excitement. It was the first sign of hope they had been given, and they were all wide-eyed and hopeful that the day may have finally come for them to leave.

"It's a helicopter," Grady said excitedly, his heart pounding wildly in his chest.

Jewel grabbed his hand, and squeezed Rudy's leg with excitement as they listened to the sound getting closer. After not seeing or hearing another outside noise that would indicate human existence beyond that camp for the last three weeks, they knew without a doubt the helicopter was there for them. They waited as the helicopter touched down in the clearing where they had all sprawled out on that first day, and then cheered and shrieked with delight when they saw the pilot flash an American Flag patch, before quickly covering it back up, and getting out of the helicopter.

"Are you Rudy?" the pilot asked coming up to one of the men. He was dressed from head to toe in a black non-distinct uniform with a head cover concealing his face.

"I'm Rudy," Rudy said coming up to the pilot to shake his hand.

"Rudy. We don't exist. You have about five minutes to get things buttoned up so we can get going. I need to blindfold all of you, and then we're going to go on a little ride. No questions. No talking. I need you to instruct your people. Can you do that?" the pilot asked as more of an order than a question.

"Of course!" Rudy said as he took control of the group and started giving orders.

The pilot and one other man had some crates they were unloading from the helicopter to carry to the dugout. "These are replacement supplies," the co-pilot said handing the crates down into the hole. "Leave them in the hideout."

Within minutes, they had replaced the hatch door, loaded themselves on the helicopter, and were lying like sardines on the floor of the helicopter blindfolded, brimming with fear and excitement. For the seven Americans, seeing a couple of highly trained American military men show up in a helicopter to carry them off, was a feeling of relief, but to Mugabo and Kinyera, it was sheer terror. It was only the trust they had developed in the other seven that made them follow suit and get on the helicopter, but it didn't happen without some coaxing, and Kinyera had to admit that he was happy to be blindfolded so he could conceal the terror he felt.

They flew for what seemed like forever before finally landing somewhere, and being instructed to not move or make a noise. "Trust me. Just lay here, be silent, and keep the blindfolds on. It's for your own protection. I wouldn't leave my fellow comrades behind. Trust in that okay?" the pilot said to them. "I'll be back shortly."

True to his word, the pilot came back several minutes later to retrieve them. None of them had moved an inch. They knew that at that point they were at the pilot's mercy anyway, and agreed to do what he said.

"Okay. I had to make sure everything was clear. Leave the blindfolds on. We're all going to take a hand and follow me," he said taking the first hand, leading the human chain out of the helicopter, and into a rather large airplane. "Watch your step."

The pilot got the nine of them seated and strapped into the airplane seats before starting in with instructions.

"You're flying to Amsterdam. You need to wait until you hear this timer go off before taking the blindfolds off. I have cameras, and I will be watching you, so don't cheat or I'll come track you down! Do you understand?" he said with a loud booming voice and a southern drawl. "Okay, I'm just kidding, but seriously, you don't want to see this. If you are questioned about it later, I need you to be able to pass a lie detector test. The less you know about what's going on right now, the better. Do you understand?" he asked sincerely this time, getting nine nods in response.

"There are suitcases up here for all of you with some items you'll need. After the timer goes off, and you remove your blindfold, then help yourself to them. There's water, liquor, and there's even some peanuts. Of course! What flight would be complete without peanuts? This is a full service operation here," he added flippantly.

"Your seat is a flotation device. If you crash, and by some miracle from God you survive, ignore the seat cushion and try to find the flares. They will not only signal a rescue plane, they can also be used to fight off sharks," he said cracking himself up, making the others laugh. "Just kidding folks! You enjoy your flight and have a nice day."

"Thank you sir!" they yelled to the man, all of them still laughing as they heard him leave.

They sat there as still as could be, and not one of them dared to peek out of their blindfold. They had seen enough. They were all wrestling with a plethora of emotions that took them to the highest of highs and the lowest of lows, all within the span of a single second that played over and over again. They sat in silence, and listened to the ticking of the timer as the plane reached higher elevations. Jewel had never let go of Grady's hand, and they sat there with just the feel of each other's skin between them, their pulses firing rapidly at one another in anticipation of their future together.

When the timer went off, nobody moved for several minutes. The quiet, peaceful flight in the cover of darkness hadn't been entirely unpleasant. Slowly, each one of them finally slipped the blindfolds off and looked around the plane in awe. It was a large jet, and aside from the pilots, there was nobody else onboard. It was packed with signs of a modern world, the likes of which they hadn't seen in a long time. Some longer than others, and some, had actually never seen the inside of a plane. Kinyera was sitting right next to Jewel, and when she saw the fear in his eyes, she just smiled at him and grabbed his hand.

Rudy was the first to get up to make his way over to the suitcases that were stacked in the first aisle. He picked the first one up and set it down on the seat, unzipping it to expose a suitcase full of clothes with a passport sitting on top. He opened it and read off the name slowly. "Jewel Esther...," he said with a little smile and a raised eyebrow, "McDonald. Please step forward and reclaim your life madam," he said waving the passport in the air.

"Mugabo Biha," Rudy said holding up the next passport and waving it, looking at Mugabo to step forward.

"Biha? What is this name?" Mugabo said confused, asking in that angry voice of a rebel that was slowly starting to soften.

"Biha! It is Biha! I remember! It is the name of our father. It is Biha," Kinyera said excitedly as he fought back tears looking at his brother.

"Kinyera Biha," Rudy said smiling at Kinyera as he handed him his Burundi passport to match his brothers.

Rudy handed out all the suitcases and all the passports, matching them all to their actual identities without aliases, including Mugabo and Kinyera whose true identities had finally been restored, complete with birth certificates. They all took turns in the bathroom, sponging off and getting dressed in the clothes that were provided to them, so they would all look clean and respectable when they landed in Amsterdam.

Jewel sighed heavily seeing herself in a mirror for the first time with her short hair. It was cut with dull scissors in a rush, but she thought it looked surprisingly well despite that. She was surprised to see that her hair had a little curl in it since it was so short, and ran her fingers through it trying to find a look she was happy with before grabbing a ball cap and pulling it down on her head. Anything beyond throwing her hair in a braid or a ponytail took more effort than she cared to think about.

They raided the galley and found dozens of small bottles filled with the liquid they craved, and sampled each one of them.

"I do not drink alcohol," Kinyera said as someone passed him one of the bottles. "Hassan made me sick to drink it. I do not like it."

"Mugabo?" Rudy said offering the bottle to him.

"I do as my brother do," he answered, still feeling unsure of the situation, clearly not understanding the idea of personal freedom just yet.

"But I salute you," Kinyera said holding up a bottle of water, nodding to all of them, urging Mugabo to do the same, "our new family and friends... you are saved us. We will be equal to you, work with you, and be free in America. One day, we will return and help another Kinyera... another Mugabo. This is how we say thanks to you."

"You saved our lives man. You don't owe us anything. Without the two of you, we wouldn't be here. You do it for yourself, and give thanks to yourself. You made this possible," Grady said giving a nod of thanks to the brothers. "The only thing you have to do is follow through with the promises you made. That much is true, but it's a gift. It'll help the both of you. You'll go to school, and you'll be able to talk to a counselor, and learn to live a different life. We'll help you, but only if you want us to."

"How will we see our father?" Mugabo finally asked, looking up at Grady with hopefulness. He suddenly had the look of a five-year-old boy who wanted his daddy, and not the look of the rebel that had terrified them that first day. The hurt in his eyes ran miles deep, but for the first time, Mugabo started to see possibilities. For the first time, the sharp swords of indoctrination that had penetrated his mind, started to drift away, and he made room for the small memory of a love that he once knew.

They gathered around the galley making one toast after another. It was a long flight to Amsterdam, and they were far too eager to sit there. They ate peanuts, and other food that had been supplied for them, and all of them told stories about the first thing they were planning to do when they got home.

"Well, I better not tell you about the first thing I'm planning," Rudy said coyly, making everyone laugh, "my wife would be pissed, but after that... I think I'd like to just sit at the kitchen table with my wife and kids, and eat a good meal. I can't wait to have them tell me about their day, or poke and tease each other the way they do. Those are the things I miss the most when I'm away."

"I think I would like to have an American cheeseburger," Kinyera said when it was his turn. "There was dis man that had come one time who talked about dis. I think I would like dis."

"I think I would like to read," Mugabo said as the next in line. "I think this would be useful."

"Ummm... surgery... and maybe a few tetanus shots for good measure," Thames joked.

Sam and Jared talked about spending time with their families.

"Merry Christmas everyone," Grady said after they had all shared their stories, raising his drink before leaning down and kissing Jewel firmly on the lips.

"Merry Christmas!" They all joined in chorus, raising their drinks in celebration.

CHAPTER 71

REUNIONS

"That was the most incredible thing I've ever witnessed Grady," Jewel said as they walked back to their room at the hotel where they were staying in Amsterdam. They had just come from the suite Mary was renting, and they witnessed the most amazing reunion between a father and his two sons that she could have ever imagined. It made everything they had been through seem worth it suddenly.

Mary and the brothers' father, Yannick, had been waiting for all of them in the suite since hearing that their plane had finally landed, and everyone gathered there before heading off to their own rooms. They would be flying back to the U.S. the next day, but they were all still feeling celebratory, hugging, and thanking everyone, and the reunion between Yannick and his sons didn't leave anyone with a single dry eye.

"Yes, I see the boys I knew. Yes, I see this," Yannick said jumping up and down, grabbing the two young men and hugging them, leaving all three of them standing there crying. It had been fourteen years since Yannick had seen his sons, but he knew them without any doubt, the way only a parent would.

They talked between themselves, in their own language, back and forth. The rest of them just stood there and watched the connection. The family resemblance left no doubt that these two young men were indeed Yannick's sons, and they watched as the two hardened and violent rebels turned into little boys again, as they hugged their father, and cried with abandon like a child would do.

"Father, I remember you," Kinyera said wiping his eyes, and taking his father's hand that had been hacked by the machete. As soon as Kinyera took his hand their eyes met, they both remembered that moment. It was the memory from a man who remembered it all too clearly, and thought of it daily as he searched for his sons, and it was the memory from a small boy who remembered seeing his father save his brother's life. "I remember Father," he sobbed, hugging him to him once again.

"I had remembered walking as a small boy, holding my father's hand. I have looked at many faces trying to see dis face, and now I know dat it was you," Mugabo said hugging his father with tears rolling down his face. "I know that you are my Father."

"My prayers have been answered," Yannick said hugging them non-stop. "Da Lord has been good to me dis day."

Yannick met everyone, and he hugged and thanked them all. He sat and listened to the story of how they came to meet Kinyera and Mugabo, and Yannick waivered back and forth between feeling sad for his sons, and feeling proud of them for the good that still lived within them, despite all the brainwashing and abuse they had endured. It was clear to see why the two young men had managed to hang onto some of the good their father instilled in them when they were children. Yannick was, in every way, the kindest, most sincere and moral man any of them had ever met.

He was a very gentle man in his mid-forties, and he already had a full head of gray hair. He wore little round glasses that sat neatly on the bridge of his nose, as if they had been custom made just for him. He was dressed in black slacks and a white button-down shirt, as he did every day of his life. His brown leather shoes were well worn, but neatly polished, and matched the old leather belt that he wore around his waist. He was slightly taller than his sons were, but he was frail looking, appearing as though he never quite got enough to eat in his life, and that was likely true. He had been working at a shelter in Rwanda before Mary came into his life, and he was always moving around getting this or that, or fixing things, or dividing his food up so others could have more. He was a man who always gave just a little too much of himself.

Yannick was an educated man who had earned a degree from Michigan State University when he was young. He had been part of a sponsorship program that allowed young men or women to go to an American college to earn a degree, with the promise of going back to their towns and villages in Burundi, to educate the youth, and give back to the community that paid their tuition. All the elders of the community who had been in a position to cast a vote, had chosen him unanimously. He always stood out as someone who was willing to help his fellow man, and nobody had any doubt that he would go back to their community, and help educate their youth.

Before the raid that decimated their village, he did just that. He taught at the school, and set up programs for young men and women to become teachers themselves. He organized church events that got people involved and excited to learn, and put them in a better position to give back to their community. Yannick had quickly become a man looked to in the community as a leader, as a counselor, and as a friend to everyone. Even through the death of his wife, who died suddenly from a deadly virus, he never took time for himself. "There's just too much need," he'd said when he came in to teach the next day.

When Mary visited his home in Rwanda the second time, to tell him about her plan to help the two young men, Yannick was on board before she ever finished her first sentence. He was beside himself with excitement. He knew that his sons had been forced to do things they would regret, and he knew they would need help. He was willing to do anything to help them, and if that meant living in the severe cold again, which he flatly detested, then that was something he was more than willing to do.

He had seen the atrocities committed by the Interahamwe. He had been a victim of it, and he knew that his sons had participated in some of it, but he also saw them as victims, taken from their homes as children, and turned into killers against their will. He knew they were violent. He knew they were uneducated. He knew they had seen things and done things that were unimaginable, but he also knew he would never give up on his sons. He smiled at them like a proud father when Grady and Jewel embellished on the stories of how they saved their lives.

When Mary came to tell him about taking the two men to America, she not only came with the promise of him reuniting with his sons, she came with a job opportunity that would allow him to work from home translating documents. He would need to translate them into the three different languages he spoke besides English, if he agreed to go to America with them. He would be editing documents, creating brochures and other documents to spread educational information about diseases, disease prevention, and other necessary information throughout the region where he was from. He would be working for the United Nations, and he immediately said yes.

Mary had explained the agreement to get the boys counseling and to provide them with an education, and Yannick thought that was a great idea. He agreed to everything, and said he would provide for the boys so they could get everything they needed. His life in Rwanda had been a constant battle between good and evil. He was happy to be leaving, and even happier to have his sons far away from there, because he knew they were going to have a hard time assimilating, and he didn't want it to be easy for them to return to the violence. His only regret would be leaving their mother's grave. She had died when Mugabo was just two, and her grave was just outside the village in Burundi the rebels raided.

"That *was* incredible Jewel, but not nearly as incredible as you," Grady said coming up behind her, swooping her up and carrying her into the shower as she still languished in the memory of the reunion. "Ya want a shower, and I want you. I think I know a way we could both be happy at the same time. We'll have our own reunion," he said pulling her shirt over her head and kissing her thoroughly.

"Okay, well now we're just standing in the shower making out. Maybe we should consider turning the water on," she said as he kissed her and pulled her pants off her before turning on the water. They stood in the shower and washed themselves, and each other. Jewel sighed with gratitude when she was finally able to shave her legs for the first time in weeks. Grady shaved his face and washed his hair thoroughly, the color fading slightly as the blond roots started showing. They finished, and hurriedly made their way to the bed. They hadn't been together for three months and they were both eager.

"I missed ya darlin'," he said as he laid her down on the bed.

"Grady, I love you," she said kissing him as he climbed on top of her.

They touched each other in ways they had both been dreaming about the last few months as they laid next to each other in the prisoner's camp, or in the dugout in Rwanda. Each touch was familiar and yet brand new, sending waves of electricity from one end of their bodies to another. There had been many days during the last few months when they wondered if they would ever see each other again, or in Jewel's case, *knowing* Grady was dead. She closed her eyes, not wanting to take a single moment for granted as she held onto him. She was getting lost in the moment when he suddenly stopped.

"Wait, I can't Jewel," he said rolling off her onto the bed beside her, hitting the pillow in frustration as he did.

"What? What are you talking about?" she said gasping, never missing a beat before climbing on top of him.

"Stop Jewel, I can't," he said pushing her off him. "I'm afraid we'll hurt the baby."

"What? We won't hurt the baby Grady. Are you insane?"

"The last time… when the miscarriage happened, we made love and everything was perfect, but then the next thing I knew you were in the bathroom covered in blood. God I want ya darlin', but if it happened again…," he said shaking his head.

"You're not going to make love to me for five months?" she asked in frustration and disbelief.

"I just want ya ta see a doctor first. Since you've been pregnant, you've been kidnapped and taken hostage by a group of armed rebels, kidnapped by an evil terrorist, gone through the stress of thinking your husband was dead, escaped captivity through an underground drug trafficking tunnel, brutally beaten in a Congolese prison, and then camped in an underground hideout for several weeks. Am I being paranoid here?" he asked sarcastically.

"Well, when you put it like that it doesn't sound like a very healthy environment for a pregnant woman, but I feel fine. If he can endure all that, then surely he can survive this," she said attempting to kiss him once again, only to have him turn away, dodging her kiss.

"I just can't darlin'. I'd never be able ta look ya in the eye again if somethin' like that happened again. Seein' ya like that, bleedin' on the bathroom floor, seein' the blood soak through and knowin' there's not a damn thing I can do ta stop it," he said shaking his head. "I just couldn't take it again."

"Oh geez," she said staring at the ceiling, understanding the point Grady was making. "Well, there's other things we can do, right?" she said propping herself up on her side seductively.

"Ya did say that ya liked it, if I recall the story of ya nearly gettin' raped by a pack of unladylike women, which I mistakenly left out of my summary of all the current events during your pregnancy," he said raising an eyebrow at her.

"Jo said that a man would go to any length to get a woman to…," she said trailing off, signaling her intentions by letting her eyes roam down his body.

"She said that did she?" he said losing his breath as she reached down between his legs.

"You first," he said rolling her over on her back and making his way down, pinning her hands with his own.

She cried out the second she felt the warmth of his mouth on her. She pressed herself harder against him anticipating every movement that brought her closer. His hands were all over her, and every sense in her body came alive all at once until she could do nothing else but tip her head back and ride the wave of pleasure that took her higher, and then deeper.

"Oh wow! That was amazing," she said laying back a minute before rolling on top of him.

This was something she had never done before, but the thought had occurred to her more than once. She had read about it, and heard her girlfriends talk about it, but Grady had never mentioned anything about it before, and so she never tried it. She met his eyes looking for a sign, but she couldn't read him as she still languished in her own pleasure.

"I don't know what to do," she finally said.

"Just do whatever feels natural ta ya darlin'," he said smiling at her, reaching up to touch her face.

"But do you want me to. I mean… do men like it like women do?" she asked feeling unsure.

"Yes, and most definitely yes, but I don't want ya ta if yer not comfortable with it. I don't want ya ta feel like I'm pushin' ya."

She kept eye contact with him while she made her way down the length of him. She could hear his heart beating faster, and she felt him catch his breath as she touched him with her tongue, lightly at first, but then with more zeal. It was a new experience in their lovemaking. She was used to them joining together and taking their pleasure at the same time, but this was different. Each time she took him deeper, he came more alive and cried louder; much like a piano would come alive as she closed her eyes and stroked each key. She owned him in that moment as he laid there with his eyes closed, begging for more until he finally let go of everything he had been holding back for months. She loved watching him as his body twisted beneath her.

"I love that I can give you that much pleasure," she finally said several minutes later.

"That was incredible Jewel. Apparently what feels natural ta ya, feels incredible ta me."

"So you like it then?" she said smiling to herself.

"Come here," he said pulling her closer to him. He could feel the mound on her stomach and ran his hands over the small bump over and over, before reaching down to kiss it lightly. "Ryan is it?" he asked looking up at her.

"Yes, his name is Ryan. When I was lying in my room at Taban's compound, I was thinking of what our baby might look like. I fell asleep thinking about it, and it was so real. It was like he was really here. He looked just like you, and when he looked up at me and grabbed my hand, I just knew that this was the baby inside of me. It was like looking into the future. It was just a small glimpse," she said closing her eyes in remembrance.

"What's his middle name then?"

"Rudy?" she said looking at him hopefully.

"Ryan Rudy?" he said several times considering the name.

"It kind of sounds like a movie stars name, doesn't it?"

"It kind of does, I like it," he said lying back to daydream a little. "Rudy will like it."

"Can you believe everything that Aunt Mary did for us? I didn't know she even cared. I almost didn't mail that letter before we left. I carried it around with me in my purse for a month, and then on impulse, I dropped it in the mail receptacle when we were walking through the airport. Can you imagine what would have happened to us if she hadn't been there?" she said shaking her head.

"The two of ya looked like ya had a good talk." He was still lying there stroking her belly.

"We did. I think we have a lot of catching up to do, and misunderstandings to clear up. But then again, I think maybe we need to just sort of move forward, you know?" she shrugged. "Who cares what happened before? None of that really matters now. All I know for sure is that Aunt Mary loves me, and she must be a wonderful person. I'm looking forward to spending more time with her."

"I think ya might need ta fight Terri off if ya have any hopes of seein' her again. The two looked pretty cozy," he said sleepily.

"I noticed that too," she said closing her eyes, both of them blissfully content to be so near each other again, and to be sleeping in an actual bed for the first time in months.

PART SIX

HOME

Chapter 72

Saying Goodbye to an Angel

Madison was glued to Grady and Jewel at the funeral. The poor child's life had been turned upside down the last few months. One night she had been lying in bed next to her dying mother, slowly drifting off to sleep, when she saw flashing lights outside, and heard police banging at their front door. They had come for Jay, but Jay had made a split decision not to go easily. He had been working in his office downstairs, but when all the commotion started, he came and got them in the bedroom, and made them go downstairs into the dining room. The dining room was in the center of their house, and it was the only room that wasn't connected to an outside wall.

They were back in the room that Madison hated the most, and her mom was so sick, as her body surrendered to the breast cancer that was slowly killing her, that just getting her there had been a feat. Madison helped her down the stairs, and once she was there, she had to lie down on the carpet between the dining room table and the wall. Madison was furious at Jay for doing anything that would make her mom uncomfortable at this stage in her life, and she let him know it.

"You're mean!" she cried at him as she sat cradling her mom's head in her lap. "She needs to be in bed!"

"Go get some pillows and blankets then, and make her more comfortable," he said, feeling a twinge of guilt as he barricaded them in the small dining room. "Hurry up!"

"Jay Geary! We have a warrant for your arrest for the kidnapping and murder of Debbie Powers, drug trafficking, murder for hire, and a whole damn laundry list of items here! You better just come on out here now," an officer yelled through the front door.

"Murder? Drug trafficking? What? What is all this Jay?" Mandi asked weakly, trying to make herself sit up as Madison brought blankets and pillows for her.

"Well, obviously it's a mistake," he said shrugging.

"Then for god's sake, answer the door and explain it to them!" Mandi demanded. "Debbie Powers? Isn't that Madison's birth mother?" she said shaking her head in confusion. It was as if the truth of what she had been trying to pretend didn't exist over the years, had suddenly forced its way into the forefront of her mind, hitting her like a ton of bricks. All the strange calls at all hours of the night, Doug, and the sudden success that Jay had that allowed them to live so comfortably; it forced her to see what she didn't want to see. She had always tried to focus on the good and get all the pessimism out. Anytime she had brought up any feelings that something wasn't right, Jay would admonish her and tell her she was crazy and paranoid. He would get angry and tell her he was offended that she would think he could be a liar, and he would scold her for being a bad person that could think such things. She had been convinced there was something wrong with her, and she tried to think more positive, and just focus on what was good.

One night, she accused him of being sneaky, and told him that she felt like there was a whole other side to him that she didn't know, and he completely lost his temper. He had to take the focus off himself by making her feel bad about herself. He accused her of being distrustful, and started bringing up things that happened years ago, anything to take the focus off himself to make her think twice about proceeding down that path. In that moment, she knew that Jay only considered something a lie if he didn't get caught, and she knew that he would do anything to protect himself from being caught. She also knew that he didn't think lying by omission was lying at all, and there didn't seem to be anyway of convincing his twisted brain that this wasn't the case.

"It's all a mistake, because the police have it out for me. They aren't here to arrest me. Believe me honey; they are here to execute me. They'll try to make it look like a justified killing, but it won't be," he said, trying to convince her that the police were just as wrong and crazy as she had been.

"Why would they do that Dad? That doesn't make any sense!" Madison said, flaring with anger as she stood toe to toe with him.

"You're just a kid. You don't know how the world works. Sit down," he said angrily.

"Jay Geary! If you don't come out, then we're coming in!" the officer yelled through the door.

"I have hostages in here! If you come through those doors, I'll kill them both!" Jay said glancing at Mandi ashamedly, bluffing, as he had absolutely no weapon in his hand, or any nearby as far as Mandi and Madison could see.

Mandi was in complete shock. The sick feelings she had felt in the pit of her stomach through the years, the years of denial, the intuition that plagued her night and day, and everything she had kept neatly tucked away in the back of her mind, was now boiling over. He had convinced her she was crazy and paranoid. She had gone to counseling, and had even gone on medication, thinking that maybe she was depressed or insane. The thought of it all made this frail, sick woman, who had wasted away to ninety pounds, suddenly come to life.

Mandi looked at the man she had loved and defended, the man she had stood behind and cared for all those years. He stood with his back to her in the doorway of the dining room. She looked at the centerpiece that stood on their dining room table, and she suddenly took action. It was a tall, slender bronze statue of a woman that she had once jokingly said would make a good weapon. She grabbed it after getting up off the floor with more energy and agility then she had been able to muster for several months. It all happened quickly. She hit Jay hard against the back of his head before Jay even had a chance to turn around, knocking him out cold.

She simply turned and gave Madison a little shrug and yelled toward the door. "Jay is out cold! I'm going to open the door," Mandi yelled as she took Madison's hand, as Madison stood there completely stunned. Mandi was always a quiet and gentle woman, even when she was perfectly healthy. She was always meek, and since she was sick, she was doubly so, and Madison had never even heard her raise her voice before, but she had suddenly turned into a five-foot two-inch Rambo.

"Mom!" she said in disbelief, as she smiled and looked at her mom in awe.

The police came in and placed handcuffs on Jay just as he was starting to come back to life. Madison led her mom to the sofa where she propped pillows around her and covered her with a warm blanket while they hauled Jay out, and read him his rights. The energy that it had taken for Mandi to knock Jay out left her completely spent, and she was barely able to keep her eyes open.

"How old are you?" the police officer finally asked Madison after she gave him an account of everything that happened.

"I'm twelve," she said feeling grown-up. She was tall for a girl that was not quite thirteen, standing at five-foot, five-inches already, but he could tell that she was young and she was scared.

"Do you have someone that you can call to come stay with you for a while; someone who could help you with your mom?" he'd asked, not wanting to leave this young girl there to care for this frail looking woman who was asleep on the couch, especially after everything that just happened.

"Yes. My Aunt Diana. I'll call her," Madison said without hesitation, having been lavished with so much love and reassurance from Diana that she felt like she had known her forever.

Diana came without hesitation, and for the first time in several months, Madison could finally just kick back and be a kid again, instead of the primary caretaker, and sole protector of her mom. Within a few days, Diana had completely cleaned the house, stocked the refrigerator, got all the household items taken care of, and helped to do everything she could to make Mandi more comfortable. She helped Madison with her homework, and insisted that she go spend some time hanging out with her friends while she took care of Mandi, which was the opposite of what Jay had been telling her to do.

She stayed for a couple weeks, and Ally brought all the kids down on a weekend after Mandi insisted, but she knew this was just too hard on her. Mandi needed to rest, and that was nearly impossible when you had a bunch of kids running around.

Being quiet is as foreign a concept to a child as closing doors, but when Diana needed to go home to take care of her children, she didn't leave without bringing in a replacement. Maggie showed up the day before Diana needed to leave, and thus the proper care and keeping of a twelve-year-old girl, who was on the verge of losing her mom, continued.

Maggie came to stay. She temporarily moved into the guest bedroom and spent her time taking care of Mandi, bonding with her grandchild, and trying to make up for the first twelve years of the girls life she missed. Madison called her "Grammy" just as all the other grandkids did, which marked the first time in her life she ever had the opportunity to use the familial term of endearment that so many children took for granted. She hadn't really gotten much time to spend with her grandparents, but she suddenly had an opportunity to get to know them in a way that most kids will never have.

Patrick, or *Grampy,* as Madison called him, came down on the weekends, and Madison was in heaven. They spoiled her rotten, taking her to go shopping, helping her with school projects, and going to all her games. Since her mom had gotten sick, nobody had gone to any of her games, and there hadn't been anyone around to ask for help with her homework.

Grammy and Grampy told her stories of her dad when he was growing up, or told stories about Diana and the kids. She loved having them there, and Mandi was thankful as well. Maggie had taken her to all of her doctor's appointments, and Maggie had managed to shelter her from Jay's reach from prison. Jay would call and call, and since Mandi had said her peace, and made it clear that she didn't want to talk to him, Maggie ran interference, screening out calls and turning off all the ringers so Mandi wouldn't startle every time the phone rang.

"What do you want me to do, and I'll do it?" Jay pleaded with her one night on the phone.

"Sign over all your parental rights so Madison can live with her family when I pass," Mandi had said as more of an order than a question. "If you don't, then she'll be in foster care for god knows how long before things get sorted out. Do this one thing for me Jay. You owe me that much."

And so, Maggie made all the arrangements for this as well. She got all the proper paperwork, and then gathered up a witness and a notary public to take the court documents to the jail for Jay to sign. It took several days of research and effort, but when Maggie finally handed the signed and notarized parental release form to Mandi, she finally felt like she could breathe easy. Maggie called Mandi's attorney as she requested, and the two of them drafted a letter so Mandi could make her wishes known that she wanted Madison to live with Grady and Jewel when she passed.

Not long after Jay broke Madison's heart by telling her that Grady was dead, Diana came and picked her up to tell her what was going on, and the two of them sat in the car and cried with an overabundance of emotions. Diana made her promise not to tell anyone that Grady was actually still alive.

"Can I at least tell Mom? She's worried about what's going to happen to me once she…," she said trailing off.

This confirmed her belief that something was indeed not right with Jay, because why else would Mandi be worried about what would happen to her once she was gone. If Jay were a good dad, she wouldn't be so worried.

"Will your mom tell your… well, will she tell Jay?" Diana asked.

"Not if I ask her not to. She was furious with him after the way he yelled at me, and told me about him being dead. I'm sure if I told her it was really important, then she wouldn't tell anyone," Madison had answered.

One day, several days before Christmas, more energy than Madison and Mandi had seen in a lifetime, descended on their household, and neither one of them could have imagined a happier Christmas under the circumstances. They all knew this was a difficult Christmas for Madison, and didn't want to leave Mandi alone or make her travel, so everyone came to them. Diana and the kids showed up, and with Maggie and Patrick already there, there suddenly seemed to be a swarm of activity that couldn't have been more welcome. Mandi was so pleased to get to witness the love that was being wrapped around her daughter that she no longer felt like she had to fight to live in her misery any longer, and died on the twenty-sixth day of December, the same day Grady made his way from Amsterdam to Denver.

Madison cried, but she was also happy not to have to see the pain that was always present on her mom's face. She sat for a long time on the edge of the bed where her mom's body was lying. She looked at the sweet smile that was on her face, and she knew her mom was finally free from pain. She knew she was finally happy and healthy, and she knew that her mom had waited to make sure she was taken care of before she left.

By the time Grady and everyone had all landed in Denver and driven to Casper, plans were already in the making per the careful instructions that Mandi had put together with Maggie and Diana's help. She had already picked out and paid for her burial plot and her casket, chosen the funeral home, and made arrangements with the church.

"Dad!" Madison cried as she ran out of the house, and he scooped her up in a big bear hug the second he stepped out of the car. They both cried, and Jewel couldn't stop herself from crying either, seeing how hard it must have been on both of them.

"Maddie! I thought about ya every day sweetheart," Grady said, holding her tight as her feet hung off the ground.

The house that was filled up with ten of them over Christmas, was now bursting at the seams as Grady, Jewel, Rudy, Kinyera, Mugabo, and Yannick descended on them. For the first time, Grady was glad the other men had gone their own separate ways, and Aunt Mary had stayed in Denver. They all stayed right there until after the funeral was over several days later, which gave them all some time to do some shopping at the mall in Casper, before heading to Buffalo where there were limited stores.

The funeral had gone nicely, but they were all a little surprised by how few people showed up from Mandi and Jay's family, and Jewel realized for the first time just how close Madison had come to growing up sad and secluded as she had, only without Troy. The ones who did come had little to say, and made little to no inquiries into where Madison would live or who would take care of her, though it must have been perfectly clear since Grady made no bones about it.

They were at each other's side constantly, and when the preacher asked if anyone would like to say a few words, Grady waited until all the others were done before standing up to say the words he had been running through his mind.

"I'm Grady McDonald. I'm Maddi's dad, and I'm pleased that I got ta know Mandi in my lifetime, and I thank God that He picked an angel like her ta raise my daughter until I could find her. I don't think it's any coincidence that God led me here right when her angel needed me ta find her," he said looking at Madison and Jewel the whole time as the newest additions to his family, Kinyera, Mugabo, and Yannick sat beside them, "and I hope I'll be as good a parent as she was."

The church was full of people that Mandi had known in the community. Everyone they met talked about how Mandi always had a kind word or a compliment for them. They talked about what a loving and caring mother she was, and how much they always disliked Jay. They hugged Madison, and came up to eagerly meet Grady, and hear stories about the adoption. Stories of who Grady was ran rampant through the church, as the obvious family resemblance stunned people who looked at the two of them together.

Some of Madison's friends from school came to comfort her, but she had surprisingly few since she had been growing up as more of a nursemaid than an actual kid, as her mother's sicknesses came and went. Rather than Jay taking care of things, he had relied mostly on Madison to care for her mother during her sicknesses. Grady couldn't wait to give her the simple life of a kid for a while, full of all the joy and complexities that came with it, and Jewel was eager to have her there as well.

Grady knew there would be a mountain of things that needed to be taken care of as far as Madison was concerned. Jay was in jail being held without bail on state and federal charges, and he likely was never getting out, which left everything to Madison. He needed to file court documents immediately to petition for permanent legal guardianship, and he would need to help decide what would be done with the house, and all of her mother's belongings. For the moment, he was anxious just to get her out of there, so when he stood next to her at the reception after the funeral and suggested they head home, she simply smiled up at him and said, "Let's go Dad."

CHAPTER 73

WAS DEBBIE POWERS MY BIRTH MOM?

"Was Debbie Powers my birth mom?" Madison asked Grady one evening when they were in the shop. Grady had his head buried under the hood of his truck, as Madison sat by nervously waiting to ask her question. He knew she was waiting to get the courage to ask him something, and so he just tinkered around until she figured out what she wanted to say.

It was early evening. Spring was starting to show its pretty face, and so the two of them had made their daily trek to the shop to spend some time together, strolling in the warm sun that was slowly making the days longer as they neared summer. He hadn't felt like going that evening, after an especially grueling day at the construction site, but he had sensed that Madison had something on her mind, and so when she asked if he was going to the shop, he said yes.

After hearing the question, Grady immediately stopped what he was doing and looked up at Madison who was sitting at his desk, casually spinning his desk chair in circles. She was a stunning girl on the verge of becoming a woman, but on this day, she looked like a small child. Her long blond hair was haphazardly braided down the middle with strands sticking out here and there, and she was wearing a pair of Jewel's old denim coveralls she always wore when she was hanging around the shop. He knew the day would come when she asked about her birth mom, but he hadn't expected her to know her name, and he was reluctant to crush the fragile little innocence he saw in the girl as she sat there and looked up at him with her big blue eyes.

"I didn't know ya knew her name," he said as he wiped his hands and came to sit with her. "Did yer mom tell ya about her?"

"Not exactly... when the police came to the door they said Jay was being arrested for the murder of Debbie Powers, and then Mom said, *Isn't that Madison's birth mother?* and so I was just wondering if it was true," she said shrugging, referring to Jay by his name the way she now thought of him.

"Wow. I didn't know ya knew about that. I thought I would tell ya down the road when ya'd had some time ta heal a bit, but since ya bring it up, I'll tell ya what

I know," he said leveling with her, since he knew that she was too smart to accept anything less than the cold hard truth.

He told her about him and Debbie growing up together and dating in high school. He told her about what happened when they broke up, and how he had never known about the pregnancy, and then he told her about the day when he learned he had a daughter, and how devastated and betrayed he felt. He tried highlighting some of the good things about Debbie, talking about her nice skin, likening it to her own so she could have something good to carry with her.

When it came time to tell Madison the truth about what he found out about the adoption, he hesitated. He didn't want to tell a twelve-year-old girl that her biological mother had sold her to Jay Geary so she could afford to pay her way through college. He had gotten the stories from a couple of her friends from back home who talked about Debbie's situation. According to Debbie, she had left with Grady to go stay with him at boot camp, but then had quickly decided to dump him. She then went to Colorado with some unknown friends she had met, but then decided to come back after a while and enroll in Chadron University.

According to Jay, whom he visited in jail, he met Debbie in a diner in Casper where she was waiting across the street from the abortion clinic. When she overheard him talking about his wife's heartbreak, because she was unable to have children, and joked about wishing he could just go buy a baby, she approached him by handing him a note to meet her outside alone. Jay wasn't clear on the details, but said he felt a moral obligation to save this unborn babies life, being Christian and all, and so he didn't hesitate, though Grady seriously doubted that Jay had any idea how a moral obligation felt.

He agreed to pay for an apartment for her, pay for all the medical bills, and give her money to attend Chadron University. Debbie didn't have much family to speak of, and her friends that she had grown up with were more than happy to have her gone. Her absence from Belle Fourche was missed about as much as New Orleans missed Hurricane Katrina, and most people thought she was wherever Grady was.

Through the years, Debbie had come back to her money tree and made demands, threatening to expose him if he didn't pay her more money, or threatening to take legal action and take Madison away. Jay was no match for Debbie Powers. She was a force that Medusa herself would have found intimidating, towering over his small stature, beaming with overconfidence. He would usually give her some money and be done with her until the next time, which usually came about every year or so.

According to police reports, Debbie played her final hand. She did a little more research and found out exactly how much money Jay had through all his illegal dealings, and she made a huge demand for millions of dollars. This time when she made her demands, she not only threatened to expose the truth about the adoption, she threatened to expose the illegal dealings behind Top Security, and Jay made the mistake of sharing this threat with Doug. It was one thing to make demands on Jay, who was largely a pushover, and quite another to threaten Doug's interests.

Of course, Jay's story was that it was all Doug, and since he was currently missing, having never returned from Africa, unable to be tracked down, and probably dead Jay hoped, Doug made a good patsy. Jay's legal defense was pinning everything on Doug, with Jay saying that everything was Doug's doing, and he was completely oblivious, thinking everything they were doing was legal. The adoption issue was another story altogether though, and Jay was laying on the Christian school boy act pretty heavily, but the fact that Debbie had turned up missing and was later found dead when Doug was documented as being halfway around the world, was a nail in his coffin.

One of the detectives had leveled with Grady and told them that they knew Jay himself hadn't committed the murder, though he would certainly be implicated in it. They knew that it was one of their shady business associates who had done the actual deed. They were waiting to expose this information until Jay's carefully woven web of lies would back him into a corner, and cause him to turn states evidence, so they could make a large sweep of their criminal organization that spanned the globe.

Grady carefully left out all the speculation, as he told his daughter what he knew. He didn't gloss it over or make excuses for anyone. He simply told her what he knew and tried to leave his personal opinions out of it, and omit any hearsay, except where Debbie was concerned, because she needed his opinion on Debbie.

"Debbie was a force. She came in so hard and so fast that ya could get swept up with her and carried off before ya had a chance ta think it through. Her mom was forty-six when she was born and her dad older still. Their kids had all gone off ta college and gotten married nearly ten years before Debbie came along, and they were pretty lax with her. I think if she'd had a better home life she could have grown up ta be President one day, but she had no guidance, and she fell off the right path," he said wanting to explain to his daughter who her biological mother was, and why she might have made the decisions she made.

"She was a pretty good friend in high school. She pretty much tailored her life ta fit mine, and I was just young and dumb enough ta be flattered by it. She went ta all my games, and would switch her class schedule around so we could be in the same ones. She was a pretty girl, and could have had her choice of boyfriends, but she chose me, and she didn't make any bones about it. She was goin' ta have me one way or another, and so... well, we just hung out. It was... convenient I guess," he said feeling a twinge of guilt saying those words as he looked at his daughter, whom he hoped wouldn't end up with a boy who dated her out of convenience. "When I broke up with her, she just kind of shrugged and acted like it was no big deal, like she could care less, but I guess she must have been about three or four months pregnant when that happened," he said meeting Madison's eyes, knowing he didn't have to explain that part again.

"Were you in the same grade?" she asked.

"Yep. We were exactly the same age. Our birthdays were within two days of each other, which is one of the reasons we were always together. When I was discharged from the Army and went home ta Belle Fourche, she came by the next day ta celebrate our birthdays, which was happenin' that weekend. She was just always right there. Always, and she could be kind of fun ta hang out with. She had a good sense of humor and was always doin' things crackin' everyone up all the time. She could be fun," he said trying to highlight some of the good things about her.

"Why did you break up with her?" she asked.

"I just needed ta move on. I felt like I should marry her and work for my dad, but it wasn't where my heart was. I wanted ta go find a life. I would have been settlin'," he shrugged.

"You shouldn't feel guilty Dad. It wasn't your fault," Madison said after they sat in silence a few moments. "I think I know you well enough to know that."

"Absolved from guilt by my daughter," Grady said laughing to himself. "I just hope ya don't date a boy just because it's convenient Maddie, and don't ever settle fer nothin'."

"All the boys in school are shorter than me, and they won't even ask me out," she said surprising Grady.

"That won't always be the case. I didn't really get tall until my sophomore year, and then I started growin'. Boys grow slower, but then they shoot up in high school. Come ta think of it, it was Debbie that used ta call me shrimp and such when we were in grade school, and then when I grew tall she suddenly took interest in me. Maybe that's the lesson here sweetheart."

"So… the ones who are mean to me now because of my height, are the ones I should stay away from later on?" she questioned.

"That seems right," he said. "Are ya havin' a hard time in school then?" he asked, having worried about her transition since she moved in with them.

"Just a few jerks. I wore that green jumpsuit the other day that Grammy bought me, and Brandon Howley called me the jolly green giant. He's always being mean to everyone," she said, narrowing her eyes in angst as she told him the story.

"Brandon Howley is it? Do I need ta come have a word with him then?"

"No Dad. He's like this much shorter than me," she said holding her hands up to show that he was about six inches shorter than her. "I could probably pound him into the ground if I wanted to, but that's only if Tina doesn't beat me to it."

"She doesn't take too kindly ta bully's, that's for sure," he said remembering the story of her punching the bully in school that was picking on her.

They sat in silence a few minutes and Grady tried not to notice as Madison wrestled with her next question.

"Dad," Madison started, reluctant to ask her next question, "do you think Jewel would… ummm, well, do you think she would mind coming to the mother-daughter pajama party that they're doing at school?"

"Maddie, come here sweetheart," he said pulling her chair closer to his so they were face-to-face. "Jewel lost both her parents when she was just eleven. She knows what it's like. She understands what yer goin' through. I'd bet my entire soul that she'd be willin' ta go ta the ends of the earth for ya. She'd be thrilled if ya asked her."

"Ummm, okay," she said unconvinced.

"She's feelin' guilty right now. She's carryin' all the blame for everything that happened in Uganda no matter how much I try ta tell her it's not her fault, and if she's feelin' a little distant, then that's why," he said taking this opportunity to try to explain to Madison why there had been some distance that had developed between them. "She thinks ya must hate her, and I'm just watchin' the two of ya dance around each other, and I don't know what ta do about it. Do ya have some hard feelin's Maddie?"

"I mean... I guess I did at first, but then I remembered that day when we were sitting around the table when Mom told you about her cancer. It was Jewel that first took my hand and told me you guys would stay if I wanted," she said wrestling with her emotions, "but then with the baby coming... I guess maybe I was thinking it would just be easier for her if I wasn't here."

"No Maddie. She wants ta grab ya and hug ya and cry with ya, but she's afraid ta do it. She has a hard time showin' her feelins sometimes, and the two of ya are misunderstandin' the other. Losin' yer mom the way ya did is bringin' up some old feelin's for her, and she's afraid that her emotions are goin' ta make it harder for ya. She's always thinkin' of ya. She's always wantin' ta buy ya the foods that ya like, or seein' an outfit and talkin' about gettin' it for ya. Trust me sweetheart, if yer feelin' like she's pullin' away from ya, it's only because she's afraid she's goin' ta pull ya under. She's tryin' ta protect ya, but if ya had a need of anything... a need ta talk or have a shoulder ta cry on, she'd drop everything ta be there for ya."

"So you think if I ask her it will make her happy?" she asked, confirming her understanding of everything he just said.

"I think she'll immediately say yes, and then her eyes will fill with tears the way they do sometimes," he said picturing it, "but then she'll grab ya and hug ya ta try and hide her emotions, before takin' yer hand in hers and thankin' ya for askin'."

Madison's eyes filled with that visible sign of relief a person gets when they were fearing bad news, but had their expectations replaced by something good instead. She peered up at Grady with a broad smile she was struggling to keep under wraps. "Do you want to put a five spot on it?" she asked playfully.

"I'd put a million spot on it if I thought ya were good for it," he said grabbing her up like a football and tickling her. "Come on now. She's probably gone ta some trouble ta make us a *nice* dinner," he said making a face of disgust when he said the word *nice*, since Jewel was not the best cook in the world, "and if ya play yer cards right, I'll sneak ya some pizza later on when she's in the bath."

"Deal!" she said smiling, looking up at her dad with complete admiration as they walked together arm in arm toward the house.

CHAPTER 74

IT'S ONLY THE BEGINNING

"Are you ever going to make love to me again?" Jewel said seductively as she leaned her head against one of the bedposts on their bed, wearing her silky nightgown, and watching him. He was lying on their bed in his underwear reading the newspaper, and she hadn't been able to keep her eyes off him as she readied herself for bed in the bathroom, catching sight of him in the reflection of the mirror.

He looked up at her then, grabbing the newspaper in one hand and casually tossed it over his shoulder to the floor, smiling at her as he did. "The doctor did say everything checked out fine," he said, holding his hand out to her to join him on their bed.

They were both up on their knees, meeting in the middle of the bed. The house was finally quiet since Yannick, Kinyera, and Mugabo had rented a small house in town, settling in down the street from where Rudy and his family were living, and Madison was spending the night with Tina. It seemed that since they arrived back home, they hadn't hardly had a moment alone. With the Biha's camping out in their living room the last couple of months, they had taken extra precaution with Madison, and had her sleeping on a mattress beside their own bed. They wanted to trust the young men, but they knew that their idea of right and wrong was different from their own, and they weren't willing to take any chances.

Madison had been given strict instructions to never be alone with them, and Grady had told them that he would gladly kill anyone that so much as harmed a hair on her head, and the young men knew he was serious. Grady hadn't let the men be alone with Madison or Jewel, and they were finally relaxed and able to rest easy in their own home. He truly felt that Kinyera and Mugabo were good men, but he also knew that they had been taught to treat women poorly. He knew they needed more time to come to learn and understand the rules of a new society, and be deprogrammed from all the horrors they had learned at the hands of the Interahamwe.

Jewel was more than halfway through her pregnancy, and they had been reassured that the miscarriage had nothing to do with Jewel or any of the problems that had plagued her mom or her grandma, but Grady hadn't been willing to take any chances. This was their first night alone, and Jewel had pulled out all the stops, putting on an off-white silky nightgown that she knew drove him crazy, especially with her swollen breasts overflowing the boundaries of the small laces in front. It was a short gown that barely covered her below the buttocks since her tummy protruded from the pregnancy, pulling it up even higher, revealing her lacey underwear. He loved the short gowns where he could see her long thin legs that he loved to run his hands down and then back up again

He softly kissed her shoulder as he pulled one strap down, and then the other, running his hands along the front of her, teasing her with his fingers. "I'm not goin' ta just make love ta ya Jewel. I'm goin ta have ya again and again until ya beg me ta stop," he said kissing her then, with an energy that she could feel tingling simultaneously in every cell in her body

"I'll never tell you to stop," she whispered as he kissed her neck, and made his way down to her breasts, laying her back on the bed as he did.

He lightly pulled at her nipples, causing her to gasp and pull him to her even harder. His hands reached down and pulled at her legs so he could position himself in the warmth he found there. They teased each other as the barrier of their clothing prevented them from going further, both of them lost in a sea of anticipation that had been threatening to consume them these last months. She could feel the hardness of him as he made the motions, simulating what was to come as he teased her further, causing her to cry out.

"What are you waiting for then?" she cried out, pulling at his underwear.

"I'll take my time darlin'. I'll have all of ya, like ya've never known before."

He rolled over on his back, pulling her up on top of him as he did. He sat up and explored her nipples with his hands before lifting the silky gown up over her head. Her nipples were round and hard, and her breasts were full, filling his hand with the warmth of her skin. He bent and took one in his mouth, exploring the hardness with his tongue while circling the other with his thumb.

When they had finally joined together, their bodies had come so fully alive, they were both wholly lost in the other, each motion giving them salvation, and taking them beyond any passion they had felt before.

She *would* beg him to stop just as he had promised, begging him to finally take what he desired and give her what she needed to finally feel full and satisfied, until the next moment when she would feel the need for him again.

"It's only the beiginnin' darlin'. It's only the beginnin'.

Epilogue

Jewel sat there with her mouth hanging open, and her heart thumping wildly in her chest, as she listened to the news anchor describe in some detail her husband's arrest, his connections to the C.I.A, his involvement with an international drug trafficking organization, his military career that was being brought into question, and the laundry list of charges he was being held on. It was only the cries coming from Ryan that startled her back into the moment, as the weight of everything that was just reported sent a shockwave through her, and nearly brought her to her knees.

She quieted him as much as she could, nursing him some more, so she could hear the political pundits discuss his involvement in killing Aaron Millet in cold blood during a trip to Alaska, and his escape from the Democratic Republic of the Congo to avoid being held on the plethora of drug trafficking charges they were accusing him of. The room was swirling around her as she stood there and heard them all arguing back and forth, as if they were all experts on the life and times of Grady McDonald, discussing all the specifics in a detail they couldn't possibly be privy to. Some were defending him, trying to interject facts that pointed to his innocence, while others presented information that would lead you to believe he was nothing more than a highly dangerous lethal weapon that the United States Military had created, and then negligently let loose on society.

Pictures of him in his military uniform from years earlier were being splashed across the screen, as if no more proof was needed to show how dangerous and menacing he was. They discussed his success as a sniper, and his extensive training, painting him as little more than a well-trained killing machine. His association with convicted felon, Jay Geary, was being introduced as further proof that he had a questionable background, and the murder of his former girlfriend, Debbie Powers, was being linked to him, with or without some degree of separation. It was as if just mentioning her death in the same paragraph proved his guilt, as those surrounding the news anchor shook their heads with judgment and concern, from the comfort of their perch on national television.

She grabbed Ryan with one hand, and fumbled to find the remote control, as one channel went to commercials, needing to see more of this breaking news. The next channel continued with even more damning terminology, with people saying things about terrorist connections and kidnappings, illegal human trafficking, and questioning whether his discharge from the military was due to his injuries, or more serious reasons that the military was trying to cover up. The house phone was ringing, and her cell phone was ringing, but she just stood there unable to move. It was as if her feet were glued to that one spot as she stood between one reality and another, unable to go back, but terrified to move forward.

Only moments before she had been sitting there quietly nursing Ryan, as she waited for Grady to call her as he had done every evening while he was in Washington D.C. The Congressional Oversight Committee that had been assembled to investigate the kidnappings that had taken place when they arrived in Uganda nearly a year earlier, had summoned him there. He had been led to believe that it was all just a matter of record and documentation, but he quickly learned that he was being railroaded and painted as a villain, but Jewel never expected this. She innocently insisted that the truth was on their side, and would win out, even as Grady sat on the other end of the phone each night and voiced his increasingly troubled concern. In the court of public opinion, he was absolutely guilty of all charges and accusations, and alarmists were calling for extreme measures, life sentences, or death penalties, and further investigations into current military practices.

The phone rang again and again, both the land line and her cell phone, but she just stood there and simply looked at them as if she had no idea what they were, and why the noise was penetrating the room so determinedly, competing with the news she was trying to listen to. Finally, she picked up her cell phone and looked at it to see who was calling, and answered it immediately when she saw the name *Uncle Rudy* across the screen; a name that gave her hope the second she saw it.

"Rudy! Are you watching this?" she asked with her voice cracking, having been sufficiently launched back into the reality that was now hers, leaving the comfort and safety of a peaceful life behind only seconds earlier.

"I'm watching it. This is crazy! What the hell is going on Jewel?"

She sat down on the couch, her eyes searching out into nowhere, looking for answers, but found nothing. "I don't know. I don't know what's going on. This doesn't make any sense."

"I'm going to have to tell the rest of the story. Everything's going to have to come out into the open. I can't just leave Grady out there to take the heat while I sit at home."

"No Rudy! That could make it all worse. We need to talk to a lawyer right now! I'm calling my Aunt Mary. I'll call you back in a minute." Jewel hung up the phone without saying goodbye or waiting for a reply. She went to her landline to dial the number, realizing that one of the missed calls was from Aunt Mary herself. Her hands were shaking as she pushed the buttons that would redial the missed call, and Aunt Mary picked up the phone immediately.

"Don't say anything Jewel. I'll be there tomorrow. Don't talk to anyone. Don't discuss anything on the phone. We'll talk tomorrow. Trust me on this," Aunt Mary said before hanging up the phone.

She looked at the phone curiously, as the line went dead, as if it just spoke a language to her that was as foreign as one that was ancient and long forgotten. She sat for a moment more, pulling something from deep within her, an anger that sprung up from the wickedness of injustice that was being thrust upon her husband. She looked down at the innocent face of her son, the one that looked so much like Grady's, and resolved herself to face and conquer the malice that was being committed against them, as accusation and speculation had already condemned him.

She calmly picked up the phone and dialed Rudy's number. "Meet me at Middle Fork. I'll be there in twenty minutes." She hung up the phone as a calm washed over her, and she gathered everything she would need for Ryan, grabbed her purse and her cell phone, and left the house to go meet Rudy.

She hummed a little song as she strapped Ryan into his car seat, unable to keep from smiling at him just a little as he cooed at her when he saw the familiar toys that hung in the backseat to keep him entertained. She realized the humming was as much for her sake as it was for his, as she feigned self-control. She was clinging to a steady center somewhere inside her that was allowing her to put one foot in front of the other, and take careful and calculating steps, even as every fiber of her being longed to pack a bag and run toward the nearest plane that would take her closer to where Grady was.

She wondered what he must be thinking, but even as it crossed her mind, she knew that he was likely sitting in some cell worried about them. She was thankful Maddie had been out horseback riding with Michael and Alisha when the story broke, and it suddenly occurred to her to run back inside and turn off the television so it wouldn't be spewing misinformation when Maddie returned home later. She rushed in, and turned the channel to the cartoon network, before turning it off when she heard the phone ring again. She grabbed it immediately and answered it, as she made her way to the window to look out at her son sitting in the car.

"Hello?"

"I have a collect call from Grady McDonald. Will you accept the charges?" the voice asked.

"Yes! Yes, I will! Grady! Oh my God Grady! What's going on?"

"Well...I didn't think you'd accept the charges if I had said it was from one Douglas Ray Howell," the deep voice said on the end of the line, sending a shiver down Jewel's spine. She had never met Doug, but she had heard plenty about him from Rudy and the other men. He had betrayed them when they assembled a team to help get her and Grady out of Uganda, after Interahamwe rebels had kidnapped them during their trip there.

"What do you want? Is there something I can do for you?" she asked a little shaken, somehow managing to keep the fear from dropping her to her knees.

"No darlin'. Not yet," he said using the term of endearment with some emphasis; the one that Grady always used, indicating that his knowledge of her was more intimate than should be possible, making the hair on her arms stand up. "Just know that I'm alive and well," he said before hanging up the phone.

ABOUT THE AUTHOR

Leslie M. Arno lives in Sheridan, Wyoming with her husband and her three children. She is currently working on the continuation of this series.

CPSIA information can be obtained at www.ICGtesting.com
Printed in the USA
LVOW08s1743140415

434538LV00019B/18/P